Legacies

"[*Legacies*] offers us strong ... with its own subset of ... beasties. . . . Old fans of L.E. Modesitt, Jr. will thrill at this new series because there is certainly enough of *Recluce* here to feel that you are back home without having to travel down the same old roads again. New fans will thrill at the prospect of being in at the start of a brand new world!"

—SFRevu.com

"The introductory novel to the latest epic fantasy from L.E. Modesitt, Jr. is a great start to what looks like will be a tremendous series . . . With the talent of Mr. Modesitt, Jr. fans will anticipate even greater insight yet filled with non-stop action and excitement as the audience explores the intricacies of the Corean Chronicles."—*Midwest Book Review*

"*Legacies* is for people who enjoy a leisurely reading experience, want to see their characters grow and like to fill in the blanks themselves rather than have the author do it for them. . . . With a likable character in an intriguing land, *Legacies* is off to a promising start."   —*Starlog*

"Solidly engrossing . . . with a robust and consistent backdrop: a satisfyingly self-contained inaugural volume that skillfully sets up the sequels."   —*Kirkus Reviews*

"Thoughtful readers will be appreciative, and the author's fans will be impressed."   —*Publishers Weekly*

Darknesses

"*Darknesses,* the second book of the Corean Chronicles, is a superb fantasy due to the abilities of L.E. Modesitt, Jr. to make a world of magic and mystical beasts seem real . . . a strong epic fantasy that will have the audience wondering where the author will take them next."

—*Midwest Book Review*

"Faster paced than *Legacies, Darknesses* is, since it concerns multiple states and their political ambitions, much more intricately plotted. Reading *Legacies* before tackling it is advisable, but because Alucius is like many other Modesitt protagonists, turning the pages to see what the author's current quiet, competent hero will do next is always a pleasure."

—*Booklist*

"A solid, well-paced sequel to *Legacies* . . . Convincing dialogue, exciting military action and a neat conclusion that leaves the door open for subsequent adventures will find fans satisfied."

—*Publishers Weekly*

❯ SCEPTERS ❮

TOR BOOKS BY L. E. MODESITT, JR.

⊁ SCEPTERS ⊁

The Third Book of the Corean Chronicles

L. E. Modesitt, Jr.

TOR®
fantasy

A TOM DOHERTY ASSOCIATES BOOK
NEW YORK

This is a work of fiction. All the characters and events portrayed in this book are either products of the author's imagination or are used fictitiously.

SCEPTERS: THE THIRD BOOK OF THE COREAN CHRONICLES

Copyright © 2004 by L. E. Modesitt, Jr.
Teaser copyright © 2005 by L. E. Modesitt, Jr.

Edited by David G. Hartwell

A Tor Book
Published by Tom Doherty Associates, LLC
175 Fifth Avenue
New York, NY 10010

www.tor-forge.com

Tor® is a registered trademark of Tom Doherty Associates, LLC.

ISBN-13: 978-0-7653-4922-4
ISBN-10: 0-7653-4922-1

First Edition: July 2004
First Mass Market Edition: September 2005

Printed in the United States of America

0   9   8   7   6   5

In memoriam:
For my father, both hero and preceptor

. . . The brave, the craven, those who do not care,
will all look back, in awe, and fail to see,
whether rich, or poor, or young, or old and frail,
what was, what is, and what is yet to be.

There is a time, and it will come, years hence,
when one will find the scepters of the day,
those scepters more and less than what they seem,
with the might to bring life itself to bay.

In those ages, then, will rise a leader,
who would reclaim the glory of the past,
and more, as he would see it, in the sun,
to make sure the dual scepters will always last.

Then too, the lamaial will rise, but once,
Where none yet will suspect, nor think to dare,
and his hidden strokes may kill aborning,
Duality of promise bright and fair.

For which will live, and which will prosper?
Who will rule the lands, in faith or treason?
One called lamaial or the one called hero,
for one would seek a triumph, the other reason.

Excerpts from:
THE LEGACY OF THE DUARCHY

I.

⊁ THE SCEPTER OF ⊁ THE PAST

1

Hyalt, Lanachrona

Light fell upon the priest. That single ray of illumination, shaped by the ancient master-carved lens in the ceiling of the long and narrow chapel hewn out of the red rock cliffs, bathed the celebrant. His green tunic and trousers, trimmed in purple, shimmered. So did the alabaster makeup that covered his face. The blue-silver threads in the black short-haired wig picked up the light, creating a halo around his face. The black boots, with inset lifts, reflected light as if they too were burnished mirrors.

A long chord echoed through the temple, but the priest did not speak until all was silent.

"When our forebears turned their backs on the True Duarchy, then the One Who Is turned away and let the Cataclysm fall upon Corus . . ." The celebrant's voice seemed to come from everywhere, yet nowhere.

More than a hundred worshippers stood with bowed heads, heads covered with black scarves of mourning. Only a handful dared to look from lowered heads toward the front of the temple.

"The Cataclysm did not have to happen. The misery and suffering did not have to come to pass. And why did it come to be? How could so many be so blind?"

The only response to his questions was silence.

"The Duarchy of Corus bestowed peace and prosperity upon all the world, for generation upon generation. Never was there so fair a realm, so just a world. Never were so blessed the peoples of a world. Never had so many benefited so much. And then, in an instant, it all vanished . . ."

In the next-to-last line of worshippers stood a dark-haired figure in gray. He was a head taller than those around him, and his face paler. The weave of the wool of his traveling cloak was somewhat finer. His head was bent slightly less than the heads of others, and his eyes never left the celebrant. The faintest hint of an amused smile appeared from time to time at the corners of his thin lips.

". . . as the Mantra of Mourning declares . . . Ice flowed from the skies. The air that had been so fair, and perfumed, became as thin and as acrid as vinegar. Streams dried in their beds, rivers in their courses, never to flow again . . . All that had been beautiful and great perished and was lost. And for what reason?"

After a momentary silence, the priest answered, "Because people were selfish and thought only of themselves. They turned their backs on the True Duarchy, and when they did so, they turned their backs on the One Who Is . . . for the Duarchy was indeed His creation . . .

". . . in this world of transitory glory, when warlord succeeds warlord, and battle follows battle, and evil follows evil, we must persevere. We must have faith in the One Who Is. We must follow the path of righteousness to restore the old truths. For only by the instrument of the True Duarchy shall we be redeemed. Only by restoring the true creation of the One Who Is shall we once more see peace and prosperity, faith and faithfulness . . ."

The traveler in gray nodded, appreciatively, and continued to listen.

". . . even today, the troubles continue. The hills to the north and west have become so dry in your lifetimes that they support nothing but twisted trees and spiky thorn, and yet the unbelievers do not see. Even here in Hyalt, where it is obvious, they do not see . . .

". . . when the only deity is gold, when the only rule is power, when the only law is that laid down by the longest blade, by the deadliest rifle, no man can be safe, and none can find security. There are no arts, no fine buildings, no wondrous words, nothing but gold and blood . . ."

The traveler continued to listen, until at last came a hymn and the concluding refrain:

". . . for the beauty of the skies and sea,
    the full return of perfect harmony,
    the blessings of the True Duarchy
    and for the One Who Will Always Be!"

After the hymn, the priest turned to the worshippers. "Praise to the One Who Is! And for His creation of the Duarchy!"

"And for His creation of the Duarchy!" repeated the congregation.

"Praise to the One Who Is! For He will come again in glory!"

"For He will come again in glory!"

"Praise to Him and His True Duarchy! For all that was and will be!"

"For all that was and will be!"

The single ray of light vanished, plunging the cavern temple into total darkness for a long moment. Then, slowly, more indirect light filtered into the temple as the skylight portals, with their gauze-covered panes, were uncovered.

The sanctuary at the front of the temple was empty.

The gray-clad traveler made his way forward, toward the side entrance leading to the chambers of the celebrant. His fingers touched briefly the outer garments over the heavy leather wallet hidden beneath his cloak and filled with golds.

2

The wind moaned over the top of Westridge, hissing through the quarasote that had grown up following the Cataclysm and that had come to dominate the arid lands of the Iron Valleys in the tens of centuries that followed. Alucius half stood in the stirrups, stretching his legs. He settled back into the saddle of the gray gelding, drank in the cool and dry morning air, and smiled to himself. He looked to the northeast out across the ridge before him, and the expanse of land empty except for quarasote and sand and red soil—and the predators and prey that were unseen, except to those who knew how to understand the Iron Valleys or to those with Talent, who could sense the lifethreads that wove the world into a unified whole.

A good summer morning, he thought, bending forward and thumping the gelding on the shoulder. "We've got a ways to go."

The lead ram was already five hundred yards—a quarter vingt—ahead of the last ewe, and they were barely four vingts out from the stead buildings.

The faint flash of green gossamer radiance washed over Alucius, and he half turned in the saddle. A single soarer hovered in the silver-green sky of morning, her wings shimmering against the sky and the sheer stone ramparts of the Aerlal Plateau to the east. The herder's eyes took in the feminine form of the soarer, then darted back to check his flock almost immediately.

He had not seen a soarer in almost two years—since he had left the hidden city. Nor had he and his Talent sensed the green radiance of one in all that time. And all the times he had seen one of the soaring winged figures had meant change—and usually trouble.

He cast forth an inquiry. *What now?*

The soarer vanished without a response. One instant, she was there. The next she was not. While she had not felt familiar, Alucius had not been close enough long enough to tell for sure if the soarer had been the one who had instructed him during his brief captivity in the hidden city.

His hand touched the hilt of the sabre at his belt. He glanced down at the rifle in its leather saddle case. Even with the massive cartridges used in a herder rifle—with casings bigger than the thumb of a large man—rifles were usually not all that effective against the kind of trouble she foreshadowed. Rifles were most useful against sandwolves and, sometimes, against sanders—and necessary, since both would prey on lone nightsheep . . . and especially on ewes and lambs. Rifles were useless against ifrits, but Alucius had never seen one near a stead—not surprising, since he'd only seen two in person in his life, three if he counted the Matrial, and he had not really even seen her.

A soarer above Westridge in the morning, reflected Alucius, was so infrequent that he almost wanted to turn back to the stead to tell Wendra about it. But what could he tell his wife, except that a soarer had appeared, then vanished without a word or gesture?

Outside of the Iron Valleys, soarers—and even sanders—had already become a myth for most of Corus, one told in tales that included the Myrmidons and alectors of the long-vanished Duarchy—the millennium recalled by most of Corus as one of peace and prosperity. Both the duration of that reign and the prosperity and fairness of the Duarchy had been lies and exaggerations of the cruelest sort, as Alucius had discovered in his battles as a Northern Guard officer, but since he had no way to prove what he had discovered—except by revealing his Talent in a world that feared and mistrusted it—the lie lived on, a comforting tale of a golden past. Some folk—especially the savants from Tempre—said the soarers were never there at all, that they were but mirages created by light and the fine, mirror-like dust worn off the quartz ridges that lined the natural parapets of the Aerlal Plateau by the endless winds. Alucius knew better. So did any of the double handful of nightsheep herders around Iron Stem.

Alucius nodded as he glanced back at his flock. Two of the nightrams edged toward each other. Their curled black horns—knife-sharp on the front edges, and strong enough to bend a sabre—glittered in the morning sun. Red eyes shone out of black faces, and the black wool that was tougher than thick leather, more valuable than gold, and covered their two-yard-long bodies and broad shoulders, gave them a massive and menacing appearance. A nightram could gut a single sandwolf, although the sandwolves were even larger, with crystal fangs more than a handspan in length, but the sandwolves hunted in packs and tried to pick off ewes and lambs, or older and weaker nightrams who strayed from the flock.

One of the nightrams pawed the ground, and Alucius could sense the antagonism between the two males. He eased the big gray gelding forward, reaching out with his Talent to project disapproval and separation. Both of the black-wooled rams looked up. Alucius could sense their frustration, but they separated. Herding nightsheep was a chancy life, and impossible, often fatal, if the herder didn't have the Talent to make his feelings known.

Alucius was fortunate to bear within him that Talent— more than fortunate, for the life of a herder suited him. That he also knew. With his crooked smile, he let his impatience flow out, spreading across the flock, chivvying the animals eastward. They needed to graze on the lands near the Aerlal Plateau—the nearer the better—if their wool were to be prime.

The nightram's black undercoat was softer than duck down, cooler than linen in summer, and warmer than sheep's wool in winter, but stronger than iron wire once it was shorn and processed into nightsilk. The wool of the outer coat was used for jackets stronger and more flexible—and far lighter—than plate mail. Under pressure, the fabric stiffened to a hardness beyond steel, hard enough to serve as armor of sorts, although its comparative thinness meant that bruises to the body so shielded were not uncommon—as Alucius well knew from his personal experience in the militia, then the Northern Guard.

The wool from the yearlings or the ewes was equally soft, but not as strong under duress, and was used for the garments of the lady-gentry of such cities as Borlan, Tempre, Krost, and Southgate. Nightsheep could make a herder a comfortable living in Iron Stem, if they and their predators didn't kill him first.

Alucius urged the gray eastward across the ground where little grew except the quarasote bushes, on whose tender new stalks the nightsheep fed. After a year's growth, the lower shoots of the bushes toughened, and after two, not even a maul-axe with a knife-sharp blade on the axe side could cut through the toughened bark, and the finger-long thorns that grew in the third year could slice through any boot leather. In its fourth year, each bush flowered with tiny silver-green blossoms. The blossoms became seed-pods that exploded across the sandy wastes in the chill of winter, and then the bush died, leaving behind dead stalks that contained too much silica to burn or to break or cut. Yet they too succumbed to the wasteland, and to the shell-beetles that devoured them. That was the harsh way of the lands beneath the Plateau and the reason why few liked Iron Stem, even those living there.

Some complained about the wind, the way it blew hard and hot through the summer and cold and bitingly dry through the winter. Some said that each wind was different and none were to be trusted. Others complained about the dryness, because little but quarasote and an occasional juniper grew in the Iron Valleys.

The same people complained that in winter there was no heat in the sun except where it struck the eternastones of the high road that ran from Eastice in the far north down through Soulend and Iron Stem and then Dekhron, and across the River Vedra, and far into the south of Lanachrona. There were other high roads, too, and while they had been traveled heavily in the days of the Duarchy, most times now only a handful of traders or travelers could be found on any of them.

Some thirty vingts to the east stood the mighty Aerlal Plateau, whose stone ramparts ran straight upward six thousand yards or more. All who had tried to climb the Plateau failed long before they reached the top. Most vanished, their bones occasionally discovered by Alucius or some other herder.

In the last years of the Duarchy, the Duarches had dumped the malcontents and worse in Iron Stem to work the iron mines and great mill, guarded by the Cadmians with their lightning-shaped blades. Later, after the Cata-

clysm and the fall of the Duarchy, the mines played out
over the millennia, and Iron Stem withered from a small
city into a small and struggling town. Then, for a long time,
all that sustained Iron Stem had been the herders from the
north, the lumber mills in Wesrigg, and the dustcat works.
There Gortal's scutters gathered the dustcat dander and
processed it into the dreamdust, which was worth more
than nightsilk in the Lanachronan cities of the south—and
far more even than that for the little that traveled the ancient roads back to Lustrea in the east.

His concentration returned to the lead nightram, even as
he wondered why the soarer had seemed to look at him and
whether Wendra had sensed the winged marvel. With a
rueful smile, he shook his head and urged the gray to catch
up to the lead rams, his eyes checking the bushes and the
hummocks for traces of wolves. Sanders left neither tracks
nor traces.

As Alucius's mount carried him eastward, his eyes
flicked back toward the long ridge that separated him from
his stead—and from Wendra. After more than three years
of marriage, skilled and Talented as Wendra was, Alucius
still fretted about leaving her.

3

Dekhron, Iron Valleys

The two men were seated in wooden armchairs before a desk in a study. On the serving table between the two were tall beakers of ale, half-full. The
summer sun beat through the glass of the closed windows,
but both men wore heavy tunics and trousers.

"I worry about the herder, still," observed the round-
faced trader in the blue tunic trimmed in dark gray. His
voice was so low that no one more than a fraction of a yard

away could have heard the words. "Have you followed him, Tarolt?"

"He returned to his stead two years ago. He has built up his flock and devoted himself to his wife and family. Has he once shown an interest in what lies beyond his stead and Iron Stem?" replied the older-looking man, his words equally muted.

"No, but he destroyed the Matrial, as well as Aellyan Edyss and more than ten pteridons. Then he traveled the Tables and killed one of ours, and came back and obliterated the Table in Tempre—although it was close to failing, in any case. And after that, he single-handedly killed more than twenty bravos who tried to ambush him. With the four hundred golds that cost . . ."

"They were only coins, Halanat, and a pittance compared to what we have gathered and will gather." The white-haired man smiled coldly. "I do believe he got the message. It took him nearly a month to recover from that, and he has, as you noted so well, scarcely looked beyond his own stead in almost two years. In that time, we have accomplished much. We have a working group here, and a new and fully functioning Table now in Salaan. We have assisted the Regent of the Matrial in finding informers, although she knows it not. We have more and more true believers, or, if you will, followers of the True Duarchy. Adarat will soon strike the first blow in the south. These followers will grow and create the necessary distraction and dissension all across Corus, all in places well away from where we operate. And we have also made a healthy profit in dealing with Adarat. Before long we will even control the Regent of the Matrial. With all that, we will be able to build more Tables and translate more true Efrans, and this world will once more be ours, as it should have been for the past millennium."

"What if the herder discovers what we have accomplished? It took much lifeforce to wrench the Table into place in Salaan, and we have not solidified . . ."

"When he has not been south of Iron Stem in two years?

That was one reason why we ensured that his wife's father is now receiving orders for his barrels. They're better and cheaper than those our traders can get here, and they will keep the herder's wife from pushing him into looking beyond their own needs. Besides, who would call us to his attention? Especially with all the other problems arising in Corus?" Tarolt's laugh carried an ironic tone.

"The older ones, the hidden ones. Or the side effects of the translations. Or sheer ill chance."

"There are few of the hidden ones, and fewer every year. In less than a handful of years, all will be gone." Tarolt frowned. "As for the translation effects . . . there is little we can do about those, would that we could, for each is a failed translation. There is always the likelihood that one will find him, because they are drawn to Talent. Still . . . he has seen sanders and soarers and sandwolves, and it may be that, even if he sees such, he will not draw the right conclusion. Or that he will wait. Remember . . . he is a man who will do what is necessary—but not unless he is forced to act. That is his greatest weakness. All we need do is to ensure that he is not forced to act. That is one reason why we have avoided . . . activities . . . near the herder steads."

"Can we continue to keep him from acting?" asked Halanat. "Especially if there are more and more wild translations around him? We must have more support from Efra. And with him that close to the Plateau and with that meddler Kustyl . . . ?"

"Kustyl could be removed."

"That would force the herder to act. Kustyl is his wife's grandsire."

Tarolt shook his head. "You make your point. Removing Kustyl would merely alert the herder. I think you have something else in mind. Exactly what?"

Halanat smiled. "The Lord-Protector is getting more and more concerned about the state of Lanachrona. The Regent of the Matrial is retaking the southernmost towns bordering Southgate. Now . . . matters are unsettled in Deforya, and it will be a season at most before the Landarch is top-

pled . . . Waleryn could suggest to the Lord-Protector that
a most able commander would be able to put down the revolt in Hyalt. A particular and most able commander."

"Why would we send him against what we are building
there? That makes little sense."

"You know that it is not important whether Adarat and
the Duarchists succeed in the coming revolt against the
rule of the Lord-Protector. What is important is the amount
of destruction and disruption there. Sensat shadow-
matched Adarat when he traveled there last year, and
Adarat is convinced that he is of Efra. He does not believe
he can be bested by any Corean steer, even a Talent-steer."

"What of it?" asked Tarolt.

"The Lord-Protector will think he is facing a local revolt. The Regent will see an opportunity to weaken
Lanachrona, and between Adarat and the herder, there will
be more disruptions . . ."

"That would put the herder overcaptain well out of the
Iron Valleys and would reduce the chance of his seeing too
much because he will be far too involved in trying to put
down the revolt, as well as worrying about his wife? That
far south, even should the ancient ones try to reach him,
they would not be able to, few and failing as they are."
Tarolt frowned. "But the Lord-Protector would scarce listen to Lord Waleryn, and if he did, he would hesitate to believe him. If he knew that Waleryn was no longer his
brother, but a shadow-Efran, he would never believe
Waleryn at all."

"He does not know that and never will. Waleryn can ensure that dispatches and information reach Marshal
Frynkel and Marshal Alyniat. He can suggest to them that
the Lord-Protector request the overcaptain—as a majer—
take command of the forces to put down the revolt in Hyalt.
The overcaptain is known to be able to do much with little,
and that will appeal to Marshal Wyerl."

"You don't want Waleryn talking to Wyerl, do you?"

"I do not wish Waleryn to spend much time with any of
the marshals, but he should not meet with Wyerl at all.

Wyerl sees too much," Halanat replied. "It is also likely
that the overcaptain will meet with the marshals. We would
not wish him to perceive any . . . influence, but especially
with Wyerl."

"You think the herder overcaptain is that perceptive?"

"More so, I fear, but if he meets with the marshals and
sees nothing . . ."

"He will not see our influence." Tarolt nodded. "There is
also a good chance he will not be able to surmount Adarat,
but if he does, the disruption will only benefit us, and by
then . . . it will be too late for him to change what must be.
And if he fails, then we have fewer worries."

"Exactly."

4

When Alucius began to herd the flock back
down Westridge, the sun was almost touching the quarasote flats to the west, its green-gold glare backlighting the
stone-walled and slate-roofed buildings of the stead so that
the walls looked almost gray, rather than reddish, and the
roofs black, rather than the dark gray they truly were. With
his Talent, Alucius could sense the web of lifethreads, the
thin black-gray lines of the nightsheep, the yellow-gold of
his mount, and the scattered thin threads that were grayjays
and scrats. With a nod affirming that there were no disruptions in that web of life, Alucius began moving the flock
toward the main shed.

He finished settling the nightsheep into the shed for the
night, having closed and bolted the shed door, then stabled
the gray. In the second stall, he was finishing grooming the
gray in the gloom that was no hindrance, not when herders
could see almost as well in low light or night as in full sunlight. At that moment, Wendra slipped into the stable.

"How was your day?" he asked, sensing the vital green

lifethread of her presence even before she stepped into sight at the end of the stall.

"The spinnerets jammed twice. I only lost about a yard of thread that couldn't be reprocessed. Your mother checked them. They may last for the summer, but we'll need another set of the control valves before harvest. If we'd known . . ."

"You could have had Grandsire order them while he was in town?"

Wendra nodded.

Alucius stepped out of the stall, closed the half door, and hugged his wife for a long moment, feeling the slight bulge of her abdomen as he did. "It's always good to see you. I'll be glad when the spinning's done and you can come out on the stead with me."

"There's still the looming," she pointed out after they released each other. "And I don't know how much longer I can ride for a full day."

"Another season, according to Mother, and I can tell if there's a problem." He laughed. "So can you, remember? And you can certainly take a day from looming now and again. The fresh air would be good for the two of you. I know you can't leave the spinning. The thread's got to be watched all the time." He paused as he waited for her to step outside the stable. Then he closed and fastened the door. "How are we doing on the solvents?"

"We should have enough for this year."

"You're letting—"

"Your mother won't let me near them, or even in the processing rooms."

"Good," Alucius said firmly, taking her arm.

They walked toward the east-facing porch of the stead dwelling. Alucius looked eastward toward the Aerial Plateau, watching as the crystals on its high west rim caught the rays of the setting sun. Directly above the crystals of the Plateau, almost lost in their radiance, was the small green point of light that was Asterta, the moon of the ancient horse goddess—or the moon of misery. Selena, the larger moon, had not yet risen.

"Where up there do you think the hidden city is?" Wendra asked.

"It's somewhere along the western edge, but it could be as far south as the part near Emal or as far north as opposite Soulend—or even Eastice. It was cold there, but that could have been because it's so much higher."

"That's hard to believe," Wendra mused.

It was almost as hard for Alucius, and he'd been the one trapped there, recovering after nearly being killed by the ifrits, then being taught by the soarers, so that he could understand and use his Talent to greater effect. "It is, until . . ."

"I know." She squeezed his hand.

"What's for supper?"

"Leftovers. We made a fowl casserole from what was left from last night."

"You didn't let her put—"

Wendra laughed. "There's no prickle in it. Plenty of other leftovers, but not prickle."

"Thank you."

"I'll remember that."

They made their way up the steps to the porch and to the north door, and then to the washroom. Alucius used the hand pump to fill the basin for Wendra, then washed up when she left to finish helping his mother. He glanced in the mirror, the reflection showing his silver-gray eyes flecked with green and the dark gray hair that had been his from birth.

By the time he was washed up, everyone else was seated at the table, and Alucius hurried to sit down.

"Which of you two?" asked Lucenda, looking at her son and then at Wendra.

"Wendra," suggested Alucius.

Wendra grinned ruefully at her husband, giving a slight shake to her head that shivered her lustrous brown hair.

The four bowed their heads.

Wendra spoke clearly. "In the name of the One Who Was, Is, and Will Be, we thank you for what we have, and

for what we have received, and for this food before us. May
this blessing fall upon both the deserving and the unde-
serving, and may both strive to do good in the world and
beyond . . ."

Once she had finished the blessing, Wendra stood and began serving the fowl casserole onto the platters, handing
them out, first to Royalt, then Lucenda, Alucius, and herself.

"The bread's fresh baked," Lucenda offered. "Wendra
said there ought to be something that wasn't a leftover."

"There wasn't enough for supper, anyway." The younger
woman's eyes sparkled as she looked at Royalt.

"Was hungry when I got back from town," grumped Alucius's grandsire. "Long hot ride. Hadn't had anything to
eat since breakfast."

"He did get a half barrel of southern rice," Lucenda said.
"That will help this winter."

"And some of the hard green apples that keep," added
Wendra.

"Ferrat had the replacement shear plates ready. Cost two
golds for each." Royalt shook his head. "Last time was
only a gold."

"That was almost four years ago," Lucenda pointed out.

"Prices shouldn't double in four years. Kustyl was
telling me that a bunch of growers near-on killed a usurer
down in Dekhron. Not the one who's one of Mairee's
cousins, but another fellow. One who clips coins before
lending them."

"That sounds like Ceannon," remarked Lucenda.

"Was him, now that I recall," said Royalt. "Never even
had to worry about usurers before. This union with
Lanachrona . . . was supposed to keep tariffs and prices
down."

"One out of two isn't bad," suggested Lucenda. "The
Lord-Protector has kept our tariffs low."

"That was because of Alucius, wasn't it?" asked Wendra
innocently.

Alucius knew the question wasn't innocent, but a gentle
reminder.

Royalt laughed. "She sure sticks up for you, Alucius."

"Who better?" Alucius grinned, but the grin faded. "You think most prices are up that much?"

"Lot of 'em," Royalt said. "Not too bad for us. Yet. Nightsilk futures are getting close to twenty-five golds a yard."

That was nearly double the highest prices of two years before, as Alucius recalled.

"That's fine for us," Lucenda pointed out, "but what about for people like Kyrial?" She glanced at Wendra.

"It's been hard for Father. Korcler told me that when he loaded the half barrels last week. Coopers don't have people coming from Tempre and Borlan to buy their barrels. Korcler did say that Father had someone who was inquiring, though." She paused. "If it weren't for Mother's sewing . . ."

Alucius nodded. He and Wendra had slipped some golds to Clerynda—Wendra's mother—but with the price of solvents and machinery and equipment rising, there was a limit to what they could do—and might be able to do in the future.

"Don't see why all this is happening," Royalt said. "No wars, no fighting. Been a little dry the past two years, but we've seen worse."

"Little things adding up?" asked Alucius.

"Could be," admitted the older man. "Kustyl said that tin ingots were double what they used to be—have to get those from Lustrea—and the purple dyes from Dramuria are way up, too. Kustyl thinks something strange is going on with the traders in Dekhron."

"Grandpa Kustyl always worries about Dekhron," Wendra pointed out.

"That's because there's a lot to worry about," said Alucius. "If not with the traders, then with Colonel Weslyn."

"You've never liked Weslyn, have you?" asked Royalt.

"Not really."

"Kustyl's not even that kind to him," replied Royalt. "Calls him a sneak. Says he smiles to your face and then poisons your ale. Always thought he was behind Clyon's death."

"I don't think he had anything to do with it, except indirectly," Alucius replied. "He's too much of a coward. Someone else had Clyon poisoned once Weslyn became the deputy commander because they knew Weslyn wouldn't do anything to upset anyone—especially the traders."

"That'd make sense. That way, no one could challenge him because he wasn't involved in Clyon's death. Then, if someone else had been deputy commander . . ."

"The militia had Dysar before him. You think he would have been any better?"

Royalt shook his head. "Traders like Ostar owned Dysar fleece and horns. Same way they do Weslyn."

"Didn't something happen to Ostar?"

"He died, like a lot of traders in the past couple of years—fires, illnesses, something like seven or eight. Ostar was one of 'em. In fact, most of those who liked Dysar are dead. They liked Weslyn, too. That's what Kustyl and I can't reckon."

"Is there anyone left?"

"Of the older ones? Tarolt, I think, and his nephew Halanat. Halanat's more like the age of Kyrial, though."

"You know either?"

"Only by name. Kustyl said he met Halanat years back. Didn't like him then. Didn't see any reason to see him again."

Alucius laughed.

"Can we stop talking about how corrupt Dekhron is?" asked Lucenda. "We can't do much about it tonight. There's still half a pie left from last night." Without waiting for an answer, she began to cut slices until she had cut the remaining apple pie into four equal sections, then passed them out on the smaller plates.

After a mouthful of the pie, Wendra looked up. "Grandpa Kustyl stopped by today."

Alucius took a swallow of ale, then grinned. "He stops by more now than he used to."

"He wants to make sure his granddaughter is taking care of herself," Lucenda said. "He's still surprised that she turned out to be a true herder."

"And now he's watching me like a prize ewe," Wendra added. "All of you were the ones who saw I was a herder. Not him."

"It was Alucius," Royalt said. "Told me to take you out on the stead."

"I'm glad I did," Alucius said.

"Don't take too much credit," Lucenda suggested.

Rather than answer that, Alucius took another bite of pie.

"You see the soarer again?" asked Royalt after a moment.

"I only saw her that one time, a week back," Alucius said.

"Used to look forward to seeing them. Now . . . don't know as I do," replied the older man. "Wouldn't want to see them gone, though. Don't see as many sanders, either."

"There's a connection there," Alucius observed.

"You keep saying that," Lucenda said, "but you've never said what it is."

"That's because—as I also keep saying—I don't know. There are a few things I don't know."

"That's good to hear," Royalt quipped dryly. "Beginning to think you're taking yourself too serious-like."

Alucius flushed.

5

The Duarchy lasted twice five hundred years, and for all those ages its eternastone high roads crossed Corus from north to south and east to west, saving only the Aerlal Plateau and the Anvils of Hel. Great carriages slipped along the roads, drawn by the tireless sandoxes. The traders' wagons followed, also pulled by sandoxes, filled with goods of every imaginable type—black night-silk from the north of Eastice, smoothed lorken planks from Hafin and Fola, the sparkling and still wines of Vyan, and the tapestries of far and fair Alustre.

The Myrmidons of Duality swept through the skies on their pteridons, carrying messages and dispatches from one end of Corus to the other, searching out rogue soarers and dispatching them to keep the skies and the ground beneath those skies safe for all. The Alectors of Justice reigned over each city, town, and hamlet, and kept the peace so that each man, each woman, and all children could walk every lane and road, every grove and grotto, and never fear for their safety. The Cadmians used their lightning-jagged blades against the barbarians of the isles and against lesser wrongdoers. The dolphin ships of the Duadmiralty kept the oceans and the coasts free from strife, piracy, and depredations.

The sun shined out of a silver-green sky and blessed the Duarchy and all its peoples under the dual scepters.

Then . . . in less than an instant, the Cataclysm struck Corus, and, in a season or less, the sandoxes sickened and vanished. The pteridons shriveled into less than dust and vanished. The rivers ran red with blood. Ice flowed from the skies. The air that had been so fair, and perfumed, became as thin and as acrid as vinegar. Streams dried in their beds, rivers in their courses, never to flow again.

Winds swept from the Aerlal Plateau with such force that all the trees to the south of the Black Cliffs were felled in a single afternoon and buried, leaving but the Moors of Yesterday. The vales of prosperity became the Sloughs of Despondency.

Fair Elcien, the western capital, sank a hundred yards into the Bright Bay, leaving but the tips of the towers above the mud that covered all. Warm and lively Ludar, the southern capital, vanished beneath the waters in an instant, and none living there were ever seen again, nor were any of the walls and towers and parks . . .

Excerpt from:
Mantra of Mourning

6

On Duadi, Wendra drove the team to Iron Stem while Alucius sat in the wagon seat beside her, watching the high road and the quarasote flats beside it. The heavy rifle was in the holder beside him. Whenever he saw the gray eternastones of the road, he had to marvel, and wonder, at the magic technology of the ancients—or the ifrits—that had created those stones, which were harder than almost any substance and which, if scarred, repaired themselves over time.

"You're thinking about the road, aren't you?" asked Wendra with a smile.

"Because I always do? There's something about it."

"It's alive, in a way, I think," she replied.

"You've never said that before."

"I hadn't thought about it."

What would make a road alive? He thought about the great high roads, especially the one through the Upper Spine Mountains into Deforya, where the ancients had cut through the very rocks of the mountains and formed a perfectly straight and unnatural canyon to carry the high road. Abruptly, he wanted to kick himself, or pound his head. It was just that he'd never considered the thought that the high road might have a form of life. But once he realized that, and what the soarer had taught him, the rest fit.

"You're upset—or worried," Wendra said. "I can feel it."

"You remember how I told you about how dead some of the lands were, especially in Deforya? That's where they have the great long high road, and that canyon—"

"Oh!" Wendra's hand went to her mouth. "You think that they—"

"I couldn't prove it, but I'd wager that the ifrits sucked the very life out of the land and poured it into the road.

They couldn't do it everywhere, or even very many places, but I'd wager that, if we looked, we'd find patches and places along the sides of the high roads that are still dead, or once were dead and still have only a little life."

"They'd do that?"

"What do you think?" Alucius gestured to the ancient spire of the tower ahead, its brilliant green stone facing visible over the low hills from several vingts to the north. "How else could they create structures that held together for so long? If you look at the high roads at night with Talent, you can see the glow. I just didn't think of them in that way." He should have, but who would have thought that anyone would squander lifeforces that way—or had that ability?

"Why would you?" asked Wendra. "We don't think that way."

Alucius just shook his head, wondering what else that obvious he had missed. He also still worried about the appearance of the soarer.

Before long, past several low rises, the warrens of the long wooden sheds of the dustcat works appeared on the east side of the road, sheds all sealed to the outside so that the dustcat dander, worth more than its weight in gems for the sensations it provided, could not escape.

"Have you ever seen Alyna?" asked Alucius.

"No. I still can't believe she agreed to be a scutter. She seemed brighter than that. Even the pleasure palace would be better than working the dustcats for Gortal. But she knew better." Wendra sighed. "How anyone . . ." Her words died away.

After passing the dustcat works, Wendra guided the wagon along the road toward the empty green stone tower and the lower building just south of it. The tower walls had remained intact, seemingly pristine and untouched, not by choice, since building materials were rare in Iron Stem, but because the ancients—rather the ifrits, Alucius knew—had used a lost technique to bond all the exterior stones together, a technique resistant to chisels, mauls, hammers, and even those with the Talent. Whether the interior had not been so protected or whether it had always been empty, Alucius did not know, only that similar towers rose all across Corus, all with vacant interiors, even without steps or interior levels. What remained of the tower was a hollow shell that rose, uselessly, nearly a hundred yards into the silver-green sky.

The pleasure palace, dubbed such generations before, was a low stone structure. The long-dead builders, some centuries back, had attempted to create a pattern in the walls by alternating those stones with the bonded blue finish with those of green. Unfortunately, after five courses of stone, they had run out of the green-faced building stones and had then used interior stones faced with yellow to alternate with the blue stones. Where the stones had come from, no one alive knew. Over the years that had followed, the yellow had faded into a sickly and uneven beige, but the blue and green had not.

As early as it was in the morning, the hitching rail outside the pleasure palace had no mounts tethered there, and the palace itself was still. Wendra drove the wagon past the empty vingt or more separating the pleasure palace from the nearest dwellings straight into Iron Stem, and then past the metal shop and its thundering hammermill, with the smell of hot iron drifting across the road and thin white smoke rising from the forge chimney.

The buildings surrounding the central square were all of two and three stories, and although mainly boarding-houses, were moderately well kept, if one ignored the peeling paint on shutters and doors. On the west side of the square were the cooper's, the chandlery, the silversmith's. On the adjoining corner was the inn, its blue-painted sign an outline of the long-vanished mining mill.

Wendra eased the team up to her father's cooperage, and Alucius jumped down and tied the horses to the post just short of the loading dock. Then the two of them entered the building, stepping into the mixed odors of oils, varnishes, and wood.

"Wendra! Alucius!" exclaimed Kyrial, beaming at his daughter. "It's good to see you both. I'd thought Lucenda might be the one picking up the barrels."

"Grandsire and Mother were kind enough to let us drive in together and handle the buying," Alucius explained.

Clerynda burst from the back room, bustling toward her daughter. "Wendra! Let me see you!"

Wendra flushed. "I'm fine."

"I know you are. You have that glow. I do hope he's a boy."

"She's a girl," Alucius said, "and she'll be a herder like her mother."

For a moment, Clerynda was silent. Then she smiled and shook her head. "Herders. You take all the surprise out of it."

Kyrial just grinned. "I wouldn't say that. The two of them just come up with different surprises."

"You look pleased, Father," observed Wendra, clearly trying to change the subject.

Kyrial smiled at his daughter. "And well I should be, Wendra, after the order I received yesterday. Fifty of the best oak barrels. Fifty!"

"Who could order that many?"

"A fellow acting as a broker for a group of traders in Dekhron. Came up with half the cost in hard golds."

"Your reputation is finally spreading, Father," offered Wendra.

"Does that mean you'll be delayed in getting us the solvent barrels?" Alucius's tone was humorous.

"Sanders, no. Yours are almost done, and your family has been my steadiest customer for years. The traders aren't asking for the first group for another two weeks, and Korcler's become a great help." Kyrial glanced at the youth who was half inside an oaken barrel, deftly using a curved plane to touch up the inside of the staves.

Korcler extricated himself and smiled sheepishly. "Sorry, Wendra. I just was afraid I'd lose track of where I was if I didn't finish."

"That's all right."

"The five full barrels are ready. They're the ones by the loading door," Kyrial said. "We'll have the half barrels and quarter barrels ready by a week from Quattri."

"Might as well get them into the wagon." Alucius turned.

"I'll help," offered Korcler. "Wendra shouldn't—"

"I'm not made of porcelain," Wendra replied. "Not for another season or two, anyway."

In the end, Korcler, Alucius, and Wendra loaded the wagon.

After the barrels were roped in place, Alucius and Wendra walked back toward the square to see what produce might be available. After they bought what they could find, they would need to drive out to the miller's.

As they walked away from the cooperage, Wendra said, "Father was pleased."

"I can see why," Alucius said. "Has he ever had such an order?"

"Not that I know, not in at least five years, and possibly ten."

"You were keeping the books before we were married, and you saw all the records?"

"Most of them. Sometimes, I'd check back to see how Mother had written in sales, especially if it happened to be something I hadn't seen." Wendra looked to Alucius. "You're worried, aren't you?"

"I shouldn't be, but I am. I can't help but wonder why he got such an order now. It could be a coincidence, I suppose."

"You don't think so."

"No. But I have no reason to think otherwise," Alucius admitted. After a moment, he smiled. "Let's see if they have any of the late peaches. Grandsire would like those."

"And you wouldn't at all?"

Alucius flushed, then shrugged helplessly.

Wendra leaned toward him and kissed him on the cheek.

7

Hieron, Madrien

The unclad redheaded woman looked at the circle of goldenstone floor tiles, ringed with black. Within the circle was a misty column—its pinkish purple barely visible. The gold-and-black circle stood out starkly against the muted green tiles of the rest of the bedchamber floor.

She took a deep breath. Then, convulsively, she took one step, and another, to place herself in the center of the black-tiled circle, forcing herself through an unseen barrier. Immediately, her entire body twisted, as if being pummeled by unseen blows. Welts appeared on her pale, freckled skin, then bruises. Her breath came in gasps, but she remained within the circle for a time, her limbs lifted and turned like a marionette's.

A good quarter glass passed before she forced her way from the circle, where she stood, slumped, breathing rapidly, outside the black tile line.

Even before she slowly walked to the dressing room, the bruises that had covered her skin began to fade—as did the freckles. By the time she stopped before the full-length mirror and took in her reflection, her skin was close to alabaster white and unmarked. Her formerly blue eyes were a bluish violet, and her red hair had darkened to a deep mahogany that was more like red-tinged black.

A cold and triumphant smile crossed her lips. "It worked," she murmured. "The old tablets were right. Regent in name only from now on."

Stepping away from the mirror, she began to don the clothing she had laid out earlier, ending with the violet tunic and trousers, the black boots, and, last, the emerald necklace.

8

Alucius stood in the shadows beside a long purple hanging draped from a stone pillar that was golden throughout—not merely gilded. Overhead, at least fifty yards above, arched a ceiling of pink marble, so precisely fitted that even his Talent could detect no sign of a join or of mortar. The same pink marble comprised the walls. Stretching a hundred yards to his right, the floor of the hall was of octagonal sections of polished gold and green marble, each section of green marble inset with an eight-pointed star of golden marble, the narrow arms of the star outlined in a thin line of brilliant metal that was neither gold nor brass.

A man stood on the dais, a tall figure with flawless alabaster skin, shimmering black hair, and deep violet eyes. He wore a tunic of brilliant green, trimmed in a deep purple, with matching trousers. His black boots were so highly polished that they appeared metallic.

Two smaller figures—a man and a woman—stood before him as he spoke. They looked like children in comparison to him, though neither was short.

Alucius listened.

"You understand nothing. More than two thousand years have passed since we departed, and you have built nothing that rivals what we left. Even with the dual scepters we left, and the libraries and the Tables, you have learned nothing. You squabble among yourselves like spoiled children. All around you were wonders, and from them you have only found ways to squander your lives."

The man lifted his head and spoke, but Alucius could not hear his words.

The ifrit in green laughed, long, melodiously, then shook his head. "There is no such thing as inherent 'right' or justice among all the worlds of the universe. The universe does not care. Its rules reward survival—and power. If you would have what you call justice, you must have the strength and the will to create it and to enforce it."

The woman spoke, and again Alucius could not hear the words.

The ifrit smiled, condescendingly, before replying. "We create grandeur and beauty, and grace. We create peerless art where there was none before. Out of mud and squalor we build such as you see. There is a price for everything. A world can live forever and be nothing—or it can become a paragon of splendor and art—and shine in brilliance for a shorter time."

The man said a few words.

"You had the chances, and you did not take them. You, like all your kind, squandered what you were given. It takes more than luck and pedestrian skill to bring your will to bear, to change what is degradation and squalor into valor and splendor. That is especially true in a world of petty and jealous men. You had the choice between being the child of the Duarchy, the one who would restore it, or the lamaial. You chose neither path, and that is a choice to do nothing . . . and nothing accomplishes nothing . . ."

Then, the great hall began to spin, and the walls began to move, closing in . . . tighter . . . and tighter . . .

Alucius sat up in the double-width bed, shivering, sweating profusely. After a moment, he blotted his steaming face.

Wendra put her hand on his shoulder. "It was only a dream. Only a dream."

"It was one of *those* dreams," Alucius said hoarsely. "One where an ifrit was explaining how we—I—had failed. I haven't had one of those . . . not since . . . the hidden city, and before."

"It was only a dream . . ." But Wendra's voice did not hold certainty.

9

Alucius and Wendra rode downhill, eastward into the gray of a late summer morning before dawn, a grayness that would soon be flooded with the golden green sun of dawn against a silver-green sky. To the west, the half-disc of Selena was paling as the sky lightened. Asterta had long since set. The flock had not spread that much so far, and that meant that, for the moment, they could ride close to each other. Before long there would be nightrams investigating away from the flock, and ewes and younger nightsheep browsing and straggling, while the farther they traveled from the stead, the greater was the likelihood of sandwolves and sanders.

Alucius looked at Wendra and couldn't help smiling.

She turned. "I like it when you look at me that way."

"I'm glad." Then, he'd looked at her that way for years, ever since he'd seen her serving ale and punch at a gathering on the porch of her grandsire's stead.

They rode for another hundred yards before Alucius guided his gray closer to Wendra's chestnut. "You know how I talked about doing something to the cartridges we used against the wild pteridons," Alucius said. "I mean when I was coming back from Deforya."

"You told me," Wendra replied. "We'd talked about it, and how the soarer had showed me something like that. You haven't talked about that in over a year. Why do you bring it up now? Was it the dream?"

"The last time I had dreams like that was before I ran into the ifrits."

"You think they might reappear?"

"I don't know. If they do, or if we see wild Talent-creatures . . . I wanted to make sure you knew how to fight them off."

"I already did . . . remember?"

"I know," he said. "But . . . I'm worried. I should have gone over it with you before. That way I'd know, and it would be something I wouldn't fret about as much." Alucius frowned, then continued, "When I think about it, it bothers me, though."

"Because we're using lifeforce?"

"Yes. It doesn't take that much, and we can draw a little from everywhere. At least, I think—I hope—that's what I did."

"Show me. I'll watch." Wendra glanced forward at the flock, then back at Alucius.

Alucius extracted a cartridge from the Northern Guard belt he had taken out that morning—for the first time in years. He held up the cartridge. Then he began to infuse it with the same kind of darkness that had brought down the pteridons so many years before. Once he felt that the cartridge was charged, he leaned toward Wendra and handed it to her.

She studied it, then handed it back. "It didn't seem to take much."

He passed a second cartridge to her. "You try."

Wendra took the cartridge. Seemingly effortlessly, she eased the darkness of lifeforce into the bullet, even making sure that none was wasted in the area of casing and powder.

"Have you been practicing that?"

"Me?" The corners of her mouth quirked. "Only a few times."

Alucius shook his head. "I didn't need to worry about that."

"I'm glad that you worry. I just don't want you to worry too much."

He laughed. "You're very good at salving my pride."

She grinned. "You're good at recognizing it."

Alucius couldn't help but smile in return, even as he hoped that she wouldn't need the skill with the cartridges anytime soon. Unhappily, he had the feeling that was a vain hope.

The slightest frown crossed his brow.

"Did I do something wrong?" asked Wendra.

"No. I was just wondering. About the darkness. I'm drawing it. So are you."

"Do you feel that we're taking it from something living? Can you tell if there's any lifeforce missing from around us?" asked Wendra.

Alucius studied the area around them and around the flock. He could not feel any difference. Then, he worked on infusing the cartridge in the rifle's firing chamber with the lifeforce darkness, trying to sense from where he was drawing that darkness.

"It's coming from everywhere, a little bit from everywhere," observed Wendra. "I'll try it again, and you watch."

As Wendra charged another cartridge, Alucius observed.

"From what I can feel," he said, "you're right."

"So that means you shouldn't worry. Not too much. I'd wager that some of that lifeforce regenerates itself within a few days, just like we do when we work hard and get tired, then sleep and eat and feel better."

Alucius glanced at the lead nightram, but the flock had not spread too much. He looked back, but the trailing ewes weren't straggling that much, not yet. "But the Talent-creatures sucked it right out of everything. Or they seemed to."

"Could that be because they're not from Corus? They're not linked to the land the way we are, or the way anything that grows here is."

"It must be." Her suggestion made sense, and he couldn't think of a better explanation. That also might be why there were so few ifrits. But the soarer had suggested that there had once been far more, hundreds of them, if not thousands.

Alucius shivered at the thought of ifrits and the wild Talent-creatures from elsewhere sucking the very life out of Corus. Yet . . . at the moment, what could he do? He didn't even know if there would be more of the creatures appearing in Corus . . . or where that might happen. There was certainly no reason for them to appear on the stead, not that he knew of.

"You look worried."

"I was just thinking about the ifrits. Not that there's anything we can do now." He looked forward, then stood in the stirrups. "One of the young rams has headed off. You want to check the stragglers?"

"I'll take care of them."

Alucius eased the gray forward. Talk of ifrits and Talent-force would have to wait.

10

Tempre, Lanachrona

The warm golden light of late afternoon poured through the west-facing window of the Southern Guard headquarters building. Three men sat around a modest circular table. The bare tabletop was inlaid with the design of a plumapple flower, and the single central pedestal leg was of aged and golden oak. The two older men wore the blue-and-cream uniforms of the Southern Guard.

The third man, younger and stockier, wore a maroon tunic cut conservatively, trimmed in black. His dark hair was smoothed back from his pale white face, and his brown eyes looked from one officer to the other. "I had heard that there has been . . . some unrest in Hyalt. When I heard that, I requested a few moments with you."

The blond marshal raised his eyebrows. "You seemed to know of the . . . unrest in Hyalt nearly as soon as we did, Lord Waleryn."

"I have my sources, Marshal."

"And what would you have of us?" asked the darker

marshal, his right eye twitching twice. "Congratulations on those sources?"

"Congratulations on mere competence, Marshal Frynkel? That would be vain, would it not?" Waleryn smiled ruefully. "No . . . you can believe it or not, but I am concerned about Lanachrona. That is why I asked to see you both."

Neither marshal bothered to conceal a look of disbelief.

Waleryn laughed. "You see? Now . . . if you most worthy officers have that view of my concerns, how then would my brother the Lord-Protector feel about what I am about to say? Assuming that he would even grant me an audience?"

"Under the circumstances, perhaps we should hear your words first," suggested Alyniat. "If you would care to enlighten us?" The fingers of his left hand tapped slowly on the wood of the conference table.

"My brother is far more noble than I am. All know that. At times, he might even be too noble." Waleryn shook his head. "I am not going to suggest anything ignoble. I do know that your forces are hard-pressed, and that the Northern Guard can offer little help to the Southern Guard. Nor will increased recruiting or conscription provide sufficient lancers and foot, not in time to deal with the unrest in Hyalt. Nor are there any mercenaries trustworthy enough to hire, even were there coins enough to pay them. Is this not true?"

"Generally," admitted Alyniat, "but should you repeat that, under the circumstances, we will deny such."

"I am not playing with words, worthy Marshals. I do not intend to use words to wound or to cause my brother or Lanachrona trouble. It has occurred to me that there is a way to deal with the unrest in Hyalt that will not weaken our forces defending Southgate and the southwest or those charged with defending Harmony."

"Oh?" Frynkel's single word expressed great doubt. The tic in his right eye twitched again.

Alyniat did not bother to speak, but his finger tapping slowed.

"My brother would not think of such, and you will see why when I explain. You may recall a certain overcaptain of the Northern Guard . . . the one who defeated ten thousand nomad barbarians with but five companies, taking over command when all above him perished?"

"Overcaptain Alucius? The Lord-Protector released him from duty in gratitude. He cannot be called back."

"What you say is absolutely correct, Marshal. But . . . what if he were *requested* to return to duty? As a favor to the Lord-Protector. Perhaps promoted to majer."

"Why would he do that?"

Waleryn smiled. "Because . . . if the Southern Guard must deal with Hyalt, the defenses of Lanachrona against the Regent of the Matrial will be weakened. Already, the Northern Guard is hard-pressed. There are not enough young men left in the Iron Valleys for more companies to be raised, not without weakening the merchants and crafters and breaking the promises the Lord-Protector has made. Now . . . I am not suggesting that the Lord-Protector break those promises. That would be most unwise, for many reasons. But surely, someone could suggest to the herder overcaptain that the Lord-Protector faces an impossible situation . . ."

Alyniat looked to Frynkel. The junior marshal nodded slightly.

"All we can say, Lord Waleryn," Alyniat said, "is that we will consider your suggestion. If upon consideration we find it has merit, we will bring it to the attention of Marshal Wyerl."

Waleryn bowed. "That is all that I could ask, Marshals, and all I sought. I trust you understand why I brought it to you. I wanted the idea considered on its merits, not upon whether it was good or bad because of its source."

"We will consider it," Alyniat repeated.

After another bow, Waleryn turned and departed.

"What do you think?" Alyniat asked after the door to the study had closed behind the departing lord.

"I worry about his sources. I would that we knew who they are."

"You think they're the ones supplying information to the Regent of the Matrial?"

"They might be. They might not be. We don't know." Frynkel shrugged. He placed the edge of his palm against his right eye for a long moment. "And Waleryn makes a crooked road look direct. That's true. But . . . he's right about our situation. If anything, it is more difficult than he has said."

Alyniat glanced toward the window and the sun low in the west. "The other thing is that Overcaptain Alucius is known to be not only an excellent commander, but one who can train lancers well and quickly. We could perhaps include some partly trained companies in his force . . ."

"You'd have to give him his own company back. Under him, that is."

"They'd probably be happy to serve under him."

"But would he agree to serve? Even as a majer?"

"He's not stupid. If his choice is to protect the Iron Valleys by serving or let them fall to the Regent, after what he's been through, he'll agree. He may not like it, but he will."

"What about the Lord-Protector? How do we convince him?"

"We don't have to." Alyniat laughed. "Wyerl has to. We just have to give Wyerl the reasons to present to the Lord-Protector."

Frynkel laughed as well, but there was an ironic bitterness in the sound.

11

   After the trip that Alucius and Wendra had made into Iron Stem, another week passed, ten long days on the stead, and Tridi dawned gray and colder than normal, more like late harvest or even fall, with gray clouds swirling in from the north, racing straight south from the Ice Sands and the Moors of Yesterday, clouds filled with water thrown as spray against the Black Cliffs of Despair and picked up by the winds. Only once had Wendra ridden out with Alucius, and the end of summer and the beginning of harvest loomed less than two weeks away.

As Alucius rode the gelding away from the stead and to the northeast up the long and gentle slope of Westridge, he found it hard to believe that more than two weeks had passed since he had seen the soarer. He had also not seen or sensed any signs of sanders, and, according to Kustyl, neither had anyone else.

Not only was he worried about what the soarer meant, but also about the dream he had had. While he did not trust anything about the ifrits, the words of the dream bothered him. Had he squandered time when he should have been doing something? But what? He couldn't very well have ridden across all Corus, using his Talent to see if people were ifrit-possessed. He had neither the time nor the golds to try such. It was not as though he possessed one of the ancient Tables, even had he dared to risk its dangers.

Because stormy weather sometimes emboldened the sandwolves, Alucius had taken two rifles with him, using the double saddle case he hadn't used more than a handful of times since he'd left the Northern Guard. He hoped he didn't have to use the rifles, but he'd rather carry them than worry because he hadn't brought them.

Once more, he studied the Plateau, then the lower hills to the north. So far, the wind was little more than a mild breeze, but the dark clouds moving in from the north suggested that before long that would change. Still, it was summer, and he couldn't afford not to graze the night-sheep, not when they needed the quarasote to produce premium nightsilk.

The wind continued mild, even after he had the flock on the eastern downslope of Westridge and headed due east through the section that had not been grazed for nearly a month. He kept the flock moving until they had covered another four vingts from the eastern edge of the long, low ridge. All the time, Alucius checked the clouds—and the wind—both with his senses and his Talent.

The flock had not been grazing the more recent, if not fresh, quarasote shoots for more than half a glass when the lead nightram lifted his head. Alucius could feel the animal's apprehension and eased the gelding forward. The gray picked his path carefully through the widely spaced quarasote bushes. While the shoots were flexible enough, the spikes at the base of those shoots could rip through hide and flesh.

Another nightram raised his head, as did several ewes. The subordinate males eased forward, shoulder to shoulder, to stand beside the leader, ready to lower their horns. The ewes edged in behind the rams, nudging the lambs to the center.

A gust of colder wind swept in from the north, then died away, but the calm lasted for only a few long moments before the chill gusts resumed, and the sky continued to darken as the clouds massed overhead and thickened.

Should he have turned back? Usually, Alucius could sense storms as violent as this one promised to be. Had he misjudged the incoming weather because of his concerns? Or was it just a Talent-spawned freak storm?

A low, almost bugling call issued from the lead ram.

Alucius could feel the presence of the sandwolves, the grayish violet rising from the south, as solid to his Talent as the wind upon his face. He turned the gray southward, toward the rear of the flock. A sudden gust of wind swirled gritty dust at the herder, but Alucius eased the gelding onward, back toward the stragglers at the rear. He slipped out the top rifle and cocked it as he continued to survey the land to the south and east.

Behind the swirling dust and grit, more than a half vingt to the east, the shifting shadows that were the sandwolves edged through the quarasote bushes as if it were twilight or dawn rather than just midmorning. Their long, crystal fangs glittered, even though there was no direct light.

Stop! Alucius threw the command out toward the nearing pack.

Several of the animals seemed to shiver, and one whimpered, dropping flat beside the silvered leaves of a third-year quarasote.

The pack leader slowed, but continued to move toward the flock. After a moment, the others followed, if more cautiously.

Danger! Stop!

Alucius could sense a whimper somewhere, as if his order had caused pain, but the pack, eight animals in all, continued to close on the nightsheep.

A young ram appeared, interposing himself between one of the flanking sandwolves and a ewe, and, without even pawing the ground, charged the sandwolf. Caught off guard by the unexpected move, the sandwolf—a younger animal than the pack leader—tried to dodge, but he was too slow, and the razored black horns of the nightram slashed deeply into his chest. The sandwolf staggered, and his legs collapsed.

In the moment of silence, Alucius lifted the rifle, sighting in on the pack leader.

Crack! The bullet slammed into the lead wolf's chest.

Crack! The second shot took another sandwolf, and Alucius recocked the rifle and aimed toward the next most visible stalker. *Crack!*

The third sandwolf dropped, then rolled and tried to struggle to its feet.

A wave of hatred, bloodlust, rage, fear—all those feelings and more—surged around the herder. The gray gelding sidestepped, then *whuffed,* then took a step back.

A long howl rose from somewhere, and Alucius could feel the pack stopping, if reluctantly.

"Easy there . . . easy . . ." Alucius had already recocked the rifle.

Abruptly, dark forms were flowing through the quarasote bushes—toward Alucius and his flock. Shapes like sanders, but not sanders. Talent-tinged shapes, shadowed in unseen purple and blue and without lifethreads.

Alucius paused just long enough to cast darkness around the remaining cartridges in his magazine before firing twice more. Each of the dark sanderlike figures he hit burst into the all-consuming blue flame he had seen only twice before—in Deforya and when leaving it.

He switched rifles and, infusing another set of cartridges with the darkness of life, quickly emptied the second. There remained only a single dark sander, which charged toward Alucius.

The herder jammed the rifle into the holder right-handed and drew the sabre with his left. As he leaned forward, he extended Talent around the blade, a darkness of green and gold, and slashed.

The shock of impact was as though he had struck stone, and his entire arm vibrated.

The dark sander seemed to shrivel.

Alucius urged the gray past the shrinking pillar of darkness, quickly enough that the blast of heat from the fire that followed only warmed him.

As the fires vanished, leaving only an oily residue on the sandy red soil, Alucius checked the flock over. One ewe—the last straggler—lay dead. So did the young sandwolf that had been caught by the younger nightram.

Alucius wondered if the younger ram had been one of Lamb's offspring.

He turned his eyes back to the ewe's body, caught by the sudden stench rising and drifting toward him. The corpse began to decompose, turning putrid even as he watched. Then, the body flared into a blue-tinged flame, and soon all that was left was oily black residue.

Alucius turned the gray, heading back toward the front of the flock, and scanned the quarasote flats with his Talent and his eyes. He could detect nothing. Even the sandwolves had slithered away—uncharacteristically leaving behind the bodies of those Alucius and the nightram had slain. He glanced down at the black crystal of the silver-framed herder's wristguard, but the wristband was neither warmer nor colder than usual. He had to wonder if Wendra had felt anything through the ring she wore that was attuned to his wristguard.

Thunder rolled overhead, and the sky darkened even more. Tiny needlelike droplets of rain began to fall, slashing out of the lowering clouds almost horizontally. Alucius squinted against the rain, wishing he had foreseen the violence of the storm.

The herder glanced from side to side, squinting through the wind and rain that had already begun to die away. Above him, the once-dark clouds were thinning rapidly, revealing a clear silver-green sky.

Alucius continued to study the ground, then the bushes stretching to the southeast, with a side glance at the low wash where the wolves had vanished, and reloaded the first rifle, then the second.

In all his years of herding, he'd never seen anything close to what had just occurred. Not in herding—only in the battles against the pteridons of Aellyan Edyss and the Talent-creatures that had attacked his forces in leaving Deforya.

He moistened his lips.

The attack made no sense whatsoever. If the ifrits were beginning another assault on Corus, why would they attack him? Why would they alert one of the few herders with true Talent to their actions? Or was the assault so far along that they could not control the appearance of the Talent-creatures?

Alucius didn't want to leave the stead. He didn't know where he could go to stop such an attack, and there wasn't anyone to whom he could turn for help—except his family—and for them all to leave the stead would likely ruin them all. He and Wendra might be able to leave . . . if they knew where to go—and what to do. Except Wendra was pregnant, and Alucius hated the thought of asking her to go anywhere into even greater danger.

Above him, the sky continued to clear.

Alucius looked to the east, to the Aerlal Plateau, but he neither saw nor felt the green radiance of a soarer . . . or anything else out of the ordinary.

12

Tempre, Lanachrona

The Lord-Protector looked down on the infant in the high-sided crib, sleeping peacefully. A smile crossed his face, and the lines in his forehead eased as he watched his son. Silently, he eased out of the nursery and back to the main sitting room, where his consort waited, seated at her writing desk.

"He's sleeping," he said.

"I told you he was sleeping." Alerya's voice was firm, but musical. "You're worrying a great deal. About your brother, still? Or the Regent of the Matrial? Or about this little revolt in Hyalt? Or is it something else?"

"About everything. Wouldn't you? Waleryn was plotting with Enyll, and he pleaded illness to avoid speaking with me for almost two months after the overcaptain killed Enyll and destroyed the Table. Waleryn still avoids me whenever he can. With the Table destroyed, no longer can I see what is happening as it does or nearly immediately. I've been reduced to receiving written reports weeks and months after events have taken place. Most of the time, it's too late to do anything. Half of what I write, it seems, finds its way to the Regent. Then, there's this revolt in Hyalt. It may be small so far, but there was no warning, and unless I do something, it will just get worse. There seem to be more of these True Duarchists everywhere. I've heard that there's another group in the hills east of Syan, but no one knows exactly where. And where am I going to find the forces to put down the trouble in Hyalt? Or Syan, if it spreads? If I take any companies from around Southgate, the Regent could retake Southgate. Yet I know nothing until it's too late."

"You miss the knowledge of the Table, don't you? And you have begun to doubt what the overcaptain told you."

"I don't doubt what he said. Or what he did. But why is it that the most useful tools are always the most dangerous? I know that Enyll would have killed us."

"Do you, Talryn? Or are you saying that to convince yourself?"

The Lord-Protector sighed. "Both, I guess. Without the Table, and with this revolt, and against the crystal spear-throwers of Madrien—how they managed to build two, I don't know—we're going to have to come to terms that aren't ideal—and quickly. Unless . . ." He shook his head.

"Unless what?"

"Wyerl suggested that I *request* that Overcaptain Alucius return to the Northern Guard. Make him a majer, at least. With one of his former companies and several partly trained companies of Southern Guards, he could handle the revolt."

"Why would he do that?" asked Alerya. "He wanted to go back to being a herder."

"Well . . . if I have to shift lancers to Hyalt, the Northern Guard is already having trouble holding its ground in the north . . ."

"Talryn! That's blackmail."

"It's true, though. I can't raise any more lancers in the Iron Valleys. Nor that many more in the rest of Lanachrona. We've conscripted everyone that we can. I'd be hard-pressed to pay for mercenaries, even if I could find any I could trust. What am I supposed to do?"

"Do you honestly think that the Regent of the Matrial—"

"Yes. We are stretched too thin, and it's not just Madrien. It's everything. The Dramurans attacked one of our vessels porting at Southgate. I just got that dispatch this morning. This afternoon I found out that the landowners of Deforya have overthrown the Landarch and replaced him with a Council of Five. They've decided to increase the road tariffs to Lustrea by half again. The Landarch was too accommodating to the needs of others, this new Council claims. What they meant was that they don't want to pay for anything themselves and keep tariffing others and oppressing all their people as they have for generations. The battles between the nomads of Ongelya and Illegea make the southern high road unsafe. That leaves the high road through Deforya and the Northern Pass, and so we're back to where we were two years ago. That means higher tariffs here. But . . . if I don't do something, we'll lose even more, just on the wine trade to the east. If we want safe trade that isn't tariffed to excess, I'll have to invade Deforya and make it part of Lanachrona. And where will I find the lancers and foot for that when I can't even find enough to hold Southgate without losing Hyalt?"

"Then . . . you must do what you must. But be generous to the overcaptain. Offer him something beyond rank." Alerya tilted her head. "Appeal to him, and offer gratitude, honor, and a stipend to his family in his absence. Pay for the stipend yourself."

Talryn laughed softly. "You are as bad as I must be."

"We all do what we must." Alerya stood.

Talryn raised his eyebrows.

"You have decided. Can you do anything more this evening?"

"No." Talryn smiled sheepishly.

"Then we should enjoy the supper Feylish has prepared. Mother also sent some of the better amber wine from the cellars."

"A good supper would help . . ."

13

Finally, the looming was mostly finished, and, on Duadi of the second week of harvest, Wendra rode out with Alucius and the flock. After the episode with the dark sanders, Alucius had taken not only to bringing two rifles but wearing his Northern Guard ammunition belt at all times while away from the stead buildings. So far, he had not had to use even one rifle, so quiet had the stead been. But that worried him as much as more sandwolf attacks would have.

Still, he enjoyed having Wendra out with him, especially on a warm and sunny day with just enough of a breeze that the sun wasn't too hot. At the same time, he had a nagging worry. After his previous experience with the strange sander, did he have any right to ask Wendra to come out with him?

"You're thinking about those dark creatures, aren't you?" called Wendra.

"I worry about whether you should be out here," he admitted.

"I've been worried about you every time you've taken the flock out alone," she countered. "When you ran into the dark sanders, my ring didn't even show that you were in trouble."

"I wasn't," he replied. "That's why you didn't feel anything."

"It's still safer with two herders."

She was right, Alucius knew, but he couldn't help worrying about her.

By midmorning, they were a good ten vingts east of the stead, and they had let the flock slow and browse its way eastward.

"How do you feel?" Alucius called across the fifty yards separating him from Wendra.

"I feel fine. It's wonderful to be out here." A smile followed Wendra's words. "It's too bad I can't come out tomorrow."

"You're going to stay at the stead and handle the last of the looming?"

"Your mother and grandsire want to go into town. They haven't been off the stead in weeks. How could I say no?"

"Knowing you, you couldn't." Alucius laughed.

After another glass, the nightsheep began to spread, and Alucius and Wendra chivvied them back into order and urged them farther eastward, toward another area where the quarasote was more dense, not that it was all that dense anywhere, but where the bushes were merely a yard or so apart as opposed to three or four.

As the nightsheep settled into grazing once more, Alucius frowned. He could feel something—almost a sense of sadness, of sorrow—that wavered at the edge of his Talent-senses. Then it was gone.

He eased the gray back toward the rear of the flock, where he urged two laggard ewes forward until they were almost up with the others, then circled back toward Wendra, letting the nightsheep graze what new quarasote shoots there were.

After another half glass, they eased the nightsheep farther east, because Alucius didn't want the quarasote overgrazed.

As he rode slowly eastward in the general direction of the Plateau, Alucius could feel the sense of sorrow growing stronger. He hadn't felt anything like that since he'd left Dereka two years earlier. He wondered. Did the feeling have anything to do with his dreams—or the earlier attack of the dark sanders?

While he had not had any vivid dreams like the one with the ifrit, he continued to have fragments of dreams—regular dreams—with the alabaster-skinned men and women dominating them, and all of them chided him for his failures to understand their right to dominance and cataloged his own shortcomings.

He looked across the flock to Wendra, then waved.

She smiled, and the expression warmed him—but only for a moment, as a sudden wave of sorrow—and then one of all too familiar purpleness—swept over him.

"Wendra!" Alucius called out. "Get your rifle, and use darkness on the cartridges. Something's coming!"

He urged the gray toward his wife, hurrying as fast as he could around the spikes of the quarasote, not wanting to injure his mount, but wanting to get closer to her.

"Do you know what it is?"

"Something else like the dark sanders," Alucius said as he reined up a yard from Wendra, where he checked his own rifles. Then he began to infuse the cartridges in each rifle with the same kind of darkness that had brought down the pteridons so many years before—and the dark sanders weeks before. He could only hope that it would work as well this time for whatever might appear. Once he felt that each bullet was so charged, he began to scan the skies and the quarasote flats for the evil purpleness that seemed ready to burst forth from somewhere.

"I can feel something out there," murmured Wendra.

The chill darkness that was overlaid with purpleness grew more and more and more oppressive as they waited— an unseen wall of stone, an avalanche of disaster, waiting to fall and sweep them away. Yet . . . what else could they do but wait, ready to act? They didn't know from where the attack might come—or if an attack would even come. Retreating in ignorance before a Talent-foe was worse than waiting.

"It feels evil, like an icy purple," murmured Wendra. "What do you think is coming?"

"I'd guess something flying, like wild pteridons, but it could be sandoxes—or something we've never seen."

With a sudden *snap,* the silver-green of the very sky itself flexed—and somehow opened—and flying blue shapes appeared less than fifty yards to the northeast of the pair. The ten-odd creatures circling in the air were purplish pteridons, smaller than those once used by the nomads and without riders. The metallic blue talons that extended from their forelegs glinted, knife-sharp.

"Start firing, now!" Alucius lifted his heavy rifle and put his first shot through the chest of the lead pteridon. The Talent-predator fluttered once, then cartwheeled out of the sky.

Wendra's rifle *crack*ed, once, twice, a third time, before a pteridon spun downward into a quarasote bush. Both bush and pteridon burst into flame.

The others began to form into a loose wedge that rose, as if preparatory to diving at the pair of herders. Alucius fired two more shots. The first missed entirely. The second caught the edge of another pteridon, which seemed to shake off the impact.

One of the pteridons ignored the formation and dived at one of the lead nightrams. The ram lifted his head, trying to twist his glittering horns to catch the predator. Both creatures exploded in bluish flame.

Alucius got off two more shots, one of which struck a pteridon, then switched rifles. "As soon as you can," he called to Wendra, "reload!"

The pteridons circled higher, and as he fired twice more, bringing down yet another pteridon, Alucius realized something else. The Talent-creatures had not been specifically hunting them. They'd been startled and surprised, and that might have been what was giving Wendra and him an edge. Still, they were dangerous creatures.

Another of the pteridons swept toward Wendra. Alucius snapped off two quick shots, and the second caught the beast on the edge of the wing. It spiraled toward one of the ewes, impaling itself on the much shorter horns of the ewe, then exploded into a column of blue flame that enveloped both.

Alucius had one cartridge left in his rifle when he realized that the sky was clear. His forehead was covered in

sweat, and he looked toward Wendra. "Some good shooting there, dear."

"Not as good as yours, but I did help, I think."

"More than a little." Alucius reached out with his Talent.
The sense of purpleness was gone, but a residual of the sorrow remained. He frowned. "We'd better check the rest of
the flock."

Wendra nodded.

From what Alucius and Wendra could tell as they circled
the flock, they had lost only the one young ram and a ewe.
While the death of both nightsheep would hurt, the damage
could have been much worse. Except, Alucius reflected,
losing even one nightsheep a week would destroy them just
as surely as a sudden disaster involving all the flock.

There were no traces of any of the wild blue pteridons,
none at all, except for the black greasy splotches on the soil
where each fallen Talent-creature had burned. No charred
scales or bones . . . nothing except the residue of intense
fires.

Alucius could sense another problem—the lack of
something. In the rough circle below where the wild pteridons had appeared, there was no life left. Even the quarasote bushes, although they looked green, were dead and
would be brown in weeks, if not days. And that was the
area from where the feeling of sorrow came.

"It's dead, isn't it?" asked Wendra. "The land around us."

Alucius nodded.

"Why . . . why did it happen here?" she asked. "Is it us?"

"I'd like to say it isn't," he replied, "but it has to be. I
can't see why, unless somehow my fights with the pteridons earlier made it easier for them to find me. But why
now? That was two years ago. And you? They never were
near you."

"It has to be you," Wendra said. "This is the second time
in a month."

"But why now?" Alucius asked again.

They looked at each other. Neither had an answer.

14

Salaan, Lanachrona

The angular man in the dark purple tunic leaned over the Recorder's Table and looked down into the transparent surface, fingerspans thick, yet so deep that the ruby mist through which he peered seemed tens of yards. The Table exuded age, as though it might have been one that remained from the score or more that had once linked the far-flung domains of the Duarchy of Corus. Only the smooth and shimmering finish on the dark lorken sides of the Table suggested that the Table was of more recent creation.

"What do you see?" demanded the round-faced trader in gray and blue.

"Somewhere, on Corus, within the former reaches of the Duarchy, years past, a lamaial was born. It might have been your herder overcaptain."

"You can't tell that? Why not? You said he had Talent."

"You know that well, Halanat. All herders have Talent. That is why they can be herders," replied the white-faced man with the purple-tinged eyes. "That has been known for years. The Table, being constructed with Talent, cannot depict those with such Talent once they have begun to exercise it. You would not want others using it on us, would you? Thus, a Table can record all steers born with the potential for Talent—or for even greater use of Talent, as with a lamaial or a hero—but Enyll never recorded those births except within the Table in Tempre . . ."

"Hero and lamaial—they sound like nonsense," the trader replied. "They're just Talent-steers."

"Ah, yes . . . myths and nonsense, created to maintain a

mystery by Recorders like me, who are translated from Efra merely for that express purpose of being obscure. The Vault was a myth, and so were the pteridons that destroyed the legions of the last Praetor, and so are the Dual Scepters."

The mockery in the Recorder's words was so edged that Halanat's eyes dropped.

The Recorder of Deeds looked up from the crystal mist of the table, purple-tinged eyes unblinkingly fixed on the trader. The mist swirling around the scene held in the Table vanished, and all that remained within the smooth black frame was an ordinary mirror, save that it was far smoother and more reflective than any such mirror produced in recent centuries in Dekhron or Tempre or any other city or town in the whole of Corus.

"All those," continued the Recorder, after a long silence, "have reappeared, save the scepters. For reasons best known to the ancients, there was never a record of where the scepters were placed, not one that we have been able to find, but they are not a myth, and they served a great purpose. As for the lamaial of the Legacy, he will remain concealed until the conflict begins. That is according to the words once carved in the Vault. Whether the ancients carved it as a warning or as a prediction, we cannot know. But you must hold in mind that those with Talent can become more than Talent-steers, and that is something that we—that you—must prevent."

"The Table is useless for that."

"Exactly. That is your job. Or have you forgotten?" The Recorder smiled indulgently.

"No, honored Trezun." The trader started to gnaw on his lip, then stopped and asked, "What about this new Praetor?"

"Young Tyren? You will not need to worry about him. Waleryn will shortly be dispatched to handle him. And to prepare for the next full translation."

"But you can show him in the Table?" The round-faced trader's words were formal, stiff, and barely avoided carrying a chill. After he had spoken, his face became impassive.

The Table came to life once more, with the ruby mist filling the glass, then displayed the image of a fair-haired man, barely out of youth, in shimmering silver and black, striding down a wide corridor flanked with tall goldenstone columns. A silvery nimbus surrounded him.

"The silver around him . . . ?"

"That shows that he could use Talent but has never called upon it."

"What is his Talent? Is it possible to tell?"

The Recorder shrugged. "The Table will not reveal what might be. We hope to avoid his discovering it until Waleryn is there to co-opt him. With the translation and Tyren, we will have two points of power and pressure."

The trader tightened his lips as he leaned forward to study the image displayed by the Table. "Can you tell me where this is?"

"Only from what appears in the Table, Halanat. It would seem to be Alustre, but that is not certain. Still, from the columns and the color of the stone . . ."

"Does your Table say whether he is the hero come at last? Or whether he will claim the Dual Scepters?"

The Recorder of Deeds laughed ironically. "Every human conqueror of the past millennium has claimed to be the hero—or denied it. Some have claimed to carry the scepter, or the Dual Scepters. Others have denied the scepters even existed. In the end, it has made little difference. Claims or no claims, what will be will be."

"That is a fine sentiment for you," said the trader slowly, "but even as a trader I cannot travel all of Corus chasing rumors. If he has something he calls the scepters, that makes matters worse, because the common folk believe that the scepters have some power. Great power, not some drizzle of vision in a mirror. Even belief in the scepters grants power."

"Vision is far from a drizzle of power, as you put it. There is much yet that you do not understand, and for a mere shadow-translation, you presume greatly. As for the people, they would do the same in any case, if it appears that their ruler is indeed powerful. This Tyren could be the hero, but any conqueror could or might be." The Recorder's tone turned colder. "In any case, he is a continent away, and you are not tasked with traveling to Lustrea. Your tasks are closer. The so-called Regent of the Matrial has two of the crystal knife-throwers and is about to take back Southgate and everything north of the Dry Coast. The Lord-Protector has lost his Table and will lose more. You must complete your work in Hyalt and Dekhron before that time comes. It must come sooner rather than later." The Recorder's purple-gray eyes met the dark-rimmed orbs of the trader.

After a moment, Halanat looked away.

15

Wendra and Alucius and Lucenda and Royalt sat around the kitchen table in the late twilight of an early harvest evening.

". . . that both may strive to do good in the world and beyond." Alucius finished the prayer.

Wendra and Lucenda stood and dished out the mutton stew with hot biscuits. Alucius immediately took some of the fresh harvest honey from the pot.

"They never grow up," Lucenda observed to Wendra. "Put honey on the table, and they're small boys again."

"And you're never girls again?" Alucius questioned.

"Never!" replied Wendra, her eyes twinkling.

"You won't win that one, Alucius," Royalt pointed out.

Alucius smiled, silently agreeing with his grandsire.

Royalt lifted his glass of ale and took a swallow. "Tastes good after a long day."

"What did you find out from Kustyl?" asked Lucenda, looking at her father.

"Ever since Alucius had that run-in with the bravos outside of Sudon," Royalt said, "Kustyl's been listening even more carefully."

Alucius nodded. "He said he thought a trader named Halanat was behind it, except that he'd known Halanat years ago, and Halanat wasn't shrewd enough, and that meant someone was directing him. He never could come up with anything."

"And you didn't want to go back to Dekhron," Royalt pointed out.

"No, I didn't," Alucius admitted. "I still don't. That's a legacy I'd rather avoid. The place is like a bucket of tar. You put one finger in, and before you know it you're stuck. I've already had enough of my life disrupted by that sort of thing." He looked at Wendra. "And I'm not too interested in ending up where I'd be forced to put on the uniform again. Especially not now."

"What did Grandpa Kustyl have to say?" asked Wendra gently.

"He had a lot to say." Royalt laughed. "He usually does."

"He's worth listening to," added Lucenda, looking at her son. "What we do here is affected too much by Dekhron— as someone once told me."

Alucius winced inside, but merely smiled.

Wendra glanced at him, and Alucius knew she understood how he felt.

"Well . . ." Royalt dragged out the word. "Kustyl was telling me that the traders in Dekhron have gotten a lot smarter. You know they've been giving those barrel contracts to your father, Wendra?"

The younger woman nodded.

"That's because they went around and checked the quality and prices of every cooper within fifty vingts of Dekhron. He came out the best."

"He is the best," Wendra averred.

"That was your grandfather's point. In his whole life, he's never seen the traders in Dekhron be that smart. They always gave the business to a friend or a cousin. They've been doing the same sort of thing with the rivermen, checking out barge transport rates. But . . . the other thing that's scary is what happened last month. A Lanachronan cloth factor decided to open a place in Dekhron and see if he could bid into the nightsilk trade . . ."

Alucius had a feeling he wouldn't like what was coming.

". . . just before he had the place ready, it caught fire. He died in the blaze. Kustyl started asking around, quietlike. Been five fires like that in the past year and a half."

"Sounds like the traders are getting organized and finding ways to kill people who get in their way," Alucius admitted. "But they've always put golds ahead of people's lives. That's what got us under Lanachronan rule."

Royalt shook his head. "It's not the same. They tried to run Dekhron the way they wanted, and sometimes they wasted golds doing it. They're not doing foolish things anymore, and there's another thing. They've started a co-operative wagon run to Borlan and down the high road to Krost. Maybe farther. Sharing the cost. They're bringing back Vyan Hills wines cheaper, and they're running them out to Dereka once a season."

"If they'd been that smart five years ago—" began Lucenda.

"It wouldn't have worked with the tariffs between the Iron Valleys and Lanachrona," Wendra said. "Father looked into it, because he heard the cost of barrels was so high in Borlan and Salaan. The tariffs cost more than the barrels."

"Kustyl told me one more thing," Royalt said slowly. "Several of the old-line traders—they've died in the past year. Three or them. Died in their sleep. Kustyl said it didn't feel right."

When a herder said something didn't feel right, he was almost always correct, Alucius knew, and Kustyl, old as he was, was certainly a herder who was no one's fool.

"Is someone trying to take over the old traders' council?" asked Lucenda.

"He doesn't know," Royalt admitted. "He just says the whole city feels strange."

Alucius's stomach tightened, but he didn't comment. All too many things were feeling strange around the Iron Valleys.

Royalt finished a large mouthful of stew before glancing at Alucius. "Lucenda said you two took the flock well east. No more creatures?"

"We didn't see or feel anything. Not a hint of anything. Haven't in more than a week. We told you that."

"You did . . . but we've never seen any Talent-creatures here, except soarers and sanders." Royalt frowned, then asked, "How are the shoots there?"

"They're good. Didn't see any sanders or sandwolves," Alucius replied. "We probably ought to take them there more in the next few weeks."

"Good idea, but we'd better have two of us with them." Royalt nodded. "Feel like it's going to be another dry winter. Been too many lately."

"How's the ramlet?" Alucius asked his mother.

"He's doing fine—for a lamb born six months too late to a mother who's got no milk. I'd appreciate it if you'd crush some more of the quartz in the morning, and if you could get it really fine. He can tell the difference."

"I'll take care of it," Alucius offered.

"I'll feed him in the morning," Wendra promised. "You both wanted to get to town early, didn't you?"

"That would help," Lucenda admitted. "The rest of the barrels are supposed to be ready, and that way Royalt and I could get one of them filled with flour at the mill . . ."

Alucius relaxed more as the conversation drifted back to the nightsheep and the stead.

Less than a glass later, after dishes had been done and the nightsheep and stables checked, Alucius closed the bedchamber door and eased off the nightsilk-covered herders' vest, slipping it into place on the clothes rack in the corner.

Wendra sat on the side of the bed and looked up at her husband. "You're worried, aren't you?"

"I am. The last time something started to look this bad, I

ended up spending four years in the militia and Northern Guard."

"You didn't say much about it looking bad," she pointed out. "Not tonight. Why not?"

"You know why, dear one," he said gently. "We have Talent-creatures and soarers showing up. We haven't seen them in years, and some are the kind no one has seen before. Now . . . something strange is happening in Dekhron as well, a different strangeness."

"You think they're connected?"

"I feel they are, but I don't know why."

"And because you don't . . . you think this will all go away?" Wendra asked, again gently.

"No. Things like this don't go away. But I don't have an answer. The last time, when the Matrites invaded, at least we could see the problem. I wasn't all that smart. I was going to save the Iron Valleys and be a hero so that I'd be respected. Well . . . my mother was right. I was a hero of sorts, and the more I did, the more people wanted to kill me. Almost all of my time in the militia and Northern Guard was away from you. I nearly got killed at least five times, and Dysar wanted to have me executed for desertion because I didn't commit suicide after I was wounded and the Matrites captured me. I guess I'm worried, too, because I feel selfish. I'd like to be a herder, a long-lived one, and spend my life with you. I've lost interest in being a hero."

"You couldn't have had this time with me," she said quietly, "not if you hadn't done what you did. We'd all be slaves to those . . . ifrits . . ." She paused. "You think that they might be behind this . . . ?"

"I . . ." Alucius almost said that he didn't know, but there was no point in that, because Wendra's Talent would tell her that he was lying. ". . . I'm worried that they are." He shrugged. "I still have the feeling I should do something, but . . . what? Just running back to Colonel Weslyn and saying there's a problem, and throwing on a uniform . . . what good will that do? Besides, I'm not sure that Weslyn isn't part of the problem. He certainly wouldn't do any-thing to solve it, not if it might cost his trader friends any golds."

"Could you go to Dekhron with Grandpa Kustyl and look around? That might tell you something."

"It might," Alucius conceded, easing off his undertunic. "I could go, if you—"

"No! You have to think . . ." He glanced at her midsec-tion. "I'll go the next time he heads down there. I will. I promise."

"You don't . . ." Then she laughed. "Sometimes it's hard, isn't it?"

"When you don't want to tell the truth? And you know the other person will know you're lying?" he asked.

"Yes . . . it can be."

She rose gracefully, stepped toward Alucius, and put a hand on each cheek, almost cradling his face. "We can't avoid the world forever, dearest."

"How about . . . just for tonight?" Alucius bent down and kissed her.

16

Dekhron, Iron Valleys

The colonel who stood behind the wide desk had broad shoulders, blond hair that was nearly half silver, and fine wrinkles running from the corners of his eyes. Those wrinkles were especially pronounced as he looked at the gilt commission in his hands, one signed and sealed by the Lord-Protector of Lanachrona. After study-ing the document, he cleared his throat gently and looked up at the senior officer in the uniform of a marshal of the Southern Guard. "Sir . . . this is rather . . . expansive."

"Yes, it is. The Lord-Protector is most thorough," replied

Marshal Frynkel. "He finds that there is less confusion that way, Colonel Weslyn."

"He is known for such," temporized Weslyn.

"Why don't you sit down?" suggested the marshal, gesturing to the colonel's chair and seating himself in the wooden straight-backed chair in front of the colonel's desk.

"Ah . . . yes, sir." The colonel laid the document on the desk before him and seated himself.

"The Lord-Protector thought that there should be no confusion, Colonel Weslyn. You have reported that you have been unable to muster more lancers or foot under the conditions set forth by the Lord-Protector, and given the parlous situation facing all of Lanachrona, the Lord-Protector thought that an inspection tour might be the best way to confirm your reports. In order to allay any suspicions by those in southern Lanachrona, you understand." The tic in Frynkel's right eye twitched.

"I understand. Especially since the union has not been that long-standing. The timing was . . . rather unexpected." Weslyn added quickly, "Then, there have been concerns in the north here, as well, about the use of the Northern Guard . . . and the costs."

"I can see that. We all bear costs in troubled times. The commission, as written, is one of those. In other times, it would not have been necessary, and the Lord-Protector would have wished it otherwise, but to send a messenger, then wait for a reply . . . there was not time, not when we expect a winter offensive by the Regent. That was another reason for the powers delegated to me. The Lord-Protector did not wish to have me beholden to messengers if I needed additional authority. That is why the commissions vest me fully with his authority in all matters. All matters," Frynkel repeated the last words.

"Might I ask . . . ?" began the colonel.

"You can ask," replied the marshal with a smile. "As I have said, I am here on an inspection tour. I will be inspecting a number of posts, including this one, the staging post in Wesrigg, and perhaps those in Soulend and on the midroad. I may or may not inspect the ones farther north and west. I may or may not make decisions on postings or use of forces, and I could make some suggestions. All that depends on what I find."

"I can see that, sir."

"I am sure you can."

"You have more than an entire company with you."

"That is true. We would not wish to burden the Northern Guard."

"You are most considerate."

"We have tried not to inconvenience you. At least not any more than necessary." Frynkel smiled once more. "That being the case, I will dispense with the formalities. To begin with, I would like to see the postings of all companies in the Northern Guard, as well as their officers."

"Now?"

"Now." Frynkel leaned back in the chair. "There are a number of matters we can discuss while you have those records gathered."

17

Alucius turned and stood at the railing of the porch, looking eastward, out over Westridge and up at the Aerlal Plateau, looking so close for all that it was a good thirty vingts away. Although the shadow of twilight covered the Iron Valleys, green-tinged light flashed from the crystal escarpments of the western edge of the Plateau.

"It's beautiful," Wendra said from beside her husband, her hand covering his where it rested on the railing.

"Beautiful . . . and sad, in a way," reflected Alucius. "To think that there's a city up there, somewhere, almost deserted, and dying. There might even be more than one, but I'd wager that all the others are completely deserted and dead."

"You don't think it was just that city?"

"No. There was too much sadness deep within the soarer, and no reason to deceive me about that. Also, we see so few soarers, yet they're a part of history and everything else. Why else is there a soarer queen for leschec?"

"Leschec's a game. There's also a sander king, and no one ever thought sanders were smart enough for that."

"Everything else in the game has proved to be real. You've even seen them all."

Wendra tilted her head. "I haven't seen an alector." A faint smile played across her lips.

Alucius shook his head. "I'm safer when I don't make big general statements."

"We all are. But you're right. There are references to alectors in the old histories."

"You've read those?"

"I used to. Grandpa Kustyl has a whole shelf of them. No one else was interested. I didn't tell anyone but him."

Alucius smiled. He'd been married to Wendra for close to five years and known her for more than three before that, and she'd never mentioned the histories. Was marriage like that, always discovering something new? "Did those histories say anything else about the soarers?"

"No. They didn't say anything about soarers or sanders. The writers mentioned the Myrmidons, the alectors, the sandoxes, the pteridons . . . even Cadmians. I always thought that was strange, especially when I was younger. I'd seen soarers and sanders, and they weren't in the books, and the creatures that were in the books were ones I'd never seen."

Alucius squeezed her hand, gently. "Some of the books I read in the quarters' libraries in Madrien said that the soarers were mythical creatures, that they didn't exist. I wondered if that was because they never lived in the south."

"They must like the cold more."

"I don't think they like it where it's warm and damp."

"There couldn't have been very many of them, ever, do you think?" asked Wendra.

"The soarer told me that Corus used to be colder and drier. There were probably more when it was. There had to have been more soarers then than there are now. I got out of the room I was in, and I saw enough to know how empty that city was. They wouldn't have built a city if there weren't enough soarers to live there." But had he seen enough? Or had he only seen what the soarer wanted him to see?

"Did she ever tell you why they were dying off?"

"No . . . only that they were, and that there were very few of them, and that before long there wouldn't be any left."

"They live a long time. So that might be a while."

Abruptly an intense green light—a line narrow as a wand—flared skyward from the Plateau, its width constant, and for a moment, as it lanced toward the small green disc of Asterta, it was brighter than the setting sun had been a fraction of a glass earlier.

"What was that?" asked Wendra.

"I don't know. I've never seen anything like that."

"You think . . . like your grandmother . . . herders?"

"The death of a soarer?" suggested Alucius. "It could be. I don't know why they would commemorate it the same way we do. We want Selena in the sky, but only Asterta is now . . ." He broke off his words, considering what the soarer had told him years before.

"What is it?"

"They helped make us what we are. You could be right. We might be following their example, except for the choice of moon."

"Asterta's green. So are soarers," Wendra pointed out. "Their lifethreads and radiance, anyway."

"I wonder . . ." mused Alucius.

"Maybe all herders are soarer's children. You are."

"So are you," he pointed out.

"Those with Talent, then." Wendra continued to look at the Plateau, but the single line of green light had vanished, and the crystal parapets of the towering Plateau were shrouded in shadow, no longer reflecting the sun.

Alucius also watched, and the porch was silent for a time.

"I wonder." Alucius paused. "The soarer said that we had been brought here by the ifrits. Did I tell you that?"

"No. You mean people? Not us, but people a long time ago?"

"Yes. She said that . . . that we were meant to be like cattle for the ifrits."

"Where did they bring people from?"

"She didn't say. She said so much that was new—I didn't ask. I should have."

"It makes sense," Wendra mused. "The ifrits feed on lifeforce, or they use it."

"That's true."

"What I don't understand is . . . well . . . most people have lifethreads that are brown or tan or amber, except herders. Most herders are black shot with green. You're green. I'm green, but we didn't used to be, did we?"

"No," he admitted. "You were black with flashes of green. I didn't know how to look at myself then, but I'd guess I was, too."

"But we're green now. Why?"

"Because . . . somehow, greater use of Talent turns the lifethread green. That's a guess, but it seems to be true. Herders with more Talent have more green in their lifethreads. Maybe it shows a greater tie to all of Corus. The soarers have been here forever . . . a long time, anyway, and they're green."

"What about the sanders?" Wendra asked.

"I never looked that closely, but I always thought of them as red-violet."

"And the ifrits are purple?"

"Both feed on lifeforce," mused Alucius. "I hadn't thought of it that way." He shook his head once more. "Then, there are a lot of things I didn't think of before I met you." He turned to face her directly, grinning.

"I'm sure you did," Wendra replied, blushing.

"Supper's ready, you two," Lucenda's voice carried out from the kitchen.

"We'll be right there," Alucius promised, taking a last look at the Plateau, wondering what other mysteries lay there, and what else he should have asked the soarer when he had had the chance.

18

Tempre, Lanachrona

As he settled into the chair across from the settee where his consort and wife was seated, the Lord-Protector looked over at the infant at Alerya's breast. He couldn't help but smile. "He's happy."

"Contented, at least. He wasn't so good earlier. Not nearly so good," replied Alerya. "How did your meetings and briefings go?"

"As well as I could expect." Talryn shook his head. "It's hard to drag things out of people when they don't like telling you bad news."

"You're most worried, are you not?"

"More than I'd ever admit to anyone but you, dearest. Nothing seems to be going right. We're close to losing Southgate. The Northern Guard has been pushed back toward Harmony. The traders have already begun to petition me about the higher tariffs being levied by the Deforyan Council. The revolt continues in Hyalt, and some of the believers have been agitating in Syan. The nomads in Ongelya slaughtered a trader's caravan. Then this business with Waleryn. He's always been difficult. You know how he was plotting with Enyll, and with all this going on, I get a note from him saying that he's on his way to Lustrea concealed as a trader, and that I'll be pleased to learn what he has discovered when he returns." Talryn snorted. "I wouldn't be surprised if he was behind half of this and was leaving before I discovered it."

"How could he be?" asked Alerya.

"I don't know. But if it were possible, he would be." Talryn stood and walked to the sideboard, from which he took out a bottle and half filled a goblet. "Would you like some?"

"If you will water it down." Alerya made a face.

"I know, but too much wine . . ." Talryn poured the ruby wine into a second goblet, then added the boiled and cooled water from the crystal decanter. "Here."

"Just set it there, beside me, dear, if you would."

Talryn set his wife's wine on the end table, then, taking his own goblet, seated himself across from her.

"Have you had any word from Frynkel? About the over-captain?" asked Alerya.

"I don't expect word anytime soon. It's a long journey."

"Do you think that the overcaptain will accept your request?"

"I hope so, especially now. I gave Frynkel some latitude in what he could offer."

"Such as?"

"Some terms that might help me a great deal." Talryn smiled, but did not say more.

"You can be . . . difficult, Talryn." Alerya smiled. "But . . . so can I . . . in my own way. Perhaps young Talus needs my company tonight."

"That's . . ."

"Blackmail?" Alerya's smile turned mischievous. "It is indeed."

Talryn began to laugh. After he stopped, he added, with a grin, "I suppose I deserved that."

"You did." She raised her eyebrows. "What terms?"

"Oh . . . Colonel Weslyn has not been exactly effective, and I don't trust him. I suggested that Frynkel offer Alucius the command of the Northern Guard if he is successful in quelling the revolt in Hyalt."

"You are a true schemer, my love." Alerya shook her head. "You know the poor overcaptain—or majer—will have to accept, if only to save his people." She frowned. "You will honor that promise if he succeeds?"

"I'd be pleased to honor it. He'll go off as a majer, and if he's successful, I'll send a full company of Southern Guards back to Dekhron with him, along with his own companies. No one could possibly complain—not too much, anyway—if I promote the greatest hero in Northern Guard history. Besides, he inspires his officers and men, and Weslyn inspires no one, except the conniving traders in Dekhron. Young as Alucius is, he'll be far better than Weslyn."

"And you'd have a much more cooperative Northern Guard? Or at least one better run and more reasonable?"

"Those were my thoughts. 'Better run' would be a great improvement." Talryn's grin broadened. "You did tell me to be generous. I hope you will be."

Alerya burst into laughter.

After a moment, so did Talryn.

19

Late on Octdi afternoon, under high gray clouds, Wendra and Alucius were nearing the eastern base of Westridge, guiding the nightsheep flock back to the stead. Wendra was riding lead, with Alucius bringing up the stragglers. After all of his precautions for the past three days, neither Alucius nor Wendra had seen any sign of any Talent-creatures or even sandwolves. Nor had Royalt on the day he had taken the flock. All they had seen or sensed were grayjays, scrats, and one or two sandsnakes.

Then, Alucius reflected to himself, they had prepared for the Talent-creatures, and usually the worst dangers and difficulties he had encountered were those for which he had not foreseen or prepared. That just seemed to be the way of the world.

"Alucius!" Wendra called back.

He looked toward her, then saw, farther west, his grandsire just below the crest of Westridge, riding downhill and toward them, far more quickly than usual. After several moments, it was clear that the older herder was heading toward Alucius.

Had something happened to his mother? Alucius forced himself to concentrate on moving the stragglers along and up toward the main body of the flock so that he wouldn't have to worry as much about them if he needed to hurry the flock. Other than that, he certainly couldn't do anything about whatever spurred Royalt on until he heard what his grandsire had to say.

As he neared Alucius, Royalt gestured toward Wendra, urging her to join them.

That made sense, because the lead ram was already on the path that led home and to the shelter of the stead barns. If any of the flock faced danger, it would be the stragglers, although most sandwolves were unlikely to attack close to a stead, especially with three herders nearby.

As Royalt neared Alucius and turned his mount to parallel Alucius and the gray, Wendra urged her mount back toward Alucius and Royalt.

"What's wrong?" Alucius asked. "Has something happened at the stead? Has something happened to Mother?"

"No one's hurt. Nothing's broken, but things are looking . . . not so good," Royalt said. "I'd like Wendra to hear what's happened."

Alucius refrained from asking again, although he wondered why Royalt didn't want to say immediately, then tell Wendra when she joined them. Both herders kept moving the stragglers up the slope, waiting until Wendra rode up on the other side of Royalt, so that the older herder rode in the middle.

"What is it?" asked Wendra.

"It's for Alucius, but I thought you both would like a little warning. There's a Southern Guard officer waiting to talk to you, Alucius. Brought more than a whole company of Southern Guards and a couple of Northern Guard scouts. Says he's a marshal. Named Frynkel." Royalt glanced at his grandson. "You know him?"

Alucius's whole body stiffened, and he tried to make his words even, measured. "There is a Marshal Frynkel. Well, he was a submarshal then. I met him. I even had dinner with him and the Lord-Protector's arms-commander. That was Marshal Wyerl. I suppose he still is."

"No . . ." murmured Wendra, so low that Alucius barely heard the word, although her body posture told him as much as that single syllable.

"Worse yet," said Royalt. "I don't like it that they're sending a marshal and one that you know personally, all the way from Lanachrona. Marshals don't ride days or weeks to see herders. Not without the kind of reason I'd rather not hear."

Alucius was sure he didn't want to hear what Frynkel had to say, either, because they wanted something, and it was likely that they thought he would have to accept, whatever it was.

"You have any idea why?" asked the older herder.

"They've got real trouble, I'd guess. But . . . why would they want me?"

"Because you're one of the best troop commanders in the north, and because Weslyn's too stupid to know it."

"He's not too stupid. He knows it. He just doesn't care for me. And the traders who back him don't like herders."

"Same thing. Officer who lets his personal feelings get in the way is second-rate. At best."

"Weslyn's not with him?"

"No. Didn't see any Northern Guard officers."

That meant that the Lord-Protector wanted something, and whatever it was, it was most likely that he didn't want the commander of the Northern Guard to know until afterward. And that would leave Alucius in a very bad position with regard to Weslyn—unless the Lord-Protector wanted

Alucius as an officer in the Southern Guard, and that could be even worse.

The three split up to herd the flock back together for the last vingt or so of the return to the stead, across the crest of Westridge and down the western side. As they came down the western side of the long rise, Alucius could make out the riders drawn up in formation between the house and the stead outbuildings, almost all of them in the blue of the Southern Guard.

When Alucius was but a few hundred yards from the formation, Royalt rode back over toward his grandson. "Wendra and I'll take care of the flock. You might as well see what he wants."

Alucius nodded and turned the gray toward the four riders at the head of the formation. He reined up several yards short of them, then bowed his head slightly. "Marshal Frynkel, it's both a surprise and an honor to see you here."

"Doubtless more a surprise than an honor," replied Frynkel. "I would request a little time alone with you, if you would not mind."

"With your having come so far, I would be happy to grant you whatever time you might need or think necessary." Alucius gestured toward the house. "Your men could stand down. There's more than enough water in the troughs, and the outside pump offers good water for water bottles." He smiled wryly. "I cannot offer to feed everyone, not on such short notice."

"We would appreciate the water." Frynkel looked to the captain mounted beside him. "If you would take care of the watering with all due care, Captain Geragt?"

"Yes, sir."

Alucius guided the gray to the pair of stone posts in front of the steps up to the house, where he dismounted and tied his mount. Frynkel followed without speaking.

Alucius turned toward the porch where Lucenda stood, her face set in an expression that Alucius had seen but once before and had hoped he would not see again.

Frynkel had dismounted and joined Alucius.

Alucius raised his voice slightly. "Marshal Frynkel, this is my mother, Lucenda. Mother, this is Marshal Frynkel. Unless matters have changed, he is one of the senior marshals of all Lanachrona."

Frynkel inclined his head. "I am honored. Your son is the finest battle commander in Corus, and the most honorable officer I have ever had the privilege of knowing."

Frynkel's words did little to remove Alucius's apprehension.

"Your words are kind, Marshal," returned Lucenda. "I will leave you to what must be done." She inclined her head, then turned, leaving the porch.

"Overcaptain Alucius," began Frynkel, "I have been personally asked by the Lord-Protector to convey a request to you."

"Why don't you come on in?" Alucius suggested. "You can tell me inside." He walked up the steps, then held the door for the marshal. After following the senior officer into the foyer, he led the way to the main room.

"Before we begin," the marshal said, "I would ask you to inspect my credentials." He extended a folder. "Please read them carefully."

Alucius took the folder, trying not to focus on the tic in Frynkel's right eye, and concentrated on studying the commission that granted Frynkel the full powers, rights, and privileges of the Lord-Protector himself in the Iron Valleys. The second document was a letter with the Lord-Protector's seal that stated that the marshal had the right and the authority to treat as necessary with, and in a manner befitting the greatest of respect for, one Alucius, former and present overcaptain of the Northern Guard. After a time, the herder handed the folder back. "If you would like to sit . . ."

"Thank you." Frynkel settled into the armchair that had been the favorite of Alucius's grandmother. "Comfortable chair."

"My family's always liked it. Especially my grandmother."

"She had good judgment." Frynkel smiled, leaning forward, his eyes directly on Alucius. "You know that the Lord-Protector owes you a great deal and that he respects you greatly." His eye twitched once.

"He must have a great need, to send you here," Alucius replied.

"He has a request of you. It is a request because he also is a man of his word, and he promised you that he would not call you or order you back to service. But the need is great, and he asked me to tell you what that need is in explaining his request." Frynkel absently smoothed back the few thin strands of black hair remaining in the center of a balding head, then pressed the edge of his palm against his right eye for a moment.

"Please do." Alucius could feel a chill settling over him. Whatever it was, the few Talent-creatures on the stead paled before what was about to happen. What bothered him most was the feeling of directness and honesty within the marshal. *That* was truly frightening.

"You may know that the Regent of the Matrial has constructed a second crystal spear-thrower. That means that there is now one in the northern reaches of Madrien and one in the south . . ."

Alucius had not known that, and he was certain that Frynkel had known he had not.

". . . the Northern Guard is struggling to hold to its gains in northern Madrien. According to Colonel Weslyn, there are few available men who can be conscripted into the Northern Guard."

"From what I know, sir, that is true. Any more conscription would wreak great harm on the Northern Valleys. There are already many crafters without sons, and, while their wives and daughters can carry on now, if too many more are lost there will be too few to pass on their crafts to the children."

Frynkel nodded. "My own inquiries have supported that. Unfortunately, events are proving most unkind. The Landarch of Deforya has been deposed by the great landowners there, and they have established a Council of Five. That Council has doubled tariffs in the east. The warring between Illegea and Ongelya has closed the southern route, and several caravans have been plundered, their traders killed. The Regent of the Matrial has retaken Fola and Dimor and is pressing southward. Somewhat over three weeks ago, a revolt erupted in Hyalt."

"And the Lord-Protector's request?" asked Alucius, dreading the response.

"While we believe that we can hold Southgate with the forces at hand, we cannot transfer more than a company or two to deal with the revolt in Hyalt. We believe that we could transfer but one company from the Northern Guard, and there are two, perhaps three, Southern Guard companies in training that could be spared. Yet, if we transfer more than those . . ." Frynkel spread his hands. "And if we do nothing, the revolt could spread and block the trading roads."

"You haven't said what the Lord-Protector would request," Alucius pointed out.

"He would request your return to duty as a majer in charge of the forces to put down the revolt in Hyalt. The revolt has been fomented by a group that advocates a return of the 'True Duarchy,' whatever that may be. Most merchants and crafters—those that can—have fled and have appealed to the Lord-Protector to restore their lands and town to them."

"I can see what the Lord-Protector would gain," Alucius replied slowly, "and I would be remiss in not appreciating his courtesy in making this a request. Still . . . that asks a great deal, not so much of me, but of my wife and family."

"The Lord-Protector understands that as well. His need is great, but so is his gratitude. He would offer not only the rank and pay of a senior majer, but also a continuing stipend, in addition to your pay, to your wife, equal to your pay, while you serve outside the Iron Valleys. He will pay that personally. He also offers his gratitude."

Alucius nodded. There had to be more. So he waited.

Frynkel leaned forward slightly, his voice lower as he spoke. "He also is deeply concerned about the future of the Northern Guard. Once you are successful in Hyalt, he would be most appreciative if you would become the commander of the Northern Guard."

"Me?"

"You." Frynkel withdrew a narrower envelope from his jacket and extended it. "This is for you."

Alucius took the envelope as though it contained a death sentence, breaking the outer seal and withdrawing the single sheet carefully.

My dear Overcaptain Alucius—
As you may have gathered, the times have become most dangerous for us all, else I would not have sent Marshal Frynkel to tender my request of you to return to service. I know that you would prefer to be a herder. You have made that most clear. I also would prefer that, rather than making this request of you.

Yet . . . we are not always allowed our choices, and the times make requests as well. The Northern Guard is not well served. By accepting my request, you can once more distinguish yourself, and in a rank that will permit no brooking of your becoming commander of the Northern Guard once you complete this mission. This letter, which I suggest you tender to your family for safekeeping, is a written promise of my faith in and gratitude toward you. . . .

The signature was that of Talryn, Lord-Protector of Lanachrona, and from what Alucius recalled from the signatures on his discharge orders, it was indeed the Lord-Protector's.

Alucius lowered the letter, folding it and slipping it back into the envelope. He could not block the shock on his face, not for a moment, and he said nothing until he felt he was more in control. "Matters are that bad?"

"They may be worse since I left Tempre," Frynkel replied. "I cannot imagine how they could have improved."

Did Alucius have a choice? A real one? Not that he could see. Finally, he nodded, and asked, "What company of the Northern Guard?"

"The Fifth, under Overcaptain Feran. That contains what remained of your Twenty-first." After a moment, Frynkel went on, "You would also receive the Lord-Protector's commission as a senior majer in the Southern Guard. That way, none could gainsay your authority over lancers from either north or south."

"That would also subject me to the authority of the Southern Guard," Alucius pointed out.

Frynkel offered a rueful chuckle. "If you accept, you would be subject to such in any case."

"True," Alucius admitted. "Could you tell me more about why this need is so great?"

Frynkel cleared his throat. "The Regent of the Matrial has become even stronger . . ."

As the marshal talked evenly about all the difficulties besetting the Lord-Protector, Alucius listened, but his own thoughts skittered around Frynkel's words as well. Truly, he had not understood fully how much the military situation had changed in Corus in the more than two years since he had left the Northern Guard. Had the ifrits somehow returned and created the changes, adverse as they were, or had human nature just taken its normal course?

His lips turned into a tight and wry smile. Did it matter?

". . . and for all these reasons, the Lord-Protector reluctantly decided to make this request of you. Will you consider such?"

Alucius let the silence drag out. Finally, he spoke. "You believe what you say, and I have found the Lord-Protector to be an honorable man. Only a man blind and deaf would conclude that he had a choice. Since I am neither, I will accept, but I cannot leave for at least a few days."

Alucius heard the faintest gasp from the kitchen—from his mother.

"We had thought that would be so. In any case, I will have to make the arrangements for Fifth Company to be recalled from Wesrigg. As I recall, they were just recently posted there in preparation to support the defenses around Arwyn."

Alucius nodded, waiting to see what else Frynkel had to say.

"Colonel Weslyn will also need to be informed of the Lord-Protector's request and orders, but it will be my pleasure to take care of that." Frynkel smiled coldly. "That will require a certain . . . firmness. But he will not learn of the Lord-Protector's eventual intent. Only the Lord-Protector, Marshal Wyerl, and I—and you—know that or will know it until just before it comes to pass."

Alucius could tell that Frynkel cared little for Colonel Weslyn. He also knew that his accepting the Lord-Protector's request was foolish and dangerous, especially since it would establish him as a rival and an enemy of Weslyn, even if Frynkel did not inform Weslyn about the Lord-Protector's future intentions for the commander of the Northern Guard.

The "request" of the Lord-Protector was intolerable. It didn't help much that the alternative was worse.

20

Alucius stood on the porch, watching as the Southern Guards rode down the lane, back toward Iron Stem, or perhaps to Wesrigg. Wendra and Royalt stood by the corral on the north side of the main sheep shed, watching as the blue-uniformed riders passed them. Absently, Alucius realized that either Wendra or Royalt had taken his gray and stabled and groomed the big gelding.

"Alucius . . ."

He turned to face his mother.

"How could you . . . ?" She looked at her son. "Haven't you done enough already?"

"I don't have any real choice," he replied. "The Northern Guard can't hold out against the Regent of the Matrial without support from the Southern Guard and the Lord-Protector, and they can't provide it."

"Can't . . . or won't?"

"Does it make any difference?" he countered.

"Will it always be this way? Will you always take on what others should do?"

Alucius didn't have an answer, not one that he wanted to voice. He'd answered once before, and it hadn't exactly helped. Instead, he just looked at her levelly.

After a moment, she dropped her eyes.

Silently, as the sun dropped behind the iron-sandy plains and quarasote flats to the west, Alucius and his mother waited and watched as the last of the Southern Guard lancers left the stead and as Royalt and Wendra walked from the corral toward them. No one spoke until all four were gathered on the southern part of the porch, just outside the door to the house.

"What did the marshal want?" asked Royalt.

"The Lord-Protector requested my return to service—as a favor," Alucius replied. "They'll promote me to majer. Senior majer."

"Senior majer? They must want you back a whole lot," said Royalt.

"You said you would, didn't you?" Wendra's voice was soft.

"How could I not accept?" replied Alucius. "If I refused, before long I'd be asked again, less politely, and I would have to fight under even less advantageous conditions . . . and without the support of the Lord-Protector."

"How bad is it?" asked Royalt.

"Worse than any of us thought, even Kustyl. The Regent of the Matrial has rallied the lancers of Madrien and come up with another crystal spear-thrower . . ." As the others listened, Alucius summarized what Marshal Frynkel had told him earlier. ". . . and everywhere there are problems. No one is going to help the Iron Valleys until they've dealt with things closer to their home. I don't like that, but that's the legacy we got from the old Council and the traders in Dekhron, and we have to deal with what is, not what we'd like."

"Always been that way." Royalt shook his head slowly. "Always will be. Too few herders, and no one else cares."

"Not until it affects them, anyway," Alucius pointed out.

"You got another problem," Royalt said. "This revolt in Hyalt. Anyone who puts it down, or tries to, isn't going to be real popular. Especially if you kill a bunch of folks. Maybe, the Lord-Protector—or his folk—have been doing something not real popular there. Could be why he wants an outsider to handle it."

"That's possible," Alucius admitted. Anything was possible. He'd already seen good and bad officers in the Southern Guard, and a few of the bad ones had been every bit as bad as Dysar, who had been the worst Alucius had encountered in the Northern Guard. It was also more than likely that the rebellion had been caused by poor administration or overtariffing. But . . . he'd just have to see.

"Better remember that for every man you kill, two will come forward to avenge him. That's the way those southerners are. Got fire for blood, and not a lot in the way of brains," Royalt said.

There was another long silence.

"I might as well get on with fixing supper. It'll be a bit late." Lucenda looked to Wendra. "I won't need help yet."

"I'll be there in a bit," Wendra replied, as Lucenda slipped through the front door, closing it behind her.

"Need to check the shed," Royalt added. "What with all the commotion, not sure I locked everything tight." He turned and headed down the steps, back toward the outbuildings, leaving Alucius and Wendra alone on the porch.

Wendra looked at Alucius, her golden-flecked green eyes meeting his silver-gray orbs.

After a moment, she said, "I know you have to do this. I could feel it."

"I don't want to," he said, taking her hands in his. "It's just . . ."

". . . that you don't have any choice. You can't fight off the Matrial's lancers by yourself, but if you help the Lord-Protector, you think there's a chance that it won't happen."

"Chance—that's a good way of putting it." Alucius uttered a sound halfway between a laugh and a snort. "I've seen how many lancers Madrien has. I don't know how this new Regent of the Matrial has managed to take over, but she has, and without the support of the Lord-Protector to block the Regent, Madrien can take the Iron Valleys in a season. Every year, we have fewer people and fewer golds . . ." He shook his head.

"Do you think the ifrits have anything to do with things getting so bad?" asked Wendra.

"I can't say. I just don't know."

"What do you *feel?*" she pursued.

"I can't say why, but I feel that they are."

"So do I. I don't want you to go. I know you have to, but . . ." Wendra's eyes were bright.

Alucius glanced at the Plateau, a grayish mass that melded with the gray clouds swirling around and above it. "I wish I knew more."

"We never do."

That was certainly true, he reflected. That had been true his entire life.

"When will you leave?" asked Wendra.

"On Londi. Marshal Frynkel will be taking care of other details."

"Informing the colonel?"

"Among other things." Alucius took the narrow envelope from within the nightsilk jacket he had never shed and handed it to Wendra. "You need to read this. It's from the Lord-Protector."

He stood and waited as she opened the envelope and read the words put to pen there.

Finally, she looked up. "Commander of the Northern Guard? Why?"

"Because things are worse than we know."

She just looked at him. "Will you accept that as well?"

"That's a road I won't reach for a while." He forced a smile. "Anyway, that would mean I would be in Dekhron, and commanders don't undertake the nasty missions."

She raised her eyebrows. "Colonel Weslyn doesn't. Colonel Clyon did. Who was the better commander?"

Alucius concealed a wince. "That road can wait. Anyway, it could be that things in Hyalt won't take that long."

Her laugh was a short bark. "Then what? The Lord-Protector will want something else . . . or you'll be tied up in trying to rebuild the Northern Guard."

"You think I should have refused?" he asked softly.

"No. It wouldn't have been right. I don't know if exactly what you will be doing is right, but I've seen the Talent-creatures, and you can't stay here and pretend they don't exist or that life will go on as before. And even if they aren't involved, Colonel Weslyn is almost as bad in his own way. I just wish you didn't have to be the one to put things right."

"I know, and I could be being sent to the wrong place . . ."

"That could be." Wendra offered a tight smile. "If that is so, then I'll have to do what you would have done."

"There are some more things I need to show you."

She just nodded, then stepped forward and put her arms around him. "You can do that . . . tomorrow."

21

Hieron, Madrien

The Regent sat on the south side of the circular ebony conference table, as had her predecessor the Matrial, with the wide glass windows behind her. The deep violet of her tunic did not quite match her eyes, but the green emerald choker glimmered as if lit from within the gems, setting off her near-alabaster skin. She leaned forward, intently listening to the officer who sat on the far side of the table.

"The Lord-Protector is overextended, especially in the north," the blond marshal said. "We have pushed the Northern Guard back from Arwyn, and we may be able to retake Harmony by winter's end."

"I had thought that was possible."

"For me, Regent, that is difficult to believe. Especially so soon after . . . the disaster. Even with the training plans and the other . . . information you have obtained."

The Regent smiled, an expression both cold and calculating and warm simultaneously. "Gold can bring forth much information, especially if offered to those with greater dreams than their abilities."

"How many . . . in all Lanachrona? Might I ask?"

"Not that many. They are not ones to be noticed. Majers and the like, high enough to know what we need to know and low enough that few would suspect them."

"I still cannot believe—"

"The lamaial vanished," replied the Regent. "We suspect that he was the overcaptain who defeated the barbarians in Deforya, but that is uncertain. What is more certain is that he is no longer in the Northern Guard. Our informants suggest that he has returned to being a herder and has no interest in arms, unless the Iron Valleys are threatened. That is not a mistake we will repeat. Anyone who has ever attacked them without all other threats removed has regretted it most bitterly." The necklace flashed, and she laughed softly, yet with a hard edge to her voice. "Even under the Duarchy, they were the last to submit and the first to rebel, and so it will be again. So . . . we will only push so far as to retake Harmony, and only as you can do so prudently with more limited forces. Can you send more lancers to the south?"

"A few more companies. Some of the auxiliaries as well."

"And the second crystal spear-thrower?"

"You wish me to use it against Southgate? That would pose some risk if the Northern Guard sends additional lancers to its forces."

"Where do you think Colonel Weslyn will find more lancers? The Lord-Protector forbid him to conscript herders, and the traders will protest if he conscripts heavily from their communities."

"So he will not have many reinforcements."

"Exactly." The Regent added, "That will allow you to place the crystal spear-throwers so that both are used against Southgate."

"We can only fire one at a time."

"I know. But if one is on the north side and one on the east . . ."

Marshal Aluyn nodded. "You wish none of the Lord-Protector's troops to escape?"

"As few as possible. Those he does not have cannot return to invade Madrien. The same is true, to a lesser degree, of the Northern Guard."

"You have risked much, Sulythya . . . Regent." Aluyn's eyes flickered to the dark hair of the Regent, hair that had once been far redder and lighter.

"Not so much as I must risk, Aluyn. Marshal. The times are changing, and we must be prepared for those changes."

"Have they changed that much, Regent? Or do we see the change we wish to see?"

"Times will change, Marshal, more than we can imagine. More than we can possibly imagine."

The slightest frown crossed Aluyn's face, then vanished, but she did not respond.

22

In the gray light of the moments just before dawn, Alucius and Wendra walked down from the house to the smaller of the two lambing sheds.

"He's doing much better. It won't be long before he can go with the flock," Wendra said. "I'll have to watch him more, though."

"Don't take him when you have the flock by yourself," Alucius suggested. "Not until he's even stronger. You'll have enough to worry about."

"I'll be careful." Wendra slid the bolt that unlocked the shed.

"That wasn't exactly a promise," Alucius observed.

"No. It wasn't." Wendra grinned. "If you're going to ride off to do what you think is best, then you can't exactly expect me to stay here and do anything but what I think is best. Can you?"

Alucius shook his head ruefully and closed the lambing shed door.

"Now," Wendra said. "What was it that you wanted to show me without your grandsire around?"

"He can't do this."

"And I can?"

"You should be able to. You can sense lifethreads. And lifeforce."

"I know. It's still hard to believe that he can't."

"Most herders can't." So far as Alucius knew, he and Wendra were the only ones who could, but that might have been because the soarers had worked with him and he'd worked with Wendra. It wasn't something that he felt comfortable sharing, except with his wife, and that, too, was a feeling. "This is something . . . I can tell you, and I can show you in a way . . . but there's no way to actually let you practice it."

"You make it sound so mysterious."

"I want you to look at the ramlet there . . . with your Talent. Look at his lifethread, really closely." Alucius concentrated his own Talent so that he could feel the reddish black lifethread of the ramlet who looked up at them from the inside pen. Already, the ramlet had the nubs of horns that would grow into razor-sharp and curled weapons, and his lifethread had thickened and strengthened over the past few weeks so that it was as strong as that of a normal ramlet—except that he'd been born out of season, and that meant a hard winter for him.

"What about it?"

"Can you see all the little threads?"

Wendra frowned. "Little threads?"

"The main lifethread is made up of smaller threads, and they're all twisted together. There's a thicker spot, just out from the body, and it's, well, usually right out from where an umbilical cord would be."

"I can feel, sort of see, really, the thicker spot."

"That's a lifethread node. If you form a kind of life-force probe, like the darkness, except it has to be more green—"

"Like this?"

A wavery greenish black probe appeared, reaching out from Wendra.

Alucius blocked it with a shield.

"Why—"

"Because," Alucius said quickly, "if you had touched that node with it, you could have severed his lifethread and killed him."

"You can *kill* that way?"

"Oh . . . yes." Alucius paused. "It's very exhausting, though. That was what I had to do against the Recorder of Deeds in Tempre, the one that the ifrit took over, and I was so tired that I could barely move. Doing too much that way could kill you. It almost did me. Bullets are better for most things, especially for Talent-creatures."

"Then why do you want me to learn this?"

"Because bullets don't always work against the ifrits. The other thing, what I was trying to tell you, is that they can also block the kind of probe that you tried if you just use it like a knife or a spear. Like I just did, except they're stronger. What you can do is use it to unravel the lifethreads at the node, because the threads are made up of smaller threads, and those are made of even smaller ones."

Wendra shivered. "They could do it to us, then?"

"I suppose so—except they never tried." Alucius frowned, trying to recall his encounters with the ifrits. No . . . they had never tried to unravel his lifethread—only to squeeze it or slash it. "They might not know how . . . or maybe they never had to worry about that."

"I'd wager on the second," Wendra replied.

So did Alucius. He cleared his throat. "That's it. I mean . . . that's what I wanted to show you and what I wanted you to know. I'd thought about it earlier, but, well, it didn't seem like you'd need it. I didn't need to use it here on the stead . . ." His words trailed off.

Wendra stepped forward and kissed him on the cheek. "I understand."

Alucius hoped so. He really should have showed her earlier, but he sometimes felt that he was always realizing what he ought to have done later than he should.

23

Dekhron, Iron Valleys

Two men sat at a corner table in the Red Ram. One was Colonel Weslyn, wearing the blue-trimmed black of the Northern Guard; the other was the round-faced trader Halanat, in his blue and gray.

"I don't like it," said Weslyn, lowering his mug to the table. "I don't."

"Why not?" asked Halanat. "This Alucius is being sent to Hyalt, and that is as far as one can get from the Iron Valleys. He's likely to cause far less difficulty there than here."

"He wasn't causing any trouble at all," replied Weslyn. "He liked being a herder, and that was fine with me. He was the kind who cared more for results than what happened later. Short-term ideals, and no thought of living with the outcome."

"Young officers are often like that."

"I can't see why the Lord-Protector would insist on sending a marshal all this way to call up an overcaptain and promote him to majer. He and his marshals never do anything without a reason, especially one that benefits them. It doesn't make sense."

"It might make great sense from their point of view," suggested the trader.

"How?"

"The Lord-Protector has a revolt on his hands. If he brings in his own Southern Guard to put it down, how does that look?"

"It has to be put down. Even I can see that."

"That's true, but no one wants the cost to fall on them. So . . . he sends a marshal up here. Didn't this Marshal

Frynkel say that he was on an inspection tour? That way the Lord-Protector can claim that he sent one of his highest officers to see about reinforcements. He can also blame Frynkel."

"For what?"

"Is this Alucius not rather . . . effective? Didn't you say once that he destroyed an entire band of brigands, something like a hundred of them—and killed every last man? The Lord-Protector may need that kind of effectiveness. Would he want to saddle one of his promising Southern Guard officers with such butchery? If it goes wrong, he can blame this Alucius without tarnishing the Southern Guard." Halanat lifted his mug and took the smallest of swallows.

"That makes sense, but it's still going to cause problems for me. He's being promoted to majer, and that's over more experienced overcaptains. Compared to them, he knows nothing." Weslyn frowned, then pulled at his chin. "That will make him one of the handful of senior officers in the Guard, and he's less than thirty years old. He's probably closer to twenty-five."

"If he is that inexperienced, then dealing with a revolt in Hyalt will prove most difficult for him. If he is disgraced or does poorly, that will not reflect badly upon you."

"And if he is lucky enough to do well?"

"Then you take the credit for originally recognizing his abilities and for recommending him to the Lord-Protector. You point out, most politely, that it was his choice to leave the Guard and not yours. If he chooses to remain active in the Northern Guard, you put him in charge of the companies fighting in northern Madrien. He was not so successful against the Matrial, you said, when he first fought her lancers."

"He was a scout. I cannot gainsay that he is an extremely good battlefield commander." Weslyn shook his head. "You have said that his family is good at business. What if he ends up here at headquarters? If he sees the accounts . . ."

"Then keep him in the battlefield and away from

Dekhron. His luck cannot last there forever, and, if it does, in another ten years, he can become Imealt's deputy, and Imealt will have to deal with the overcaptain."

"Majer," Weslyn corrected. "Like it or not, he's now a majer."

"That is, if he survives," Halanat replied. "Rebellions are most chancy affairs. One never knows from what direction come the arrows and slings—or shots."

"Most chancy." Weslyn nodded. "At least, after he heads south, he will not be my problem, and the Southern Guard will make the payroll for him and for Fifth Company while they are south of the River Vedra. At least, that will help." He paused. "The real loss is Overcaptain Feran. Good solid officer . . ."

24

Late on Decdi afternoon, Royalt met Alucius when the younger herder was leaving the nightsheep shed after having brought the flock in and settled them for the night.

Alucius nodded to his grandsire. "You look worried. Is everything all right?"

"Things around here are fine. Been thinking. You'll be leaving in the morning, and I wanted to talk a few things over with you before that." Royalt paused. "You don't mind, do you?"

"You've seen more than I have," Alucius replied. "I can use any thoughts you have." He slid the last bolt into place, then turned to walk toward the stead house. "And you usually have a few."

Royalt fell in beside him. "They're sending you to put down a revolt. That's what this marshal said, and he came all the way from Tempre to ask you? That seem strange to you?"

Alucius laughed. "You know it's strange. I know it's strange. I just don't think I could refuse."

"That's right." Royalt paused, then asked, "You ever think about why people get up in arms, especially when the ruler's not that bad?"

"Well . . . either the local authorities haven't done well or there's something that they don't understand . . . or it's not local at all, and someone's stirring up trouble."

"Could be all three," suggested Royalt. "Before you start shooting these so-called rebels, you need to find out what started the trouble first . . . You know, one of the things that caused all the trouble back with the Reillies . . . maybe even was what led to your Da's death . . . that was that the Council and Colonel Dyalar never asked what had gotten the Reillies all riled up. Dyalar didn't even ask, just sent out a bunch of companies and started shooting. That's one way to shut down a revolt—just kill every last one. Problem is that if you miss anyone, then they're going to come back and try to kill you and your side. Just keeps going. Sometimes, with some folk, there's no other way. But . . . doesn't hurt to see if there's another way. Lord-Protector doesn't much care, I'd guess, how you handle it, so long as everyone gets their property and stuff back and the trouble-makers are taken care of."

"Probably not," Alucius agreed.

"Thing is . . . they wouldn't be calling you in if it were all that easy. Means they think some folks are going to get killed. Could be that's what they want."

"I think the Lord-Protector is looking for a way to get peace for a long time, and he doesn't know where else to turn. That doesn't mean the Southern Guard thinks the way he does. I'd wager that they just don't want to have to take lancers from anywhere else, and they don't want the blame laid on them."

"Glad to see you understand that." Royalt barked a short laugh. "You solve this without a lot of bodies, and everyone's going to say that anyone could have done what you did. You kill a lot of folk, and the Southern Guard'll come back in and tell everyone you didn't have to do that, and everyone will behave for a while just so they don't bring you back. And the Lord-Protector will thank you and send you back here. You'll be known as the Butcher of Hyalt for so long as you live, and so long as you're alive, no one's going to do much in Hyalt to upset the Lord-Protector. So you'll have all sorts coming up here to do you in."

"You don't make it sound easy."

"I'm probably not telling you anything you don't already know, but someone has to tell you, just in case you hadn't thought about it."

"Some of it, I had thought about. Hadn't thought about people trying to kill me long after it was all over."

"Alucius . . . nothing is ever all over. Nothing," Royalt repeated firmly.

Those words—"nothing is ever all over"—echoed in his thoughts as he continued to walk toward the stead house, listening to his grandsire.

25

On Londi morning, well before dawn, after Alucius had turned in the wide bed and wrapped his arms around Wendra one last time, he slowly swung into a sitting position. He looked back at her, taking in her face and the warmth within her. He swallowed, thinking of what lay ahead of him.

She slid into a sitting position beside him, leaning against his shoulder for a time, and Alucius rested his head against hers.

Finally, he turned and kissed her once more. "I'd better get ready."

She smiled. "You said that earlier."

"I know. But it's later now." Alucius stood and made his way out of the bedroom to the washroom across the hall.

The water was cold, but not so frigid as it would become as fall followed harvest, and especially when the cold winter of the north descended upon the stead. After he washed and shaved, he returned to the bedroom, where he donned the nightsilk undergarments, then the blue-trimmed black uniform of a Northern Guard officer—with the silver insignia of an overcaptain, since he had none for a majer.

Wendra had already dressed and made her way to the kitchen, where she and Lucenda had breakfast waiting for him.

"Riders a ways out on the lane," announced Royalt, entering the kitchen. "You're getting an escort this time."

"They want to make sure he doesn't change his mind," said Lucenda, her voice hard. "Not that he will."

"Now . . . Lucenda," offered Royalt. "Not as though he's got any choice. We don't either, not these days."

"I know that. I don't have to like it." She turned to Alucius, her voice softening. "You'd better eat. You've got a long ride."

"Longer than I'd like," he admitted, seating himself at the end of the table with his back to the archway into the main room.

Wendra nodded, sitting down to his right.

Alucius ate the egg toast and ham quietly and quickly, glancing occasionally at Wendra, who ate almost mechanically.

"Pretty clear that they want to get you south quicklike," observed Royalt after a mouthful of his ham. "Lord-Protector must have his hands full and then some."

"He should have kept them off us," replied Lucenda tartly.

"Sad as that is," countered Royalt, "we're better off under him than we were with the last Council."

"Self-centered gold-grubbers, and those were the best of the lot."

"We herders knew that years ago. Just that no one listened to us." Royalt took a swallow of the cider. "Always that way. Greed usually drowns common sense."

"Can't swim the rivers of trouble wearing gold armor," added Lucenda.

Alucius and Wendra traded knowing glances. Royalt winked in their direction when Lucenda turned back to the hot stove.

When he had finished eating, Alucius stood and walked to the window. "They're about here. Better get my gear."

He turned and headed toward the rear of the house, and Wendra followed. In the comparative privacy of their bedroom, he embraced Wendra one more time, with another lingering kiss.

"You be careful," he whispered. "You and Alendra."

"Shhh . . ."

Alucius understood the age-old taboo against using the name of an unborn child, but he had to voice her name at least once before he left. "Both of you take care."

"You, too."

Reluctantly, he released her and lifted the saddlebags that held a nightsilk vest and his cold weather riding jacket, as well as his other uniforms and gear—and the nightsilk skull mask that had proved useful in the past.

Lucenda had vanished from the kitchen when Alucius walked back through with Wendra, but Alucius had half expected that, knowing his mother had trouble with his leaving. She always had, from his first conscription.

Royalt nodded to his grandson. "Just remember to think it through."

"I'll try." Alucius gave his grandsire a smile, and with both rifles in hand and Wendra by his side, he walked out of the house and down toward the stable. The lead riders of the Southern Guard were less than a hundred yards from the stead when the two herders entered the stable.

Alucius saddled the gray quickly but methodically, strapped his gear behind the saddle, and set the rifles in the double holsters. Then he turned. Even as he put his arms around Wendra, hers were around him.

"I love you," he whispered. "Take care of both of you."

"I love you, too. We want you back."

In time, too short a time, Alucius led his mount out into the cloudy morning. Wendra remained by the stable door.

What looked to be two squads of mounted Southern Guards stood in formation behind two officers—Captain Geragt and Marshal Frynkel.

Frynkel rode forward and reined up short of Alucius. "I thought you might have trouble getting these." The marshal leaned forward and extended his hand.

"Thank you." Alucius took the majer's insignia, slipping them into a pocket for a moment while he removed those of an overcaptain, then replaced the old insignia with the new. Then he swung up into the saddle. "If your men would like to water your mounts . . ."

"Ah . . . I had them take that liberty. I trusted that you wouldn't mind." Frynkel's voice was apologetic.

"That's fine." Alucius nodded. "Then we're ready."

Frynkel nodded to Geragt, then eased his mount up beside Alucius's gray.

"Eighth company!" ordered the captain. "Forward!"

Alucius kept his eyes on Wendra until he was past the stable and could no longer see her without contorting himself in the saddle.

Once they were on the lane, headed out to the main road, Frynkel looked at Alucius and at the double rifle holder, as well as the pair of heavy rifles resting there. His eyes moved to the pack set behind the gray's saddle. "There wouldn't be an ammunition belt in there, by any chance?"

"There just might be, sir." Alucius smiled.

"Fifth Company, Northern Guard, was supposed to have reached Dekhron last night. Overcaptain Feran conveys his regards." Frynkel chuckled. "He also said that he hoped that this campaign would be less adventurous than the last time he served under you."

"We can hope that we don't run into pteridons and sky-lances," Alucius said. "But I'd like your thoughts on this revolt. From what I've seen, the Lord-Protector is a good ruler. So why are people up in arms against him?"

"We don't know. Not for certain. They're rebels who were living in the hills to the southwest of Hyalt. They showed up with weapons and mounts on a Decdi morning at dawn, attacked the two squads of Southern Guards left there, and slaughtered them to the last man. Some of the wealthier merchants and crafters managed to escape. They reported that the insurgents, or the invaders, numbered more than three hundred armed men. They're mostly followers of a cult that believes in the return of the True Duarchy, whatever that might mean."

"A new duarchy under their guidance," suggested Alucius.

"That well might be."

"Wasn't there a post, a fortified one, at Hyalt?" Alucius recalled having breakfast, years before, with an overcaptain stationed there. The man had seemed a good sort, and Talent usually allowed a good judgment of character.

"There was never a hint of trouble. The gates have been open there for years. They were open that morning." Frynkel shrugged.

Royalt had definitely been right, Alucius reflected. "And what sort of support will I get from the Southern Guard?"

"Two or three companies of new lancers just out of training, with a handful of experienced squad leaders and some junior captains, one who's never seen a battle. You'll pick them up in Krost, where they're winding up training."

"You have great confidence in me."

"As I heard the story, you took an entire company of green forced conscripts, broke them free of the Matrial's collars, trained them, and bested four companies of the Matrial's best. For an officer who can do that, this should not be all that hard." A smile played around the marshal's lips. "Of course, I could have heard the story wrong."

"You heard it mostly right. Except we didn't really best four companies. We evaded two and attacked the other two.

We just fought well enough to break through them and get home to the Iron Valleys."

"An officer who doesn't listen to the stories about himself. That's even rarer than a good battlefield commander, and you're both."

"I did what had to be done," Alucius said.

"That's what all good commanders say."

"And bad ones as well," replied the younger officer.

Frynkel laughed, then went on conversationally. "I was asking around, Majer, and I was told an interesting story. After you were released from duty as an overcaptain and were headed back home, you were attacked by brigands. Some twenty of them. A senior squad leader said that you'd been badly injured, but that you'd killed all twenty. Not one brigand survived, he said." The marshal looked at Alucius. "How true is that?"

Alucius shrugged. "I killed most of them. I don't know how many others there might have been because I wasn't in very good shape at the end."

"Amazing story. And no one ever tried to find out why twenty brigands were sent after you?"

"Not that I know. At that point, I was still recovering and just wanted to get home. Nothing like that ever happened again. There wasn't much reason to stir things up."

"And no one ever mentioned it to you? Even indirectly?"

"No one, except family here on the stead, of course."

"Hmmm . . . You never heard from Colonel Weslyn about the matter?"

"No, sir. Then, I was no longer on the active rolls. I am certain that the colonel has had other more pressing concerns. How did you find him?"

"He was most pleasant, although somewhat puzzled at my inspection tour. That was another reason for my trip through the Iron Valleys."

"He has always been most pleasant," Alucius said politely.

"So far as I could tell, he has never been in command in any skirmish or battle."

"That is something I didn't know."

"He had served two years as a captain sometime ago," Frynkel continued, "and then headed the guards for a trader—Halanat was the name, I believe. After the death of a Majer Dysar, about which I understand you have some knowledge—the Traders' Council prevailed upon Colonel Clyon to name him as the assistant commander. Certain irregularities were then removed from the records. I assume you know what occurred after that."

"Colonel Clyon's strange illness and death? Yes." Alucius wondered what irregularities had occurred. "As a captain in the field, I would not have heard about irregularities in Dekhron."

"You were doubtless concerned about more pressing matters—such as surviving brigand attacks. I was led to believe that a young trader died under rather mysterious circumstances following the death of Colonel Clyon's youngest daughter."

"And the young trader was the son of Halanat?"

"No. He was the son of a man called Ostar."

Alucius kept his nod to himself. No wonder the Iron Valleys had been forced to accept annexation by and union with Lanachrona. The Traders' Council had had far too little interest in anything but their own personal schemes and machinations. But then, the Lord-Protector and the Southern Guard had their schemes and machinations, and Alucius could only hope that their goals were somewhat more noble.

"I haven't paid that much attention to what has been happening outside of the Iron Valleys," Alucius said. "If you would not mind, since we do have some time on the road, I would appreciate anything that you could tell me that might bear in any way, however indirect, upon my commission . . ."

Frynkel turned in the saddle and looked at the captain who rode behind them. "Geragt . . . move up closer. It won't hurt you to hear all this." Then he cleared his throat and began. "The simplest way to begin is . . . Nothing is going quite right. Not disastrously wrong, not yet, anyway. I'll start in the east. We have some scattered reports that the new Praetor of Alustre is continuing to increase his forces . . ."

Alucius listened intently, hoping somehow that what he heard would prove even more useful than Frynkel intended.

26

The ride to Dekhron was long, even on the roads of the ancients, and the two squads were forced to stop on the first night at Sudon, then continue on the next morning to Dekhron. There had been but a handful of squad leaders and officers at the training base at Sudon who knew Alucius personally, but all had seemingly heard of him and his past achievements—and by the time he had finished breakfast on Duadi, the newly promoted majer was relieved to mount up and be back on the road to Dekhron.

The clouds of Londi had been replaced by a clear silver-green sky, with a crisp but light wind out of the northwest. The golden grain in the fields to the west of the eternastone road bent slightly to the wind.

Neither Alucius nor Frynkel spoke much until they were a good five vingts away from Sudon and back on the main road south.

"You have quite a reputation, even today," observed the marshal. "That is most interesting."

"Why do you think that is interesting, sir?" asked Alucius.

"When all are doing deeds that are honorable and heroic, there are few with reputations that are heroic, and even fewer stories. The deeds are told quietly, as if necessary, and then all go out and do what they must."

"You seem to be suggesting that there are not enough heroic deeds in the Northern Guard."

"Not exactly, Majer. Those who are true heroes are the men who do what must be done, with fear in their hearts and full understanding of the odds and risks they face. That is what you have done, and I would wager that most of those in your companies also did the same. When you were decorated by the Landarch of Deforya, as I recall, you did not wear the Star of Gallantry. Nor do you now, nor the Star of Honor."

"There were many who deserved those stars, Marshal. Many of them did not live, but they deserved them as much as I."

"You said that to the Lord-Protector, did you not?"

"Yes, sir."

"And how did your men speak of what you did?"

"I don't recall that they did, sir. Most of them did not wish to speak of what we did at all."

"That was my point. When a fighting force must look only to past heroics and not to present deeds and duties, all is not as it should be."

"And what of the Southern Guard?"

"I fear that you are also a hero there, if not of quite such great dimensions." Frynkel laughed softly. "Still . . . it is a rare man who has been a hero for three lands before he has reached his thirtieth year, and even rarer for him to have survived those heroics."

"I was extraordinarily fortunate." As he replied, Alucius could not help but wonder what had happened over the past two years, and how Lanachrona had gotten into such a situation.

"You doubtless were, and let us hope that such fortune continues. We all could benefit from such." Frynkel smiled. "Now . . . I should tell you more about the geography of the hills to the southwest of Hyalt."

Alucius nodded, listening.

27

Alustre, Lustrea

The man who sat in the unadorned silver chair on the dais wore the silver-and-black jacket of the Praetor with the matching silver trousers. He scowled, the expression making his youthful face ugly rather than older. Although he tossed his head slightly, his short and pale blond hair did not move at all. Neither did his black eyes, which remained fixed on the two men in the tunics of Praetorian Engineers.

"You have been working for nearly two years in Prosp, and you can report nothing beyond this?" He lifted a thin sheaf of paper.

"Honored Praetor Tyren," replied the taller and broader engineer, his eyes still downcast, "it took more than half a year to clean out the rubble, sir. You instructed us to be most careful and to try to salvage all that we could. We took the utmost care."

"There was no sign of Vestor?"

"Ah . . . his clothes and possessions were there, lying on the floor, as if he had vanished and they had fallen on the floor. There was a pistollike weapon, but nothing like anything we'd seen before. It was crushed, and we've been working to see if we can replicate it."

"Why not just repair it?" Tyren's voice carried untarnished sarcasm.

"It was destroyed beyond all repair."

For a moment, there was silence before the Praetor spoke again. "In this report, you claim that the Table was unbroken. How could that be when two stories of building stones collapsed over it so that nothing was left but a heap of rock?"

"Sir, that was what we found. The Table was untouched. The stones that collapsed on it cracked and broke, but there is not a scratch upon it. As you instructed, we rebuilt the structure around it, but with greater reinforcements."

"Have you had any success with the Table?"

"No, sir. It has a faint glow in pitch darkness, but we can find neither the source of the glow nor an explanation for why it might glow."

"There are no records of what Vestor did?"

"Ah . . . yes, honored Praetor . . . he did leave some records and notes . . ." replied the slimmer and shorter engineer.

"Then why have you not used them to decipher the mysteries of the Table?"

"We cannot read them," confessed the slim engineer. "They appear to be in the ancient Duarchial script, and there is no one alive who can read such."

"If there is no one alive who can read it, just how did Vestor learn it well enough to write it?"

"We don't know, sir," admitted the broader man. "He never talked to anyone about what he was doing. There are some notebooks, older ones that date to several years back, and those were written in Lustrean, and we have used those to reconstruct one crystal tank. We have been successful in rebuilding one of the light-knives similar to those that were successful against the pteridons of the nomads."

"Partly successful," corrected Tyren.

"Yes, Praetor."

"You call yourselves engineers." Tyren snorted. "You might as well call my staff of office one of the Scepters of the Duarchy. A name does not make it so. You may go. Endeavor to learn something more from the Table, if you would. And continue to construct more of the light-knives."

"Yes, honored Praetor."

Neither man met the eyes of the Praetor. They both bowed and retreated from the receiving hall.

28

Under a clear silver-green sky, with the sun just nearing its noontime zenith, Frynkel, Geragt, and Alucius rode side by side on the eternastone road toward Dekhron. Behind them rode two squads of Southern Guards. They had just passed the stone announcing that the former capital of the once-independent Iron Valleys lay but two vingts ahead.

"Majer?" Frynkel said.

"Yes, sir?"

"You will need to present yourself to Colonel Weslyn. Since you now report to the Lord-Protector and are under my direct command, that is merely a courtesy and a formality, but a prudent one. As I mentioned earlier, your pay and that of the companies under you, including Fifth Company, will also be borne by the Southern Guards, as will all supplies and equipment once you leave Dekhron."

"The colonel cannot be too displeased with that."

Frynkel offered a crooked smile. "About the golds, no. As I am certain you have considered, he is likely to be less pleased that one of his inactive overcaptains has been promoted to one of the highest ranks in the Northern Guard without his approval and that the same officer will be under the command of and working with the senior officers of the Southern Guard. He also will have thought out that your reputation is both impeccable and unassailable."

"In short," replied Alucius, "he will be most polite, most courteous, and doubtless would not be grieved in the slightest if lightning struck me or some other unlikely calamity occurred."

"That would be a good working assumption, although, if he is as I suspect, he would probably not wish any calamity upon you until after you complete your duties in Hyalt."

Alucius understood that all too well, because the Lord-Protector might well continue the operation in Hyalt with Feran, and Feran's success—and long-standing career—would make Feran an even greater threat to the colonel.

Before that long, they neared the outskirts of Dekhron. The town itself seemed little changed from Alucius's last time there, more than two years earlier. The houses were crowded together and built of the same uneven mixtures of stones scavenged generations earlier from even older buildings. Few of the shutters and doors were painted, and on more than half of those the paint was chipped or peeling, or both. Most of the side streets were of packed clay swirled with red dust. Only the eternastone of the high road seemed fresh and new, if also dusty, and it was older than everything else, Alucius reflected.

As they neared Northern Guard headquarters, Alucius squared himself in the saddle. He couldn't honestly say that he was looking forward to seeing Colonel Weslyn again.

The headquarters complex was also unchanged, not that Alucius had expected much change in two years. The stone wall enclosed a square half a vingt on a side, and stables, barracks, and officers' quarters were all of dressed lime-stone, with split-slate roofs on all the buildings and stone pavement covering all the courtyard spaces.

The two troopers on sentry duty stiffened as the column approached.

"Marshal, Majer . . . welcome to Guard headquarters," called out the older trooper.

"Thank you," replied Frynkel and Alucius, almost simultaneously.

". . . was the majer?" murmured the younger sentry, in a voice almost too low to be heard.

"The one with the dark gray hair? That's Overcaptain Alucius. Majer, it looks like now. He's the one who killed a thousand barbarians by himself, then was sander-near killed in an ambush and still took fifty brigands down and rode ten kays holding his guts in. Brother served under him. Best troop commander ever . . ."

"Oh . . ."

As Alucius reined up before the main headquarters building, he smiled. There had only been twenty brigands in the ambush, and it had taken weeks for him to recover.

"You've got quite a reputation, Alucius," Frynkel murmured with a smile. "The impressive thing is that most of it's true."

"Maybe a little."

The marshal shook his head. "Go ahead and see the colonel. I'll meet with him after you do, while you're getting things settled with Overcaptain Feran and Fifth Company."

Alucius dismounted, then tied the gray to the stone post before opening the worn oak door and stepping into the anteroom outside Colonel Weslyn's spaces. A ranker looked up, momentarily surprised, taking in the uniform and the majer's insignia. "Oh, sir, you must be Majer Alucius."

"That's right. I'm here to see Colonel Weslyn."

"I'm sure he'll be glad to see you, sir. He was asked to meet with the new Traders' Council this afternoon, and he hoped you'd get here before it got too late." The ranker rose. "If you'd just wait a moment, sir, I'll let him know you're here."

"Thank you." Alucius offered a pleasant smile, concealing a frown at the extreme deference. Was that because the ranker feared him—thinking that he had a direct link to the Lord-Protector?

The ranker slipped through the door into the colonel's study, closing the door behind him, but reappearing almost immediately in the anteroom. "Please go in, sir."

Alucius nodded and stepped through the door, in turn closing it behind him.

The tall and broad-shouldered colonel was already standing behind the wide desk. "It's been a while, Majer," offered Weslyn, gesturing to one of the chairs across from him and reseating himself. "You're looking good . . . and very fit."

"Thank you." Alucius settled into one of the chairs across from Weslyn. He noted that the colonel's thick hair now contained more silver than blond, and a welter of fine lines extended from the corners of his eyes. His Talent sense also showed that the colonel's lifethread was normal—the same amber brown, without the second purpled thread that was the sign of ifrit possession. But . . . there was the faintest hint of purpleness, as if Weslyn had been near an ifrit or influenced by one. That realization hit Alucius like a wall of cold water, and he was silent for a long moment.

Yet, there was little he could do about that, not at the moment. He had no way of knowing if Weslyn had simply met an ifrit, not even recognizing it, or was a marginal agent of the ifrits. And what was he going to do? Tell Frynkel that ifrits existed and that, because Weslyn had been near one, Alucius would have to back out of the mission to Hyalt?

He tried to use his Talent to get a better feel about the vague purpleness that hovered around Weslyn's lifethread, but the feeling was so dispersed that he had no way of tracking it or knowing if Weslyn were even aware of being influenced. Or, in fact, if the senior officer was being affected.

"You've been tasked with a rather important mission by the Lord-Protector," Weslyn finally said. "How well you do will certainly reflect on the entire Northern Guard." The colonel's smile was warm and professional, and Alucius trusted it little.

"I do understand that, and that was something I had to think over. Yet, if I rejected a request from the Lord-Protector," Alucius replied, "that would not have spoken well for either the Iron Valleys or the Northern Guard." He offered a disarming smile and a shrug. "So I thought that the best course was to accept."

"Ah, yes. If one faces difficult situations, it is always better to try and fail than fail to try."

"But it is far better to try and to succeed," Alucius replied politely. "That is my goal. As it has always been."

"You've been most fortunate in that, and the Guard sincerely hopes that fortune will continue to follow you."

Alucius could sense that Weslyn was suggesting luck as the reason for Alucius's past success almost to annoy the younger officer. So he forced another smile. "We will certainly welcome luck, but we won't be relying on good fortune. It's safer that way."

"That it is. Let us hope you have that fortune as well."

Alucius paused slightly, then asked, "Could I ask how the Lord-Protector's campaign to the west is coming?"

Weslyn tilted his head, offering a hearty smile, the false one that Alucius had disliked from the first time he'd seen it. "The campaign is progressing entirely as planned. I am sure that the marshal can tell you whatever else you wish to know on your way to Tempre. I assume he will be returning there with you."

In short, Alucius decided, the advances were stalled in the northwest, and Weslyn wouldn't know about the southwest, and the colonel wasn't about to admit anything. "I'm glad to hear that." He smiled politely again.

Weslyn returned the smile. "I do appreciate your courtesy in stopping to see me."

"I could do no less," Alucius replied. "Not for a commander who has always been most supportive and who has spoken so eloquently on behalf of the Guard." That sentence did not quite choke Alucius, although it was certainly true to the letter of the words.

Weslyn paused, as if he had not quite expected the answer, before replying. "We wish you the very best in your efforts in Hyalt. I will not keep you. I know you have much to do." He rose from behind the desk.

Alucius stood quickly as well. "Thank you." He paused, then asked quickly, "I had heard you would be meeting with the Traders' Council. Is this a new council? I had thought the old one . . ." He let the words drift off.

"Oh . . . this is just a group of traders who decided to meet because they felt they needed to act together in these troubled times."

"Thank you. I hadn't heard about that." Alucius bowed his head briefly. "By your leave, sir?"

Weslyn nodded, and Alucius left the study, closing the door gently behind him.

Feran was actually standing outside the colonel's office, talking to Marshal Frynkel. ". . . worried some about the ammunition . . . hard to get south of the Vedra . . . larger bore . . ."

"We made provisions for that . . ."

Both men broke off speaking and turned toward Alucius.

Feran didn't look much older . . . not to Alucius. He had the same brown hair, except with a touch more gray, the same deep lines radiating from the corners of his eyes, gray eyes that still held the hint of a twinkle, and a sense of not taking everything in life too seriously—only the important matters. He smiled warmly. "Alucius . . . or should I say 'Majer'?"

"Feran . . . it's good to see you. And you did make overcaptain."

The older Northern Guard officer laughed. "Not much before you made majer, I think."

Alucius looked to Marshal Frynkel.

The marshal nodded. "He also holds a temporary commission as an overcaptain in the Southern Guard. It ensures a clear chain of command."

That made sense to Alucius. It also suggested a difficult campaign.

"After you and Overcaptain Feran have taken care of what you need, and after I say a few more words to Colonel Weslyn, I'd like to suggest that the three of us and Captain Geragt have supper at the Red Ram," said the marshal. "Say, a glass from now?"

Alucius looked to Feran.

Feran nodded.

"Yes, sir," Alucius told Frynkel.

"I'll see you outside the senior officers' quarters then." Frynkel turned and walked past the ranker straight to Weslyn's door, opening it and letting himself in.

Feran smothered a smile.

"Why don't we go on outside?" suggested Alucius.

"Sir? Majer Alucius?" interjected the ranker. "You have the second of the senior officers' rooms, between the marshal and Overcaptain Feran."

"Thank you."

Alucius didn't say more until they were outside the building, and he had untied his mount and walked the gray toward the stables. Then he looked at Feran. "What's really happening out west?"

"We're about to get our asses handed to us, unless winter comes early." Feran shook his head. "Most of the men are relieved to be headed south."

"Is this . . . Regent that good a commander? I can't believe . . . all the collared troops would fight . . ."

"We've invaded them. The past fades pretty quick when your enemies are at your doorstep. We're seen as Lanachronans now. That doesn't help."

"Do you think she has gotten the collars working again?" Alucius didn't see how that was possible, since he'd destroyed the giant crystal that controlled them, but he supposed stranger things had happened. And the Regent had to have done something to rally Madrien.

"We didn't have enough close combat to tell. They still wore them. Couldn't tell if they were working. No one's said anything, and they were tough enough when they did have collars before." Feran shrugged.

"You at full strength?" asked Alucius.

"To the man. The last five just arrived from Sudon this morning."

"How many are just out of training?"

"It's not too bad. Twelve, and I've spread them out through all five squads. All the squad leaders are pretty good." He laughed. "They should be. You trained half of them."

Alucius led the mount toward the open stable door. An ostler hurried up. "Sir . . . can I help?"

"In a moment, after I get him stalled and unloaded." Alucius smiled at the youthful stable hand. "Any possibility of some extra grain? He's had a long ride."

"Yes, sir. We can manage that. Oh . . . you're in the third stall there, sir."

Alucius ended up unsaddling and grooming the gray while he talked to Feran.

". . . heard there was another of those crystal spear-throwers . . ."

". . . we were on the midroad . . . said they used it some-times to throw back the attack on Arwyn . . . another rea-son why the men aren't that upset about going south and not facing the Regent's lancers . . ."

"What about the squad leaders you got from Twenty-first Company? Egyl and Faisyn . . ."

Feran smiled. "Egyl's Fifth Company's senior squad leader, and Faisyn has first squad, and Zerdial fifth. Sawyn got sent to Eighth Company . . . doing fine. Anslym . . . he got sent to Twelfth. They got hit hard at Arwyn. He . . . didn't make it."

"Sorry to hear about that . . ."

"We all were. Problem is that Dyabal wasn't that good a captain."

Alucius frowned. "Dyabal?"

"Dysar's youngest brother—stepbrother really."

Alucius nodded. Somehow, that figured.

Before all that long, or so it seemed to Alucius, he had stowed his gear in the second room on the upper level of the quarters, the same room he had had once before—a good six yards by four, with a double-width bed, a large writing desk, twin wall lamps, an armoire, a weapons rack, boot trees, and an attached washroom. All of that was a far cry from where he had started years before as a conscript in a long barracks with over a hundred other lancers.

Feran was waiting outside when Alucius finished wash-ing up.

"First time I've been put up in the fancy quarters," Feran said.

"It's only the second time here for me."

"They have to for you," Feran pointed out. "You know that you're the fourth-ranking officer in the entire Northern Guard?"

"Fourth-ranking?"

"There's Weslyn, and his deputy—"

"Is that still Imealt?"

Feran nodded and continued, "and there's Majer Lujat. He's in charge of everything in North Madrien."

"How is he? I've never met him."

"Not bad. Not quite so good as you in sensing what's happening in a battle, but he listens to his captains and squad leaders, especially the senior squad leaders, because a lot of the captains aren't that good."

"Why not?"

"Weslyn picked them," Feran said dryly. "Anyway, Majer Lujat's got a good feel for what companies can do what."

"And he's still in command?"

"The colonel has to report results to the Lord-Protector," Feran said dryly. "And Majer Lujat is only about three years from a full stipend. He's made it clear that he has no interest in serving in Dekhron."

"Smart man," murmured Alucius.

"I thought you were, until I heard you'd agreed to this," Feran said, the faintest smile appearing in his eyes.

"I didn't see that I had much of a real choice. If the Lord-Protector has to shift—"

"I know. Same tale, told again. No support, and the Guard pulls back to defend the southern part of the Iron Valleys. You herders get squeezed again." After a moment, Feran asked. "How's your wife?"

"Lovely . . . helpful, and more able than I'd ever have believed." Alucius almost had said that Wendra was more Talented. He'd have to get back into the habit of being more closed-mouthed now that he was off the stead.

"Can't tell you're still in love or anything."

Alucius flushed.

Feran laughed. "Wager you brought writing paper."

"That's not even a wager. I just hope I'll have time to write." And that the messages actually get to Wendra, he added silently.

"Here comes the marshal."

Alucius turned. Although Frynkel had a smile on his face, as did Geragt, Alucius could sense anger in the marshal.

"It's been a long day, a very long day," Frynkel said. "Time for a good ale."

"I'd agree," Alucius replied.

He found himself walking beside the marshal, who was clearly disinclined to talk, with Feran and Geragt following.

Less than a hundred yards south of the post, the Red Ram was an old redstone building set on the corner, with ancient and narrow windows. The graying Elyset met them at the door. She smiled professionally.

Alucius inclined his head to the proprietress, projecting warmth and friendliness, as he had done once years before. "It's good to see you again." He grinned. "You suggested the quail the last time. Is it still the tastiest thing you have?"

Elyset laughed. "Majer or not, you're still a trooper. Don't have any quail today. No pheasant, either, but the noodles and fowl are good." She turned to Frynkel with a smile. "We don't see marshals often, and I've seen you more than a few times in the past week. Best we get you seated." She led the way toward the corner beside a cold hearth covered with a wicker screen. "Be quiet here this evening."

Frynkel took the seat in the corner, and Alucius sat to his left, across from Feran.

Instead of a server coming to the table, Elyset stayed. "Expect you know the drinks—ale, lager, wine. Right now, we've got stew. Always stew. Lamb cutlets, and the Vedra chicken with the heavy noodles. And lymbyl."

"I'll have ale and lymbyl," Frynkel said. "And the heavy dark bread."

Alucius had never liked the eel-like lymbyl. "The ale . . . and you suggested the fowl and noodles. Is that the Vedra chicken?"

"That's it. You want it?"

"Yes, with the dark bread, too."

Feran and Geragt both opted for the chicken, and Feran took ale, but Geragt asked for wine.

The drinks arrived almost as soon as Elyset left, brought by a taller and younger woman.

Frynkel lifted his ale. "To a successful campaign."

"To a successful campaign," echoed the other officers.

Even as he repeated the words, Alucius wondered how one judged a campaign against a revolt or a rebellion as successful, but he merely took a swallow of the ale and waited to see what else the marshal might offer.

"You know this won't be the usual campaign," Frynkel said after a long swallow of ale.

"I imagine not," Alucius replied. "Dead people don't pay tariffs, and if the rebels believe deeply, you either have to kill very few or all of them."

A puzzled expression flitted across Geragt's face. Feran offered the hint of an amused smile.

Frynkel chuckled. "You've been thinking." He turned toward Geragt. "He's right. If the rebels believe deeply that the Lord-Protector is wrong or evil, for every man that the majer kills, two others will take up arms. That's because the deaths will prove to others that the Lord-Protector is evil."

"Or something like that," murmured Feran under his breath.

"Needless to say, it couldn't have come at a worse time, which is why it did," added the marshal, lifting his right hand to his eye to calm it. "We not only have to fight the Regent, but attacks on Southgate by Dramurian warships, and unrest by our own merchants who want tariffs lowered because the costs of all goods traded anywhere outside of Lanachrona are going up. Of course, we need higher tariffs to protect the merchants and traders, but they don't see that."

"Why is all this happening now?" asked Feran.

"Because people take advantage of weakness, I'd judge," replied Frynkel. "The True Duarchists have been preaching against the Lord-Protector of Lanachrona for generations. There was a small revolt there when the Lord Talryn's grandsire was Lord-Protector. They waited until they thought the time was right, when they thought that the Lord-Protector couldn't bring many troops to Hyalt. It could be they figured he might well ignore it, because it's out of the way."

"So why didn't he, sir?" pressed Feran politely.

"Out of the way or not, it sets an example. The dryland spice traders of Soupat might decide they'd like to be independent. Or the mountaineers near Indyor. The Deforyan Council has already decided to impose exorbitant tariffs on our traders. Who knows what would be next?"

"Where did they come up with the golds for weapons and ammunition?" asked Alucius. "Does anyone know?"

"No," admitted Frynkel. "We went through all the trading records, but that doesn't mean much."

"Not if someone wanted to hide it," Alucius said. "Or if they were smuggled in from Madrien."

"It is shorter from Madrien, and the Regent of the Matrial will try anything to weaken Lanachrona," mused the marshal.

"Would these True Duarchists accept weapons from Madrien?" asked Feran.

"Who's to say that they'd even know where the weapons came from? They're the same standard that we use—not as heavy as those monsters you in the Northern Guard carry—but they could come from any number of gunsmiths. I doubt that the Duarchists care in the slightest." Frynkel followed the words with a dry laugh.

The more Alucius heard, the more everything seemed to make sense—and the more he felt he was missing something. He decided to follow his grandsire's advice once more, and listen as much as he could and say as little as possible.

He took another small swallow of the ale. It, at least, was good.

29

Early on Tridi, just after the Northern Guard muster, Alucius sat mounted on the gray as Fifth Company formed up on the north side of the courtyard. Eighth Company of the Southern Guard was forming up on the other side, south of the headquarters building.

Alucius watched and listened while Feran addressed Fifth Company. Mounted beside and slightly back of Feran was the senior squad leader—Egyl—who'd been Alucius's senior squad leader after Longyl had been killed battling the nomads led by Aellyan Edyss. Alucius wondered how many other men he'd recognize.

". . . be leaving shortly, but there will be a brief inspection by Majer Alucius. Full open ranks!"

"Full open ranks!" repeated Egyl, his voice booming across the courtyard. "Ready for inspection!"

"Fifth Company stands ready for inspection, sir," Feran reported.

"Thank you, Overcaptain." Alucius guided his gray along the first rank of first squad, followed by Feran, then by Egyl.

Alucius couldn't help but note the square-faced first squad scout. "Waris . . . you ready for this?"

"Yes, sir!"

The fifth trooper was also a man he recalled. "Skant. Are you ready for warmer weather than we had in Emal?"

"Yes, sir . . . so long as it's not too hot."

As he rode through the open ranks of Fifth Company, he managed to recall more than a few names and incidents, including Reltyr, who had suffered more than a few problems with an unfaithful wife when Twenty-first Company had been stationed at Emal before the annexation. Although the inspection seemed to take a long time, only slightly more than a half glass had passed by the time he returned to the front of the Fifth Company.

"That was good, sir," Feran said quietly. "You got most of them."

"And the ones I didn't will be wondering why I didn't . . ."

"Better they're wondering than thinking you don't remember anyone."

Alucius hoped so. He eased his gray away from Feran. "I'll let the marshal know we're ready."

Feran grinned. "Sir . . . you're supposed to have me send someone."

Alucius shrugged helplessly. "I have to get back to being an officer and not a herder."

The overcaptain turned. "Egyl . . . send one of the scouts to inform the marshal that Majer Alucius and Fifth Company stand ready to depart."

"Yes, sir."

Alucius glanced toward the headquarters building, but he did not see Colonel Wesyln. That was not surprising. Doubtless the colonel was on the south side, seeing Marshal Frynkel off. Alucius couldn't help but wonder whether Weslyn knew that Frynkel neither cared for him nor respected him. He supposed the colonel knew. Weslyn was too astute in playing the political currents not to know. That was one aspect of being a Northern Guard officer that Alucius could easily have done without, although his Talent was extraordinarily useful in sensing those types of undercurrents.

"They'll be waiting," Feran suggested.

"No doubt of that. They probably didn't do an inspection, although I wouldn't have put it past the marshal."

"I wouldn't, either."

Shortly after Waris returned from delivering the message, from the far side of the courtyard on the south side of the headquarters building came the command, "Eighth Company! Forward!"

"We'll hold till Eighth Company clears the gates," Alucius said.

Feran nodded.

Before too long, Alucius inclined his head to Feran.

"Fifth Company! Forward!"

As he and Feran led Fifth Company, from behind the last riders Alucius could hear the wheels of the supply wagons on the stone pavement of the courtyard. The sound of iron on stone diminished once the wagons rolled out through the gate and onto the hard-packed clay of the avenue that led eastward to the eternastone road south through Dekhron.

The buildings in Dekhron were similar to those in Iron Stem, mostly built of salvaged stone, and with either tile or slate roofs. Too many of the shutters had peeling paint, or none at all. While a number of the older dwellings nearest the river piers were two or even three stories in height, they looked even more run-down, as if they were boarding-houses for the poorer dock and river workers.

The trading buildings near the center of Dekhron had been better maintained, and several sported fresh paint and clean glass windows. Still, Dekhron appeared quieter than the last time Alucius had been there—with but a handful of people on the streets—and that surprised him, after having heard from Kyrial and Kustyl that trade had recently picked up in the river town.

At the eastern end of the avenue, Eighth Company turned south onto the eternastone high road, and Alucius and Fifth Company followed, riding past the last several blocks before the river.

The high road leaving Dekhron and leading to the bridge reminded Alucius of Hieron, because the cause-way leading to the bridge had been built long before the trade section of the town beside the river. Several inclined roads had been constructed later to connect to the eternastone pavement. As Alucius rode up the causeway

out of Dekhron, the sound of hoofs from the Eighth
Company ahead of him echoed off the eternastone pavement and side walls of the ancient Duarchial bridge over
the River Vedra. It was a bridge Alucius might have
called grand years before, arching over the river and
standing out against the low dwellings of Salaan on the
south side of the river. But, after having seen the massive
and graceful structures over the Vedra at Hieron, or the
stone canyon through the Upper Spine Mountains, the
bridge he crossed seemed more of a marvel as a part of a
system of highways and bridges that had endured for
thousands of years—a dark marvel, because he was one
of the very few who knew the cost that system had imposed on Corus.

The bridge itself held a roadway twice the width of the
high road, but without the dividing curb of the larger
bridges Alucius had seen in Madrien. The stone guard-
house on the southern side still had not been torn down, as
Feran had done to the one in Emal more than two years before, and that also troubled Alucius. From Alucius's point
of view, such remnants of the near-open former hostilities
between the Iron Valleys and Lanachrona would best have
been removed as soon as possible.

Just beyond the southern end of the bridge, to the left,
had been the Southern Guard fort. Alucius glanced eastward. The center and building and the barracks and stables
remained, but the glass was gone from the windows, and
stones had been knocked out of the stable walls and removed. He looked away, shaking his head.

"What is it?" asked Feran.

"The Southern Guard—just packed up and left their fort.
There won't be anything left in another year or two except
rubble. It seems like such a waste."

"They don't want to spend the golds to keep it up, and
who would buy it?"

"I know." It was another thing that bothered Alucius.
Too much was getting more run-down. But there wasn't
anything he could do about that. Instead, he looked ahead

to the high road, diverging gradually from the River Vedra as it headed southwest, and he thought of the long ride ahead, each glass carrying him farther from the stead, from Wendra, and from their daughter.

30

Two long days later found the two companies on the high road at the place where it once more met the River Vedra.

"Marshal's picking up the pace," Feran noted.

"It's only about a glass to the post here." Alucius studied the steads and fields, taking in the two rivers, the Vyana to his left, running westward through the lower fields to the south, and the Vedra to his right. Before all that long, even through the dust raised by Eighth Company, the walls of Borlan Post appeared on the right side of the high road ahead, set on the higher triangle of land formed by the junction of the River Vedra and the River Vyana.

Fifth Company followed Eighth up the cracked pavement of the side road to the post, slowing and then halting for a time just outside the gates—gates without sentries, Alucius noted.

From somewhere ahead, Alucius heard a greeting. "Marshal Frynkel, welcome to Borlan Post! You do us honor, and we offer all that we can to ease your journey."

Alucius recalled similar words, delivered in a similar tone, and he wondered if Majer Ebuin still remained at Borlan.

Fragments of Frynkel's response drifted back.

"... appreciate the welcome, Majer ... your courtesy and support ... most welcome ... two full companies ... Majer Alucius ... Northern Guard ... may recall him ... Overcaptain Feran ..."

The blond majer—who was indeed Ebuin—remained

outside the post headquarters building, waiting for Alucius and Fifth Company, while the marshal and Eighth Company had moved on toward the stables.

"Majer." Alucius inclined his head as he reined up once more. "I'm pleased to see you. This is Overcaptain Feran, in command of Fifth Company."

"It's good to see you again, Majer . . . and to meet you, Overcaptain."

Feran nodded.

"Are you now the post commandant?" Alucius asked politely.

Ebuin nodded. "I am. Captain-colonel Yermyn was stipended in the spring, and Borlan Post will be reduced to a travel post under a captain at the turn of the year. I'll remain here until the changeover."

Alucius hadn't really considered that the annexation of the Iron Valleys would also have had a wide-ranging impact on Lanachrona, but it certainly made no sense to retain a large outpost at Borlan now that the northern side of the Vedra was part of Lanachrona. In fact, as he considered it, he had to wonder why the reduction had not occurred earlier. "Do you know where you'll be posted then?"

Ebuin shrugged. "Best we get your men." He raised a hand, and a Southern Guard stepped forward from behind him. "Squad Leader Henthyn can help get your squad leaders oriented. You know where the officers' stable is. Marshal Frynkel will be taking the commandant's quarters, and that will allow each of you a room in the visiting officers's quarters."

"Thank you."

Alucius and Feran rode to the stables, where they unsaddled and groomed their mounts. Then Alucius—carrying his rifles and saddlebags—led the way to the structure behind the headquarters building, climbing up the steps to the upper level. As he recalled, their rooms would be the last three—all sharing a single washroom.

Alucius had the end room, slightly larger but still modest, with a bed for one, a writing desk, boot and weapons racks, and a narrow armoire.

While Feran checked on Fifth Company, Alucius used the cool water in the washroom to clean up, then to wash out one uniform and one set of nightsilk undergarments. After dressing in his other uniform, he made his way down the steps. Then he stopped. What was he going to do? He'd only get in Feran's way, and the older officer knew his duties, probably far better than Alucius did at the moment.

Alucius climbed back up the steps and reentered his temporary quarters. He seated himself at the writing desk. Here he was, a majer in charge of one company and shortly to be in charge of three or four, and he'd never thought about exactly how he was going to handle things. He hadn't been given any instruction or ideas, either from the marshal or from Colonel Weslyn, and he needed to set up some sort of structure to run three or four companies, and one that didn't take many lancers.

He was still jotting down notes when Feran knocked on the door to the quarters.

"Majer . . . the marshal has asked us to join him for supper . . ."

Alucius quickly stood. He had most of his ideas down in rough form, not that there were all that many.

"What were you doing?" asked Feran, as Alucius stepped out of his quarters.

"Trying to figure out how to run three or four companies without riding over my own mount."

"You've done that before."

"Ride over my own mount? Several times, at least."

Feran frowned. "You were in charge of all the companies on the way back from Deforya."

"We didn't have to do all that much except ride west on the highway," Alucius pointed out dryly. He started down the steps to the lower level. "That didn't take much skill. Here, we're going to be trying to put down a rebellion, and I'd guess that's going to mean different companies in different places."

"So . . . what do you have in mind?"

"There's a chain of command, and you're next in line. Frynkel's taken care of that by making sure you have a commission in both the Northern and Southern Guard." He stopped as they neared the mess. "We can go over it later."

Feran nodded.

The marshal and Captain Geragt were standing in the small mess, with its three tables, talking in low voices with Ebuin as Feran and Alucius arrived.

". . . kind who will do what needs to be done . . ."

". . . seemed that kind before . . ."

Frynkel broke off his words to Ebuin and cleared his throat. "Now that we're all here . . ."

Ebuin gestured to Frynkel. "Marshal . . . we're not formal here. If you would do the honors?"

With a nod, the marshal took a seat at the larger circular table, the only one set. Following the marshal, Alucius seated himself, followed by Ebuin and Feran, then by Geragt.

"As I once told Majer Alucius," Ebuin said, "the ale is good. It's one of the best parts of meals here, and that's why there are two pitchers set out." He took the pitcher and filled the beaker before the marshal.

Ebuin kept looking at Frynkel, and Alucius could sense that, for all Ebuin's outward heartiness, the majer was fretting about something.

A server appeared and set two large platters in the center of the circular table. The first held long slices of meat covered with brown sauce, garnished with lime slices. The second held glazed and fried rice.

"Whistlepig?" asked Alucius, although he thought he recognized the dish.

Feran looked at Alucius quizzically.

"It's one of the specialties of Borlan," replied the other majer. "They're like scrats, except much larger and tamer, and taste like fowl."

The marshal served himself, as did the others in turn.

As he ate, Alucius decided, once more, that despite what

Ebuin said, whistlepig was not so good as fowl, especially not so good as the Vedra chicken at the Red Ram, but far better than much he had eaten over the years.

"Have you received any dispatches from Krost or Tempre that would be of interest?" Frynkel glanced at Ebuin.

"There have been very few. Arms-Commander Wyerl will be shifting the Southern Guard out of all the outposts along the Vedra east of Tempre, except here at Borlan, by the turn of the year."

"They'll all go west?" suggested Alucius.

"More than likely," Frynkel replied. "Not that I've been told yet. What else?"

"All lancers in either Northern or Southern Guard whose service is due to expire at the turn of winter or spring have been extended another season, until more trainees are ready. As possible, they will be used in training assignments."

Feran frowned, as did Geragt.

Alucius had doubts about whether such assignments would really be offered, especially for the Northern Guard.

"Such refreshingly cheerful news," Frynkel said sardonically. "And how are the crops here in Borlan?"

"I wouldn't know, sir. Not for certain, but there's not too much complaining."

The marshal turned to Alucius. "Majer, you've heard about the overthrow of the Landarch by the large landowners of Deforya. You are certainly the most experienced officer to serve there in many years. What do you make of that?"

Alucius took a small swallow of ale before replying. "The Landarch was trying to balance the needs of his land against the demands of the landowners. You may have read my report on the structure of the Deforyan Lancers. Most of their overcaptains are the younger sons of the large landowners. The undercaptains and captains come from the crafters and less prosperous merchants. That means that those with wealth control the water supply through the aqueducts, the lancers through their officers, and trade and business through their golds."

"Then why did the Landarch not fall years before?" asked Ebuin.

"It's only a guess, but I would judge that his power lay in the long tradition of the Landarchy and in the distrust between landowners. They felt they needed someone who was beholden to all the landowners and not to any one of them."

"Why would you judge the landowners overthrew him now?" Frynkel's words expressed mild curiosity.

"You would be more aware of the current situation than I am," Alucius replied, "but I would guess that they overthrew him because he understood what was happening and tried to move Deforya to face those troubles, and the landowners were opposed to the changes . . ."

"Go on," encouraged Frynkel.

Alucius shrugged. "I don't know for certain, but only a few of the senior officers in the Lancers seemed to understand anything they didn't want to, or anything new. They could have cultivated more land, but instead they seemed to force people into Dereka, almost as if they wanted to keep them poor. They refused to believe in the pteridons until they were flaming thousands of lancers. Times are changing in Corus. The Praetor of Lustrea was preparing to take over the nomad grasslands, and now that Aellyan Edyss is dead and the nomads are fragmented and blocking trade on the southern route, he probably will resume that effort. If that is the case, the Landarch might assess a slightly higher tariff on the northern pass, but he would be aware that too high a tariff would not be well received by his neighbors. The landowners would not care. They would only see the chance to shift the tariff burden farther away from themselves and onto someone else." Alucius paused for another swallow of ale. "That is but a guess, and probably a poor one at that."

Frynkel nodded slowly, then glanced to Feran. "What do you think, Overcaptain?"

"I think Majer Alucius is being charitable. The landowners would suck the life out of the stones in the mountains and the grass in the plains if they could make a copper more. Their sons treat the junior officers like ignorant rankers when the juniormost officers know more than the senior officers."

"Majer Ebuin?" prompted Frynkel.

"I know less than either of these worthy officers . . ."

"You still must have an opinion."

Ebuin tilted his head, thinking for a time. "It is always easier to blame someone else. The Matrial blamed Lanachrona. The Dramurians blame us now. Deforya has slowly become less and less prosperous. I would say that it was easier for the landowners to blame the Landarch. The only way to keep him from refuting their charges was to topple him before he could. That is but my best guess, sir."

"You majers are most cautious. Overcaptain Feran is more direct." Frynkel laughed softly. "Rank can make one cautious. That is not always a virtue." He laughed again. "I learned that the hard way, many years ago when I was an overcaptain in charge of a small border post near Chronant . . ."

Alucius forced himself to listen intently.

Much later, after several more stories from the marshal and one from Ebuin, Alucius returned to his quarters for the night. After bolting the door, he used his belt striker to light the wall lamp over the writing desk. He set aside the sheets of paper holding his thoughts on organization and began a letter to Wendra.

When he finished, more than a glass later, he reread what he had set down, eyes skimming through the words.

My dearest—
I am writing this from Borlan. As you doubtless know, little eventful has happened, for which I am grateful. I did meet with Colonel Weslyn in Dekhron, and he is as he always has been, most po-lite and gracious in his speech. It was good to see Feran again, and some of the men I had commanded several years back . . .

We leave in the morning for Krost, where we are to meet the rest of the force I will be commanding. We have no new tidings of what may have occurred in Hyalt or elsewhere . . .

I would that matters were not as they are, and that we were together on the stead. I look forward to completing my tasks so that I may return to you.

Then he signed and sealed it. In the morning he would see what arrangements he could make for his letter to Wendra to be carried to Iron Stem by one of the regular dispatch riders. Of course, it would cost half a silver, and there wasn't that great a guarantee, but it was worth the coin. He just recalled his regrets when he'd been captured by the Matrite forces and had never written a single letter home.

31

Dekhron, Iron Valleys

The stocky man turned from the shelves of the library as the door opened and a white-haired man in black entered. "Tarolt."

"I see you are perusing the volumes again. For references to the scepters, I presume?"

"I thought that it would not hurt to look, as I could. I have completed my other assignments. Or what of them that I can do at the moment."

"The scepters might be helpful, Sensat, but they have already accomplished what was necessary a thousand years ago." Tarolt's voice was firm and cold.

"Are we sure that those tensions remain as necessary? Without the locators . . ."

"They do, else none of the Tables would have worked all

these years. I have calibrated the new Table, and Trezun has rechecked the measurements. It is so. We do not *need* the scepters."

"There are still possible lamaials—Tyren in Alustre and the herder—and if they find the scepters . . ."

Tarolt silenced Sensat with a gesture. "The only one with any hint of true Talent about whom we need worry is the herder. He is on the way to Hyalt. Adarat has been warned that the northern officer with the dark gray hair is the lamaial. That will fire the believers even more, and the herder will have more than enough to handle, because he has not been in service for years and never in such a situation."

"But if he hears of the scepters . . .?"

"How would he even know about the scepters and what they are? Also, it is most unlikely that the ancient ones can support him there in Hyalt—or that they will try. Still, it would be good to uncover the scepters, but not at the expense of preparing for what must be." He looked hard at Sensat. "Just how much progress can you report on your primary duties?"

"Adarat has the Hyalt area organized and under firm control. There are already five companies of Cadmians in training. The believers of the True Duarchy have been told that a northerner is being sent against them, a lamaial who will kill them to stop the return of the One Who Is and the peace of the Duarchy to come. They have been assured that they are the chosen ones to restore the Duarchy and to destroy all who would oppose them in returning hope to Corus," offered the pale-faced and stocky man in the maroon tunic. "Adarat has also sent weapons to Syan as well, but we have fewer believers there."

"Whose fault is that?" asked Tarolt.

"There are few of us yet here. All this has taken some considerable planning and effort, since there are no longer Tables in Tempre and Hyalt . . . and since we have not yet been able to reactivate the one in Soupat. It will be much easier when one more translation is complete."

"It is always easier with more Efrans, but full translations are still difficult and risky . . . and few on Efra wish to take that risk. Too few, and they do not understand the greater dangers. Like all those in comfort, they do not wish to understand. But . . . that was why you agreed and why you were translated here," replied Tarolt. "To assist as required to create the unrest and chaos that will make a new Duarchy seem paradise by comparison. And to facilitate the events necessary to rebuild the grid. Never forget that."

"Yes, fieldmaster."

"Tarolt . . . always Tarolt."

Sensat swallowed before replying. "Yes, Tarolt."

32

Two and a half days had passed since the four officers and the two horse companies had left Borlan and taken the eternastone road south to Krost. Although it was early afternoon, a gray overcast blocked the sun and had since midmorning. There was no wind, leaving a sullen feel to the day, one that, to Alucius, promised little good. Yet, what could happen now? The two companies rode southward through low, rolling hills with prosperous steads on each side and occasional small towns. There was almost no possibility of encountering hostile lancers, not when the nearest forces were those of the Regent more than three hundred vingts to the west—as an eagle might fly—and twice that by even the high roads.

Then, from nowhere, a crimson emptiness flared through Alucius's wristguard. He glanced down involuntarily. Wendra? What had happened?

But the guard remained warm and gave no other indication.

He frowned and studied the road ahead of him. He tried to use his Talent to probe the wristguard's crystal, yet all it revealed was that Wendra was alive and healthy—all it could reveal. He could only take that as a sign that she and Alendra were well.

Suddenly, Alucius found himself almost shivering, yet he wasn't really cold. He was wearing nightsilk undergarments and a riding jacket, and it wasn't winter, but harvest. Harvest was warm in Lanachrona, even on an overcast day, especially without any wind.

Another quarter vingt went by, and the wristguard revealed nothing else. Then Fifth Company followed Eighth Company through a road cut made ages earlier. Even the walls were of eternastone, rising a good three yards above Alucius's head at the point where the roadbed was in the center of the ridge. As Alucius neared the southern end of the cut, he glanced over his shoulder, noting that the ridge, unlike the other hills, seemed to stretch as far as the eye could see, both to the northwest and to the southeast.

As the road shoulders dropped level with the road itself, another crimson emptiness, far more overwhelming, washed over and around him, and not from his wristguard. This was a Talent-sensed void—the same emptiness that he had felt on the high road back from Dereka. He turned to Feran, riding beside him. "Order ready rifles."

Feran started, but only for a moment, before replying, "Yes, sir," then turned to Egyl. "Ready rifles! Pass it back."

"Ah . . . yes, sir. Ready rifles. Fifth Company! Ready rifles!"

Alucius then added, "If you'd order your four best marksmen up here."

"Egyl . . ." Feran began.

"Waris, Makyr, Solsyt, Tonak, forward!"

"Put two of them on each shoulder, about three yards ahead of us." Alucius had no idea what exactly was coming, but it had the feel of a reddish purple Talent, all too much like the wild pteridons, and he wasn't about to wait to see what it might be. If nothing showed up, he'd pass it off as a drill. He didn't think they'd be that fortunate. He infused the cartridges in his own rifles with darkness, then did the same to those in the loops in his belt. He waited to say more until the four lancers rode up.

"I'd like you four to take a position ahead of the company. Be prepared to fire, at my direct command."

"Yes, sir."

"Two on each side," Feran added.

"Yes, sir."

As the four rode past Alucius, Feran, and Egyl, Alucius reached out with his Talent and began to infuse the cartridges in each of their rifles with the same kind of darkness that he had used.

The chill and unseen red-purple darkness became more and more oppressive as the company continued southward. Alucius felt as though an unseen avalanche was building behind the gray clouds above, a sweep of *something* ready to crash down upon them. Yet . . . what more could he do? Tell the marshal that they were facing a danger he could not describe, could not identify, and could not even explain?

All he could do was to ready his first rifle and slowly infuse the cartridges of the lancers in the first squad with darkness. More than that he could not do, except study the skies ahead and the terrain beside the high road as he rode. Even so, he felt shaky after drawing on so much darkness.

They had ridden only a few hundred yards farther when the entire sky flashed purple—but only to Alucius's Talent, and then on both sides of the eternastone road the sky shivered, with lines of black lightning flashing down and then vanishing. To the east Alucius took in ten creatures from a nightmare—or from wherever the ifrits came. Each was more than four times the size of a draft horse, with massive shoulders, a long triangular horn, and scales that shimmered purple. The oversized mouths boasted crystal fangs a yard long.

"Friggin' monsters!"

"Sow's belly!"

". . . same as back then . . ."

Alucius glanced to the west, where another set of identical creatures had appeared, then swung up his own rifle. "Fifth Company! Halt! Out oblique and hold! Prepare to fire. Fire!"

"Fifth Company! Out oblique and hold! Fire at will!" echoed Feran and Egyl.

Aiming to the east, because that grouping of Talent-creatures seemed closer, Alucius put his first shot through the forehead of the horned creature in the middle. As the creature collapsed with a *thud* that shook the ground, then flared into a column of flame, another lithe creature sprang from behind the monster. The second looked vaguely like a dustcat, except that it was a shimmering black, and far swifter—and with longer fangs and claws.

Alucius's second shot missed the black dustcat, and the third only struck it in the hindquarters, but it flailed forward, hissing, until a shot from someone else turned it into a small blue-flame pyre.

The remaining horned Talent-beasts—or wild sandoxes—lowered their heads and rumbled forward, their bulk sending vibrations through the ground itself. Alucius fired the last shot in his first rifle at the foremost of the sandoxes, bringing it down as bluish flames erupted from the wound, but from behind the fallen sandox sprang a pair of the black dustcats.

Before him, the four marksmen fired deliberately, and one of the dustcats exploded in the same bluish flames, but the remaining dustcat streaked toward Tonak with incredible speed. Somehow, the lancer managed to get off a shot at point-blank range, but so close that for a moment he appeared enveloped in blue flame.

"Eighth Company! Forward!"

As the Southern Guards tried to ride away from the attack, three of the horned sandoxes swept through the rear squad. Bodies flew in all directions, each encased in blue flames.

Because he could do nothing for the Southern Guards

without firing directly into them, Alucius switched rifles and looked westward, targeting another of the wild sandoxes, then the dustcat that followed the fall of the massive beast. He paused for an instant to squeeze more darkness into the cartridges of the rifle Waris carried as the lancer reloaded, then raised his second rifle to aim at the nearest beast. While the shot struck, and bluish flames issued from the beast's shoulder, it swerved and stumbled toward the last rank of Eighth Company, exploding in a gout of flame that engulfed two Southern Guards.

Alucius fired at another of the beasts—and hit it. A blast of blue flame washed toward the left side of Fifth Company's first squad. While Alucius could feel the heat, the flames died short of the lancers. He targeted two more of the cats, but it took three shots to get the second.

"Watch the cats!" Alucius ordered, trying to infuse the cartridges of the marksmen and of the lancers around him with blackness as he reloaded the second rifle.

Another horned beast flared into blue flame, just at the edge of the eternastone, but at the rear of Eighth Company.

Alucius snapped off another shot and was rewarded with another blue explosion. Then he concentrated on three cats that streaked toward first squad.

The last one skidded to a halt less than a yard from the western edge of the road, flaring into a sudden blue flame. Even before those flames died away, more of the black cat-creatures appeared, striking the column from all angles, coming in low and slashing at the legs of mounts and men.

Alucius forced himself to concentrate on two things—his own shooting and supplying darkness to the cartridges of those around him. In time—how long it was Alucius didn't know—he shot the last cat, then lowered his rifle.

For all the chaos and the slashing attacks, there were fewer bodies strewn on the shoulder of the highway and amid the column than Alucius had feared—at least among Fifth Company. He looked ahead and could see charred bodies of both Southern Guards and their mounts, perhaps as many as two full squads along a half-vingt stretch of eternastone.

Alucius surveyed the fields on both sides of the road. In places, the wooden rail fences had been burned through, and in others merely broken. There was no sign of any of the creatures, save for large patches of burned ground and the black smoke that rose in thin trails from the seared ground on both sides of the eternastone road.

"Have Egyl find out our casualties and report back," Alucius told Feran. "I'm sure the marshal will want to know—when we catch up to them."

"Egyl?"

"He's already headed back, sir," called Elbard.

"Thank you." Feran looked at Alucius and said in a lower voice, "This was worse than coming out of Deforya."

Alucius nodded, his face bleak. "More of the sandoxes, and I've never seen anything quite like those cats."

"Quite like?" Feran's eyebrows lifted.

"They looked like jet-black dustcats." Alucius forced himself to reload both rifles, overriding the trembling in his fingers. Only then did he holster the rifles and take a long swallow from his water bottle. He realized that he felt light-headed . . . and very tired. He pushed the tiredness away.

"I'd hoped that all we'd have to deal with would be an-gry peasants and religious zealots," Feran said, "not more Talent-creatures from the time of the Duarchy."

"The marshal said they wanted to bring back the True Duarchy," Alucius said. "I hope these weren't what they had in mind."

Feran snorted. "People don't know when they're well-off." After a moment, he added, "You don't really think this had anything to do with the rebellion in Hyalt?"

"I don't know. I don't know how it could, but they've got priests of some sort, and Aellyan Edyss found a way to call up pteridons. Maybe these rebels could too . . ." Alucius shrugged, turning in the saddle to look back northward along the road. He could see Egyl riding toward them.

"Majer . . . you know I never liked it when you said things like that the last time you had an impossible assignment."

"I know, Feran. I don't like having those thoughts, either. But why would anyone bring Talent-creatures against us in the middle of Lanachrona? If the Regent could summon those, I'm certain she'd use them against our forces actually in Madrien."

"Same thing'd be true of the Deforyan Council or the Praetor," Feran pointed out.

Alucius did not mention the other possibility—that the ifrits were to blame—because he couldn't prove that they even existed, let alone that they had sent the creatures against the two companies. Yet that possibility was as likely as the priests of the True Duarchy having unleashed the beasts.

Egyl reined up. "Sir, Majer . . . we lost four men in fifth squad at the rear, and two others in second squad. Ten men with burns, but it looks like they'll be all right."

"Mounts?" asked Feran. "Supply wagons?"

"They didn't go after the wagons, and anytime they got one of our men, they got the mount, too."

"Do what you can, and let me know when we're ready to ride on," Feran said.

"Won't be long, sir. There's . . . well . . . not much left if one of those things got a man. Just a greasy black patch."

Alucius looked forward again, southward along the road. Eighth Company appeared to have halted about a vingt south of Fifth Company and was regrouping. As he watched, he could see a rider moving away from the rear of the Southern Guard column and northward toward Fifth Company.

"I think I'll ride forward and see the marshal," Alucius told Feran. "Once you've got things settled, have Fifth Company rejoin Eighth."

"Yes, sir." Feran offered a ragged grin. "Better you than me meeting with the marshal, sir."

"Thank you," Alucius replied dryly, easing the gelding forward.

As Alucius rode southward, he ate some travel bread, and that helped with the dizziness. He also counted more than twenty charred patches on the stones and the roadside, but, as had been the case with the nightsheep killed by the Talent-pteridons, the corpses had vanished or burned away.

Some of the Southern Guards glanced at him as he rode past them toward the front of the column, but they were silent, almost as if stunned.

"Marshal, sir," Alucius said, reining up two yards short of the senior officer.

"Majer." Frynkel nodded, paused for a moment, before asking, "What were your losses?"

"Six men dead, ten burned, but not badly."

"Eighth Company lost almost thirty, most in the last two squads." The marshal's eyes fixed on Alucius. "You didn't have your men charge those creatures. Why not?"

"We'd already found that didn't work. On the way back from Deforya. It was in my report, sir. If they touch a lancer, he usually bursts into flame. It's not a good idea to get too close. They're also faster than a mount. Massed fire works better." Alucius waited.

"I thought it might be something like that." Frynkel tightened his lips. "Have your force rejoin us. I'll debrief you tonight at the way station at Ghetyr."

"Yes, sir." Alucius turned the gray back northward and rode on the eastern edge of the stone pavement, past Eighth Company and toward Fifth. He was not looking forward to discussing the attack with the marshal. Not at all. And he still worried about Wendra, and why there had been a flash just before the Talent-creatures had appeared around him.

33

North of Iron Stem, Iron Valleys

Wendra reined up at the top of a low rise. The hazy clouds overhead cut off most of the heat from the afternoon sun, but since there was no wind, she had left her herder's jacket open. To the west, still almost fifteen vingts away, was the base of the Aerlal Plateau. The top of the Plateau was lost in hazy clouds.

Cloudy weather, especially stormy weather, often encouraged greater sandwolf stalking of the nightsheep, but usually light clouds did not. Still, Wendra continued to study the gradual slope below her, and especially the wash farther to the southeast.

Most of the flock was but fifty yards downslope from where she viewed the nightsheep. Somewhat farther to the north were three young nightrams that sparred with each other, not for dominance, but for practice for the time when they would fight in earnest, unless stopped by Wendra or Royalt. After making sure that the sparring was only that, Wendra turned and studied the slope to her right where a handful of older ewes grazed and moved slowly toward the main body of the flock.

From nowhere, a shivering line of reddish purple flared to her left. She had not seen it, but sensed it and turned in the saddle, drawing her rifle out of its holder as she did. Almost as quickly, as she eased her mount around, she infused the cartridges in the magazine and chamber with darkness.

Four dark forms swarmed over the ridge to the north of her, moving swiftly on a line between the three young nightrams and Wendra. As if sensing the purple-dark sanders, shadowed in unseen blue and without lifethreads, the three nightrams turned and formed a vee facing the on-coming danger.

Carefully, Wendra squeezed off her first shot, aimed at the lead sander. Her aim was true, and she targeted the second. But the first flared into a pillar of fire, and the force of that flare of blue flames pushed the second sideways. Then the remaining three turned southward and began to sprint toward Wendra.

She squeezed off a third shot and then a fourth, and the second sander fell. With her fifth shot so did the third.

But the last Talent-sander was less than twenty yards from Wendra, and she doubted that she could reload in time.

Desperately, she threw out a line of Talent-fire. The sander reeled back, but remained upright. She tried a second probe, but the sander struggled forward.

Did she need bullets for lifeforce darkness?

With the Talent-sander less than ten yards from her, Wendra formed another Talent-probe, this one tipped with as much darkness as she could gather, and thrust it as hard as she could at the oncoming creature. As she did, she knew that what she tried *had* to work . . . or she would turn into a mass of blue flames.

Less than a yard from her, the dark sander halted, as if stopped by a wall, shuddered, and then seemed to shrivel.

Wendra urged the chestnut sideways and back away from the slowly toppling and shrinking form that abruptly burst into flame. Warmth cascaded across her left side, warmth that faded as she and her mount moved away from the Talent-fire.

Wendra reined up, studying the slope. She was shivering and breathing heavily, but there were no sandwolves and none of the dark sanders remaining, only four trails of thin black smoke rising in the still air from four patches of oily black residue on the sandy red soil.

Belatedly, and silently berating herself for being so slow, Wendra reloaded the rifle.

As she slipped the last cartridge into the magazine, an-

other single sharp purple feeling jabbed at her from somewhere, and was gone.

Wendra glanced around quickly, but the hazy clouds
above the stead remained unchanged. The three younger
nightrams had eased back to the main flock, and the ewes
had closed up, with the rams forming a loose perimeter
around the flock. But, so far as she could see or Talent-
sense, there were neither sanders, nor soarers, nor sandwolves. Nor were there any more of the strange
Talent-creatures.

She continued to watch and sense, but nothing happened, and the nightsheep began to graze once more, if
cautiously. So why had she felt the stab of purpled emptiness *after* she had killed the dark sanders that had not felt
like sanders?

After a moment, she eased off the glove on her left hand
and studied the black crystal of the herder's ring. She
sensed nothing, but she knew she had felt *something*. Or
had Alucius felt something?

The crystal was warm, and there was no sense of danger
or pain, as had been the case when he had been injured.
She replaced her glove and studied the flock.

Alucius was all right. Of that she was confident. But she
still worried, both about him and about the dark sanders—
and why they had come after her. Because they were replacing the older, more greenish sanders? Or because she
had become more adept with Talent? Or both?

34

Before even thinking about seeking out the
marshal for debriefing, Alucius made sure that Fifth Company was settled into the way station at Ghetyr—two buildings within a stockade with a well and watering troughs.

The lancers' barracks consisted of little more than a long shed with straw mattresses on plank platforms. At the west end of the barracks were the officers' quarters—six cubicles without doors. Each officer's cubicle had a bunk platform with a straw mattress, a stool, and two planks attached to the wall and supported by timbers to serve as a writing desk. The other building was the long stable, with a roof that had seen far better days and probably leaked.

After having groomed the gray and left his gear in one cubicle, Alucius went to find Marshal Frynkel. The marshal was not in the barracks building or in the stable. Alucius found both the marshal and Captain Geragt standing in the last light of a setting sun in the northeast corner of the stockade, well away from anyone else. Alucius stopped a good five yards away.

"Majer, come and join us," Frynkel called.

"I didn't wish to intrude, sir."

"You aren't. We were talking about those . . . creatures."

"Wild sandoxes. Or Talent-infused sandoxes," Alucius said as he joined the other two.

"You think so?"

"They're close to the ancient illustrations, except for the horns," Alucius said. "They're bigger, too, I think."

"You'd run across both types of creatures before?"

"No, sir. We were attacked by wild pteridons and wild sandoxes on the return from Deforya. Until today, I'd never seen those giant black cats."

"They look familiar . . . somehow," mused Frynkel.

"They look like a dustcat might, if it were larger and black, with longer claws."

"Thank you. I knew I'd seen a drawing or something like them." Frynkel nodded, as if relieved to recall the similarity. "Why do you think the creatures are supported by Talent or magic or whatever?"

"Well . . ." Alucius paused for a moment before continuing. "Because they have a feel that's similar, but not the same, to soarers and sanders—and to the pteridons that Aellyan Edyss had. And they react the same way as the pteridons did when they were killed—exploding in those blue flames." He tilted his head. "It could be something else. I don't know for certain, but that's what they seem to be."

"I must admit . . . when I read your report several years ago . . . I had some doubts about your encounter on the return from Dereka." Frynkel laughed harshly. "I would rather have not had to confirm personally that such creatures do exist."

Geragt offered an affirming nod.

Frynkel looked at the Southern Guard captain. "If you wouldn't mind inquiring about whether the cooks are going to fix something, or whether we're on field rations . . .?"

"Yes, sir. I'll see what I can find out." With a smile of relief, Geragt nodded, turned, and departed.

Geragt's sense of relief confirmed for Alucius his feeling that Frynkel had not been totally pleased with Geragt about something, probably his handling of the Talent-creatures.

Frynkel waited until the other officer was well away before speaking again. "Majer, as I mentioned earlier, I noticed that you and your men were ready for those creatures. I also noted that the shots from Eighth Company seemed to have little effect."

"Yes, sir. Part of that was because I'm a herder. We learn to listen to our feelings. I felt something was going to happen. I couldn't have said what. So I called a drill for a formation I'd found useful on the Deforyan campaign. That was to bring forward the best marksmen so that they would be in position. I'd have to say that the reason our shots had more effect was that we use larger shells. They don't carry as far as those used by the Southern Guard, but we found them to be more effective against the pteridons at Dereka."

Frynkel chuckled. "Why is it that everything you say makes perfect sense, and that I'm certain that I'm still not getting the full story?"

"Because you're not," Alucius admitted. "I can't explain to you why I feel what I do." That was absolutely true, but not in the way that Alucius hoped Frynkel would take it. "I don't think any herder could explain why we feel what we do. We've survived because of what we can sense and feel. That's one reason why the Northern Guard has used those off of herder steads as scouts for generations. But it's not a skill that necessarily works well as part of a larger organization. Can you imagine my trying to explain to you that I have *feelings* that you should heed? In the middle of a battle?"

This time, the marshal laughed more loudly. "I see your point. I also see why the Lord-Protector wanted you in charge of a force. You need the freedom to follow those feelings, and he needs the ability not to be directly responsible." He paused. "How did you manage with Majer Draspyr?"

For a moment, Alucius was lost, not following the marshal's question, before he caught the connection between it and the majer who had led the combined expedition into Deforya years earlier. "I acted, then explained. Majer Draspyr needed results, sir."

"I suppose that's why—" Frynkel broke off his sentence. "Never mind that. Can you explain why those creatures appeared in the middle of Lanachrona and attacked us?"

"Explain? No, sir. I suppose it's possible that the priests or whoever is behind the rebels of the True Duarchy found a way to call up these creatures and send them against their enemies. How they would know where we are or how to send them against us I have no idea." Alucius thought the idea was possible, but he doubted that was the reason, or the sole reason, behind the appearance of the Talent-creatures. Yet he also didn't see why the ifrits would send such Talent-creatures against Alucius himself when he was leading a force large enough to destroy the beasts.

"Neither do I, but that makes more sense than anything else. I don't like it, and the Lord-Protector will like it even less."

Alucius could imagine that. The Lord-Protector had more than enough problems already.

"It still doesn't tell us why this is happening now. Do you have any thoughts on that, Majer?"

"Something's happening. It has been going on since

Aellyan Edyss and the pteridons. It could have started before that, but it's been more obvious in the past few years.
There were the pteridons used by Edyss, and there were
those that attacked us on the Deforyan road. Herders in the
Iron Valleys have reported strange kinds of sanders on the
steads. The Regent of the Matrial came up with the crystal
spear-thrower. There are probably other things I don't
know that you do. According to the histories, none of these
things has happened since the Cataclysm." Alucius
shrugged. "It means something. I just don't know what."
Again, what he said was true. He didn't *know*, but he had a
feeling that it was all tied to the ifrits, if he could but figure
out how and why.

"You talk about feelings, Majer. What do you feel?"

Alucius thought for a moment. "It could be that the True
Duarchists are right, that the times are changing again, and
that there could be another duarchy."

"Is that what you feel?"

Alucius forced a laugh. "I feel that the times are changing. That's what I feel. How or why . . . I couldn't say."

Frynkel nodded slowly. "There are limits to those herder
feelings."

"Yes, sir. That's why we don't say much."

"I can see that."

"Sir," called Geragt. "The cooks are working on a
stew . . . but it will be more than a glass."

"Well . . . come on and join us. We might as well go over
tomorrow's ride."

Alucius had no illusions that the marshal had given up
on trying to see if he could use Alucius's senses as a
herder to discover more about the dangers facing
Lanachrona and the Lord-Protector. Frynkel wasn't the
kind to give up.

35

At Marshal Frynkel's request, on Londi midmorning, Alucius rode at the head of the column beside the marshal. The sky had cleared and was a brilliant silver-green. A pleasantly warm breeze wafted out of the southwest. Asterta was well above the horizon, but barely visible against the brightness of the sky.

Frynkel spoke softly, and he did not look at Alucius. "Several years ago, I talked to an overcaptain of the Northern Guard before a dinner at Arms-Commander Wyerl's home. He seemed intelligent, hardworking, knowledgeable, and extremely skilled in the use of weapons. He was tactful and could disagree so graciously that it was hard to get angry with him. Then, he went to an audience with the Lord-Protector and vanished. Now . . . this has been known to happen, I hate to admit. The difference was that the Lord-Protector was not relieved, but quietly upset. Several weeks later, the officer returned, unshaven, unkempt, and several other matters came to light. First, there was an explosion in the chamber of the Recorder of Deeds, and the Recorder died. Second, the health of the Lord-Protector's consort improved greatly, against all medical advice and understanding, and third, the overcaptain was rewarded and discharged as he had requested."

Alucius remained silent, wondering where Frynkel was leading.

"The Lord-Protector has expressed concern about not having the information that the Table once provided, but he has not raged over its absence, even though its lack has created many difficulties for him. Now . . . we are seeing many manifestations of great Talent in Corus—and the Lord-Protector agreed to the recommendation that the Northern Guard officer be requested to return to duty . . ."

Recommendation? Who could have made that recommendation? Alucius wondered, then decided to gamble. He turned in the saddle. "Why did you recommend that?"

Frynkel smiled. "Someone else made the suggestion. I thought myself wise enough to recognize its wisdom. Does who brought up the idea matter?"

"It might," Alucius replied, trying to think through the situation. Neither the Lord-Protector nor the arms-commander would need to recommend anything to Frynkel, and who else even knew what had happened?

"I had thought that myself, but we examined the idea closely, Marshal Alyniat and I did, and we thought it was good enough to bring before the arms-commander."

Alucius almost froze in the saddle as he considered the most likely person to have made that recommendation.

"You look a bit . . . pensive, Majer," mused Frynkel, his tone verging on the ironic.

Alucius focused his senses and Talent upon the marshal before he spoke again. "Might I ask if the one who suggested this was Waleryn, the brother of the Lord-Protector?"

"Why would he come to us?" replied Frynkel.

Because Waleryn must have wanted me away from the Iron Valleys, Alucius wanted to say, and that meant that the Lord-Protector's brother had been more deeply involved with the ifrits than Alucius had realized. Instead of revealing that, Alucius merely said, "You would know that far better than I, Marshal."

"And I had to ask myself," the marshal went on, as if he had not asked Alucius anything, "why would the Lord-Protector so readily accept the mere hope of services of a relatively obscure officer, enough to send a marshal on a journey of some five hundred vingts?"

Alucius waited, glancing at the long and straight road ahead, and at the scouts who rode a half vingt ahead.

Frynkel turned in the saddle, fixing his deep black eyes on Alucius.

"It wasn't a hope, Marshal," Alucius answered. "If we wish to be honest, I must point out that it would have been foolish, if not idiotic, for me to refuse that request. You know that, and so do I."

"Ah . . ." Frynkel continued. "That is even more to the point. And how does a former officer who is a herder know this?"

"Because he is a herder. Because the prices of nightsilk reveal more than any talk by officers or officials. Prices and their future contracts do not lie." *Not for long,* Alucius temporized silently.

For a moment, Frynkel was silent.

"People tend to forget that herders operate a business that relies not only upon unique animals, but also upon equipment and processes with very high operating costs. We have to look to the seasons and years ahead. A herder who does not will lose his stead."

"In that case, to what do you, as both herder and officer, ascribe your presence here? And mine?"

"More than a few people of power wish me here," Alucius replied. "That is most clear and does not require any great foresight."

"And why would they wish you here?" Frynkel pursued.

"The Lord-Protector and, I presume, the arms-commander wish me here because they trust I can deal with the revolt in a way that will not weaken Lanachrona's defenses against the Regent of the Matrial."

"And what of others? Say, Lord Waleryn, since you did mention him."

"He wishes me here for his own purposes, which are not those of the Lord-Protector."

"I see you share the high opinion of Lord Waleryn held by a few others."

Alucius did not respond, since he had not actually been asked a question.

"What purposes might be ascribed to Lord Waleryn?"

"Anything that might enhance his stature or power."

"So he wishes you to fail, you think?"

"He may, but I would think he would prefer that I succeed, and that he judges my success will achieve the result he desires."

"For a comparatively young officer, you are cynical, Majer. Now . . . there is one other matter that has troubled me. The matter of the Table. The Table seemed impervious to most damage. If the records are correct, on more than one occasion over the centuries, large blocks of stone fell on it, yet it showed no damage. Then, seemingly for no reason at all, it exploded. And you returned to the palace. Equally striking is the fact that the destruction of the Table was taken so calmly by the Lord-Protector."

Alucius shrugged. "I only met the Lord-Protector briefly, but he struck me as a man who would not brood or rage over what he could not control." He hoped—vainly, he suspected—that the marshal would not continue his probing for the rest of the journey to Tempre.

"That may be, but what role did you play in the Table's destruction?"

"Just how could I destroy something that had lasted centuries?" Alucius laughed. "You do me far too much honor, Marshal. I am a herder. I do know a little about Talent. All herders do, but I know nothing about how such a Table might work, and, in truth, I did not even know such a thing existed before I came to Tempre."

"I had hoped you would. There were reports that you were the one who dragged Lord Waleryn to safety when the Table exploded."

"I can tell you in all honesty," Alucius replied, "that I do not know how a Table works, but I pledged the Lord-Protector that I would say nothing to anyone about the task he assigned me. I can say that he did not task me with anything involving the Table or its use."

"So he did have a task for you."

Alucius nodded.

"And you will not say more?"

"Not unless the Lord-Protector requests that I do, and I would not do so unless he did so in person."

"You are indeed cynical, Majer." Frynkel shook his head, then gestured to his left at the long expanse of rolling meadows, with grass still green, despite the harvest season. "Now . . . do you know why that expanse to our left is called The Folds?"

"I had not heard the name, sir."

"It's called that because in the early years of Lanachrona all the herders gathered their herds and flocks to winter over . . ."

Alucius refrained from taking a deep breath. The ride to Krost was long, and getting longer.

36

Alucius spent at least half of each of the next four travel days riding with the marshal, who had come up with what seemed hundreds of ways to approach the same set of questions—just what had Alucius been doing for the Lord-Protector and what did it have to do with the destroyed Table?

On two of the nights, the companies had slept out on very hard ground, in areas posted for lancers. South of Borlan the flatlands had turned into rolling hills that were far more lush, and in the bottomland between the hills were more meadows still green even in early harvest. The fields were bringing forth beans, maize, oilseeds, and the hillsides carried vingt upon vingt of almond orchards. The wooden stead houses and outbuildings were as well kept and numerous as Alucius recalled, and the high-road traffic was even thicker than he remembered.

With the warmer and moister air, Alucius had gone back to drinking more and more from his water bottles, and by late afternoon, his uniform was damper than he would have liked from all the perspiration.

Late on Quinti afternoon, Alucius, Feran, and Fifth

Company, following Eighth Company, were approaching Krost from the north, nearing the post where he was supposed to add two recently trained companies to his force. Southeast of Krost were the hills covered in rows of staked green vines, the northernmost of the wine-producing Vyan Hills, as Alucius recalled. Directly ahead was the crossroads where the two high roads intersected. At the crossroads, they would turn west to reach Krost Post.

"How good do you think these trainees are?" asked Feran.

"Not so good as they should be," replied Alucius. "Nor as good as they will be, between the two of us." He grinned and turned in the saddle. "And Egyl."

"Sir . . ." protested the senior squad leader.

Alucius gave an exaggerated shrug before turning back to look at Feran.

"You're going to have another problem . . . sir," Feran ventured.

"The way you tacked on the honorific, *overcaptain*, says I'm going to have a significant problem. Pray tell me." Alucius smiled.

Feran smiled back. "They're barely more than trainees. They don't know squat about anything. They've been told for years that the Northern Guard is a ragtag outfit of herders who had to be bailed out by the Lord-Protector." Feran held up his left hand. "We know it's not true, and probably whoever's been training them lately hasn't been saying that, but I'd wager that's what they all believe."

"You're probably right. I've been thinking about that. It's going to be hard on the trainees, but we'll set that right."

"Oh? Just like that, sir?"

"Just like that," Alucius replied. "We'll run a company-on-company exercise, and we'll use rattan blades, and you'll let it be known to Fifth Company the way the trainees probably feel. Or Egyl and the squad leaders will."

Feran winced.

"And then, I'll take on whoever thinks he's the best blade in the trainees."

"What if he's really good, a former duelist?"

"I doubt I'll have to. Someone that good won't be in with trainees. If he is, I'll cheat," Alucius said bluntly. "He won't know it, though."

"Whatever happened to that innocent young officer who believed in doing the right thing?"

"I still believe in doing the right thing. I hope I'm not quite so naive." Alucius looked southward, taking in the three tall chimneys that marked the glassworks, then, to the southeast, south of the other high road, the odd-shaped hill that had been cut away for the sand that fed the glassworks.

"Then, there's hope for us all." Feran laughed sardonically.

Ahead of Fifth Company, the marshal and Eighth Company had reached the crossroads in the center of Krost and turned westward. Fifth Company followed along the high roads that ran amid the old buildings, several as much as four stories tall.

The marshal had clearly sent someone ahead to announce their arrival because, once they followed Eighth Company through the wide stone gates of Krost Post, just west of the city, a full squad was lined up to welcome them, with a senior squad leader in the front. Alucius, Feran, and Fifth Company had reined up barely inside the gates of the post when three officers in blue-and-cream uniforms hurried out into the paved courtyard and stiffened before Marshal Frynkel.

Almost as quickly, a young-faced Southern Guard captain hurried at not quite a run past Eighth Company and came to attention opposite Alucius. "Captain Zenosyr, sirs. The captain-colonel asked me to make sure you and your men are settled in."

"Captain-colonel Jesopyr?" asked Alucius.

"No, sir. He was sent to Madrien in command of three companies. Captain-colonel Jorynst is post commander."

"I'm Majer Alucius, and this is Overcaptain Feran. He commands Fifth Company."

"Majer, Overcaptain." Zenosyr bowed his head briefly, then smiled and gestured. "You must have had a long ride. The front section of the stable is set aside for your lancers. I'll just walk with you. It's not that far."

Alucius refrained from saying that he'd been at Krost Post before, and merely nodded.

Fifth Company followed the captain to the massive stable, which had spaces for close to four hundred mounts. It was far more crowded than the last time Alucius had passed through, and only about a quarter of the stalls were vacant. The other stable appeared almost as full. From the stable, while Feran dealt with the squad leaders, Alucius carried his gear back across the courtyard, following the young captain to a two-story graystone structure a good hundred yards in length and up a set of steps to the upper level containing the officers' quarters.

Zenosyr opened the third door. "These are a colonel's quarters, but as a force commander with three companies, you rate them. If there's anything you need, let me know."

"I will, Captain, but I think it's unlikely."

"The captain-colonel would request your presence at the supper honoring the marshal in about a glass and a half."

"I'll be there."

Once the captain left, Alucius frowned, thinking. It was clear that the captain had no real idea who Alucius was, other than another majer. While Alucius was well aware that fame vanished quickly, he would have thought that someone might have briefed the captain, and he had to wonder why it had not been done.

He glanced around the room—a good ten yards by four—with an antique desk, a double-width bed of equally ancient vintage, a double armoire, a carved weapons-and-boot rack, wide, shuttered windows, and an attached washroom. It could have been the same room he'd been in before, although he thought that room had been closer to the headquarters building.

He decided to get cleaned up. He could puzzle over the strangeness as he did. First, he racked his weapons and hung up his clothes and gear before heading to the washroom with the tub and the spigot that provided ample volumes of lukewarm water. When he had finished washing himself, he washed out dirty uniforms and garments, then dressed and seated himself at the antique desk.

The last times he had passed through, the post that could have held between ten and fifteen full companies had housed only a company or a company and a half in residence. Now, it was more than half-full, but the honest Captain-colonel Jesopyr was gone. Had all the officers been transferred? That might explain why no one knew Alucius. Abruptly, he laughed. Why would anyone have cause to know him? "You're taking yourself too seriously," he said in a low voice to himself.

With a smile, he set to work writing out the exercises he planned to use to test the Southern Guard companies he would be commanding. He was still writing when there was a knock on the door.

"Alucius?" called Feran.

"Come on in."

The older officer slipped inside the quarters. "Not bad. It's about twice the size of my pantry." He paused. "We are supposed to add two companies here, aren't we? Wasn't that what you told me?"

"That's what the marshal told me."

"That captain's senior squad leader wanted to know if we were being sent west to fight the Matrites. I said that we had another fighting assignment. He just nodded."

"Captain Zenosyr didn't seem to know who I was and why we were here. I didn't tell him. I thought it might be more interesting to see what happens at supper." Alucius closed the folder that held his draft plans and orders, pushed back the armless desk chair, and stood.

"I never did like that word," Feran replied.

"Interesting?"

"Things are always interesting around you. No offense,

most honored Majer, but too often interesting just means dangerous."

"I know. But . . . if the officers here don't know, that's for a reason."

"I'd say it's because the marshal didn't want it known that those companies would be serving under a Northern Guard officer. I'd feel better if I knew why."

"Would you?" Alucius raised his eyebrows, then laughed. "We'd at least know what we're up against, besides a revolt. We might find out more at supper."

"I wouldn't wager on that."

"Neither would I, but we shouldn't keep the captain-colonel and the marshal waiting." Alucius followed Feran out of the room and closed the door behind him.

Zenosyr was standing in the courtyard below, outside the building that held both officers' quarters and the officers' mess. Young as the man looked, Alucius realized that he himself was only a few years older than the captain, if that.

The two Northern Guard officers followed the captain in through the double oak doors and down a short hallway floored in blue-and-white marble tiles shaped like diamonds. Although the mess itself had space for a good twenty tables, a single long table was set up with white linen and cutlery and with places for fifteen officers.

Perhaps ten Southern Guard officers were standing around the marshal, talking quietly, if insistently. Only a single officer, a majer who looked vaguely familiar to Alucius, even looked toward Alucius and Feran, and he glanced away quickly.

"Captain-colonel Jorynst, here are our Northern Guard officers," said the marshal more loudly, looking toward Alucius. "Majer Alucius and Overcaptain Feran."

"Welcome to Krost Post," offered Captain-colonel Jorynst, a square-faced man with thin brown hair and bright green eyes. "You'll pardon me if I don't attempt to introduce everyone at the moment."

Alucius just nodded an affirmation, smiling politely, adding, "We're pleased to be here."

"Now that everyone is here . . ." Jorynst gestured toward the head of the table. "If you would do the honor, Marshal . . . Majer Alucius?" The colonel nodded at the seat to the marshal's left while moving to the one to the right. The other majer sat beside Jorynst, while Feran was to Alucius's left, with the three other overcaptains next on each side of the table, followed by the captains.

Alucius noted that Zenosyr was the most junior captain, sitting at the last position on the left side of the table.

"In following the noble tradition set by my predecessor," Jorynst began, standing and moving to the table against the wall behind him, "I am pleased to offer one of the best white wines, that is, the best that the mess can afford." With a laugh, he uncorked one and then two of the amber-colored bottles, half-filling the marshal's goblet. Then he handed the bottle to a steward in white, who continued down the table filling the officers' goblets.

Once the goblets all held the near-colorless wine, the colonel looked to the marshal.

Frynkel smiled politely and raised his goblet. "To the officers of the Southern and Northern Guards, and to their triumphs, wherever they may be."

Alucius raised his goblet to the toast, then took a small sip of the wine. It was far better than anything he had tasted in recent years—since the last time he had been in "old" Lanachrona.

Three troopers in white jackets appeared, quickly setting plates before each officer. On each plate was fish fileted into thin strips and covered with a yellow glaze. As he had expected, the first course was lemon-almond oarfish.

"Majer Alucius," said Jorynst after a time of silence, "this is Majer Fedosyr. He's my deputy here. In addition to being most efficient and organized, he's also quite adept with the sabre and other weapons."

Fedosyr—Alucius now recalled the man from when he had passed through Krost before. That was why Fedosyr had seemed familiar, and from Alucius's covert scrutiny of the other officers at the table, he thought that Fedosyr was the only officer he had met before. "We met most briefly several years ago. It's good to see you again."

"And you, too," Fedosyr replied.

Alucius could sense a darkness about the other majer, and a darkness that he thought might bear a hint of purpleness, but that was so faint a feeling he wasn't certain. But he did not recall that darkness from their previous meeting. At the same time, the colonel showed neither darkness nor light, nor any spark of Talent. He was a senior officer probably on his last command.

"The colonel mentioned your efficiency. From that, I take it that you are in charge of the training going on here," Alucius ventured.

"The colonel has allowed me to do what I can—"

"Nonsense!" interjected Jorynst. "He's good at it, and he's in charge of it all. I just approve everything. What's the use of good officers if you don't have them do what they're good at?"

"Precisely," said Frynkel. "That is the nature of command, to use the tools best fitted for the tasks at hand." He looked directly at Alucius. "You, the colonel, and I will meet in the morning to discuss such weighty matters. They can wait until then." He lifted his goblet. "In the meantime, this wine is a tool for a good meal." He laughed and took a swallow.

A very small swallow, Alucius noted, which was in keeping with the effective prohibition on discussing why Alucius was at Krost Post.

After the fish came a marinated lamb, with spices that gave it an aftertaste that was too close to prickle for Alucius to enjoy it, especially given too-heavy lace potatoes smothered in cheese. With the heavy food also came light conversation—or conversation that avoided why Alucius was in Krost.

". . . say that this Council in Deforya won't last long . . ."

". . . could be . . . go through several before they realize . . ."

Alucius understood that. The Council hadn't wanted to accept reality and had toppled the Landarch. If they accepted reality, they'd be toppled. If they didn't, reality would force their hand, and they'd be toppled—somewhat later. His lips quirked into an ironic smile, but he continued to listen more than talk.

". . . Denorst's cousin says that the grapes are going to be the best in years . . ."

". . . liked that red he had last time we were there . . ."

". . . still think that the bays handle the cold better . . . coats are thicker . . ."

". . . hard to find a good farrier . . ."

In time, the marshal smiled and stood, and slipped away. Shortly thereafter, so did Alucius and Feran. Neither spoke until they were outside the door to Alucius's quarters and Alucius had opened the door.

"What was all that about?" asked Feran quietly, stepping into Alucius's quarters and closing the door. "The marshal as much as ordered us not to talk about why we're here."

"I don't know," Alucius admitted. "But I didn't want to say why we're here, not if the marshal and the captain-colonel didn't want to talk about it."

"I can see that. Why didn't he?"

"Something's wrong here, and . . ." Alucius had almost said that he felt Majer Fedosyr was the problem, but he didn't know that. ". . . I don't think anyone wants to face it. It could be that they resent my coming in here, that it's somehow a glove across the face."

"It wouldn't have to be," Feran said, "but it hasn't been handled right."

"Or someone doesn't want it handled right," Alucius suggested.

"There's a lot of that," Feran pointed out.

"There always has been. We saw that in the militia, even when Clyon was colonel. People want things the way they want them, not the way that would be best." Alucius shook his head and laughed softly and ironically.

"That doesn't even count the problem of knowing what is best."

"You're right about that."

"We won't get to the bottom of this tonight. I'm supposed to meet with the marshal and the colonel in the morning. They may not have wanted to say anything until they had a chance to meet. You're the deputy commander of this force. I'd like you to get both Southern Guard companies out on the maneuver field one glass after muster. I should be there by then, but if not, just tell everyone that those are my orders, and that I'll be there as soon as I can be."

"What about Fifth Company?"

"Tell them they can take the day off, but to get their gear in shape. The mounts need the rest anyway. We'll bring them into this on Septi. That's when they'll earn their pay."

"You don't make things easy."

"I'd prefer to do things more gently. It won't work. So . . . what I'm suggesting will be easier than trying to talk everyone into cooperating. I can tell that none of the officers are in the mood to be cooperative. So . . . we establish that we're in charge, and then we go after cooperation after that."

"I hope it's that simple."

So did Alucius.

37

Hieron, Madrien

The Regent stood between the conference table and the wide windows that displayed the southern part of Hieron as well as the southern quarter of the Park of the Matrial. Her violet eyes followed the east range high road southward to the point where it vanished into the harvest haze. Then she turned to the marshal. "You say that the second crystal spear-thrower should have reached the forces moving south from Dimor?"

"Yes, Regent," replied Marshal Aluyn. "Unless something unusual has occurred, they should be ready to begin the assault."

"I would not like that."

"Nor would we, Regent. But the Lord-Protector cannot bring any more lancers into the south."

"Cannot or will not?" asked the Regent.

"If he does, he risks losing the north more quickly or even his own south. If the revolt in Hyalt spreads to Syan, Soupat will be cut off, and that will limit the lead available to the Lanachronans, both for their bullets and their crystal trade."

"How are your efforts proceeding in that?"

"There are more weapons being shipped into Hyalt along the old Coast Range trails, and the revolt there continues to grow."

The Regent nodded, then asked, "And the torques? How many have we repowered?"

"We have concentrated on repowering those of former captives and those in and around Hieron."

"How many, Aluyn?"

"Less than a quarter. It takes time. We only have a few truly Talented officers. The new crystal is not as strong, not yet. We dare not send any recently trained captive lancers too far from places where we have Talent-officers."

"The crystal grows more powerful with each day."

"The Talent-officers have noted that, but you ordered us to concentrate on retaking the south."

"I did. That I did." The Regent nodded. "You may go. Let me know when we have word on our progress."

The marshal bowed. "Yes, Regent."

After the conference room door closed behind the departing marshal, the Regent turned back to the windows.

She looked southward in the golden light of the time just before sunset. Her fingers touched, briefly, the dark green emeralds of the choker. The gems flared deep within at her touch, and her smile hardened.

38

Sexdi morning, immediately after breakfast and morning muster, found Alucius in Captain-colonel Jorynst's study along with Marshal Frynkel. The three sat around a circular conference table in one corner of the study, a corner flanked by two man-high bookcases filled with leather-bound volumes. As he shifted his weight in the wooden armchair, Alucius couldn't help but notice that all the volumes were dusty, as were the bookshelves themselves.

"The marshal was telling me that you were attacked by strange creatures on the road south to Krost," offered the colonel. "Never heard of such a thing." He looked directly at Alucius.

"It was a surprise to us," Alucius replied. "I've never heard of anyone being attacked on a road like that. Not in the middle of Lanachrona, certainly."

"It happened to you and not to anyone else," said the colonel. "You were not terribly successful in protecting the Eighth Company, successful as you may have been with your own lancers. Command is not about protecting just one part of a force; it requires one to handle all the companies as one."

"That is true, Colonel," Alucius replied as politely as he could, despite the growing rage seething within him. What business did Jorynst have in chastising him? "At that time, I was only in command of Fifth Company, and I did not receive any orders from Marshal Frynkel."

"Shouldn't need orders for that. Your job was to protect the marshal."

Alucius debated for a moment, deciding whether to point out that he was not and had never been under the colonel's command. He decided against doing so and said calmly, "That was what we did. We stayed and fought the beasts. We killed them all, and that way none of them reached the marshal."

"You didn't do that much for the fourth and fifth squads of Eighth Company, now, did you?"

Alucius could not figure out why the colonel was attacking him—and why the marshal was allowing it—except that it was clear Frynkel had always had his own agenda. Alucius tried again, keeping his voice level. "We did the best we could, sir, and we did keep the other Eighth Company squads from taking casualties."

"That still left some thirty dead and wounded—almost a third of Eighth Company."

From what Alucius could sense, the colonel was angry, but Alucius couldn't figure out why. Jorynst hadn't been there. Eighth Company did not belong to Krost Post, but was stationed out of Tempre, according to the marshal. So Alucius just waited, without saying more.

"Your pardon, Marshal," offered Jorynst, nodding to Frynkel and turning back to Alucius, "but many strange things have happened around you, Majer, and you have an extremely high rate of casualties. I will do as ordered and place the Twenty-eighth and Thirty-fifth Companies under your command, but I cannot say that I am pleased. I am not pleased at all, and I cannot understand why this step is necessary. But I am a faithful officer and will do as directed."

Deciding that the abuse had gone far enough, Alucius forced a polite smile. "Then, Colonel, we feel exactly the same way. The last Southern Guard officer under whom I served managed to lose almost his entire company to the last man, and I was forced to watch as tactics I thought were unsuitable were employed. I managed to defeat an enemy that outnumbered our forces by close to ten to one. It is true that we suffered casualties in the range of thirty to forty percent, but that was far better than Majer Draspyr's ninety-eight percent. I am here at the request of the Lord-Protector. I did not ask to be here, and I did not ask to be sent to put down an internal domestic revolt in Lanachrona, a revolt with which the Iron Valleys have no connection. Because I, too, am a good and faithful officer, as always, I will do my very best. In the past, it's been far better than the Southern Guard has managed."

Jorynst's eyes almost bulged out, and he opened his mouth, then closed it. Finally, he spoke. "You . . . that is . . . insubordination . . ."

"Yes, sir," Alucius replied. "If telling the facts as they are constitutes insubordination, then I am insubordinate."

"I cannot believe that you—" began Jorynst.

"Colonel . . ." Marshal Frynkel said, firmly. "Majer Alucius is a Northern Guard officer. His record is impeccable. He is the only man in the history of Corus to receive the highest decorations from Deforya, Lanachrona, and the Iron Valleys simultaneously. He is also the only officer ever to engineer an escape from Madrien and, with less than a company of half-trained recruits, defeat between four and six experienced companies. He prefers the truth in a less varnished fashion and speaks more directly than the subordinates to whom you are accustomed. You may note that he replied most courteously and politely in his manner of speech time after time, when you were the one who was abusive. You took offense to what he said, and to the substance of what he said, I fear there is no rebuttal." Frynkel smiled coldly and turned to Alucius. "What are your training plans, Majer?"

"Do they need any more training?" asked Jorynst. "The Twenty-eighth and Thirty-fifth Companies have been preparing since we received word from the arms-commander."

Alucius couldn't believe that the colonel was still objecting. Was he that stubborn? Or was he just trying to set up Alucius? "We'll need at least several days to work with them and to assess—"

"They're good lancers—" said Jorynst.

"I'm certain that they are," the marshal interjected, "but the majer needs to work with them to make sure that the command structure works and to know how they do what they do, and they need to know how the Northern Guards do what they do."

"I suppose that's true . . ." The colonel's words were grudging.

"Colonel," Frynkel said almost amiably, "Majer Alucius understands his task. We should let him get on with it. There are a few matters that we need to discuss." Frynkel looked at Alucius. "If you wouldn't mind, Majer." After the briefest pause, he extended a folder. "Here are the rosters and squad assignments for your new companies. Your command begins as of now."

"Yes, sir." Alucius didn't mention that Feran had probably already established that command. He stood. "By your leave, Marshal?" He did not look at Jorynst.

"You have my leave, Majer."

Alucius left, closing the door behind him. He paused, but heard nothing, then stepped past the ranker seated at the desk in the anteroom. He wished he knew exactly what game the marshal was playing, but by the end of the meeting it had been clear to Alucius that the marshal had used Alucius against the colonel and had been quietly pleased. Alucius didn't like being used that way, but there was little he could do until he knew more.

He made his way to the armory, where he arranged for three hundred rattan blades to be ready on the following morning. Then he hurried to the stable, where the gray was waiting, already saddled. He took several moments to study the rosters, and then slipped them inside his tunic before leading the gelding out and mounting.

The post seemed quiet as he rode out past the sentries, who barely acknowledged his departure. Feran and the two Southern Guard captains were waiting for him at the edge of the flat dusty maneuver field to the west of the wall of Krost Post.

"Overcaptain, captains . . . I apologize, but the marshal had a few matters to discuss." Alucius offered a smile he did not feel. "I'm Majer Alucius, and I see that you've met your deputy commander, Overcaptain Feran."

"Yes, sir."

Alucius studied the two captains. One was dark-haired and painfully young. The other was at least ten years older, with a rugged face, short-cut blond hair, and a thin red scar across his forehead. Alucius looked at the older captain. "You're Jultyr?"

"Yes, sir."

"Were you in one of the companies that patrolled the Coast Range against the Matrial?"

"Yes, sir."

Alucius could detect the faintest puzzlement in the captain's response, but continued, "Did you ever wonder why the Matrites never sent out patrols of less than what seemed to be a half squad?"

"I hadn't thought about it, sir."

"We'll talk about that sometime, Captain." Alucius offered a smile as he projected a hint of warmth and trustworthiness at Jultyr. Then he turned to the second captain. "Captain Deotyr?"

"Yes, sir."

"How long have you been in service?"

"Just a year, sir."

"Good," Alucius said ambiguously. "I understand you two have been working your companies hard. I also suspect that neither of you is thrilled to be assigned to a command where you know little or nothing about your commanding officer. Has anyone briefed you on our mission?"

There was a flicker of eye contact between the two captains. Jultyr's jaw tightened, and he said nothing.

After a silence, Deotyr spoke. "We heard that we might have to do something about the revolt in Hyalt."

"That's correct. Contrary to what may have been passed

around," Alucius said easily, "I'm not interested in putting down a revolt by killing large numbers of people. That's a very last resort. Dead people don't produce goods. They don't pay tariffs, and their friends and relatives have even more reasons to revolt and try to kill lancers. That said, I won't hesitate to use force, if necessary, but I'd prefer other tactics first."

"Other tactics, sir?" blurted Deotyr.

"We'll discuss those later. We'll have plenty of time on the ride to Hyalt. This morning, we're going to go through some exercises to see just how your lancers operate and how good they are at what. This afternoon, we'll be adding some squad and company maneuvers and formations that are not used widely in the Southern Guard but that will have some application in Hyalt. Then, tomorrow, we'll begin some squad-on-squad drills against Fifth Company. Fifth Company is a very experienced outfit, and we can't afford any serious casualties. So . . . for any contact drills, I've arranged for rattan wands. You'll pick those up from the armory tomorrow after muster."

"Rattan?" blurted Deotyr.

"Captain," Alucius replied patiently. "We have to integrate tactics, techniques, and maneuvers. While basic mounted commands are similar from force to force, they are not identical, and tactics vary widely. There's a great possibility for miscommunication to begin with, and miscommunication with edged weapons is not desirable. Neither is conducting evaluation exercises and blade training without using weapons."

"Yes, sir."

"For this morning's maneuvers, I'll go with Captain Deotyr and Twenty-eighth Company." Alucius looked at Deotyr directly. "I'll give you the commands I want you to order. That will let me see how your company operates. Overcaptain Feran will do the same with Captain Jultyr and Thirty-fifth Company. Now . . . if you'd return to your companies and brief your squad leaders."

Alucius remained on the gray beside Feran, using his Talent to boost his listening as the two captains rode back to their ranked companies.

"Rattan . . ." murmured Deotyr. "Don't believe it . . ."

So far as Alucius could tell, Jultyr said nothing. After a moment, Alucius looked to Feran.

"Jultyr has an idea of what's coming," Feran said. "The other one . . ." He shook his head.

"I know," Alucius said. "I know."

Once he was sure that Deotyr had had time to brief his squad leaders, he rode toward Twenty-eighth Company.

The rest of the day was a blur, with exercise after exercise, and only a two-glass break between morning and afternoon sessions. By the time Alucius released the two companies—only slightly past midafternoon, because he had not wanted to put too much strain on the mounts—both trainee companies had learned, in general terms, the additional oblique maneuvers that Alucius had brought back from his captivity in Madrien and adapted for Northern Guard use, as well as a few others that had been used only by the Fifth and Twenty-first Companies of the Northern Guard.

At some point, Alucius wanted to send off a letter to Wendra. That was all he could do to reassure her that he was thinking about her and Alendra, but he had a great deal of planning to do. Also, he was well aware that anything he wrote and dispatched from Krost Post would have to be short and say little beyond expressing his affection.

As he rode back to the stable, dust-covered, tired, and hoarse, he couldn't help but wonder what the marshal and the colonel had discussed and how it would all play out.

39

Septi morning was cloudy but dry, and as
he reined up the gray on the maneuver field, waiting for
Captain Deotyr and Captain Jultyr, Alucius could almost
feel the resentment from a least some of the lancers in the
two Southern Guard companies as they formed up—carrying the rattan wands. He had not talked with Marshal
Frynkel, as had decided that it would be better for the marshal to seek him out than to seek out Frynkel immediately.
Alucius's orders did not mention a specific time when he
was to leave for Hyalt, and he did not want to leave until he
and Fifth Company had had more time working with the
two Southern Guard companies.

Within moments, Feran had brought his mount up beside Alucius. "Fifth Company is ready, sir."

"Thank you. Do all your squad leaders know what's necessary?" Alucius asked quietly.

"All I had to tell them was that the Southern Guard was
most unimpressed with the Northern Guard." Feran's voice
was dry. "I did add that the Southern Guards didn't seem to
understand that you were trying to protect them, and that it
might be wise to reinforce that point. Show the southern
boys that they needed that protection."

Alucius nodded slowly. "Good. I wish it were some
other way, but Colonel Jorynst's attitude has made this
more difficult than it had to be."

"You mean that he can't believe that we're fit to command good southern men? Sir?" Feran snorted.

"Something like that."

"How do you want to handle today?" asked the overcaptain.

"Might as well start with squad-on-squad. One set of
squads at a time, so the others can watch. Alternate. Your

first squad against first squad of Twenty-eighth, second squad against second squad of Thirty-fifth until we go through five drills. Then, we'll take a break. Say a half glass, but we'll see. Then, we'll reverse the order . . . Your first squad against the first squad of Thirty-fifth . . . That will mean your men have to work twice as hard."

"They can handle that."

Alucius remained on the gray, watching and waiting as Deotyr and Jultyr formed up their companies, then rode forward.

"Twenty-eighth Company, present and accounted for, sir."

"Thirty-fifth Company, present and accounted for, sir."

"Fifth Company, present and accounted for, sir," added Feran.

Alucius accepted the reports with a nod, then said, "Good morning, Overcaptain, captains."

"Good morning, sir."

"We'll be doing squad-on-squad drills this morning . . ." As Alucius explained, he studied the three officers. ". . . and once we've had a run-through of the first five skirmishes, the men will get a break, while I debrief you on each squad's performance. Then, you'll get some time to work out things with each squad and squad leader, and a break for rations and water. Then, we'll go through another set of squad-on-squad skirmishes . . ." As he finished the outline of the day's training exercises, it seemed to Alucius that Jultyr's attitude combined understanding with resignation. Deotyr seemed resentful and bewildered. Feran managed to conceal an ironic amusement.

After he dismissed the captains to make ready, Alucius rode farther toward the center of the maneuver area so that he could watch more closely.

"First squad, Fifth Company, ready, sir!" called Feran.

"First squad, Twenty-eighth Company, ready, sir!"

"Commence exercise!" Alucius ordered.

He watched intently as the first squad from Fifth Company wheeled, then rode toward the first squad of Twenty-eighth Company. Within moments, most of the recent trainees were either rocked back in their saddles, had lost their rattan wands, or had suffered blows that would have been crippling had they faced lancers with real sabres. Alucius had anticipated that some additional training would be necessary, but he had not expected such a poor showing.

He let the skirmish go on for a time, long enough that it was clear to most that those raw lancers in Twenty-eighth Company would have been slaughtered.

Then he rode toward the swirling melee, raising his voice and projecting command, "Break it off! Now!"

"Re-form! First squad break and re-form!" came the command from Faisyn.

"Re-form!" echoed the squad leader from Twenty-eighth Company.

Alucius watched, but it appeared as though all of first squad still held their wands.

After the dust settled, and the two first squads had cleared the center area, Alucius called out. "Second squads! To the center of the field. . . . Commence exercise!"

Once more, the results of the quick skirmish were overwhelmingly in favor of Fifth Company's second squad, but the lancers of Thirty-fifth Company's second squad generally managed to hang on to their weapons, and a few even parried or landed blows of their own.

Alucius tried not to frown as the morning wore on, but the pattern set in the first two skirmishes held consistent for the last three. Twenty-eighth Company was hopelessly overmatched, while Thirty-fifth resembled trained raw lancers.

As the last of the morning drills broke off and the two fifth squads re-formed, Alucius caught sight of a Southern Guard officer riding away from the maneuver field. He wasn't certain, but he thought the man was Fedosyr, and he wondered exactly why the other had been watching the drills.

Alucius made a mental note to himself about Majer Fedosyr as he rode toward Twenty-eighth Company, loosely formed up in the northwest corner of the field.

He began his debrief with Captain Deotyr and the first squad leader. "Captain, squad leader . . . the first thing that I noticed was that too many lancers in your squad were leaning back in their saddles . . ." After going over the general observations, he moved on to specific points.

Then he repeated the process with Captain Jultyr.

After that Alucius called a break. The companies dismounted, tying their horses to the railings on the east and west sides of the maneuver field.

Alucius turned his own gray to the northeast, where he reined up at the very north end of the railing. There he dismounted and took a long swallow from one of his water bottles. Shortly, Feran joined him.

"What do you think?" Alucius asked the older officer.

"Thirty-fifth Company will be all right. Jultyr's solid. Not outstanding, but solid. Twenty-eighth Company . . ." Feran shook his head.

"They've made it harder for us," Alucius suggested. "Normally, you just rotate replacements into an existing company. Except for the squad leaders and captains, they've formed two complete companies out of trainees. So we get to train them, and when it's all over they either get two trained and experienced companies, or they haven't lost an existing company."

"Why do we always get deals like this, sir?"

"Because a lot of the Southern Guard doesn't like the Northern Guard. We cost them a lot of lancers and officers over the years, and they haven't forgotten—or forgiven."

"Have we?" asked Feran with a laugh.

"We haven't forgotten, but I hope we've enough sense to put it behind us." Alucius fished out some hard travel bread and chewed on it, wondering just how many more difficulties that he hadn't anticipated would raise their heads.

After the midday break, the afternoon skirmishes went in much the same way as the morning, except that Twenty-eighth Company's results were even worse, with two lancers breaking their sword arms. On the other hand, Thirty-fifth Company's three squads did a slightly better job against Fifth Company and also managed to hold discipline and a semblance of ranks.

Alucius went through another long series of debriefs with the captains and their squad leaders, and it was well past midafternoon when he finished those and ordered the companies to form up.

"How do you think they'll react to today?" Feran asked.

"You probably know better than I do," Alucius replied. "What do you think?"

"My guess is that the trainees—I guess they're lancers now . . . they'll start to accept the fact that they have something to learn. The captains, I don't know. Deotyr will do what you want, but he won't give much leadership. Jultyr . . . he can probably lead, but I can't tell whether he'll make it hard or not."

"It's your job, for now, to find out and see what it will take with Jultyr," Alucius said.

"I was afraid you'd say that."

"And one other thing . . ." Alucius smiled tiredly. "Once everyone is formed up, I'm going to announce a complete gear inspection in one glass. That includes Fifth Company."

Feran smiled in return. "Fifth Company should be set. I held one yesterday."

"The others may be set, but . . ."

"You don't think so."

"I'd like to think so," Alucius said.

He waited for a bit longer, before ordering, "Captains, forward!"

The three officers rode from before their companies, reining up in a line three yards short of Alucius.

"Captains, Overcaptain."

"Yes, sir."

"You and your men have a glass and a half to get set for a complete mount and gear inspection outside the barracks. Uniform will be standard field dress. Gear will be full deployment equipment. That includes all officers and men in all three companies."

"Yes, sir."

"That will be all."

After the three turned their mounts, Alucius listened as they rode back to their companies.

". . . think he is . . ." muttered Deotyr.

". . . he's in command, Deotyr . . . better realize that . . ." answered Jultyr. "He's got a nasty job to do, and we're the ones . . ."

A nasty job indeed, Alucius reflected, as he turned the gray back to the stable, but nasty jobs seemed to be his legacy.

40

On Octdi morning, a day with hazy clouds rather than the heavy overcast of the previous day, Alucius had just led out the gray from the stable, but had not mounted. He and Feran stood by their mounts.

"You still intend to work with Twenty-eighth Company?" Feran asked.

"For now. You seem to be working things out with Jultyr."

"He's seen enough to realize what you are. He also asked. I told him you'd entered service really young and been a militia scout, a Matrite captive, and then a squad leader, and all the militia history." Feran smiled. "I think he was more impressed that you were a squad leader for the Matrial and escaped."

"If that's what he likes, that's fine."

"If I might ask . . ." Feran began, . . ."about the inspections?"

"The same as the drills. Sloppy gear in Twenty-eighth, what you'd expect of decent raw lancers in Thirty-fifth." Alucius could sense someone coming, and he turned to see Marshal Frynkel walking alone across the paved courtyard of the post toward them. Alucius waited, hiding a smile as Feran eased away.

"Majer?"

Alucius looked at the marshal. "Sir?"

"I have been talking with Majer Fedosyr. He is rather distraught about your exercises of yesterday. Most distraught, I would say."

"Sir?"

"He feels that it was highly unfair to place lancers just out of training against a battle-tested company of veterans."

"I would agree with the majer, sir," Alucius replied. "That was exactly why I did it. Battle isn't a question of fairness. It's a question of who's more skillful and who's better trained and better led. The sooner these new lancers understand that they're no match for experienced lancers, the sooner they'll be ready to listen and to learn."

"I had told the majer that I thought that was your rationale." A faint smile crossed the marshal's face. "He feels that you may have an image of all Southern Guards as being less . . . able."

While Alucius harbored some suspicions along those lines, he wasn't about to voice them. "I don't believe I've ever said or even hinted that, sir."

"Nonetheless, the majer is quite concerned."

"I appreciate his concerns, but I need to have these lancers ready to accept more rigorous training and understand why it's necessary."

"In fact, the majer would like to uphold the ability of the Southern Guard in a demonstration match against you."

"Is that necessary?" Alucius asked cautiously. Although he'd mentioned to Feran the possibility of such a match against the best blade in the two companies, he'd decided against it as unnecessary when the skirmish exercises had turned out the way that they had.

"The majer believes it is necessary, and since he does, and since it is likely that many follow his views, I fear I must concur."

"Yes, sir. When does the majer suggest that this take place?"

"Within the glass. Here in the courtyard. He does not wish to disrupt your training schedule unduly, but he feels that for you to proceed under a misapprehension would not be wise."

"I can understand misapprehensions, sir."

"Majer Fedosyr is considered one of the best blades in the Southern Guard, and he would like to demonstrate that the Southern Guard is indeed expert with weapons. He would like to have all the lancers in the post watching."

"If you feel it necessary, I would be more than happy to engage in such a demonstration with Majer Fedosyr," Alucius replied. "Our exercises have been using rattan blades . . ."

"I believe that Majer Fedosyr might find that . . . less than satisfactory." Frynkel frowned. "Yet I would find it disturbing if you were unable to carry out the Lord-Protector's wishes."

Alucius ignored the presumption implied by the marshal. "Perhaps you could suggest to Majer Fedosyr that we begin with rattan, and that if he finds rattan unsatisfactory, we could resume with our own sabres."

"He might be amenable to that. In half a glass?"

"Yes, sir."

After the marshal turned and walked back toward the headquarters building, Alucius walked the gray back inside the stable and stalled the big gelding. Feran followed, also with his own mount. Alucius did not unsaddle his mount, but left the stall carrying the rattan wand. He stopped in the open space beyond the stall as Feran approached.

"Fedosyr's looking for an excuse to kill or disable you," Feran said in a low voice. "Humiliate you at least."

"Whatever makes you think that of the most honorable majer?"

"My high opinion of him, I guess," Feran replied, deadpan.

"I thought it might be something like that."

"What will you do?"

"Begin by acting in the most honorable way and assume that he won't. Then only appear to act honorably while doing what's necessary."

"You're using a lot of words."

"How about: Wait until he tries something dirty, then do it worse before he can?"

"I like that better," Feran said.

"I'm also going to my quarters for a few moments. I'll be back shortly. I need to get a few things."

"Good idea."

Alucius walked quickly from the stable to his quarters, where he stripped off his tunic and donned the padded nightsilk vest that had stood him in such good stead in the past. He'd end up sweating profusely by the time everything was over, but that was a price he was more than willing to pay, especially given his distrust of Fedosyr. Then he made his way back to the stable.

Feran was not there, but returned shortly. "You're wearing the vest, aren't you?"

"Wouldn't you?"

"Might be a good idea to wear it all the time around these sandsnakes."

Alucius laughed.

"I told Jultyr and Deotyr to have their men form up in a square in the courtyard to watch the demonstration suggested by the marshal. Also told Fifth Company."

"Was there any reaction?"

Feran's lips quirked. "Egyl suggested that the marshal must not care much for Majer Fedosyr. Either that, or he didn't understand herders."

"It could be both. We'll see."

"The other companies are already forming up—Eighth Company and the two others stationed here."

The last thing Alucius wanted was a sabre match in front of five hundred lancers, but upon reflection, he couldn't say that he was surprised. He spent the next quarter glass doing some stretching and bending exercises. Then, he picked up his rattan wand and walked out toward the open square area formed by the gathered lancers. There were indeed at least five companies arrayed in the post courtyard.

Alucius stopped at the southern edge of the open space, in front of Fifth Company. He still wore his sabre in the belt scabbard. The murmurs of low voices filled the area with a low, whispering rumble.

Majer Fedosyr was already out in the courtyard, standing beside the marshal. As soon as Frynkel caught sight of Alucius, he said a few words to Fedosyr. Then the marshall stepped into the center of the area flanked with lancers. The murmurs died away.

"We're very fortunate to have two exceptional officers here at Krost Post. Many of you know Majer Fedosyr, who is renowned for his skill with a blade and for his long and devoted career in the Southern Guard. Majer Alucius of the Northern Guard is also renowned and highly decorated. They will be demonstrating skill with weapons." The marshal nodded and stepped back.

With the rattan wand in hand, Alucius moved forward into the open space, smiling, but listening to the murmurs from the ranked lancers.

"Except for that gray hair . . . looks younger n' a fresh captain . . ."

". . . think he's all that good?"

". . . no one's as good as Majer Fedosyr . . ."

". . . say that this majer decorated for bravery everywhere . . ."

". . . doesn't make him a good blade . . ."

Alucius agreed with that, but bravery didn't make a man a poor blade, either.

After a moment, Fedosyr stepped away from where he had stood beside the marshal on the northern side of the rough square.

Alucius studied the majer closely. Fedosyr was a big man, a fraction of a span taller than Alucius and well muscled, but not fat, and he carried himself with a certain litheness. Fedosyr was not ifrit-possessed, but Alucius was sure now that he could detect the faintest hint of purpleness to the man's lifethread—much as he had felt with Colonel Weslyn. Yet the colonel and the majer had never met. Of that, Alucius was most certain.

Alucius stopped a good yard short of Fedosyr and bowed slightly. "Majer."

"I applaud your caution in suggesting rattan, Majer, if not your confidence," said Fedosyr.

"I am most cautious, Majer," Alucius replied politely.

"That is obvious." Fedosyr raised his wand.

Alucius matched the gesture, reading with eyes and Talent the next move. He began the parry almost as Fedosyr eased to one side and swept in from Alucius's right.

For the first moments, Alucius reacted and observed. To him, it was obvious that he was faster than Fedosyr and able to anticipate.

Fedosyr seemed to stumble, going down slightly into not quite a crouch. Alucius sensed the feint and gave the faintest hint of trying to test Fedosyr's less protected side. Fedosyr came out of the crouch in a focused attack, but Alucius had anticipated the attack and struck.

In an instant, Fedosyr's wand lay on the ground.

"You couldn't do that with real weapons," the Southern Guard officer said.

"Actually, it would be easier with a real sabre," Alucius replied. As soon as the words were out of his mouth, he wished he could take them back, realizing that Fedosyr was so hotheaded that he would take them as a challenge.

"Then we should try real sabres." Even before he finished the words, Fedosyr's hand went to the sabre at his side. He kicked the rattan wand away, and a lancer ran up and took it away.

Alucius stepped back, then half threw, half slid the rattan wand across the pavement stones of the courtyard in the general direction of Feran. His own sabre was in his left hand before the wand scraped across the stones to stop short of Feran's feet.

Fedosyr's sabre glinted in weak morning light, polished

and clearly sharpened to a razor edge. A duelist's edge, Alucius noted, as brought his own blade into a careful guard.

The Southern Guard majer attacked, furiously but deliberately, keeping himself well balanced.

Alucius circled away, easily parrying or slipping the other's blade, not giving any openings.

"You see . . . not so easy with *real* blades," Fedosyr murmured.

It wasn't, not when Alucius didn't really want to injure or kill the other man. He continued to parry and defend, his own sabre weaving a defense that Fedosyr could not penetrate.

As the moments passed, Fedosyr's attacks grew sharper. Then for a moment, the taller man eased back, far enough back that Alucius did not press. Fedosyr blotted his forehead with the back of his sleeve, then his hand dropped to his belt, as if to wipe the sweat away. Except Alucius could sense that Fedosyr had something in his hand.

The Southern Guard officer held his free hand out more to the side, as if to balance himself, then rushed Alucius.

Alucius could sense the colorless powder that flew toward his face and eyes almost from the moment that Fedosyr released it. Instead of parrying or blocking the other's thrust, Alucius darted sideways—but only for an instant. Even so, Alucius could feel the burning on the side of his neck where some of the colorless powder had grazed him.

Fedosyr hesitated for a moment, as if unsure whether his powder had done its work, and in that instant, Alucius attacked—for the first time. At the last instant, Alucius turned the blade. Even so, there was a dull crack of bones breaking as the flat of the sabre slammed across Fedosyr's wrist.

The polished sabre clanked on the stones.

"I apologize, Majer," Alucius said quietly, "but I don't like duelist's tricks."

Fedosyr's face had drained of color. He just looked at

Alucius blankly for a moment. Then his left hand darted toward his belt.

Alucius took two steps forward before Fedosyr managed to fire one shot from the small pistol. The shell slammed into the left side of Alucius's chest, not quite at the shoulder, staggering him, but he managed to hang on to the sabre just long enough for his right hand to grab it and use it to slash back across Fedosyr's neck.

Fedosyr didn't even look surprised as his lifeless body slumped to the ground.

Alucius forced himself to bend down and wipe his blade on Fedosyr's tunic. He straightened and sheathed the sabre. Then he walked slowly toward the marshal.

". . . shit . . . how could the majer miss?"

". . . didn't   miss . . . see   how   Majer   Alucius staggered . . ."

". . . took the shot and then killed Fedosyr . . . with his other hand . . ."

"Must have been a duelist . . ."

". . . never seen someone do that . . ."

Alucius stopped short of the marshal. Frynkel's face was impassive.

"Sir, I regret the last, but I could not afford to allow Majer Fedosyr the opportunity for another shot. By your leave, I would like to get on with the training."

"You have my leave, Majer. I will ensure that Majer Fedosyr's kin know that he died in overextending himself during a training exercise, one in which he disobeyed Guard policies."

"As you see fit, sir." Alucius had to struggle to keep the anger out of his voice and wasn't sure he had.

Frynkel waited, then said, "You may go, Majer."

"Yes, sir." Alucius stepped back and turned.

Feran met him on the far side of the open space. "I'd forgotten how good you are with both hands."

"It helps at times."

"How badly—" The overcaptain's eyes flicked toward Alucius's shoulder.

"I'll be bruised on the left side of my chest," Alucius said in a low voice, "and probably from elbow to shoulder. Better that none of them know that."

"It'll be a long day."

"It's already been too long. Have all three companies mount and form up here." Alucius turned and walked toward the stable. The lancers parted, leaving a wide aisle. Only when he was past them did the whispers begin.

". . . made Fedosyr look like a recruit . . ."

". . . see why they wanted him . . ."

". . . wiped his blade on his tunic . . ."

". . . looked like he wanted to kill the marshal, too . . ."

After he reached the stable, Alucius checked his chest. The vest and the nightsilk undergarments had done their work. Nothing was broken, but the bruises were already beginning.

After blotting his sweating forehead, taking a long swallow of water from one of his bottles, and readjusting his uniform, Alucius waited a quarter of a glass before he led the gray from the stable out into the courtyard. He mounted and rode to the front of the formation. There he looked at Feran, Captain Deotyr, and Captain Jultyr. He waited for a moment before he raised his voice for all of them to hear. "We'll head out to the maneuver field. Once we're there, we'll break down into two-on-two drills, trainees against Fifth Company. And you will use rattan. You'll have enough bruises to prove that it's no toy. Tomorrow, we'll go back to working on the squad level . . ."

As he finished his instructions, Alucius couldn't help but wonder if there weren't an easier way to convince people than with some form of force. He also hoped he could keep moving without betraying the pain and stiffness that was spreading from the impact of Fedosyr's bullet.

41

Stiff and sore after finishing the last training exercises on Octdi, Alucius walked into the headquarters building. The marshal had sent a lancer with a message requesting Alucius's presence when his training duties were finished for the day. Alucius anticipated nothing good from the meeting.

Alucius looked at the ranker behind the desk. "The marshal requested my presence."

The lancer bolted to his feet. "Yes, sir. He's in the colonel's study, sir. He's expecting you, sir."

"Thank you." Alucius doubted that he'd ever gotten three "sirs" from a Southern Guard before. It was truly amazing what the application of skill and force could achieve when common sense and courtesy could not prevail. He opened the door and stepped into the study, expecting both the marshal and the colonel, but Frynkel was alone.

"Please close the door and have a seat, Majer."

Alucius sat down cautiously.

From behind the colonel's desk, Frynkel looked at Alucius. "Captain-colonel Omaryk had said that you were not only an officer, but a warrior-leader."

It took Alucius a moment to recall that Omaryk had been one of those who had debriefed him in Tempre years before. "Warrior-leader, sir?"

Frynkel laughed wryly. "That's why you've led so much from the front."

"I've had trouble leading any other way, sir."

"Just remember this, Majer. All the great war leaders led from the front. Most of them died. There were less than a handful that didn't die in battle, and they founded empires and saved lands."

There wasn't much Alucius could say to that or wanted to. So he remained silent.

"I've spent most of the day cleaning up the mess that Majer Fedosyr created. Or rather, explaining that he had overreached himself. I found the pouch of acid-dust. He had more in his quarters. How did you manage to escape that?"

"I saw him reach for something. It seemed likely that it would be thrown at either my face or my feet."

"You saw that while you were fighting?"

"Yes, sir."

"You see more than you tell."

"Everyone does, sir."

Frynkel shook his head.

"I haven't seen the colonel," Alucius ventured, trying to shift the subject and probe as well.

"I doubt that you will, since he has left Krost Post for his family home in Syan. I asked for and accepted his resignation. He had enough service for a stipend."

"So I was a tool for that?"

"Let us say that you helped. It was most useful to be able to point out that Jorynst did not recognize your past contributions. It was even more useful to be able to cite his failure to understand casualty figures. That allowed me to note that a once-distinguished officer had apparently suffered a loss of mental faculties by denying verified and published figures and events." Frynkel's smile was both wry and cold. "I did make sure that several lancers made copies for the files and for dispatches."

Alucius understood that. Those lancers would spread the word. There was no way to stop that, and Frynkel certainly hadn't wanted it stopped. "And Majer Fedosyr? Was that part of the plan?"

"Majer Fedosyr has always had an excessive opinion of himself, as well as well-placed friends in Tempre. They have always been rather forceful supporters. I hadn't realized that he had a hidden pistol or that he was foolish enough to use it. If he had killed you, he would have been court-martialed and executed. That would have solved that problem, but I certainly wouldn't have wanted to pay that price to get rid of him." Frynkel looked at Alucius. "You didn't have to kill him. He would have been court-martialed. Why did you?"

"I wasn't certain of that, sir, and my grandsire always told me that a man who gave a sander or a sandsnake a second chance was a fool and deserved what he got. Majer Fedosyr was a sandsnake, and I felt that it was likely that he'd have gotten away with what he did if I hadn't acted then and there."

"You may be right, but we'll never know."

Alucius wasn't about to point out that there had been too much risk in letting Fedosyr live.

"You made a point with all those lancers. You also set a personal standard that could be hard to live up to."

"I can't say that I'd thought about that, sir. I did what I thought was right."

"The Lord-Protector told me that you always did. He also said that such officers were to be used sparingly. The right is too powerful a weapon for frequent use." Frynkel looked directly at Alucius for a long moment. "I'm leaving tomorrow for Tempre. Overcaptain Nybor is temporarily in charge of Krost Post, with orders to support you fully. Even without my orders, I doubt you would have difficulty." Frynkel paused. "Your orders allow you some latitude in when you leave. When you do, you are to proceed directly to Hyalt and not to go to Tempre."

"I had thought so."

"You also have complete discretion in Hyalt, and that means that you will be fully accountable."

Alucius understood that message as well. Hyalt was another opportunity for total personal disaster.

"When do you intend to leave?" asked the marshal.

"Londi. I'd thought we'd take a measured pace, with mounted drills every morning and individual weapons practice and drills every evening. The individual practice won't tire the mounts, and if I can instill good habits in tired men, they'll hold."

"You and Overcaptain Féran make a good team."

"He's very solid and very practical, sir."

"That seems to be a trait of the north. Along with ruthless idealism implemented pragmatically."

"For all the procedural niceties, sir, I did not ask for this assignment."

"I know. It is recorded as my suggestion to the Lord-Protector. If you're successful, we both will profit."

Alucius didn't see how having to follow Colonel Weslyn would be any great profit to him or to his family—or the stead. He could see all too easily the disasters that would follow if he succeeded to command of the Northern Guard—let alone those that awaited him if he failed earlier.

"I've been away from Tempre too long," Frynkel continued. "Marshal Wyerl has requested my return so that he can leave to take personal command of the Lord-Protector's forces defending Southgate and the trade highways."

Alucius nodded.

"I wish you well, Majer, for both of our sakes, and trust I will see you in Tempre before too long, reporting your success in dealing with the rebels."

While Alucius understood that the marshal wanted to end the meeting, there were too many unanswered questions. "Sir . . . there are a few matters . . ."

"Yes?"

"Supplies. The post at Hyalt has been taken. It's unlikely that we can count on local support for rations or feed, at least not much past the south of Tempre. I'd like to request some supply wagons . . ."

"In Lanachrona?"

"Especially in Lanachrona, sir. I would doubt that the Lord-Protector would wish us to forage off his own people . . ."

Frynkel took a deep breath. "We can make arrangements. What else?"

"More information. There are maps, but the only reports we have are a season old. What kind of weapons and mounts do they have? How many are there? Where did they come from?"

Frynkel shook his head. "You have all the information I have. That's all the information anyone in Lanachrona has. We sent in scouts. Not a one returned. Since the first traders and crafters fled, no one else has appeared coming north or east out of Hyalt."

"No one?"

"No one."

"You expect me, with three companies, to deal with something like this?"

"I never told you it would be easy, Majer. The Lord-Protector is stretched thin everywhere."

Just how thin Alucius had not realized. He took a slow breath.

All in all, he spent another half glass with the marshal before finally saying, "Thank you, sir. We'll do all that we can and appreciate your support." He paused, then asked, "By your leave, sir?"

"You have my leave and best wishes."

Alucius rose, trying to make the movement fluid, when he felt anything but graceful. Frynkel said nothing more as Alucius left the study.

He walked back across the courtyard to his quarters, thinking. Frynkel had used him to solve a problem at Krost Post, exactly as the Lord-Protector was planning to do in Hyalt. That underscored his own problem. He had more planning to consider so that he was not merely re-acting when he reached Hyalt, and that meant some intensive study of the maps of the area around Hyalt. The lack of information bothered him, because it strongly suggested the ifrits might be involved. But how could he tell?

He smiled, faintly, ironically. There was one simple aspect to the day's events. Now that Fedosyr and Jorynst were gone from Krost, Alucius could finish his letter to

Wendra and send it off. Again, he pushed aside his worries about her and Alendra. He doubted he'd be sending many dispatches from Hyalt, and for a glass or two of the evening ahead, he didn't want to think deeply about what lay ahead, even if he would have to in the glasses and days before him.

42

Dekhron, Iron Valleys

Even in harvest, it is chill here," observed Sensat, closing the shutters against the twilight. He moved to the iron stove set against the outside wall of the study, where he opened the stove door and thrust in a generous shovelful of coal before setting the shovel against the hearth wall and propping it against the base of the scuttle.

"Acorus is a cold world," replied Tarolt. "You knew that."

"Knowing it in one's mind and feeling the chill seeping into your bones on all but the warmest of summer days are two different matters." Sensat pulled one of the chairs closer to the stove and seated himself. "It's not just the chill. It's everything." He gestured at the shelves and the books set upon them. "This, this is one of the largest collections of what passes for knowledge in all of Corus. The paintings, they are as child's drawings. The sculpture is crude, raw, unfinished. The buildings are low and squat. Save for the handful of towers surviving from the Duarchy, nothing soars. Nothing challenges the eye or the spirit."

"If you miss Efra so much, you could chance a return."

"And risk becoming a wild translation? One world-translation in a lifetime is quite enough." Sensat took a deep breath. "Can I not miss the soaring spires of Deconar? Or the high domes of Peshmenat? Can I not regret not having listened more intently to the lilting compositions of Ghefari?"

"You can. I miss them as well," Tarolt replied. "But there will be no spires in the future, no music for the ages, no domes that span the skies . . . not if we do not complete and strengthen the grid. Not if we do not prevent the ancient ones and their tools from again acting against us."

"Always the ancient ones . . ."

"Once-powerful pastoralists, who would try to pass their lack of ambition on to dull steers." Tarolt shook his head. "Steers who have no concept of art, of architecture, of beauty. They would leave their world a dull mudball drying in the eternity of time, accomplishing nothing, striving for nothing, becoming nothing."

Sensat stood and walked to the stove, opening the door and adding more coal. "You're right. I'm still cold, though."

"Dull steers worthy only of providing the lifeforce for achievement and glory," Tarolt said quietly. "Remember that."

43

Under the soft light of the wall lamp in his quarters, Alucius leaned back in the old wooden chair, ignoring the creaking as his weight shifted, and blotted his forehead. The night was as warm as some summer days on the stead, and he doubted that he'd ever get used to the heat of the south. Places like Hyalt and Soupat—or Southgate—were even warmer. He glanced over at the nightsilk skull mask that lay folded on the corner of the desk. Wearing it in the current weather, even at night, would leave him a mass of sweat. Still . . . it might prove useful at some point.

After taking a swallow from the water bottle he had set on the corner of the desk, he eased back forward, studying the map, his eyes following the narrow roads to the west of Hyalt. The map didn't show how high the hills were, or how steeply they might climb into the eastern side of the Coast Range, but from the way the roads curved on the map, it was clear to Alucius that the terrain was anything but level. After a time, he took the calipers and began to measure the distances, writing them down on a sheet of brown paper.

He had to hope that the maps he had been studying were indeed correct, or mostly so. He'd learned over the years that few were totally accurate, but if the roads he had measured and studied went roughly where the map said they did, then he could at least attempt the strategy he had in mind. Then, too, he told himself, once he got to Hyalt, he might have to rethink everything.

Would there be more of the strange Talent-creatures in Hyalt? Or was it too far south for them? Or did it matter? While the soarers did not appear in the south, he had the feeling that the creatures associated with the ifrits would not be limited by heat.

No one seemed to know much about the revolt in Hyalt, except that the followers of the True Duarchy had appeared with weapons early on an end-day morning and slaughtered an unprepared and badly outnumbered garrison. Alucius had decided that a thorough reconnaissance was the first step, including staying well away from the town of Hyalt in the beginning. The more information he could gather before acting, the better.

His lips quirked into a half smile. He already had a reputation for being almost impulsive and ruthless, and he wasn't sure that he was truly either. Ruthless? The ifrits had been ruthless.

He paused. Did every effective officer rationalize his actions that way? Did the ifrits?

After a long silence, he returned to studying the map and making notes.

When he was finished with the maps for the night, he'd write some more on the letter to Wendra. It was always more pleasant to end the day—or night—thinking of her.

44

Alucius studied the small hall in which he found himself, a vacant space ten yards long and half that in width. The walls were of pink marble with a tinge of purple, and at intervals of five yards half pillars were set within the marble—or against the stone. Alucius could not tell which. The stone pillars were of goldenstone, not gilded, but golden throughout. Overhead, slightly more than five yards above him, curved a ceiling of the same pink marble. All of the stone was so precisely fitted that his Talent could detect no sign of joints or of mortar. The floor was of octagonal sections of polished gold and green marble, each section of green marble inset with an eight-pointed star of golden marble, with the narrow arms of the star outlined in a thin line of brilliant—and unfamiliar—metal.

The walls seemed to have shifted, and Alucius glanced around. There was no one but him in the chamber, and there were no wall hangings. He realized that he had not seen a doorway, and he turned to look behind him. There was no entrance there, either.

How had he gotten into the chamber? He did not see a Table anywhere.

Again, there was the sense that the walls had shifted, and Alucius tried to figure out what had happened. He studied the chamber. It was smaller—now only eight yards in length and four wide.

He took two steps forward and looked back. Nothing had changed, and there were still no doors anywhere.

The walls shifted once more, and now the chamber was but five by two and a half yards, and the ceiling was less than four yards above him.

He reached out and touched the marble of the wall, cold, but not freezing. As he withdrew his hand, the walls shifted once more, then again almost immediately, so that he was standing in a chamber smaller than a cell, surrounded by hard stone less than a yard away.

He tried to reach out with his Talent, to find a way out, but he could sense nothing but stone, hard stone.

The walls shifted again, so that he had to turn sideways. Sweat poured down his forehead. He had to get out . . . somehow. He had to—

Alucius bolted upright in the wide bed in the senior officers' quarters. The sudden movement sent twinges through his aching body. Sweat was indeed streaming from his face and chest. He swung his feet over the side of the bed and stood slowly. He walked to the window, looking out into the darkness, but he still felt closed in. So he turned and made his way to the door. He opened it wide and stepped out into the darkness, breathing the cool air deeply.

After several moments, he finally turned and stepped back into the quarters, closing the door gently. He walked slowly back to the bed, where he lowered himself to sit on the edge, all too aware that many of his bruises had a ways to go before they stopped aching. As he sat on the edge of the bed, he used the back of his hand to blot the cooling sweat from his forehead.

He'd never had a dream quite like that, with the walls closing in on him, but he had to admit that in some ways, that had been how he'd felt in having to agree to the Lord-Protector's "request."

After a time, he stood and walked around the room, still trying to cool off, still wondering what else lay behind the walled-in feeling.

45

The three companies left Krost Post promptly after breakfast on Londi morning, even before the post's muster. By then, most of Alucius's bruises had turned vivid shades of yellow and purple, and while the worst of the aching had subsided, he was still stiff. He hadn't had another wall dream, for which he was thankful, and he'd written out a simple command structure and selected his three lancer messengers. He'd studied the maps of the Hyalt area and made some initial plans. He'd also sent off another letter to Wendra, and he could only hope that all was going well on the stead. His wristguard showed that she was healthy, and that was good. After his meeting with the marshal, he'd also managed to obtain not only the supplies, but also a large amount of blasting powder—and the wagons and teams to carry them.

Because he also had decided to spend part of each day riding with each of the company commanders, he was riding at the head of Twenty-eighth Company with Deotyr, at the front of the column on the high road that ran all the way to the coast in Madrien. They would turn southward in something less than a week, onto the high road to Hyalt, days before they could have reached the Coast Range, let alone Madrien.

The midharvest sky was hazy, without actual clouds, and windless, making the morning seem warmer and dustier than it was. Still, one advantage of the eternastone roads was that there was far less dust raised, and that meant the company bringing up the rear didn't have to breathe nearly so much dust and grit as on the back roads.

"Captain . . ." Alucius began, once they were settled into an easy riding rhythm, "I haven't had much of a chance to talk to you and Captain Jultyr. I was wondering. Where are you from?"

"Cersonna, sir."

"I'm not that familiar with many of the places in Lanachrona beyond Tempre, Krost, and those along the River Vedra. Where is Cersonna?"

"It's on the high road to Indyor, just east of where the road crosses the Vyana," replied the young dark-haired captain. "There's not much there, except for cattle and grasslands."

"How did you come to join the Southern Guard, then?"

"When you come from a cattle-running family, and you're the youngest of five, your choices aren't what they might be elsewhere."

Alucius nodded. "You can't split lands and a herd that many ways."

"The lands mostly. We're not as dry as places like Soupat or Hyalt, from what they say. A square will only graze so many head. That's over time, but if you overgraze one year, unless you're lucky to get a monsoon winter, you'll have to sell off part of the herd the next, or they'll all lose weight, maybe starve." Deotyr paused. "You're a herder, though. Isn't it the same for nightsheep?"

"They graze quarasote, not grass, but it's like that in a way. If they don't get the better quarasote, their wool isn't as strong, and that cuts its value, but it doesn't cut the processing costs. They probably won't starve, but the herder running them might." After a moment, he asked, "What's the biggest danger to your cattle? On the steads, we're always on the lookout for sandwolves and sanders, but I've heard that there aren't many south of the Vedra."

"No, sir. The snakes get a few, but grassdogs are the problem. They run in packs, and they can take down a straggler in moments . . ."

Alucius listened, letting Deotyr enlighten him on the details of cattle-running in eastern Lanachrona.

In time, the junior officer looked at Alucius. "Sir . . .

they say that you've been in battles all over Corus and wounded many times . . ."

"And you want to know if it's true—or how much is true?" Alucius smiled. "I started out as a scout in the Iron Valley Militia . . ." He tried to summarize the campaigns and the wounds quickly. ". . . I guess that makes something like three times where I wasn't expected to live and three other times where I had minor wounds. I've been in fights in every land west of the Spine of Corus except Ongelya." Alucius didn't include the fourth severe injury, where the soarer had nursed him back to health, or his times in Lustrea, fighting the ifrit engineer.

Deotyr was silent, so silent that the loudest sound was that of hoofs on the eternastone road.

Alucius decided not to push. He had almost two weeks of riding before they reached Hyalt.

After a time, the young captain cleared his throat. "Sir . . . what can we expect in Hyalt?"

"Trouble," Alucius said with an ironic laugh. "The kind that always happens when people think they're so right that they can't believe that anyone else could be right or be better at what they do." He waited a moment before he added. "Like Majer Fedosyr."

"Majer Fedosyr? Sir . . ."

"That seems so unlike a revolt? It's an example. The Northern Guard fought Lanachrona to a standstill twice. That's history. The Iron Valleys agreed to union with Lanachrona not because they were defeated in battle, but because they had no golds left to pay the militia or to purchase supplies. Because Lanachrona took over the Iron Valleys, the majer wanted to believe that the Northern Guard was somehow deficient in its training and arms skills. He could not force himself to acknowledge that it was otherwise. Because he could not, he broke every rule for a demonstration match. He even threw acid-dust at my face. People who can't judge their beliefs against what happens in the world around them, who cannot see what is . . . they're much like Majer Fedosyr. The True

Duarchists believe that a duarchy that has not ruled in thousands of years will provide a better life for them than the Lord-Protector. Yet the Lord-Protector is one of the more enlightened and intelligent rulers in Corus. One only has to ride through other lands to see this. But the True Duarchists have yet to see this, and it is most unlikely that they will."

"I thought folk in the Iron Valleys don't care much for the Lord-Protector."

"Most probably don't, but they haven't seen the alternatives. There are problems in Lanachrona. There are problems everywhere, but there seem to be far fewer here than in other lands. That's one reason why we'll need to be very cautious in approaching Hyalt."

"Because you don't think there should have been a revolt?"

"From the few reports we have, it isn't really a revolt. It's more like a local invasion by the True Duarchists. Most of the local people had to flee, but no one else has since then. That suggests either a number of armed rebels or local support—or both. The duarchists had rifles and blades and the training to use them. They struck at a time designed to take the local garrison by surprise. That doesn't sound like discontented subjects so much as someone trying to make it seem like a revolt."

"Who would . . . the Regent of the Matrial, you think?"

"That's the most likely possibility, but we won't know until we can scout out the situation." Alucius didn't want to mention the missing scouts. Not yet.

"How do you . . . what do you plan?"

"To do what they don't expect, where they do not expect it, and in ways that they don't."

"That sounds . . . difficult, sir."

"It will be. It's better than the other approaches. They're impossible."

"Can you give us some idea . . . ?"

"We won't be riding in on the high road, not for the last twenty vingts or so. We're also going to try to create doubt about the abilities of the duarchists. All kinds of doubt. If we do, that will make our job much easier." Alucius smiled politely. "I'll be going over the details with all of the officers together as we get closer to Hyalt, and some of the training exercises we'll be doing along the way are designed to work with the tactics we'll be using."

Deotyr nodded slowly, as if at least some of what Alucius said were new to him and needed further consideration.

That was what Alucius wanted. He shifted his weight in the saddle, a saddle that would get harder than he liked before they arrived near Hyalt, and reached for his water bottle. Early in the day as it still was, it was hotter than he would have liked. Then again, everywhere south of Dekhron was warmer than he preferred.

46

On Tridi midafternoon, Alucius was riding at the head of Thirty-fifth Company with Captain Jultyr. The fields on both sides of the road, beyond the wooden rail fences, held growers and their hands and families, all of whom were involved in harvesting a range of crops—from maize to some sort of beans, and a type of oilseed. They were busy enough that only a handful of youngsters even bothered to look at the passing lancers.

"You've seen quite a bit in your time with the Guard," Alucius said. "You came up through the ranks."

"Yes, sir." Jultyr did not quite look at Alucius, as seemed to be the case on most of the occasions when Alucius had ridden with the older captain.

"How long did you serve with the forces against the Matrites?"

"About four years, sir."

"What did you think of their abilities?"

There was a pause before Jultyr spoke. "Some were

good. A company here or there was real good. Most weren't as good as we were."

"You have any thoughts on why that might be?" Alucius found himself waiting and forcing himself to be patient while Jultyr considered his answer.

"Couldn't say for sure, sir, but they seemed to do better on the squad level. Thought they had better squad leaders than officers. Some of their auxiliary companies were good, too." Jultyr looked to Alucius. "You think that might be so?"

"They don't have any officers who are men. So the highest a good man can go is senior squad leader. Some of those I knew were very good. Their officers . . . a handful were good, but the best ones were more likely to get killed. Their strategy was generally better than either that of the Northern or Southern Guard, but their tactics and battle-field leadership weren't so good."

"You think we have better officers and better tactics . . . they have better squad leaders and strategy?" questioned Jultyr.

"Overall . . . probably. Both have officers who are good, and both have officers not so good, though. We know that's true in any fighting force."

Jultyr nodded.

"According to your record," Alucius said, "the Guard promoted you from senior squad leader to captain directly. That's not done often, I know."

"It happens, sir."

"I know." Alucius laughed. "I didn't expect it when it happened to me."

"Suppose I had hoped," Jultyr said after a silence. "Never think it will happen to you. Doesn't happen often in the Southern Guard."

"It doesn't happen that often in the Northern Guard, either. Overcaptain Feran and I are about the only two officers who are still serving that I know who came up that way."

"The overcaptain said you'd faced down the deputy commander of the Northern Guard for your men. Stood alone in front of a whole company."

Alucius wondered where Feran had learned that, since it was something Alucius had never mentioned to anyone outside his family. "Just did what I thought was right."

Jultyr nodded. Another silence followed.

Alucius glanced back at the four supply wagons that followed the lancers, thinking about his conversation with Marshal Frynkel about the wagons. He wondered if he shouldn't have pressed for even more supplies.

"You think that these duarchists have any connection with the Regent, sir?"

"I don't know," Alucius replied, "but I'm sure that the Matrites will take advantage of them any way possible. At the very least, I'd guess their weapons are coming through Madrien. I don't see where else they could come from."

"Could be more lancers or troopers in Hyalt than you've heard," suggested Jultyr.

"That's why we won't be heading all the way to Hyalt. We'll take some of the back roads and circle around the town. We need to see what we can find out before we decide on a final strategy."

"Sir . . . how soon in that match before you knew you were a better blade than Majer Fedosyr?"

"I had some doubts about his ability," Alucius said slowly, "when I heard that he was opposed to using rattan wands."

"He never meant it as a practice match."

"No."

"You knew that?"

"Not for certain until I saw his sabre. Then it was pretty clear. He had it polished and the edge ground to razor sharpness. That's a duelist's blade, not a working lancer's blade. Then, I had my doubts he'd ever really been a working lancer." Alucius forced a laugh. "I haven't spent as much time in the field as you and Feran have, but I know that, and that's why I try to listen to experienced officers and squad leaders. But all the years I have spent in service have been in the field. I'm sure you notice which senior officers understand and which don't."

For the first time, Jultyr laughed, softly and briefly. "Yes, sir."

Alucius continued to ask gentle questions, continually reminding himself to allow the captain time to reply and not to hurry him, trying also not to say too much about his own past.

47

Tempre, Lanachrona

In the indirect light of late afternoon, the three marshals sat in straight-backed chairs upholstered in deep blue and trimmed in gold. Facing them across the severe dark oak table desk was the Lord-Protector. The polished desktop was bare.

"Why don't we know what is happening in Hyalt?" The Lord-Protector's eyes traveled from marshal to marshal, from Frynkel to Wyerl to Alyniat, before snapping back to the arms-commander.

"We have no recent information, sir," admitted Wyerl.

"No one has left Hyalt since the last of the traders and their families fled almost a season ago," added the blond Marshal Alyniat. "Not that we've been able to find, under the circumstances."

"And you have sent no scouts?"

"We sent several," Wyerl said slowly. "None of them returned. While we would have preferred to provide Majer Alucius with more information, it seemed imprudent to keep sending men to their deaths for nothing. We have few enough good scouts remaining as it is."

"You expect me to believe that no one has left Hyalt? In a season?"

"They have blocked the roads, sir, and fortified those points. We told you that when we discovered that had occurred. You told us not to send lancers to tear down the barricades, but to leave that to Majer Alucius." Wyerl glanced toward Frynkel.

"Majer Alucius has yet to reach Hyalt," offered the balding marshal. "He is within a day or two of the city, I would judge." Both eyes blinked rapidly for a moment, and Frynkel pressed the side of his palm against the right one.

"We guess . . . we judge." The Lord-Protector snorted. "We assume, but we do not *know*. How can we prevail when we know so little? We have no Table. Your scouts cannot tell us what is happening in our own land, and they cannot reach us with what is happening in Madrien until it is too late to do anything."

"That is true, sir," Wyerl replied. "Very true."

"I am supposed to rule without information? You are supposed to decide where our lancers should be when we do not know where our enemies may be or how many of them may be where?"

"We know where the Regent's forces are," Alyniat pointed out, "and how many she brings to bear in each area."

The Lord-Protector ignored the statement and turned to Wyerl. "When do you leave?"

"Tomorrow, unless you wish it otherwise, sir."

"All I wish is your success—and that of Majer Alucius—so that we may return Lanachrona to a land of not only prosperity, but peace."

"Majer Alucius is most likely to be outnumbered, sir," Frynkel said quietly. "He could be badly overmatched."

"Thankfully, that has not been a problem for him in the past, and we must hope that it will not be one now," Wyerl commented. "He has a very different style."

"I do not see it as different," replied the Lord-Protector. "He fights only when he must, and then he does his best to destroy all of the enemy so that he does not have to fight them again. Had we been able to do that in Madrien, we would not now be fretting about where and when the Regent will strike."

None of the three marshals responded, but waited for the Lord-Protector to speak again.

After the silence had dragged out, he stood. "If you would continue to keep me informed . . . You may go."

"Yes, sir." The three marshals rose as one.

After they had left him alone in the study, the Lord-Protector turned and walked to the window gazing to the northwest at the twin green towers, a legacy of the Duarchy.

"Have rulers always had to act knowing so little?" he mused half aloud into the empty room.

There was no answer.

48

For another week—ten long days—Alucius and the three companies rode, almost due west for the first five days. The next five days, they rode south on the eterna-stone road that ran from Tempre in the north to Hyalt in the south. The night after heading south, Alucius had once more dreamed about the chamber with the walls closing in, and again he woke up sweating. Clearly he felt hemmed in, but there was little enough he could do besides being aware and doing his best.

On Quattri, just as the sun had almost reached its zenith, Alucius realized what had been nagging at him for the past few glasses. They had seen no one heading north the entire morning. Not a soul. While the road was supposedly less traveled than many others, it was part of the trading "square" of high roads that linked the five major cities in western Lanachrona.

On either side of the high road was a vingt or so of low scrub brush, little of it over knee-high. Each bush or plant was surrounded by an empty area of reddish sand. To the east, the brush gradually gave way to rolling grasslands, but the harvest tan grass was sparse, and in places the brownish red soil showed through. To the west were hills that rose no more than fifty to a hundred yards above the high road. A patchwork of reddish sand, brush, and junipers covered the slopes.

The last Southern Guard way station had been two days earlier, manned by but a half squad, and Alucius had his scouts out not only on the eternastone road ahead but also on the few side roads. Another set of scouts paralleled the main road, riding through the scrub brush roughly half a vingt to each side. Not a single scout had seen anyone since they had broken camp that morning.

"This is a trading road, isn't it?" Alucius asked Feran, riding beside him.

"They say it is."

"We haven't seen any traders or anyone at all. There were more people on the road from Salaan to Dereka."

"You're saying that there's trouble ahead." Feran laughed. "We knew that already."

"It's not just trouble, but the kind of trouble. Everywhere else where I've been around fighting, people move. Some flock in to make a quick coin, and some flee. Marshal Frynkel couldn't provide any information about this revolt. No one has found out anything since the first traders fled, and that was more than a season ago. Just how likely is that?"

"Likely or not, honored Majer, that's the way it is."

"Exactly. But it means we need to know more before we go charging into Hyalt." Alucius looked at the road ahead and the lancer scout who was headed back toward Alucius at close to a gallop.

Alucius turned to his left, looking at Dhaget, one of his three courier/ messengers. "Send back word for all the companies to halt and have Captain Deotyr and Captain Jultyr join me."

"Yes, sir."

Alucius turned back toward Feran. "Have Fifth Company halt and take a break."

"Fifth Company! Column halt!"

"Company halt!" Egyl echoed Feran's command.

Both officers waited until Waris reined up short of them.

"Sir . . . there's a barricade ahead. It's a pile of stones and logs on both sides of the road, and a log set on a post so it can block the road. Troopers, or something like 'em, in maroon tunics."

"Did they see you?" asked Alucius.

"Don't think so, sir."

"How far ahead?"

"Three vingts, give or take a few hundred yards."

"How many troopers were there?"

"Looked to be a half squad or so. They had some merchant's wagon. Didn't see the merchant, though. Also had maybe ten mounts saddled and ready to go."

Alucius frowned. "Call in the other scouts. Station them on the road a vingt to the south to stand watch for now. Then report back here."

"Yes, sir."

While Alucius waited for the other two officers to join them, he took out the map from the top of his left saddle-bag and unfolded it, studying it and checking distances, looking up and comparing what the map showed to what he saw, as he had done periodically for the last several days.

"Sir?" offered Jultyr, riding up and halting on the edge of the road beyond Feran.

"There's a roadblock ahead. When Deotyr gets here, we'll go over the next steps."

"Yes, sir." Jultyr nodded.

Within moments, Deotyr reined up beside the other captain.

Alucius lowered the map. "The scouts have reported a fortified roadblock about three vingts ahead, with half a squad of mounted armsmen. There's no way to tell yet if they're actually trained lancers. We could take this barricade, possibly without many casualties. But we'd still be more than twenty vingts from Hyalt, and they'd know that we were here. I'd rather they didn't know until we've learned more, and until we can make an attack with the advantage of surprise.

"We're going to head back north for about five vingts. We passed a road, more like a trail, back there. It runs south between the hills just west of us and another line of higher hills farther west. We'll only take it far enough to find a good bivouac. Then, we'll start scouting in earnest. I'll tell you now, but you also need to make sure that the scouts know it. The Southern Guard lost a number of scouts here. So, at first, I don't want your men trying to get too close. I'd rather have sketchy information than none."

Deotyr glanced to Jultyr, then back to Alucius.

"You have a question, Captain Deotyr?"

"Not exactly, sir. Ah . . . it's just . . . wouldn't they know the back roads?"

"I'm certain that some of them do. But they're expecting any lancers to come straight down the road. The way the roadblock is set up, it's not a defense against a company of lancers. If there are any defenses, those defenses are farther south. The barricade is set up so that even if we did manage to capture everyone there, it would be obvious from a distance that it had been overrun. I'd rather not announce our presence over a roadblock and ten or twenty men."

"Ah, yes, sir."

"If you're right, Captain," Alucius went on, "and you well may be, we could run into larger forces on the back roads. Now . . . we know that they're somewhere and armed. Right now, do they know we're here?"

"No, sir, probably not, sir."

"Not yet, I hope," Alucius replied. "So, if we run into another force on the back roads, who has the advantage of surprise?"

Deotyr nodded, if grudgingly.

"If our scouts are good, we might even be able to set up an ambush for them." And if he and the companies were lucky, Alucius added to himself. "Twenty-eighth Company will take the lead on the way back to the side road, and I'll be riding with you. Overcaptain Feran and Fifth Company will ride rearguard, just in case we have been spotted. Once we find a defensible bivouac, we'll send out scouts, possibly for several days."

Alucius's eyes went from officer to officer, ending with Deotyr. "Is that clear?"

"Yes, sir."

"Then let's get moving." Alucius gestured to Waris, who had reined up a good five yards away. "Is there any sign of the rebels?"

"No, sir. Everyone's where you ordered."

"Have half of them hang back and watch the rear, and you and Elbard move up with us. We're going north, then west. After you tell the other two, you two join up with me, and I'll brief you on what we need."

"Yes, sir." Waris eased his mount away.

At least, the scouts weren't second-guessing him. Alucius kept a smile on his face as he turned the gray and rode back along the road with Captain Deotyr.

49

Alustre, Lustrea

The slightly stocky, dark-haired traveler, flanked by two Praetorian guards, bowed to the man who sat in the unadorned silver chair on the dais. "Honored Praetor Tyren."

"You provided most interesting materials, stranger."

"Waleryn, Praetor. Lord Waleryn of Lanachrona."

"Why are you here?"

"Because my brother fears me, and a ruler who fears his brother is not one that it is wise to remain close beside."

"And I should trust a man who would betray his brother? If indeed you are that man."

"I am not here to betray my brother. I am here because my brother does not trust me, and I would work with a ruler who can use what I know. That is far different from offering to betray a brother. That I do not offer. I offer the knowledge—"

"And if I were to torture you for that?"

"Sure as the week has ten days, you would lose what else I have to offer—freely." Waleryn laughed. "Almost freely."

"Almost?"

"I ask for good quarters and a modest stipend. Very modest. Less than the engineer received."

"What engineer?"

"The one who provided you and your sire with the light-knives. The light-knives whose secrets I also know."

"Why should I do this?"

"Because it is in your interest, Praetor, and because you lose nothing by seeing if I am who and what I claim."

"Can you prove what you say?"

"I can offer you more proof than you can believe." Waleryn smiled. "The engineer's spaces have not been touched. There is a Table-like mirror hidden within those spaces. I can find the mirror and call up a scene in that mirror." He paused. "Will that suffice?"

"We shall see." The young Praetor nodded to the guards. "Take him to the entry of Vestor's work area. Then . . . let him guide us from there."

In addition to the two guards flanking Waleryn, four others guarded the Praetor as the eight men walked from the audience hall to the second floor of the south wing of the Praetorian palace. They halted before an archway. One took a key and opened the door.

Once he was released, Waleryn stepped forward, walking past the main workbench, then to the empty crystal tanks, where he eased around the last tank to the smaller workbench in the corner, tucked away out of sight—a bench slightly dusty and clearly unused for some time.

Waleryn studied the small workbench for a moment, then slid back the green quartz surface to reveal a polished and silvered metal circle recessed beneath the oak that held the quartz top. "Here is the mirror of which I spoke."

One of the guards stepped forward, then nodded to the Praetor, who stood well back of the crystal tanks.

The Praetor moved past the tanks, but only far enough so that he could see the mirror. "Proceed."

Waleryn took several deep breaths. After a time he concentrated, staring deeply into the ruby mists that appeared, tinged somehow with both purple and pink. Shortly, the mists cleared and revealed the audience hall in Tempre, where the Lord-Protector sat upon a white onyx throne, with a blue crystal glittering at the spire at the top of the back of the throne.

"Another, if you will."

Waleryn concentrated, this time bringing up an image of the audience hall they had so recently departed, where one of the remaining guards was talking to another.

A smile crossed the Praetor's lips.

The amber crystal set in a small metal fitting beside the mirror began to glow, and Waleryn stepped back. "That is all it will do for now."

The image vanished, revealing once more just the metal, now slightly tarnished, as if by fire.

"Why could you not see more?" asked the Praetor.

"This mirror is not a Table," Waleryn explained. "Had the engineer made it of glass, already it would have shattered. For a Table to work, it must be linked within the earth, as is the one in Prosp."

"Is? The building collapsed in the earthquake and destroyed that Table."

Waleryn smiled.

"You dispute that?"

"The Table that he constructed in Prosp was buried by the collapse of the building, but it is untouched."

"How could that be?" asked the Praetor.

"The Tables are linked within the earth. So long as the links are not destroyed, a Table cannot be damaged." Waleryn smiled once more. "Why don't you send someone to Prosp to see? If you have not already. Or send me with them. Or come with us."

Tyren frowned.

"Would you not like to have the information that your sire had?" asked Waleryn. "To see what is happening throughout Lustrea without waiting days or weeks for dispatches? Knowing what did happen without having to trust others, when you do not know whom to trust? That is the beginning of what I provide. Just the beginning."

"And you wish just a modest stipend?"

"And the means to continue the engineer's work, so that you and all Lustrea may benefit." Waleryn bowed his head slightly. "And I, of course, if to a lesser extent."

After a moment, Tyren nodded. "We will allow you those privileges, but you will be watched for a time. Closely watched. I trust you understand."

Waleryn bowed again. "I do, honored Praetor. How could it be otherwise?"

50

In the late afternoon, Alucius studied the camp. Situated on a low hillcrest, it lay a good five vingts to the west of the high road—as an eagle flew—and about five vingts south of where the scouts had sighted the rebel roadblock. The northern slopes of the hill were more heavily wooded, but the mixed firs, cedars, and junipers grew out of steep and rocky broken ground that offered a slow, steep, and treacherous climb for a rider, and much of the lower ground held spiky thornbush. To the west was a long, sloping ridge, mostly open, and the east offered a bluff nearly fifteen yards above a narrow stream. To the south, the ground sloped more gradually toward the narrow road—dirt and barely wide enough for two men riding abreast.

From the hillcrest, there was enough of a vista that the lookouts Alucius had ordered posted could see dust from the roads while riders were still several vingts away. On the ride from the high road, Alucius and the scouts had seen few tracks in the dusty road, and those had been of single riders and carts, not even large wagons. On their ride south and west, they had passed close to a score of long-abandoned steads set on the side of hills that looked too arid to support much of anything.

While the camp was being established, Alucius had dispatched Elbard and Waris to scout farther to the south and east. Even as far away as three to four vingts south, the two had found no sign of riders or posts, or much of anything, nor any sign of recent movement of lancers or large numbers of mounts. That bothered Alucius. Was he being too cautious? Should he have pressed farther south? Or was he missing something?

It could just have been that the hilly land was too dry. Alucius doubted that the lancers could have foraged off the land, even had he wanted them to. The trees were mainly low junipers and twisted cedars, with largish patches of spiky thornbush, and the grass, although long in places, was already brown and sparse, certainly not enough for more than three hundred mounts for long.

"Cookfires?" asked Feran from where he stood to the left of Alucius.

"Small ones, but only if they can find dry wood that doesn't smoke much," Alucius replied. "If you'd pass that on to Deotyr and Jultyr."

"I'll do that. I'd already said that was likely."

"You ought to be the one in charge." Alucius smiled faintly. In many areas, Feran was well ahead of Alucius.

"No, thank you. I'm fine on the day-to-day things. You're much better in battles and fights."

Alucius had his doubts, but only replied, "Good thing we're both here." He lifted his eyes toward the south-southeast, in the direction of Hyalt, supposedly fifteen vingts away. He saw nothing but more of the same cedar-

and juniper-covered hills. His Talent had revealed no one nearby except for those of his own force and few enough animals. Those were mainly grayjays and rodents of various kinds.

"Rather neither one of us had to be," Feran grumbled. "Sir." He brushed back a lock of the graying brown hair.

"I didn't exactly want to ride halfway across Corus, either. It's just that the alternatives were worse."

"Why is it always that way?"

"It's not," Alucius replied with a laugh. "It's just that way for us."

"You are so cheerful, most honored Majer."

"I know." Alucius's voice turned somber. "How many really good scouts do you have? Besides Elbard and Waris?"

"One, maybe two."

"Is there anyone from the other companies?"

"Jultyr says that one of his shows promise. Was raised in the Vyan Hills. Father was a warden for some wealthy landowner. Son tracked poachers for a while."

"No one else?"

Feran laughed.

"We'll do what we can, then. I'll want them all out early, well before dawn. We need a quick picture of what's out between five and ten vingts, not so much near the high road, but along the hills. There are bound to be steads closer to the main road, but we need to know what might be along the back route."

"One thing that bothers me," Feran said slowly. "There's no one out here, but there are roads."

"I don't know for certain," Alucius replied, "but you saw all those abandoned places."

Feran nodded.

"There used to be more people who lived out here. Like the northlands, I'd wager it's gotten drier and drier until holders couldn't make it here. You also saw some of those hillsides, with all the stumps? They're still logging the land, and probably most of the roads out here are used for that."

"You think so?"

"I don't know what to think, but it makes sense. Whether I'm right is another question." Alucius could only hope he had reached the right conclusion, and not just about the deserted state of the hillside lands. Time—and the scouting reports—would tell that.

51

The scouts departed well before dawn, briefed as well as Alucius knew how, and he stood silently as they rode southward. Feran stood beside him. Alucius just watched, long after the four had disappeared into the predawn grayness.

"You'd rather be scouting, wouldn't you?" asked Feran.

"It's hard, just watching." Alucius glanced toward the east, but the sky had not brightened with the immediate welling of light that heralded sunrise. "Harder than I realized."

"That's the problem of being in command. It's harder for you than for anyone else."

Alucius suspected he knew what Feran was suggesting, but he wasn't sure he wanted to admit it. "Oh?"

"You're a better scout than anyone you sent out. You're a better lancer than anyone you command. You're a better company captain than the rest of us. But you're not sure that you're a better force commander. And you have to be the best." Feran shook his head. "Me . . . I just want to be good enough to survive in one piece. I'm happy to follow you because you don't do too many stupid things, and you won't put men in any danger you wouldn't face yourself, and you like to tilt the odds in your favor."

"You're so encouraging, Feran."

"Admit it . . . Majer."

Alucius laughed ironically. "You know me too well. I

probably am a better scout. I'm a herder, and I have more experience than most scouts."

"More experience than just about all of them. You've fought and scouted for every land in the west of Corus."

Alucius knew that was true, but it was the Talent-abilities that made the difference. He still recalled Geran, the older scout he had worked with in the Iron Valley Militia. Geran had no Talent and yet could read the land as if it had been laid out in a book. Alucius still needed his Talent to do that.

"You have to remember one thing . . . Majer." Feran's voice was low.

"What's that?"

"No matter how good you are, you can't do everything. You can't scout and command at the same time. You can't always lead the charge and also hang back to see where you should move companies . . ."

"I suppose I needed that reminder." Alucius still wished he were out with the scouts. He grinned briefly. "Thank you."

"My pleasure, sir." Feran returned the grin.

As Alucius walked back toward the center of the camp, he had to wonder. How did a man ever know when he'd reached the limit of his abilities? The Lord-Protector had chosen Alucius because of what he'd done mostly as a company captain, and as an individual operating alone. Could he really command three companies effectively? He took a deep breath. All he could do was listen, learn, and do his best.

Light began to flood across the hilltop, and for a moment the sky overhead was white-silver before darkening into a bright and cloudless silver-green. There had been no rain at all since Alucius had left Dekhron, and that had been the longest time he had spent in Lanachrona without rain. Was that another sign that times were changing—or just coincidence? He laughed softly. Not everything was because of the ifrits and the soarers. At least, he didn't think so.

While he waited for the scouts to return, he ran through

a set of drills with Twenty-eighth Company, then with Thirty-fifth Company.

Despite the drills and the debriefing of the captains, the morning passed slowly, without any sign of riders on the back roads near the encampment. Late morning arrived before the first scout returned—Jultyr's Rakalt.

Alucius hurried down from the hillcrest to meet the scout halfway up the south slope. He had the lancer—a rangy young man with a narrow face and deep-set and intent green eyes—dismount and have some water for the short time it took to summon the other officers. Then he looked at Rakalt. "Tell us what you found out, Rakalt."

"I followed the wider road west, like you said, sir." Rakalt met Alucius's eyes, then swallowed. "It keeps going west, like you thought. Two or three vingts from here, it crosses a dry creek, then turns northwest. Half a vingt farther, it splits. The road going north is rutted, but they're real old ruts. Doesn't look like anyone travels it. I didn't see any new tracks. The left fork goes southwest. Not many riders and wagons there, but some recent tracks in the dust. I followed it close to five vingts, like you said, sir. By then it was heading close to due south. There's nothing there, sir. Just bare hillsides. They've logged off everything. Gullies everywhere. Won't support more 'n rats and birds, maybe not that. Now . . . the tops of the hills on the east side of the road, they got some trees, same firs and junipers."

"What about the road itself?" asked Alucius. "Could you tell who was using it?"

"Mostly single riders, looked like. Might have been patrols, but the shoes weren't always the same, not like ours." Rakalt tilted his head. "Had to be patrols. Only one set of tracks at a time."

Alucius continued to ask questions, with Feran occasionally adding one or two of his own.

"How steep were the hills to the east of the road?"

"How sturdy were the bridges?"

"Did you see any dwellings or any smoke?"

"Did any of the hillsides look liked they'd been logged recently . . . ?"

After another quarter glass of questions—and answers from Rakalt—Alucius paused, wondering what he'd overlooked. He took a swallow from his water bottle, as much because he wasn't used to talking that much as that the day was warm. He looked to Feran. "Anything else you can think of?"

"No, sir." Feran's smile was ragged. "Wish I could."

Alucius looked to Jultyr.

"Ah . . . yes, sir . . . just one."

"Go ahead," Alucius said.

"Rakalt . . . sounds funny . . . but did you smell anything strange . . . anywhere?" Jultyr's words were firm.

The scout squinted, cocking his head again. "Smells? No, sir . . . don't recall anything like that. No strange smells."

Alucius nodded. He'd have to remember that one. It made a lot of sense. As he turned back toward the scout, he heard a shout from the south hillside.

"Majer! Dust on the main road—lots of riders, sir!"

Alucius whirled and looked to the south. There were actually two clouds of dust—one a thin and barely visible plume, less than a vingt from the bottom of the slope leading to the camp, and the second a larger cloud perhaps half a vingt south of that—a scout pursued by a squad or more of the local lancers or armsmen. So much for surprise—the idea flashed through Alucius's thoughts even as he raised his voice.

"Twenty-eighth Company! Mount up and form on me! Fifth Company! Mount up. Flank Twenty-eighth Company to the west! Thirty-fifth Company, mount-up and flank Twenty-eighth Company to the east."

Alucius hurried toward the tieline that held his gray gelding. Even after running uphill on foot to get his mount, he was mounted and halfway back down the hillside before the first of Twenty-eighth Company's lancers began to

form up. After scanning the hillside once again, he rode
lower until he was only about a hundred fifty yards from
the road, and with the slope as gentle as it was, only about
six yards above the road's surface. The position, like everything, was a compromise. He wanted his men close enough
to deliver withering fire, but in a location where the enemy
would have to charge uphill.

"Form up here!" he called upslope.

Feran and Fifth Company had already formed up farther
uphill, and the other two companies were moving into position east of Fifth Company.

"Forward, and form on a line with the majer!" ordered
Feran.

Alucius glanced toward the road. The trailing cloud of
dust was closing on the scout, but it looked as though the
scout would reach the camp before his pursuers could at-
tain a position to allow any accurate rifle shots—and any
shots would be almost a matter of luck with the twisting of
the road and its uneven surface.

"Fifth Company in position, sir!"

"Thirty-fifth Company, sir!"

"Twenty-eighth Company, sir!"

Alucius turned in the saddle toward Feran. "Stagger and
angle them to get a clear line of fire from all files."

"Yes, sir."

Then he turned to Jultyr and repeated the command. By
then, Deotyr had Twenty-eighth Company in even ranks.

Alucius addressed Deotyr. "Captain, put them in a staggered right oblique formation."

"Yes, sir." Deotyr turned in the saddle "Twenty-eighth
Company! Staggered right oblique."

The senior squad leader echoed the command, and
Twenty-eighth Company shifted into a mounted firing position. Alucius rode over closer to Deotyr. "If they turn or
break, I'll order Twenty-eighth Company into pursuit. Be
ready for that if it comes."

"Yes, sir."

Alucius eased the gray back to the west, reining up just at the point where Fifth and Twenty-eighth Companies joined. He looked westward, studying the empty section of road below and waiting. He reminded himself that the Lanachronan rifles carried a ten-shot magazine and had a longer range than the Northern Guard's weapons. He continued to watch the road, even as he extended his Talent senses. There was no sign of any Talent, but the trailing riders were too far away for him to detect fainter Talent-usage.

Another quarter of a glass passed. Finally, a single rider emerged from the last turn of the road before the straight section that extended to the base of the hillside where Alucius's forces were arrayed.

"All companies!" Alucius ordered. "Rifles ready. Fire at my command."

"Rifles ready."

As the rider neared the encampment, less than a hundred yards from the base of the slope, Alucius recognized Waris, despite the dust-coated uniform. Behind him rode nearly two squads of lancers in loose-fitting maroon tunics.

The rebel lancers fired occasional shots at Waris, but all seemed to fall short or wide. But they were closing slowly on the scout so that, when Waris reached the foot of the slope, the oncoming rebel lancers were but three hundred yards behind him. The scout eased his mount uphill and toward the Guard companies.

Alucius waved Waris past. "Go on." He waited until the oncoming lancers were within fifty yards of the base of the hill. Then he ordered, "Fire at will!"

"Fire at will!"

A series of rapid *cracks* came from Twenty-eighth Company, then from Thirty-fifth Company. The deeper-sounding reports from the heavier Northern Guard rifles were more deliberate.

Only a handful of shots from the first volley struck. Alucius saw one rebel lurch in the saddle and another pitch sideways. He lifted his own rifle and fired carefully. His first shot struck a man in the shoulder. His second took another rebel out of his saddle.

A squad leader rode first among the maroon-clad lancers, flourishing a blade half again as long as a lancer sabre. Despite the continuing fire from the Lanachronan forces, he charged to the end of the road, then upslope toward Alucius.

Alucius targeted the man, and his first shot slammed through the man's left shoulder. The rebel remained in the saddle, still brandishing his long blade. Alucius paused only for a moment before putting a second shot into the man's chest, slightly to the left of his breastbone. Still clutching the blade, the man was less than fifty yards from Alucius before the majer's last shot smashed a gaping hole in the attacker's forehead.

As quickly as he could, Alucius switched rifles. He took slightly longer with each shot, trying for head shots as much as possible. He knew what he was seeing couldn't be happening, but it looked like almost nothing besides a head shot, one through the heart, or enough fire to dismember one of the rebel lancers was enough to stop one.

He felt as though he were fumbling every time he reloaded, but he had the rifle up quickly enough and continued to fire. He kept reloading and firing, watching rebel lancers fall. In time, he got only one shot off after reloading when he realized that there was no one moving downslope.

"Hold your fire!" he ordered.

"Hold your fire!"

As the last rifle reports died away, Alucius glanced downhill. From what he could see, only a handful of his force had been killed or wounded. Then, he looked at the thirty-odd bodies strewn on the hillside. There were several loose and riderless mounts, but not one rebel had slowed or turned back.

After a moment, Alucius rode slowly downhill, shaking his head, seeing the gaping wounds in every body. Yet he could sense only the faintest touch of Talent—certainly not enough to have kept men who were dying or already dead moving forward in an attack.

Feran had been generous earlier, because this time Alucius had been stupid. He'd been lucky to lose so few men. He should have had them in trenches or embankments, or behind trees. He'd thought that the attackers would have turned and retreated, given their far fewer numbers, and he'd wanted to be able to pursue them. Then again, the ground was so hard it would have been impossible to have dug effective trenches . . . but his tactics had still been stupid.

Near the bottom of the hill, he turned the gray and started back upslope. "Overcaptain, captains, report as you can!"

He continued toward Feran and Fifth Company, reining up short of the overcaptain.

Feran offered a ragged smile.

Alucius shrugged, adding in a voice low enough that only Feran could hear, "We were lucky this time. I've never seen anything like that."

"Haven't either. They using Talent?"

"Just the littlest trace of it. Shouldn't have made any difference."

"That's scary," Feran murmured.

Alucius had to agree, if silently. It had taken the mass fire of three companies for almost half a glass.

Egyl reined up, waiting. Both officers looked to him.

"Two dead, sirs, three wounded."

"Thank you, Egyl," Alucius replied.

"Yes, sir." Egyl turned his mount.

While Egyl hadn't felt or expressed reproach, Alucius knew that the senior squad leader had every right to do so.

"Any captives?" Alucius asked.

"No, sir."

Alucius looked down at the fallen rebels, then at Feran. "Can you take care of the dead? Have them checked for anything that would tell us something. Just two burial pits for the rebels, one for mounts, the other for men. Draw some men from each of the companies."

"I'll take care of it."

"Thank you. We'll meet later," Alucius told Feran, before turning his mount eastward toward the center of Twenty-eighth Company. Deotyr and Jultyr had drawn up their mounts side by side.

"Three dead, four wounded. Only one seriously, sir," reported Deotyr.

"Two wounded. Not serious. We weren't in their line of fire," offered Jultyr.

For that Alucius was grateful.

"Were there any survivors? Any captives?"

Both captains exchanged glances, then looked at Alucius. "No, sir."

Alucius managed not to frown. "Thank you. Overcaptain Feran will be drawing some men from each of you for a burial and disposal detail."

"Yes, sir."

"Take care of what you need to handle. Dismissed." Alucius raised his voice. "All companies, stand down, except for burial and disposal detail."

The first skirmish of the campaign was over, and he should have felt relieved. His force had killed more than thirty attackers and lost only five men. But . . . he'd misjudged the situation, and had there been twice as many attackers, the results would have been far different. The faint touch of Talent indicated something besides ifrit involvement, but what? He pursed his lips. There had been no survivors, and none of the attackers had tried to retreat. There was so much he didn't know.

He looked around, searching for Waris, to find out what the scout might have discovered, only to see the scout standing grooming his mount less than fifty yards away.

"Officers forward! Without your mounts."

Alucius eased the gray up to Waris. "We'll need your report, Waris."

Waris was still covered in dust, and his mount had clearly been pushed earlier, although the scout had brushed out the dust from the roan's coat, but there were still traces of sweat. Waris looked at Alucius. "Had to push him hard to get clear, sir. Saved my ass, he did." After a pause, he added, "Looks like you had a little trouble here, too."

"We did," Alucius replied. "That's why we need to hear what you found out. We'll be down there by the cedar."

"Yes, sir."

Alucius rode his gray back to the tieline, where he tethered the gelding. Then he walked partway downhill to an area shaded by the low but broad cedar he had pointed out to Waris and waited for the others to join him. His eyes looked downhill, taking in the fallen men and the lancers searching and dragging bodies to the west, where part of the hill had slumped, leaving an easier disposal site.

He looked up as the two captains and Feran rejoined him. "Waris will be here in a moment."

"Elbard and Chorat are still missing," Feran said.

Alucius could only hope they had been delayed.

Waris walked downhill and stopped short of the half circle of officers. After a moment, he began. "They sent three lancers after me, sir, and I took out all three. Didn't change anything. Hadn't gotten a vingt away when they had another three after me. Almost half a squad after one scout? Don't understand that, sir."

Alucius gestured to the slope below them. "They sent a squad and a half against three companies. Not one turned back."

Waris shook his head slowly.

"If they had so many after you," asked Alucius, "how did you escape?"

Waris grinned. "Figured if we got far enough away from their camp, they wouldn't know to send more. I shot 'em, one after the other. They can't shoot as well as my one-armed grandmother."

"Before you got rousted out, what did you find?"

"Took the narrow dirt road, sir, like you told me. Three vingts south of here, it forks. One fork goes mostly south, maybe a little east, and the other heads due west. Tracks on both, but, well, couldn't tell you, except I thought I ought to see about the west fork first. Follows the bottom of a ridge-line little less than two vingts through trees sort of spaced like the ones here. Goes pretty straight, though. Ends in an open space. Lucky I stopped in the trees. Was trying to see what was there, and saw some smoke ahead. So I circled around the clearing and eased up the hillside. Couldn't get too close 'cause the whole slope is covered in that spiky thorn stuff. But . . . got high enough to get a pretty good view. It's almost like a lancer post, sir. They got long sheds like barracks, and even stables. They're on a flat. Behind them, there's something dug or carved into the rock of the hillside."

"Are there any places from where you could mount an attack?" asked Alucius.

"In two places," the scout added. "There's a lower meadow to the east of whatever's dug into the cliff, and there's an upper meadow to the southwest. You might be able to come over the top of the hill, but then it's like a cliff coming down . . . have to do that on foot. They've also got a perimeter cleared on the west side of the hill, posts every hundred yards or so. That was where I got seen."

"Do they have any walls or palisades?"

"Not much. They don't need them. They've got a gate across the road to Hyalt—think it must be the road to Hyalt, anyway. It's a good, wide, packed road . . . got walls on each side of the gate for maybe a hundred yards. Beyond that, you've got those thorn thickets and rough ground. If one doesn't get you or your mount, seems like the other would."

"How many lancers are there?" asked Feran.

"Couldn't say for sure, sir. I'd guess maybe two companies. Could be more if they've got barracks in the caves. Couldn't be too many more, though, because all the mounts are stabled. Stables might hold three hundred."

"We'll need to find out if they've got other outposts," Alucius said to Feran. "Somehow." He looked at Waris. "Did you see many wagons?"

Close to another glass passed before Alucius was satisfied that he'd learned everything that he could from Waris. Even so, he suspected he'd missed things.

After they finished debriefing Waris, Alucius and Feran walked to the hillcrest. There they settled on two low boulders, slowly eating travel bread and hard cheese, washing the heavy food down with swallows from their water bottles.

"Some ways, this is worse than Deforya," mused Feran. "There, we knew what we were up against. Here . . ." He shook his head.

"The more we discover, the worse it gets. Is that what you mean?" asked Alucius.

"That charge . . . the lancers chasing Waris . . ." Feran smiled faintly. "He sounded like you. Could be that's what we need."

Alucius didn't feel like pursuing that. Was the only solution to kill more than your enemy? "We really need to know more. I hope the other scouts can find out more."

"It's early yet, and we've gotten two back already," Feran said.

"We're missing two, still. Elbard . . . and your other one . . ."

"Chorat. He begged me to let him do it."

"He had the area to the south and east of Hyalt."

"You don't think he's coming back."

"We'll have to see." Inside, Alucius worried whether either of the remaining scouts would return.

After the two finished eating, Feran headed down to check on the burial detail and Alucius walked the perimeter of the encampment, using his Talent, directing it outward to sense if anyone might be stalking or scouting them. He found no signs of outsiders to the east, south, or west, and a good glass later, he was standing a full fifty yards below the crest on the north side of the hill, trying to make sure that no one was sneaking up from the least obvious side, but there was no one there. There weren't even many rodents, and few enough birds. He turned and began to walk back uphill.

He looked up as a lancer hurried downhill. "Sir! Overcaptain Feran needs you, sir. Elbard's back, and he's wounded bad, sir."

"Show me!" Alucius hurried after the young lancer, back over the hillcrest and another hundred yards downhill.

Elbard lay stretched on a ground cloth. A lancer Alucius didn't know had bound the scout's shoulder and chest, and Feran stood there, his face impassive, listening.

Alucius let his Talent range over the wounded scout as he listened.

". . . one moment . . . was watching the town . . . next thing, I was . . . almost like sleeping . . . except I was awake, but I didn't hear anything . . . never heard the rifle . . . pain of the bullet . . . guess broke the spell . . . just a boy . . . standing there . . . wore a sloppy maroon uniform . . . must have walked up to me . . . no more . . . fifty yards . . . Shot . . . never heard him . . . Hurt like . . . managed to get a shot off . . . didn't miss . . ." A hollow laugh came from Elbard. "Boy . . . he looked surprised. Managed to get to my mount . . . Suppose . . . shouldn't gone all the way to Hyalt . . . where the road led . . ."

Slowly, the majer reached out with his Talent, strengthening the lifethread, and doing what else he could to knit bones and muscles together. Alucius's vision was blurring by the time he finished.

Elbard looked to be sleeping.

"I think he'll make it," Alucius said hoarsely. He looked at the lancer who had bound the wounds. "Let me or Overcaptain Feran know when he wakes."

"Yes, sir."

Alucius began to walk slowly back uphill and away from the group around Elbard.

Accompanying Alucius, Feran looked back at the scout, then to the majer. His voice was low as he spoke. "That takes a lot out of you, doesn't it?"

Alucius debated denying it, then shrugged tiredly. Feran already knew; he'd known for years, even if they'd never spoken of it. "I can only do one or two a day, if that, and nothing else. It's useless in a battle."

"They say . . . you can't heal yourself, can you?"

"No. I think I heal a little faster than most people, but Talent doesn't work that way."

"Why . . ."

"Because he's a good scout. Because we need to know what else he found out." And because, Alucius had to admit to himself, he felt guilty for sending Elbard out into trouble. "What he ran into—it sounds like . . . some kind of Talent. I've never heard of anything like that, though."

"Nothing herders can do?"

"Not that I know of," Alucius admitted.

"That would explain why none of Frynkel's scouts got back."

"It might."

"You think there's more?" asked Feran.

"I don't know, but . . ."

"They wouldn't send us—or you—unless it was something tough," Feran pointed out.

"There's one thing that doesn't make much sense. Weslyn was totally opposed to my being sent here."

Feran laughed. "That makes perfect sense. When you were a herder, you were out of the Guard. Now, you're a majer. You pull this out, and you're the Lord-Protector's favorite. Even I can tell that Marshal Frynkel despises Weslyn, and—"

"We'd better think more about how to pull this off," Alucius said quickly. "Tomorrow, we'll send a messenger back to the last manned post, letting the marshal know about it." He could hear the reluctance in his voice. "We'll also have to request more ammunition."

"You don't like that," observed Feran.

"No . . . but he and the Lord-Protector should know."

"Elbard was the only one who felt this. Are you sure . . . ?"

"We sent out four scouts. One hasn't returned. Two got chased back, and one of them got Talent-spelled and wounded. Frynkel sent at least a few. None of them got back. What does that tell you?"

Feran offered a bitter chuckle. "They got some sort of

Talent watching over them. Is that what you're thinking?"

"What else could it be?" After a moment, Alucius added, "Unless it's something worse."

"You know of anything worse?"

"The return of the True Duarchy." Alucius forced a wry dryness into his voice.

Feran nodded.

"Let's get the captains and go over the maps." Alucius turned and headed back toward the tielines and his mount, and the saddlebags that held the maps.

As he walked, he went over the questions in his mind.

The rebels knew where he and his force were—at least in general terms. They might not know exactly where, since there had been no survivors of the attack, but he had one missing scout, presumably dead, and one who had been wounded and one who had left a trail of bodies. If he kept the three companies where they were, he'd need to have them dig in, and the hillside wasn't that suited to digging in. On the other hand, he knew far too little about the land and the people, and who controlled what—and how. Every move, every ride, was into the unknown. But . . . he reflected . . . from what he'd seen, the rebel lancers weren't that good. They were only fanatics. Only?

He laughed softly to himself.

He knew more about attacking than defending—a great deal more. His forces would have to move on.

52

Alustre, Lustrea

The man in the silver cloak and matching trousers walked up the stone steps of the ancient covered arena toward what had once been the Duarch's box. Beside and behind him were two quints of guards, wearing silver-gray trousers and tunics. Each of the ten guards bore a brace of two-shot pistols and a gladius. The covered arena was dimly lit, the only light coming through the arched windows that were covered with grime.

A stocky man in dark blue stood beside a device that resembled a cannon, save that what would have been the barrel was composed of crystals set in holders and connected by silver wire and that the armored square body, three yards long and slightly less than two wide, rested on four ironbound wheels, rather than the two wheels and trunnion mounting used for cannon. He bowed. "As you requested, all is ready, Praetor."

"How does it work, Waleryn?"

"Very well, Praetor." The stocky figure smiled, drawing his lips into a pleasant expression belied by the coldness in his eyes.

"Then proceed to show us, if you will." The Praetor turned to look at the center of the arena, where several battered statues had been placed. Armor had been strapped on two of the horsemen. In addition to the statues, there was a shield wall, looking as it might in battle, except that the shields had been fastened together rather than held by soldiers.

Waleryn stepped up to the device and drew down a lever. The faintest humming sounded, thin, high, and intense enough that several of the guards stiffened. After a moment, a line of blue-green fire—or light—flashed from the crystal barrel, light so intense that the Praetor was forced to close his eyes.

When Tyren could see again, the center of the arena contained nothing except an oval of rough glass from which rose heat waves, as in the southern deserts.

The Praetor hid a swallow. "Very impressive. How far will it reach?"

"At the moment, this one has a range of just less than a vingt—say, eighteen hundred yards."

"How often can you use it?"

"It takes about a tenth of a glass to recharge, but if I adjust the aperture, it could destroy a line of troops three hundred yards across and fifty deep."

"What *makes* it work? And keep the explanation simple this time."

"The essence that supports the Talent . . . it infuses all of Corus, all of the oceans and the air as well. It is a force, like fire, except it cannot be seen but through its manifestations." Waleryn took the white leather gloves that he held in his right hand and gently used the fingertips to brush away a fleck of something that had appeared on his lower left sleeve. "The crystals inside the tube barrel concentrate and refine this essence into elemental force, call it a fire, that will burn anything."

"Anything?" The slender Praetor laughed, a cool and mocking sound. "That is claiming much."

"Oh, there is more to it than that. Because it draws and concentrates this essence, it can reduce the power of those with the Talent who might oppose you and your forces."

"How many of these can you fabricate?"

"The materials are most costly, as you know."

"You had said it would be easier after the first few."

"Easier, yes . . . but not that much less costly."

"Hmmm . . . fabricate another five. That way we will have two for each force crossing the Spine of Corus." The Praetor smiled. "I am sure that you can manage that, *Lord* Waleryn."

"Your Mightiness is too kind." Waleryn bowed again, his gesture nearly as mocking as the words of the Praetor.

"If these devices prove their worth in the campaigns ahead, you can look to great rewards, perhaps even, shall we say, the prefectship over Lanachrona." Tyren nodded and turned.

Two of the guards remained flanking Waleryn for several moments, until the Praetor had entered the ancient tunnel that led back to the underground carriageway. Then, they too departed, leaving Waleryn standing beside his weapon.

The eyes of the Lanachronan lord flashed purplish for a moment, watching the departing guards, but he said nothing at all, before tapping the bell beside the projector to summon his engineers-in-training.

53

At dawn on Septi, the three companies were on the move, headed westward and following the road that Rakalt had scouted the day before. From the maps and from what the scouts had discovered, Alucius was fairly certain that the one rebel camp was to the east of the road they traveled, perhaps by as little as a vingt, certainly no more than two. If the maps were correct, he noted to himself from where he rode at the head of the force, beside Feran.

Elbard was better, although he was riding in one of the supply wagons, and he had told Alucius and Feran more about Hyalt itself—a town rather than a city, and one that had seemed half-deserted, but with maroon-clad armsmen seemingly on every street, at least of those that the scout had seen from his hilltop vantage point before he'd been Talent-spelled. Alucius didn't like the thought that the rebels had enough men to place so many in the town itself, and he had to wonder from where all of them had come. To that question, like so many others, he had no answer.

Alucius had worked with Feran and the fifth squad of Fifth Company the night before, with cloth taken from the downed rebel lancers and some of the gunpowder from the Southern Guard wagon. While gunpowder exploded, it also burned, and that was what Alucius had in mind. He'd decided against sending a messenger north immediately, because, once he'd thought about what he could report and request, he determined that no one would believe him, and, even if they did, they wouldn't understand the danger that he could explain—and he couldn't explain about the ifrits. That was something no one would believe, especially since he had not seen a one, just their influence and traces.

"Better to be moving, rather than sitting and waiting," Feran said.

"I feel better on the move, too, but I'd like to know more about where we're moving," Alucius replied dryly.

"Even when you do know, you really don't."

Feran was probably right about that, too, reflected Alucius. So often, knowledge could be an illusion, particularly if the knowledge wasn't firsthand and hard-won.

"I've been thinking about the scouts," Alucius said. "What if we just sent patrols down the roads, maybe full squads as patrols?"

"You don't think they'd just pick them off?"

"Not at first. They'd have to send out squads and patrol all the roads. I'd like to learn more about this place."

"If what you have planned for today goes right, they might do that tomorrow."

"Where?" asked Alucius. "Even if they have two other camps and six companies, they don't know where we'll be. If the lancers we fought the other day are any example, we'll do better at picking them off here and there. We'll attack, then move back to the way station and get refreshed and resupplied." He should have adopted that approach to begin with, but he'd never dealt with anything like the situation in Hyalt before. Then again, he doubted anyone had.

He looked at the hills to the northwest. The stump-covered and gullied ground looked tired, with its intermittent low bushes and sparse grass. Even to his Talent, it felt tired. Could land feel tired? According to what the soarer had told him years before, whole worlds got tired, and the ifrits made that happen more quickly. But how long did worlds last? Or did the worlds continue on as lifeless lumps once the spirit of life was exhausted?

"You look grim," Feran observed, his voice cheerful. "We haven't even seen anyone. Isn't that better than another skirmish right off?"

"I was just thinking."

"That can be dangerous," Feran said lightly.

Alucius chuckled, then observed, "There weren't any survivors. No one tried to escape. I've never seen that."

"Haven't either. Could just have been the way things happened there."

"Could be."

"You don't sound convinced."

"Are you?"

Feran shook his head.

Ahead, the road began a long and gentle turn more to the south. To the west, beyond the rolling hills, was another set of higher, redder, and drier hills, and in the dim hazy distance, the peaks of the Coast Range, marking the old boundary between Lanachrona and Madrien. To the east was a short flat stretch of meadow, although the grass was also sparse, before the ground rose into juniper- and cedar-sprinkled hills.

As the companies rode southward, and as the sun crept over the hills to the east, Alucius continued to study the road and the area to the east. After another two vingts, the road turned due south, then angled sharply westward. As he neared the curve, Alucius turned to Feran. "We'll stop at the turn there."

"Column, halt! Pass it back!"

"Column halt!"

Fifth Company came to a halt, followed by Thirty-fifth and Twenty-eighth Companies.

"You're going to lead the squad, aren't you?" asked Feran.

Alucius had debated himself, back and forth, on whether he should lead the fire detail. In the end, he'd decided he would do so. One reason was simple enough—if necessary, he could use his Talent to touch off the powder. "I know it will work, and they're more likely to get back." Alucius smiled. "If you thought I was wrong, you'd say something."

"I don't like it, but you're probably right." Feran

snorted. "I've been worried about this duty from the beginning, and I still am."

"So am I, but that's another question. We'll be as quick as we can." Alucius turned the gray. "Fifth squad forward!"

Nineteen men rode forward along the edge of the narrow road, led by Zerdial. The once-youthful-looking and thin squad leader was harder than when Alucius had first made him a squad leader, and the thinness had become a tough angularity. The squad leader reined up.

"Zerdial, your squad set? With all the burn bags?"

"Yes, sir."

"Let's head out, then, along that trail until we reach that outcropping to the southeast. One scout two hundred yards ahead."

"Yes, sir. Orlant, you take scout."

Once Orlant was past him, Alucius turned the gray off the road and along the narrow trail following the scout. Zerdial and the rest of fifth squad followed.

For the first several hundred yards the trail was almost flat. Then it swung south between two cedars and angled back east, up the side of the hill in a gradual climb. Although Orlant was well forward, Alucius scanned the trail in front as well as the sparse woods on all sides. For the first half glass, he could detect almost nothing except some grayjays and rodents. As they neared the top of the first rise, through the trees, Alucius could see a thin trail of smoke to the east against the early-morning sky, beyond an even steeper line of hills.

The squad drew up at the ridge crest, with Orlant and another scout posted out from the squad, while Alucius spent several moments checking his maps and studying the two narrow trails. Then he nodded. "The left one. It should bring us up on the north side of the camp, and if Waris's reports were right, we could come out on a low bluff."

The trail wound down, then back up and farther to the north before turning back to the southeast. To cover perhaps a vingt as an eagle flew took close to three vingts on the trail, and it was late midmorning when they stopped again.

To the south beyond the thicker junipers where Alucius had ordered the stop and just over the ridgeline above them, Alucius could sense both people and *something* that was similar to an ifrit, but wasn't, a vague dark purpleness. What could be like an ifrit, but not? He decided that question could wait. As he scanned with his Talent, he looked at the maps once more, not that he needed them, but he wasn't about to explain that he didn't. He raised his eyes to Zerdial.

"The camp is almost due south, over that ridge. We'll ride up through the trees and stop just short of the top. Then I'll move forward and study the layout quickly and come back with instructions on who will use their burn bags where."

"Yes, sir." Zerdial turned in the saddle. "Follow the major, and keep it quiet."

Alucius eased the gray from behind the junipers and started up the uneven slope. He reined up about twenty yards from the crest. There he dismounted and handed the gray's reins to Orlant. Carrying one rifle, he made his way up the slope, moving sideways as well, until he reached the crest at a point just behind an ancient cedar. Keeping low, he eased up behind the cedar's trunk and studied what lay below.

Several grayjays squawked, but then flew westward.

The camp was almost exactly the way that Waris had described it—or rather, Waris had described it accurately. Alucius studied the lines of vegetation and the trees and spiky thorns particularly. All but one area could be reached from cover, and the wind was from the west, which should fan the flames downhill into the areas of dry spiky thornbush. Alucius set down his rifle and took out the map, marking the spots for each two-man team.

Then he spent more time using his Talent. He could detect no one in the heights above the camp—not a single patrol or sentry. That suggested a lack of solid military training, or something else. The darkish purple that was visible only to Talent seemed to be centered in the cave area that was to his right and farther south, but there was a thin miasma over the entire camp. For Alucius, that was as good as an announcement that the ifrits were involved. It was also useless as an explanation of anything to anyone else. He couldn't exactly explain the evil behind beings that no one else had seen and no one else alive could explain—except for Wendra and the ifrits and their allies and servants.

Finally, he slipped back down to the waiting squad.

"Gather round." As the squad circled around Alucius, he began. "We're just to the north of the camp, and it's below us, set against a curve in the bluffs. Each of you is to fuse your burn bags and place them so that the areas of brush and thorn catch fire. That will take away part of their defenses so that we can attack later from more points. It might also keep them guessing. Once you get things burning, return to the juniper grove down below here. We'll reassemble there. Anyone who's not back in a glass will have to find his own way back. Is that understood? Now . . . I'll explain to each team where your targets are . . ." Using the map and his own study of the camp, he described each target area to each two-man team. When he was finished, he looked at Zerdial. "Let's go."

He remounted the gray and rode eastward, keeping below the crest of the ridge but still scanning with his Talent. He picked up more rodents, including tree-rats, and the grayjays, and several larger animals—a mountain cat, he thought, and several deer—but no sentries or patrols. That absence continued to worry him.

Alucius had given himself the farthest and the trickiest assignment, the one to the east, just above the broadest section of spiky thorn—but the area most vulnerable to an attack by lancers if there were no thorns. It was also the closest to the camp, and the one area most likely to have patrols.

A good vingt to the east and south, Alucius reined up below the ridgeline, although it was more of a plateau running to a drop-off holding the spiky thorns than a ridge. From what he could see and sense, the only guard was one stationed at the end of the palisade running out from the gate at the narrow east road entrance.

Alucius dismounted and tied the gray to the only tree nearby, a bent juniper. He took the three burn bags from behind the saddle and slung them over his shoulder. Then, rifle in hand, and moving in a low crouch, he eased along the gentle slope toward the drop-off. He crawled the last few yards until he was stretched behind a low bush. From there, he looked at the spiky thorn below. It was farther away than he had realized, a good fifty yards to the south of the base of the low bluff, and the area was open and exposed enough that to drop down the two-yard irregular rocky and sandy slope, then move close enough to make sure that the spiky thorn caught fire, would leave him totally exposed to the sentry—and anyone else who might be alerted.

The sentry was not especially alert, but he did scan the area where Alucius lay.

Alucius looked westward and uphill, watching.

One thin trail of smoke appeared, then another. Shortly, there was a third.

"Fire!" The call was faint, but Alucius could make it out. He lifted his rifle and waited.

Finally, the guard turned to look to the west, moving enough away from the wooden pillars of his sentry box so that Alucius had a clear shot. At that distance, it took him two shots, but with the yelling from the camp, no one noticed—for the moment—the sentry slump out of sight.

At that instant, Alucius left the rifle and scuttled over the edge of the drop-off, scrambling down the sandy and rocky slope, then ran toward the wall of spiky thorn.

Striker in hand, he lit the fuse of the first burn bag and hurled it to the south. The second went straight in front of him, to the southwest, and the third flew to the west-southwest. He paused for a moment, using his Talent, but he could feel that all three bags were burning fiercely. He also sensed no one nearby.

He ran back toward the bluff, scrabbling up the slope, grabbed his rifle, then hurried across the near flat until he reached his mount. A quick glance to the west showed that more fires were appearing around the rebel camp. From the south, Alucius could hear a bell clanging as he untied the gray and mounted.

He rode back westward at a quick walk. There was a wind, light and out of the southeast. Alucius wasn't sure what, if any, effect the wind would have, but he could see the smoke welling up from the south in more and more places, and the air around him began to smell smoky as well.

As he neared the rendezvous point, Alucius began to sense other men coming from the south. They had to have been climbing straight up from the camp below, but near the rendezvous point, that climb was close to a hundred yards of near-vertical face.

"Zerdial! Is everyone here?"

"Yes, sir!"

Alucius almost ordered them to depart. Instead, realizing that a half squad or so of rebels had reached the top of the bluff and that those rebels were almost at the ridgeline, he snapped. "Oblique firing line to the south! Now!"

Despite the irregular command, fifth squad formed up.

"Rifles ready!"

Alucius watched the ridgetop until, within moments, nine men in maroon charged over the top on foot and down toward fifth squad, raising their rifles as they ran.

"Fire at will!"

Twenty rifles fired almost as one. Four men dropped where they stood. Two others, blood streaming across faces and tunics, staggered forward. Three others sprinted toward the lancers as if nothing could touch them, shooting wildly. Fifth squad continued to fire.

Alucius held his own fire, looking to the ridgeline. Two

more armsmen in maroon appeared, and they too hurried downslope, both of them headed directly toward Alucius.

Alucius lifted his own rifle, aimed, and fired. The bullet struck the first of the remaining two armsmen in the forehead, and he pitched forward onto the trail. Alucius hit the second man in the shoulder, but the rebel still tried to aim his weapon at Alucius until Alucius's third shot silenced him.

Alucius had thought about taking captives or prisoners, but the way the rebels fought so far, trying that would have been near-suicidal for any lancer who tried. He turned the gray toward fifth squad. One lancer was on the ground.

Zerdial shook his head.

"Get him over his mount," Alucius ordered. "We need to get out of here before any more of them show up." He could sense others climbing the escarpment behind the rebel camp, but they would not reach the top for another quarter glass, he judged. Already, the sky was filling with the hazy smoke from the fires below, and he could smell the burning thorn plants.

In moments, the dead lancer—Hylik—was fastened over his saddle, and fifth squad was on the trail back to meet up with the other companies.

As they rode westward along the trail, Alucius frowned, thinking. What was going on in Hyalt? It was one thing for a single armsman to try an ambush or to fight back when cornered, but to try a suicidal charge against mounted lancers on an open trail? To climb a hundred yards up an escarpment and attack a larger force without even trying to use cover?

Behind him, the fires continued to burn, sending smoke higher and higher, and from what he could see looking backward, it appeared as though some of the fires had spread from the spiky thorn patches into the cedar and juniper groves as well.

Midafternoon came and went before Alucius and fifth squad rode across the last few hundred yards to the road, passing Waris, standing scout on the trail.

"Anyone come this way?" asked Alucius.

"No, sir. No one on the trail but you, and no one at all on the road. Spooky, if you ask me."

The more Alucius saw of Hyalt, the spookier it was.

As Alucius rode up, Feran gestured toward the east. "You were successful, I see."

"We got the fires set. We didn't stay to see if they burned the way we planned. We took out close to a squad of defenders. They attacked exactly the same way—just a blind rush at us, firing their rifles. We lost Hylik. An unfortunate and lucky shot. The rebel was running full speed downhill."

"They weren't good shots?"

"Except that one shot . . . no."

Alucius looked back to the east, where the hilltops were a mass of fire. Gray and black smoke rose into the hazy sky. With the harvest dryness of the spiky thornbushes, when the fires burned out, the thorn cover that had protected the approaches from the west and northeast would be gone. So might some of the log walls and palisades, although Alucius doubted that the heat would be intense enough for long enough to fire heavy logs.

54

On Septi night, the three companies had made camp some five vingts directly southwest of the rebel encampment, but a distance closer to fifteen by the roads, if the maps were accurate. Even so, there had been a glow in the sky for a time after sunset.

Octdi morning dawned hazy, and the scent of smoke remained in the air, carried by a gentle breeze out of the north. Shortly after dawn, the lancers were back on the road that had turned southeast and would eventually circle Hyalt to the south, then to the east—that was, if the maps were correct. So far they had been, and the reports from the lancers scouting the road ahead had confirmed that for the next few vingts, at least, the road and the map agreed.

The road dust and dirt showed signs of patrols, but only by a few riders and not by squads or larger groups. As he rode at the head of the column beside Captain Jultyr, Alucius wondered how soon it would be before that changed.

"You think the rebels will come after us?" asked Jultyr almost idly, as if to open conversation.

"After what you've seen so far . . . what do you think?" countered Alucius gently.

"They seem like hornets. You know what I mean. You hit the nest, and they all take off, all at once. Never seen an outfit charge like that squad the other day. Not even the Matrites. Have you, sir?"

"No." Alucius shook his head. "Even the grassland nomads didn't do that, not where every man charged superior weapons and positions without taking some evasive action or using cover."

"Word is that there's Talent here."

"There is. I'm a herder, and I think any herder would feel what I've felt. Nothing like it anywhere I've been." Alucius offered a laugh, partly forced. "It hasn't stopped them from getting killed." He would have said more, except he could see a lancer scout riding toward them, almost at a gallop.

Alucius kept riding, waiting until the scout—Hikal, used only for road scouting—pulled in and swung his mount into a walk beside Alucius.

"Sir . . ."

"Lancers headed our way?" asked Alucius.

"Yes, sir. Looks to be a full company ahead—same maroon uniforms—and they're riding hard this way."

"How hard?"

The youngish Hikal flushed. "Quick trot, but they've got their rifles at the ready."

"How far are they?"

"Two vingts, sir. No more than three."

"What else?"

"They're quiet, sir. Real quiet. No talking. No singing. They're just riding. Seems strange."

"They see you?"

"Don't think so, but I moved back quick."

"Any wagons or any foot with them?"

"No, sir. Just looked to be a company of horse. That's all."

Silently, for a moment, Alucius studied the terrain. To the left of the road were lowlands, ground that would have been marshland with more rain and perhaps once had been. To the right were the same rolling hills, with only a gentle slope and the heavier grass that seemed to grow closer to Hyalt. A line of thorn olives that might once have been a windbreak blocked a clear view of the road to the south, but there was no sign of the stead that might have planted the windbreak.

Alucius turned to Roncar, one of his messengers, riding just behind Jultyr and him.

"Call the other officers forward."

"Yes, sir."

While he waited for Roncar to get word to Feran and Deotyr, Alucius went over the lay of the land again, matching what he saw against what he had in mind.

Once Feran and Deotyr had ridden up, Alucius ordered the column to halt.

Then, facing the other three officers, he began to explain. "We've got a rebel company headed toward us. They're in battle dress and looking for a fight, according to the scouts. We'll give them one." Alucius paused, letting the words sink in before continuing.

"We'll form an arc. Fifth Company will take the forward part—right behind the trees over to the right. Then Thirty-fifth Company, running from the flank of Fifth to within twenty yards of the road. Twenty-eighth will cover a span of about fifty yards, centered on the road. Staggered formations so that every lancer can fire. And targeted shooting—each man in each company aiming at his counterpart. I don't want a hundred rifles aimed on the first rank. When the rebels come around the curve, all companies will open fire at my command. We'll take down as many of their men as we can until they get abreast of the trees. I'll order 'Cease, fire,' and Fifth Company will charge through. If a second charge is necessary, I'll call on Thirty-fifth Company. Twenty-eighth Company is to hold the road and allow none of the enemy through. I'll be with Fifth Company." Alucius looked from Feran to Jultyr, then to Deotyr. "Is that clear?"

"Yes, sir."

"Form up as directed."

Alucius and Fifth Company continued on the road for another hundred yards before swinging southward over the rough land that had once been pasture, but now looked merely neglected.

"Column halt! Left oblique! Stagger spacing!" Feran called out. "Ready rifles!"

Fifth Company re-formed swiftly into a staggered double file firing line by companies. Alucius looked back to see that the other two companies were also formed up as he had ordered. Then he looked to the southeast to the point where the road curved more to the east, just past the windbreak of thorn olives. There was no visual sign of the rebels, although he could sense riders farther away through his Talent.

A quarter glass passed. The feeling of the oncoming riders was stronger, and that feeling held the vague purple overtones detected by his Talent, but the riders had not yet appeared on the small section of road visible from where Alucius waited on the gray gelding.

Abruptly a pair of riders appeared at the end of the curved section of the road, riding westward. Within moments, the forward part of a column of maroon-uniformed lancers also came into view. Neither of the outriders looked to the side as they rode forward.

Then, one of the riders stopped just short of the windbreak, and the other turned and rode back toward the column.

"You think we'll need to charge them?" asked Feran, his voice low.

"They'll regroup and charge us," Alucius predicted.

Yet, for almost a tenth of a glass, nothing happened. The single outrider remained in the middle of the road, looking straight in the direction of Twenty-eighth Company, seemingly ignoring Fifth Company and Thirty-fifth Company, and the column of rebel lancers continued to ride closer, but neither faster nor more slowly, until they were within yards of the eastern end of the thorn olive windbreak.

Then there was a single barked command that Alucius could not make out, and the entire column, still in two files, began to gallop pell-mell down the road toward Twenty-eighth Company, totally ignoring Fifth Company and Thirty-fifth Company.

"Prepare to fire!" Alucius judged the distance, waiting.

The rebels were within fifty yards of the nearest lancers in Fifth Company when Alucius ordered, "Fire at will!"

"Fire at will!"

The command echoed down the ranks of the companies, followed immediately by the sounds of rifles, first the heavier weapons of Fifth Company, then the sharper sounds of the Lanachronan rifles.

At the first volley, close to twenty rebels sagged in their saddles or toppled onto the dusty road, but the rebel column charged past Fifth Company.

Alucius almost wanted to call off the attack as the veterans of Fifth Company picked off rebel lancer after rebel lancer. The shots from the Thirty-fifth and Twenty-eighth Companies rained more destruction on those remaining.

The remaining rebels, less than a squad's worth, now unsheathing blades, were less than a hundred yards from Twenty-eighth Company.

"Cease fire! Cease fire! Fifth Company, charge!" Alucius slipped his rifle into its case and drew his sabre.

The sound of rifles died away, to be replaced with the drumming thunder of hoofs on the weary pastureland and road as Alucius led the charge toward the depleted rebels.

He would have expected the rebel lancers in the rear ranks to have turned as he and the lancers from Fifth Company bore down on them from behind. Not a one did.

Alucius cut down two men from behind, his guts churning as he did.

Within moments, not a single rebel remained mounted. One rebel, his arm mangled, struggled to his feet and raised a blade, staggering toward a Guard lancer looking the other way.

Crack! A single rifle shot brought the rebel down.

Alucius glanced to see Egyl holding his rifle.

Several more shots rang out, cutting down rebels who tried to bring blades or rifles from standing or sitting positions on the road. Then there were no more shots.

"Fifth Company! Re-form on me!" ordered Feran.

A good thirty rebel mounts milled among bodies and the Fifth Company lancers as they moved to the southwest side of the road.

"Captain Jultyr! Set a detail to capture the rebel mounts!" Alucius called out.

"Yes, sir. Third squad! Get those mounts and form them up behind fifth squad."

Feran eased up beside Alucius. "One man got a shallow slash. No other casualties."

"No casualties in Thirty-fifth Company," reported Jultyr, riding by and supervising his third squad.

"Thank you." Alucius paused for a moment. "Well done."

As the chaos began to sort itself out, Alucius glanced from the fallen rebels, bodies strewn everywhere, and the riderless mounts to Captain Deotyr, who rode toward him.

"Two men killed, sir, three wounded. No captives."

"Thank you, Captain. You did well to hold there."

Neither Thirty-fifth Company nor Fifth Company had suffered any casualties. None at all. Twenty-eighth had lost two more lancers, and three others had taken wounds from which they should recover. Alucius's force had been through three skirmishes, or perhaps a small battle and two skirmishes, and he'd lost something like ten men, with slightly more than that wounded, and they had killed close to two hundred rebels. So why was he so worried?

Because, once again, the rebels had fought to the death? In the heat of battle, Alucius hadn't wanted to order a capture, not when it would have risked his own men in such an effort to capture a fanatic.

Deotyr remained motionless, looking at Alucius.

"You're wondering why I set the companies as I did?" Alucius asked.

"No, sir . . . well . . ." Deotyr didn't quite meet Alucius's eyes.

"There were several reasons. First, Twenty-eighth Company had taken the most casualties before today." Alucius offered a bitter laugh. "I put your company farther away than Thirty-fifth, with the hope that you wouldn't suffer as many casualties. I was wrong. The rebels seem to attack directly along the road."

"I don't think any of us would have seen that, sir."

Alucius should have, but he let that pass. "Second, Fifth Company is more experienced, and third, your rifles have more range."

"More range?"

Alucius repressed a sigh. "Captain, your rifles are smaller bore. They're more accurate over a longer range, and your magazines carry twice as many cartridges. Because your men aren't as experienced, putting them where I did equalized the rates of fire."

Deotyr nodded, and Alucius could see the understanding. The captain turned his mount back toward Twenty-eighth Company.

Alucius surveyed the bodies on the road again. They'd need to search them, at least quickly, and salvage ammunition and supplies—and see if there were any written orders.

He had ridden to Hyalt thinking that he would not enter

the area and immediately start killing people. He snorted softly to himself. He hadn't. He'd gotten near Hyalt, and the rebels or invaders or whatever they were had started attacking his forces, leaving him no choice but slaughter.

But why?

He had no idea, and he certainly didn't like being put in positions where he had no choice but slaughter. Before they entered another skirmish he needed a captive—if he could get one, somehow. He had no doubts that there would be another skirmish or another fight.

He looked back at the bodies once more.

55

Octdi morning dawned with clouds and a light drizzle, barely enough to wet the dust on the road, but enough to make the southern late-harvest warmth feel uncomfortably muggy, at least to Alucius, especially as he was wearing his nightsilk undergarments as well as the nightsilk herder's vest under his tunic. Despite the moisture, the air still held the odor of wood and thornbush smoke, acrid and penetrating.

The sentries had seen no one on the road through the night or in the morning, but Alucius was concerned enough that he had the companies on the road within a glass past dawn on the gray morning. According to the maps, the road they traveled would join another road in four to five vingts, and from Alucius's observations and calculations, that road was probably the one that led to the rebel camp they had surrounded with fire. The merged road turned northeast toward Hyalt. For the first several vingts, they had seen nothing, and the handful of steads they passed were empty. They showed signs of having been deserted, not in the past few days, but several weeks earlier.

Alucius considered that the whole situation was upside

down. He and his Guard companies were Lanachronan, but they were having to act as though they were invaders in their own land, and anyone away from the main force was definitely at risk. What was worse was that Alucius still knew very little about why this had happened, except that somehow the ifrits were involved. That didn't make much sense, so far as he could determine, because Hyalt was as far as one could get—with the possible exception of Soupat—from other major towns and cities in Lanachrona. It wasn't on the direct route to anywhere, such as cities like Borlan or Indyor, and even the Regent of the Matrial couldn't have gotten to Hyalt by any major high road directly. There were no ifrit ruins or, so far as stories went, no rumors of a Table that might have been of use to the ifrits—unless there was one hidden somewhere. Yet matters were as they were, and Alucius had had few enough real choices.

What was worse was that his efforts at individual scouting had lost him one scout, wounded another, and gotten another chased for vingts. On the other hand, anytime that they had encountered or found larger numbers of rebels it had been in a fighting situation where, when the dust had finally settled, there had been no survivors because any living rebel would keep trying to kill lancers until the rebel died.

Alucius turned in the saddle toward Feran. "I'd like to send Waris out with some other lancers to see if they can scout that road up to the rebel camp—not too far—and capture a messenger—if they use them."

"Capture?"

"We have to get some information. There haven't been small groups of rebels or stead holders anywhere that we've been so far. If we can't capture a messenger, then maybe on the road toward Hyalt we can find a stead or two with someone there and find out something."

"Wouldn't hurt," Feran agreed, turning in the saddle. "Waris!"

Within moments, the scout had ridden forward, and Alucius had edged the gray to the right shoulder of the road, so that the three could ride abreast.

"The majer has a job for you," Feran said.

"Yes, sir?"

Alucius looked at Waris. "The task is simple. Accomplishing it won't be. We need a captive lancer or armsman, one in good enough shape to answer questions. There's a road ahead, a little over four vingts away, and it joins this one, and then the two run to Hyalt. The other road starts at the camp you scouted. There ought to be messengers or some travel along there. If there are just large parties, report back, and we'll try something else. Oh, and pick two or three others you think can help you."

The scout looked to Feran. "Overcaptain, sir?"

"Anyone but squad leaders or wounded."

In less than a quarter glass, Waris and three other lancers had ridden off, ahead of the main force, past the scouts and outriders ahead of the column.

A good glass passed, and the scouts had reported nothing, and while they had passed another five steads, all had been abandoned in the same fashion as those they had passed earlier. Then, the figure of Waris appeared, followed by four other mounts. Three held riders, and the fourth had a figure strapped across a saddle.

"Column halt!" Alucius ordered.

"Column halt," echoed back along the line of lancers.

Waris rode slowly toward Alucius, then reined up. "We got a captive, sir."

"Was it difficult?"

"Wasn't too hard." A weary smile crossed the scout's lips. "We ended up shooting two. This one, we shot the mount, then shot him in the leg before he could get to his rifle. Took two of us to disarm him, and all of us to tie him up."

Alucius wasn't surprised. Dismayed, but not surprised, as he looked at the prisoner, slung across the saddle of the mount behind Waris, hands tied behind his back, feet trussed together, and a gag tied across his mouth.

"Sorry, sir. We had to tie him like that. He just tries to bite, kick, anything . . ."

"Get him off the mount. Set him on the stones there." Alucius gestured toward a rough heap of stones that once might have been a stile across a sagging and neglected fence.

"Yes, sir."

Alucius dismounted and handed the gray's reins to Fewal, one of his messengers, then waited as the three lancers carried the bound captive to the stones and propped him against the bowed middle railing of the fence.

"Did he say anything? Before you gagged him?"

"Nothing. Maybe he doesn't speak Lanachronan."

Alucius studied the captive. As he looked closely, he could Talent-sense what resembled a fine purplish mesh net that fit the captive like a glove. For a time, he just studied it until he could find the purplish nodes that held it. Once he found those, it was but an instant, and the net vanished.

The captive fainted.

"Sir . . . ?"

"He'll be fine in a few moments. You can ungag him now."

It wasn't that long before the man looked up, an expression that was clearly fear as he took in Alucius and the uniform that he wore.

Alucius pressed forward the feeling that the captive should be helpful . . . cooperative. There was no sense of resistance. After a moment, he asked, "Could you tell me your name?"

The man looked at Alucius, wide-eyed, then lowered his gaze. "Escadt, sir. Of the Cadmians."

"What are the Cadmians?"

"We are. The Cadmians are the lancers of the prophet and the True Duarchy."

"Why were you ordered to attack us?"

"You are the evil northerners. You will keep the Duarchy from returning. All the land will die, and all our families will starve and perish without the Duarchy."

Alucius glanced at Feran.

"Why would we do that? We're all part of Lanachrona."

"You are the lamaial of evil, the one who will use treason to destroy all that is good."

"Who told you this?"

· "The prophet Adarat. He is the servant of the True Duarchy. He said that the man with the dark gray hair, the one who is not old, he is the lamaial. Adarat knows what is and what will be."

Alucius had his doubts about that. "Who told Adarat this?"

"He knows. He is the servant of the True Duarchy."

That line of questioning wouldn't help, Alucius reflected. "How long has Adarat been in Hyalt?"

"He has been here forever."

"Forever?"

The rebel shrugged. "The Temple of the Duarchy has been here so long as any can remember, and there has always been a prophet, and the prophet has always been Adarat."

Alucius couldn't see much point in pursuing that. "How many camps with armed men are there around Hyalt? With Cadmians?"

"I have heard that there are two. I only know of one, myself."

"Where is the other one?"

"I do not know for sure."

"Where do you think it is?"

The rebel shrugged. "They say it is on the Hill of the Dead to the northeast of Hyalt."

"How many companies are there?"

"I do not know."

"How many lancers were there at your camp?"

"I do not know."

"How many do you guess that there were?"

"Three hundred. That was before you northerners killed so many."

"Until you attacked us, we never attacked or fired upon you," Alucius pointed out. "Why did you attack us?"

"Because you are evil, and you would destroy the good of the True Duarchy."

Alucius kept proving to himself that there was little point in following that line of questioning. "What is in the cave in the hillside?"

"It is not a cave. It is the Temple of the True Duarchy."

"Is that where Adarat is?"

"I do not know . . ."

"Does it have a Table of power?"

"I do not know."

"Have you seen a Table there?"

"No, sir."

"How many people remain in Hyalt?"

"I do not know . . ."

Even after almost half a glass of questioning, Alucius had learned only slightly more. The captive seemed to know very little beyond declaring the goodness of the Duarchy to come and the evilness of Alucius and his "northerners."

Finally, Alucius nodded to Feran. "That's all for now. Keep him tied up, but don't gag him unless he causes trouble."

"Egyl?"

"Yes, sir. We'll take care of it."

Midmorning came and went, and they reached where the roads joined, but saw no one and no signs of rebels. The air remained damp and more misty than actually drizzling. None of the scouts had seen any traces of another large body of rebels, and Alucius decided to continue northeast on the road toward Hyalt for the next three or fourth vingts, until they reached what the maps showed as a narrow hill road that actually connected with the road where his force had first camped north of Hyalt. Alucius didn't plan to take that road all the way back, but he liked the idea of having a way out, if necessary.

In midafternoon, the company saw the first stead that was actually occupied, and within a quarter of a glass, Alucius was facing a round-faced older man with unruly curly gray hair and shoulders stooped from years of toil, a man of perhaps forty, whom the scouts had brought in. The stead holder trembled as he stood on the side of the road and looked at Alucius. The majer could sense the fear pouring from the man—as well as the faintest trace of the purplish miasma that seemed to touch all the people in Hyalt—or all those with whom Alucius had come in contact. He dissolved the purplish miasmatic net and tried to extend a sense of reassurance with his Talent, but the holder shivered even more.

"Is that your stead?"

"Yes . . . sir."

"Is your family there?"

"Spare them, sir . . . I beg you, spare them."

"I have no intention of harming either you or them. I'm just trying to find out what has happened here in Hyalt in the last month."

The holder said nothing.

"What did happen?"

"The prophet Adarat sent his disciples to disperse the lancers of evil. They refused to leave, and they were killed."

"Did you see this?"

"That is what the prophet said, and a prophet of the True Duarchy always tells the truth."

"What about the traders and the crafters?"

"Some of them fled. Those who would not accept the True Duarchy, but fleeing will avail them little. Before long, all of Corus will prosper under the return of the Duarchy."

"Why has no one left Hyalt in more than a month?"

"Why would anyone wish to leave when the True Duarchy is about to return?" A vaguely puzzled expression crossed the man's thin face.

"How do you know that?"

"The prophet Adarat said so. He is the servant of the True Duarchy. He knows what is and what will be."

"Why do you fear us?"

"You are the evil northerners. You will try to keep the Duarchy from returning. All the land will die, and all our families will starve and perish without the Duarchy."

Alucius glanced at Feran, then back to the holder. "How do you know this? How do you know that this Adarat tells you the truth? Have you seen anyone besides him who would bring back the Duarchy?"

"You are the lamaial of evil, the one who is old before his time, the one who will use treason to destroy all that is good."

"Have you seen anything that would prove this?"

"I know what I know, and the prophet Adarat knows what is and what will be."

Alucius tried a few more questions, but the answers were invariably the same. Adarat was the prophet, and Adarat knew what was to be. Finally, he looked to the lancers standing five yards away, beside the rail fence. "Take him back to his stead. Let him go, but make sure you take care of yourselves."

"Yes, sir."

The holder did not look back as he was led away under the low clouds that had promised rain and delivered but an occasional drizzle.

"Even the lancers of the Matrial weren't that bad," mused Alucius.

"Coming from you, sir," Feran replied, "that doesn't make me feel especially good."

Alucius walked slowly to the gray, untethered his mount from the rail fence, and remounted. He looked to Feran. "I don't think we'll get more answers, but we ought to try a few more holders, or their wives."

The overcaptain nodded.

Another two glasses later, after getting almost identical answers from two holders and the widow of a third, Alucius brought his force to a halt while he composed a message to Marshal Frynkel, one that summarized events so far, emphasizing the fanaticism of the rebels. Then he dispatched Hikal, along with two other lancers, northward to the last way station, from where the dispatch riders could take it to Tempre and the marshal. He told the three to remain at the way station until the force returned or until he sent orders, since he had no idea where his force might be in a few days.

Then, after seeing the three off, he ordered his force westward and then northwest, along the road he had mapped out earlier.

Feran, riding beside Alucius, cleared his throat.

Alucius turned in the saddle.

"I have bad feelings about this," Feran said slowly. "Especially when you send off messengers like that."

"That makes two of us." Alucius looked down the road, angling northwest away from Hyalt. "We'll avoid Hyalt itself for now. Then we'll find another hilltop campsite for tonight. Tomorrow, we'll locate the other rebel camp." Alucius couldn't bring himself to call them Cadmians, no matter what they called themselves. "Then, we'll see what we can work out to get rid of them both. I want to find out about the other camp or camps first, but I'd like to take down the Temple of the True Duarchy, and this Adarat, before we even try to deal with the town."

Feran nodded. "That makes sense."

It made sense to Alucius as well, but whether it was the right tactic was another question.

56

In the warm, damp, and dark air, Alucius was stretched out on his bedroll, not under it. He was tired, but not sleepy. Or not sleepy enough to drift off when lying on relatively hard ground. The cedar- and juniper-branch ends under the bedroll helped, but not really enough, not with all the thoughts going through his head.

Setting up another camp hadn't been that difficult, and the hilltop was more defensible than the others from which he had to choose. That was good and necessary, given that they were in the hills less than ten vingts to the west-southwest of Hyalt, although the hillsides were rocky and rugged. Yet, after encountering the one messenger patrol, they had seen no more rebels, and he had sensed nearby none of the purple-linked Talent he had felt from the rebel encampment to the north and west.

Adarat had to be an ifrit, or strongly influenced or linked to them. Could ifrits be killed with Talent-darkened bullets, the way the Talent-creatures could be? Or could they only be destroyed in the way he had killed the Recorder and the engineer, through direct use of Talent energy from Alucius himself? Should he just attack the first camp? Or should he finish finding out what he could about all the camps and rebels? Why were the ifrits trying to establish a foothold in Hyalt? What role did the Regent of the Matrial play? How many more of the Talent-influenced lancers were there? What had really happened in Hyalt so that no one left? What was it about whatever Talent Adarat had used that left the rebels and stead holders still believing in the True Duarchy? Did that kind of Talent-use change what people believed forever?

The questions going through his mind seemed endless, and then he thought about Wendra. She had to be fine; the wristguard would have let him know if she were not.

Finally, forcing himself to recognize that he had answers for neither worries nor questions that evening, he closed his eyes.

His sleep was restless.

"Sir?"

"What?" Alucius shook his head, then sat up in his bedroll. He couldn't have slept that long. He looked through the darkness at the face of the lancer standing a yard away, his herder's nightsight telling him that the sentry was Noer. "What is it?"

"The prisoner killed himself."

"How?" Alucius stiffened. "He was still tied up, wasn't he?"

The young lancer grimaced. "Yes, sir. Hands behind his back. Guess he found a rock with a sharp edge. Just kept sawing at his wrists when no one was looking. Blood everywhere. Never made a sound. Don't know how he did it."

Alucius shivered. How on earth could a man do that? Why on earth? Because he still believed in the prophet? Or because he realized that he'd been deceived and had lost everything?

57

Alucius didn't feel as though he'd slept at all when he finally rose before dawn on Novdi morning. He'd had the wall dream again, with the same ifritlike stone walls closing in on him, with no doors and windows. Once more, he'd awakened in the middle of the night, sweating, and it had taken him a while to cool off and get back to sleep—and to push away the sense of being walled in by his own actions. Now, every part of his body felt stiff and sore, or so it seemed as he rose and stretched, his eyes taking in the campsite, where most lancers still slumbered.

He looked up. The clouds and drizzle of the previous day had been replaced with a thin fog, but he could see a clear sky above the low-lying whiteness that drifted in patches around and over the hilltop camp. He had barely gotten himself together when a call echoed through the white-fogged gray of the moments before dawn.

"Rebels on the road!"

"Companies form up! In ranks! On foot!" Alucius bellowed. "South facing!"

He found Feran less than ten yards away. "Have Fifth

Company take the center. Put them in kneeling or prone positions. We'll take fewer shots that way."

"Yes, sir."

Alucius could tell Feran agreed with that, and he merely added, "I'll try to find Deotyr and Jultyr. If you see them first, convey my orders."

"Yes, sir."

Alucius found both captains heading toward him, and he relayed the same orders, ending with, "Twenty-eighth Company take the west flank, Thirty-fifth the east. And tell your men to keep down and make every shot count."

"Yes, sir."

As the three companies formed up, Alucius took a position in the center of the formation that followed the curve of the hill. He had both his rifles with him and his ammunition belt.

For almost a quarter of a glass, there were no sounds from the road. Then, a handful of shots echoed through the thin fog. Alucius heard a bullet smash into a juniper slightly uphill and five yards to his right. He couldn't say that he was surprised that the rebels were trying to use the fog as cover for an attack, but he didn't understand the comparatively few shots being fired. His Talent-senses indicated that at least a company of rebels was moving uphill through the fog, still mounted, but the fog was thicker along the lower-lying road, and while Alucius could sense the attackers, he could not see them. He was just thankful that he had ordered the sentries be stationed even farther away from the campsite than he had in the past.

He wondered. Were other rebels sneaking up on other sides of the campsite?

His Talent-senses showed nothing, except for the force moving uphill toward them. He held his first rifle ready, because his ears could hear the sounds of hoofs on soil below, seemingly magnified by the fog.

"Prepare to fire!" he ordered.

"Prepare to fire!"

Less than fifty yards below him, the first maroon-clad

lancer trotted his mount out of the patchy fog, in a place where the whiteness had thinned.

"Fire at will!"

Alucius squeezed off his first shot, and the lancer dropped, knocked from his saddle by the force of the bullet from the herder's heavy rifle.

Along the line, there were other scattered shots, but not many, and then, for another quarter glass, there was comparative silence across the hillside. Alucius could sense the rebels below, holding a rough line in a fog that was slowly thinning under a sun that had finally risen. After taking the lull as a chance to reload, Alucius looked skyward. Above, he could see patches of silver-green sky, patches that were becoming more frequent.

Alucius sensed movement below.

"Prepare to fire!" The command was unnecessary, technically, but he used it as a warning.

"Prepare to fire!" The echoes of the officers' repetitions had barely died away when rebel lancers and their mounts burst out of the fog below. Most did not seem to be using rifles, but charged uphill swinging blades of various lengths.

The rifles of the defenders *crack*ed and even thundered, and rebel after rebel went down, as did many of the mounts. Alucius fired methodically, going through the first rifle, then the second. The attackers thinned. He reloaded one rifle quickly and barely managed to get off two shots at near-point-blank range at a rebel who was less than ten yards away. Somewhere below, a man was moaning, and to the west a horse screamed. At least, it sounded like a wounded horse.

Alucius swallowed. He waited, and kept waiting, but not another rebel lancer appeared.

Slowly, he used his Talent to scan the hillside. He could sense some badly wounded figures, but none mounted.

"Hold your positions!" he ordered.

The time passed, and the fog continued to thin rapidly until, a half a glass later, only wisps remained, not enough to conceal the carnage of fallen men and mounts below.

"Fifth Company, take cover and advance! Five yards at a time!"

He knew the caution was not necessary, but there was no other way to convey to the lancers that the hillside contained no further danger.

A glass later, Alucius was checking the gray and his gear, ready to mount. He heard a mount approaching and turned.

Egyl reined up short of Alucius, followed by Feran.

"Yes, Egyl?"

"We did a quick search of the bodies, sir, like you ordered."

"What did you find?"

"Sir . . . a lot of those lancers were either barely more than boys or they were graybeards. Most of them didn't have rifles, and the blades were mostly old and of all sorts. Their tunics hardly matched, up close."

"The rebels in the other attacks weren't like that, were they?" asked Alucius, although he already knew the answer.

"No, sir."

"You think this was some sort of feint?"

Egyl glanced downhill. "Don't know what to think, sir."

"Thank you," Alucius said. "We'll be leaving shortly."

"Yes, sir. I'll tell the men."

Feran remained, waiting until Egyl had ridden out of easy earshot. "Do you think we've worn them down to that few?"

"No, but I couldn't say why," Alucius admitted. "They were sent against us for a reason, but I can't figure out why. What worries me most about this prophet is that he's willing to have hundreds of lancers slaughtered for whatever his goals are. Anyone who does that . . ."

"Maybe *that* is his goal," Feran suggested.

"To have us create so much carnage that it undermines the Lord-Protector's rule?"

"Can you think of another reason?"

The only ones Alucius could think of were even worse. "We'd better get moving."

Nothing was going the way he'd thought it might, and

yet . . . what else could he have done? Even rusty blades and the few mismatched rifles would have killed all too many of his lancers had he done nothing. And retreating without fighting would have undermined the Lord-Protector's rule and authority even more than the carnage Alucius found himself creating.

58

Salaan, Lanachrona

Tarolt and the angular Recorder sat on opposite sides of the circular table. A pitcher of clear liquid rested on a silver tray halfway between them.

The Recorder took a sip of the liquid, setting down the crystal goblet. "I miss Efra. Even more than the towers against the golden sky, or the perfumes of summer, I miss the food. It was an art in itself, firetails marinated in the liqueurs of Serela and stuffed with dauflin, grilled to perfection so that each bite melted . . ."

"There is much to miss . . . but even more that will vanish if we do not succeed. As always, we must create a new and greater Efra."

The Recorder nodded somberly.

"What does the Table show of the events in Hyalt, Trezun?" asked Tarolt, after a silence.

Trezun fingered the base of the goblet, purple eyes burning out of his pale white face. "Adarat has taken the shadow most successfully . . . or, I should say, the shadow has taken him most successfully. He has maneuvered the majer into an impossible position, and one in which, even if Majer Alucius succeeds in subduing the 'revolt,' the Lord-Protector's authority will be undermined greatly, and he will be regarded as a barbarous butcher."

"Or he will be condemned all across Corus for having

unleashed the butcher of the north on the hapless steers of Hyalt." Tarolt laughed. "Even those worthless steers will play their part."

"This Alucius is far better than you think, as an arms-commander, Tarolt," observed the Recorder. "He could be back in Dekhron before spring, and that would not be for the best. The grid will not be fully ready by then, and we cannot accept mass translations without a fully powered grid. Waleryn is having to proceed more slowly with the Praetor, and that will delay the next translation."

"He is proceeding, is he not?"

"His work is going well, if not quite so quickly as we had planned."

"It never does, not when one must deal with steers. Even translated Talent-steers are often less than satisfactory."

"How is Halanat?" asked Trezun.

"He is better than many, and his trading has provided the golds we need." Tarolt paused and took a swallow from his own goblet. "We might be able to make other matters work for us. The Regent of the Matrial is likely to break through the lancers of the Lord-Protector. She will hold Southgate by the turn of the new year, if not within weeks. What if she sends that troublesome Marshal Aluyn against Tempre with one of the crystal spear-throwers?"

"You think that the Lord-Protector would send Majer Alucius against the spear-thrower?"

"If Wyerl is dead, what will Marshal Frynkel recommend? What other choices will he have, if he must save Tempre?" Tarolt's white eyebrows rose. "Or to hold Southgate, if the Regent is less successful."

"I will see what we can do with the sub-crystal to plant those thoughts." The Recorder paused. "I still cannot determine what created it, but we can use it as though it were a Table."

"That is secondary to its use . . . for now. You have some time."

"The Regent is already mostly ours, and the idea makes sense. The Lord-Protector will always threaten her. The

Matrial did not attack, and look what happened to her. The Regent will see that kind of reason."

"As do all the steers, she will accept what is plausible," said Tarolt. "Especially if it fits her inner desires. That is always the key to persuasion and manipulation—plausible appeal to desire."

The Recorder's fingers touched the base of his goblet, but his eyes were a world away.

59

It was just past midafternoon on a cooler and hazy Decdi when Twenty-eighth Company, leading the column, turned onto the eternastone road that would take the entire force two days northward to the manned way station. Once there, Alucius wanted his lancers—and their mounts—to get some rest. He also wanted to see if there was any information on what else was happening in Lanachrona.

He'd managed to get a few more reports on the town of Hyalt and the other camp from the scouts—without losing any more. Waris had reported that the town appeared half deserted, and Rakalt had confirmed that a second camp did exist northeast of Hyalt, with stables and barracks for three or four companies.

Even after going over the reports with the scouts, Alucius had very mixed feelings about moving away from Hyalt. Part of him said that he should have just plowed in and attacked the two camps, and part of him worried that he knew too little. The first part of the campaign had certainly not been a failure. The three companies had effectively killed almost four rebel horse companies, reduced the natural defenses of the major enemy staging camp, and determined the bases of the forces opposing him, with relatively light losses—except in terms of ammunition. In the end, ammunition had been the deciding factor. While he had enough for a few more fights, he doubted he had cartridges sufficient for attacks on both rebel camps. For that reason, he'd also finally sent a second messenger ahead, directly to Tempre, to request more ammunition, along with a more complete report on events to date and on the general situation in the Hyalt area—or what he and the scouts had been able to observe.

He'd also come away with close to fifty spare mounts, some of which were so poor as to be useless, but perhaps those could be sold for other purposes.

He still fretted about the last rebel attack and the use of boys and graybeards. Was it a diversion, or had it been designed, as Feran had suggested, to destroy support for the Lord-Protector? Or for something else that he had not even thought about? His lips tightened. However it had been meant, the result had been to make his task harder, because the killing of boys and old men would create more resentment and anger against the Lord-Protector. What also worried him was that there was even more behind that strategy.

Neither Alucius nor Deotyr said much for a good half glass after they started directly north. The lands on both sides of the road might once have been meadows or pastures, but they had long been untended and held a preponderance of thornbushes, with only scattered areas of true grasslands. Then, Alucius reflected, the area around Hyalt seemed partial to thornbushes.

"How long will we be at the way station, sir?" asked Deotyr finally.

"Four days—that's what I'd planned on, but that depends on how soon we get the ammunition."

"We had a wagon full of it, sir, didn't we?"

"We did, but about half of that was for Fifth Company, because the larger cartridges are hard to get in lower Lanachrona. We wouldn't have enough for an attack on the rebel camps, not if they send lancers at us the way they have."

"It's almost a slaughter, the way they attack," mused Deotyr.

"Only so long as we have bullets and space between us," Alucius said dryly. "With their numbers, a more equal fight wouldn't be something you'd look forward to, would you?"

"Ah . . . no, sir."

"Majer!" The shout came from a lancer riding along the side of the high road from the rear.

"Here!" Alucius gestured, although it should have been unnecessary, since, while heading Twenty-eighth Company, he was the only rider in the black and blue of the Northern Guard.

The lancer was Skant, and he eased his mount beside Alucius. "There's lancers moving up on us from the south, really pushing their mounts. They're less than half a vingt back. Overcaptain Feran wants to know if he should engage."

Alucius did not reply, but glanced northward. Perhaps three-quarters of a vingt ahead, the road passed through a stone-walled cut in a low rise that ran east and west in both directions so far as he could see. He strained to sense what might lie ahead. Was there a sense of a vague purpleness? He glanced at the road cut, then stood in the stirrups and half turned to look back southward. There were no hills or obstructions to vision on either side of the road to the south—except the knee-high to waist-high thornbushes that were even thicker than they had been farther south. His nightsheep could have taken care of those—although it wouldn't have done their wool any good.

Alucius settled back into the saddle, looking at Skant. "Tell the overcaptain that we'll ride on about another half vingt and halt the column. Have him move the wagons to the middle of the column. I'll have Thirty-fifth Company move out beyond the road to provide additional fire. He's to engage as he sees fit once we halt. I'll hold Twenty-eighth Company in reserve."

An expression of concern and puzzlement crossed Deotyr's face, but the captain said nothing.

"Half a vingt and we halt," said Skant. "Wagons to the middle. He can engage, and Thirty-fifth will move out to the flanks with covering fire."

"That's right, Skant."

"Yes, sir." The lancer turned his mount and rode back along the shoulder.

After a moment, Deotyr spoke. "Sir?"

"Why did I only offer Thirty-fifth as covering fire? Look ahead. See that rise? Don't you think it's strange that we're being attacked from the south as we near that?"

"You think they'll attack from the north as well?"

"I don't know. If they don't, there will be time to pull Twenty-eighth out, but once a company's off the road here, with all that thorn, it takes time to re-form, especially if the rebels come charging down the road. But if I don't send Thirty-fifth off road and out, they don't have any angle to provide covering fire."

Deotyr nodded.

After riding back and providing Jultyr with detailed instructions, Alucius hurried back northward to rejoin Deotyr and Twenty-eighth Company. He kept studying the road, both to the north and south. Before long he could sense riders on both sections, but only about a company in each direction. Again, that didn't seem to make much sense, but Adarat or whoever was commanding might be thinking that the surprise of a rear attack would be sufficient. Like everything else in Hyalt, the situation bothered Alucius.

The three Lanachronan companies covered the thousand yards, and the rebels to the north remained concealed. Alucius waited longer, another three hundred yards, until the column reached a point where the ground beyond the road on each side formed an almost imperceptible rise that was mostly clear of the thornbush.

"Column, halt!" Alucius ordered. "Thirty-fifth Company! To the flanks!" He turned to Deotyr. "Captain. Have Twenty-eighth form into a staggered front from five yards out from the shoulder of the road on one side to five on the other side. If you get a rebel attack, don't open fire until they're within a hundred yards unless they're moving at gallop. In that case, you'd better start firing at a hundred and fifty yards. Is that clear?"

"Yes, sir."

"I'm moving back to the center so that I can see what's happening on both sides."

"Yes, sir."

Not without misgivings, Alucius moved back toward the middle of the formation until he was within yards of Jultyr and to the slightly higher ground beyond the east shoulder of the road, trying to see and sense what was happening both to the north and the south.

Feran spread Fifth Company and waited until the rebels were within a hundred yards. Then Fifth Company opened fire. Although he could not see them, Alucius could feel the waves of death and the purple miasma that dissolved with each death. He could also sense the rebel forces to the north, moving southward into the shadows of the road cut ahead, as well as several wagons. The wagons bothered him, but he couldn't determine why or what they contained.

"Rebels to the north!" The call echoed from one of Twenty-eighth Company's outriders, galloping southward. "They're forming up on the road."

"Twenty-eighth Company, hold!" came Deotyr's command. "Rifles ready. Prepare to fire."

Alucius half nodded. He noted that the northern force of rebels was still a good four hundred yards away. Then he turned his Talent to the south once more.

This time the rebels attacking Fifth Company did not continue to charge blindly forward. After the shock of the first volleys shredded through their ranks, they turned their mounts and rode off the road, half east and half west. That worried Alucius, especially when he saw that they were re-forming two hundred yards away. He turned the gray and shifted his study to the north, where the oncoming maroon-clad rebels were less than two hundred yards out from Twenty-eighth Company.

From the north, it seemed, a burst of crimson emptiness flashed over Alucius, along with a momentary, but intense, chill. He forced himself to infuse the shells in his rifles with darkness, even as he had the first rifle out of the holder, his eyes scanning the skies and the land beyond the road. He forced himself to ignore what happened to the north—at least for the moment.

A wild pteridon appeared some seventy yards to the southwest, almost a hundred yards into the sky. Alucius could tell that it was about to dive directly at him, even before it half folded its wings.

He concentrated on the pteridon, squeezing off one shot, then a second.

A ball of blue flame exploded from where the Talent-creature had been and plummeted into a thornbush, which exploded in flame.

Alucius turned, catching sight of something else, a single horned sandox lumbering toward the eastern flank of Jultyr's lancers.

It took Alucius a single shot, but the creature had appeared so close to the last of the lancers that the bluish flames surged over the outermost lancer, enveloping him in flames. His screams were brief, but Alucius shuddered. He continued to search for more of the Talent-creatures even as he heard Deotyr's command.

"Twenty-eighth Company! Fire at will!"

The *cracks* of shots from north and south echoed around Alucius as he searched for another Talent-creature, and he almost missed the pteridon coming in from the north.

"Look out!" someone yelled.

He twisted in the saddle and used the last two shots in the first rifle to hit the pteridon, but once more the bluish firebolt resulting from his successful shot flared downward, barreling into the chest of a lancer's mount. The man, quick of thought, jumped clear, but the horse's scream was agonizing.

His second rifle out, Alucius scanned land and sky, but the crimson emptiness, that legacy of the Duarches, was gone.

The rebel company from the north continued to ride southward, lancers falling to the fire of Deotyr's men, until the rebels were less than thirty yards from Twenty-eighth Company. Abruptly, at that moment, a single long trumpet blast came from somewhere. The single note wavered but held. As one, the rebel lancers who had attacked from the north threw down their rifles, turned their mounts, and galloped back along the eternastone road, back to the north.

"After them!" ordered Deotyr.

Alucius wheeled the gray as Twenty-eighth Company rode in pursuit of the fleeing rebels. Should he countermand the order? How?

From the slight ridge on the side of the road, Alucius looked northward, watching as Twenty-eighth Company closed on the rebels, feeling that something was not right.

Why were they fleeing, when they had never done so before?

The rebels neared the road cut made by the ancient road through the low rolling hill. There, Alucius saw a low line of what appeared to be packed clay that ran from one side of the road to the other, and the road behind the clay appeared to be shiny. Something splashed from the hoofs of the mounts of the retreating rebel riders.

At that instant, he *knew*. He forced himself to ignore the bullets from the south, and concentrated on extending a thin golden green line of fire northward, toward the liquid in the road cut. His thinnest of lines of Talent-fire touched the liquid held behind the miniature dikes at the same moment that the leading riders of Twenty-eighth Company crossed the first one.

Whhhssst! A flare of flame erupted from the eternastones, bathing at least half the rebels in flames, turning them and their mounts into living torches. The first three or four ranks of Twenty-eighth Company's first squad also flared into flame.

Alucius's guts twisted. But there was little more he could do, not after Deotyr had ordered the charge.

He twisted in the saddle, looking south, but with the fiery gout to the north, the remaining rebels turned their mounts and fled, pell-mell, south.

"Fifth Company! Thirty-fifth Company! Re-form! Forward!" Alucius urged the gray forward and onto the road, riding northward quickly.

Deotyr had re-formed Twenty-eighth Company, well back from the wall of flame.

The few remaining rebel lancers rode eastward along the ridge. They were already a vingt away when Alucius neared Twenty-eighth Company. His Talent sensed no one nearby besides his own force—no one living. Both a single glance and his senses told him that there was enough of the oil or whatever it was to turn the dead mounts and men into little more than ashes, and the fire might well continue for at least a glass.

He could feel his entire body beginning to shake, and his eyesight blurring. He forced himself to steady his hands as he fumbled out the water bottle and drank, then unwrapped some travel bread for a quick bite. What else could he have done? He didn't know any way to have stopped the conflagration, and if he'd simply waited, he might have lost all of Twenty-eighth Company. Why hadn't he seen what was coming more clearly?

He shook his head. He'd known something was wrong. He never would have ordered the charge, but, as Feran had said, he couldn't be everywhere. No one else could have dealt with the pteridons.

His hands were still shaking as he took another bite of travel bread. Was his shakiness his reaction to the flame trap? Or was it overuse of Talent? Had he used that much Talent? He decided that it had taken more effort than he had realized to extend his Talent to fire the oil or whatever had been used to create the deadly flames. But his decision to use Talent still troubled him, much as he could see no other alternative.

By the time he finally reached Twenty-eighth Company, the blurred vision and the shaking had subsided. Alucius kept his face impassive as he reined up close to Deotyr.

The captain's countenance was ashen.

"Captain?"

"Yes, sir . . ."

"Casualties?"

"Twelve men dead, sir, three others burned, two wounded."

Before Deotyr could say any more, Alucius spoke. "I don't recall ordering a charge. But what is done is done. We'll talk about it later." Alucius dared not say more, not with the rage seething inside him at Deotyr's stupidity.

"Yes, sir."

"Finish forming up. We'll have to circle the road cut on the west. We'll probably have trouble with the wagons. Pick a detail to help with them." Alucius glanced at the low flames still flickering from the road cut ahead. He could feel the heat. As he turned to head back to check with Jultyr and Feran, he just wished he could turn away from the stench of burned flesh.

Alucius rode back southward, both to meet with Jultyr and to avoid saying anything he would later regret.

As Alucius neared the older captain, Jultyr studied Alucius's face before speaking. For a moment, Jultyr did not speak. Then he said, "One man dead, sir. One man wounded, sir. Looks to recover."

"Thank you. You handled your company well, Captain."

"Thank you, sir."

"Majer!" called another voice—that of Feran.

Alucius turned his mount and waited for Feran to join them.

"Just two men wounded. One took a shot to the shoulder," Feran reported. "The other took a bullet in the calf."

"Fifth Company did well," Alucius said. "As always."

He could feel some of the anger subsiding. "Twenty-eighth Company lost twelve men, had five wounded." His words came out flat.

"Lucky that the rebels set that fire too early," observed Jultyr.

"They probably didn't plan it that way." Feran looked hard at Alucius.

Alucius knew Feran understood, and he merely replied, "I wish they'd been even earlier. Twenty-eighth's first squad didn't deserve that."

"Captain Deotyr?" asked Feran.

"He may have gotten singed, but he was just far enough back."

"What was that stuff? Do you know, sir?" asked Jultyr.

"Some kind of oil, maybe the kind that you can find in pitch ponds. It was dark and shiny, but not too thick. Their mounts splashed some of it before it caught fire." Alucius gestured to the road ahead and the low rise. "We'll have to ride around. I told Captain Deotyr to form a detail to help with the wagons."

"Ah . . . the men . . . ?"

"It's still burning. There won't be anything left but ashes. There's not much we can do."

Jultyr shook his head. "What a horrible . . . way to go."

Alucius agreed, but he wasn't sure that any way to die was good, notwithstanding all the legends of glorious heroism. Dead was dead.

60

In the dim light of early evening, Alucius and Deotyr stood at the edge of the camp, little more than rows of lancers and bedrolls on a low rise twenty-some vingts north of Hyalt and less than half a vingt to the west of the high road. All the campsite had to recommend itself was a creek with cold and clear water that ran along the bottom of the swale to the north of the rise, and the slight elevation of the low hill—and the fact that men and mounts needed the rest and that there had been nothing better in vingts.

In the eastern sky, halfway to the zenith, was the small green disc of Asterta. That the moon of misery shone down on Deotyr and Alucius was entirely appropriate, although the dark-haired young captain was obviously unaware of that coincidence as he shifted his weight from one boot to the other.

"I said that we would discuss the events of the afternoon later. I did not say that we would dismiss them." Alucius kept his voice mild. "Why did you order the charge?"

"They had thrown down their rifles, and they were re-treating in disorder, sir. It seemed like the best tactic."

"Did I tell you to engage them?"

"No, sir."

"Did you hear me relay orders to Overcaptain Feran granting him the leeway to engage the rebels?"

"Yes, sir."

"Did I give you similar orders?"

"Ah . . . no, sir."

"But I didn't forbid you to order a charge, either," Alucius pointed out. "That's the first lesson, Captain. Discretion always rests with the company commander, but so does responsibility for the use of that discretion. If you choose to ignore orders, and there may be a *very* few times that you should, or if you decide to take an initiative, you should have a very good reason for doing so. You should have a definite plan for what you intend to do, and you should understand the situation in which you find yourself." Alucius paused only briefly. "Explain to me why you thought charging this particular fleeing enemy was a good tactic."

There was a long silence.

"Come, Captain . . . if you did not have a good reason

when you ordered the charge, and if you cannot come up with a good reason after having thought about it all afternoon . . . why exactly did you give that order?"

"I just . . . well, sir, it felt like the thing to do. I can't explain why."

Alucius nodded slowly. "I've done that myself. But there's a problem with that. If you can't explain why you did what you did, even afterward, then you didn't have a good reason. Now . . . consider this. We've fought the rebels a number of times. Before this afternoon, have they ever retreated?"

"No, sir."

"Did you ask yourself *why* they were retreating? They didn't just turn and break. They turned just before reaching the company, and they were ordered to retreat by the sound of a horn. That signal alone should have told you that the action was planned."

"Did you see that, sir?"

"As soon as I heard that horn signal, I knew that whatever they were doing was planned, but I was too far away to countermand your orders, Captain. I thought that trying to do so from a distance could have created even greater confusion and left the company scattered and even more vulnerable." Alucius let the silence drag out for a time. "You were extremely fortunate to have lost only twelve men. Had they set that oil on fire a few moments later, most of Twenty-eighth Company would have died." Alucius did not hammer home the point that Deotyr would have been among the dead. Nor did he voice his own regrets that his own options had been constricted by his own limitations. "You need to know what your own company can do. You also have to be aware of what your enemy has done, what he can do, and what he might do."

"Yes, sir." Deotyr's look at Alucius was almost accusing, as if Alucius were responsible.

Alucius *was* responsible. He hadn't given Deotyr clear enough orders, or orders that could not have been misunderstood. Yet, in one respect, he shouldn't have had to give such orders. In another, he should have known that Deotyr was too inexperienced. But it was better not to say that. And, in the end, for whatever happened Alucius would be the one held responsible.

"Captain. I could have given you orders to stand fast no matter what happened. And what would have happened if another company of rebels had appeared? Or if one of those pteridons had crashed into the ammunition wagon and set it on fire? Every order is a balance. If I make the order too firm, that can be as deadly as making it too general."

"Pteridons?"

"The Fifth and Thirty-fifth Companies were attacked by them, along with the rebels. That's why I moved southward. When they're fatally wounded, they explode in nasty bluish flames. You might ask Jultyr about them. Fifth and Thirty-fifth Companies had as many casualties from them as from the rebel lancers."

Alucius still had no idea why the pteridons had appeared when they did, or why there had been so few that afternoon, compared to the larger numbers on the previous occasions. He wished he knew if other forces or herders had been attacked, but he had an uneasy feeling that there had been few, if any, such attacks where he—or perhaps Wendra—had not been present. But he had a hard time believing that someone would send such beasts after someone as insignificant as he was.

Deotyr frowned.

Alucius wrenched his thoughts away from the Talent-creatures and spoke slowly. "We all have to learn, and we all learn different lessons, and sometimes the only way to learn is painful." That he knew all too well. "You'll remember this. It might be difficult to forget it. Just get into the habit of asking yourself why the enemy is doing something. Or why I do things the way I do. And you can ask me afterward why I did it. You learn from this, and you'll be a better officer. Every good lancer force rests on the quality of its officers, and quality comes from training and learning and improving." Alucius offered a smile, one he hoped was both encouraging and slightly sad. "Neither one of us can undo what's been done. We can only learn from it and go on."

Against the whispers and murmurs of the conversations of the camp, almost like a harvest wind, Deotyr was silent for a time before speaking. "Sir . . . is all . . . I mean . . . the rebels . . ."

Alucius laughed gently. "I've never seen anything like this. Most other forces I've fought against have much more able lancers, but you could stop them. These rebels will keep riding until they're dead in the saddle. It's the first time we've gotten low on ammunition with so few casualties, but that's why we're moving back to resupply. Without more ammunition, we can't mount an attack on their bases."

After the afternoon's attack, Alucius was even more convinced of the necessity of that resupply—and it wouldn't hurt for him to rethink things once more. He almost laughed out loud at his caution. Did command do that to once-impetuous young officers?

61

Tempre, Lanachrona

The gray morning light did little to brighten the Lord-Protector's study or the faces of the three men seated within it.

Marshal Alyniat sat at one corner of the dark oak table desk, the fingers of his left hand quietly drumming on the wood, while Frynkel sat at the other corner. A single dispatch lay on the polished desktop where the Lord-Protector had set it.

"Majer Alucius has been in the Hyalt area perhaps a

week," the Lord-Protector said slowly. "He has destroyed four companies of rebel lancers with minimal losses, except ammunition, and that is to be expected."

"That is what he reports," acknowledged Alyniat. "He has sent two dispatches."

"If that is what he reports," replied the Lord-Protector coolly, "then that is what has happened. Unlike some officers' reports, his I can trust. That presents another question."

The two marshals waited.

"Exactly how did this prophet Adarat manage to create two military camps and arm and uniform more than four companies without the Southern Guard even noticing it until the local garrison was overcome and killed?"

"If we knew the answer to that, Lord-Protector," replied Alyniat deferentially, "it would not have happened."

"However it happened, I have lost. The question is only how much. If the majer can destroy this prophet and his followers, I lose only my respect, the gratitude of many subjects, and I will gain a reputation not as a just ruler, but one to be feared. I do not think I need to spell out what I will lose if he fails."

Neither marshal spoke for a moment.

After the silence had drawn out for a time, Frynkel finally replied, "In these times, it is not entirely without benefit to be a ruler to be feared."

"That is true," Talryn stated. "But is it to the credit of the Southern Guard that it takes a herder majer from the north to accomplish even that?"

Another silence filled the room.

"Get him the ammunition, and send it on the way by noon, even if you have to strip every arsenal and company in Tempre." The Lord-Protector paused before asking, "How fares the defense of Southgate?"

"The latest reports say that the defenses are firm, and that Marshal Wyerl has pushed the Matrites back north of Zalt. There have been no changes in the positions of forces between Fola and Southgate. That is acceptable, under the circumstances." Alyniat glanced at Frynkel.

"The last company from Borlan is between Krost and here, and will join the companies released from Indyor. That will provide four more companies of lancers that could be used against the Regent as necessary."

"And the training?"

"There are lancers enough to fill four companies in training at Krost. They have just begun, and we will lose a quarter of them in training. They will not be prepared to fight until spring," Frynkel replied. "We should have less trouble at Krost, now."

"For which, again, you can thank the majer. Perhaps, if he succeeds in Hyalt, I should make him a marshal."

The faintest hint of a wince crossed Alyniat's face, and the subdued finger drumming ceased.

"Oh . . . don't worry about that," Talryn said wryly. "He's too smart to accept it, and if I offered it, I'd end up losing half my officers within a year. That, too, is a sorry state of affairs." He glanced at Alyniat, and added, "Especially under the circumstances, Marshal Alyniat. I trust you two will continue to work to remedy those circumstances."

Alyniat's face stiffened slightly at the Lord-Protector's use of the phrase "under the circumstances." Then, he replied, "Yes, sir."

"That's all. One of you send me a messenger confirming that the ammunition is on the way."

"Yes, sir."

The Lord-Protector rose.

So did the marshals, bowing, then departing the study.

62

In the glow of the oil lamp set in a bronze wall bracket, the five officers sat around the single table in what passed for the officers' mess in the Ceazan way station. Four were from Alucius's force. The fifth was Korow, the gray-bearded undercaptain in charge of the station. His pale green eyes moved slowly from officer to officer, but kept returning to the gray-haired and young-faced Alucius.

Alucius took a long swallow of water from the chipped crockery mug. "We'll give the men another two days to rest and check gear." The men didn't need the rest so much as the mounts did, but both men and mounts could stand the time away from the strangeness around Hyalt. He also would leave the more seriously wounded, such as Elbard, to recover at the way station.

"You haven't said much, sir," offered Jultyr. "Not about what's happened in Hyalt."

"That's true. I haven't." Alucius paused. "I'd like your thoughts first. Then, I'll say what I think."

A faint smile crossed Feran's lips, and Alucius knew that was because Alucius had never been known for being reticent among other officers.

No one spoke for a time.

Then Feran cleared his throat. "Something's happening. It didn't start when we rode into Hyalt. It didn't even start when we left Dekhron. There were pteridons when we fought the nomads in Deforya. That was more than three years ago. The Matrial started using the crystal spearthrower before that. This revolt . . . whatever it is . . . is part of it. These rebels don't act like any lancers I ever saw anywhere." The overcaptain shrugged. "That's all."

After another silence, Alucius looked to Jultyr.

"Don't know what to say, sir. Never seen anything like it. Couldn't say where any of them came from. They don't look or act like any folk from Lanachrona, and I've served in almost every post in the land."

"Captain Deotyr?" Alucius prompted.

The dark-haired young officer moistened his lips.

Alucius waited.

"Sir . . . where are they getting all the lancers? We . . . well . . . the Lord-Protector has trouble raising enough from all across Lanachrona, and we must have killed . . .

what . . . five companies' worth, and they still have more . . ." Deotyr's words trailed off.

"That's a very good question," Alucius replied. "I have an idea, but we won't know until we finish what we were sent to do." He paused, then continued. "The scouts have reported that Hyalt is half deserted, and we've seen that many of the steads have been abandoned. We've captured mounts, though many aren't that good, and some have their coats worn from harnesses and collars. We don't know as much as I'd like, but it looks like this prophet Adarat has used some form of Talent to persuade people to leave their homes and steads and serve him as lancers, and perhaps in many other ways as well.

"Even so, if that's true," Alucius continued, "whatever this is, it's not a rebellion or a revolt. Rebels don't have standardized uniforms within weeks. They don't have lancers who can still ride with wounds that should have left them dead. They don't have Talent-wielders powerful enough to enchant scouts from a distance."

"You think it's an invasion?" asked Deotyr.

"I don't know. If I had to guess, I'd say it's a Talent-invasion, with the Talent-wielder coming from somewhere else and getting some supplies from there, but using the local men and boys as fodder."

"Who could be behind it?" pressed Deotyr.

"The Regent?" asked Jultyr.

"It's possible," said Alucius, even though he doubted that it could be the Regent. From what he could tell, it had to be the ifrits, and he could only hint at that.

"You don't think so, do you?" said Feran.

"I don't know what's behind it. It could be the Regent of the Matrial, but I think it's something else. What that something is . . . that's another question, but the way we were attacked by Talent-creatures near Hyalt, then earlier north of Krost, and all the feeling of Talent all around Hyalt . . ." Alucius shook his head. "Don't you think that if the Regent of the Matrial had that kind of power, our lancers would be taking terrible losses in Madrien and getting pushed out of Southgate?"

"Maybe they are," suggested Jultyr. "We wouldn't know, would we?"

Alucius let a rueful laugh escape. "You could be right. We wouldn't know."

"If that happened, can't have happened too long ago," offered Korow. "We get the dispatches here, two, three days after Tempre. Nothing in them. Can't see why they'd hide something like that. 'Sides, if they did, still be something about lancer companies being formed or moved." The older undercaptain stopped and pulled at his chin. "Come to think of it, one of the dispatch riders said they've got more companies in training at Krost, and something about the companies being moved out of Indyor and being sent west."

Alucius put the most faith in the dispatch riders. If anyone outside of the marshals and the Lord-Protector would know, the dispatch riders would.

"If it's the Regent, then we're on our own, Majer, aren't we?" asked Jultyr.

"We knew that already," Alucius said wryly.

"But where did the Regent get all this Talent?" asked Deotyr, the tone in his voice one between exasperation and annoyance.

Alucius shrugged. "We don't know what caused the Cataclysm or the fall of the Duarchy. We don't even know how the Duarchy came to be. All we know is that something strange is happening that doesn't seem to have happened before, and it's been happening all over Corus. The prophet could be a wild Talent-wielder who's convinced everyone from merchants to local holders that the Duarchy will come again and gotten them to provide uniforms and supplies. Proclaiming that the True Duarchy will come doesn't mean that it will, no matter how many in Hyalt believe it. Under those conditions, the Regent of the Matrial would be happy to supply weapons to keep the Lord-Protector and Lanachrona occupied elsewhere. Even the Dramurians might do that. We can't deal with the Matrial or the Dramurians or whoever. Our job is to stop whatever's happening in Hyalt."

"What do you have in mind, sir?" asked Feran.

"Make a strike at the camp we hit with the fires, first. That's likely to be the headquarters camp from what we've learned so far. Then strike the other camp. If we destroy this so-called prophet's forces, we'll find it easier to strike at him—if he's even alive after we finish." Alucius cleared his throat and took another swallow of water. "I thought the men could use a break before we made that kind of strike. We should be getting supplies tomorrow, but, if we don't get any more supplies, we'll take whatever extra ammunition Korow can spare and head off the morning after tomorrow."

"You don't want to wait, then?" asked Deotyr.

"Not too much longer than we have," Alucius admitted. "I'd thought we could find out more than we have. We didn't. Sometimes, you just can't get any more information. When that happens, you have to act, because you won't get any more until they're attacking you, and you're better off acting instead of reacting."

"Still think it's strange," mused Deotyr.

"It is strange. It may well get stranger if we don't put a stop to it," Alucius pointed out. He didn't point out that they were also better off dealing with the prophet before the Regent of the Matrial became even more involved—if she were involved in the first place. If the prophet happened to be an ifrit, early action was also better. He just hoped the ammunition arrived—and before long.

63

North of Iron Stem, Iron Valleys

As she reined up the chestnut outside the stable in the late afternoon of a cold harvest day, Wendra swung out of the saddle gracefully, despite her growing midsection.

"You won't be able to keep that up for much longer," offered Lucenda, walking over from the processing shed.

"I'm good for another month, maybe two," insisted Wendra, leading the chestnut mare inside the stable and into the second stall. "The baby's fine, and you know that the longer I can ride, the easier the delivery." She grinned. "That's what you told me."

"I didn't mean spending the entire day in the saddle. I wasn't talking about riding herd on the flock." Lucenda looked over the end of the stall at the younger woman. "You look tired. You shouldn't be taking the flock so often."

"I'm only taking them every other day," Wendra said. "It's not that. There were more of those . . . creatures . . . those pteridons. They appeared maybe two glasses ago, on the way back."

"Did they—"

"I shot both of them. They didn't get any of the flock. One came close to a lamb, but I dropped it onto a quarasote bush. They both went up in that blue flame." Wendra racked the saddle and then shook her head. "I never thought I'd see anything that could burn quarasote."

"I don't like your being out there, not with those . . . creatures."

Wendra looked at the older woman, then lowered her voice. "You know Royalt can't do anything about the pteridons or the black sanders. Besides, they don't show up that often."

"That's the third time since summer."

"Fourth," Wendra admitted. "But there were only two, and now that I'm carrying two rifles, it's easier."

"You're getting those golds from the Lord-Protector. We could afford to lose one or two ewes, and it wouldn't be so bad now."

"They're helpful, but not enough to replace more than a ram, if we could," Wendra pointed out. "I'd rather save the golds for later, when we really need them."

Lucenda offered a wan smile. "You're a herder—just like your grandsire. And Alucius."

"I'm a herder, and I won't give it up. You and Alucius gave that to me, and the flock will be here, and so will the stead, when he comes back." She paused. "I know he's all right, but I wish we'd hear more. It's been two weeks since his last letter. He said it would be hard to send them after he left Krost, but I worry."

"Knowing Alucius, he worries about you."

"He doesn't need to. He's the one who's in danger." Wendra continued to curry the chestnut. "Rebels will be shooting at him."

"Whereas you merely have to fight off Talent-creatures the likes of which haven't been seen since before the Cataclysm—another legacy of the Duarches." Lucenda snorted.

"The times are changing," Wendra said.

"You sound like Alucius."

"He's right."

"He was almost always right," Lucenda said, her voice holding a mixture of sadness and wistfulness. "I can remember when he saved Lamb. He looked up at me, and he said, 'He'll get well. You'll see. He will.' Then he went to sleep."

"That's Alucius."

"As a mother, it's frightening. He always saw so much

more. He didn't always know what it meant, but he saw it."
Lucenda's eyes fixed on Wendra. "Your daughter . . . she'll
be like that, and then you'll understand."

"I've thought that," Wendra admitted. "Especially at
those times when I've wakened and seen Alucius sleep,
and he looks so childlike."

Lucenda looked as though she might say more. Then she
laughed softly. "I need to check on supper. Come on in
when you can."

After Lucenda left, Wendra continued to brush the
chestnut, her eyes open but focused far to the south.

64

Octdi found the column of lancers riding
back southward on the high road away from Ceazan and
toward Hyalt. Although he did not expect to find traces of
the rebels until the next day, Alucius was still using both
his Talent and his eyesight to scan the road and the terrain
to either side, seeking any trace of the purpleness that
marked the rebels or any sign of dust in the dry harvest
season that was but days away from fall. Soon the weather
would turn colder, even in southern Lanachrona, if not
nearly so cold as autumn days would be in the Iron Valleys.

Through the morning Alucius rode with Twenty-eighth
Company, and midmorning came and went. At noon, he ordered Thirty-fifth Company forward and rode with Jultyr.
They had ridden more than a glass, passing but a few pleas-
antries, before Jultyr cleared his throat.

Alucius waited.

"The marshals sent that ammunition real quick, sir."

"My dispatch explained the problem, at least as well as I
could."

"I've seen colonels, sir, didn't get supplies that fast."

"The Lord-Protector has a problem. The sooner we get the ammunition, the sooner we can deal with it."

"You don't think there's any other way?"

Alucius laughed softly. "I don't know that the rebels gave us much choice. They attacked us first on several occasions. Do you think there was anything else we could have done?"

"No, sir."

"Do you think we ought to strike the hill camp first or the one northeast of town?"

Jultyr considered.

Alucius waited once more.

"I'd say the hill camp, sir. You hit the town camp, and they'll be ready for the second attack. Be harder to get word from the hills back to the other camp. Also, you hit the town camp, and folks could run to the other one. Make the second attack harder, and we might have to kill women and children." Jultyr shrugged. "Might have to, anyway."

"We might."

"Still can't figure why they don't like the Lord-Protector. Never did anything to these folks. Nothing. Garrison here was mostly those with injuries of the kind that wouldn't heal, serving last year or two before getting a stipend." Jultyr paused. "This True Duarchy thing . . . might not be as good as the old one. Who's to say the old one was that good? All we got is stories and legends and a few roads and buildings. Doesn't tell what living there was like."

"Legends don't tell everything," Alucius replied mildly.

"Folks remember what they want to. Could be good. Could be bad." Jultyr cocked his head, thinking. "My grandda . . . he told stories. Never told a happy one. My grandmam, she never told a sad one. Spent near-on fifty years together. Funny . . . lived the same life. Sure saw it different—or told it different."

"People are like that."

Jultyr frowned. "Except these rebels. They all act the

same . . . do the same. Folks in their right minds aren't like that."

"This prophet is using some kind of Talent to change their minds."

"That's hard on folks, hard on us."

Alucius nodded. Whatever happened was going to be hard on everyone. He scanned the road ahead once more, then the thornbush-covered rises on each side.

65

On a cool and cloudy Londi, just past noon, Alucius, Feran, Jultyr, and Deotyr stood to one side of the ashes of a cookfire, halfway down the slope of the hillside camp less than five vingts from the eastern approach to the western camp of the Hyalt rebels.

Facing them were Rakalt and Waris, the two best remaining scouts. Given the earlier scouting problems, Alucius was both pleased and relieved that the pair had returned, although Elbard remained at the way station and was healing well. For that, at least, Alucius was grateful.

"Sir . . . you know we burned all those trees around their camp—and the spiky thorns," said Waris.

"I was there," Alucius pointed out.

"The trees that we burned—they're still black, but there's fresh green spiky thorn everywhere that was burned—looks even bigger and thicker."

"You're sure about that?" asked Feran.

Jultyr and Deotyr exchanged glances.

"Cut off a piece. Tough, too." Waris produced a half-yard length of a greenish brown thorn branch.

Even as the scout extended it, and Alucius took the thorny length, he had to repress a shudder at the faint hint of purple and black that his Talent detected. Someone—either an ifrit or an ifrit-possessed Lanachronan—had bled

off the very life-essence of people to spur or fuel the unnatural growth of the spiky thornbushes. "It's like this all
the way around the camp?"

"Looked to be, sir." Waris glanced toward Rakalt.

"Far as I could tell, sir," added the second scout.

"What about the palisades and the walls? Have they
been reinforced?"

"No, sir."

"Are the gates kept closed, or are they open some of the
time?"

"Only the same two, sir, and they were both open.
Didn't look like they were ever closed, maybe except at
night. Maybe not then."

"Did you see any lancers, besides those doing sentry
duty?"

"There were some walking around, sir, but I didn't see
any drills or anything," replied Waris.

"They don't have a maneuver ground or anything like
that, either," added Rakalt. "Only place that the ground is
packed or dug up is the road."

"Did you see any sign of digging, pits, stakes . . . ?"

"No, sir, and the way the ground is . . . be hard to dis-
guise that."

"What about that cave?"

"Couldn't see anything new there, sir. Just looks like a
big square arch carved into the stone of the bluff. Be hard
to take, if they all got inside, but they couldn't shoot from
there without being exposed themselves. No embrasures or
windows cut in the stone. Just that arch."

"And a skylight slit of some sort," added Waris.

Feran and Alucius kept asking questions, but little had
changed, except for the regrowth of the thorns. That nothing had changed bothered Alucius, and he kept wondering
what he was missing.

Finally, he cleared his throat and said to the scouts,
"Thank you. If there's anything else, I'll find you."

"Yes, sir."

Alucius waited until the two scouts were a good ten

yards away before lowering his voice and speaking to the other officers. "We'll attack at dawn tomorrow, just the way we'd planned. The sun will be in their eyes."

"What if they attack us before that?" asked Deotyr.

"Then we'll kill them here and attack in the morning," Alucius replied. "That means that they'll have fewer defenders. They've got to be weaker than before. They've lost something like five companies, and they can't have that many more, not unless they're cramming lancers into those buildings like chickens in a coop."

"They might, sir," Feran replied deferentially. "Some chickens have more brains than some of those lancers."

Alucius managed not to laugh, but he couldn't help smiling. Neither could Jultyr. Deotyr just looked down at the ground.

"Post two sets of sentries, one set a good vingt out on the approach roads. Captain Deotyr could be right about a late-afternoon or evening attack. And have your men sleep with their weapons loaded."

"Yes, sir."

As the other officers moved back to relay the information to their squad leaders, Alucius took out the thornbush section that Waris had brought back. He studied it with distaste, then slowly used his Talent to separate the brownish lifethread energy, already fading, from the greenery. Abruptly, the entire length turned black, then shriveled into ash.

The majer nodded to himself. If he had to, he could remove the thornbushes, and with a little misdirection, no one but Feran would know exactly what happened. His guts tightened.

"What happened to that spike-thorn?" asked Feran, walking toward Alucius. "One moment you were holding it, and the next it was gone."

"It died."

Feran raised his eyebrows, then frowned. "You were upset when Waris gave you that spiky thorn. Tough plant. Or was it something else?"

"It's not the plant," Alucius replied in a low voice. "Plants regrow after fire. That's the way it is. They don't grow twice as big across whole hillsides with one small rainstorm in only two weeks. Someone used Talent, more than a little." Alucius wasn't about to tell Feran what else his own Talent had revealed.

"Using Talent to rebuild thorns?" Feran frowned, the fine lines radiating from his eyes deepening. "Must have more than a few with Talent there. You still want to go through with this attack?"

"Better now than later, when there might be more with Talent," Alucius replied.

Feran's laugh was harsh. "I liked the world a lot better before Talent started coming back all over the place."

"Makes you think about whether the Duarchy was as great as the legends say."

"If this prophet's any example, I'll take the way things were before."

"I don't think there's any way to go back," Alucius said dryly.

"You're always saying things like that, most honored Majer," Feran replied. "You know what I hate about that?"

"What?"

"You're usually right."

They both laughed, Alucius as much at the dry irony in Feran's tone as at the words themselves.

66

Alucius stood on the crest of the hill as if frozen, his legs anchored to the sandy soil. He tried to lift one leg, then the other, but neither would move. The three-quarter disc of Selena cast an eerie purplish white light across the night hillside, and Alucius strained to hear the sounds of the night. There were none, just a dead silence.

A purplish pink mist swirled across the road, which was barely more than a dirt track at the base of the hill, at first just intermittently blocking his view of the road itself, but slowly thickening until he could no longer see the road or the ground on either side. Slowly, ever so slowly, the purplish pink mist began to thicken even more, and rise, so that it crept up the hillside, obscuring the lower parts of the hill, then obliterating them from view. The higher the mist rose, and the closer it drew to Alucius, the colder he felt.

Abruptly, Alucius woke with a start. He glanced around, but the encampment was still. Totally still. Even the horses, secured on tielines on the western end of the encampment, had not stirred, and usually there was some unrest among the more skittish mounts when things were not going well.

After a moment, he pulled on his boots, clumsily, as if his hands and legs had been asleep, and as if neither was fully awake yet. He struggled to his feet. Even standing was an effort, but with each movement he felt less constrained. *Constrained?*

He shook his head. Even his thoughts were slow.

He had to force himself to use his Talent, something that he hadn't had to do in years. His Talent was so much a part of him that its use was usually like using his arms or his sight.

Somewhere down below was something . . . something woven out of Talent, out of ifritlike Talent, with the purplish tint that he associated with them.

His first reaction was to sound an alert, but he paused, even as he bent down and eased one of his rifles out of its case, then the second.

He glanced to his right, where Feran lay sleeping, but the older officer was breathing so lightly that his form barely moved. With both rifles, one in each hand, he eased toward Feran's sleeping form. "Feran?"

He bent down and repeated, "Feran?"

The overcaptain did not stir, and Alucius could sense the

faintest fog of purple surrounding Feran's head. Abruptly, Alucius focused a Talent-probe. The faintest touch of the probe, and the fog dissolved.

"Feran?"

"What . . ." The other's voice was hoarse, as if unused.

"We're about to be attacked . . . everyone's been put to sleep with Talent."

"Talent?" Feran sounded as confused as Alucius had felt when he'd awakened.

"Talent, from the prophet," Alucius replied.

Feran convulsed erect, kicking back his blanket and groping for his boots. "Son of a misbegotten sow . . ."

"We need to get Fifth Company awake, quietly. I'm afraid that if we try to wake everyone at once, they'll rush us, and . . . we won't have enough steady rifles."

"You had to do something, didn't you? Herder stuff." Feran pulled on his boots.

Alucius ignored the question as he used his Talent to take in the riders who were dismounting out of sight on the mist-swirled road below. "You ready?"

Feran stood. "Let's go."

The two started with Egyl, and then Alucius just stood at the edge of the line of bedrolls and used his Talent to dissolve the purplish mist around each man, while the squad leader quietly explained.

Then he eased downhill with Faisyn and Fifth Company's first squad.

"They'll be coming up on both sides of the path, on foot," Alucius whispered to Faisyn. "We want to hold fire until they're close."

"We can do that."

While Alucius stationed himself in a prone position, with two of the lancers abreast the path, Faisyn slipped from one lancer to the next, whispering the instructions.

Second squad arrived before Faisyn returned, and Alucius passed on the orders. Those hadn't reached every lancer when figures began to appear below them. No more than twenty rebels in dark tunics and trousers eased up the hillside in silence, slipping from juniper to juniper.

Alucius forced himself to wait until the first man was less than twenty yards away.

He squeezed the trigger and ordered, "Now! Fire! Fire at will."

The hillside flared into fire.

Almost half the attackers went down under the first few volleys, but a number of them struggled to reach rifles or blades even as they were dying. Some crawled forward, others struggled with weapons suddenly too heavy to lift.

Alucius kept shooting. Anyone who looked to be possibly dangerous, already wounded or not, was a target.

Within half a glass, the hillside below was quiet once more.

Alucius reached out with his Talent, trying to determine whether another attack was likely, but from what he could sense, there was no one alive on the road below, except for perhaps a squad of riders a half vingt south, heading at a quick trot down the dirt road away from Alucius and in the general direction of the rebel encampment.

"Faisyn . . . if you'd hold first squad in readiness for a bit longer."

"Yes, sir."

Alucius eased himself up into a sitting position and then stood, looking for Feran and finding the older officer twenty yards to the west. He walked toward Feran.

"Didn't lose anyone here," Feran said.

"I worry about the sentries."

"So do I. Sent Egyl and fourth squad to check on them." Feran coughed. "Frigging sleep spell . . . slimy bastard . . ."

"It wasn't exactly a spell . . ."

"Same thing, no matter what you call it."

Alucius shrugged. In practical terms, Feran was right. He glanced uphill, where, with the deaths of the attackers and the departure of the prophet or whoever had used Talent to create the stuporous sleep, the purplish sleep miasma began to dissipate, and the more normal sounds of a camp rustled through the night.

Feran stood and stretched. "Do you think . . . ?"

"They're gone. You can have them stand down, except for first squad, say for another half glass. If we don't hear or sense anything, they can turn back in then, too."

"I'll let them know. Egyl's checking on the sentries."

No sooner had Feran left than Jultyr was beside Alucius. "Sir . . . thought I heard shots . . . said you were down here."

"You did. The rebels tried another attack. Fifth Company drove them back."

Jultyr yawned. "Never . . . slept through firefight before . . ."

"We might have had some help. Everyone was sleepy."

"Talent?" asked the older captain.

"I think so."

"Sneaky bastards . . . tomorrow can't come soon enough."

Both officers turned at the footsteps nearing.

Egyl walked slowly out of the gloom and shadows of the scattered junipers toward Alucius. "We lost the outer sentries. They slit their throats. All four of them."

"The others?"

"No, sir. They're sleepy, still. Should be all right."

"We won't post any more that far out. Not tonight."

"Yes, sir." Egyl slipped uphill.

Jultyr looked at Alucius. "Never fought anything like this."

"I don't know that anyone has." Alucius bent and lifted his rifles, carrying one in each hand. "I'll see you in the morning."

"Yes, sir."

As he eased away from Jultyr, trying to find a little space to think, Alucius tried to consider what had happened and what he had planned. Should he still order the attack at dawn? The question was whether to attack immediately . . . or to wait.

Alucius had never liked waiting, but he had to wonder if the commander of the rebels had wagered on that. Then, if he didn't attack, how many more men would he lose to something like the sleep compulsion? And how much rest would he and everyone else lose trying to make sure they weren't surprised again?

For better or worse, he would attack in the morning.

67

Alucius hadn't slept that well when he heard the voice. "Sir? It's two glasses before dawn."

"Thank you." He rolled out of his bedroll tiredly, then eased on his boots. After a time, he slowly stood, yawning. The night had been all too short, but unless they stopped the prophet Adarat, every night could be like the last—and some night he'd be too tired to protect his men . . . or himself.

After washing up with the water in the bucket that he'd gotten the night before, he pulled himself together for the day ahead, finishing up rolling up blankets and bedroll and walking to the tielines. There he saddled the gray and strapped his gear in place. He went over both rifles, making sure they were fully loaded. Finally, before mounting, he checked to make sure the nightsilk skull mask that he had not used in years was safely well inside his undergarments. It wasn't something he wore often, and almost never when leading lancers, but it had proven useful in cold weather and on solo scouting missions . . . and upon a few other occasions.

Then he mounted and rode slowly down the gentler section of the hillside to the flat bottom between hills that held the rutted dirt road where the three companies were forming up in the predawn darkness. In the gloom on the west side of the road, amid the scent of dust and cedars, he listened as lancers and their mounts made their way into formation.

"... hate early rides ..."

"You hate all rides, Bakka ..."

"... friggin' long night ... now we're supposed to fight?"

"... we don't fight, and you'll have more long nights ..."

"Almost wish we were freezing our butts around Harmony."

"Not me. Matrites can shoot better."

"... take shots any day to this Talent crap ..."

"... rebels are scary ... not all there ..."

"... better that than Matrites who are all there."

Alucius just hoped that lancer was correct. When he sensed Feran moving to the head of the column, he eased the gelding from the shadows and toward the overcaptain. "Good morning."

"It's not morning yet, and it's not that good ... sir," Feran said, his voice cheerful even though his words were not.

"We have some problems you haven't told me?"

"Besides last night? Not yet." Feran chuckled mournfully. "You know how much I like mornings, and this is before morning. I'm not a herder. I left the family holding just so I didn't have to get up before the sun."

"It'll be up in a glass or so."

"More like two. This is *night,* not morning. I can't see in the dark the way you herders can."

Even as Alucius laughed at Feran's mournful tone, he wondered what it would be like for night to be a barrier to seeing. He only experienced something like that a few times, in caves or ruins where there was absolutely no light. He turned the gray as a lancer rode along the shoulder of the road from the north.

"Majer, sir?"

"Here."

"Captain Jultyr reports that Thirty-fifth Company is present and accounted for and ready to go, sir."

"Thank you. Tell the captain that we'll be riding shortly."

"Yes, sir."

As the lancer turned his mount, Feran coughed, then said, "Fifth Company is ready, sir. Should have reported that earlier."

"You're always ready."

"With you, Majer, it pays."

The two waited, their mounts in the road just south of where Fifth Company had formed, waiting for the report from Twenty-eighth Company. It felt as though a quarter glass had gone by before a squad leader appeared out of the gloom, but Alucius knew that far less time had passed.

"Twenty-eighth Company, present and accounted for."

"Thank you. We'll be departing momentarily."

"Yes, sir."

Alucius turned to Feran. "Column, forward!"

The order echoed through the darkness. As the words died away, the sound of hoofs on hard dirt replaced them, and the three companies began to ride southward.

They covered almost three vingts before the darkness began to lighten, with the hint of gray rising above the low hills just to the east of the road. Along the way, Alucius munched some travel bread and cheese, washing it down with water. He could tell that a number of the Fifth Company lancers did as well.

"What are you going to do about the spiky thornbush?" asked Feran.

"Nothing. Not unless I have to. I don't think they'll be expecting a dawn attack. Except for setting those fires, we haven't made a single attack, and we haven't been moving near Hyalt this early. Also, they don't seem to be very alert. If the gates are still open, I'm going to take out the sentries, and we'll just ride in. If they've actually closed the gates, then we'll set a few fires, and ride around the walls and then in."

"You really don't think they'll have the walls heavily guarded, do you?" asked Feran.

"One of the failures of great power is that you can rely on it too much."

"You're being mysterious again."

"When I was first a scout, I was assigned to an older scout. He wasn't a herder. He didn't have the faintest trace of Talent. He was one of the best scouts I ever knew, far better than I was. He looked at everything and fit it together. That's the problem with relying on Talent alone. This prophet is relying on Talent, and he has no real regard for his lancers. You can tell that by the way he spends them. The gates were loosely guarded the first time we scouted them, and that was after they knew we were here. They won't be that well guarded today," Alucius predicted.

"I hope you're right."

Alucius wasn't sure what he hoped, because lightly guarded gates meant a confidence in some other power, presumably great power, and he wasn't certain he wanted to face that kind of power.

Another half vingt passed, and the sky lightened further, enough to see the recent hoofprints in the dust, prints only from the night before, Alucius judged. Then, they reached the last turn in the narrow road before it headed due west toward the rebel camp.

"Column, halt!"

Once the force halted, Alucius ordered, "Ready rifles. Silent riding."

Then the files split, one on each shoulder of the road, leaving the center open.

They rode another vingt before halting. The lead riders of each file stopped short of the last cover before the open meadow in front of the entry road and gates that lay open two hundred yards away.

Feran looked across the open road to Alucius.

Alucius looked back over his shoulder, waiting. He pointed to the east.

Feran nodded, and they waited until the orange-white light of the sun spilled over the horizon, then above the low eastern hills, flat and directly into the eyes of the sentry, if the man was even looking eastward.

Alucius eased the gray forward until he was barely clear of the squat cedar that was one of the last before the open space in front of the walls. He halted the gelding and, raising his rifle, using sight and Talent, took aim on the rebel guard in the boxlike sentry post by the gate.

Crack!

The rebel slumped from sight.

With the single shot as the signal, without a word, Fifth Company led the way—not a charge, but a mounted fast walk, up the narrow road and across the open space short of the palisades. The other two companies followed.

Beyond the palisades and the gates, a dark purpleness slumbered, silent and present, but not so much waiting, as just *there*. Alucius held his Talent and his rifle ready as he led the force across the meadow toward the open gates. With his Talent, he could sense only one other form near the gates, and that rebel was sleeping in the other sentry guard box. Alucius kept his attention focused on the sleeping rebel, as well as on the road past the open gates and into the encampment.

Step by step, the mounts and the lancers they carried neared the gate. They were less than twenty yards from the gates when the sleeping sentry bolted upright.

Alucius had been waiting. His first shot went into the sentry's shoulder, and the second into the man's chest. The striker in the sentry's hand made a muted *clang* as it struck the watch bell.

"Column, forward!" Alucius snapped, urging the gelding forward toward the still-open gates.

Fifth Company responded, and after several moments, so did the other two companies.

As he rode inside the now-unguarded gates, Alucius kept scanning for defenders, but he could neither see nor sense any at the palisades. So he continued to ride, with Fifth Company immediately behind him, up the gentle slope of the road to the upper level, where the barracks and stables were—on the flat just east of the temple carved out of the bluff.

As he rode over the low crest of the approach road and onto the flat, Alucius studied the one-story barracks—two unpainted, plank-sided dwellings, each fifty yards long and ten wide, each with a roof sloped down from a high rear wall to a lower front wall. The handful of windows had shutters, also unpainted, but no glass.

The watch bell from the south gate began to clang, repeatedly and almost desperately.

"Lancers! Lancers inside the gates!" someone yelled.

"Fifth Company! Firing line abreast, double file!" Feran ordered.

As Fifth Company re-formed, rifles aimed at the barracks, Alucius continued to scan the flat and the bluff area beyond, where the prophet had to be, from the swirling purpleness that had begun to billow from the square arch cut into the reddish sandstone.

Less than a hundred men in the maroon tunics stumbled from the long and crude barracks, and a third might have held rifles. The others held blades or spears. All the rebels were dusted with the purple miasma, and all began to run toward the mounted lancers of Fifth Company.

"Fifth Company! Fire at will!"

The first volley took down a good third of the rebel attackers.

At the same time, Alucius could see a goodly number of rebels leaving the western end of the barracks and running toward the temple carved into the bluff. Then he had to concentrate on the six rebels sprinting toward him.

It took him two shots to down the one rebel with a rifle, because the man bobbed irregularly as he ran toward Alucius. The bobbing not only made it hard for Alucius to target the man, but also made it difficult for him to aim accurately at Alucius or any of the mounted Northern Guard.

Alucius slipped the first rifle into the holder and drew the second one, firing at another tall rebel sprinting toward him. The man sprawled on the dirt, then struggled to his knees, and lurched upright, blood pouring from the hole in his guts, less than five yards from the Northern Guard majer. Alucius put another bullet into the man, killing him. He shifted aim to another rebel, one within yards of driving a long poleaxe into Bakka from the right, while Bakka was using his sabre to slash down an attacker to his left.

For the next half glass, rifles fired, and sabres rose and fell.

Then there was silence across the flat.

From what Alucius could determine with his Talent, the only remaining living lancers were those of his force—and those rebels who had fled into the temple carved out of the hillside. As he considered what to do next, a purple miasma flared from the temple, unseen except with Talent, washing over the northern end of Fifth Company, those in fifth squad. Abruptly, a good ten lancers slumped in their saddles.

Alucius could sense that at least one, possibly two men, were dead.

"All companies, pull back a hundred yards! Now!"

"Pull back and re-form!"

The orders echoed across the open space between the barracks and stables and the cutaway bluff that held the temple within. Alucius eased the gray across to the lancers who had been struck. Two were indeed dead.

Feran rode toward Alucius. "Talent, Majer?"

"A nasty form of it."

Between the two of them and Zerdial, the fifth squad leader, they managed to get mounts and lancers, dead and alive, back away from the temple.

Alucius looked to Feran, then to Deotyr and Jultyr. "I'd judge there might be a hundred lancers inside. Overcaptain Feran will take charge of rotating companies covering the main entrance to the temple there. One company should be enough. A second company will be standing by.

The third will see if they have any supplies and ammunition we can use."

"Yes, sir."

"I'm going to see what we can do about this prophet." Alucius turned the gelding back toward the temple, reining up to one side, about twenty yards away, in a position where he could not be fired at unless one of the rebels actually stepped outside the archway.

When the second wave of purple flared forth, conelike, from the temple archway, Alucius countered with his own net of golden green. The two meshed, and minute pinlights of brilliance, visible to all the lancers, flashed across the morning.

Alucius waited for the next attack from the ifrit/prophet.

The third wave collapsed fifty yards from the temple archway, well short of any of the lancers.

Doubting that there would be another Talent attack soon, Alucius studied the square arch of the temple, both with sight and Talent senses. The archway itself was clear, with a stone-walled corridor three yards wide and close to three high running back some four yards before opening onto an antechamber of sorts. The corridor walls were smooth, without projections or niches. Behind them were rebels, armed and waiting.

There was no way to enter the temple, not that Alucius could sense, without getting caught in the stone-walled corridor. There was also no way to plant any of his powder deep enough to bring down the temple without subjecting anyone trying to murderous fire.

He turned the gray and rode back toward Feran.

"They can't get out, and we can't get in," observed the overcaptain. "Not without losing a lot of men."

Alucius beckoned to Waris, on the end of first squad's formation.

The scout slipped his mount out of formation and toward Alucius. "Sir?"

"You've scouted this twice. Is there any other way in besides that archway?"

"Not for people, sir. There's a slit above in that angled line of stone, sir," observed Waris. "It's sort of a skylight. You can't see it from here, but it's there."

"How wide is it?"

"Maybe a third of a yard, half at most. Two yards long, I'd guess."

"I may see if I can get up there," Alucius said.

Feran raised his eyebrows, as if to ask "Why?"

"There's a Talent-wielder in there. If we leave him, we're no better off than we were, or we won't be in a few weeks. If we try to rush him, we lose more lancers than all that we've lost this far. I'll need some rope, though, and Waris and Rakalt to help me."

"What . . . if I might inquire, sir . . ." asked Feran deferentially, "did you have in mind?"

"I thought I'd use one of the heavy shells and a rifle," Alucius replied. "If no one thinks I can get up there, I'd at least like to try a shot at him. If not that, then if I start shooting maybe I can panic the rebels inside to try to escape."

"You don't think they'll surrender?"

"Has anyone surrendered?" Alucius countered.

"Couldn't anyone else . . . ?" asked Jultyr slowly.

"We don't have any other herders," Feran replied. "You saw what happened when the lancers got too close to the temple. The majer's right about his being the only one who can do this."

There was the faintest murmur of "Oh . . ." from Deotyr.

Alucius hoped no one asked about the scouts. While he could protect them, he didn't want to explain that. "I'd like to do this fairly quickly. That last Talent-blast showed he was weaker, and I'd like to catch him before he regains too much strength." He reached inside his tunic and pulled out the skull mask, working it into place.

Feran summoned Waris and Rakalt, and they rode up as Alucius turned the gray. "Where do you suggest we start?"

"To the right, just past that funny-looking fir," replied Waris. "I've got some rope, maybe twenty yards. Will that be enough?"

"It'll have to be." Alucius angled the gray toward the fir, and the two scouts followed him.

"What's the majer doing?"

". . . going after the prophet, they say . . ."

". . . hope he gets him . . ."

". . . only officer I know who does the dirty stuff . . ."

". . . if I had those bars, wouldn't catch me . . ."

". . . could be why he has 'em so young . . ."

It could be, reflected Alucius, just plain stupidity. But he had to at least get up there and look and see what he could do. He couldn't leave the prophet, and he didn't have the time and supplies for a long, drawn-out siege, not when he had no idea how many supplies might have been stockpiled in the temple cave for how long. And he certainly didn't want to sacrifice lancers from a force that was already too small for the tasks assigned.

That didn't leave many choices.

He dismounted behind the fir and tied the gray to a stubby cedar root. Then, with his rifle slung over his shoulder, he and the two others began to climb the side of what was too steep to be a hill and not steep enough to be a bluff. Between the boulders, the sand-covered red sandstone made the footing treacherous, and more than a few times Alucius could feel his boots slipping. Riding boots were not designed for climbing.

Every so often Alucius paused, not only to catch his breath but to use his Talent to check on Adarat, but the purple shadow presence remained within the hillside temple. Alucius continued to climb, boulder by boulder, using roots and rocks.

Every so often a few shots rang out below, but they were from Fifth Company, and Alucius judged that Feran was having the lancers fire occasionally to keep the rebels thinking about the Guard troopers and not about what else might be happening—like Alucius on his fool's errand.

"Sir . . ." called Waris from behind Alucius. "The roof part is just ahead, over that line of rocks."

Alucius studied the line of rocks, realizing belatedly that

the stonework had actually been laid, but that the mortar had been mixed with red sand to conceal the unnatural origin.

"Why . . . if you don't mind, sir . . . Rakalt and I ought to climb past you, then move up to those boulders at the bottom of the higher cliff there. If you attach the rope around your waist . . ."

"I won't fall too far if the roof gives way under me?"

"Or . . . if anything else happens, sir . . ."

Like getting shot, Alucius thought to himself. "You're right. I'll just move here, and you two can climb by me." He watched as the two scouts made their way up to him.

Waris scrambled a half yard or so beyond Alucius, his boots slipping and dislodging more sand before he anchored himself on a darkish red stone. From there, he handed Alucius one end of the rope.

Alucius fastened it around his chest, then said in a low voice, "I'll wait until you two are in position."

Waris nodded. After Rakalt climbed past Alucius, the two continued upward for another five yards, then began to move westward.

While Alucius waited for them to position themselves, he used his Talent to scan the area ahead of him. He could sense nothing new, but the purplish miasma filling the temple below seemed clearer and nearer.

Roughly a quarter of a glass passed before Waris waved and gently tugged the rope. Alucius waved back, then resumed his own climb toward the course of stone that Waris had identified.

When he reached it, he smiled faintly. The stones were slightly corbeled and extended almost two yards above him. He had to edge eastward, practically to the end of the rope and to the sheer drop-off below, before he could find footing and a true isolated projecting stone that gave him solid enough footing so that he could edge his way upward. Between the rifle and the rope, every step worried him, and he was panting and sweating heavily when he finally sat astraddle the artificial stone course.

He caught his breath before he eased to the inside of the

roof wall. The stones below and beyond the course of stone that Waris had called to Alucius's attention were not natural at all, but more like thin sheets of stone layered into an arch. With one hand on the stone ridge, Alucius put his boot on one of the roof stones nearest to him. It felt solid. He took another step, and nothing happened.

As Alucius made his way up the arched stone roof, Waris kept the rope fairly taut.

Alucius was almost upon the open stone slit before he saw it, much as Waris had described it. As he dropped into a crouch, he could sense the purpleness below, and its overtones of what he could only describe as evil, almost like individual nets linked by tiny purplish nodes.

Alucius reached out with his Talent, and touched one of the nodes with a point of golden green—herder/soarer Talent. With but the barest pressure from Alucius, the golden green leapt from point to point along the purple net, and abruptly, with an unheard rending sound, the purple miasma shredded.

The entire temple shuddered, if only slightly, just enough that Alucius could feel the stone beneath his boots moving and his body swaying.

He steadied himself and studied the skylight. Beneath it and inside the temple there were actually shutters that could cover the opening, presumably in case of rain. Through the skylight he could see the temple far below, with more than a hundred rebels in maroon, and below the western end of the skylight, against the wall, he could see steps.

As he looked at the steps and wall, his rifle in hand, a man walked up the last steps to a landing, where there was a rope and pulley, probably to operate the skylight shutters. The man wore maroon silk and radiated the purpleness of an ifrit as he stood on the landing of the steps, little more than five yards below Alucius. He looked up and spoke. "I thought there might be one of the lamaials beyond. You reached too far, Talent-steer, when you entered here. You will not return to the north, lamaial."

A bolt of purple force flashed toward Alucius.

Awkwardly, because he felt off-balance, Alucius flung up one of his own shields, and purpleness flared around him.

"Frig! . . . See that?" Rakalt's voice was incredulous.

Another blast of purple flared toward Alucius, not quite so strong as the first. As the flare subsided, Alucius refocused his Talent senses on the prophet.

Adarat was not an ifrit like the Recorder of Deeds in Tempre or the engineer had been. That Alucius could sense. The prophet had but one lifethread, not the twined and twisted double lifethread. But the thread was different— brown shadowed with purple, a dark and strong purple.

"You have some ability, Talent-steer," Adarat said. "But not enough."

"Why have you turned them all into slaves?" Alucius asked, even as he prepared his own Talent-thrust.

"Slaves? They are to serve the coming Duarchy. That is a mission of glory!"

An even stronger blast of purpleness flashed from Adarat.

Alucious let it sheet past him. "You're as much a slave as they are."

"Never! I am the prophet." Adarat reached for a long black tube.

Alucius had no idea what the device was, but he'd seen some of the ifrits' weapons and scarcely wanted to find out. He struck with his Talent-probe, aiming for the node that linked body and lifethread.

Adarat flung another purple blast, even as purple and brown shreds exploded outward from the prophet's body. The black tube spun out of Adarat's hands and began to fall end over end toward the floor of the temple below.

Alucius rocked back on his heels, then managed to recover his balance.

"You will not succeed . . ." Adarat's words were strained, little above a whisper. "Neither you nor your ancient ones will prevail against the glory of Efra . . ."

Efra?

In the moment that Alucius took in the strange word, he could see Adarat slump.

Crummmpppttt! Below Alucius was an explosion that shook the entire hillside. Cracks appeared in the red rock on which he stood, and the stone edges of the skylight began to crack, then fragment. Pieces began to break away and fall into the temple.

He scrambled sideways, pulling himself along the rope and away from the center of the temple roof, trying to bound over the stones crumbling beneath him as more and more of the roof stones of the temple cracked and began to crumble even under his boots.

He could feel Waris and Rakalt trying to reel in the rope.

Then something smashed into his shoulder, and blackness rolled over him.

68

North of Iron Stem, Iron Valleys

In early afternoon, the three sat around the kitchen table, ignoring the chill wind that whipped around the stone walls of the stead dwelling, trying to rattle the snug-shuttered windows and tight-fitted doors. The gale-force winds of the first full storm of fall battered the walls, as they had since the middle of the night before. Warmth radiated from the iron stove.

Wendra stiffened, her face paling. "Oh . . ."

"You're too early," Lucenda said. "I told you about riding—"

"It's not that. I'm fine. Alucius . . . he's hurt."

Both Royalt and Lucenda looked hard at Wendra.

"It was like a fall . . . it wasn't Talent . . . he's alive . . ."

"He's too good a rider to fall," Royalt said, "not unless he was shot, and you'd feel that."

"They could have shot his mount from under him," Lucenda pointed out.

For a time, no one spoke.

"He's alive . . . he feels stronger . . . but he's still hurt. He's badly hurt." Wendra's lips tightened. "He can't do this alone. He can't. How can I help when I'm five hundred vingts away?"

"You're helping him by being the herder," Royalt said slowly. "He won't have anything to come back to without you."

"He has you," Wendra said slowly, the pallor in her face lifting.

Royalt shook his head. "There's only the two of you—you and Alucius—who can handle those new Talent-beasts. They'd turn me into blue flame before I'd have two shots off, and not one of my shots'd do a thing. Without you, Alucius wouldn't have anything."

For the first time, Wendra's eyes misted. She blotted them. "It's not what you think. It's not. I'm trapped. If I go to him, he could lose the stead, and that's almost everything for him. In a way, then, I'd lose him. If I don't, I could also lose him."

Royalt nodded slowly.

Wendra looked at her husband's grandsire for a time. Finally, she smiled wearily, a crooked expression, and lifted the mug before her to her lips.

69

Alucius opened his eyes. He could see stars. Had he been hit that hard? With what? His entire back felt numb, but without the sharpness of a specific wound. He thought he was lying on some sort of pallet, but he wasn't sure. He squinted. There were stars against darkness . . .

and the half disc of Selena. He was lying on the ground, hard ground, and it was night.

"Don't move," said a voice.

"I'm . . . not. What happened?"

"The whole cave . . . exploded, and it just fell away from under you, sir. We thought you'd gone with the cave."

Alucius could make out the lancer's face, but not well enough in the dim light to put a name to it. Or had he been hurt worse, somehow, and he couldn't remember names and faces?

"How is he?" came another voice—Feran's.

"I'm not so bad as you think," Alucius replied.

"That's still bad," retorted Feran, moving into Alucius's sight.

"Why am I out here?"

"We didn't want to move you. Besides, the barracks are like a hog pen. Never saw such filth."

That didn't surprise Alucius. Under the prophet's Talent-spell, many of the enslaved lancers had shown little initiative.

Feran bent down to study Alucius. "Good thing you and Waris worked out the rope, except that you were dangling there in the middle of nothing and a bunch of rock bounced down and hit you. A couple were a lot bigger than you are. Waris and Rakalt did their best, but they had a hard time getting you down. We lost a bunch of lancers to stone shrapnel when that temple blew. The whole front exploded, sent stone everywhere."

"How many did we lose?"

"All told . . . thirty or so. About half came from Fifth Company and half from Thirty-fifth. There aren't enough rebels left to fill a squad. We figured there must have been at least fifty inside there."

"Closer to a hundred and fifty—and their prophet. He's dead. I killed him." Alucius wasn't about to say how. "That's when the place blew. Somehow, he'd Talent-linked himself to a bunch of powder, and when he died, it set off the powder. Could have been something else, but I don't know what." That was what Alucius had thought, but there wasn't any way to prove that—or disprove it—not that he knew, and it didn't matter. The effect had been the same. Despite the explosion of the temple, Alucius had to wonder about Adarat. The prophet had been either too strong or too weak, but with the pain that ebbed and flowed through and around him, Alucius lost track of why he'd thought that.

"Nasty bastard to the end," said Feran.

Alucius wiggled his fingers. They were slightly numb, but they moved. He tried the same with his toes. He lifted his left arm. It was sore, but it also moved. He tried his right arm. A wall of fire and pain slammed into him, and he barely managed to lower it, rather than let it fall onto the ground, which he knew would have hurt even worse. "I'm pretty sore . . . don't think anything's broken . . ."

"How would you know?"

Rather than answer immediately, Alucius used his Talent to look at himself, bit by bit. Finally, his eyes met Feran's. "Nothing's broken. Everything's bruised on my back side and on my right. Need to roll over. Need some help."

"Are you sure?"

"All the weight on the bruises doesn't help."

"The pressure might keep it from hurting more."

"Help me roll over. To the left . . ."

Feran knelt beside Alucius.

As Feran helped him turn, another wall of pain slammed into Alucius, worse than the first. When he woke again, lying on his stomach, Feran was sitting on the ground, watching.

"I told you, Majer."

Alucius wanted to laugh. "You . . . did . . ."

"You're not going anywhere real fast, even if nothing's broken."

"I can feel that, but I heal fast. In a week, I'll be able to ride."

"Do you think we should wait a week?"

"No . . ." Alucius paused. "Without the prophet around, you could handle the other camp."

"You're sure that there's not another Talent-wielder?"

"I haven't seen any signs of one, but if there is . . . we can wait."

"Just the same to you, sir, I'd like to finish off these rebels before something else happens. I'll take Twenty-eighth Company with Fifth tomorrow, and half of Thirty-fifth, and we'll finish off the other camp. Without their prophet, it'll be a slaughter job. Unless you've got any objections."

Alucius thought. He knew that Feran wanted his approval, possibly because the older officer didn't believe that Alucius was not more severely injured. "Scout it first. Then, if you still think so . . . go ahead. Without the prophet, they might surrender, but you'll have to be careful. Shoot first, if you've got any questions." He wasn't feeling all that charitable, not lying on whatever he was, and he had a great deal less sympathy for the people of Hyalt than when he had first arrived in the area. He still hadn't figured out exactly who or what the prophet had been, except that he hadn't been an ifrit—exactly—but he'd been more than merely influenced.

Alucius was finding it hard to keep his eyes open, and that sort of speculation and deduction would have to wait.

Feran said something, but the words slipped away as a grayish darkness crept over Alucius.

70

When Alucius struggled into awareness once again, it was morning, or he thought it was. He lay on a pallet in a small room, his head propped up slightly with folded blankets. A lancer sat on a stool, his face not quite bored, but impassive from long glasses of inactivity. The lower part of the lancer's right tunic sleeve had been cut away, and he wore a heavy dressing on his forearm.

"How . . . long?" Alucius managed, his voice raspy. His head throbbed. In fact, almost his entire body throbbed.

"Yes,   sir . . . Ah . . . it's   Quattri . . . around   mid-afternoon." The man stood and hurried toward the pallet, extending a water bottle, left-handed, with a slight awkwardness. "It's your water bottle, sir. The overcaptain said you needed to drink as much as you could."

Alucius managed to reach across his body with his left hand and take the water bottle. He only spilled a small amount on his face as he drank.

The lancer watched.

Alucius eased his hand holding the water bottle down until it rested on the pallet beside his leg. "I'll keep it for a bit."

"Yes, sir."

"Did Overcaptain Feran head out this morning?"

"Yes, sir. He left two squads and those of us wounded. And the wagons."

"Were there any rebels left alive?"

"Seven of 'em, sir. That's all. Were more, but a some of 'em did crazy things, like slitting their wrists or cutting their own throats. The rest . . . well, the overcaptain had 'em tied up so as they wouldn't hurt themselves. Said once you were better, you'd be wanting to talk to them."

Alucius glanced around the room. Moving his head intensified the throbbing that had started to fade after he drank the water.

The lancer followed his eyes. "This was the cleanest place around. Only had to move junk out and swept it down good. The rest of 'em . . . well, everyone'd rather sleep outside."

"Has anything else strange happened?"

The wounded man cocked his head. "No, sir. I mean, no more rebels, and the weather hasn't changed much, maybe a bit windier." He paused. "Castav . . . he did say that all the new growth of the thornbushes was turnin' black, suddenlike . . . maybe tried to grow back too soon. Said he'd never seen bushes turn so quick."

Alucius had a good idea why that was happening. That growth had been forced, and with Adarat's death, there was nothing to bind the life force into the thornbushes. He lifted the water bottle slowly and drank some more.

He hated being hurt, not being able to be in complete charge of his body.

Then why do you keep doing things where it's likely to happen? asked a voice inside his skull.

Because the alternatives seemed worse, he answered himself. The problem was that he was using that response too much. All too much.

71

By midday on Quinti, Feran had still not returned. From what Alucius could see through the open shutters of the single window, the sky was only slightly hazy, and there was little wind. That he could feel even from his pallet. He had been able to use the makeshift chamber pot, thankfully, and eat some bread and cheese, and move, if slowly. But he worried about the missing forces. Had there been another Talent-wielder? Or a better-trained force in Hyalt?

Alucius kept fretting and stewing.

When his latest lancer aide and guard left for a moment, after Alucius had assured him that he would be fine alone for just a few moments, Alucius struggled into a sitting position on the side of the pallet, then levered himself along it until he was close enough to reach his clothes and boots. Donning the trousers wasn't that hard, but even the first boot was an effort. He'd just managed to get the second one on when the lancer stepped through the doorless arch.

"Sir!"

"I'll go mad if I lie here any longer," Alucius said. "Can you help me with the tunic?"

"But . . . sir . . ."

"Just help me with the tunic."

The right arm had to go first, because he didn't have much of a range of motion without feeling close to excruciating pain, and his forehead was damp with sweat by the time he walked slowly from the room and outside. He spotted a bench against the side of the barracks, less than fifty feet away. Walking the fifty feet felt as though it took as much effort as running ten times that would have if he had been healthy.

Several lancers turned and watched.

". . . see why . . . say he's tough . . . hurt . . . no one else'd be alive. A day and he's walkin' . . ."

". . . not real steady . . ."

". . . you'd be flat . . . mountain fell on him, and he's walking . . . You try that."

". . . survived . . . so?"

". . . *he* went in there . . . hundred and fifty lancers in there, and their prophet . . . don't know how he did it, but he killed 'em all . . . How many commanders you know do that? They'd send us and get us all killed . . ."

That might be, reflected Alucius, *but I'm beginning to understand what Frynkel said about leading from the front.* How many more times could he do it and survive?

He settled onto the bench, his back against the plank wall, and waited. He just hoped he didn't have to wait all that long, and that his forces would return without too many casualties.

His thoughts drifted back to Adarat, the prophet. The man hadn't been like any human Talent-wielder Alucius had encountered and hadn't seemed to know what he was doing, but he was stronger than any of the Matrial's Talent-officers. Yet he'd been totally unaware of the vulnerability of his lifethread—and that hadn't been like any of the

ifrits. What exactly had created Adarat? The thought that
the ifrits could create—or change—someone into an
Adarat—that worried Alucius.

Even with the wristguard's warm pulse that told him
Wendra was healthy, he couldn't help worrying about Wendra and Alendra, and whether he could finish with the rebellion and return to Iron Stem before Alendra was born.

For all the worries, he must have dozed off for a time,
because he awakened to the sound of hoofs on the hard
dirt. He had to hope that the riders were his force, because
he was in no shape to lift or use a rifle, and there wasn't
one handy for him to use even if he had been able to shoot.

Feran rode in at the head of Fifth Company, his eyes
scanning the handful of wounded lancers who were watching. His eyes took in Alucius, and he rode over toward the
majer. "As soon as I get them settled, I'll be back. We
didn't take any casualties, but there's a lot of work ahead."

"When you have time," Alucius replied. As the lancers
rode by, he watched. A number looked at him, and several,
including Bakka and Waris, nodded.

Almost half a glass passed before Feran reappeared,
walking quickly from the direction of the stables. He
stopped several yards short of Alucius and surveyed his
commander.

"You shouldn't be up," Feran observed. "I've seen
corpses left in the sun for a week looking better. Sir and
Majer."

"It wasn't doing me any good to lie on that pallet and
fret. What happened?"

"Not much. They had a few sentries, but they just stood
there. We killed maybe fifty rebels before we realized that
they weren't fighting and before I could order a stop to the
shooting. That was the problem. Half of their lancers . . .
they'd follow a direct order . . . but otherwise . . . they'd
just stand there." Feran shook his head. "Maybe fifty . . .
quarter of those left, they'd already killed themselves
when we got there. Some just died, not a mark on 'em."

Alucius thought he understood the reason for Feran's delay in returning. "What did you do?"

"What could I do? No point in shooting them. Sent Thirty-fifth Company into Hyalt. Had Jultyr be real cautious. He didn't need to be. The place is a mess. Mostly woman and girls, small boys. They all look hungry. We put the rebel lancers who were left into saddles and rode 'em into town. Turned them over to the women, and told the women that they were in charge. A couple seemed to understand."

"We'll have to help them get better organized," Alucius said.

"I figured that." Feran shook his head. "Town'll never be the same. Not for years."

"Maybe. The women did all right in Madrien. We'll just have to see if we can get them started. Make sure that they tear down those roadblocks, and maybe do some beginning training for a patrol of some sort to keep order."

"Who's going to be a problem?" asked Feran.

"Outsiders," Alucius said. "We'll also have to make sure our own men don't take advantage of them . . . the women."

Feran lifted his eyebrows. "After this?"

"After this," Alucius said, "if our men abuse the women, the Lord-Protector will be in the position of not only having ordered us to butcher the men, but to abuse and rape the women. Do any of your men want to be called the rapists of the north? How long do you think we'd last in the south of Lanachrona with that kind of reputation? And even if we could ride back to the Iron Valleys because all the Southern Guards are tied up with the Regent . . . do you want to risk it? What will happen to that stipend you've been struggling for?"

"I'm not sure . . . one or two . . ." Feran offered.

"One or two we can survive, if there aren't any more. Make it really simple. First, it's wrong. Rebels or not, they're our people. Second, we killed all the guilty ones. Hurting the women is just punishing them again for what their husbands and sons did, and they're going to suffer enough for years. Third . . . if I discover another man who does anything from this moment on, I'll kill him personally, weak as I am. And if any officer doesn't enforce this, I'll send him back to the Lord-Protector with a recommendation for discharge or worse."

"That won't help the Lord-Protector all that much," Feran pointed out.

"Probably not," Alucius replied. "But I'd like to keep our lancers as lancers, not barbarians. My orders are more for their good than for the poor bastards left in Hyalt."

"You don't think we're done after we finish here?"

"No. Even if we head straight back to the Iron Valleys, we'll still have to deal with the Regent there. And they'll put the Southern Guard companies right into the battle order in the southwest. They might get a week's rest. If they're lucky."

"I can see you're as cheerful as ever." Feran laughed harshly. "I suppose that's a good sign."

"Tomorrow, we'll move into Hyalt and see what we can do."

"Tomorrow, sir, we'll move into Hyalt, and you'll just give the orders and watch." Feran smiled. "You don't have to do everything personally."

Not everything, Alucius thought, but more than he'd ever wished.

72

Alustre, Lustrea

Waleryn stood above the corner workbench that all had ignored until he had arrived at the Praetor's palace. After checking the hidden metal mirror that acted as a Table-viewer—if but for short periods of time—

he opened the book that had been concealed in the chamber beneath the mirror.

He looked at the first page quickly, nodding to himself, as well as at the second and third. He continued flicking through the pages until he reached one near the end. A smile crossed his lips as he viewed Vestor's notes.

"Good."

After closing the book and replacing it in the small chamber, he straightened and stepped from the smaller workbench to the crystal tanks, all in use. His eyes closed for a moment, and the air took on a purplish tint, just for an instant. Then Waleryn walked to the far side of the second tank and, from another recess, extracted a device resembling an antique gunpowder pistol.

The design was far more ancient, with the barrel a crystal discharge formulator and the butt holding the crystal light-charges. Waleryn removed one of the butt plates and slipped two small amber crystals into the receivers, then replaced the plate and set the weapon in the belt holster on his right side.

One by one, he checked the crystal tanks, nodding as he finished with each.

Then he walked to the far end of the workshop, where a tripod held an oblong device. The shorter and wider end held a pair of padded grips. Above and between the grips was a flat metallic mirror, not quite the size of a man's palm. The longer section ended in a circle of pale orange crystals, each crystal extending the length of a finger from the shimmering silvered metal.

"What is that?" Tyren stood five yards away, well to the side of where the five crystals pointed. The Praetor was flanked by four guards, each with a gladius in a scabbard on his left and a double-barreled pistol in a holster on his right.

"You needn't worry, Praetor," Waleryn replied cheerfully. "This is not a weapon."

"Then why did you construct it?" Tyren frowned. "Your efforts are not without significant cost."

"To find an ancient weapon of even greater power. It is designed to send forth . . . vibrations would be the best word. The vibrations will echo from the ancient weapon and return. They will provide an image in the mirror that will enable me to locate exactly where the weapon might be."

"What ancient weapon do you seek that is so much more powerful than those you and your predecessor have already created?" Curiosity had crept into the Praetor's voice.

"You might have heard of the Scepters of the Day. Some called them the Scepters of the Duarches. There were two, and one is hidden somewhere in Lustrea. Or so it is said."

"Isn't that just a legend?"

"Some would claim that everything your engineer created and everything I am constructing are only legends. Are they? Or would you rather dismiss the crystal light lances as legend and ride into battle trusting in lances and uncertain rifles?"

"Your point is made, Lord Waleryn." Tyren's voice was dry. "Just how powerful is this scepter? And how much more will it cost me for you to find it?"

"It will cost you nothing more. As I have time, and as I travel, I will use the device. It will take little time. The scepter was powerful enough that it was the tool that created the Tables and made the Duarchy possible. Do you not think that a few golds and a little time are worth seeking it? That search will not slow the production of more and better weapons."

"So long as it does not."

"Have you decided whether I might go to Prosp and see if the Table there still functions?"

Tyren slowly nodded. "You will go with a detachment of Praetorian Guards, and you will keep me closely informed of your progress."

Waleryn bowed. "It would be my pleasure, and in my interest, and yours."

"That it would be." Tyren nodded brusquely, then turned.

Waleryn waited until the Praetor had departed before he turned his violet-purple eyes back to the locator.

73

Even by Octdi, Alucius could barely walk, let alone ride. His entire body was sore and bruised, and already turning purplish green in far too many places. He was going to have another scar, this one angled across his forehead. He had no recollection of how he had gotten that, especially since he had been wearing the skull mask, now tucked safely inside his tunic once more.

He and the officers had taken over a dwelling a block off the main square in Hyalt, not the largest available, but sizable, and apparently vacant, as were many in the town, and less than a hundred yards from the inn and stables where Alucius had put Fifth Company. The two Southern Guard companies were at work making the camp just northeast of Hyalt habitable, since the old Southern Guard garrison was far too small and was in even worse condition. For the sake of the Lord-Protector, Alucius had thought that the less the people of Hyalt saw of the Southern Guard, the better. He had also dispatched a messenger to Tempre outlining the results of the campaign thus far, noted his quartering arrangements, and indicated that it might be as much as several weeks before they could leave Hyalt and return to Tempre.

With all that done, late on that Octdi morning Alucius still had to work not to grimace as he mounted the gelding under a gray sky that threatened rain. After mounting, he eased the gray in the direction of the main square. Beside him rode Waris, and behind them were four other lancers. Feran had suggested a half squad, at least, but Alucius had decided that five lancers were more than enough, either for a show of strength or for any protection he might need in his present condition.

From the three-story dwelling that had belonged to a merchant of some sort, Alucius and his lancers rode northward as he began to inspect Hyalt. No matter how accurate Feran's, Rakalt's, and Waris's reports might be, their words did not convey the "feel" of Hyalt.

All the streets entering the main square were paved, but the north– south main boulevard, as a part of the ancient high road, was of eternastone, and Alucius had decided to begin with the square, then spiral outward, to take in as much as he could.

The central square was a stone-paved expanse a hundred yards on a side. In the center was a stone platform, raised a yard above the surrounding pavement, without walls or railings. The stone looked to be a gold-tinged marble whose edges had softened over the years. Both the center of the square and the platform itself were vacant. Not a single horse was tied to the hitching rails and posts in front of the buildings fronting the square. Alucius slowed the gray and studied each structure as he passed. The goldsmith's shop was boarded shut, as was the adjoining coppersmith's shop. The cotton factor's door was ajar, and Alucius thought he heard voices, but one set of shutters had been ripped away and lay on the narrow porch beside the door. Past the empty alley was a fuller's shop, but that door was closed. Next came a cooperage, and that door was open, and Alucius could smell the charcoal of a forge.

"Most of the crafters and all of the merchants left," Waris said.

Alucius nodded. That agreed with what he thought— that Adarat had not been an ifrit, or one of a weaker sort. It also suggested that there could not be too many ifrits in Corus, not if what Adarat had done represented the work of one being who was less than an ifrit. Alucius still did not understand what the ifrits had hoped to accomplish in Hyalt, and he had the feeling that riding around Hyalt would not add much to his understanding of the secretive and illusive ifrits, but it would offer him insights on what needed to be done for the people.

The inn was the only building around the square that

showed activity, but that was because Fifth Company was quartered there.

Alucius kept riding, trying to ignore the soreness throughout his body, and after his second spirallike widening circuit around the square, he slowed his mount again as he rode toward a wall that had once been whitewashed but which now needed stucco in too many places and fresh whitewash everywhere. He could hear two women talking. One was sobbing between words.

Alucius used his Talent, trying to pick up the words.

"Why . . . why . . . they killed our husbands . . . our sons . . . what did they do?"

"What harm did the prophet do?"

What could Alucius say to such words, when people had not seen the evidence before their eyes? When people believed, they could not see what had happened. They saw what they wanted to have seen.

". . . have nothing . . . nothing at all . . . no horses, no sheep, no goats . . . no sons . . ."

". . . followed the prophet and the lamaial struck him down . . . and we will never see the True Duarchy and its prosperity . . ."

"We will never see our sons, and for that I grieve far more . . ."

Alucius held in a wince. He had crushed the revolt—or the invasion. He'd done it only by the very method that he knew would cause the Lord-Protector unrest, discontent, and lasting resentment. And Alucius had had absolutely no choice—not that he could see. From the first moment he and his force had arrived, they had been attacked, time after time, by Talent-washed rebels who had fought poorly, but to the death.

And he still had no idea why, not when so much death could only ruin a land, not bring the kind of prosperity that the prophet had promised. The only thing he had learned—really—had been in Adarat's last words, ". . . Neither you nor your ancient ones will prevail against the glory of Efra . . ."

Was Efra the true name of the world from which the ifrits

had come? And did that pronunciation mean that somewhere on Corus another contingent of ifrits had appeared?

Alucius kept riding and watching and taking in what he saw—and worrying.

74

Salaan, Lanachrona

The Table displayed the image of a reddish hillside, the eastern side of which appeared to have been cut away, with the section that had been cut away heaped full of all sizes of boulders of redstone and sandstone. To the east of the jumbled stone were several long and low unpainted structures.

The Recorder looked up from the Table, and the scene that had been before him and Tarolt vanished. "The majer has triumphed over Adarat and his Cadmians."

"You expected otherwise, Trezun? Those steers were not real Cadmians. Adarat was but a shadow-Efran, certainly capable enough against un-Talented steers, but the majer is more than that. Even so, he almost did not survive. He will not last against a true Efran."

"That would seem to be so," the Recorder replied.

"It was not exactly a triumph for the majer and the Lord-Protector," Tarolt pointed out. "Hyalt lies in ruins, and we have most of the golds. The larger part of the men and boys are dead, and all Corus will know the Lord-Protector as the butcher of Hyalt. That is something that we can make sure all the world knows." With a smile, Tarolt stepped back from the Table.

"What of the majer? If he comes back to Dekhron, especially as commander of the Northern Guard . . . ?"

"We have already taken steps to forestall that. It is likely he will go to Southgate."

"Do you think the Lord-Protector will countenance that?"

"The Lord-Protector cannot object to what he does not know. Overcaptain Deen has proved most helpful in conveying ideas to the marshals. He is so guileless and thinks he is so clever. That is a weakness of so many steers. More important, this Alucius could not withstand the crystal spear-thrower before, and there are two in place there. Even if he can rally the Lord-Protector's troops and defeat the Regent, what does he gain?"

"A substantial victory," suggested Trezun.

"That kind of victory is a triumph for us. The Lord-Protector has little more than half the lancers he did two seasons ago. The southwest of Corus is weakened and ready to accept any kind of peace after five years of bleeding warfare. Majer Alucius cannot win without creating even more death and destruction, and that is what we need. He can only triumph through destruction, and that paves the way for us. People do not wish glorious and destructive battles. They wish peace and prosperity, and so long as the cost is deferred, they will not look beyond tomorrow."

"What of Waleryn?"

Tarolt frowned. "You have great interest there. I hope that his building the locator will not interfere—"

"I instilled strong conditions that it should not interfere—"

"You and Sensat and your concern about the scepters."

"*We* do not *need* them, but if we have them, then no lamaial or ancient one can use them," Trezun pointed out.

"You have a point. Not the best, but a point, so long as it does not interfere with the plan and the next translation. We must have more true Efrans here . . . and yet so few wish to take the risk."

"When between a third and half perish? Or become wild translations without thought or cognizance? Can you blame them?"

"When our future is at stake? Yes . . . I can. And I will.

Far more will perish if we do not receive greater support. Yet each wishes another to take the risk."

"You were about to tell me how you think Waleryn will affect matters." Trezun spoke quickly. "Does he have the shadow matrices that he will require? One suitable for Tyren?"

"He has ten, and three would seem to match what he has scanned of the Praetor, within acceptable parameters. He has also reported that the Praetor is coming to Prosp to inspect the Table—before he heads to Passera to ready his forces for the invasion of Deforya."

"Deforya it will be, then. That will create enough disruption for the next year, at least."

"Waleryn is well on the way to positioning Tyren so that the Praetor will ask to use the Table . . . Once that happens, in time, the Praetor will change his plans and concentrate on taking Deforya. The landowners will have to fight, and they will lose. Then Tyren will overreach himself and go south, and the plains will be filled with chaos . . ."

"He could head more directly west into Lanachrona."

"He could, and if Majer Alucius survives, no doubt we would have a larger and even bloodier series of battles."

"And what will happen if . . . just if . . . Majer Alucius does survive and prosper? He seems to have the luck of the hero or the lamaial."

"Ah . . . that is the beauty of it," Tarolt replied. "The Regent must still reclaim Harmony and Klamat. More unrest and destruction. Tyren will build larger armies and rampage westward. While that goes on, few will notice what we do and what we build, or that they act against themselves. Let them struggle with their rifles and blades. Their puny rifles and blades."

75

By Duadi morning, there were people, mostly women, on the streets of Hyalt, and some carts of produce had appeared. The two roadblocks across the high roads had been torn down, and Feran was working with a group of younger and huskier women to create the core of a mounted city patrol. There were enough spare mounts for that.

By midmorning, Alucius was sitting in the council chamber of Hyalt, a block off the main square, interviewing women who seemed to have some courage and intelligence, trying to use his Talent to find a handful to administer the crippled town. After glancing over at Bakka, who held a marker, with a short stack of paper before him on the table, Alucius tried not to shift his weight too obviously in the chair as he waited for the next group of women to file into the chamber.

Four more women stepped inside the chamber, ushered by four lancers.

An older gray-haired woman studied Alucius from the moment she entered the hall. So did a blonde woman, although her observations came from a lowered head and half-averted eyes. A black-haired, good-looking woman with ruby lips surveyed Alucius and smiled. Unlike the others, she looked well fed.

Alucius cleared his throat. "Whatever happened here in Hyalt is over. What remains is to rebuild the town and maintain order. Under the authority of the Lord-Protector, I am talking to anyone who might be useful in this." He paused, looking for reactions.

"We're so fortunate to have your assistance," began the attractive woman.

Alucius almost winced at the feeling of hypocrisy and greed that radiated from her, but he inquired politely, "Your name?"

"Sanaval, sir."

Alucius turned to the lancer guards. "Take Sanaval and lock her away with the others we're sending north."

The woman's mouth opened, almost wordlessly, as two of the lancers moved to flank her.

"Every syllable you said was false and deceptive," Alucius replied. "Hyalt doesn't need your kind right now. Take her away."

"Who are you to judge?" asked the stern-faced, gray-haired woman.

"I'm judging because someone has to administer Hyalt, and we need to find people who can, because that is not our task."

"Was your task just to bring down death on our men and sons?" asked the thin red-haired woman, almost hissing the words at Alucius.

He turned, and his eyes flashed. He tried to keep from exploding with a rage that had appeared within him, seemingly from nowhere. "Your men were so weak that they gave up their families, gave up their work, and gave up their brains. They attacked the Lord-Protector's scouts. They killed traders bringing in goods, perhaps even food. We did not ride here to bring death. We rode here to discover why the people of Hyalt were driving out merchants and crafters and killing strangers. When we got here, we, too, were attacked. Unlike the others, we could fight back." Alucius's eyes fixed on the angry woman, and he projected both power and assurance, trying to keep anger out of the sending. "There has been enough killing. There has been too much. I *am* choosing—from among your people—who will administer Hyalt. Do you want to run in fear from every man on a horse with a sword or a rifle?"

The woman shrank back, and Alucius turned his attention back to the gray-haired woman.

"They were fools," she admitted. "Did that give you the right to kill them?"

"Not until they tried to kill us and every other stranger," Alucius replied. "Not until they refused to talk and only attacked. Do you think that was right? Was it smart?"

"No. I am only a woman who sells vegetables and fruits from a cart."

"Do you still have vegetables and fruits to sell?"

"Yes." The admission was wary.

"Then you have more sense than most in Hyalt," Alucius said dryly. "What is your name?"

"Isaya."

Alucius nodded to Bakka, who inscribed the woman's name.

"Where do you live?"

"Off north road. You'd know. Your men near-dragged me here."

"Can you run the market square? Make sure what's sold is good?"

"Depends. Can't tell someone how many coins to charge . . ."

"No. What's charged has to be between buyer and seller. But Hyalt doesn't need spoiled meat or weeviled grain being sold as good."

"Might be able to do that . . . if we've got that patrol you promised . . ."

Alucius nodded. Probably half of what he was trying to do wouldn't work, but if he could put together some sort of organization, maybe the women could sort it out themselves as fall progressed into winter. He only knew that he had to try, and that if he sorted out the truly rotten apples, or as many as he could, they might have a chance.

His eyes turned to the nervous blonde woman. "What do you do?"

"I'm a seamstress . . . Leastwise, I was . . ."

Alucius wondered how many more glasses and days he'd have to work on trying to give the ruined town a chance at putting itself back together. It could take seasons to do it right, but he didn't have seasons. Besides, in the end, what was done rested on the survivors in Hyalt.

But he was still angry about how matters had turned out.

76

By Sexdi, Alucius was feeling somewhat better, enough for a ride back out to the western camp of the prophet and the site of the ruined temple. Feran insisted on accompanying Alucius with the fourth and fifth squads of Fifth Company. Behind the squads came a wagon, one filled with axes, bars, rock hammers, and other tools, as well as some barrels of powder.

As they passed the open and abandoned south gates of the encampment, with a cool and blustery wind whipping around them, announcing the arrival of a cold fall season, Feran glanced at Alucius. "You really think that you'll find useful supplies under all that rock?"

"I hope so," replied Alucius.

"I know you. You have to be more than hoping."

"There's one thing we haven't resolved, and I should have thought of it earlier," Alucius mused, his eyes taking in the rubbled base of the hillside that had held the temple.

"Just one?" asked Feran, his tone dry.

"What happened to all the golds in Hyalt? No one seems to have any, and yet people left things hurrying to leave. There were others who said they gave everything to the prophet. But no one left Hyalt after the first weeks, and we haven't found any strongboxes, nothing."

"Oh . . . you think . . . ?"

"I don't know, but it's worth looking into, and I really didn't want to say much. If the acting council has some golds, they can buy some food."

"You wouldn't send it to the Lord-Protector?"

"Why? What good would that do? If we find anything, we'll dole some of it out to the most needy families who are left. Not that the coins won't end up in certain pockets before long . . . " Alucius snorted. "But it does more good spread around. If we can find anything."

"If you find much, some of the men would think they should have some."

"I'm sure they would," Alucius replied.

"You don't think so?"

"We'll worry about that if we find anything. I'm hoping we can at least find some supplies, perhaps some ammunition or some flour or dried or salted meat. That's always useful."

"You'd give that away, too?"

Alucius shook his head. "Lancers have a right to eat. They deserve that."

"Aren't you splitting hairs?"

The majer laughed. "You really think that there's a huge treasure out here, don't you?"

"I could hope," Feran replied good-naturedly.

"Let's see." Alucius had his doubts, but there had to be *something*.

They rode past the barracks and past the small building where Feran had placed Alucius after the explosion and toward the ruined hillside. Alucius reined up the gray almost at the base of the rubble of irregular chunks of sandstone and redstone.

As the lancers in fourth squad unloaded the gear from the wagon, Alucius studied the rubble with his Talent. As he had suspected—or hoped—with his Talent he could sense an area to the south of the main temple that seemed to hold goods. He rode southward another ten yards, then motioned for a lancer to climb up onto a smaller pile of stone.

"If you can lever away the slab on top . . ." Alucius studied the rock, then nodded. "You see that dark patch there?"

The lancer with the rock hammer and chisel nodded.

"Put the chisel just below it . . . no . . . a little to the right. There's a fracture there somewhere."

The lancer worked at it for almost a tenth of a glass, then leapt up and stepped back. With a long and slow *craaackk,* the sheet of sandy rock split, and the lower half slid off the rounded redstone below, breaking into smaller fragments.

Just underneath the remaining slab, Alucius could see the square corner of a passageway. "There!" He gestured.

"How'd he know that . . . ?" came a murmur from somewhere.

"You don't want to know . . ."

"Clear the rock away from the doorway," Alucius ordered.

While he wanted to help, he forced himself to watch as lancers cleared away the remaining rock. That took more than three glasses, and he was grateful that the day was cool and breezy. The efforts also reminded him that finding out things and coming up with ideas were far easier than the grunt work necessary to implement those ideas.

Once the last bits of rubble had been removed, it was clear that the tunnel deeper into the hillside had not been touched by the effects of the blast set off by Adarat.

Alucius dismounted, then gestured to the lancers with the pry bars and hammers. "You all did the work. We'll go in together." He pointed to Kasaff, who had single-handedly moved large chunks of the rubble. "Do you want to lead the way?"

Kasaff grinned. "Just so you're right there, sir."

"Smart lancer," Alucius quipped.

Laughter rumbled across the squad.

Alucius stepped into the passageway, stone smoothed years before, certainly not at all recently, and walked toward the door on his left.

The first room was but half-full and contained several barrels of dried and salted beef, almost ten huge wedges of hard cheese, and more than a score of barrels of flour. There was one barrel of dried fruit and what looked to be a barrel of wine.

The second room held, unsurprisingly, cases of ammunition, but not a single rifle.

The third room, well to the back, was locked, with the large lock attached to a heavy hasp.

"Need a hammer, like as a whole forge, to cut that," offered Kasaff.

Alucius slipped out his belt knife and stepped toward the lock. "Maybe not." He stood so that no one behind him could see what he was doing and pretended to work at the keyhole with the point of the knife, as he wrestled with the internal workings of the lock with his Talent.

How long that took, he wasn't certain, but his face was dripping sweat when the lock popped open. He stepped back, handing the open lock to Quesal. Before trying the door lever, he cast a Talent-probe into the room behind the door, but he could sense nothing in the nature of an obvious trap. Then, he opened the door and let it swing wide.

The room was small, a strong room no more than three yards on a side, with but three chests side by side on a crude waist-high bench. The chests were closed, but not locked.

Again, pausing, Alucius extended his Talent, but aside from a lingering trace of ifrit purple, there was no sign of anything besides wood and metal.

He opened the first chest. Less than half-full, it contained golds, but not an extraordinary number for the treasure taken from a city—certainly no more than a thousand coins, if that. The second chest held the silvers, and there were perhaps slightly more than a thousand. The last chest was almost empty, holding only a hundred or so coppers.

Alucius stood by the chests, letting every lancer who wanted to come down the passageway and look at them. Then, once the chests were loaded onto the wagon, he assembled the two squads and began to speak to them.

"I had all of you look at the chests. I wanted you to see what was there. I'd like to tell the others what we found, but I also want you to understand what we did not find." He paused. "We did not find all that was stolen from Hyalt. Nor will we. It is spread across Corus. Think of this.

"What we found is what is left. It seems large, but it is not, not for the wealth of a large town. It is not enough to pay the payroll of the Northern Guard for a season. I doubt if it would pay the Southern Guard for a month. Without these coins, the people of Hyalt will starve this winter. Even with them, many will die. The coins will go back to the people from whom they came because the coins were stolen from them, and taking them from here would only make us no better than those we defeated. Worse, it would make us thieves as well. That's all."

He turned the gray and gestured to Feran.

"Column! Forward!"

After they had ridden out through the abandoned gates, Feran looked at Alucius. "Some of them still won't like it."

"I know they won't."

"They'll say you're a rich herder, and you can afford it, and they can't."

Alucius's laugh was bitter, but there was little he could say that anyone would understand. He was well-off, but not wealthy. He'd been blackmailed into commanding a force on an unpopular mission, leaving his family to fight off Talent-creatures without him—but saying all of that would convince no one. He just knew that starving people in order to line lancers' pockets was wrong. The people well might perish anyway, but he wasn't about to make matters worse than they had to be.

77

Alucius walked into the Hyalt council chambers in midafternoon on Octdi. The two women and the wiry white-haired man who sat along one side of the long table looked up at him.

"I just thought I'd see how you were doing," Alucius said politely.

"The coin will help," offered Asala, the younger woman, perhaps the age of Alucius's mother.

"That was all?" asked Birtraf. "Much more was given to him, I would judge."

"That was all. I'd guess that he had to pay high prices for the weapons and ammunition, and for the uniforms. Were there any traders who came here with large wagons?"

"There were several. They came on the road from Syan, and their wagons bore the symbol of a silver wheel. I had not seen them before the last spring."

"They probably have most of the coin." Traders from the east, or the north? Ones that no one had seen before? Could they have come all the way from Lustrea? Or could they have been the traders who had become more active in Dekhron? Kustyl had said that they had become far more adventurous and effective. Were they somehow tied in with the ifrits? But why would ifrits need coin?

"Majer . . . how long do you intend to remain in Hyalt?"

"I would judge that it will not be long. I sent my report to Tempre a week ago. That's one reason why we have tried to get as much done as we could."

"For a conqueror, Majer, you have wielded a light lash. I wish that I could say more," offered Asala.

"I'll take that as a compliment," Alucius said. "I only wish that none here had followed Adarat."

"So do we," replied Birtraf, "but where was the Lord-Protector when we needed protection against a false prophet? Waging an unnecessary war in Madrien?"

Alucius had to struggle to bite back a harsh retort. He paused, then replied, "There are always false prophets, and no ruler can protect his people from foolishness." He forced a polite smile. "If you have no more questions . . ."

None of the three offered a word.

"Then, good day. I will let you know when we will be departing." Alucius nodded, turned, and left the chamber.

Why did people always resent a ruler, despite expecting him to protect them from their own stupidity? Then, he reflected, Adarat had used Talent to get people to act against their wills. But what ruler could detect that, let alone fight it?

Alucius walked back to the unofficial officers' quarters as fast as he could. Not that there was any rush, but because it was yet another way of working out his sore muscles, although the majority of his bruises had faded into a pale yellow and purple.

Two Southern Guard lancers stood waiting inside the foyer of the dwelling. Both stiffened to attention as Alucius entered.

"Majer, sir!" snapped the older, extending an envelope. "A dispatch from Marshal Frynkel, sir."

Alucius took the envelope, forcing a pleasant smile. "Thank you. Our quarters, for now, are in the inn on the square. Once I've read this, I'll have a response. It's not likely to be immediate."

"Yes, sir." The dispatch rider cleared his throat. "We're to wait for a response."

"I'm sure that waiting at the inn will prove far more comfortable. You've had a long and a hard ride. I'll make sure you know as soon as my reply is ready."

"Yes, sir."

Neither dispatch rider said a word even after they had stepped outside. Alucius took the still-sealed envelope through the archway into the front parlor and study. There, he used his belt knife to slit the end of the envelope. There were two pages inside. The first sheet was a dispatch addressed to Alucius. He began to read.

Majer Alucius—
Congratulations and our deepest appreciation for your most effective efforts. Your report on the resolution of the unrest in Hyalt was most welcome news to the Lord-Protector, and he has asked me to convey his great and deep appreciation for your efforts . . .

Alucius stiffened. When someone else was conveying appreciation, there was trouble ahead, or words that he needed to peruse most carefully. He continued reading.

He was also most pleased at the comparatively low casualties, for which you are also to be most highly commended, for qualified lancers are most urgently needed.

I must regretfully inform you that the Regent of the Matrial has undertaken a massive assault against our forces surrounding Southgate and that Marshal Wyerl has perished in battles to the north of Southgate in the defense of the city and the port. Marshal Alyniat has taken over the defenses and has rushed all available lancers westward to combat her forces and crystal spear-throwers.

In this time of crisis, when all the lands east of Madrien are threatened, the Lord-Protector requests that you complete what you can within the next two days in setting Hyalt back on the proper path toward rebuilding. Upon that timely conclusion, he would ask your sufferance to take your force to Zalt and from there to Southgate, to place yourself and your companies under the command of Marshal Alyniat or the commanding marshal, of course, as you see fit as a loyal officer of the Northern Guard.

If you choose to accept this request, the attached formal orders are yours to use as necessary.

The dispatch was signed by Marshal Frynkel, Acting Arms-Commander of Lanachrona.

Alucius looked at the last few words, once more, before rereading the entire sheet. Then he took out the second sheet and read it. Those orders directed him to report to Marshal Alyniat or the commanding marshal. If he found no marshal in command, he was to coordinate with the officer in charge at his own discretion. That, in itself, was frightening.

It also made him more than a little angry. He had a wife who was expecting a child, and once more he was being forced into riding off and solving another problem that wasn't of his making. And if he didn't, both Wendra and Alendra—and most of the Iron Valleys—would probably suffer.

"What is it?"

Alucius looked up to see Feran standing in the archway to the study.

"I heard that we'd gotten some dispatch riders," Feran offered. "I'd hoped we'd get some word on when we could head back to Dekhron."

"That might be a little difficult," Alucius said. "We've been 'requested' to try to save the Lord-Protector in Southgate."

"What? He's not in Southgate, is he?"

"No . . . but the Regent of the Matrial is pressing toward the city, and Marshal Wyerl has been killed. Alyniat has taken over command there, and Frynkel is now Arms-Commander of Lanachrona."

"Smells worse than a putrefying sow's belly . . ." muttered Feran. "Do we have any choices?"

"It's *only* a request." Alucius snorted. "Yes, we could choose to ignore it or decline it. Then what?"

"We'd stay alive," Feran suggested. "We wouldn't get chopped up in a war between a desperate ruler and a crazy woman."

"What about the two Southern Guard Companies? They'd get sent there right away and get chopped up. And where would that stipend of yours go when they discharged you on the spot when we got back to Dekhron?"

"You could refuse . . . you don't need a stipend," Feran pointed out.

"I could, and the Lord-Protector could pull every company of Northern Guards south to save Southgate or even Tempre, if it comes to that. It might, because the Regent has two of those spear-throwers and is using them both in

the south. Then, within seasons, if not weeks, I'd have neither family nor stead, either because we'd be overrun or
we'd have no one to sell nightsilk to."

"Majer . . ." Feran's voice carried a trace of resignation
with the irony. "You're always pointing out these small un-
pleasantnesses. You won't even let me entertain a brief
dream that someone might keep their word or reward us for
a job well done."

"Desperate rulers don't reward anyone."

"I know." Feran shook his head. "We'll ride out on
Decdi."

"Londi. According to this, we get two full days to complete our work, and if we're headed west, we need every
moment to make sure we're ready." Alucius also needed to
write a final report on Hyalt—and he wanted to make sure
that the Lord-Protector knew about the merchants with the
silver wheel emblem who had skimmed off golds from the
prophet's coffers.

Feran nodded slowly.

Alucius had no idea what it took to get ready to fight
something like a crystal spear-thrower. He certainly hadn't
been that successful the first time. But then, he hadn't
known much about Talent.

Would what he had learned help? He had no doubt that
he'd find out. His lips tightened, and he had to take a deep
breath in order to try to relax some. The tension didn't help
his still-sore muscles.

78

  Londi morning was cool, almost chilly,
with a misty drizzle drifting in from the northwest off the
distant Coast Range. Four Fifth Company lancers waited in
front of the quarters as Alucius strapped his gear behind
the gray's saddle and then mounted, easing his mount be-

side Feran. Then the two rode toward the main square, where Fifth Company was already forming up.

Alucius, as a matter of habit, used his Talent to scan the area, but even with the reduced population of Hyalt, there were far too many bodies for his skills to sort out any who might be dangerous. All he could determine was that there were no ordered groups anywhere around the square—except for Fifth Company.

"I'd be a lot happier to leave here if we were headed north of the Vedra, north and east especially," Feran said quietly.

"So would we all. Life isn't always that accommodating."

"You mean rulers aren't," Feran suggested.

Alucius offered a wry smile and a nod.

The two officers reined up on the north end of the square, waiting for the last of the squad leaders to report to Egyl.

"Fourth squad, present and accounted for."

"Fifth squad, present and accounted for."

Egyl turned and rode the few yards to Feran, reining up and reporting, "Fifth Company, present and accounted for, sir. Ready to ride."

"Thank you," Feran said, turning to Alucius. "Ready to ride, Majer."

"Let's go."

"Fifth Company! By squads! Forward!"

Fifth Company rode at a comfortable walk out of the square on the ancient eternastone pavement that was the high road north toward Tempre. Six days ahead lay the intersection with the southwest high road to Zalt—and Southgate beyond.

A block out of the square, on the left side of the wide street that was also the high road, stood the three members of the temporary council, watching as the lancers passed. Not a one spoke or gestured as Fifth Company passed.

"Not terribly friendly," Feran observed.

"I don't know as I would be, were I in their boots," observed Alucius. "We killed hundreds of their husbands and sons and brothers. To them, it doesn't matter that we didn't have much of a choice."

"Suppose they didn't, either." Feran shook his head. "Talent's a bad thing all around. Seems like you and the other herders are the only ones ever used it right. Everyone else is using it to kill or conquer or enslave someone else. What's the difference with herders?"

Before answering, Alucius surveyed the dwellings and shops on both sides of the avenue. More than half still appeared deserted, but even those that seemed to hold inhabitants were run-down, with stucco chipped away, and dingy walls whose whitewash had long since turned to yellowed white or pinkish white. The dilapidation had clearly existed for years before the prophet had taken hold of Hyalt.

Had the decline of Hyalt, and the poverty that had crept in, made the prophet's efforts that much easier? Or had he been there all along, undermining the town's prosperity? Or had the latest prophet been the one? When they were all called Adarat, how could he tell? Alucius hadn't been able to get a straight answer from anyone, and doubted that he ever would. Or that anyone would.

"I don't know as herders are any different from other folks in how they feel," Alucius said slowly. "Except in one thing. They love the land and being one with it. The land is more important than they are. It's bigger than they are. Maybe that makes a difference, believing in something bigger than golds, or a dwelling, or power over people."

"You think that's true of *all* herders?"

"No," Alucius admitted. "Only those that survive as herders."

"You've never wanted to be a lancer, have you?"

"Only because I wanted to keep the stead."

"That's the hold they have over you—the land, isn't it?"

"For a herder, that's a powerful hold," Alucius pointed out. The image of the Aerlal Plateau rising in the east, over the endless vingts of sand and quarasote, appeared in his mind, and he wished he were there with Wendra, with the flock, and with his family. He took a slow, deep breath. If he did not succeed in the weeks ahead, he would not ever have that opportunity.

"If all rulers were herders, then, maybe we wouldn't have all this fighting." Feran's words were light, but not quite humorous.

"Who knows?" Alucius countered. "It won't ever happen."

"Probably not," Feran agreed.

Alucius did not reply. As he rode northward through the light drizzle toward the camp where they would pick up the Southern Guard companies, Alucius could not help but think about Hyalt and what had happened there. One man, had appeared, something other than a man but less than the ifrits he had seen, and he had turned a functioning town, not the most prosperous, but not the poorest or meanest, either, into a collection of followers without wills. Was that what the temptation of Talent in its strongest manifestations led to?

79

The drizzle and the mist had lasted for two days, then dissipated during the morning after the three companies had left the manned way station at Ceazan, along with Elbard and some of the wounded likely to recover over the ride to Southgate. Alucius had also sent off his final report on Hyalt from there, along with an apologetic letter to Wendra, explaining only that he had been ordered to deal with other matters that affected their future and safety, and that he was most unhappy to be away from the stead at such length.

Four days later, they had turned onto the west high road, then a half day later southwest onto the high road that would lead through the Coast Range and into what had been southern Madrien, eventually to Zalt, then to Southgate. Two days after starting southwest on the high road to the coast, under a cool fall sun, they were nearing the eastern side of the Coast Range. Thirty-fifth Company was in the van, and Alucius rode beside Jultyr.

"You know . . . things in Hyalt could have turned really nasty, especially that night when that prophet used Talent to put everyone into a deep sleep." Jultyr frowned. "How did you and the overcaptain manage to wake up?"

"I had a nightmare about being unable to move," Alucius admitted. "It took a long time to wake up. It took longer to rouse enough lancers to fight off the attack. If they'd brought a full company . . . things would have been very bad." Just how bad, Alucius had considered more than a few times. He'd also wondered about how he would ever deal with the ifrits if he ever had to face more than one at a time.

"Good thing they didn't," affirmed Jultyr. "Can't say I'm all that pleased to be heading west so soon. A lot of the men are going to have the wrong idea about fighting from dealing with the rebels."

"That blade cuts two ways. The Matrites fight better than the rebels, and they have better weapons and training, but most of them won't keep coming with wounds gaping open."

"That's true," mused Jultyr. "What about that knife-thrower? Have you seen that?"

"Yes. It's more like a spear-thrower. It fires a stream of crystal spears about a half yard long. One time they chopped away a hill with it and flushed out a whole company of foot."

"You were there?"

"That was when they invaded the Iron Valleys." Alucius decided against mentioning that he'd been wounded and captured in the battle to destroy the weapon. Or that he only had the vaguest idea of how the weapon had been destroyed.

"They've got two of them now. That was what Dostak said. Wager that they're both near Southgate."

"I won't take that wager."

"That's the problem with being a lancer," Jultyr went on. "You do a good job, and what happens? They give you something worse." The older captain shook his head. "You can't risk doing a bad job, 'cause that might kill you, but sometimes the lancers who survive doing it badly make out better than the good ones. They get assigned to trade stations or as orderlies somewhere."

"There's some truth in that." Alucius shifted his weight in the saddle. Most of the time now, he didn't notice the residual stiffness and soreness, but every so often something twinged, reminding him that he still wasn't fully healed.

"More 'n a little," said Jultyr. "You been awarded every decoration in three lands, and here you are, headed back against the Matrites. You did too good a job, sir. Look where it got you."

"We did the job in Hyalt," Alucius replied, ignoring the references to his previous accomplishments. "It took all three companies. Any less, and the prophet would have overrun us."

"We won't be running into much Talent with the Matrites, do you think?"

"They didn't have much before. We can hope that they don't now." Two crystal spear-throwers would be more than enough to cause misery and death. Of that, Alucius was certain.

80

Tempre, Lanachrona

The Lord-Protector stepped past the guards into his private apartments, throwing the door bolt behind him. His boot heels echoed on the marble of the foyer, carrying ahead of him into the sitting room where Alerya sat with young Talus in her lap, both mother and son bathed in the warm glow from the lamps set on the end tables on either side of the love seat.

"Here comes your father . . . can you say, 'Da!'?" Alerya turned toward the Lord-Protector, but did not rise.

Talus smiled and gurgled.

Alerya's smile faded as she beheld Talryn's face. "I'm sorry. Whatever it is, it must have been a very bad day."

"They're all bad now, except when I'm with you." The Lord-Protector smiled warmly at his consort and son, but the smile faded. He stepped forward to the love seat, then bent down and scooped his son from his consort's arms. "How's my boy? Did you have a good day?" His arms enfolded his son.

"He's usually good. He was a little fussy. I think he might be getting his first teeth." Alerya stood. "Would you like some wine?"

"I'd like the whole decanter, but I'd pay for it later." Talryn smiled once more at Talus. "Wouldn't I, young fellow?" He shifted his son to his shoulder, patting his back. "It's good to see you in such fine fettle."

"Talryn . . . he just ate . . ."

Alerya's voice died away with Talus's satisfied burp.

"Oh, dear . . . that was a good tunic," Alerya said, taking Talus back and handing the Lord-Protector a square of white cotton. "Perhaps . . . if you hurry . . ."

Talryn laughed, taking the cloth and doing what he could to wipe away the damage. "At least, he doesn't know any better. Unlike my marshals and advisors."

After folding the soiled cloth and setting it on the nearest end table, the Lord-Protector moved to the side table, where he stood and poured half a glass of a deep red wine into the waiting goblet.

"Do you want to tell me?" Alerya asked.

"Who else can I tell? Honestly, that is?" He took a sip of the wine. "You recall Majer Alucius?"

"The herder majer, the one you owe?"

"You won't ever fail to remind me of that, will you?"

"No. I feel we owe him even more, but I cannot say why, and it is not wise for a ruler to forget what he owes and to whom."

"You're right, dear. That is why I am not in the best of moods. I found out that Frynkel, that paragon of duty, used my seal and ordered Majer Alucius to Southgate." Talryn set his goblet on the side table.

"Frynkel did what?" asked Alerya. "I can't believe he sent an order under your seal without your approval. How could he? How could he dare?"

"It wasn't exactly an order. He was more clever than that. It was a request from me. A request, almost begging. He was quite proud of it. Oh . . . sometimes, the legacies that we bear."

"What will you do?"

"What he expects. A reprimand and dismissal for him if Majer Alucius succeeds, and Frynkel's execution if Alucius fails."

"He would expect execution?"

"He might. He might not. It is a measure of our situation that he would do this, knowing how I feel. No matter how desperate the situation . . . Frynkel deserves execution. At the least, I should sign my own requests, do my own treachery." Talryn's voice was cold. "Yet . . . there is no one half so well qualified as Frynkel left."

"Can't you change the order?"

"Majer Alucius is almost in Zalt. What will happen will happen."

"You really are desperate, dearest, aren't you?"

"I have no more lancers to spend. I've lost my best marshal. For all I know, I've already lost Alyniat as well."

"Couldn't you just have the lancers retreat to the old borders?"

"I could. Then I would have to have them fight the Matrites there without Majer Alucius. Perhaps in weeks at worst, in a year at best. And I would have both those crystal spear-throwers sent at Tempre. The Regent is far worse than the Matrial was . . . far worse." Talryn laughed. "That is why one removes a ruler at some risk. One never knows who may succeed. Not that I had the slightest to do with the mysterious death of the Matrial."

"It is unlikely that the majer can save our forces, is it not?"

"Unlikely, yes. It is not impossible. He has accomplished the impossible before. More than once, I suspect. It is indeed impossible to hold on to Southgate and the southern high road without him. And that is what is so miserable and unfortunate about Marshal Frynkel's 'request' under my seal. I suppose I'm as angry at my own weakness as at his actions. Frynkel knows that I hesitate to do the less than honorable, and he knew that we could not delay, not and have any hope of success in saving Southgate."

"Is it that vital?"

"The Praetor of Lustrea is building up his forces to take Illegea and Ongelya, then Deforya. Or perhaps the other way around. When all is done, there will be but two lands controlling Corus. We will be one of them, or we will be dead." Talryn shrugged. "I did not create this situation. The Matrial and the old Praetor and perhaps Aellyan Edyss shoved the first stones out of their positions and began the avalanche, even before I became Lord-Protector. I have been dealing with what they began, and my choices have always been few."

"They are all dead. Does that not tell you something?"

"Yes, my dear. It tells me that I must be most careful." He eased Talus from Alerya's arms and into his own. "It tells me that I must enjoy those loves and pleasures that I have, for each season may be the last." He gently wrapped his arms around his son for several moments, then straightened and let Alerya take Talus. "I suppose we should eat. There is little need to suffer hunger as well."

"Talus will be up for a time."

"He can stay with us, can he not?"

Alerya smiled softly. "Of course."

The three walked toward the small private dining room.

81

On a Septi afternoon, seven days after starting through the Coast Range, Alucius was riding with Feran at the head of the column. His past knowledge of the back roads and old lumber camps in the Coast Range and the western hills below had proved useful in finding several encampments with some shelter and water. He'd never mentioned it, just sent out scouts to various places, and most of them had reported what he had recalled.

Now, the valley holding Zalt spread out before them to the west.

"You can see Senob Post to the right of the high road, just before this road intersects with the range road from the north. Senob was what they called it then, anyway." Even without standing in the stirrups, Alucius could make out the redstone walls, high enough to be visible from at least four vingts away. "The town is all in the northwest quarter of where the two high roads join. The range road ends about a hundred yards beyond the junction. I always wondered if the builders had meant to go farther south and had been working on the road when the Cataclysm struck."

Feran looked at him.

"I was stationed here once," Alucius said. "Remember?"

"I knew you were a Matrite captive squad leader. You never said where."

"Here and in Hieron, but just for a short time there."

"Then you know more about what's west?"

Alucius shook his head. "I know most of the back roads between Zalt and the old border to the east, but I never went farther west than a few vingts from Zalt. I know the road north from here, but not the coast road." He turned in the saddle. "Egyl? Were you always in the north?"

"Yes, sir. Except the one time we went to Hafin. So far

as I know, none of the veterans you brought back were ever in the south."

"Thank you." Alucius turned back to Feran.

"Are you sure that all these places aren't what turned your hair gray?" Feran's expression and tone were deadpan, but Alucius could sense the amusement behind the lack of expression.

"No. I was just born worried. Herders are, you know."

"For someone so worried, you're awfully eager to get into nasty positions."

"That's only to avoid nastier ones," Alucius quipped back.

"You're still an optimist, I see."

"Always."

As they neared the former Senob Post, the road flattened, and they rode past weathered earthen berms to the south—the site of a former Southern Guard attack base, one that Alucius remembered all too well. His lips curled into a faint and ironic smile.

Before that long, they were approaching the post itself, almost a vingt east of where the high roads intersected. The post had walls half a vingt on a side and four yards high. The heavy timbered gates were bound with dark iron and were open. Each was only about three yards wide. The paving stones of the approach lane and the courtyard were dusty, and there were faint streaks of rust on the huge iron hinges of the gates. As he rode through the gates, Alucius scanned the second, inner gates, designed to be closed by sliding forward along channels in the stone paving. He could see all too much sand and grit in the channels, and those channels had always been clean when Alucius was a Matrite squad leader.

They had barely reined up in the wide, stone-paved courtyard when four lancers and a gray-haired colonel appeared, moving quickly.

Alucius recognized him. "Colonel Jesopyr. Majer Alucius. We're under orders to Southgate and Marshal Alyniat."

"Majer Alucius! I had heard that we might be seeing

some reinforcements headed to Southgate, but I hadn't expected you. And a majer now!" Jesopyr beamed. "Not that you're not most welcome. Most welcome."

Alucius smiled wryly. "We have three companies here, the Fifth from the Northern Guard, and the Twenty-eighth and Thirty-fifth from the Southern Guard. The Lord-Protector prevailed upon me."

"I imagine he did." Jesopyr looked to Feran and back to Alucius. "You and your overcaptain will be our honored guests for the evening meal. You'd be our guests in any case, but you're most honored. It's scarcely every day we have the only officer who's won the stars of three nations and lived to tell of it. I even have a few bottles of a good vintage left."

"We'll enjoy that. As I said, we've got three companies here. Can you handle that?"

"We're down to three squads. I doubt you'll be a problem. Jeron and Ghujil here will help get your men settled. The officers' quarters aren't bad, and they're in the wing just ahead. There aren't any senior officers' quarters, so pick whatever empty rooms suit you."

"Thank you."

The two lancers stepped forward.

"The stables are ahead and to the right," Alucius said.

"Column, forward!"

Alucius left Feran and the captains to sort out quarters for the lancers and squad leaders. After unsaddling and grooming the gray, he quickly took one of the vacant officer's rooms—he had the feeling it had once been Captain Dynae's, the commander of Thirty-second Company when Alucius had been a Matrite lancer—and headed for the library, on the off chance that some of the maps might have been left, at least the older ones.

As he walked down the stone-floored corridor, he couldn't help but note that the floors were dusty and had lost the gleaming polish of the days when he'd been a Matrite lancer and later a squad leader. Most of the wall lamps were missing from their brackets, and the walls showed smears here and there that Captain Hyrlui would never have tolerated when she had commanded the Matrite outpost. Alucius shook his head. How the years had changed things.

At the end of the corridor, he stopped, then stepped toward the door behind which there had once been a library. He pressed on the lever, and the door opened. He stepped inside, closing the door behind him and looking across the shelves. From what he could tell, the library remained much as he recalled, with even the map racks in one corner. Some of the shelves were emptier than he remembered, but it appeared as though most of the books remained. Alucius found it hard to believe that the library had been left, but then, books were heavy and on short notice hard to burn. Also, they were all written in Madrien, and the library was close to the officers' quarters, which might have discouraged wanton vandalism.

Alucius found that one of the wall lamps actually had oil, and between his belt knife and his Talent, got it clean enough to burn. He put it in the sconce over the desk he'd used years before to study maps, and lit it. Then he began to search for what he needed, stacking the most likely maps and books on one side of the desk.

The first thing he needed to find was to see if the way stations on the highway to Southgate were shown anywhere. Then, he wanted to see if there were topographical maps of the hills around Southgate. He thought there might be, because there had been such maps for all of Madrien, clearly copies of more ancient ones, but most topography didn't change that rapidly.

Almost two glasses passed before the door opened.

Feran peered in the doorway. "Someone said you might be here. What are you doing?"

Alucius did not look up. "Studying the maps for the areas to the west."

"How did you— You've used this library before?"

"Years ago. I hoped it was still here."

Feran stopped and picked up one of the dusty volumes,

opening it, then setting it down. "It's in Madrien . . . I guess."

"They all are," Alucius said absently, jotting down the vingtage between back roads on the northeast sector outside Southgate.

"You read Madrien, too?"

"I learned when I was here."

"I should have known . . ." Feran shook his head. "I suppose you've read every book in here."

"No. Some of them. Pretty near all the histories and map books. Some of the tactics manuals."

"We're supposed to be in the mess before long. The colonel seems fond of you."

"I like him. He's honest and says what he means. They were smart to put him in charge of the outpost here." Alucius jotted down the last of the figures. "I may have to take some of these maps. No one else seems to have known they were here."

"How would they?"

"They could have looked," Alucius suggested, rising from behind the map desk. "Let me go wash up, and I'll join you in a moment."

"You keep thinking that the rest of us should be as bright as you are, Majer, reading and speaking three languages, and . . . whatever . . ." Feran snorted. "We aren't. We're just poor lancer officers who didn't want to be crafters or holders, slaving until we died."

Alucius stopped. He looked at Feran. "I'm sorry. I shouldn't have been short."

"You weren't short . . . but sometimes you forget . . ." Feran left the words hanging.

"I won't be long."

As he headed for the washroom, Alucius considered Feran's words. He certainly didn't think he was that much brighter than most officers. There was so much he didn't know, and it made sense to figure out as much as possible before it was too late. But he had been born with advantages—his grandsire, for one, and his mother, for another.

And he'd gained another advantage with Wendra. Feran was right. Most lancers were in either the Northern Guard or Southern Guard because their alternatives were worse. The Guard life was better than what they had known. For Alucius, it was to be handled as a means to holding on to what he had outside the Guard, and his life outside the Guard was better than in it.

He washed quickly and was relieved to get a smile from Feran when he rejoined the older officer outside the mess.

"The colonel said something about good wine?" asked Feran.

"He offered very good wine when he was in charge of Krost Post."

"I could use some."

"Sirs?"

Alucius turned to see Deotyr and Jultyr walking down the inside corridor toward them.

The four entered the mess together to find Colonel Jesopyr and a captain waiting.

"Colonel," offered Alucius.

"Majer. This is a treat for Captain Kuttyr and me," added the colonel. "These days, our mess usually is just the two of us."

"We're happy to enlarge your table," Alucius declared. "In fact, we'll be here for another day, if at all possible. We've been on the road for nearly two weeks, and—"

"Say no more! You and your men are more than welcome." Jesopyr walked to the table against the wall. There he picked up one of the ten or so amber-colored bottles set at the back. He twisted the corkscrew, then pulled out the cork. "This is one of the best reds. That is," he added apologetically, "one of the best reds that a Southern Guard officer could cart here." He opened a second bottle as well, then gestured. "Do be seated. Majer . . . here, Overcaptain . . . You captains sit where you want."

Jesopyr stepped back to the table and half filled the plain glass goblet before Alucius, then filled the other five goblets, emptying the first bottle in the process. Then he lifted his own goblet. "To our guests. May they travel to South-gate in health and once more serve the cause of freedom both effectively and successfully, and may we see them all upon their safe return."

"Thank you." Alucius lifted his own goblet. "And to your hospitality."

The wine was good, but even Alucius could tell it was not as good as what the colonel had been able to offer at Krost years earlier. Then, it was far better than anything Alucius had tasted in some time, except for the white wine at Krost on the way to Hyalt.

"The food is somewhat plainer here," the colonel said.

A pair of troopers in white jackets appeared. The plates they set before each officer held a single round slice of something, covered with a dark glaze.

"Cactus heart, with berry glaze," explained Jesopyr. "No one in Madrien knows how good it is, and so we have it to ourselves."

Alucius wondered if it tasted like prickle, and took a small slice to begin with. He was relieved that it was melonlike in taste, if somewhat crunchy.

"If I might ask, Majer . . . did you have the opportunity to stop at Krost Post?"

"We did, sir. That was where Twenty-eighth and Thirty-fifth Companies joined us. We did some joint training there with Captain Deotyr and Jultyr." Alucius inclined his head in the direction of the two captains. "Colonel Jorynst had said you'd been posted west, but he didn't seem to know where."

"Jorynst wouldn't know where his head was if it weren't attached, and that assistant of his, Fedosyr, wasn't any better. I tried to get Fedosyr discharged, but headquarters would never listen. Had friends in Tempre, I guess. I never was much for that." Jesopyr snorted. "Thought he was a duelist. Always provoking quarrels. Best thing about being sent here was leaving him behind."

Feran was having trouble concealing a smile, Alucius realized.

"Did you see Fedosyr?" asked the colonel, looking at Alucius.

"Yes, sir."

"I have the feeling I'm missing something, Majer, and, knowing you, it's something I might enjoy." Jesopyr turned to Feran. "The majer can be quite reticent about his own accomplishments. Perhaps you could enlighten me."

Feran looked at Alucius, then gave the slightest of shrugs. "Majer Alucius felt that the new companies did not understand the capabilities of a trained lancer company. He issued all three companies rattan wands and held exercises. Majer Fedosyr took some offense and insisted on a personal demonstration match with Majer Alucius. Marshal Frynkel was at Krost Post and also insisted on the demonstration. Majer Alucius disarmed Majer Fedosyr quickly with rattan. Fedosyr claimed that the rattan was at fault and insisted on true sabres. Majer Alucius disarmed him even faster. Majer Fedosyr pulled a hidden pistol and shot Majer Alucius. Majer Alucius, although wounded, killed Majer Fedosyr with one slash."

"Better death than the sandsnake deserved," Jesopyr replied. "Officers like that give the Guard a bad name. Where was what's his name—Jorynst—during all this?"

"He was absent," Alucius said, "but Marshal Frynkel accepted his resignation the next morning."

"Would have loved to see it." The colonel laughed. The laugh died out. "That Frynkel . . . if he weren't so devoted to Lanachrona, he'd be as bad as Fedosyr. Probably set the whole thing up to get rid of them both so that he could claim to Fedosyr's friends that the snake did himself in. Fedosyr did, of course. From what they say, not an officer in three lands can match you, Majer."

"I've been fortunate," Alucius demurred.

"Ha! You're the kind who makes his own luck. So . . . after they carted off Fedosyr's miserable carcass, what happened?"

"We rode to Hyalt and destroyed the prophet and his rebels," Alucius said. "We were trying to get the town back together when we received the Lord-Protector's request. So here we are."

"Just like that? Like you rode to Deforya and killed four thousand nomads?"

"The rebels were a little easier," Alucius admitted.

Jesopyr looked to Feran. "Overcaptain?"

"The rebels were easier, sir," Feran replied. "The majer brought down a mountain on them, but he had to be on top of it to do it, and . . . well, he was laid up for a day or two. Not like a month when he got flamed by the pteridons he killed."

"Always love to see a fighting officer . . ."

While Alucius enjoyed Jesopyr's frank openness and hospitality, he wanted to change the subject, and quickly. "What can you tell us about the fighting around Southgate? And here?"

"None of it's good. Not so bad as it could be . . ." Jesopyr waited as the lancer servers cleared the empty plates and replaced them with cleaner larger plates, then brought in several serving platters. "Mountain antelope, and had to make do with rice and some other stuff . . ."

Knowing the colonel, Alucius was certain that the dish would be more than just making do. "You were saying, sir?"

"Oh . . . two Southern Guard companies holding on just south of Dimor. Matrites used one of their knife-throwers to level the gates of the compound there. Once they took the place back . . . it seems like nothing much else happened. The Matrites repaired the garrison and added some lancers and foot, but what they did with that cursed weapon . . . who knows? I don't know how long those two companies can hold the road up there, because Marshal Alyniat pulled the other four to Southgate. Could be that the Regent just left enough to keep Dimor and sent all the rest of her companies south to take Southgate. Now that they've got two of those Talent-cursed knife-throwers here in the south to attack Southgate, it's going to be a mess.

We've had to pull back. Wyerl had Fola, lock, stock, and hogshead, and then they surprised him with one of the knife-throwers. Cut down him and four companies in moments. Said that the air was a bloody fog . . ."

Alucius had seen that in the battles for Soulend. He'd hoped never to see it again.

". . . had to pull back, of course. We still hold the southwest high road, and Alyniat's in command now. Reports are that the Matrites are pulling most of their lancers out of the north, riding them south in preparation for the battle to take Southgate. We don't know how many, but it's more than we've got." Jesopyr shrugged. "That's what I've gotten from the dispatches and the dispatch riders."

"Do you know if they have any Talent-wielders as well?" asked Feran.

"No one's said anything like that. Why?"

"Well . . . there seems to be some of that happening. This prophet in Hyalt was a Talent-wielder," Feran explained.

"Ah . . . that's why they brought in you northerners. Herders are better at fighting Talent. You have to deal with those creatures . . . what are they?"

"Sandwolves and sanders," Alucius said.

"Talent—that's not good." Jesopyr took another sip of wine, then a bite of his antelope before continuing. "No . . . we haven't heard about the Matrites using Talent. Unless those knife-throwers are somehow powered by Talent."

"They're not," Alucius said. "They're nasty enough that you'd think so, but they're copies of ancient weapons."

"Hope they don't come up with more of those. What we've got kills enough."

Alucius could agree with that, silently, as he took another sip of the wine, continuing to listen to the colonel.

82

In the dim light cast by a single oil lamp set in a battered bronze wall sconce, the stocky figure in dark blue studied the oblong Table that stood in the middle of the underground room, a room whose stone walls had been reinforced with goldenstone pillars salvaged from elsewhere. Then, he stepped up to the edge of the Table, and his brow furrowed. A faint purplish glow appeared in the center of the Table, coming from a single purple point of light, then slowly expanded until the entire surface of the Table glowed purple.

Waleryn took a deep breath. The glow vanished. He blotted his damp forehead and stood before the Table, continuing to breathe deeply.

After a time, he looked down at the Table once more. This time, the glow that suffused the Table was even. With the faintest of smiles, he concentrated.

Above the surface of the Table, a grid appeared. A handful of sections were in purple, but the majority were red. Waleryn studied the grid. Then, another small section changed from red to purple. A moment later, the entire grid vanished.

Waleryn nodded and looked into the reflective surface of the Table, where crimson mists appeared.

An image appeared, that of a dark-haired and pale-faced man, an image that, in the Table, carried a purplish tinge. The image was that of Trezun. Trezun's eyes widened slightly, and then he smiled.

In turn, Waleryn smiled, and concentrated.

A miniature image of the grid that he had called up moments earlier appeared, seemingly deep within the Table.

Waleryn looked at the image in the Table—that of Trezun—and made a gesture.

Trezun nodded and extended a long-fingered hand. The grid shimmered and vanished.

Both figures smiled.

Then the Table blanked, returning to its silvery reflective surface.

Waleryn took a long, deep breath, then blotted his forehead, before turning away from the Table, which continued to glow after he left the chamber.

83

After leaving Zalt, Alucius and the three companies rode for another five days. As they crossed the warm and dry grasslands southwest of Zalt, lands that verged on desert, he was glad that he had insisted on taking an extra day of rest at Zalt for the lancers—and their mounts. He was also grateful for the maps and his studies of them, because he was able to plan their stops to take advantage of the former Matrite way stations—and their wells. Both way stations and wells were useful in the lands to the southwest, especially during fall, because, as Alucius recalled, the early weeks of autumn were especially dry. The rains would not come until close to the turn of the new year—and winter.

In the late morning on Tridi, Rakalt came riding back down the high road, pulling his mount in beside Alucius.

"What is it?" asked Alucius.

"Looked to be Southern Guard scouts, sir. Except it's a full squad, almost a road patrol."

"It probably is. They may be worried that the Matrites are coming this way. We'd better bring out the banners, fly them up front in the van." Alucius turned to Feran. "I think it would be best if Fifth Company moved into the middle, and we brought Thirty-fifth Company to the fore. Best we have Southern Guard uniforms up front and in the rear."

"What happened to the trusting young officer I once knew?" asked Feran.

"He vanished about five injuries ago," replied Alucius. "He also still doesn't fully trust the intelligence of some Southern Guards."

"That's wise."

"Column, halt!"

The order echoed back. Shortly, Thirty-fifth Company had taken the van, and Jultyr rode beside Alucius. The two standard-bearers were a good fifty yards ahead, and Alucius had pulled back the scouts to only two hundred yards before the standards.

Before long in the distance on the high road, Alucius could see riders. Their approach was slow, and cautious, and it was a good half a glass before the Southern Guard squad leader reined up short of Alucius, who had halted his companies. The squad leader, with a fifteen-man squad drawn up farther back, was plainly confused at seeing both the Northern and Southern Guard banners, and a Northern Guard majer at the head of a Southern Guard force.

"Majer Alucius, squad leader. I've been dispatched personally by the Lord-Protector to report to Marshal Alyniat with these three companies."

"Sir . . . I'm sure you'll be more than welcome."

"I've fought here before. That's one reason why the Lord-Protector sent me," Alucius said. While his words weren't totally accurate, he didn't feel like trying to explain in detail.

"Yes, sir." The man still looked bewildered.

"I'm the one who fought the barbarians in Deforya several years back. Because I've worked with the Southern Guard, and there aren't any more Southern Guard lancers to send besides these companies, the Lord-Protector sent me." Alucius used his Talent to project reassurance.

The squad leader glanced to Jultyr, and his face relaxed, probably even before the Talent fully affected him.

"We just finished putting down the revolt in Hyalt, Kisner," Jultyr explained. "The majer took out over a hundred by himself. Dropped a mountain on them. Set the charges and took 'em out."

"The revolt's over?"

"It's dead. So are about a thousand rebels," Jultyr pointed out.

"Good to hear one problem's out of the way," Kisner said.

"What does it look like ahead?" Alucius asked.

"The Matrites are pouring south from everywhere in the north."

"Where is Marshal Alyniat?"

"We're just a road patrol, sir. Out here to make sure they're not flanking us. Last time we heard, the marshal was at the Fola high road fort. That's about fifteen vingts north of the city."

Thirteen and a half vingts, according to Alucius's calculations. "Then that's where we'll be heading. Is the northeast ring road still clear?"

The squad leader's face again reflected surprise. "Ah . . . yes, sir."

"That will make it easier to get to the marshal."

"Yes, sirs." Kisner nodded. "Wish you luck. We need to check farther east. Road back toward Southgate is clear. Least it was earlier, back five vingts."

"Thank you, squad leader," Alucius said. "Best on your patrol."

After a last nod, Kisner and his squad headed eastward, along the shoulder of the high road and past the three companies.

Once the patrol squad was well away, Jultyr cleared his throat. "I apologize, sir, for that explanation. Seemed the only way to make it simple. Kisner's a good man, but . . . he's a fighting lancer. Known him for years."

Alucius understood. "Thank you. It made it easier." He had no doubts that dealing with Alyniat would be much harder, especially if he intended to keep his companies from being squandered in useless fighting.

84

Midmorning on Qattri brought Alucius and his force to the Southern Guard encampment that surrounded the southeast high road fort.

Along the way, Alucius had decided on his approach. There was no sense in merely putting himself and his companies under the command of some colonel and being ordered to destroy as many Matrites as possible. Not when the crystal spear-throwers remained. Without them, as events had proved twice, the Matrites could be handled. With them, the odds were too great that the Lanachronans would lose everything and be pushed out of Southgate—if not slaughtered in massive numbers. So Alucius and his companies had to destroy the replicas of the ancient weapons, if only to avoid being among those slaughtered by them.

That meant the companies had to get Alucius close enough that he could destroy the weapons. How? That he didn't know, but he did know that when the sanders had attacked the Matrites in Soulend, the sanders had used Talent of some sort to destroy the first crystal spear-thrower. So it could be done. He had to hold on to that thought. The soarers had told him—and shown him—that he could do what they did, and they could do more than the sanders. His problem was that he didn't know how . . . and would have to learn by trying.

According to the maps and histories that Alucius had studied, Southgate was surrounded by an irregular arc of hills, and the early seltyrs of Southgate had used slave labor to build up the low spots between the hills and create a stone ring road linking the small hillside forts set at regular intervals along the road. There were two main forts, the one where the southwest high road intersected the ring road, and the one to the west where the coastal—or Fola—high road intersected the ring road.

When Alucius and his force neared the ring road around Southgate, just about midmorning, he could see the road cut ahead. To the right, on the ridge crest, was a large stone-walled fort. To the left was a smaller one. Thick walls ran down from each fort to massive gates, ironbound gates, open for the moment, as Alucius's force rode closer.

A single rider rode toward them, pausing and talking to the banner bearers, and then riding toward Alucius and Jultyr. The rider was a senior squad leader, and Alucius could sense his anxiety as he neared the column.

"Column, halt!" Alucius waited.

"Sir? Your orders, sir?"

Alucius rode forward, and tendered the orders.

The squad leader read them, before handing them back. "Sir . . . you'll have to wait a moment. Undercaptain Girynst will be right here."

"We've got a ways to go, squad leader." Alucius could sense some apprehension, and tension, but nothing he would have considered dangerous—but he still worried.

"Yes, sir. I know, sir."

The squad leader rode back and disappeared into the fortifications surrounding the gates, which remained open.

Alucius studied the hills or ridges that stretched northwest and southeast from the high road. The hills themselves looked like ramparts, even without walls upon them. Then he switched his attention to the gates, but nothing happened except that an undercaptain rode out toward them—alone.

"Sir, your name?"

"Majer Alucius, Northern Guard, commanding Fifth Company, Northern Guard, and Twenty-eighth and Thirty-fifth Companies of the Southern Guard."

"Might I see your orders again, sir?"

Curbing his irritation, Alucius handed the orders back over.

The undercaptain read the orders, then checked the seals

against something he carried, and the orders against something else before handing the orders back. "I apologize, sir, but orders are orders, sir."

"I understand." Alucius understood that people felt that way, but had he or any inventive commander wanted to get through the Lanachronan defenses, there were far easier ways. The ring road was lightly defended most of its length, as opposed to the fortified points at the high road intersections.

"Do you know where you're headed, sir?"

"Only generally, Undercaptain. I know we're supposed to report directly to Marshal Alyniat, and that the ring road west will take us to the coast road fort, and that's where he is and we're supposed to be."

"Yes, sir. You ride through the gates here, and then, about a half vingt beyond them, you take the stone road to the right. At the top of the hill it joins the ring road, and you turn left—that's west—and keep going for . . . well, it's close to fifteen vingts."

"Thank you."

"Yes, sir."

Alucius nodded to Jultyr.

"Column, forward!"

Thirty-fifth Company rode forward, followed by the other two companies and the supply wagons. Passing the massive gates was almost like riding through a stone-walled trench, somehow oppressive, with ancient walls that had to have been built centuries before by the seltyrs of Southgate, or even by the Dramurian lords who had held Southgate before them. Alucius could sense the hidden lancers with rifles and was more than glad to have his forces through the walled road gap and riding uphill to the ridgeline hill road.

Once he reached the ridge top, and the main ring road on the northwest side of the road cut and the high road, Alucius looked back and studied the layout. The ring road split on each side of the road cut, one segment ending at a small fort on the east side of the high road, and a second segment angling gradually down to meet the high road a good half vingt to the south. The same pattern existed on the west side, where Alucius was, except that the one segment provided the entry to the larger ring road fort. The ring road itself was eight yards wide, and the stones showed signs of age, being worn down in spots, and in others showing shallow grooves from years of use by iron-tired wagons. On the flatter land below the larger road fort were tielines and tents—and mounts and men—possibly fifteen companies, if not twenty.

The hills on which the ring road had been built were covered with brown grass waving in the light breeze and occasional patches of scrub oak, but clearly, to Alucius's eyes, they had been kept clear of trees and taller vegetation. With the two banners before the companies, after the interrogation by the undercaptain, no one at the eastern fort had even come out as Alucius had ridden past. While a respite would have been welcome, he knew all too well that some colonel would try to order him where he didn't want to go. That would happen soon enough, Alucius knew.

The ring road from the east slowly swung from angling northwest to heading due west and then, after more than ten vingts, began to descend along a ridge toward the fort guarding the coast high road leading into Southgate. Even from more than a vingt away, Alucius could see the tents and tielines of the Southern Guard on the back side of the hill and in the valley to the south of the ring road.

"Must be fifty companies here, sir," observed Jultyr, riding to Alucius's left.

"And twenty to the east." Alucius took a deep swallow from his water bottle. The afternoon sun beat down on him through a clear sky, providing a warmth that reminded him just how far south he had come.

As they neared the fort itself, Alucius saw that the ring road again followed the same pattern as with the more eastern fort. The thick walls overlooked a road cut where the high road passed between two sides of the ridge. The

stonework and fortifications that ran down the sides of the
cut to the massive gates—as well as the gates themselves—
had obviously been built after the high road, since none of
their construction was eternastone.

Alucius and his force were no more than two hundred
yards from the stone gates to the road fort when several
riders made their way up the angled section of the ring
road from the camp area below the ring road and to the
left. A captain and a colonel were followed by two
lancers.

"You want to stop, Majer?"

"Not until they're almost on us."

They only covered another fifty yards before Alucius ordered, "Column, halt!"

Then he waited as the colonel reined up five yards away.

"Good to see you, Majer. Colonel Hubar. You'll be under my command, and—"

"No, sir," Alucius smiled politely. "My orders place me
directly under the marshal and no one else. If Marshal Alyniat is not here, or is unable to command, I've been ac-
corded equal command status with the remaining senior
officer." Alucius held out the sheet with the orders. "These
are very specific."

"I don't think you understand, Majer. All officers are directed to report to the marshal. You should know that. But
seeing as you're from the Northern Guard . . ."

"Sir, I'd like to suggest that you read these orders."
Alucius tried to project a sense of reasonableness he
didn't feel.

"Majer, I've read orders for years. They're all the same,
and I really don't have time to debate about it. You're under
my command."

"No, sir. In the north, we read orders before we decide."
Alucius smiled pleasantly.

"Majer . . . I must insist."

"Colonel, I must defer. I've read my orders, and you
haven't."

"You're subordinate . . . and you'll behave . . ."

Alucius reached out with his Talent and squeezed the colonel's lifethread, very gently.

The man turned red, then blue. After a moment, he looked at Alucius, fear and anger warring on his face.

"I'm not arguing, Colonel. I'm carrying out the Lord-Protector's orders. Now . . . can you direct me toward the marshal?"

"You . . ."

"For what it's worth, I'm the third most senior officer in the Northern Guard. We're not exactly blessed with colonels and marshals. The Lord-Protector knows that, and he personally requested my presence here. Now . . . Marshal Alyniat?"

"You can't take Southern Guards . . ."

"I also hold a commission in the Southern Guard. Would you like to see that?" Alucius's voice was like ice, and he projected absolute power and authority.

The colonel looked coldly at Alucius. "I suppose you have some experience."

Alucius sighed, loudly. "I'm Majer Alucius. For what it's also worth, I'm the one who destroyed Aellyan Edyss. I'm the one who got the last Star of Honor from the Lord-Protector, and I'm the one who just squashed the revolt in Hyalt. And if you put up one more objection, you'll be answering to both the marshal and the Lord-Protector—if there are enough pieces of you left for either to find." Alucius couldn't quite contain the rage he was trying to suppress, despite his efforts to remain civil.

The colonel's face turned ashen. For a moment, he just swallowed. Finally, he spoke. "I apologize, Majer. I spoke in haste. We're very hard-pressed here."

"I understand," Alucius replied, far more gently. "That's why we made haste to get here, and that's why we were given a special assignment. I doubt you or your men would want it. Marshal Alyniat?"

"He's . . ." The colonel took a deep breath. "He's in the fort. Second level."

As they rode on, Alucius could hear a few of the low murmurs, first from the captain,

". . . who . . . he think he is?"

". . . just who he said . . . be either dead or untouchable in a week . . ."

Alucius suspected the first was more likely, but death was certain if he did not stick to his own plans.

Then came the murmurs from Thirty-fifth Company, so low that he could not have heard them without Talent.

". . . never seen that before . . . colonel turned white . . ."

". . . beginning to see why they sent him . . ."

". . . colonel . . . he'll never forgive . . ."

". . . last majer and colonel tangled with him . . . one's stipended . . . other's dead . . ."

Alucius had to wonder how someone in the ranks knew that Jorynst had been stipended out, but then, as a ranker, he'd known more than a few things officers had wished he hadn't.

"The Northern Guard doesn't like fools, does it?" asked Jultyr.

"We've had our share of them," Alucius said dryly. "That's why I don't care for them. That's also why I left active service."

"Is it true . . . you're the third highest officer in the Northern Guard?"

"Actually, I was talking faster than I thought," Alucius admitted. "I'm the fourth most senior."

Jultyr chuckled. "That'd make you a majer-colonel or a submarshal in the Southern Guard."

"We're a little smaller. Just twenty companies of lancers." Alucius considered. "But the Iron Valleys were only about a quarter the size of Lanachrona before the union."

The west road fort had not been built to house large numbers of lancers or their mounts. Even before he reached the gates, Alucius could tell that the stables could not have held more than a company, and the narrow barracks perhaps twice that. The walls were of an old graystone, and there were more than a few places where stones had been replaced. Then, as Alucius recalled, at least three different lands had ruled Southgate in the past five centuries.

The courtyard looked to be so small that he ordered the column to halt just outside the gates and rode inside with Rakalt. Once inside, he dismounted, leaving the gray's reins with the scout. He walked up the two steps and through the archway.

Once there, Alucius didn't wait for a reaction, but used his Talent to pour authority at the two lancers standing guard duty just inside the narrow arch.

"I'm looking for Marshal Alyniat. Is he on the second level?"

"Ah . . . yes, sir. But . . ."

"Thank you." Alucius reached the second level, a long marshaling hall. Groups of officers were gathered around tables. One was piled high with maps.

A quick study indicated that the only guarded door was halfway down the hall on the west side, and Alucius set out with a purposeful stride. He almost made it to the pair of guards before he was intercepted by a tall black-haired colonel.

"The marshal's busy . . . Majer."

"I'm certain he is, Colonel." Alucius smiled pleasantly. "My name is Alucius. The Lord-Protector sent me here to provide special assistance to the marshal. I think you should usher me in." Alucius projected friendly firmness, and some authority.

"I said he was busy." Impatience colored the colonel's words, and Alucius could tell the man was put off by the assumption of authority. "Field majers report to Colonel Hubar."

"I'm not a field majer, Colonel," Alucius said politely. "I was sent by the Lord-Protector to report to Marshal Alyniat for a special mission." He showed the orders.

"He said he was not to be disturbed." The colonel ignored the sheet.

"Colonel, why don't you announce me, and we'll see." Alucius didn't know what else to project. It had been a long ride, even the last part from Zalt, and he wasn't thinking as well or as quickly as he should have been. And he could feel his blood beginning to boil at yet another insistent and overbearing colonel.

"Majer . . . we're going to be under attack tomorrow, the next day at the latest."

"That's why you should announce me, Colonel." Alucius was getting very tired of imperious colonels, but he told himself that they were probably tired of arrogant and pushy majers. "If you would, please?"

"Come back late this afternoon."

"It won't wait that long, Colonel. He needs to know that I'm here, and why. It won't take long, but he should know."

"I said later, Majer."

Alucius touched the man's lifethreads hard enough for the colonel to topple forward onto the hard stones. Then he looked at the two guards. "I'd appreciate it if you'd announce me."

The two exchanged looks.

"Majer Alucius, from the Lord-Protector," Alucius supplied. "Just say that. If he doesn't want to see me, I'll leave."

"Ah . . . sir. Know you asked not to be disturbed, but there's a Majer Alucius. Northern Guard, sir. Says he's from the Lord-Protector."

"Show him in."

Alucius smiled, but he held his Talent ready as he stepped through the door that the surprised guard opened.

Amazingly, Alyniat was alone in the small chamber. He turned from the window and smiled. "Majer! I had hoped . . . What happened in Hyalt?"

"The prophet had five companies. We destroyed most of his men, but the revolt isn't anymore. We set up a council of the older women and a few graybeards. Almost no one else was left. Then we set out for Southgate."

"You make it sound easy."

"Getting here, after we finished in Hyalt, was easy. Get-

ting to see you wasn't. I've pushed my way past two of
your colonels. One wanted to shunt me and my forces—"

"Forces?"

"I've got three companies with me, but they're for a special mission."

Alyniat raised his eyebrows.

"Taking out the crystal spear-throwers."

After a split second, the marshal began to laugh, shaking
his head. "Only you . . . a majer . . . taking on colonels . . ."

Alucius smiled. "The Lord-Protector sent specific orders. I report only to you. If anything happens to you, I'm
on equal footing with your successor." Alucius extended
the order sheet.

Alyniat read through the sheet and handed it back, nodding thoughtfully. "It doesn't mention that mission."

"Do you think that the Lord-Protector would put that in
writing, or Marshal Frynkel? The level of authority . . ."

"Frynkel never did like paper trails . . . and under these
circumstances . . ." Alyniat pursed his lips, then ran his
thin fingers through his silvering blond hair. "How do you
propose this mission?" The fingers of his left hand began
to tap on the table, if intermittently.

"There are two of the spear-throwers, I've been told. It
seemed to me that we'd try to deal with the one posing the
most difficulty first. But . . . we just got here, and I've no
idea of the tactical situation."

"We're stretched too thin. They're coming down the
high road from Fola." Alyniat coughed, then cleared his
throat. "They could attack as early as tomorrow, or wait for
days. My best judgment is that they'll attack either Sexdi
or Septi. They haven't waited long when they've attacked
before."

"They'll have to move the spear-thrower into position.
It's heavy."

"What do you know about it?" asked Alyniat.

"The projectiles are more like short spears, half a yard
long, and made of a hard crystal. They can fire in any direction, but only in one direction at a time. They can turn it

across a field so that it slices through everything in its path. It can dig through earthworks, and even thin stone walls. Those take time, though."

"You've fought against them before."

"Yes."

"How do you propose to take something that fearsome out? If I might ask?"

"Very carefully," Alucius replied. "To do it, it will have to be operating, and that means we'll need to do some scouting to find out exactly where it is and will be. I'd guess it will be used to lead an assault."

"Do you need all three companies?"

"Do you want me to take out the spear-thrower, sir?"

"Fair enough." Alyniat lifted his thin blond eyebrows. "You mentioned some difficulty with colonels . . . What colonels and what difficulty? I should know."

"Hubar was the first. He was difficult, but not impossible, not after I explained to him that . . . well . . . who I was and why he really shouldn't get involved. I don't know the second. Tall, with black hair. He was just outside here. Kept telling me that you weren't to be disturbed. I offered to go away if he announced me and you told me to depart or come back or whatever. He wouldn't announce me."

"Do I want to know how you got announced?"

"He fainted and fell onto the stones. Might have broken his nose."

"You didn't touch him?"

"No, sir." *Not physically,* Alucius qualified to himself.

The marshal shook his head. "You're hard on our officers, Majer."

"Just the stupid ones, sir. We don't have time for that."

"You don't have time for that. We in southern Lanachrona need to put up with some of it, because if we eliminated them all right now we couldn't fill their billets. They're already complaining that I've elevated too many senior squad leaders to captain. It won't help me, but it might help the marshals to come. Enough of that."

Alyniat walked to the door, but did not open it. "Was Colonel Sarthat the one who tried to stop the majer?"

"Yes, sir."

"If he's well enough, send him in."

Several moments passed before the door opened and Sarthat walked in, holding a cloth to his nose, a very bloodied cloth. He did not look at Alucius.

"Sarthat."

"Yes, sir?"

"Did you ask to see the majer's orders?"

"No, sir."

"Why not?"

"Every majer wants to see you, sir. Everything is urgent . . ."

"How many are Northern Guard majers?" Alyniat paused. "I'll make this very clear. As I am certain he told you, Majer Alucius is here on a special mission. His orders make him the equal of any officer here, except me. He is to be given every assistance, no matter what you feel personally. This is not because I am favoring him. If he succeeds, we will win. If he fails, it is likely he will be dead, as will many of our officers and men. In case you don't recall, Majer Alucius is the one who defeated over a hundred companies of nomads and those Talent-pteridons in Deforya several years ago. He took command when the senior officers were killed, and he managed that with three companies. He got the Star of Honor for that. He just put down the rebellion in Hyalt with three companies. He's used to doing the impossible. His methods are not suited to regular chains of command. Don't make it harder on him. The Lord-Protector, Marshal Frynkel, and I all would take it amiss—if you lived that long."

"Yes, sir."

Alucius looked at the colonel, who was both chastened and furious beneath his frozen features. "I'm a herder, Colonel. I can sense every feeling you have before you can recognize it yourself. I don't want your job. I don't want your authority, and I didn't really want to hurt you. I've ridden over a thousand vingts in the last two seasons, and I did it at the Lord-Protector's personal request. I have no desire to remain in southern Lanachrona. I just want to do what I was sent to do so that I can go back to the Iron Valleys and not worry about the Regent of the Matrial."

Some, but not all, of Sarthat's rage subsided, followed by a sense that perhaps all was not lost. At least, that was how Alucius read him.

Alyniat cleared his throat. "Make sure that his companies have a bivouacking space, and feed and water for their mounts, and standard rations for the lancers."

"Yes, sir."

"There's no mess here," Alyniat added, "but officer's rations are laid out before morning muster, and at the sixth glass of the afternoon."

"Thank you, sir."

"You know Captain-colonel Omaryk?" asked the marshal.

"I've met him before, sir."

"He's in charge of intelligence . . . the third table in the hall. I'll make sure he knows that you'll be seeing him. When do you expect . . . ?"

"Overcaptain Feran can handle billeting, sir. The sooner I know . . ."

Alyniat nodded. "You introduce the overcaptain to Colonel Sarthat, and by the time you get back, Omaryk will be expecting you."

"Yes, sir."

"And, Majer . . . I expect a short verbal report in the morning, just after muster. Very short."

"Yes, sir." Alucius understood Alyniat's last words, and the reasons for them.

He and Sarthat left the small chamber and walked silently to the south end of the marshaling hall, then down the steps and out to where the companies waited. Rakalt rode behind them, leading Alucius's mount.

Feran had moved up to the front, his mount beside Jultyr's.

"Colonel, this is Overcaptain Feran. Feran, the colonel will be working with us to arrange space, feed, and water, and whatever else he can. You'll have to stand in for me. I'm expected to meet with Captain-colonel Omaryk."

"Yes, sir."

Alucius turned to Sarthat. "I apologize, Colonel, and I appreciate your aid and forbearance."

"I understand, Majer. We're fortunate to have you."

As Alucius walked back to the main building of the fort, he understood all too well that Sarthat's forbearance would vanish the moment Alucius was vulnerable in any way. With some people, that was always the way they operated. His legs hurt slightly as he made his way back up the stone steps and along the side of the hall, looking for Omaryk. It had been a long day, after many other long days. The captain-colonel was at the third table, but it was the third table from the north end.

Alucius stepped toward the older officer.

"Ah . . . the warrior-leader." As Alucius recalled him, Captain-colonel Omaryk still had freckles and a long narrow face. The red hair was thinning and washed with silver, and there were dark circles under his eyes.

"Just a majer, sir."

"You were never just anything, Majer. Technically, with those orders, you're probably a breveted sub-marshal. Now . . . what do you need to know?"

"Where the closest spear-thrower is . . . how many sand wagons are following it, if there are easy places to get sand near where you think they'll station it for the attack here . . . I'm sure you've thought all that out."

"I have, as best I could. Only you and the marshal have asked." Omaryk nodded thoughtfully. "Will nightsilk protect you against the spears?"

"Against one or two . . . it might, but they're fired with such force and so quickly that you don't usually get hit with one or two. The impacts would probably end up breaking every bone in my body."

Omaryk spread out a small map. "The last position we

could see, and the scouts hád to use a long-glass for it, the wagons were ten vingts north. They'd stopped at the dry creek here . . ."

"Sand. I didn't see any just to the north."

"We don't know of any. Now . . . there are three knolls where they would have a clear line of fire at the fort and the defenses . . ."

Despite his tiredness and his doubts about the Matrites being obliging enough to attack where the Southern Guard forces were, Alucius forced himself to follow every word Omaryk spoke, and to relate mentally each position to the map.

85

On Quinti, Alucius was up before dawn, riding along the ring road on the far side of the coast road gap and fortifications. He rode alone because he wanted a better feeling for the land, the emplacements, and even for any sense of Talent. He also rode by himself because he had felt so hemmed in by everything, by so many lancers and officers all around, by the situation, and by the feeling that he was being pushed toward something whether he wanted to go or not. He laughed softly. He'd chosen to be pushed, even if he'd had little real choice. Perhaps that was what upset him—the feeling that even his choices were constricted so tightly that they weren't really choices, but a matter of picking the lesser evil.

The first thing he felt as he rode out was a sense of deadness underneath the land. The land hé saw, the grasses, the animals—their lifeforces were much the same as anywhere, but somewhere, around two to three yards beneath the surface, there was little life, as if it had once been wiped away. Whatever had happened had taken place a long time ago, certainly at least at the time of the Cataclysm, if not before.

He rode slowly looking toward the north and the north-west, but he saw little except for the land and what lay upon it and the Lanachronan patrols and sentries. Someone must have passed some word about the Northern Guards, because while guards scrutinized him, not a one chal-lenged him. Nowhere did he sense any form of Talent, nor the lifethreads of large numbers of lancers—except where the Lanachronan forces were posted along the ring road. The ring road itself remained stone-paved as it slowly arced to the southwest, but less than two vingts to the west-southwest of where it intersected the coastal high road, it narrowed from roughly eight yards to slightly less than six.

Alucius continued to worry about the unspoken Lanachro-nan assumption that the Matrites would attack the fortified points on the ring road. In some ways, that made sense—if the Matrite goal was to reduce the fortifications and destroy the Lanachronan forces. If Alucius had been designing the attack, he would have simply bypassed the fortifications, taken the city, then attacked from inside the ring road. The crystal spear-throwers were only marginally useful against heavy stone, but highly effective against everything else.

On the other hand, he reflected, the spear-throwers were so heavy that they had to be moved on solid surfaces, and he doubted that they could be pulled up any steep incline. That meant that they would either use the high road or find a good side road that would allow them to move to a posi-tion where the ring road was low in comparison to the sur-rounding land.

Four vingts to the west of the coast road intersection he found a likely possibility. The ring road had been cut across a long ridge that angled northwest, descending on a gradual angle from the ring road. There were steep gullies on either side of the ridge until it was more than a vingt away from the ring road. At the road itself, those gullies had been filled in to create both a wall and a support for the road. The base of the ridge was three vingts to the northwest, and only a few hundred yards across a flat expanse separated the lower end of the ridge from a narrow dirt road that looked to angle off the coastal high road several vingts to the north.

The whole distance could be covered at night, and by the time the Matrites were discovered, unless sentries were posted down the ridge, they could hold the ring road. If they used one of the spear-throwers to isolate the Lanachronan forces, they could send forces to take Southgate bit by bit, and eventually force either a Lanachronan pullout and retreat or the destruction of most of the Lanachronan forces.

Alucius spent almost half a glass studying the ridge, determining how his forces might flank a possible assault in a way that would offer minimal exposure to the spear-thrower.

On the way back, he stopped on the west side of the high road from the main road fort. For a time, he looked down at the heavy stone walls and iron-timbered gates that felt ancient and had to have been constructed centuries before, if not even earlier. After studying the fortifications, he doubted that the gates and walls would see any action.

Then he rode down the connecting ring road segment, across the high road, and up the eastern traverse to the main road fort, where he tied the gray outside and made his way inside and up the stairs to the marshaling hall and to the door to Marshal Alyniat's small study.

"Majer Alucius, reporting to Marshal Alyniat, as ordered personally by the marshal."

"Sir, let me see if he's ready to see you." The guard turned and relayed Alucius's statement word for word.

"Have him wait."

The words were muffled, but clear in intent.

Although he could sense no one inside the chamber with the marshal, Alucius ended up waiting more than half a glass. After his acts of the day before, he had half expected something like that, foolish as it seemed to him.

At the sound of a single rap on the inside of the door, the guard turned to Alucius. "He's ready to see you, sir."

"Thank you."

Alucius opened the door and stepped inside, closing the door behind him.

The marshal looked up from the table desk and the maps spread across it. "I'd have preferred to see you immediately," Alyniat said with an open smile, and a sense of amusement, "but this is Lanachrona, and if I did not make you wait some, under the circumstances, every officer would be trying your techniques, Majer."

"They might have some difficulty with that, sir. They're not herders."

Alyniat laughed. "That would not stop them from trying. And this morning was a good morning for games, because the reports from the scouts show that the Matrites will not reach the area within several vingts of the ring road before late afternoon."

"Yes, sir. Have they seen the heavy wagons and the sand wagons that follow them?"

"I asked for that information. There are two such wagons. One is coming down the Fola road. The other is on the road from Zalt. They must have used another road to bypass our forces. The weapon on the Zalt road was used to take out half a company whose captain thought that he was attacking a Matrite supply caravan. I would have reprimanded him for not understanding the instructions, but since he's dead, I'll merely be passing on the information at officer's call this morning. You will be here, and, for now, you're a brevet majer-colonel." Alyniat turned to his writing table and picked up the two collar insignia—a four-pointed star crossed with a single sabre. "Those are Southern Guard insignia, but I can only brevet you in the Southern Guard. The sabre point is to the outside."

"Thank you, sir."

"You'll perform to the rank, I'm certain." Alyniat's wry smile dropped away. "I don't need details, but I'm presuming that, as with all your other accomplishments, you'll need your force to get you to the point where you and some of your Northern Guards can actually do what needs to be done."

"Effectively . . . yes, sir."

"That's one aspect of your demeanor you should keep, Colonel. There's nothing saved by indirection, except confusion. Do you need any special supplies?"

"No, sir. We could use some extra grain for the mounts, if it can be spared. They've ridden a long ways in a short time. But . . . sir, I've done some scouting, and I have some concerns that the Matrites may not attack directly from the high roads."

"That's possible. Where do you think they might attack?"

"I don't know all the possibilities, sir, but there's a ridge some four vingts to the southwest on the ring road. The slope is flat enough, and the ground looks hard enough that they could attack from there."

"Four vingts? I know the place. I have my doubts that they would move that far from the forts. They don't just want the city. They want to smash us."

"Yes, sir."

"You have that doubting agreement, Colonel. I'll make you a wager. You post a watch there, and I'll wager that they'll see nothing."

"If I have your approval, sir, I'll take that wager."

Alyniat laughed. "I'll tell the other colonels that you'll be watching special areas for unusual activities. But . . . if we get attacked elsewhere, I want your forces ready to support or do what you need to do to take out the crystal spear-throwers."

"Yes, sir. Except that we can only attack one at a time, and I can't break off dealing with one crystal spear-thrower to deal with another."

Alyniat frowned, then nodded, his fingers drumming on the table for several moments before he spoke. "I can't gainsay that. I just hope we don't need you in two places at once."

So did Alucius.

"I'll make sure that the majer of quartermasters takes care of the feed. You were out riding this morning. Did you find anything else that I should know?"

"Not yet, sir."

"Report to me every morning until we move into actual fighting. Is there anything else?"

"No, sir."

"You may go. Until officers' call."

"Yes, sir."

Less than half a glass later, Alucius stood at the north end of the marshaling hall, in the front rank with two older majer-colonels, neither of whom he had met.

Alyniat stood in front of the close to fifty officers. He began speaking without preambles. "First . . . the Matrite forces were still more than fifteen vingts to the north as of midafternoon yesterday, and the latest reports show that they have moved less than five vingts southward . . . appears that both crystal spear-throwers are being moved . . . Colonel Alucius has joined our forces with three companies trained to deal with them . . . His force has ridden from Hyalt . . . defeated the prophet there and put down the revolt . . . only group so equipped, and can only deal with one at a time . . . will need to step up scouting as the Matrites approach . . .

"That's all for the moment. Colonel Cyrosyr and Colonel Korynst—I'll brief you each individually immediately after dismissal. I've already briefed Colonel Alucius."

Just like that, Alyniat had announced that Alucius was one of the top three colonels in the force, without even directly saying so. The faintest smile crossed Alucius's lips. Alyniat's actions reminded Alucius that he had much to learn about the politics of lancer operations, but he wouldn't worry about those aspects greatly—not until he'd dealt with the Matrites' spear-throwers. If he didn't find a way to destroy the two supremely lethal weapons, he certainly wouldn't have to worry about the political aspects of anything.

86

Sexdi was much the same as Quinti had been, with no sign of the Matrites from the ring road. Alucius checked his maps and sent Waris, Elbard, Rakalt, and Bakka to check the ring road for other possible Matrite attack points. None found others as promising as the one Alucius located, but they did not go farther east than the intersection with the road to Zalt. While a second major attack might well take place farther east, he could cover only so much of the ring road from where they were stationed. He could only hope that any obvious movement of even more Matrite lancers and the spear-throwers would precede such an attack. The reports that Alyniat provided indicated that the bulk of the Matrite forces remained near the two main high roads.

That could and would change, Alucius was convinced, but until it did, he saw no point in moving his own forces blindly. They could use a day of not riding, and so could their mounts. In the meantime, he also established a scouting pattern and rotation for the ridge area, then worked out a rough pattern of attack—if the Matrites did as he thought they might.

As Alyniat had wagered, the main Matrite force moved slowly down the high roads toward Southgate, so slowly that, by sunset on Sexdi, the main body was still on the coastal high road, a good seven vingts north of the ring road. A slightly smaller Matrite force was on the southwest high road six vingts northeast. Had Alucius been planning an attack of the sort he had envisioned, the Matrites were close to where he would have been. So far as Alucius could determine, there was no absolute proof that the Matrites would attack either as he had expected or as Alyniat had, but Alucius was wagering that the Matrites would not begin with a direct assault.

While the two other senior colonels had small rooms in the road fort, Alucius had decided to sleep in the field, where he could rouse and move his forces quickly.

His plan was based on what he had seen and learned years before. The spear-thrower had felt totally dead until it was put into operation, and that meant that Alucius couldn't count on using his Talent against it until the Matrites powered up the weapon. He didn't know when that might be, but it was likely that wouldn't happen until the weapon was close to the ring road. He hoped his guesses were correct. He'd planned his attack that way, although the details of what he intended were not something he was sharing, beyond telling his officers and squad leaders that there was a special attack force. He wasn't saying that he was the attack force.

On Sexdi evening, he'd gone over the contingent battle plans with his officers until he was certain they understood. He hoped they did, but he was uncertain about Deotyr.

He finally drifted off into sleep, a restless sleep.

In time, he struggled awake, only to find himself in a hall, one with pink marble walls, tinged with purple, walls with half pillars of goldenstone set at regular intervals. Above him was an arched ceiling of the same pink marble. So precisely were all the stones set that he could detect neither joints nor mortar. He looked down. As he somehow had known, octagonal sections of polished gold and green marble composed the floor, with each section of green marble inset with an eight-pointed star of golden marble.

When he looked up, the walls had shifted.

Alucius's eyes flicked from one wall to another, but he was alone in the chamber, a chamber without wall hangings . . . or doors . . . or windows. He whirled, but there were no exits behind him, either.

Had he gotten into the chamber through a Table? He did not see or sense one anywhere.

The walls shifted once more, inward, leaving the chamber far smaller, less than seven yards long and three wide. He stepped forward and glanced back over his shoulder. Nothing had changed. There were still no doors anywhere.

The walls shifted yet again, leaving the chamber less than four by two and a half yards, with the ceiling less than a yard above him.

He lifted his arms to touch the cold marble walls. Before he could lower them, the walls pressed in, forcing his hands inward toward his body, leaving him standing in a space more confined than a cell, with hard stone inexorably contracting toward him.

He reached out with his Talent, to find an escape, but could sense nothing but stone, hard stone that went on endlessly beyond the immediate surface of the marble walls.

Sweat poured down his forehead. He had to get out . . . somehow. He had to—

Alucius bolted upright in his bedroll. Despite the cold night air, he was sweating, almost feverishly. He blotted his forehead, then quickly extended his Talent.

Was someone attacking? Had the sentries been affected?

His breathing slowed as he understood that, for the moment, all was quiet, and that only Lanachronan forces were gathered nearby.

Why the dream now? Because he felt even more trapped by events?

He took a long slow breath. He needed to relax, to get some sleep. Tomorrow, or the next day, he'd have a battle to fight, and he wouldn't do well without rest.

He lay back on the bedroll, trying to think of calming thoughts, of the stead . . . and of Wendra. That didn't help, because he began to worry—about her and Alendra, and he had the growing feeling that he might not be able to make it back to Iron Stem before Alendra was due. Nothing was going as he had hoped—or anyone had planned. The knowledge that wars usually went that way didn't help either, not as he tried to find sleep.

87

A horn sounded somewhere, as if both distant, yet nearby. Alucius turned over in the bedroll, trying to shut out the sound.

"Sir!"

Alucius struggled out of the depths of exhaustion. "What . . . ?"

"Majer . . . Colonel, I mean. Bakka sent word that there's a bunch of Matrites moving toward that ridge. Says there's a company or more and some wagons."

Alucius bolted into a sitting position. "What time—"

"It's maybe two glasses before dawn, sir."

"Wake up the captains and have them rouse everyone. They need to be ready to ride in a quarter glass."

"Yes, sir."

In the mild chill of the dry night air, under a clear sky with only the greenish half-disc of Asterta in the heavens, Alucius pulled on his boots, checked his nightsilk vest, and then pulled the nightsilk skull mask into place. His men had seen it before, and he'd need it with what he planned. He gathered his rifles, saddled the gray, mounted, and rode toward the area where the companies would form up.

Feran was already there.

"You think this will work?" asked the older officer.

"Until we try . . . I can't say."

Feran laughed softly. "It had better, because if it doesn't, I'll be in charge, and there's no way I want to explain to Alyniat. Or Weslyn."

At the sound of riders, both Northern Guard officers turned, expecting Jultyr and Deotyr, but an unfamiliar captain in the blue of the Southern Guard appeared, outlined by the torch carried by the lancer riding with him. "What's going on here?"

Alucius rode forward until the light fell on him. "We've gotten word that our target's moving into place. Once we're certain, we'll be letting the marshal know."

The officer's eyes took in the insignia, but his eyes lingered on the skull mask. "Ah . . . yes, sir, Colonel. Sorry to bother you, sir."

"I understand, Captain. Carry on."

"Yes, sir."

No sooner had the watch captain disappeared into the darkness than Jultyr rode up, followed by Deotyr.

"We don't have much time," Alucius began. "The plan is the same as we discussed last night. We'll move into position and wait for them to begin the attack. Then the attack group will move on the crystal spear-thrower. If the group is successful, the spear-thrower will fail. That's when you get the order to attack the forces around the weapon."

"Sir?" asked Deotyr.

"Why attack, if it's not working? Because they could fix it, and we'd be in the same position in another few weeks or months, and they'd have even more lancers surrounding it. We need to capture it or make sure it's destroyed. That's why we have half a squad carrying gunpowder. Now . . . when we get to the ridge we're taking down, and that's not the one where the Matrites are coming up, remember, we'll go in this order—Fifth Company, Twenty-eighth Company, and Thirty-fifth Company. That's the way we'll form up now."

"Yes, sir."

Despite Alucius's impatience, it was almost a tenth of a glass before the three companies were on the ring road, climbing the western segment, and heading west through the darkness.

They had traveled slightly more than a vingt, Alucius judged, when Waris appeared out of the darkness.

"Sir!" The scout eased his mount beside Alucius.

"Yes, Waris?"

"Like you thought, sir. They put four companies on the coastal high road, where that dirt road leaves the high road."

"What about the rest?"

"They look to be headed south, even past the ridge." Waris's voice contained puzzlement.

"That far south?" asked Feran.

"It could be an ambush," Alucius suggested. "The Matrites attack farther to the south, as if trying to take the city . . ."

"And when the marshal tries to shift his lancers . . . ?" suggested Feran.

"The spear-thrower takes care of them. Or they could just be trying to take the city and using the spear-thrower as a way to keep the Southern Guard from reaching them directly. If the marshal doesn't use the ring road but the high road, the Matrites take the ring road, and then all the Southern Guard is trapped inside the ring road."

Alucius turned to Fewal, who had been riding behind him with Dhaget and Roncar. "You ride to the fort. Try to get the message to Marshal Alyniat that the Matrites are moving to attack here with the crystal spear-thrower and that another force is continuing southward outside the ring road. Tell him that we're moving against the spear-thrower, but that will take all our forces."

"Yes, sir."

Once Fewal had left, Alucius turned back to Waris. "You and Rakalt head down the narrow ridge, the one we're taking. Halfway down, short of where we'll move into the gulch, and keep an eye out."

"Yes, sir." Waris urged his mount away from the column and was joined by Rakalt a hundred yards ahead, beyond the lancers' clear sight in the darkness, but not beyond Alucius's vision or the range of his Talent.

As he kept riding westward, Alucius let his Talent study the darkness to the north and west. He stiffened in the saddle, not because of the weave of lifethreads from all the lancers on both sides, but because of what he had not expected. Fine pink threads from the Matrite forces soared to the north, in the direction of Hieron. While Alucius had the feeling that not every Matrite lancer wore a silver torque, there were enough that the combined luminescence of those evil-feeling pink threads seemed to cast a purplish pink light. That pinkish cast was unseen and unfelt, except to those who could see it with Talent.

As with the first time he had truly seen not only lifewebs, but torque-threads filling the sky, Alucius was silent for a long moment, taking in the subtle weave that filled the entire darkening skies with the warp and weft of intertwining lifewebs, webs that somehow never touched. Against the soft rightness of the living web, the purplish pink was shudderingly wrong, an oppressive chain weighing on the lifethread of each man or woman who wore a collar. Alucius half wondered how he had survived such a collar for so long.

Feran cleared his throat. "You're worried about something. What?"

Alucius smiled wryly. He'd betrayed too much in his surprise. "There's a feeling out there." He *knew* that he had destroyed the crystal that controlled the torques—and the Matrial. Or rather, the destruction of the crystal had destroyed the Matrial. Had the Regent rediscovered that secret and created another crystal?

"And what exactly is that feeling?" asked Feran.

"They've repowered the torques, the silver collars of the Matrial. I can feel it from here."

"Told you this was all part of something bigger," murmured the older man.

"I agreed with you." Although he had wondered about how the Matrites were forcing their attacks, he hadn't thought about the torques in some time. Were they connected with the ifrits? Or was he just trying to find a pattern that didn't exist?

They rode another vingt, past several small watch posts, where Alucius had to identify himself, before they reached the section of the ring road where Bakka waited.

"Sir . . . Waris says there's no one on this ridge below. He also says that you'd better take it slow down the path."

"Thank you. We will." Alucius turned. "Single file! Silent riding. Follow me!"

He turned the gray off the ring road and down onto the steep and narrow path that wound northward, a path difficult enough to travel in the light. But that was why he was riding first, Alucius told himself. Still, traveling the path in the darkness, under only the light of the stars and the tiny half-disc of Asterta, was safer than waiting on the ring road and facing the spear-thrower.

Half a glass passed, and Alucius had traveled only less than a third of the way down the path to where the ridge flattened, and where the lancers could move more quickly to the southwest and the ancient black lava ledge that would conceal them from the Matrites once the sky lightened. He forced himself to be patient and keep moving.

Another half glass passed, and Alucius could sense the Matrite forces and the wagons on the ridge to the south, but they seemed to be moving more slowly than he had anticipated. He allowed himself the hope that moving their heavy equipment upslope, even up a gentle dirt road, had proved more time-consuming than the Matrite commanders had calculated. He could also sense the heavy wagon, the one carrying the spear-thrower, and behind it the wagons carrying the sand that fed it. All four wagons were below where Alucius intended to place his own forces.

The faintest tinge of gray was coloring the sky above the ring road when the last of Thirty-fifth Company's lancers rode into position behind the ledge. Alucius let himself heave a sigh of relief. At the very least, the companies were shielded from direct fire from the crystal spear-thrower, and the Matrites were only slightly uphill of his men, if on the adjoining ridge. His men would have to sweep down another two hundred yards to reach the swale that connected the two ridges, but farther down there was no cover for them.

Alucius dismounted and handed the gray's reins to Dhaget, then turned and looked up at Feran, who lay in a notch in the lava, from where he could view the adjoining ridge. "You'll have to watch the crystal spear-thrower. No one moves until you're satisfied that it's disabled."

"I think I can manage that."

"Good." With one rifle in hand, Alucius walked downslope a good hundred yards, still behind the lava.

There, half concealed by Talent, and half by his own dark uniform, Alucius climbed over the now-much-lower lava and dropped to the hard ground on the other side. Keeping low, he tried to move down into the gully and back upward. He was sweating heavily and panting by the time he pulled himself over the rim of the gully on the south side. He felt like anyone could have heard him a vingt away, but there were neither Matrite foot or lancers within a hundred yards.

He forced himself to pause and let his breathing subside before he began to move in a crouch uphill through the lightening darkness and toward where the heavy wagon had stopped. He could sense that a group of engineers had gathered around the wagon and begun to dig into the hillside, as if to level the wagon somewhat.

How close would he have to get to use his Talent? Was the weapon powered up enough so that he could?

He let his Talent range toward the device.

The weapon was inert . . . dead . . . unpowered, and Alucius could not bring enough Talent force or lifeforce to do anything to the assemblage of wires and crystals and other components that he had neither words nor knowledge to describe.

Below him, he could hear a voice.

"There's a Talent-wielder somewhere up here."

Alucius's lips tightened. He should have expected a Matrite Talent-officer. He should have, especially protecting the spear-thrower.

"Aim to your right more. Just sweep the area."

In the darkness, Alucius scrambled toward the edge of the gully, dropping into a ditchlike depression just short of a far deeper drop-off.

Shots pierced the predawn gray, and he could sense the bullets a fraction of a yard above his head. Lying there, with more bullets passing above him, he extended a Talent-probe downhill, seeking the brighter lifethread of the Talent officer.

She was riding uphill in his direction, with a small squad, calling out instructions. Those instructions were far too accurate.

Alucius would have preferred to use his rifle, but the Matrite shots were so close that lifting his head could have been fatal. Doing nothing was also likely to be fatal before very long.

He extended the Talent-probe toward the officer, seeking the lifethread nodes. Her main node was unprotected, and he twisted. An unseen spray of brown and green was followed by the fall of her lifeless body from the saddle.

"Talent-wielder got her!"

"Keep shooting!"

"Where? There's no one anywhere."

"Got to be somewhere!"

A sheet of bullets passed overhead. Alucius resisted the urge to fire back and, keeping on the precarious edge of the gully, began to crawl, then scramble uphill. Going in a half crawl, half crouch was hard on his legs, his feet, and his lungs, and he kept having to stop to catch his breath. The rifle felt like a long, heavy weight. The sky was turning from deep black green to dark silver green by the time Alucius had scrabbled his way uphill another three hundred yards.

He tried once more with his Talent to explore the spear-thrower, but it was still depowered. He was also stretching to reach it with his Talent.

The small squad that had been with the Talent officer had begun to move forward toward a point just below where Alucius had almost been shot, but they were moving too carefully, he thought, to be able to track him before he got into position to do something about the crystal spear-thrower.

He kept moving, making another fifty yards, so that he was at the edge of the gully, flat on his stomach on a slope that was steep enough that he would slide down into a fifty-yard drop if he moved incautiously or lost his footholds. Although his Talent was supposed to be shielding him from view from below, he felt horribly exposed.

The sense of a *crack* echoed around him, and he could feel the energy building from the spear-thrower, which was positioned only a half vingt below the ring road, with its discharge formulator pointed at the road itself.

"There they are!"

A single trumpet blast echoed across the ridge from the ring road, and a company of Southern Guards appeared and charged downhill.

Alucius winced. He hadn't even begun to try to work out how to deal with the weapon. A nimbus of pinkish energy flared up around the spear-thrower, followed by a humming that quickly rose to a high-pitched whine and abruptly stopped. With the end of the whining, miniature crystalline spears formed a yard beyond the crystal muzzle of the device, then flashed outward so quickly that sunbeams seemed to radiate from the weapon rather than crystal projectiles. The deadly spray struck the center of the oncoming lancers, disintegrating them into a pinkish spray.

Alucius forced himself to ignore the wave of death and concentrate on the weapon itself, extending a Talent-probe. The probe was repelled from the nimbus of unseen pinkish light, repelled by the strength of that light. Alucius forced himself to probe around the weapon; but the only place where the shield did not extend was that point where the spears seemed to form before they were accelerated outward.

He turned his probe and extended it behind the formation point.

The shock of raw power slammed back through his probe with such force that Alucius had to release the probe and concentrate on keeping his balance to avoid slipping, then sliding, to the drop-off below him.

His shield wavered in the effort.

"There's someone up there!"

He managed to get his balance back and recover the Talent shield.

"Where?"

"Up there, below the machine on the side."

Another wave of Southern Guards vanished in pinkish spray, and their deaths washed across Alucius. He swallowed and tried to get his concentration back.

What about using the rifle, wrapping lifeforce around the bullets?

He crawled upward and forward until he could just ease the rifle over the edge of the rim of the gully. Then he focused on infusing the bullets with lifeforce. He aimed at the spear-thrower, narrowing his concentration, and squeezed the trigger, once, twice, three times.

A brief flare of energy flashed from the side of the spear-thrower with each impact, but there was no sense that even one of the bullets had had any real effect on the Matrite weapon.

A line of bullets plowed into the rim of the gully less than five yards below him.

What could Alucius do? The soarers said that everything had nodes. Could he find something like a node in the weapon, something that would undo a key part?

He extended his Talent probe again, this time keeping it flexible.

There were no nodes—not like those of people or ifrits. But there were hard diamondlike glittering Talentlike points that rotated around the point where the spears were formed. Alucius tried to slow them in their rotation, but that was like trying to halt a huge iron wagon wheel headed downhill. If he hung on, he'd be crushed.

What if he pushed it faster?

He lent his strength to try to hurry the diamond nodes.

Suddenly, the tiniest thread trailed from one diamond node, and Alucius grasped it with his probe and began to pull it. The node unraveled, and the following node shifted, as if to try to take the place of the first, and additional smaller threads appeared.

Alucius could suddenly feel the discharge formulator, hard and impervious crystal, begin to sag, as if melting. He used his probe to tug at more and more of the threads.

Then . . . a surge of power, seemingly rising from everywhere, poured into the spear-thrower.

Alucius dropped his probe and concentrated on forming a greenish Talent-shield around himself, barely getting it over himself when a roar of flame and force exploded from the spear-thrower.

Metal and crystal exploded everywhere, and in all directions, scything outward.

So much death followed the destruction of the weapon that for several long moments, Alucius was numb, deaf, blind. He just lay under his shields, waiting for the patter of metal and crystal rain to stop.

Then he began to inch his body upward and over the top edge of the gully.

"Companies! Forward!" came Feran's order from below on the adjoining ridge.

Slowly, Alucius stood and surveyed the flat ridge before him. The explosion had scythed crystal and death through the Matrite force and through the few remaining Southern Guards who had attempted to attack the spear-thrower before Alucius could disable it. He had to swallow hard to keep from retching. Everywhere were small gobbets of things—flesh, wood, metal, brush, dirt, and all were pinkish. He looked down. There was even a pinkish film on his own boots.

The destruction had created a circle only a vingt or so in diameter, and there were still two companies or more of Matrites lower on the ridge. Feran's charge had caught them while they were still stunned by the devastation.

Rifle in hand, Alucius began to walk down the ridge.

He'd covered about two hundred yards when three riders appeared leading his gray. Dhaget was in the lead, and Alucius was more than glad to see him.

"Sir! Thought you might like a mount!"

Alucius swung into the saddle, but by the time he had

ridden down toward the fighting, the few surviving Matrites had pulled clear and were riding southward hard. A sense of more regret and anger washed over him. He wished he'd been able to be part of the attack, to wield his sabre somehow, tired as he was. But the Matrites had retreated so quickly that pursuing would have been stupidity. Besides, there was still another spear-thrower to destroy.

Feran had ordered a recall, and the three companies reformed as Alucius neared. Alucius reined up short of the overcaptain.

Feran looked at Alucius. Alucius knew he was a sight, black skull mask still in place, with smears of blood and other things across his uniform. Jultyr and Deotyr rode up within moments. All three officers looked at Alucius.

"Sir, we engaged and broke off as ordered. Fifth Company, three dead, five wounded."

"Sir, Thirty-fifth Company, ten dead, eight wounded."

"Twenty-eighth Company, seven dead, six wounded."

"Thank you. We'll ride straight up to the ring road, banners ahead."

"Banners forward, column, forward!"

Feran rode up beside Alucius. "How did you manage to escape that?"

"I was hanging over the side of the gully when it exploded."

"I won't ask about the rest, Colonel."

"You don't want to know," Alucius said tiredly. Belatedly, he realized that he hadn't fired a single shot from his rifle at any of the Matrites—just three useless shots at the spear-thrower.

"I learned that a long time ago. How many Matrite companies were there up there?"

"Three . . . could have been four. There was a Southern Guard company, too. Most of them had been killed before . . ." Alucius shook his head, reaching down to take the rifle out and reload it. He should have done that sooner.

Again, behind him, he could hear the murmurs.

". . . walked out of that . . ."

". . . blood all over him . . . none of it his . . ."

Except, Alucius thought, *I'm responsible for all the blood.*

88

Even before they had reached the top of the ridge and the ring road, Alucius sent Roncar ahead to the main road fort to report the total destruction of one crystal spear-thrower and three Matrite companies. He'd also worried off the skull mask and slipped it inside his tunic. At the top of the ridge and the edge of the ring road, a Southern Guard squad leader rode forward from the handful of lancers that remained from his company.

"Sir?" The squad leader's eyes took in the insignia and the blood streaks across Alucius's uniform. "Colonel, sir?"

"Yes?"

"Do you have any orders for us, sir? Majer Storynst and Captain Chelopyr . . . they got taken out by that spear-thrower . . . most of the companies, too." His eyes narrowed. "You were the one walking across the ridge, sir?"

"I was the one," Alucius replied hurriedly, taking in the no more than two squads remaining from what had to have been two companies. "For right now, you'd better patrol this area. You see that road down there? That offers the Matrites easy access to the ring road. We need to be heading east to deal with the other spear-thrower, and someone needs to make sure that they don't change their position and try this approach again. I'll let the marshal know that you're here. What company?"

"Seventeenth and Nineteenth, sir. What's left of them."

"If you see any sign of more Matrite forces, send a messenger to the marshal."

"Yes, sir."

As he finished speaking, Alucius could feel his body shaking all over. Once his force had all reached the ring road and formed up in a column heading eastward, he managed a long swallow from his water bottle and began to eat some hard travel bread, followed by some salted almonds they had gotten from the quartermaster.

They'd traveled less than a vingt when Alucius could see another body of riders moving toward them at a quick trot. By then he'd eaten and drunk enough that most of the shakiness had subsided.

"Banners forward!"

Before long, Alucius was reined up opposite another colonel.

"The Matrites are attacking on the south ends of the ring road, both east and west," said the captain-colonel, a man Alucius had seen at officers' call but had not met. "Are you sure, sir, that you should be headed east?"

Alucius fixed the other with silver-gray eyes that turned metal-hard. "We've been fighting since well before dawn, Colonel. We've destroyed one of the crystal spear-throwers, and we're riding toward the other one to see what we can do before it slaughters most of the Lanachronan forces on the east side of Southgate."

For the first time, the older colonel's eyes took in the blood and gore on the Northern Guard uniforms. His eyes did not quite meet those of Alucius. "Ah . . . yes, sir."

"Two Southern Guard companies attacked the spear-thrower prematurely, before we could take it out. There are fewer than two squads left. They've mounted a patrol there, to watch for any other Matrite companies. You can obtain the details from them, if you'd like. The longer we delay, the more Southern Guards will die. Good day, Colonel."

"Good day, sir."

Alucius moved to the right side of the road. "Single file, until we pass!"

"Single file."

Neither Feran nor Alucius spoke until they were past the four companies of Southern Guards.

"Idiots . . ." Alucius finally muttered. "Told Alyniat that they wouldn't do a frontal assault. Told him we shouldn't do any against the spear-throwers. No wonder they're losing what they'd held."

"It makes you wonder," Feran returned. "You still think supporting the Lord-Protector is that good an idea?"

"Good? No. Better than all the alternatives? Yes."

"You're being so optimistic again, Colonel." Feran's voice dripped irony.

"I have to be. The Regent has figured out how to power those silver torques, and that's worse than anything in Lanachrona."

"If only those idiot traders in Dekhron had been willing to spend a few thousand more golds five years ago . . . I'd wager that they still don't understand."

"You'd win. Most of them are dead, one way or another."

"Figures." Feran snorted. "Left us alive with a mess to clean up."

They rode on for a vingt and a half before seeing another force ahead, seemingly smaller than the first, but also hurrying southward.

An overcaptain rode forward, took one look at Alucius and inclined his head. "Permission to pass, single file, sir?"

"Permission granted, overcaptain," Alucius replied.

Alucius kept track as the two sets of lancers passed each other, and from what he saw, the overcaptain had two companies with him.

Over the next two vingts, they saw no more Southern Guards, except for the scattered handfuls on ring road patrol. By the time Alucius and his forces neared the coastal high road, it was still early morning.

Even from the west side of the road cut overlooking the high road, Alucius could tell that the Southern Guard encampment was deserted, except for scattered riders and wagons. Cook fires were out, and even the main road fort

looked to have fewer lancers around and within the courtyard.

"They've sent most everyone south," Feran suggested.

"Where they'll arrive tired and suffer unnecessary casualties." Alucius stretched in the saddle. "We'll take a break
for a glass. Make sure everyone eats and that the mounts
are fed and watered. If you and the captains can weasel or
beg more supplies quickly, do it."

"You're not thinking . . . ?"

"I still think we can pull out some sort of a victory, but it
won't be easy, and finding supplies later is going to be
tough."

"Getting them any way is tough."

"That's true," Alucius agreed. "Break for a glass. No
more than a glass and a half." He reined up, trying not to
think about what lay to the southeast.

89

While the three companies had taken a
break and the officers had worked at getting more supplies,
Alucius had gone to see if Marshal Alyniat had remained.
But the marshal had reportedly headed southeast to direct
the battles there, leaving but a junior captain and some
messengers to relay information.

Still, well before midmorning, Alucius and his lancers
were back in the saddle again, this time headed east toward
the other high road and its fort. They'd found little enough
in the way of supplies, except travel bread and more cartridges for the Southern Guards. Another fight or two, and
Fifth Company would be out of ammunition, but Alucius
would have to worry about that later.

The stillness of the early morning had given way to a
cool wind out of the southeast, a wind that, for all its mild-

ness, carried a hint of late fall or winter rawness. On the entire stretch of ring road between the two major road forts, they passed no one, except the handful of sentries. Most of them looked worried.

After another break for rations and water at the eastern road fort, also largely deserted, they crossed the southeastern high road and followed the ring road as it curved southward. To the southwest, Alucius could see thunderclouds building. The storms did not seem to be moving eastward but were hanging over the coast that he had yet to see.

"You knew they wouldn't attack the road forts, didn't you?" Feran asked after a long period of silence.

"I didn't *know*. I just thought it was unlikely. The Matrites don't usually fight as well, but in my experience they also don't make obviously stupid attacks. Attacking the road forts first would have been both obvious and stupid."

"Are you trying to become arms-commander of all Lanachrona?" Feran's tone was humorous.

"Legacies, no! I just want to get rid of the crystal spearthrowers and head back to the Iron Valleys. Sooner rather than later."

"And what if the Lord-Protector has another one of his 'requests'? He doesn't seem inclined to let us go that easily."

Alucius groaned. "It would have to be awfully convincing to make me stay . . . or ask Fifth Company to."

"I'll remind you of that . . . Colonel."

"I have no doubts about that," Alucius replied.

"Good." Feran grinned, but the expression faded quickly.

They rode south on the ring road for four glasses before reaching the southeast high road and another near-deserted Southern Guard encampment. After a half-glass break, they continued southward for close to another two glasses, to the outskirts of an encampment centered on a small road fort—a circular stone structure no more than ten yards in diameter and with walls not quite three yards high.

A young-faced captain was stationed north of the encampment, mounted, with two lancers beside him. One held a thin sheaf of papers.

"Column, halt!" Alucius ordered before riding forward, the late-afternoon sun slanting into his eyes.

"Sir?"

"Colonel Alucius, with the Fifth Northern Guard and Twenty-eighth and Thirty-fifth Southern Guard."

"Yes, sir." The captain looked at the lancer with the papers.

"Black."

"The black area is yours, Colonel. Straight ahead and then downhill to the right. You'll see the black banners on poles. There should be rations and water barrels there."

"Thank you."

After they had passed the captain, Feran turned to Alucius. "I don't like it when they've got everything organized this way. It makes me feel like they've got a surprise I won't like. More than one."

"They probably do."

"You're being optimistic again, Colonel."

"Comes from my cheerful nature."

As they headed down the long and gradual slope westward from the ring road, following a path recently created by hundreds of mounts before them, both officers could see the open space marked out with four poles, each with a strip of black cloth. On a ground cloth were what looked to be some form of rations. Five large barrels were also set out at intervals. A single Southern Guard was stationed there.

Alucius had barely reined up at the edge of the area, and had not even had a chance to dismount, before he saw Roncar riding toward him. The lancer's narrow face showed both concern and relief. "Sir!"

"What is it, Roncar?"

"Marshal Alyniat wants to see you. Right now, sir."

"Where is he?"

"He's in the tent, sir, there on the hill, just below the fort. He said that he wanted to see you as soon as you arrived."

Alucius turned the gray.

"Remember, Colonel," Feran called. "A very good reason."

"I'll remember that, Overcaptain."

Roncar eased his mount up beside Alucius. "The Matrites are only about five vingts south of here, sir. They hold the entire ring road from there to the ocean, and they've been moving north a few hundred yards at a time. They've used the other spear-thrower, and they haven't lost many lancers. The marshal's scouts say that they haven't moved toward the city, but they could at any time. After you smashed the crystal spear-thrower in the west, the companies he sent west have kept the ring road there, so there's not much danger yet of being attacked from the north and west on the ring road."

"Thank you. Do you know what the Southern Guard casualties are?"

"No one's saying, sir. Besides the two companies that they lost on the ridge, I've heard words that Colonel Cyrosyr and his force of six companies had been wiped out almost to the last man. Less than two squads remaining."

That didn't surprise Alucius, but he had hoped that they wouldn't have to deal with the spear-thrower immediately. That hope appeared less and less likely.

He reined up short of the lancers surrounding the tent, dismounted, and handed the gray's reins to Roncar.

An undercaptain stood beside the guards. "Colonel Alucius?"

Alucius nodded. "We just rode in."

"The marshal's in the tent, sir. Just go on in. He said to send you in whenever you got here."

"Thank you, Undercaptain." As Alucius stepped past the lancers, he caught the slightest whisper from the lancers well to the side.

". . . see all the blood . . ."

". . . you expect? That one's a fighting commander . . ."

Stupid commander as well? Alucius wondered as he lifted the tent flap and stepped inside into an area no more than three yards by four.

Alyniat was sitting on a stool before a small table strewn with maps. A lock of hair more silver than blond fell across his forehead, and the circles under his eyes were deep and black. He looked up from the maps at Alucius, taking in the bloodied uniform.

"Sir," Alucius said.

"You've made decent time, Colonel. I received your report about destroying the crystal spear-thrower and the annihilation of four to five Matrite companies." Alyniat paused. "I hate to sound ungrateful, but . . . couldn't you have found some way to capture it, Colonel? It would have been so much more useful to us that way, especially under the circumstances."

For some reason, Alyniat's phrasing of "under the circumstances" grated on Alucius. "I'm sure it would have been, sir," Alucius replied. "It's not designed to be captured."

"Not designed to be captured?"

"I can't explain, sir, but it's like . . . like gunpowder shielded by flame. You break through the flame, and the gunpowder explodes."

"Use the equivalent of water, perhaps . . ."

"I can only try."

"If you don't capture one, only destroy them, what's to prevent them from building more?"

"It takes years to do that, sir, and I understand it's most costly. If they even can."

"Even can?" Alyniat raised his eyebrows.

"The last time one was destroyed, there was only one engineer who knew enough to re-create it. It takes special equipment. I don't know if he is still alive."

"Are you certain you can't find a way to capture one?"

Alucius considered for a moment. Was there any way he could have stopped the device? Just stopped it? Finally, he spoke. "I couldn't find any way with the first one. I'll certainly keep that possibility open, sir, when we try to deal with the second one."

"I'd be most grateful if you would. Our losses are not inconsiderable."

"Where is the second one?"

"Oh . . . about five vingts south of here, moving toward us. We're trying to slow them down with rifle fire from behind berms and the like, but the terrain here is far flatter than on the west side of Southgate. As you know, attacking it directly is foolish and fatal. They're advancing up the ring road with it as a spearhead. They haven't sent companies into Southgate yet, but if they can reach where we are now, we'll have to consider pulling out of Southgate."

"As soon as the men get something to eat, and the mounts get some feed and water, we'll head south," Alucius said.

"That might be for the best."

Best for whom? It might be best for the Lanachronans and perhaps the people of Southgate, but it wasn't likely to be easy on Alucius and his forces. "Yes, sir."

"Colonel?"

"Sir?"

"We've lost enough lancers that, even if you do destroy another five Matrite companies and the spear-thrower, no one will be calling you a hero."

"Sir . . . I came here because I was asked to come. I didn't come to be a hero. And, sir, I didn't ask for that the last three times I've bailed out Lanachrona. Good day, Marshal." Alucius turned and slipped out of the tent. As he mounted the gray and rode back toward his companies, he knew he shouldn't have reacted so strongly, but all he wanted to do was to destroy the spear-thrower and return to the Iron Valleys. Even being colonel of the Northern Guard would be a pleasure compared to dealing with the politics of Lanachrona and the Southern Guard. And if his reaction to Alyniat made sure he wouldn't be colonel . . . well, that was fine, too.

He was still seething when he reined up near Feran and dismounted, slipping the feed bag for the gray into place—

a feed bag that Feran had thoughtfully readied.

"You're angry," Feran observed. "What happened?"

"The marshal suggested that even if we destroyed another five Matrite companies and the crystal spear-thrower, we wouldn't be heroes. He also wanted to know why we couldn't capture the weapon, rather than destroying it. 'That would have been so much more useful, Colonel.'" Alucius's mockery of Alyniat's words was edged.

"And you still want to go after it?"

"If we don't destroy it, we'll end up in a worse mess, and one that will have us fighting for our lives across the Iron Valleys, possibly in weeks, certainly in months." Alucius lifted his water bottle. It was empty. "Legacies! I need to refill the water bottles and get something to eat. How soon can we move out?"

"As soon as your water bottles are full and the gray has some water," Feran replied. "Waris was nosing around, and the rumors are that the Matrites are less than five vingts south and moving forward behind the spear-thrower."

"That's what the marshal said."

"Sir!"

Alucius turned. A lancer rode toward him bearing a small keg. The lancer was Skant.

"Got a keg. Used to have ale, but I drew the water myself."

"Thank you, Skant. I appreciate that." Alucius looked to Roncar. "Did you have a chance to refill your water bottles?"

"Yes, sir. But thank you, sir."

With Skant holding the keg, Alucius refilled all three bottles and replaced them in their holders.

Within a quarter glass, the three companies were riding south on the ring road. As he rode southward, Alucius took out the maps and studied them once more. Unlike the northern section of the ring road, or the western and southwestern sections, the ring road to the east and south was much lower, rising less than ten yards above the arid rolling plains to the east. Even the lands inside the road were almost equally flat. That gave whoever held the road a tremendous advantage.

No matter how he looked at it, Alucius could come up with only one plan. He turned to Feran. "Do we still have spades?"

"About ten in the ammunition wagon."

"That will do."

"Earthworks won't stand for long against the spear-thrower. You know that."

"I know. But they'll last just long enough." Alucius went on to explain. "I want enough lancers to be firing at the Matrites that they don't study what's off to the side of the road where it looks clear."

"You're thinking of being out front?"

Alucius shrugged. "I can't see anything else that will work. Can you?"

"One of these days, someone's going to shoot you."

"They already have, you might recall. Several times."

"You might not survive it the next time."

Alucius laughed. "Anything else I can come up with means they get more shots at me."

They'd ridden slightly less than a vingt when they saw about ten lancers moving slowly toward them in single file. All were wounded and splattered with blood.

"Waris . . . if you could find out how far from here the fighting is?"

"Yes, sir." The scout rode ahead to meet the retreating and wounded lancers before they reached Alucius and his companies.

Waris returned shortly, as the wounded lancers moved single file on the west side of the road past Alucius's forces. The scout turned his mount to ride alongside Alucius and Feran.

"The Matrites are a little more than three vingts ahead, according to the roadstones," Waris reported. "There's a Southern Guard force of about four companies maybe a vingt and a half in front of us, near the next set of sentry boxes."

Alucius checked his maps. "That should do." He wondered who was in command of the Southern Guard forces.

A vingt later, Alucius found out.

The dark-haired colonel who rode toward the column looked familiar—Hubar. Alucius held in a tight smile. He shouldn't have been so hard on the man. Now, he'd probably end up paying something in return. At least, it wasn't Sarthat. That . . . that would really have made things difficult.

"Colonel Hubar."

Hubar looked at Alucius, taking in the majer-colonel's insignia on Alucius's tunic collar. "So . . . you think you can pull this out, Colonel?" The contempt in the older man's voice was barely veiled.

"I won't know until we try, will we?" Alucius paused but briefly, then added, "We did manage to destroy the other crystal spear-thrower at around dawn this morning, and we've been making our way here ever since."

Hubar studied Alucius and his uniform. "I suppose that explains the blood."

"We also managed to kill about five companies of Matrites."

Hubar looked at Alucius. "What do you want from us? I'd prefer no frontal charges, sir."

"I don't want any. They'd just get lancers killed here." Alucius gestured to the small stone watch posts on each side of the road. "We'll be setting up a line of earthworks here, ten yards on either side of the road. A trench deep enough to protect a lancer from stray bullets."

"That won't—"

"I know. It won't stop the spear-thrower once it gets within a few hundred yards. But my lancers will be firing at a greater distance than that." Alucius turned in the saddle and gestured to the low rise to the west and back north almost a quarter vingt. "I'd like most of your force formed up on that knoll—in a way that's visible for at least two vingts."

Hubar frowned.

"I don't want them to attack. I want the Matrites to be watching them. I'd like your men to fire at the Matrites near the edge of your range and keep it up until my lancers start firing. Then your men can pull back. They can use the back side of the knoll as cover and circle back to the ring road, if necessary. If we're successful, though, they should be prepared to join our companies in a full attack on the remaining Matrites. The Matrites should be disorganized, and the more lancers we can bring to bear, the fewer survivors they'll have."

"Fewer survivors?" Hubar's mouth remained slightly open.

"Neither the Lord-Protector nor Marshal Alyniat nor I want to fight this war again anytime soon. Wars are hard to fight without troops."

"Yes, sir. That's *if* you and your men destroy or disable the spear-thrower."

"That's correct. You can watch Overcaptain Feran."

"What about you?"

"I'm part of the team assigned to destroy the spear-thrower. It takes a herder, and I'm the only one left around here."

Hubar nodded slowly. "We'll form up now."

"Thank you."

Hubar nodded brusquely, then rode back toward the ranked companies. Shortly, they began to angle down the slope on the western side of the road.

Alucius turned to Jultyr and Deotyr. "You see what Colonel Hubar's doing?"

"Yes, sir."

"There's a similar rise out to the east, but it's forward of where we are. You're to place your companies in staggered firing order there. As soon as the Matrites come within the edge of your range, I want you to start firing on them. At that distance, I know you won't hit many, but I want you to keep firing until it looks like they're about to turn the spear-thrower on you. Then pull back about half a vingt and take what cover you can behind that next rise. If everything goes as before, something will happen to the spear-thrower, and that's when you'll join with Fifth Company and charge the survivors. Is that clear?"

"Sir . . . did you mean that about slaughtering them all?"

"I should have been more clear. If someone's down, disarmed, and disabled, don't bother with them. But no quarter for anyone who's fighting. There's no need to slaughter anyone who can't fight or isn't fighting."

"Yes, sir." Deotyr looked relieved.

"I told Hubar that because without those kinds of orders he won't understand the kind of battle we're in. Captains, go ahead out to that rise and form up."

"Yes, sir." Jultyr and Deotyr replied almost simultaneously, then turned their mounts back toward their companies.

"Now," Alucius continued, "I need two spades. Dhaget, get the spades and join Fewal and Roncar and me farther south on the road." He turned to Feran. "Overcaptain, can you get the trenches dug here? Do you think that two lines will be enough? Staggered so that the lancers firing won't get hit by the ones behind them?"

"We can do that, sir."

"You'll start firing, slowly at first, once the Southern Guard companies pull back. I want the Matrites worried about rifle fire. But make sure you pull back before that spear-thrower can reach you."

"Yes, sir," Feran replied. "How long after that . . . ?"

"I don't know. I don't know its range. It's less than a vingt, but how close it will have to get, that I don't know." Alucius looked southward past the stone sentry boxes. "We'd better find what we need."

He urged the gray forward, riding roughly half a vingt farther south before reining up. From the inner shoulder of the ring road he studied the ground, using his Talent, finally finding a spot on the slope about twenty yards to the west of the road, and as the ground slanted, perhaps three or four yards lower than the edge of the ring road. He dismounted, handing the gray's reins to Fewal and walking down the slope. Finally, he nodded.

He only had to wait a few moments more before Dhaget rode up with the shovels.

"There's some rock here, but dig right behind it, only about a yard and a half wide and two yards long."

"How deep, sir?" asked Roncar, who, along with Dhaget, had dismounted and brought a shovel down to where Alucius stood.

"I'd like at least a yard."

As his messengers dug, Alucius watched the road to the south, where in the distance he could see riders and a dark-ish blob above a wagon, most probably the spear-thrower. Occasionally, he heard the sound of a rifle, but that could have come from anywhere.

It was almost half a glass later before the slit trench was finished to Alucius's satisfaction. He pulled out the top rifle from the saddle case and looked at the three messengers. "Same as before. Once the spear-thrower's gone, and it looks halfway clear, see if you can get to me with a mount."

"Yes, sir."

"Now, you need to get back before the Matrites get close enough to see exactly where you are." Alucius settled into the trench, listening as the sound of hoofs receded.

For a quarter of a glass, he watched the sky, but the hazy silver green looked the same everywhere, and the thunder-clouds to the south had seemingly never crossed the coast. Then he used his Talent to explore the ground around him. As he'd discovered earlier, there was a "dead" layer per-haps three or four yards beneath him, suggesting that what-ever had killed everything in that section of ground had occurred before the ring road had been built, perhaps hun-dreds if not thousands of years before.

Then he extended his Talent senses once more, noting that his Southern Guard companies were in position, as were Colonel Hubar's forces, and that the Matrites were little more than a vingt to the south. Shortly, the rifles of the Twenty-eighth and Thirty-fifth Companies opened fire, a solid series of volleys.

The Matrites did not return fire, but Alucius also could not sense any power in the crystal spear-thrower. He frowned. Were they using it as a bluff? Or trying to avoid using it too much?

The volleys from the two Southern Guard companies continued, and Alucius could feel the occasional wound or death from the Matrite companies flanking and following the spear-thrower.

Volleys began from Hubar's Southern Guard companies, and still the spear-thrower had not been powered up.

The heavier bullets from Fifth Company began to fly over Alucius's head, and Hubar's lancers began to pull back.

Craaackk . . . Energy began to build rapidly within the approaching spear-thrower.

Alucius swallowed, hoping that Jultyr and Deotyr would drop back before the spear-thrower reached full power, and the Matrites turned it northeast toward them.

He could sense the lancers of his two Southern Guard companies pulling back, but the spear-thrower also seemed to be casting its deadly weapons toward them. Alucius took a breath as he sensed the spears falling short—mostly. He could also sense a death or two.

Hubar's Southern Guards continued to pull back, and Alucius hoped that they hadn't been too late in retreating.

He had to ignore those and concentrate on the weapon itself, extending his own Talent-probe in a way to avoid the shielding nimbus of unseen pinkish light that englobed the spear-thrower—except at the point where the spears formed and were accelerated outward.

There he twisted his Talent-probe toward the glittering Talentlike diamond nodes that rotated around the spear-formation point. Recalling his promise to Alyniat, he tried to tease out one of the threads he knew were within the node, but the node remained solid. This time, he tried to trace out the forces that propelled the nodes, but there were no threads there, at least none that were unprotected by the pinkish shield.

Then he tried twisting one of the nodes, but his Talent-probe couldn't budge it. He tried opening it with dark life-force, spinning it, but the nodes kept moving, and every so often a swath of crystal spears flew somewhere.

By then Alucius could sense that the spear-thrower was less than five hundred yards away and beginning to scythe its spears toward Fifth Company. With the lancers just back of it, it wouldn't be long before a Talent-officer spotted him. Alucius certainly couldn't assume that there wouldn't be one.

With a deep breath, he returned to what he knew worked, lending his strength to speeding the diamond nodes in their rotation. As before, after a rotation and a half or so, the tiniest thread spun out from one diamond node. Alucius Talent-grasped it and tugged. The node began to unravel, then vanished in a flashing spray of thread. The following node shifted forward, and all the nodes began to trail threads. Alucius grasped them all and tugged with all his Talent-force.

The hard and previous impervious crystal of the discharge formulator sagged, and pinkish force built behind it, followed by an even greater surge of power from somewhere beyond poured into the spear-thrower.

Alucius flattened himself on the bottom of his trench and dropped a greenish Talent-shield around himself. The ground, the shield, and he were shaken violently. A blast of flame roared overhead, with metal and crystal scything through the late-afternoon air.

More death and destruction followed. For a time, Alucius just lay in the bottom of the trench, half-covered with dust and dirt that had fallen on him—or his shield. He stayed flat until he was certain that the rain of metal and crystal had stopped.

Then he began to inch himself upward, letting his senses range outward.

There were still almost two companies of Matrite lancers a half vingt south of where the crystal spear-thrower had been. Alucius could also tell that a good half company of Hubar's lancers had been struck down.

With all the dirt around him, he had to half dig his way out of the trench, and it took him two attempts to struggle out of the dirt and onto his knees beside the trench. He looked northward. Fifth Company was formed and riding toward him.

He stood, and as he held his rifle and watched Dhaget leading the gray toward him, he tried not to think about Frynkel's observation on leading from the front.

"There's the colonel!"

Alucius mounted quickly, but Fifth Company was well past by the time he was back on the road, surveying the carnage. Twenty-eighth and Thirty-fifth Companies were moving up smartly from the east, with Thirty-fifth a good hundred yards ahead of Deotyr and his men. To the south, from what he'd seen and sensed, the Matrite forces were more disorganized than those in the west had been—but there were also more of them.

Hubar's lancers were still milling around to the northwest of the fight, as if there were no officers to give orders. "Idiots!" he mumbled quietly. "Just sit there like targets."

Sheathing the rifle and drawing his sabre, Alucius urged the gray forward, moving just behind Fifth Company's fifth squad. He felt as though he should have been leading the charge, rather than following it. He could sense the impacts as the Northern Guard lancers slammed into the near-motionless Matrites.

Alucius swung the gray out to the left and found himself attacked by two Matrites. A wave of red fury surged over him at the mere sight of the two attackers, and he pressed the gray toward them. He slipped the first wild slash and countered with enough force that his sabre slammed the Matrite's weapon from his hand and cut deeply into the man. Alucius finished him with a quick cut and twisted in the saddle to parry the violent cut of the big woman who had attacked while he was dealing with the first Matrite. Almost contemptuously, with a strength he had not known he had, he deflected her blade and slash-thrust through her neck.

He moved forward, taking another Matrite from behind with a single cut, just before the man was about to take down a Northern Guard, also from behind.

In a moment of calm, Alucius glanced to the southeast, where a full Matrite company charged up the hill toward the rear of Thirty-fifth Company, engaged in hand-to-hand with the remnants of the last Matrite companies. He looked north where two or three of Twenty-eighth Company's squads were re-forming—a command of which Alucius approved.

He rode partway down the slope and called out, "Twenty-eighth Company! On me!"

"On the colonel!" Deotyr echoed.

"Forward!"

Alucius once more urged the gray forward as the Twenty-eighth Company lancers fell in behind him. He found himself alone at the point of attack, and the red fury took him as his sabre became a shimmering circle of death, with lancers scrambling back from his berserk rage. Behind him and to both sides, Twenty-eighth Company crashed into the Matrites who had thought to surprise Thirty-fifth Company and had been themselves surprised, if only by the speed and fury of Alucius and those who followed.

A horn doublet sounded.

Alucius glanced around, finding himself nearly alone—except, five yards to the east, a Matrite squad had appeared, halted, and raised rifles.

Even before Alucius sensed the line of fire flaring toward him, he urged the gray forward, then, instinctively, raised his sabre, as if to block whatever it was, knowing that the gesture was futile as a huge unseen hammer struck him and flung him from the saddle.

His last thought, with the blackness sweeping over him, as he struggled to stay in the saddle, was that Frynkel had been right. Leading from the front could get him killed.

90

North of Iron Stem, Iron Valleys

The three sat in the main room. Wendra leaned back slightly in the rocking chair, her feet on the lower hassock. Lucenda had taken the end of the couch closest to Wendra. A book lay in Lucenda's lap, closed with a leather marker in it.

Wendra looked blankly at the wall to the right of the hearth.

"Can you tell how he is?" Lucenda.

Wendra shook her head. "I should have gone south. I should have."

"You're due in a few weeks. Then what would you do?" asked Lucenda. "You can ride. No one can gainsay that, but having a babe on the road . . . that's not wise."

"What's wise, anymore?" Wendra's lips tightened into a near-cynical smile. "Alucius was doing what he thought best. Now . . ."

"If he's alive after three days, and the crystal's not fading, he'll recover," Lucenda said.

"I worry that he'll be . . . Alucius isn't a man to sit around . . ."

"He won't sit," interjected Royalt, standing in the archway from the kitchen. "Herders don't. Hulius lost both legs. Still herded until he was near ninety. Fudalt . . ."

"Father . . . we know you're all indestructible, but Wendra doesn't need to think about things like that. Besides, Alucius will be all right. That's that." Lucenda straightened.

"Kustyl'll be bringing the goats tomorrow, Septi at the latest," Royalt announced.

"We don't need goats," Lucenda said.

"Maybe yes, maybe no. Kustyl's insisting. They're a gift."

"But . . ." Lucenda glanced at Wendra.

"His Mairee had trouble nursing," Royalt said. "He figures Wendra won't, but Mairee insists, just in case. Says we can always use them if we get another lamb that turns motherless or if one has twins."

"Grandmother's always been like that," Wendra said. "That's why her cellar has everything in it. Grandfather says it's less trouble to store the extras than to argue about it."

"Wise man," observed Lucenda.

Wendra stiffened.

"Alucius?" asked Lucenda.

"Just a little cramp . . . the kind that sort of exercises things," Wendra said. "She's just fine."

"You still think you'll call her Alendra?"

"That's what we'd agreed on, and I still like it," replied Wendra, shifting her weight in the chair. "I feel like a ewe with twins."

"You're small. I was out to here with Alucius." Lucenda placed her hand a third of a yard in front of her still-slender waist.

"I know that. But I don't feel small. Especially when she kicks."

"She'll be a healthy one, no matter," Royalt observed.

"She'll be big, we think," Wendra said, "more like Alucius."

"She'll be beautiful, whatever size she is," added Lucenda.

Wendra's eyes dropped to the black crystal of the herder's ring. "He's still strong."

"Alucius was meant for great things," Lucenda mused. "He'll be back, strong and healthy. He's a soarer's child."

"But he's suffered so much already," Wendra said quietly.

"The great ones do," Royalt said in a low voice.

Lucenda shot a glance at her father, but Wendra only smiled sadly, her eyes focused far beyond the wall before her.

91

A reddish pink haze enveloped Alucius. At times it was redder and more painful, and at other times a trace of cooling golden green crept in. Then the haze was barely pink, and he merely felt as though he had been staked out in the summer sun, rather than placed on a bonfire. Every time he started to feel even slightly cooler, the redness and heat and pain returned, and when he tried to lift his arms to ward off the unseen sun, he could not.

He could sense water or liquid going down his throat, and even that hurt, and the water cooled him not at all.

In time, the haze faded enough that he could make out a figure looking down at him.

"Colonel . . . ? Can you hear me?"

"Yes . . ." Alucius half mumbled, half croaked.

"That's good. You were badly injured, but you're going to be all right. It's going to take some time. Just try to relax."

Relax? When he alternated between burning and merely being overheated?

Even that simple thought was enough to plunge him back into the pinkish fog, the pink that he'd come to dislike so much.

When he woke again, he could see more clearly. He was in a moderately wide bed in a small room with a window. A heavy splint was strapped around his right forearm. There was gray and rain, he thought, beyond the window, but the white walls of his room helped in keeping the gray at bay.

Within a short time, a heavyset, gray-haired woman in pale gray appeared beside his bed. For a time, she looked down at him. Then she smiled, almost sadly. "You will recover. It will take time."

Alucius couldn't place her accent or her speech. It was somewhere between Madrien and Lanachronan. "How long . . . ?"

"You have been here more than a week. They did not think you would live. You have two broken ribs, two cracked ribs, a broken arm, and your chest was so badly bruised that it was bloody from your neck to your waist. So was your right thigh. Even nightsilk cannot save someone who has lost that much blood to bruising."

"You're cheerful," Alucius rasped.

"Much of the bruising has already healed. I have not told anyone how badly you were injured."

"Thank you."

"You are a child of the ancients. We have not seen one in many years." She extended a mug. "You should drink. This will help with the healing."

Alucius drank, and in time, drained the mug.

"You're from Southgate?" he asked.

"From Dramur, years ago. Here I became the healer to the Seltyr Benjir. He knew I did not wish to return to Dramur, and he let me escape when the Lanachronans came. Now . . . you must rest. You have many vingts yet to travel."

With the same sad smile, she stepped back. Alucius could feel the reddish darkness creeping over him, but it was not so hot this time.

For the next few days, he drifted in and out of sleep, mostly.

One afternoon, he woke to see a figure in a Northern Guard uniform sitting on a stool beside his bed.

"What . . . who . . ." His voice felt and sounded like his vocal cords had been filled with sandstone and grit, but that seemed to be the case every time he woke.

"Waris, sir. You were hurt pretty bad, they say, but it looks like everything is healing all right. Healers don't know why, but that doesn't matter."

"Matrites . . . ?"

L. E. MODESITT, JR.

"You smashed 'em, sir, you and the overcaptain . . . broke their whole center. Captain Deotyr, he'd never seen you fight in battle. Said you took out a whole squad by yourself, the ones going after Thirty-fifth Company. The other Southern Guard companies got it together enough after that. We slaughtered half of 'em. Maybe more. Captain Deotyr . . . he saw that they'd set up an ambush just to try to get you . . . he fought like a madman. All of Twenty-eighth Company did . . . they were pretty good this time. Never thought I'd see that, not after those days back in Krost, but they were good . . .

"Word is that the Matrites have moved back to Hafin. Colonel Faurad took back Dimor, too. The whole south of Madrien is back under the Lord-Protector's control. Matrites don't do so good without those spear-throwers."

"That was . . . the idea."

"Overcaptain Feran, he's got everything organized. We even got a wagon of the right kind of ammunition yesterday. Been a little worried about that. Didn't have much left after the big fight on the ring road."

"Any word on going home?"

"You don't worry about that, sir. Overcaptain says we don't go until you go. Besides, we got a few others need to heal, too. More 'n a few, actually. About twenty."

Alucius didn't really want to ask about casualties. "How many didn't make it?"

Waris looked away, then back at Alucius. "Both battles . . . we lost thirty. Thirty-fifth Company lost thirty-five, Twenty-eighth almost forty."

Alucius winced, and pain shot through his entire body. "Too . . . many."

"No, sir. Most Southern Guard outfits, they lost fifty, sixty, out of every hundred. Matrites lost eighty. Figure we're lucky." Waris stood. "Healer said I shouldn't stay long, sir, but wanted you to know everyone's glad you were in charge, want to see you back soon."

"Thank you."

"You take care, sir."

After Waris left, Alucius looked at the window and the grayness beyond. In winter in Southgate, was there ever sunlight?

All told, Fifth Company had taken roughly forty percent casualties . . . and that was the lowest by half? What was happening? How had the Lord-Protector and the Regent ever gotten themselves into positions where such carnage was necessary? And why?

The grayness of the day merged with the hot grayness of sleep before he ever found an answer.

92

Hieron, Madrien

The Regent stood to the right of the conference table. Because of the rain and mist that fell outside the wide glass window, only the southern quarter of the Park of the Matrial was visible. The southern part of Hieron had been swallowed by gray mist and rain. The Regent's violet eyes fixed on the officer who had just entered the chamber.

"I have read your report, Marshal Benyal. I am not pleased. We no longer have either crystal spear-thrower?"

"We don't even have the pieces of either, Regent." The marshal's voice was flat and level. Her eyes met those of the Regent.

"How could that possibly happen? How could both explode in the same campaign? In the same battle?"

"We don't know. The first one exploded as well after a period of use, as you may recall. It may be that the weapon does not hold up well for prolonged use."

"I find that hard to believe. A weapon whose parts endured for more than two millennia explodes after a few weeks of use?"

"There is another possibility. We do know that there was one company of Northern Guards in the battle. This is the first time they've been sent south. We're fairly certain that we killed their commander."

"What does that have to do with the crystal spear-thrower? If anything?" Scorn colored the Regent's voice.

"Only this. The first spear-thrower failed and partly exploded in the battle for Soulend against the Northern Guard. They were the Iron Valley Militia then, but there may be a lamaial among their officers. That was why we targeted the officer at Southgate. Even if the spear-throwers were destroyed, we would not wish to suffer a lamaial to live."

"The lamaials—always a lamaial." The Regent glared at the marshal. "And the pieces? What of them?"

"Both weapons exploded into small fragments. The detonations killed almost ten companies and cleared the areas where they exploded. Without the lancers, we could not recover what scraps there were, but the reports we did receive indicate that there were few fragments larger than palm-sized."

"How soon can we build another?"

"We cannot. Not at present. The plans for the formulator assemblies were lost when the engineer's revolt failed."

"One section . . . we are missing the plans for one section, and you can do nothing. Could not anyone have studied that section and created plans?"

"We had two working spear-throwers. Had we tried to take one apart and determine its construction, there was a good chance that we would have lost that one and still not been able to determine how it was built."

"I *will* get you those plans, Marshal. You *will* find an engineer to build another spear-thrower. And you will make sure that we retain the ability to build others. Is that clear?"

"Yes, Regent. Perfectly clear."

"Good. I am most tired of explaining the obvious time and time again." After a pause, the Regent gestured. "You may go."

Benyal bowed and turned, her face remaining impassive under the steel gray hair.

93

Alucius shifted his weight in the padded chair. His eyes dropped to the heavy splint on his right arm. He still hadn't figured out how he'd broken his right forearm. He remembered throwing up his left, sabre in hand, and being hammered out of the saddle. Had he broken the right in falling?

The healer had said that it had been broken by rifle fire against the nightsilk of his undergarments. He could recall seeing all the rifles aimed at him. But why? How had the Matrites even known he was there? Or were they shooting at all commanders? Was that why there weren't any bright ones left in the Southern Guard? That sort of tactics would certainly explain many things.

He tried to ignore all the aches. If he lay flat in bed, his ribs didn't hurt so much, but he had to cough and had trouble breathing easily. If he sat propped up in the chair or in bed, his chest and ribs hurt more. No matter what position he assumed, something hurt. In the end, he decided that he'd deal with the pain of the ribs and use the chair as much as he could. He forced himself to stand and walk around the room at least once a glass, but he was careful to keep a hand on something to steady himself.

As he had improved, Alucius had discovered that he—along with other wounded officers—had been put in a villa that years before had belonged to a wealthy factor. He was one of the few with a room to himself, one of the privileges of rank, he had gathered.

He was reading, or trying to read, a history of Southgate, but he found sometimes he had to go over the words several times. That might have been because the book had been written in Dramurian, which was related, but not too closely, to Madrien. Outside the window, the sun was shining, the first sunny day he could recall since he'd been truly awake after his injuries, and the window was ajar, letting in a cool refreshing breeze that almost took away the sour smells that drifted into Alucius's room from the other rooms and halls.

He concentrated on the words before him.

> . . . in the time of Seltyr Alijir, the harbor walls were strengthened and thickened. The hills around the city, at a distance of fifteen vingts from the square, were leveled at a height of thirty yards above the lands surrounding to the west of the coastal high road and ten yards to the east . . .

"You're looking better," observed Feran, moving into the small white-walled room.

"Better than when?"

"I've come by a few times, but you weren't in any shape to remember."

"That was most of the first two weeks. Another week, and they say I'll be able to move to some sort of regular senior officers' quarters."

Feran settled onto the stool across from Alucius. "They just want to get you out of here."

"How's Fifth Company doing?"

"I've got them back into a training routine. We're doing the same thing with Twenty-eighth and Thirty-fifth Companies. No one's shifted command of them. I thought it'd be a shame to see everything they learned lost."

"I see you share my high opinion of certain Southern Guard practices," Alucius said cheerfully, ignoring the twinges in his ribs.

"You were too charitable, Colonel." Feran snorted.

"What now?"

"Nothing. That's the problem. They either ought to strike a peace of some sort with the Regent or take Hafin and Salcer. That would cut their supply lines and make it harder on the Regent."

"It also would put the most productive lands of Madrien in the hands of Lanachrona." Alucius frowned. "I wouldn't blame the Lord-Protector, though. The Matrites never would sue for peace or accept it on anyone else's terms. I doubt that the Lord-Protector has enough lancers to make another assault. Waris told me that the casualty rates were something like fifty percent in the Southern Guard."

"Higher for some companies. Makes us look pretty good," Feran said.

How could his forces have the lowest rates by far with casualties running well over thirty percent? "No one can keep fighting for long with those kinds of casualties."

"They've been doing it for a couple of years, they tell me. Not so many big battles, but smaller fights with those kinds of casualties."

"That's going to hurt the Matrites more."

"How do you figure that?" asked Feran.

"They've got more women in arms. Dead women don't have children. Also means they'll have more trouble with men—and they'll have to keep using those torques."

"It looks like a standoff to me," Feran suggested. "The Lanachronans have to travel farther and hold longer supply lines, and they're fighting on less familiar territory, but their lancer ranks fight better. The Matrites have a more compact land to defend now, and they're better marshaled and led, but their lancers aren't as good. Oh . . . and the Lanachronans are going to lose you when we head home, and that won't help."

"They're losing you, too."

"Everything I learned . . . I learned from you."

"That's hardly true, and I'm still making mistakes—like getting ambushed."

"That was stupid," Feran said amiably.

"Very stupid," Alucius agreed.

"No. Stupid of the Matrites. After the first volley, they were all set up like clay targets. Don't think one of those snipers escaped. They all got killed, and that left them surrounded. Twenty-eighth Company butchered them. And you survived."

"I wasn't sure about that for a time."

"No one was, but I figured that if you could make it through the first days, you'd come all the way back."

"I appreciate your confidence."

"I did take one liberty." Feran looked down.

"Liberty?" Alucius didn't have the faintest idea of what Feran meant.

"Figured that your being a herder and all, your Wendra'd probably sense you were hurt. So we sent off a letter dispatch to her. Told her you'd been hurt badly, but looked like you'd recover fully. Also told her you'd been made a temporary colonel. Just hope it gets there."

Alucius smiled. "Thank you. I appreciate that. I can't tell you how much."

"Knew you were worried. Times you were talking to her, or about her . . ." Feran looked sheepish. "You cared that much, all those letters you wrote . . . thought she ought to know."

"I can't thank . . ." Alucius yawned, in spite of himself.

"That's my signal to go." Feran smiled and stood.

"Thank you for coming by."

"We took turns."

"Turns?"

"While you were unconscious, first week, someone was here every moment."

Alucius swallowed.

"We all know that as many of us made it through as did was because of you. Every man does."

Alucius was speechless.

"Get some rest, Colonel." Feran grinned, then stepped out of the room.

94

Prosp, Lustrea

Waleryn glanced at the image in the polished surface of the Table, his own image looking back up at him, that of a Lanachronan lord in the uniform of a Praetorian Engineer. His lips quirked into a crooked smile. He straightened and waited.

Around him, the recently cleared chamber was clean of dust and grit, but the walls and pillars remained bare. Besides the Table, a workbench set against the wall, a tall stool, and several wooden crates were the only objects within the reinforced stone walls of the chamber.

"Engineer? The Praetor will be here shortly."

"I await him with pleasure," replied Waleryn, turning from the Table.

Two of the Praetorian Guards stepped into the Table chamber. The taller walked around the Table and opened the drawers in the chest, closing them after his inspection. The shorter lifted the tops of the crates, one by one, replacing them. Their inspection complete, they stationed themselves on each side of the door.

Waleryn continued to stand by the Table, waiting.

A quarter glass passed, then another quarter, before the sound of boots announced the arrival of more Guards and the Praetor. Two more Guards entered the Table chamber, followed by Tyren, wearing a black cloak trimmed in silver, over the shimmering silver tunic and trousers of the Praetor.

"I trust this will be worth a detour, Engineer." Tyren's voice was curt. "Show us."

"If you would step forward and behold the Table, most

honored Praetor," offered Waleryn, "I can show you what is happening this very moment at any locale in Corus."

"Perhaps . . . no, a wise man does not look too deeply into his personal life." Tyren laughed. "Such temptation, but one best resisted. Show me something of the so-called Council of Five in Dereka. If you can."

"That can be." Waleryn looked into the table, and the silver reflection of the two men vanished, to be replaced by swirling ruby mists. Immediately, the mists vanished, replaced with a view of an audience hall. On the dais at one end of the hall was a table in the shape of a semicircle, and on the arced side sat five men in high-backed gilt chairs, facing two lancer officers in ornate gold and crimson uniforms.

The view showed the backs of the officers and the faces of the Council. All five faces radiated displeasure.

"They are not happy." Tyren sounded pleased. "And they should not be, not with our legions marshaled in Passera to begin the campaign once the worst of the snows on the Spine of Corus melt."

Dampness formed on Waleryn's forehead as an unseen set of purpled arms rose out of the Table and slowly embraced Tyren.

"What . . ." Tyren fell silent.

"They . . . the Council . . . is threatening some sort of punishment. That is clear," offered Waleryn. "It may be that they do not believe the reports of your legions." He glanced at the immobile form of the young blond Praetor, whose hands and arms were knotted, gripping the edge of the Table. "Then . . . they may be looking for someone to blame for their own foolishness." More sweat beaded on Waleryn's forehead.

The figure of the Praetor remained unspeaking . . . although his face contorted, moving rapidly from expression to expression, and his eyes appeared close to bulging from his forehead.

"They . . . they are letting them depart . . . Yes . . . as you request, Praetor," Waleryn spoke. "An image of the

Lord-Protector . . . In a moment, for it takes time to displace one image and seek another."

Suddenly, the Praetor's face smoothed, and a wide smile appeared. "Yes . . . we should see that image, Engineer. You should follow the Lord-Protector closely. After Dereka, Tempre will be our next conquest." The hearty laugh that followed carried a chill undertone. "And . . . you shall come with me, so far as Vysta, where you will proceed to Norda. You will have all the supplies you require to rebuild yet another Table."

"Yes, Praetor." Waleryn bowed his head, concealing the smile of triumph.

95

Alucius sat in the armchair in front of the window, overlooking a rain-slicked stone courtyard. Outside, the sky was leaden gray, much the way he felt. His eyes dropped to the history in his lap.

"Colonel . . ."

Alucius looked up to see Alyniat standing in the doorway. "Marshal. I hadn't expected you."

"After my last comments, under the circumstances, I imagine not." A crooked smile crossed Alyniat's lips.

"Or after mine," Alucius admitted.

"Yours were deserved. Mine were not. I have to admit that I was wrong, Colonel," Alyniat said, a trace of a smile still hovering at the corners of his lips. "That's a hard thing for marshals."

"Sir?"

"The stories of your exploits have crossed the entire Southern Guard. You walked through the crystal spears . . . you single-handedly killed five companies of Matrites . . . it took an entire squad of Matrites firing at you from point-blank range to bring you down . . ."

That part, Alucius reflected, was the only one that actually contained a grain of truth.

". . . you saved two companies by charging an entire Matrite force alone . . ." Alyniat shrugged. "I also came to apologize."

"Sir . . . you did the best anyone could in those circumstances . . ."

"Except for you, Colonel."

Alucius laughed. "I wasn't that bright. I almost got killed riding into a trap that I should have seen."

"By doing it, you rallied five companies into routing almost ten and putting Southgate back under the Lord-Protector's control. Everything changed after you destroyed the second crystal spear-thrower. I got a rather graphic report from Captain Vyarinst. He interviewed two whole squads of lancers because he couldn't believe what he had been hearing."

Alucius tried not to wince.

"They all said the same thing," Alyniat continued, inexorably. "The crystal spear-thrower exploded, and you rose out of the ground and mounted your horse. You caught up with the company that had charged past you and rallied another company to follow you. Single-handedly, you cut down an entire Matrite squad, taking blows that would have felled a lesser man—"

"Matrite squads are only eight men, sir."

"I'm not at all sure that changes much, Colonel," Alyniat replied, smiling broadly. "Then, you charged a squad clearly sent to assassinate you, and you killed two of them with a sabre you flung just before you were struck with something like twenty bullets. That was how many they found flattened against your nightsilk."

"I just did what had to be done."

"Do you want to tell me how you destroyed that construct of evil?"

"Let's just say that I put myself where I could fling charges under it. That was the trench."

Alyniat laughed, then shook his head. "It's a good thing you actually had requested blasting powder."

"We did, you know."

"Colonel . . . your account makes perfect sense. I doubt strongly that what really happened would make sense, or would make anyone very happy. Marshal Frynkel, the Lord-Protector, and I are just grateful that you and your lancers managed to accomplish the impossible . . . again. Once you are well enough to ride, you may return to Tempre, at your convenience, where the Lord-Protector wishes to see you, then return to your Iron Valleys."

"What about Twenty-eighth and Thirty-fifth Companies?"

"Your question does you credit, but it is, again, a measure of your abilities." Alyniat's smile turned crooked. "I cannot send them to the Iron Valleys. They will return with you so far as Tempre. Both companies have been recommended for commendation as distinguished units, and they will receive a month's furlough in recognition of that, and a half month's pay as an additional bonus. More than that, we cannot do."

Alucius understood. "Thank you. They fought well, and they've learned much."

"So have their officers." Alyniat paused. "Captain Deotyr observed that were you in command of the Northern Guard, Lanachrona would never have to worry about its northern borders."

"I fear he rates me too highly," Alucius demurred. "He is young. There are many capable officers in the Northern and Southern Guard."

"Capable, yes. Outstanding, no."

Alucius didn't want to deal with that.

"Just as a matter of simple justice," Alyniat added, "your back pay was adjusted to that of a colonel from the date Marshal Frynkel sealed your orders to Southgate. Under the circumstances, that seemed only fair."

"Thank you, sir."

"Thank *you*, Colonel. Without you and your men, we would be fleeing to Tempre this very moment. I am most happy to be able to reward those who have broken the threat of the Regent."

Alucius decided against mentioning the repowering of the torques.

"I will see you before long, and before you return to Tempre."

"Yes, sir."

With a friendly smile, the marshal departed.

Alucius had sensed that most of what Alyniat had said was what the man felt, except that the marshal would also be relieved when Alucius left. Would it always be that way? That people wanted him to accomplish the impossible, then were glad to see him go?

Alucius looked to the window. Would he really be able to return to the Iron Valleys? Without some other hidden "request" or obligation? Would the Lord-Protector honor his promise to promote Alucius to commander of the Northern Guard? Did Alucius really want that?

He looked down at the history of Southgate that lay in his lap, then back at the dreary winter sky outside the window. He had no answers, none that were clear to him.

96

Salaan, Lanachrona

The two men walked toward the building set in the low hills to the southwest of Salaan, a building of recent construction that half burrowed into a hill that was but one segment of a long ridge that extended vingts both to the northeast and southwest.

"For all your efforts, the majer survived, except he is a colonel now," observed Trezun.

"He barely survived, you said, and it will be weeks, if not a season or more, before he can leave Southgate," replied the white-haired and pale-faced Tarolt.

"With his Talent, it will be weeks, not seasons, and he will be stronger for all that he has been through. That is one of the dangers of failing to eliminate him."

"What is your concern? The injuries prove that he is but mortal. He has yet to face a fully translated Efran." Tarolt laughed. "The devastation and casualties he has created could not have been better. Hyalt is a shadow of its former self. The Regent is bleeding Madrien to a husk, and the Lord-Protector is doing little better with his own land. People are getting poorer and more dissatisfied, and none dare voice their anger. Neither ruler understands what is happening. That is as we had planned."

"Majer . . . Colonel Alucius . . . he should have died more than five times. The last two, there were not even any ancient ones around."

"My dear Recorder, the colonel is doing us far more good alive than were he dead. He raises hopes, and thousands have died. What will they do once he has departed? They will be bereft of that hope."

"I question that." Trezun stepped into the front hall of the Table building. "Hyalt is rebuilding, and unless you are willing to send Sensat back there and find another Talent-steer to shadow-match, we will see no gain there."

"Oh . . . but we have. Already, all of Lanachrona and much of Madrien wearies of war and of endless casualties. At the very least, who in Hyalt is left to oppose the new duarchy? All they wish is to tend their gardens in peace, and that we can give them." Tarolt followed Trezun into the room with the conference table. "And what of Waleryn? Has he located the scepters?" Irony tinged Tarolt's words.

"He has moved most expeditiously. After he arrived in Prosp and cleared the fallen building from the Table, he re-activated the Table and added its power to the grid." Trezun smiled. "He just sent a message. We have shadow-matched the Praetor, and he is supplying Waleryn and dispatching him to Norda to rebuild the Table there."

"That will take time. It is a three-week ride from Prosp to Norda in good weather."

"You had said that we needed more Tables."

"Lasylt has been pressing," admitted Tarolt. "And the duarchists of Dulka?"

"That proceeds as well. Without another Table powering the grid, we will have to send someone there by the high roads."

"Once the Table in Norda is operating . . ."

"We may need one more, yet."

"That will come . . . all is going well, and the colonel is not going anywhere in the next few weeks. Even were he recovered this moment, he would face a journey of weeks to return to the Iron Valleys."

"Then what? What if Weslyn is right to fear that the majer will be placed in Northern Guard headquarters?"

"Majer . . . Colonel Alucius does not wish to be a Northern Guard. What motivated him to accept the Lord-Protector's request was fear that he would lose his stead to the Regent, not ambition to become a majer or a colonel. No matter what happens, we do not lose. If Alucius goes back to herding, the situation in the south will continue to worsen, and the conflict between the Lord-Protector and the Regent will seesaw back and forth with greater casualties and more unrest, and Alucius can and will do nothing. If he becomes the deputy to Weslyn, that will tear the Guard apart and create even more unrest in Dekhron. That will lead to less effective lancers in the north of Madrien. If he replaces Weslyn, Halanat will turn the traders against him, and that will create great discontent and a revolt of sorts here." Tarolt shrugged. "It matters not. The unrest will grow, and so will the support for the peace and prosperity of a new duarchy."

"Led by our shadowed Praetor?"

"That would be best, but the Regent would serve if

something goes ill with Tyren. It is best to keep multiple options available. We will use whatever tools are at hand. If the majer ends up in the right place, we could even translate him and create a duarchy here."

"I think that is unlikely."

"Unlikely? Yes . . . but stranger things have occurred." Tarolt smiled. "They have indeed."

97

Another week passed, and Alucius had moved to a second villa, down the road from the one where he had first started to recover. The villa itself was on the outskirts of Southgate, perched on a low hill. From the writing desk in front of the narrow window in his room at the rear of the second floor, Alucius could look out at a large, walled courtyard, with a fountain that no longer held water, and vines and trees in planters adjacent to the walls. The lemon and lime trees seemed to be healthy, and there was fruit on their branches. The grapevines were bare and without grapes, but it was early winter, even if it did not seem to freeze in Southgate. From what Alucius could tell, the walls of both the villa and the courtyard were stone covered in stucco and painted a bluish white that had faded to grayish white in places. Gray dust had gathered in the northern corners of the courtyard.

On another cloudy Tridi afternoon, he was seated before the small writing desk in the modest quarters, taking a short break and looking down at the courtyard, then out at the heavy gray clouds that were too high to deliver rain. After a time, he took a deep breath and dropped his eyes to the papers on the wood before him. He'd been writing out his own report to Marshal Frynkel and the Lord-Protector. No doubt the marshal already had reports, but there was some information that the Lord-Protector needed, and that Alucius doubted would be passed along—not from what he had seen. Still, necessary as reports might be, writing them was not something he enjoyed, especially at the moment. With his right arm still in the splint, while he was left-handed, writing was still slower with only one hand. His eyes began to look back over the key phrases and paragraphs of draft conclusions that followed his chronological report of what had happened to his force since they had left Hyalt.

. . . Matrites try to avoid attacking fixed positions, and do so only when they have weapons or other clear advantages. This tendency has apparently been overlooked by many Southern Guard officers . . .

"Letters? Or reports?" came a voice from the door.

Alucius turned. Feran stood there, wearing a lancer riding jacket over his uniform.

"Reports. I sent off a letter to Wendra yesterday."

"At least you've got your priorities in order. You think you're up to riding?"

"For a while, anyway, and it would be good to get out of here."

"I thought it might, and it's easier if I just show up with a mount."

Alucius stacked the sheets of the incomplete report and weighted them down with a book of Southgate history he had been puzzling through. Then he stood and moved to the pegs set into the white-plastered walls of the room where his few clothes hung and took down the nightsilk riding jacket, carefully closing it over the sling so that his right sleeve hung down empty. "Be glad when I can take off the splint."

"Has the healer said when?"

"Not before next week. I'll have to be careful and wear a brace."

Feran laughed. "You look pretty good for a man who ought to be dead."

"The ribs are still sore." Alucius walked toward the door. He followed Feran down the wide tile steps of the grand staircase that rose from the entry hall and out into the front courtyard. The afternoon was cool and moist, not raining or misting, but there were few scents in the air, just dampness and moldy vegetation.

The mount Feran had brought for Alucius was a chestnut. Alucius glanced at the overcaptain.

"Your gray," Feran said slowly, "he took as many bullets as you did. More probably, and mounts don't wear nightsilk."

For a moment, Alucius just stood there. Then, he mounted, easily, even one-handed—another skill he could attribute to his grandsire. As he settled into the saddle, he couldn't help but consider that the gray had been the third mount he'd lost in combat, one way or another. He reached down and patted the big chestnut. "Where to?"

"I thought you might like to see some of Southgate, since you almost died defending it."

"Lead on. You have to know more about it than I do."

The gates to the villa were of weathered timbers, but not ironbound, and had been left open. Neither of the two Southern Guard lancers on guard duty even looked in Alucius's direction as the two officers rode out. Feran turned right, heading southward along a road paved with square reddish stone.

Alucius followed, glancing ahead. So far as he could see, every dwelling was like the villa he had left, in that each was surrounded by a white stucco-finished wall so that the street was, in effect, walled, with a raised space for walking on each side. But the sidewalks were only a yard in width and the street but five. With the walls for the houses almost three yards high, even in the saddle Alucius felt closed in. Cross streets were just as narrow, and seemed to be set about a hundred yards apart.

"Are all the streets like this?"

"Most of them, except in the center of Southgate, or out beyond the city walls."

"How far are we from the high road?"

"About two vingts. Both high roads end at the city walls. The closest is the southwest high road. That's about two vingts to the east of here. Your villa's less than a quarter vingt from the north wall."

"The high roads don't come into Southgate?"

"Not that I know. Never thought about that, though. Wonder why they don't," mused Feran.

Alucius wondered as well. "The walls are about ten vingts inside the ring road, and the roads end at the walls."

Feran nodded.

As they rode southward past dwellings that were far smaller than those around the villa, Alucius became aware of what he had sensed before—except the feeling was far more pronounced. Beneath everything was the pervading sense of deadness, the lack of life in the deeper soil.

Under the gray clouds, the street was vacant. Alucius could sense people in the dwellings, but he saw only two people on the sidewalk—two white-haired women in shapeless gray coats and trousers—and no other riders. "Not many people out."

"There never are. A few more in the early morning, and a bunch out on Septi—that's market day. Looks almost normal then."

The street crossed a stone bridge that arched only slightly over a stone-lined and paved streambed. A trickle of muddy water meandered across the ten-yard-wide stone base of the oversized ditch. On the far side of the bridge, the houses were yet smaller, and their walls replaced the courtyard walls. No windows opened onto the street, only narrow wooden gates.

They rode for at least another two vingts, past more of the small dwellings, interspersed upon occasion with rows of small shops. There, Alucius did see people, but they all avoided looking at the two officers.

"Center of Southgate's ahead, across the inner ring," Feran announced.

Inner ring? Alucius decided against asking, at least until he saw it.

The street down which they had ridden came to a cross street, clearly the inner ring of which Feran had spoken, because Alucius could see that it arced in both directions. The pavement was smooth gray granite, and it was, unlike the other streets, a good thirty yards in width. Alucius looked both east and west, but he saw no riders on the inner ring.

On the far side of the ring was what appeared to be a walled palace, with four graceful stone towers, each set at the corner of walls that formed a trapezoid. Alucius judged that the "base" of the wall facing him was roughly a half vingt long. He looked to the right, then to the left. From what he could tell, there were a number of such "palaces" set in a circle inside the inner ring. Alucius lost count at eleven. "How many are there?"

"Thirteen, I'm told. They form a circle around the central square, except it's round."

Feran and Alucius crossed the inner ring.

As they rode past the four-yard-high stone walls, Alucius could sense no life within them. "Doesn't anyone live there now?"

"No. They gutted them and stuffed everything on ships and went to Dramuria once it was clear that the Lord-Protector would take the city. Didn't leave a gold or a statue or much of anything. That's what Sholosyn said."

"Just abandoned the people?"

Feran nodded.

Alucius studied the walls, definitely ancient, but not eternastone. He also realized that the grounds enclosed by each palace were enormous, because they rode almost a vingt before coming to the next turn in the wall. That meant that each trapezoid was roughly a half vingt across the larger base, a vingt in depth, and something like two-fifths of a vingt across the shorter base.

"They all face onto the square. See?"

The center square of Southgate was . . . different. That

was the only word that came to Alucius's mind. To begin with, in the center was a circle of absolutely white stone, a circle that was a third of a yard above the surrounding gray stone paving and was roughly one hundred yards in diameter. Except for its dead-white color, to Alucius's Talent and eyes, the stone looked and felt like the harder gray granite. There were no decorations on the circle—just the circle itself. Ten yards out from the white circle there were four stellae of exactly the same dimensions, each also of the white granite, and each placed at a cardinal point of the compass.

Alucius turned the chestnut. Feran was right. In the middle of the wall of each palace that faced the "square" was an arched gate. Most were now open or ajar. After slowly looking in both directions, overwhelmed in a way by the empty grandeur of the abandoned palaces, Alucius turned his mount back toward the inner area, conscious of the fact that they were the only ones in sight.

Slowly, he reached out gingerly with his Talent to examine the whitestone circle. He shuddered. The stone, only the whitestone, was dead, dead in the same sense that the layer in the ground beneath Southgate was dead. He rode toward the nearest stele, noting that something had been carved upon it.

"Southgate's been here for a long time, from what those buildings look like," observed Feran, keeping pace with Alucius.

"A long time." Alucius rode closer to the stele, catching sight of a series of scenes sculpted into the stone. He reined up less than a yard from the stele and began to study the scenes. The bottom row showed men toiling—building a wall, building a ship, plowing a field, presumably set outside the city walls. The three images above that showed men riding, hunting, and fighting another force. There was a single wider image above those—it showed thirteen men seated at a table, each holding a scepter. Alucius looked more closely. Standing directly in the center, in back of the seated men, was a sculpted figure that resembled the ifrit in his infrequent dreams—the same features, although the stone did not convey the stark whiteness of the skin, the purple eyes, or the jet-black hair. That figure stood behind the center seltyr, the only one who sat on something resembling a throne. The ifrit figure was not threatening, not carrying a weapon, just there.

Alucius frowned.

"What is it?" asked Feran.

"Just thinking. This is an old city, perhaps as old as Tempre or Dereka, or as old as Iron Stem or Dekhron."

"Most cities in Corus are old." Feran laughed. "Who ever heard of a new city?"

"This city has no eternastone and no green towers within the walls."

"So?"

"Name me another city that doesn't. Even Iron Stem has a green tower. Dekhron has eternastone roads and the bridge. Tempre and Dereka have buildings and towers. So does Krost. The others at least have eternastone roads running through them."

Feran didn't reply for several moments.

"And there's no one in this central area," Alucius added. "Not a beggar, not a thief. No one."

"It means something, but what? That everyone hated the seltyrs so much that they don't ever want to be here? The palaces had to be for the seltyrs. Could be that they took everything, and there's nothing left to loot."

"It could be," Alucius agreed. He was beginning to feel a little dizzy at times. He looked at Feran. "We ought to head back."

"Are you all right? You're a little pale. Maybe we shouldn't have ridden this far."

"It's only a few vingts. I'll be fine." Alucius turned the chestnut.

As he rode back, he was conscious that he was weaker than he'd thought, and that he'd probably ridden farther than he should have. But he wasn't going to get any stronger doing nothing. And he hated being weak.

He was also conscious that Southgate was more—and less—than it seemed, and that he was too tired to figure out what he was missing. He'd have to sleep on it.

"You're tired."

"A little," Alucius admitted.

"It's not that far."

Alucius managed a smile. He would ride back, and he wouldn't fall out of the saddle. No matter what.

98

On Quattri, sometime in the dimness before dawn, Alucius woke abruptly, pain slashing from his wristguard through his arm. So sudden was the feeling that he was disoriented. After several moments, he struggled awake and into a sitting position, but the pain had vanished. He touched his forearm gently, but there was no soreness, and he'd been far less bruised there than across his chest.

He puzzled over the sudden pain, wondering, when another contracting pain radiating from the herder's wristguard, followed by a flash of lifeforce from the black crystal.

Wendra . . . what was happening to her?

He swallowed. It had to be. She was in labor. She was having their daughter . . . and he was a thousand vingts away. He should have been there. And he might have been . . . if only, if only he hadn't thought that he had no choices. Or if only he hadn't been struck down.

Another of the hazards of leading from the front? Or of feeling indispensable?

Another wave of pain washed over his forearm, slightly removed, perhaps because he now understood what it was. Yet, even removed . . . it was far from pleasant, especially when his own tender muscles tightened involuntarily.

If he were with Wendra, then he knew he would have been able to help if anything went wrong. That would have been something beneficial and lifegiving from his Talent. But . . . from afar, there was nothing he could do, nothing but wait, and watch and sense the crystal . . . and hope that she and Alendra would both be all right.

He eased his way from his bed to the window, pulling back the shutters and looking out into the darkness. He saw nothing, but he did not need to see.

All he could do now was wait and hope.

99

By Octdi morning, as he sat at the writing desk, trying to write a letter to Wendra, Alucius was certain that she was well and that, by extension, so was Alendra. He just had to hope that everything else was going well for her, Alendra, and the stead.

"Sir?" A Southern Guard squad leader had knocked on the door and stood there.

Alucius set the pen in the holder, turned, then rose. "Yes?"

"Begging your pardon, Colonel sir, Marshal Alyniat was wondering if you would be willing to ride out to meet with him at his headquarters."

Alucius used his Talent to study the man, but could detect neither malice nor deception—just apprehension. "I'd be happy to see the marshal. My mount is in the stable here, but I'll need a little help saddling him." He looked down at his still-splinted arm.

"Yes, sir. We can help."

Alucius could see that there was indeed help when he made his way down the stairs and out to the stable and discovered that he had an escort of half a squad. Two of them had already groomed and saddled the chestnut.

"Thought you wouldn't mind, sir," said the Southern Guard lancer who had led out Alucius's mount.

"Not these days. Thank you." Alucius still could mount easily, and did so.

They rode out the villa gates two abreast, Alucius to the right of the squad leader.

"Have you seen any more of the Matrites in the last week?" Alucius asked, after a time, as they turned off the street and through the gates in the city wall, and onto the high road to Fola—and the Southern Guard encampment—if it still happened to be there.

"No, sir. Not around here. They say they've pulled back to Hafin and Salcer. 'Course, that's just until they build up their forces. They'll be back. Always have been, anyways."

Alucius was afraid the squad leader was all too right in his assessment. "It seems that way."

Still worried about Wendra and Alendra, he said little on the nearly ten-kay ride out to the road fort. Most of the companies that had been camped around the main road fort were no longer there. Some, like Alucius's three companies, had been quartered in Southgate. Others, he suspected, had been moved northward or to Zalt and other posts closer to the Matrite forces. He could see only what looked to be two companies in bivouac on the slope below the stone fort.

Alucius reined up outside the arched entrance inside the fort.

"We'll just wait for you, sir."

"Thank you." Alucius dismounted and made his way past the sentries.

". . . hard to believe . . . say he's killed something like three thousand men personally . . ."

Alucius tried not to wince. The number was either far too high or far too low, depending on what one meant by "personally."

He had to take the stairs more slowly than usual, and he could feel the eyes on him as he walked along the west side of the marshaling hall. With his Talent, he could even catch a few phrases.

". . . three/four weeks, walking . . ."

". . . Foysyr said he's seen dead men looked better . . . blood everywhere . . ."

". . . good thing he's ours . . ."

". . . good thing for the marshal . . . otherwise, he'd have ended up blood soup like Wyerl . . ."

Alucius stopped outside Alyniat's doorway.

"Just a moment, sir." The lancer turned. "Colonel Alucius is here, sir."

"Have him come in."

The marshal stood as Alucius walked in. "Colonel. Please take a seat." The circles remained under Alyniat's eyes, but they were not quite so black, and his silver blond hair was longer and disheveled. He brushed it back off his forehead as he reseated himself behind the stack of maps.

"Colonel . . . you look well."

"Thank you." Alucius wasn't about to mention that he was still sore in too many spots, especially around his ribs.

"How long before you can ride?"

"I'm riding now," Alucius pointed out. "The healer thinks I can trade the heavy splint for a brace early next week, and I could certainly ride then. It will be a while longer before I can lift a blade or handle a rifle."

"But you could ride back to Tempre next week?"

"If I don't have to fight." Alucius smiled politely. "Are you saying that I actually might be able to return to the Iron Valleys?"

Alyniat stood momentarily and extended a sealed envelope. "This arrived late last night."

Alucius took the envelope, broke the double seal, and began to read.

Colonel Alucius—
The Lord-Protector was most gratified to hear of your successes in destroying the Matrite spear-throwers and distressed to have learned of the extent of your injuries. Later reports of your progress have cheered him greatly, and he would like to extend an

invitation for you and your three companies to return to Tempre at your earliest convenience, but not earlier than prudent in your recovery. He extends his personal best wishes, and hopes for your early and complete recovery, as does the Lady Alerya.

You will, of course, be honored once more, and the Lord-Protector would hope that you would accept an invitation to supper in his private apartments once you have returned to Tempre . . . .

The missive was signed by Frynkel and bore both his seal and that of the Lord-Protector.

Alucius understood clearly the last paragraph—both the honor and the likely conditions that might come with it. He looked to the marshal.

"I also received a letter, saying that you would receive a request to return to Tempre with all three companies, and that you would be honored upon that return. Is that . . . ?"

"Yes, sir. Whenever I feel that I can ride." Alucius smiled faintly. "I'd say next week, once the heavy splint is off." It wasn't really the splint, but he hoped that his ribs would be better by then. Only two of them ached any longer—most of the time. At times, all four did.

"That would be good." Alyniat paused. "I will offer my own thanks once more, Colonel. In addition to the destruction of the crystal spear-throwers, you and your companies accounted for the deaths of more than ten Matrite companies. Your actions have changed the entire balance of power here in the southwest. For that, both personally and professionally, I am most grateful."

"Thank you, sir. I am sorry that there was no way to capture either weapon. The way that they were built meant that they could not be disabled—only destroyed." Alucius cleared his throat. "That's not quite accurate. They could be captured, but only when they were not in use, and we could never get close enough with sufficient force when they were not in use."

"Do you think they could build another?"

"I would judge it is possible. It will take at least a year, and possibly longer, based on what I know."

"A year . . ." mused Alyniat. "Two at most."

"You could prepare . . ."

"How?" Alyniat's eyes fixed on Alucius.

"The spear-thrower is not terribly effective against stone. Rebuild the gates to your key forts so that the spear-thrower cannot be used against anything wooden. Perhaps a stone wall ten yards in front of the gates and wide enough that the spear-thrower could not be used at an angle. It cannot be used without a great deal of sand. That suggests that it will be most effective in the north in warmer weather. Also, the Matrites are not nearly so effective in small groups. I would send raider groups into their territories and pick off as many patrols as possible. The greater the losses now, the longer before they can build up the forces necessary to protect a spear-thrower for its use." Alucius almost shrugged, but managed to stop the gesture—knowing that it would have been painful.

"What else?"

"If . . . if they do rebuild one, it cannot travel quickly except by the high roads because it is so heavy. If you control the high roads south, you can restrict its use." All of what Alucius said seemed simple and direct enough to him.

The marshal nodded. "All very simple, but effective. Like you."

"I'm too young and inexperienced as a commander to attempt anything terribly complicated."

Alyniat laughed. "Don't, even when you're more experienced. Complicated plans just have more ways to go wrong."

Alucius had already thought that, and had decided against saying so.

"I won't keep you longer, Colonel." Alyniat paused. "By the way, do you know that you're the youngest majer-colonel in the history of the Southern Guard?"

"No . . . I didn't." Alucius wasn't surprised. He was too

young to be a colonel, but Marshal Frynkel and the Lord-Protector had needed him—and needed him to be independent, and so had Alyniat. "But you had a great deal to do with that."

"I did." A wry smile crossed the face of the blond marshal. "Promoting you was far easier than arguing and took less time. I figured that I couldn't lose."

"I'd be either dead or successful. Dead, the rank wouldn't have mattered, and if we were successful, who would challenge your decision? And, either way, since I'm a Northern Guard officer, you wouldn't have to deal with any problems that followed."

"That's one of the things I like about you, Colonel." Alyniat chuckled. "You're an idealist, but a very realistic one." He stepped toward the door. "You can choose when you leave, but I would appreciate your letting me know."

Alucius rose from the chair. "You can be assured that I will, Marshal."

Even though his ribs were beginning to ache more, he forced himself to leave the fort at a measured pace without betraying the growing pain. He still needed more rest than usual—a great deal more. As he mounted the chestnut, he just hoped that he'd improve more by the middle of the next week.

100

The following Quinti, two mornings after the healer had replaced the splint with a removable brace, Alucius and Feran and what remained of the three companies rode out of Southgate headed for Tempre. No one saw them off, and there were no fanfares or much of anything else, for which Alucius was grateful. The wristguard showed that Wendra was healthy. Although he knew there was no way he could have gotten any messages, he still wished he could have gotten some word.

Five days later, they reached Zalt, but Colonel Jesopyr had been sent north to take charge of rebuilding and refortifying the post at Dimor. While Captain Kuttyr was most pleasant and helpful, Alucius had to admit that he missed Jesopyr.

A week later—ten long days—they were less than five vingts out of Tempre, and Alucius was riding at the front of the column with Jultyr and Thirty-fifth Company. The day before, Alucius had sent Fewal and Rakalt ahead with a message to Southern Guard headquarters announcing their impending arrival. The last thing he wanted was to show up with three companies that no one had counted upon—although he doubted barracks space would be a problem, not with the majority of companies still in the southwest. Alucius wasn't sure whether to call the area the southwest, southwest Lanachrona, south Madrien, or old Madrien, and he'd seen all four terms used in dispatches. So he'd opted to use the semineutral "southwest" in his reports to Marshal Frynkel.

Alucius was tired, and his ribs and arm had begun to throb, as had happened later in the day on most of the journey northeast toward the capital city of Lanachrona.

"What do you think will happen in Tempre, sir?" asked Jultyr.

"Not all that much. The Lord-Protector will commend everyone, thank me personally, give you furlough, and send us back to the Iron Valleys. They'll send you replacements, give you some training, and in a season, you'll be back in the southwest. Two seasons, if you're fortunate."

"As Overcaptain Feran says, sir, you're most optimistic."

"Rulers have needs. They seldom care what ours are. If they're good, they'll try to do something to meet ours, but whatever they do won't compromise what they need."

"Suppose not, sir."

"They won't stay rulers if they don't look out for the

country first." Alucius did not say more because he saw riders ahead.

Those riders were four Southern Guards, waiting on the east side of the high road. The four caught sight of the banners and straightened in the saddle before riding toward Alucius and Jultyr.

"Colonel Alucius?"

"Yes."

"Marshal Frynkel sent us out to meet you. Your quarters and barracks are arranged, and Captain Wasenyr will be briefing you on the ceremony."

"Ceremony?" asked Alucius.

"Yes, sir. All three companies will receive the Lord-Protector's unit commendation."

Alucius could sense Jultyr's concealed amusement.

"They don't give many of those, sir. That's because it comes with two weeks' pay for every lancer as a bonus."

"That's good to know," Alucius replied. "Lead on."

As the four lancers swung in front of the banners at the front of the column, Alucius turned to Jultyr and shrugged.

"We were cheap at the price," Jultyr said dryly. "Still, the men will appreciate it. They'll make sure to pay it before we get any replacements."

Alucius couldn't help smiling at the veteran's assessment.

The sun was low in the west, shining through a hazy sky and offering only slight warmth by the time the four lancers escorting Alucius and the three companies turned off the high road and then onto the Avenue of the Palace.

Looking down the Avenue and through the space between the two green towers that dated back to the Duarchy, Alucius could see across the River Vedra to the southernmost part of the Westerhills. Unlike the northern Westerhills, where the trees were junipers and pines spread widely on rocky and sandy ground, the trees north of Tempre were mixed pine and softwoods growing far more closely together.

As they neared the palace itself, with the stone-walled

gardens of the Lord-Protector on their right, the lancers turned right on the avenue fronting both the palace and the headquarters complex of the Southern Guard. Behind both structures to the north was a long ridge that extended to the river in the west and well into the distance to the east. There were no structures on the top third of the ridge.

Alucius, getting more sore by the moment, shifted his weight in the saddle as they neared the gray granite walls of the Southern Guard headquarters, modest in size against the low hills directly behind the gray buildings. As before, when he had been in Tempre, there were but four guards flanking the gateposts. The guards looked up briefly, possibly surprised to see such a long column of riders. Behind them, the main headquarters building rose four stories, with clean gray walls looming over the paving stones that covered the space inside the walls. The exception was the small walled garden set forward of the squared-off portico that was the main entrance.

The four lancers rode around the east side of the building and into the rear courtyard, a space cut out of the hillside, with the stables to the right, and barracks and quarters behind, but forward of a stone wall that rose almost fifteen yards. They continued turning, toward the portico that marked the rear entrance. Standing on the steps above the mounting blocks were several figures in Southern Guard uniforms. As they rode closer, Alucius recognized Marshal Frynkel, but not the captain with him, nor the lancers behind the two officers.

The lancers reined up, and Alucius ordered, "Column, halt!"

Frynkel stepped forward. "Colonel Alucius, Overcaptain Feran, Captain Jultyr, Captain Deotyr, and all the lancers of the Fifth, Twenty-eighth, and Thirty-fifth Companies . . . welcome to Tempre and Southern Guard headquarters. Your efforts can truly be said to have been critical in saving Lanachrona, and for that you will be recognized and rewarded at an official ceremony on Duadi. Later, Captain Wasenyr will go over the details with you."

442   L. E. MODESITT, JR.

Frynkel inclined his head to the dark-bearded young captain standing back and to his left. "On behalf of the Lord-Protector, I wanted to welcome you all to Tempre." A nod from the marshal clearly ended the welcome.

Alucius inclined his head. "We thank you, Marshal, and the Lord-Protector. We are pleased that we have been of service."

Frynkel stepped forward. "Colonel, I would appreciate the honor of your company and that of Overcaptain Feran at supper this evening."

"We would be pleased."

"Good. Captain Wasenyr will fill you in." Frynkel's smile was pleasant, but Alucius could sense the tiredness behind the expression. "I'll let you get your men and yourselves settled."

"Thank you, sir."

The lancer escorts urged their mounts into a slow walk.

"Forward," Alucius ordered.

Once the three companies were drawn up outside the stables, Wasenyr and three squad leaders met them.

"Colonel," offered the bearded captain, "the squad leaders will show your companies what sections of the stables are assigned, and the barracks areas. Once you've taken care of what you need to here, I'd be pleased to escort you and your officers to your quarters." A lopsided smile followed. "You may have noticed that we're somewhat understaffed here from the way things were in the past."

"With so many companies in the southwest, I thought that might be the case." Alucius dismounted, somewhat stiffly.

"Do you need—"

"I'm just stiff from riding." Alucius was stiff from riding, but his ribs were also bothering him, and the brace on his forearm, under his sleeve and riding jacket, was chafing his skin.

"I should tell you that the ceremony will be one glass after morning muster on Duadi—at the rear portico. It won't take that long, and regular travel uniforms are appropriate, but your men won't need to saddle up. Just form on foot. If you'd be there a quarter glass before they form up, I'll let you know if there are any changes."

"That's fine. Is there anything else?"

"Not right now, sir."

Alucius nodded and led the chestnut into the stables. When he had finished with stabling and grooming the chestnut, more slowly than usual, he was the last to join Feran and Captain Wasenyr outside the stable.

"I took a moment to show the captains their quarters. I hope you—"

"That's fine," Alucius said.

The walk back to the main building was even longer than Alucius recalled, especially carrying his own gear. Once inside the main building, Wasenyr led the way up a wide stone staircase. "Both of your quarters are on the third level. Yours are on the east end, Overcaptain Feran, and yours are on the west end, Colonel. We'll get the colonel settled first, if you don't mind, sir," Wasenyr said to Feran.

"That would be best." Feran grinned at Alucius.

Alucius wondered if he'd get the same quarters he'd had before.

At the third level, they turned left, past a pair of Southern Guards with blue braid on their shoulders, similar to that worn by Wasenyr. Wasenyr stopped at the next-to-last set of double doors. He opened the door with a shining brass key and handed it to Alucius.

The foyer inside was tiled in blue and gold. Through a square archway was a sitting room ten yards in width and fifteen in length, the long side containing three wide windows that opened on a view of the Lord-Protector's golden cream palace. In the sitting room were a dark blue upholstered settee, two matching armchairs, a carved cherry desk set against the north wall, with an equally imposing and matching carved desk chair. Five wall lamps were spaced around the chamber. In the center of the floor was a dark blue carpet bearing a design of intertwined eight-pointed green stars outlined in gold.

Alucius could see that the quarters were a mirror image of those where he had stayed before, with few differences in furnishings or decor.

"The bedchamber is over here . . ."

The bedchamber was small only by comparison to the sitting room. It also had a view of the palace, with a high triple-width bed and two matching armoires. Alucius set down his saddlebags and laid the rifles on the weapons rack most gratefully. Beyond the bedchamber was the bath chamber. The tub there was carved out of a single marble block, with two spigots of shimmering bronze.

"I assume you'd like your uniforms cleaned. If you let one of the orderlies know after you get back from supper tonight, they can have them cleaned and pressed before noon tomorrow."

"That would be helpful," Alucius said politely.

"Majer Keiryn will escort you to dinner in about two glasses." Wasenyr glanced around. "I believe . . . is there anything . . . ?"

"No. You've been most helpful." Alucius turned to Feran. The overcaptain's face held a bemused expression. "I'll see you then. I'm sure your quarters will be similar to these."

"Oh, yes, sir. Almost the same, except his look out to the east."

Once the two had left, Alucius walked back into the bath chamber and turned one of the spigots, hoping the water was at least warmish. It was warm, but not hot.

He took his time bathing and cleaning up, and laying out clothes to be cleaned later. After a season on the road, he intended to take full advantage of the amenities available.

Majer Keiryn—the same Keiryn who had accomplished the same task once before, tall and redheaded—arrived almost exactly two glasses later, accompanied by Feran. Keiryn escorted them down two levels and to the eastern end of the headquarters building to the exact same private dining room where Alucius had dined three years earlier with Wyerl and Alyniat. The single circular table was covered in a shimmering white linen, with blue linen napkins. Each of the four places was set with silver cutlery, platters and plates of cream porcelain rimmed in gold and blue, and with two goblets set before each of the four diners. On a side table were several bottles of wine in the amber bottles.

"Marshal Frynkel should be joining us shortly." Keiryn paused.

"He's the only one in Tempre right now?" asked Alucius. "The only marshal?"

"Yes, sir. Really one of the few senior officers here. Marshal Alyniat took most of the senior colonels, too. You're probably the third-ranking officer in Tempre right now, behind Marshal Frynkel and Majer-colonel Dytryl."

And the youngest colonel in Lanachrona, Alucius reflected . . . so long as he held the rank.

"The marshals aren't promoting many majers to colonel?" asked Feran.

Keiryn frowned, tilting his head slightly, pausing before he replied, "No. I think Colonel Alucius is the only promotion I know of in the last year. I know that Marshal Frynkel noted that when he received the dispatch from Marshal Alyniat." Keiryn offered an embarrassed smile. "I shouldn't have mentioned that, but . . . it is true."

"I'm sorry I'm late," came a voice from the doorway as Frynkel stepped into the small dining room. "I lost track of time." The marshal smiled as warmly as Alucius had seen. "I can't tell you how happy I am to see you both, especially you, Colonel."

Alucius could sense that, pleased as Frynkel was, the marshal seemed almost more relieved than pleased.

"I had to send a message to the Lord-Protector confirming your safe arrival and telling him about the ceremony on Duadi." Frynkel gestured to the table. "Please be seated."

As soon as the four officers were gathered around the table, a single orderly appeared and immediately poured a pale amber wine from one of the bottles into the smaller goblet in front of each officer.

Frynkel lifted his goblet. "To our guests."

"With our gratitude for your hospitality," Alucius replied, lifting his own goblet. Feran lifted his as well.

The orderly vanished, then reappeared to set a small plate atop the one before each diner. On the small plate was a pastry no more than the width of three fingers.

"Cavern mushrooms in pastry. Very delicate and tasty," offered Frynkel, taking a bite after speaking.

Alucius wasn't sure that he didn't like the flaky pastry better than the filling, but even the mushrooms were better than cactus or prickle.

Frynkel began to speak. He did not look directly at Alucius. "I'll need to meet with you tomorrow, Alucius, but that's almost a formality. Still . . . debriefings are one of those necessities." He smiled. "It's a pity, in some ways, that you're here in winter. You're used to colder winters than ours, of course, but the gardens aren't in bloom, and the river's far too cold for sailing . . ."

To Alucius, it was more than clear that Frynkel was both fulfilling a duty and avoiding discussing anything bearing on what had happened in Hyalt or around Southgate. Given Alucius's own tiredness and sore muscles, that was probably just as well.

He sipped the wine and listened.

101

Slightly after midmorning on Lundi, Alucius sat in a comfortable wooden armchair on the other side of a table desk, behind which sat Marshal Frynkel.

Frynkel looked across the desk at Alucius. Once again, his eyes were dark-rimmed, and the right one twitched. Absently, the marshal pressed against it with the side of his palm.

"You'll be meeting with the Lord-Protector at the fourth glass past noon tomorrow. Captain Wasenyr will escort you."

"Yes, sir."

"It was his request. He has been most impressed with your accomplishments." Frynkel paused. "For all that you did, we're far from winning the war against the Regent of the Matrial. I gather you understand that."

"We've regained the territory that was lost. Perhaps more," suggested Alucius.

"The Regent of the Matrial is still a problem. We suggested a truce. She refused. Her answer was that she will continue to fight until Southgate and all of the south and Harmony and all of the north are returned. She also demanded ten thousand golds in reparations, to be paid immediately."

"Madrien never held Southgate."

"That doesn't seem to matter to her." Frynkel paused. "What do you know about this Regent?"

"Almost nothing."

"We know less than you do," Frynkel said. "That's even if you know nothing beyond your time in Madrien. She was a marshal named Sulythya, and everyone else decided to obey her. We don't know why. Do you?"

"You know I escaped Madrien when the Matrial vanished and the torques failed. The Regent or someone under her has managed to repower some of those torques."

Frynkel fixed his eyes on Alucius. The tic in his right eye twitched more rapidly. "That's something you know as a herder?"

Alucius nodded. "If I get close to them, I can feel them."

"Could she repower them all?"

"I don't know," Alucius admitted. "It took me by surprise."

"Hmmm." Frynkel frowned. "Does Marshal Alyniat know this?"

"He might. He might not. I didn't recognize what the feeling was until I was on the way back to Tempre," lied Alucius. "So I thought I'd tell you."

"Convenient," suggested Frynkel.

"You have to remember that I wasn't in very good shape after those battles, and I wasn't thinking my best," Alucius pointed out. "We did destroy the crystal spear-throwers."

"Yes . . . Marshal Alyniat did note my circumspection in giving you only verbal orders for that," replied the marshal.

"I thought that our best efforts would be to handle what the regular Southern Guard could not, sir."

"Your initiative was commendable." Frynkel's laugh was almost a bark. "You'll be better off in Dekhron, Colonel."

"If that is what the Lord-Protector wishes, Marshal."

"I doubt any of us *wish* that, Colonel. We all recognize that your presence in Dekhron is necessary so long as Madrien remains a threat."

Both Lanachrona and Madrien were threats to the Iron Valleys, Alucius thought, but Madrien was the greater and more immediate danger. "Is that the only threat?"

"Candidly . . . no," admitted Frynkel. "We've received reports that the young Praetor of Lustrea is rebuilding his forces. It's likely that he will make an effort to annex Deforya within the next year or so. Or the grasslands of Illegea and Ongelya—or all three."

"If he chooses to do so, and the Lord-Protector does not send any support, he will succeed."

"Do you think we should aid Deforya?"

"Not so long as the landowners hold power. They cannot control the people except through water and fear, and they will not spend the coins necessary for an effective fighting force. Nor will that force ever be well commanded."

"Water? How does that control the people?"

"All the water in Deforya comes from the great ancient aqueducts. Whoever holds the aqueducts controls the water. Without water . . ." The point was obvious to Alucius, so obvious that he'd seen it as a fresh overcaptain years before.

"I'm glad to know that you agree with the Lord-Protector's decisions."

"I did not know the Lord-Protector's decision," Alucius said mildly, wondering why Frynkel had such an edge behind his questions. "How could I? I only know what I saw when I was there."

"You took a great deal upon yourself," Frynkel suggested.

Alucius did not reply for a time, considering. Finally, he replied. "I had few choices. Even before I reported to Marshal Alyniat, there were colonels trying to order me around, trying to waste my forces on what would have been useless attacks or defenses."

"Useless? The defense of Southgate was useless?"

"No, sir. Direct attacks on any force with a spear-thrower or any defenses against one, unless you happen to be behind a thick stone wall, are useless."

"And you didn't attack directly, Colonel?"

"No, sir. We used stealth to obtain an explosive result." What Alucius said was true, but not in the way he hoped Frynkel would take it.

"How did you manage that?"

"As I wrote you, sir."

Frynkel pressed his twitching eye with his left hand. "Ah, yes. Your report. I should get around to reading that."

Alucius was confused. Frynkel was lying about the report. But if he had read it, why would he say he hadn't?

"How dangerous are you to the Lord-Protector?" questioned the marshal.

Alucius laughed. "I'm not at all dangerous to him. He's the only real chance we herders have to keep our way of life."

Frynkel nodded. "How dangerous are you to the Southern Guard?"

"Not at all. Though some senior officers might feel otherwise."

"A number apparently do. Colonel Hubar protested your high-handed actions. Colonel Sarthat has demanded that you be stripped of rank and executed for assaulting a senior officer."

"I never even raised a hand against the colonel," Alucius said.

"He claims you used some herder skill to throw him to the floor and break his nose."

"Exactly how many Matrites did Colonel Sarthat kill? How many crystal spear-throwers did he destroy? How many bullets did he take?" Alucius's words turned icy. "You suggested, sir, that you and Marshal Alyniat and the Lord-Protector needed results. You requested, and you promised. I kept my word. I delivered. How many of those who have complained have delivered?" Alucius's eyes blazed.

A reluctant smile crossed Frynkel's face. "None of them, as you know. That was why Marshal Alyniat breveted you on the spot. That's been protested, also. All of those protests have been denied. I'd like to send Sarthat against the Matrites, but I don't want to lose scarce lancers with him. Hubar dispatched his protest before he was killed."

"And you've been pressing me . . . just to see how I react?"

"Mostly. And to give you a feeling of just how unreasonable people in authority can be. That also goes for factors or merchants who feel they have authority. You'll have to face them as commander of the Northern Guard."

Alucius nodded. If the Lord-Protector still offered that, Alucius would need to ask for some additional authority for the position.

"There are still times when it pays to say that you understand someone's concerns and that you'll look into them," Frynkel said. "Most people aren't reasonable. They think they are, and they rationalize what they want, but they're selfish. We all are. It's a wise man who knows what his own selfishnesses are and who can set them aside."

"That's difficult."

"No. For you, it's clear that it's not. In a sense, that's one of the greatest problems you'll face. You have fewer delusions than most. I'm not certain that you understand just how many delusions most people have. Most people are more like Majer Fedosyr than like you, although they usually aren't so direct as to cross blades. People have an image of themselves, and they'll do almost anything to maintain that image. I wouldn't be that surprised if Colonel Hubar just managed to get himself killed because you did too much damage to the image he had of himself."

That was something Alucius hadn't even considered.

"Now . . . the official ceremony is tomorrow, and I'll present the commendations on behalf of the Lord-Protector." Frynkel paused. "You *do* have to wear this one, Colonel, at least on your dress uniform. It's sufficient, and you're wise not to wear the stars. That's becoming modesty. In late afternoon, you'll have your audience with the Lord-Protector, and then you'll have an early supper with him. After that . . ." The marshal shrugged. "I don't know. I'm sure you'll be returning to Dekhron fairly soon, but that's in the hands of the Lord-Protector."

"I can see that."

"That's all I have." Frynkel stood. "By the way, your rank as a majer-colonel in the Southern Guard has been made permanent."

"Thank you, sir." Alucius rose.

"Don't thank me. For all that you've done, you'll go through at least as much holding the rank as getting it. Until tomorrow."

Alucius inclined his head. "Until then." As he left Frynkel's study, the older officer's words reverberated through his thoughts. While he doubted that he could take more wounds than he'd already taken and survive, that hadn't been what Frynkel had meant. In a way, he appreciated the example that Frynkel had presented without warning, because it had illustrated how suddenly people changed from reasonable to less reasonable as something dear to them was threatened.

102

After the meeting with Frynkel, Alucius had met with Feran and the two captains, then spent much of the day arranging for everything from riding rations to replacement uniforms. Every single item had to be obtained from somewhere else, and each required a different form. By the end of Lundi, Alucius was exhausted, and his ribs had begun to ache once more.

He and Feran had a quiet supper in the senior officers' mess, bringing the two captains as guests. When supper was over, Alucius excused himself and retired to his quarters. There, he wrote a lengthy letter to Wendra and climbed into the overlarge bed.

Lundi had not been a short day, and before long Alucius was asleep.

When he woke, it was still dark. He struggled out of the bed and toward the bath chamber. But when he stepped through the doorway, he found himself in the hall with the pinkish marble walls, tinged with purple. The half pillars of goldenstone seemed larger than before, and the ceiling, if of the same pink marble, was lower. All the stonework was precise, so precise that even with Talent, he could detect neither joints nor mortar. His bare feet felt chill on the polished stone floor.

He looked down at the octagonal sections of green marble and their inset eight-pointed stars of golden marble, but when his eyes lifted, the walls had shifted closer to him. Again, he could discover no windows, no doors, and the walls began to press in on him.

In moments, the cold marble walls were inexorably contracting toward him, viselike, and not even his Talent could find him a way out.

Sweat poured down his forehead. He had to get out . . . somehow. He had to—

Alucius shuddered . . . and found himself standing beside the bed in the senior officers' quarters. His forehead was soaked. In fact, he was damp all over.

Why was he still having the dream? He was in Tempre, and, presumably, after his audience with the Lord-Protector, would be headed back to the Iron Valleys, either to Dekhron or to Iron Stem.

Or was it because he feared going to Dehkron, of being hemmed in there as colonel? Or because no matter what he did, no matter how successful he was, he still seemed to have no choices, and those he did have just restricted him further?

What could he do to change that?

He would have to do something. He had to . . . Didn't he?

. He took a slow, deep breath, and blotted his forehead with the back of his forearm, ignoring the twinges in his ribs.

103

On Duadi morning, Alucius stood just north of the rear portico to Southern Guard headquarters, at the front of the lancers of the three companies, waiting for Marshal Frynkel to appear. The other three officers stood in a row behind him, with Feran in the center. Captain Wasenyr and Majer Keiryn stood on the top of the steps of the portico.

"Think we'll have to wait long, sir?" asked Feran.

"He'll be on time, or close to it," Alucius suggested.

Almost as Alucius finished his words, the marshal appeared from the archway off the portico and moved forward to the edge of the steps. From there he surveyed the lancers formed up below.

"Ceremonies should not be too short or too long," Frynkel began. "If they are too short, the importance of what they reward is lost. Too long, and that importance is trivialized by boredom." He paused. "I will try to be neither too short nor too long."

Alucius wondered how one judged whether something was too short or long, or did Frynkel just gauge the reaction as he proceeded?

"It is not often that three companies are sent out to do a task that others have judged impossible. It is even less often that they succeed in accomplishing the task. It is less often than that that they do so and return. It is unheard of for three companies to do that twice, and in less than a season . . ."

Frynkel went on to summarize what the three companies had done in both Hyalt and in Southgate, clearly using Alucius's reports as the basis for his remarks. Then he added a few words about the unit commendation and about how few lancer companies received the award.

". . . These were not only notable achievements, but were achievements absolutely necessary to preserve Lanachrona as a land of freedom and prosperity, and achievements most worthy of special attention and honor. For this reason, you all unreservedly deserve the commendation of the Lord-Protector and will be awarded that commendation. In addition, because lancers cannot live on words alone, the commendation also comes with a bonus of two weeks' pay, which you will receive on your next payday." Frynkel permitted himself a smile. "And in keeping with my promise to be neither too terse nor too verbose, I will close by saying that both the Lord-Protector and I appreciate your efforts. We commend you for efforts well-done and honorable, and we are greatly honored by your service, accomplishments, and dedication. Well and bravely done!"

Frynkel inclined his head to the lancers below and to the officers. "Carry on." He turned and reentered the headquarters building.

Alucius turned. "Dismissed to company officers."

"Dismissed to squad leaders."

The three officers eased toward Alucius.

"The men'll like the bonus," Deotyr said.

"Half of 'em will have it spent before they get it," Jultyr suggested.

"Half of them?" asked Feran so sardonically that all the others laughed.

"They'll still have the commendation when the coins are gone," Alucius pointed out, "but for now they can enjoy the coin."

"And they will."

"So will I," Feran said. "We get the same bonus. I know. I asked."

Alucius couldn't help smiling. "That's all for now. I won't know more about what we're doing until after I meet with the Lord-Protector this afternoon. I'll let you know tomorrow morning—if I know—before muster."

After Jultyr and Deotyr left, Feran waited, then asked, "Do you really think we'll be headed back?"

"I think it's very likely."

"Why? Because they don't like us making them look bad?"

"Twenty-eighth and Thirty-fifth Companies did well, and they were little more than recruits. I don't think the Southern Guard lancers are bad. Not so good as ours, but better than most other lands."

"You know what you're saying, honored Colonel, don't you?"

Alucius raised his eyebrows. "That they've got too many political officers? Yes. Marshal Alyniat said he'd taken a great amount of criticism for promoting senior squad leaders to captain and stipending off colonels, and not promoting majers."

"He's got the right idea. Whether it will last beyond him is another question."

Alucius nodded.

The two turned and walked toward the barracks.

Alucius conducted an informal inspection, something he

had often done, but not recently, for obvious reasons, then spent a good glass in the stables with Feran, assessing the state of their mounts. He wanted a solid sense of what Fifth Company needed before he met with the Lord-Protector. Then he went back to his quarters to write down his observations and what he and Feran had determined was necessary for the return to the Iron Valleys. While he might never mention them to the Lord-Protector, he would need to request those items from someone, and while he had what he needed in mind, he began to write a draft of those needs.

Before all that long, or so it seemed, Captain Wasenyr had appeared to escort him to the palace, and the two walked back down to the stables.

"What happened to Captain Deen?" Alucius asked, recalling the rather charming verbose captain who had last briefed him on an audience with the Lord-Protector.

"Deen?" Captain Wasenyr frowned, then nodded. "He's an overcaptain now, works for Majer Ashynst. Talks to people, gathers ideas . . . I think that's what he does . . ."

Deen had been good at talking, but Alucius had his doubts about his listening.

"You've had an audience with the Lord-Protector, Colonel, and you're on the preferred list. You really don't need much briefing. Captain-colonel Ratyf is still the director of appointments. You know that no weapons are allowed in the audience chamber, except for your sabre. It's considered a ceremonial weapon. Your audience is private. Almost all with Guard officers are these days."

Once they reached the stables and mounted, the two officers rode around the east side of the building and through the outer gates. From there, they turned right. Their mounts carried them westward toward the river and the Grand Piers and green towers that lay beyond the Lord-Protector's palace.

Alucius glanced at the gardens that flanked both sides of the boulevard. Despite the winter season, the grass was green, as were the hedges, even those trimmed into the shapes of animals, but the flowers that he had seen before were absent. Guards in cream-shaded uniforms were posted at intervals along the low stone walls bordering the boulevard, and others walked along the stone paths, but Alucius had the sense that there were fewer guards than before. He also saw only a single woman with a child, and one couple. It might have been the cooler weather, but the gardens were far less attended than upon his previous visit.

"You are familiar with the Lord-Protectors' gardens?" inquired Captain Wasenyr.

"I saw them on my last visit. They look as well kept as then, but fewer people are enjoying them."

"That might be so. These are harder times for all."

Ahead of them, beyond both the gardens and the palace, the green towers flanking the Grand Piers were clearly visible, spires identical to the one in Iron Stem and those in Dereka.

Alucius took a last look at the gardens as he rode past the wall on the right side of the boulevard, a stone wall a good four yards high, which marked the beginning of the palace grounds. On the left side, the gardens—although divided by the Avenue of the Palace running northward from the high road—continued westward to the Grand Piers.

"Here, sir." Captain Wasenyr gestured to the first entrance.

The palace entryway was a portico only slightly larger than that of the entry to Southern Guard headquarters. Waiting for them was a half squad of guards in dark blue uniforms trimmed with silver. There were also two stable-boys standing by as the two officers reined up. At the top of the steps above the mounting blocks stood another captain. Like Captain Wasenyr, he wore blue braid across his shoulders. Alucius felt he had met the man on his last visit but did not recall his name.

Captain Wasenyr did not dismount. "I leave you here, sir."

"Thank you, Captain."

"Yes, sir."

Alucius dismounted, handing the chestnut's reins to a stableboy.

The graying captain stepped down to meet Alucius. "Captain Alfaryl, Colonel. Captain-colonel Ratyf asked me to escort you."

"Thank you." Alucius was glad the captain had offered his name. "It's been more than three years, but you were my escort the last time, weren't you?"

"Yes, sir. I think so."

Alucius laughed. "You must escort hundreds of officers and others. This is but my second audience."

"That's more than all but the marshals usually get, sir."

Not having a ready reply to that, Alucius followed Alfaryl through the double stone arches. Beyond the arches was a square vaulted entry hall that rose a good ten yards overhead and measured fifteen yards on a side. Light poured through the high clerestory windows on the south side. The polished granite floor was inlaid with long strips of blue marble, creating a blue-edged diamond pattern.

Captain Alfaryl led Alucius through the middle of three square arches into a corridor that stretched a good forty yards. After less than twenty yards they turned left into a short corridor, at the end of which was a set of high double doors. In front of the doors stood four guards in blue and silver. Silently, the one in the center opened a door, holding it as Alucius and the captain stepped through. Just as silently, the door closed behind them.

Beyond the door was a large chamber, with a number of settees and upholstered armchairs, and with blue-and-cream hangings. Thick carpets, in blue and cream, stretched over the granite floor. Several portraits hung on the light-wood-paneled walls. All were of men, past Lord-Protectors. The chamber was empty, except for Alucius, Captain Alfaryl, and the captain-colonel who walked toward them.

"Captain-colonel Ratyf," said Alfaryl, "Majer-colonel Alucius."

"Ah . . . yes. It is good to see you again, sir. The Lord-

Protector is most looking forward to seeing you. I will tell him you're here." The captain-colonel vanished through a small doorway, then returned nearly instantaneously. "Do enter, sir."

Alucius turned to Alfaryl. "Thank you."

"My pleasure, sir."

Alucius followed Ratyf's gesture and stepped through the larger door in the rear of the waiting chamber.

The captain-colonel held the door and announced in a deep voice, "Colonel Alucius of the Northern Guard."

After entering the audience hall, Alucius heard the door click shut behind him.

Nothing had changed from the last time Alucius had been in the hall. It remained not that much larger than the corridor leading to the waiting chamber, and the golden-stone walls were draped with the same rich blue hangings, and light-torches were everywhere. The polished white marble floor was patterned with the same blue stone as in the outer entry hall, but the pattern was that of smaller oblongs.

"Greetings, Colonel. Once more, you've accomplished the impossible." The Lord-Protector stepped away from the white onyx throne, whose high stone back rose into a spire, at the tip of which was a shimmering blue crystal star.

"We have done our best to accede to your requests, sir." Alucius moved forward, stopping short of the dais on which the slender dark-haired man in the severe blue violet tunic stood.

"You have apparently rendered me yet another service that I cannot fully repay on a request of you that I cannot acknowledge in full—not publicly."

"Neither of us had a choice, sir. Not really."

The Lord-Protector Talryn smiled, spoke, his words carrying a trace of a laugh. "That is one of the ironies of power and position. The greater each of these is, the fewer real and wise choices there are, and yet there is the illusion that those who have power and position have an immense range of choice."

Alucius smiled in return. "They do, sir. They have an immense range of choice to make mistakes."

Talryn broke into a deep laugh. When he finally stopped, he shook his head. "When you were on your way to Hyalt, I read Marshal Frynkel's report about what occurred in Krost. Later, your report on Hyalt was most revealing, and so were Marshal Alyniat's and your reports on the events that took place in Southgate.

"I would that I could enjoy and utilize your services here in Tempre, but, for many reasons, that would not be wise. Lanachrona is too old and the Southern Guard too traditional for a colonel of your directness. Nor would the Iron Valleys or the Northern Guard be well served. They need you, and I need you there." The Lord-Protector extended an envelope, then a pair of insignia. "You are hereby promoted permanently to majer-colonel in the Southern Guard, and colonel in the Northern Guard. The Lord-Protector's acceptance of Colonel Weslyn's request to be stipended is enclosed, along with your orders and appointment as commandant of the Northern Guard. Your orders allow you to make any and all changes you deem necessary within the structure of the Northern Guard, but they do not provide you with any additional powers of conscription, nor do they change my standing order against conscription of herders . . ."

"Sir . . ." Alucius stopped. The Lord-Protector was right.

"Do you have any thoughts or requests?"

"Yes, sir." Alucius did have thoughts, one in particular.

The Lord-Protector's eyebrows rose. "Yes . . ."

"I believe that the Northern Guard headquarters should be moved from Dekhron. While Lanachrona and the Iron Valleys were contending with each other, that placement was sensible. I fear that for the years to come, the greater threat will be in the west."

"You think Iron Stem, perhaps?" A smile curled into the corners of the Lord-Protector's mouth.

"Yes, sir. If that would seem too self-serving, then I would suggest Wesrigg. There is already an outpost there.

But Iron Stem would be better, because it is the junction of the two high roads, north and west."

The Lord-Protector nodded. "I can see that. Would you move the entire Guard from Dekhron?"

"Yes, sir. For many reasons."

"That will cost golds, Colonel."

"Yes, sir. It will. At first. Later, it will be less costly. Far less costly. And I have another request."

"Another?" The mock astonishment was colored with amusement.

"I would like an order closing the dustcat establishment in Iron Stem."

This time, puzzlement appeared on Talryn's face.

"I would close every such establishment anywhere. It is a filthy and degrading addiction." Alucius shrugged. "That would not work. It would only crop up elsewhere. But requiring Gortal to move his establishment from Iron Stem will disrupt some of that trouble . . . and I would not wish that establishment near the Northern Guard."

"How would you handle that?"

"If I have the authority, it will occur." Alucius's voice was cold.

"You may have the authority for both—with a single proviso. You may not announce either until after the turn of spring. We will discuss, if by dispatch, how to make these changes, and you and Marshal Frynkel will work out the details."

Alucius nodded. "Yes, sir."

"Have you any other official requests?"

Alucius caught the slight emphasis on "official."

"No, sir."

"Then, you have my leave to return to Dekhron as you see fit, but no later than a week from now. You will take both Southern Guard companies, with some replacement lancers, and I would appreciate your efforts at ensuring they get training. Once you are certain that you have full control of the Northern Guard, you can detach those companies and send them back to Tempre." Talryn offered the quickest of grins. "You can also promise them a month of furlough once they return. Now . . ." The Lord-Protector reached back and lifted a bell, ringing it gently. "I have my own request."

"Sir?"

"My consort and wife, the Lady Alerya, has requested that you join us for an early supper. I believe you were informed of the supper, but not by whom the request was made." Talryn rose and announced to the seemingly empty audience hall, "The audiences are concluded for the day."

Alucius followed the Lord-Protector into the chamber off the audience hall, up the private circular stairs to the upper level, and out into a hallway. Across the archway from the stairs was a set of double doors, before which were stationed two guards.

Talryn opened one door, but gestured for Alucius to step into the private foyer before following. On the other side of the foyer and through an archway, in the sitting room on the love seat set between two end tables, was a young woman. She held a small child, barely more than an infant, in her lap. She rose as Alucius and the Lord-Protector entered the room.

"Colonel Alucius, this is my wife and consort, the Lady Alerya—and my son Talus."

Alucius bowed to the slender young woman who carried the child, perhaps six months of age, already with the dark brown hair and eyes of his sire. "Lady." He straightened.

Alerya looked straight at Alucius, then she inclined her head . . . and smiled. "I thought as much. It was not a dream, was it?"

Alucius debated. "No, lady, but it is best treated as one. Healing by herders is not well thought of."

Talryn looked at Alucius. "You . . ."

"I could have denied it, and who would have known?"

"But . . . so many could benefit . . ."

Alucius shook his head. "So few . . . it takes much time and energy. It cannot be done often, and it is often not successful. You have treated fairly with the Iron Valleys—and the herders. Far more fairly than have the traders of Dekhron. Call it the reward you most deserved, and I am pleased to have been able to have done so."

The Lord-Protector was silent, clearly both relieved and angered simultaneously.

"He has given more than he has received, Talryn. Far more. Do not ask more. Ever." Alerya's voice was soft, but Alucius could sense the steel behind it.

Talryn laughed, softly and ruefully. "My commander of the north and my consort. Truly, I am well served." He inclined his head to Alucius. "My lady is correct. I can never fully repay you, but I will heed you. I do ask that you do not leave me bereft of your advice."

"Mine is no better than that of many," Alucius replied, "but I will do as you request."

Talryn laughed again. "It is better that I do not request, but allow you to use your judgment."

"Before we dine, I have but one question of a prying nature," Alerya offered, "but I must ask."

Alucius couldn't help but respect the Lord-Protector's consort. "I will answer as I can."

"Talus . . . did you . . . ?"

"No. I healed you. That was all. I had hoped."

"Thank you." Alerya's smile was broad.

Alucius could sense a great relief from Talryn, and for that he was grateful for Alerya's question.

"Should I ask how you managed that?"

"You can ask, sir, but I can only say that it was tied in with the Recorder."

"We should eat, Talryn, before Talus gets terribly fussy."

Alucius looked at the boy, and the slightest wave of sadness swept over him. He had not yet even seen Alendra.

"We should indeed." With a smile, the Lord-Protector turned toward a set of open doors that revealed a small dining room.

As he entered, Alucius could not help but see that it was set for only three, and he was placed on one side, while Talryn and Alerya sat at either end. Alerya still held Talus, who was making a determined effort to grasp and gnaw on the blue linen cloth that covered the table.

"This is a personal supper," Talryn said. "No Lord-Protectors or colonels."

"And no tactics." Alerya took a sip of wine as soon as the steward poured it. "I trust you will not mind, but I will eat and drink as I can, else I may get little nourishment."

"Go ahead, my dear."

"Please," added Alucius. "You spend much time with him, I see."

"Most of every day. I have seen too many children raised by servants and tutors, and then parents wonder why their child shares none of their values and understandings." She took another sip of the red wine. "I am most fortunate that my lord understands and that this is something we can do."

"You can do," Talryn said.

"You spend much more time with him than did your sire with you."

"You set a good example, my lady," Talryn laughed.

"Talryn has talked about herders and the north. Would you tell me what it is like, truly like, to be a herder?"

Alucius smiled. "I can tell you what I feel, and some things. To tell it all would take far longer than we have."

"Tell what you can, if you would."

"There is a feel about being a herder, and about the land and the nightsheep. One of my first memories was when I saw a ramlet who had been abandoned, and I persuaded him to take a bottle. I was very young, perhaps four or five . . ." Alucius continued with the story of Lamb, still slightly amazed that he was having a private supper with the two.

II.

⊁THE SCEPTER OF⊁
THE PRESENT

104

The noon sun was mostly obscured by a hazy sky, and a bitter wind blew out of the northeast from the Aerlal Plateau as Alucius and his companies neared the southern edge of Salaan and the scattered huts of the small holders who scrabbled out an existence on the dry ridges south of the River Vedra. The trip back had been long, and the only thing that Alucius could say for it was that he had healed—mostly, although he still wore the brace on his right forearm—and that no forces and no Talent-creatures had attacked them.

One of the wagons carried the pay chests for the entire coming spring season for the Northern Guard, as well as a chest for supplies, possibly because Marshal Frynkel had seen the advantage of escorting so much gold with three companies. Another carried barrels of dried southern fruit—a gift of sorts to Fifth Company and the Northern Guard from the Lord-Protector's consort.

Alucius was looking forward to seeing Wendra, although he had no idea when that might be, not when he had to relieve Colonel Weslyn. He had no doubt that delivering that dispatch from the Lord-Protector would be anything but pleasant. In the past, however, the colonel had always been courteous—then had acted covertly in one fashion or another. Given Weslyn's closeness to the traders of Dekhron, Alucius could be certain that once the colonel left the Guard, Alucius would face all manner of difficulties with a number of the traders, if not with all of them. That excessive influence of the traders was just another reason why he wanted to move Northern Guard headquarters to Iron Stem.

He had finally received a letter from Wendra just before he'd left Tempre, assuring him that both she and Alendra were doing well, as was the stead. She'd also mentioned obliquely that the additional coins he had arranged for— the bonus paid to her—had gone to purchase a ram and a ewe from her cousin Kyrtus's flock. Knowing Wendra, she'd probably played on her cousin's fondness for her to get a good price. Along the way, he'd sent her several letters saying that he was headed back, but that he might have to spend a few days in Dekhron debriefing Colonel Weslyn, since, as she knew, that had been requested, along with other details, by the Lord-Protector. That was as much as he dared put in ink.

And . . . in the days before he had ridden out of Tempre, he'd had meetings, with Frynkel, with the supply chief of the Southern Guard, and with his own officers. Both captains and Feran had hardly seemed surprised at the Lord-Protector's decision to make Alucius commander of the Northern Guard, but the captains had been surprised at the decision for them to accompany Alucius to Dekhron. Neither was that unhappy, because it ensured that they would not be posted to Southgate or the west any sooner than early summer and perhaps even much later.

Twice on the ride back to Dekhron, he'd had the dream of the walls closing in on him. Was that the feeling that being the head of the Northern Guard was a trap? But why, then, were the walls those of an ifrit palace?

The one good thing about the length of the ride was that, for the most part, Alucius felt almost back to normal as he neared Dekhron.

Feran rode beside Alucius. "How do you want to handle telling Weslyn?"

"I think it ought to be quick, and that we ought to take charge of everything pretty much as quickly as possible."

"Close the gates?"

"No . . . but have the companies set up to control the post. I suppose a few men ought to come in with me, armed and ready. I can't believe he'd try something, but . . ." Alucius shrugged.

"He's a sandsnake, and I'll have a squad ready."

Alucius nodded. "Then, after I deliver the Lord-Protector's dispatch, just gather the officers. After that, we'll figure out how to tell all the lancers. We'll have to send dispatches to all the posts and companies. For now, you're going to be my assistant. Then you're going to be deputy."

"You didn't ask me, sir."

"I didn't. I'm not giving you the chance to say no." Alucius grinned. "Besides, it means a bigger stipend."

"If I live to collect it."

"You will."

The wind grew more and more chill, and stronger, as they rode through Salaan. Once they crossed the ancient eternas-tone bridge and entered Dekhron, the patches of ice and the dirty granular snow that had blown into side yards, alleys, and shaded areas beside houses and buildings confirmed that they were in the north and that it was winter. As Alucius turned the chestnut westward off the high road and onto the avenue leading to Northern Guard headquarters, he glanced northward, where dark clouds obscured the Aerlal Plateau. With the wind out of the northeast, Dekhron would see more snow by late afternoon, certainly by nightfall.

"Forgot how cold it was, even this far south," observed Feran.

Alucius smiled. He didn't mind the cold, not nearly so much as the heat of the south.

"You herders. Must have fires in your blood." Feran glanced ahead, toward the open gates of the post. "Better get ready." He turned in the saddle. "Fifth Company, rifles ready."

"Rifles ready!" The command echoed back along the column.

The two sentries at the gates looked up as they saw the uniforms of Fifth Company. Those eyes widened as they saw the uncased rifles and the two companies of Southern Guards that followed.

"Colonel Alucius, returning from Tempre," Alucius announced.

"Yes, sir."

Once inside, the commands continued. "Fifth squad. Cordon off the armory!"

"Yes, sir. Fifth squad!" Zerdial's voice rang out. "To the armory."

". . . Twenty-eighth Company . . . cordon the barracks!"

"Twenty-eighth Company! By squads . . ."

Feran motioned to Faisyn, then leaned over closer to the squad leader and spoke in a low voice for a time. Alucius wondered, but he was tired and didn't want to expend the Talent-effort. Besides, he trusted them both, and they'd both saved his life at different times.

"First four, you'll accompany me and the colonel," Faisyn ordered, dismounting and tying his mount. "With rifles."

Alucius gave Feran a weary smile.

"It's safer that way," replied the overcaptain.

Alucius dismounted and walked up the steps into the headquarters building, carrying the orders and dispatches from the Lord-Protector.

Faisyn and four lancers from first squad followed, carrying rifles.

The ranker at the table outside the colonel's study looked up. He swallowed as he saw Alucius. "Majer . . . we hadn't heard."

Alucius smiled. "It's Colonel, now."

The man paled.

"Is Colonel Weslyn in his study?"

"Ah . . . yes, sir. But . . . well . . . he and Majer Imealt . . ."

"That's fine." Alucius walked to Weslyn's door and eased it open.

Both officers were seated, Weslyn behind his desk, Imealt in front of it, and both turned.

"I'd asked not—" Weslyn broke off as Alucius stepped into the study, leaving the door open.

Alucius extended the sealed envelope to the silver-haired colonel. "It's from the Lord-Protector. He asked that it be the first thing I deliver on my return."

"Oh . . . ?" Weslyn did not rise as he took the envelope. Belatedly, his eyes flicked to the insignia on Alucius's collar. "Greetings, and congratulations, Colonel."

"It might be best if you read the Lord-Protector's dispatch," Alucius said.

"When I get a moment . . . right now . . . Majer Imealt and I . . ."

"Now." Alucius smiled politely.

"I am your commander—"

"No, Colonel. The Lord-Protector has accepted your resignation."

Alucius could hear the door opening wider behind him, but he could sense that Faisyn had been the one to ease the door fully open.

Imealt paled, his eyes darting to the door. "There are armed lancers out there, Colonel."

"Just a precaution," Alucius said. "There are also two companies of Southern Guards out there, as well as Fifth Company."

Weslyn looked at the seals on the envelope. "Were it anyone but you, Colonel, I'd have doubts about the seals. You wouldn't stoop to that." There was the slightest edge to his words. "Might I ask why?"

Alucius smiled wanly. "It was his idea."

At that, Weslyn laughed, a low laugh, half-rueful, and half-bitter. "It would be, wouldn't it?" He opened the envelope, carefully avoiding the seals, and extracted the single ornate sheet. He read it, slowly, carefully. Then he looked up. "Congratulations, Colonel. You're in command. It's not what it seems, or what you think."

Alucius nodded. "I've known that for years."

"Nothing is. Nightsilk doesn't protect what it doesn't cover, Colonel." Weslyn held a pistol, clearly aimed at Alucius's head.

There was also a pistol in Imealt's left hand.

Alucius stepped back, as if in astonishment, but also to his left.

"Fire!" he snapped, throwing himself sideways and down, and flinging up his left arm across his face.

Something hammered into his upper arm.

Shots smashed past Alucius, one after the other.

Neither Imealt nor Weslyn even had the time to look astonished. Both pitched forward.

Then Faisyn and two lancers were in the study.

"Sir?"

Alucius rose, slowly. He could barely move his left arm, but nothing was broken. He could tell that. He stepped forward and looked at the two dead officers. "My upper arm is going to be sore for a time." He wanted to shake his head or bang his head against the wall. He'd known that Weslyn hadn't been trustworthy, as he had known Fedosyr had been untrustworthy. He'd even taken steps to protect himself. Yet . . . when he'd walked into the study, he hadn't quite believed that Weslyn would try treachery immediately. He'd really expected it later. Not with pistols at the moment. He should have, but he supposed that he'd thought that there were some depths to which officers could not sink. He'd been wrong.

Feran appeared in the doorway. "Sir? Are you all right?"

"I'll be fine. I just . . . I still couldn't believe . . ." Alucius used his right arm to gesture to the two dead officers. "They pulled pistols and tried to shoot me."

"They did shoot him, sir," offered Faisyn. "Without the nightsilk . . ."

"I'd still be alive, but my upper arm wouldn't be in good shape," Alucius admitted. "It won't be much use for days, anyway." After dusting himself off with his right hand, awkwardly, he looked at the two bodies. "Leave them where they are for now." He turned and walked out of the study. The ranker who had been sitting at the desk was standing against the wall with two lancers watching him.

"We thought he might be like the other two snakes," Faisyn said.

"What's your name, lancer?" Alucius asked.

"Nadalt, sir." The round-faced man kept looking from Alucius to the lancers with rifles.

"What was the colonel so afraid of that he carried a pistol and tried to shoot me?"

"I don't know, sir."

The apprehension behind the man's voice and his feelings prompted Alucius to rephrase the question. "What is your best thought as to what the colonel feared, Nadalt?"

"He . . . he . . . I really don't know for sure, sir . . ."

"I didn't ask for certainty. Or do you want to be court-martialed for being part of this mutiny?"

"Mutiny? No, sir."

Alucius waited.

"I don't know, sir . . . except . . . well . . . in the last couple of years, he never stayed in the commander's quarters upstairs, and he has a big house on the west end of town, and . . . his wife, she died more 'n three years ago, and he had to borrow money to settle things, and then two years ago . . . he bought the house when the trader Ostar died . . . used to be Ostar's house . . ."

"What other officers are here in Dekhron?"

"Well, sir, there's Captain Yusalt. He's in charge of Seventh Company—that's the only company here these days. Overcaptain Shalgyr is the Guard quartermaster, but . . . I think I saw him hurry out the back gate just a few moments after . . . after you met with the colonel . . ." Nadalt paused. "Overcaptain Sanasus, he runs the dispatch riders and messengers, and all the wagons and teams—and the mounts here. He arranges for the pay chests to be sent to the outposts. Oh . . . and Undercaptain Komur. He's in charge of all the maintenance and equipment here at the post, and I guess everything else that no one else does."

As he made a mental note of the names, Alucius had the definite feeling that he wouldn't be seeing Overcaptain Shalgyr anytime soon. The overcaptain had used the foot gate, the one that led to the Red Ram, among other places in Dekhron.

"Sir . . . ?" Feran glanced toward Nadalt.

"Confine him somewhere until we get things sorted out," Alucius said tiredly. "We might as well call in the officers, those who are left here . . . right now, and tell them all what happened." He looked at Feran. "You're the acting deputy commander."

"You aren't giving me a choice?"

"Not right now," Alucius said. "I wasn't given one, as I recall."

Feran barked a laugh. "Faisyn . . . have Egyl find some squad leaders, and have them request the officers join the colonel here immediately."

"Yes, sir."

Nadalt glanced from Alucius to Feran. The ranker's shoulders seemed to droop.

"Where's the roster of all lancers stationed here?" Alucius asked Nadalt.

"It's there . . . the black folder on the right, sir. The first pages are headquarters. The others are listed by post after that."

Alucius walked to the narrow desk and lifted the folder, opening it and beginning to read the names, counting as he did. The officer's names on the roster agreed with what Nadalt had said. He skimmed through the pages, frowning as he reached the end. "Only eighteen companies?"

"Yes, sir. The colonel disbanded Nineteenth and Twentieth Companies in early fall. He said we didn't have the coins to supply and pay them. But . . . no one was released, not really. They were just transferred to other companies, and the officers replaced others."

"Did the colonel inform Marshal Frynkel or the Lord-Protector?"

"I . . . ah . . . I wouldn't know, sir."

"Do you know of any messages or dispatches that he sent making that known?"

"No, sir."

"Is it likely that you would not know?"

"No, sir." Nadalt's voice contained even greater dejection.

Alucius turned to see an angular and graying overcaptain step through the front doorway.

"Colonel . . . Colonel Alucius?"

Alucius recognized the older man, who was somewhere between forty and fifty, as he recalled. "Yes, Sanasus. I'm back. If you'd just wait a moment until the others arrive."

"Yes, sir."

Alucius turned his attention back to Nadalt. "So . . . how likely is it that Colonel Weslyn actually informed Tempre of his actions in reducing the number of Guard companies?"

"Ah . . . not very likely, sir."

"And did he notify the Lord-Protector that the payroll needed to be reduced?"

"Ah . . . not that I know of, sir."

Alucius turned as the last two officers walked into the open space inside the doorway. He recognized Undercaptain Komur—a wiry and short man with a weathered and tanned face. The blond and stocky officer behind him had to be Captain Yusalt, younger than the other two but still probably several years older than Alucius.

Alucius studied the three with his Talent, trying to gather impressions, even as he began to speak. "I appreciate your rapid arrival here. I wouldn't be surprised if word is all over the post, but if it is not, I thought you should know before I talk to all the lancers. The Lord-Protector was concerned that matters here in the headquarters of the Northern Guard were not as they should be. You may recall that Marshal Frynkel was here in early harvest conducting an inspection tour." Alucius paused, letting the words sink in.

Sanasus nodded slightly, as did Komur. Yusalt looked confused and radiated that confusion.

"You may know that I was requested to take Fifth Company and two others to Hyalt to put down a revolt. We did so, then were ordered to the defense of Southgate. Our three companies managed to destroy both crystal spear-throwers. The Matrites were pushed back. We were summoned to Tempre, and there, we were awarded the Lord-Protector's unit commendation and dispatched here. I was ordered to relieve Colonel Weslyn. When I delivered the Lord-Protector's acceptance of Colonel Weslyn's resignation, the colonel and the majer both drew pistols and attempted to shoot me."

Yusalt's confusion turned to shock, while Sanasus nodded once more. A thin and crooked smile came to Komur's face.

"Fortunately, Overcaptain Feran was less trusting than I, and had sent in several armed troopers. I survived. The colonel and the majer did not. The Lord-Protector had been concerned about certain irregularities in the Northern Guard. I think that the fact that the colonel's initial reaction was to shoot a fellow officer suggests those concerns were well-founded. I would also note that Overcaptain Shalgyr immediately rode out of the outpost."

"'Course he would, sir," said Komur. "Never let any of us see the ledgers. Wouldn't even let me buy grease myself."

"Before we proceed further, I'd like each of you to look into the colonel's study and also look at the dispatches and orders that I brought with me. You might also note that I was entrusted with the pay chests for the next two seasons. Those are in the guarded wagon out in the courtyard."

Overcaptain Sanasus nodded. "I will look, as you suggested, sir, but I have no doubts that matters are as you stated. They may be even worse."

Alucius could sense that Sanasus believed what he said.

"But . . . Colonel Weslyn . . . he was the commander," Yusalt protested. "Why . . ."

"To pay for that big house," suggested Komur. "And all those wines from Vyan, and to pay off his trader friends."

Alucius stepped back as the three officers walked toward the colonel's study.

The fact that two of the three had known something was wrong was encouraging. The fact that they had not been able to do anything—or not dared to—was more than discouraging.

The last thing Alucius wanted to do was to determine the extent of the damage and how badly supplied, provisioned, and led the Northern Guard might be—and those had to be among his very first tasks. After making sure that all the Guard knew of the change in command and leadership.

He looked bleakly toward the open door into the colonel's study.

105

North of Iron Stem, Iron Valleys

Wendra settled into the rocking chair, set at an angle to the iron stove of the main room. Outside, the wind moaned softly, and despite the closed shutters, the floor was chill from what of the biting cold had seeped into the stead dwelling.

"Little woman . . . you need to sleep."

A small fist waved, as if in protest.

"You do." Wendra began to rock slowly, looking down at her daughter in the quiet of the late evening. Then she began to sing the old song, the child's rhyme that she had always preferred sung to spoken, the one that linked her husband and her daughter.

"Londi's child is fair of face.
Duadi's child knows his place.
Tridi's child is wise in years,
but Quatti's must conquer fears.
Quinti's daughter will prove strong,
while Sexdi's knows right from wrong.
Septi's child is free and giving,

but Octdi's will work hard in living.
Novdi's child must watch for woe,
while Decdi's child has far to go.
"But the soarer's child praise the most,
for she will rout the sanders' host,
and raise the lost banners high
under the green and silver sky."

By the last words, Alendra's fist had relaxed, and her eyes were closed, her breathing even.

Wendra smiled, murmuring softly, "Another soarer's child . . ."

Her eyes lifted to the east, toward the Plateau she could not see through walls and shuttered windows. Then, slowly, she rose from the rocking chair, careful not to wake the sleeping Alendra as she carried her daughter toward her cradle.

106

As he tried to gather himself together, to think about what else he should be doing, Alucius stood for a moment outside the colonel's study. Then he stiffened and looked toward Dhaget. "Can you get Overcaptain Feran for me?"

"Yes, sir." Dhaget headed for the door to the courtyard.

"No one's left the post except Overcaptain Shalgyr, have they?" Alucius asked the nearest lancer.

Fewal looked toward Roncar. "That'd be hard to say, sir. We don't have a roster . . ."

Alucius nodded. It had been a foolish question, and he should have thought before asking it. He'd have to try to avoid that sort of thing. Commanders didn't ask stupid questions, not if they wanted to stay commanders.

Feran hurried through the doorway. "You wanted me, sir?"

Alucius looked at Sanasus. "Do you know where Colonel Weslyn's house is?"

Sanasus blinked. "His house?"

"The big one Undercaptain Komur mentioned. The one where he just might have all the golds he took from the Guard."

"Yes, sir. I mean, it's less than a vingt from here."

Alucius looked at Feran.

"Two squads, you think?" asked Feran.

"That should do it. We need to hurry . . . and find a mount for Overcaptain Sanasus. Shalgyr may have headed there. He may not have, but I don't want those golds vanishing, if they're there at all." He paused. "You'd better stay here and keep a hold on things."

Feran nodded, then hurried back outside.

"Golds? You think . . . ?" Sanasus closed his mouth.

"I don't know, but if we wait very long, we'll never know." Alucius was just hoping that he wasn't already too late. "If you'd stand by here, Komur . . . and you come on with us, Overcaptain . . ."

"Yes, sir." A certain tone of resignation tinged Sanasus's voice.

Alucius hurried back outside and mounted the chestnut.

"Third and fourth squads will accompany you, Colonel," Feran announced. "Holgart will act as senior squad leader."

"Sir, we're ready," announced Holgart. "There's a spare mount here for the overcaptain."

Sanasus mounted quickly enough that only Alucius was likely enough to have sensed his reluctance.

"Which way?" asked Alucius.

"Out the gates. Turn right, then west at the next cross street."

The ride was indeed short, less than three-quarters of a vingt, Alucius judged, before they reined up before a large two-story dwelling, a good twenty yards wide and close to twice that in depth. There was a stable to the right rear, and a wide front porch enclosed with a carved and painted pillared railing. A set of stone steps rose from the graveled walk to the porch. A wide single door with a stained-glass window was centered in the middle of the main floor. The house itself was of graystone, with black shutters trimmed in white. The roof was gray slate, and all the windows were wide, the shutters open. Thin trails of gray smoke circled from both chimneys.

All in all, a grand house, especially for a Northern Guard officer, Alucius judged.

"Best let me knock, sir," Holgart suggested. "You've taken enough shots."

"Be careful."

"That I will."

Four troopers stood with rifles leveled at the door as the squad leader used the heavy bronze knocker to rap smartly on the plate beneath.

The heavyset blond man who opened the door stood stock-still for a moment. Finally, he spoke, "What's . . . what is the meaning of this? The colonel will have your miserable hides for carpets."

"I'd not be thinking so, sir," offered Holgart. "Seeing as Weslyn's no longer colonel, by the order of the Lord-Protector. Colonel Alucius is the new commander of the Northern Guard. We're here to recover the property stolen by Weslyn."

"Stolen?" The blond man, presumably Weslyn's son, from his size and coloration, started to close the door.

Holgart wedged his big boot in the doorway and leveled his rifle at the man's midsection. "I do believe you'd best be opening the door and coming right out here on the porch."

The man looked out at the two squads of troopers, then at Alucius, with the colonel's insignia on his collar. He let the door open and stepped out.

"Degurt, you and the others secure the house! Report when it's secure."

Alucius could tell with his Talent that the house was vacant, but said nothing.

"There's no one here but me right now." The blond man looked at Alucius, who had dismounted and walked to the steps at the bottom of the porch. "This is disgraceful. My father still has some influence . . . You will answer for this."

"I'm sure I will," Alucius admitted. "But I'll have even more to answer for if I don't recover everything that's been stolen. The Lord-Protector's not terribly sympathetic to theft by officers, especially now."

"Theft? That's a serious charge . . . Colonel. My father is a good officer."

"That remains to be seen. If we find nothing, then you will have my deepest apologies, but we will be looking. You are?"

"Your apologies? Your apologies? You'll offer more than that."

"I'd like your name, if you wouldn't mind," Alucius said.

"Lynat."

"Lynat, if I am mistaken, you will have my apologies."

"If you're mistaken, and you are, my father will have your head."

"That's highly unlikely. He tried to kill me in sight of a half score witnesses. He and Majer Imealt died in the attempt."

Lynat paled.

"Sir, the house is clear."

"Good." Alucius turned to Lynat. "I'll try to make as little disturbance as possible. Please accompany us." He motioned to Sanasus. "You, too, Overcaptain."

After using the boot scraper and brush, Alucius stepped into the front foyer, its floor tiled in ceramic tile, with a geometric design in dark green, black, and silver. A Deforyan-style chest, with a gilt-edged mirror, stood on the left, a wall-hung, oak-backed row of bronze garment hooks on the right. The archway to the left led to a study, and Alucius stepped inside, using his Talent to search the desk and cabinets, but they held little besides papers. The bookcase under the side window held four shelves of leather-bound volumes.

Alucius nodded and crossed the foyer to the front parlor, with its two upholstered love seats, four armchairs, and two matching sideboards—well designed and exquisitely crafted. The dining room held a long cherry table and twelve chairs, with both a large and small sideboard, and a carving table, all of matching design. The chairs had blue and gold brocade upholstery. Behind the dining room and to the right, the kitchen boasted an indoor pump and a large iron stove, as well as a pantry that was a good three yards by two. The rear laundry room was just that. Alucius noted the doorway to the cellar stairs.

"We'll check the cellar last," he said mildly, watching Lynat. He wasn't at all surprised at Lynat's worry and fear when he mentioned the cellar. "Let's go upstairs."

Alucius briefly checked the three smaller bedrooms first. One was disordered and clearly Lynat's. The only thing Alucius found there were two Guard sabres and a pair of rifles.

"Not exactly proper," he said, setting the weapons on the end of the unmade bed, "but not something to be that concerned about." He turned to Sanasus. "Still . . . would you make a note of the serial numbers on those?"

"Yes, sir."

The largest bedroom was in the northwest corner. The only thing of interest there was a small chest set on the chest of drawers. Alucius pretended to take a key, but actually used his Talent to open the small lock.

"Where did you—"

Alucius opened the chest. Inside were perhaps twenty golds.

"Overcaptain . . . note that there were twenty golds in the chest in the colonel's bedchamber."

Lynat frowned, clearly puzzled as Alucius relocked the chest.

Then Alucius led the way back down to the locked door to the cellar. He looked at Lynat. "Would you care to unlock it?"

"I don't have a key. You'll have to break it down if you

want to open it." A certain smugness permeated Lynat's voice.

"Oh, I think not." Again, Alucius stepped forward and took out a key, the one to his own quarters. He stepped to the door, close enough that no one could see, and used his Talent on the lock. It was a heavy lock, and he was perspiring slightly when he finally turned the lever and opened the door.

Below was dark.

Alucius let Holgart step forward with a striker to light the lamp on the wall. Then he went down the stairs. Lynat followed, reluctantly.

On one side of the open space were several rows of barrels, all with markings showing receipt by the Guard. On the other side, neatly set in racks, were more than two hundred bottles of wine.

"Overcaptain, if you would note all the barrels and their contents."

"Yes, sir," replied Sanasus.

"And make a note of the number of bottles of wine."

On a rack on the west wall were four rifles, all Guard issue, as well as another four sabres.

Alucius surveyed the clay-floored room slowly, using his Talent. Then he nodded. The stone walls in the center, ostensibly the support for the fireplaces above, actually concealed a single room. He moved toward the stones, seeming to inspect each area, but in fact using his Talent to find the hidden doorway and access.

"Here. Yes." The door opened.

As it did, Alucius could hear the hard swallow from Lynat.

Inside the small room was a built-in cabinet against one stone wall. On top of the cabinet were two locked chests. Before addressing the chests, Alucius checked the cabinet. It held a number of items, such as an antique compass, some tarnished silver buttons, and a small jewelry case in which were a golden necklace with a single emerald, two gold rings, and a diamond-shaped golden brooch with small diamonds at each corner. Alucius replaced the jewelry case quickly, thinking of Wendra as he did.

He straightened and took a deep breath. There were no signs of keys to the chest locks. So . . . he would have to use Talent.

In time, both chests stood open. Each was filled with golds, and the majority were fresh-minted Lanachronan pieces, similar to those sent in the payroll and supply chests that Alucius had brought in the wagon from Tempre.

"Sanasus?"

"Yes, sir?"

"Would you kindly go up to the study and write out a receipt to Lynat here, for two chests filled with Lanachronan golds, presumed diverted from the Northern Guard treasury, and taken pending further investigation."

"You . . . had better count them, sir."

The last thing Alucius wanted to do was to count the golds, but he could see the overcaptain's point. "You're right. Lynat, you and I will count them, and you will sign the receipt once we agree on the numbers."

Lynat looked as if he wished to protest, but finally only nodded.

In the end, one chest contained exactly two hundred golds, the other precisely one hundred sixty-one—the total an astounding amount for a man who had not had a coin to his name six years earlier, and whose highest monthly pay was but four golds.

Sanasus had also added several lines to the receipt, indicating that the Guard had noted, but not taken, six rifles and six sabres, five barrels of flour, two of rice, two of potatoes, and three of dried fruit, and that the Guard had neither damaged nor removed any other property or goods on the premises.

Alucius signed two copies of the receipt, as did Lynat, then left one copy with Weslyn's son.

"I'll be sending lancers and a wagon to reclaim the barrels in the cellar. Your father had the right to use them so long as he was colonel, but they're not his property. They belong to the Guard."

"I understand that, Colonel." Lynat's words were cold. "You do what you must."

"I will, but I deeply wish it had not been necessary."

Lynat said nothing.

Alucius nodded. "We'll not trouble you more, except for the barrels."

The blond man offered the slightest nod, then watched as the two officers and the lancers left.

"Now what do you think, Sanasus?" asked Alucius, as they rode back eastward toward Guard headquarters.

"Worse than I feared, Colonel."

"We may have to use those golds, but we'll hold off, if we can, until I get word from Marshal Frynkel and the Lord-Protector. Tomorrow, you'll have to go back and reclaim the barrels of supplies. That's too much to let go, but we didn't have a wagon today."

"Yes, sir."

"Don't worry. You can take a squad of lancers."

"You think the barrels will still be there?"

"If they're not, Lynat could be in as much trouble as his father." Then, if matters turned sour, so could Alucius. Raiding a private house to reclaim stolen property wasn't exactly the way to start out as the new commander of the Northern Guard. But then, allowing three hundred sixty-one golds to vanish from the accounts wouldn't have been exactly to his credit. Either way, he had troubles.

"Oh . . . we'll need to get new locks for the strong rooms and put these chests in there."

"Yes, sir."

No one spoke for the rest of the ride back to headquarters. Overhead, the sky darkened, and flakes of snow began to fall.

Feran was waiting as Alucius dismounted. "What did you find?"

"Outside of six Northern Guard rifles and sabres, barrels of flour, rice, potatoes, and dried fruit, all marked for the

Guard, not much. Except two chests with something like three hundred sixty golds, two-thirds of them fresh-minted Lanachronan coins."

"That many? Seems stupid."

"They were in a hidden strong room in the cellar," Alucius added.

Feran nodded. "You have this way of finding hidden rooms and passages."

Alucius started to shrug, but the pain in his arm stopped the gesture almost before he started. "We do what we can."

The rest of the afternoon was a blur to Alucius. He and Feran finished briefing the officers and had them tell their own lancers. Then Alucius addressed all the lancers briefly, stressing not only the irregularities noted by Marshal Frynkel, but that Alucius himself had started as a militia scout and that his family still lived in Iron Stem. After the address, they reworked the post watch schedules and installed some of the more dependable lancers from Fifth Company to take over Nadalt's duties. Then Alucius inspected the entire post, yard by yard. Somewhere along the way, he ate some cheese and travel bread.

It was well after sunset when Komur accompanied Alucius up to the commander's post quarters.

"Hope you didn't mind, sir," Komur said as he opened the door to the upper-level quarters, "but while you were organizing things, I took the liberty of having my crew pack up Colonel Weslyn's few things and clean up the quarters best we could on short notice. Linens are clean, if spare." He lit the oil lamp in the front foyer.

Alucius walked from the small foyer into a large sitting room, with a modest and ancient coal stove that radiated heat. Komur also lit a lamp, one of a pair set on a side table. Off the sitting room to the right was a study, with dark oak shelves built into the walls, and even with books taking up perhaps half the shelf space. The wide writing table was empty and was set so that it overlooked the side courtyard. Alucius turned and crossed the sitting room to a large dining room, with a table capable of seating ten to fifteen people.

Behind the dining room was the kitchen, and an alcove and a table for more intimate meals. A large coal stove dominated the kitchen, also radiating warmth, and Alucius was glad to see that there was a rear pantry and an outside exit that led to a separate rear staircase. He retraced his steps to the sitting room and the double doors that led to a rear hall and one small bedroom, a bathing chamber with a jakes, and a larger master bedchamber, a good five yards by eight. The dark hangings were over the windows, leaving the chamber gloomy, and although he could see well enough, he lit a wall lamp for the warmth of the illumination.

The windows all had inside shutters, as well as deep blue hangings that could be untied and allowed to cover shutters and windows. The floors were polished dark oak, covered with large carpets of what looked to be a Dramurian design, with intricate interweavings of geometric patterns. Sections of the carpets in the bedchamber, the sitting room, and the dining room had worn places, and there were a few ancient spots and frayed edges.

Still . . . the quarters, with some more cleaning, were most livable and far better than any officers' quarters where Alucius had been permanently stationed. While compared to Alucius's stead house, the quarters were small, but they were not cramped.

As Nadalt had told Alucius, Weslyn hadn't used the commandant's quarters much. That was also clear from the fact that Komur had been able to remove Weslyn's possessions so quickly.

"These seem quite livable," Alucius said to the undercaptain. "I appreciate your efforts, especially under the circumstances." He winced as he realized that he'd used Alyniat's phrase, the one that had grated on him.

"Begging your pardon, Colonel, but I'd a scrubbed the floors on my own knees to get back a fighting commander."

Alucius smiled. "I know something about fighting. I fear that I'll need your help in other matters. I've had but a short stint running a small outpost and some experience running a stead, but nothing like running a headquarters post."

"That's what we're here for, sir."

"Good." Alucius offered a gentle laugh. "I'll need all your expertise and advice." He paused. "Thank you again."

"Glad to be of service, sir. Now, tomorrow, we'll be making sure that everything here works as it should . . ."

"The quarters are fine for now. I'm more concerned about the post, especially if there were recommendations you made that were not taken."

"There were a few." Komur smiled crookedly. "Some of them we managed anyway.'

"We'll talk tomorrow about the others," Alucius promised.

"Yes, sir."

Komur had barely left and closed the door when there was a knock.

Alucius could sense Feran. "Come on in."

The older officer stepped inside and glanced around. "Nice quarters. I've never been up here before."

"Neither had I," Alucius admitted. "You'll pardon me if I sit down." He tried several chairs, finally settling on an overstuffed armchair that looked uncomfortable—and wasn't.

Feran sat across from him in a straight-backed chair.

"What have you found out so far?" Alucius asked.

"Shalgyr kept the ledgers, and he left them. He was probably running for his life."

"I wouldn't have executed him," Alucius said.

"I know that. So did Shalgyr, probably, but he left anyway," Feran said.

"So . . . the mess is worse than we thought, and there's someone else involved," mused Alucius. After a moment, he laughed. "I'm tired. Of course, there had to be someone else involved, and it has to be one of the factors or traders. Or several. Finding out who won't be hard. Neither will proving that Weslyn was corrupt. But I'd wager that there won't be anything in the post that points directly at anyone but Shalgyr and Weslyn, and that Shalgyr is either in Lanachrona or already dead."

"He was smart enough to run and not try for the stables. Seven will get you ten that he's across the river and moving south."

"We're going to have to review all the supply accounts, all the pay accounts . . . just about everything. And count what's in the strong room and certify it," Alucius said. "That's just the beginning. I need to have personal talks with those three—Komur, Sanasus, and Yusalt—but I wanted to read their files first."

"Komur and Sanasus seem solid enough. Yusalt doesn't know much."

"I know. That bothers me." Alucius held back a yawn. "But before I do that, we'll have to send dispatches to all posts, notifying them, and also saying that Shalgyr is a fugitive."

"I told you that being commander wouldn't be what anyone thought," Feran said. "You'd better use that Talent to keep looking over your shoulder—and everywhere else."

"Now look who's being the cheerful one."

"I'm just telling you what I see." Feran's laugh was rueful.

"You're right." Alucius stifled a yawn. "I'm not thinking that well. I need to get some sleep." If he could.

After Feran left, Alucius unpacked his gear and washed out his dirty undergarments and uniforms. He managed to find a dusty washtub and was thankful that there was a pump in the kitchen. Only after that did he settle himself down at the writing desk in the study off the sitting room and begin to write Wendra.

Dearest,
I am at last back in the Iron Valleys and find myself as colonel and commander of the Northern Guard. I fear matters here in Dekhron are far worse than any of us had thought. The colonel and his deputy are dead. They tried to shoot me when I presented the

Lord-Protector's dispatch accepting Colonel Weslyn's resignation. Their reaction leaves me with
some considerable concern about what I will discover in the days ahead.

While I would most dearly love to ride to Iron Stem
to see you and Alendra, under the current circumstances, leaving Dekhron until these matters are resolved is not possible. Nor would it be wise, either
for the Guard or for me. I am going to need all the insight and assistance I can garner, and yet I dare not
leave Dekhron. Not until matters are far more settled, at the least. Do you think that your grandsire
would be willing to ride here and offer me his insights? I would also love to have yours, but not at the
expense of Alendra and the stead.

I will write more soon, but know that you are always
in my heart and in my thoughts . . .

He signed the letter and sealed it, then stood. He did
need sleep, and the days ahead would be long indeed.

107

By just before noon on Quattri, Alucius had
sent off his interim report to Marshal Frynkel and the
Lord-Protector, which included the results of the search of
Colonel Weslyn's dwelling. Then he dictated, revised, and
signed the last dispatches for the last Northern Guard
outposts—those at Eastice and Klamat. Sanasus took them
off to the waiting dispatch rider. Each dispatch had contained the identical summary of the Lord-Protector's concerns, a short summary of the previous day's events,
including the discovery of significant supplies and golds

from Northern Guard accounts found in Colonel Weslyn's dwelling, and a message from Alucius affirming his support for the long-standing traditions of the Guard and his pledge to follow the shining examples of such past commanders as Colonel Clyon. He dared not promise more than that until he understood the situation far better. With the copy of the interim report to Marshal Frynkel, he'd sent a note with the promise to report more as he discovered the details of what Weslyn had been concealing.

He did wish that he could have written the dispatches in his own hand, but by the time he had just signed the last dispatch, his fingers were numb, not because there had been so many, but because of the swelling in his upper arm. No sooner had he been able to take the brace off one arm than the other was injured, if not so severely. He stood from behind the desk that had been Weslyn's, and Clyon's before Weslyn. Alucius was determined to remember the study and the furnishings as Clyon's. He looked down at the desk and the four officers' files there—those of Sanasus, Komur, Yusalt, and Shalgyr.

"What do you intend now?" asked Feran.

"I need to meet with the officers. I'll start with Yusalt. Could someone find him?"

"I think we can manage that." Feran stepped out of the study.

Alucius picked up the officer's file on top—Yusalt's—and began to read, ignoring the whistle of the wind and the cold air seeping through the window. Flakes of snow swirled in the courtyard outside, adding to the light dusting Dekhron had received the evening before.

Yusalt came from Fiente, a town on the north side of the River Vedra roughly two-thirds of the way to Emal from Dekhron. He hadn't served at all as a conscript or as a regular lancer, but had been placed with Fifteenth Company as an undercaptain for two years, then spent another year as an undercaptain with Sixth Company.

Alucius frowned. He couldn't say that he recalled Yusalt when Sixth Company had been at Pyret trying to fend off the first Matrite invasion of the Iron Valleys. A year and a half ago, Yusalt had been promoted to captain and been given command of Seventh Company when it had been rotated off duty at Soulend, and he'd been at Dekhron ever since with Seventh Company. Fiente? Alucius had his own ideas, but he'd have to see if he were jumping to unwarranted conclusions. He continued to read through the single line reports on the captain, entries that noted very little except Yusalt's presence and submissions of his own reports.

Before long, Yusalt appeared at the door to the study. He stiffened. "Sir? You requested my presence?"

"I did. Come on in and sit down." Alucius settled into the wooden chair behind the desk. He waited until the junior officer seated himself, then studied him for a time. There was no sign of ifrit presence. "You're from Fiente, I see. Your family has been there a long time, I take it?"

"Yes, sir." Yusalt looked at Alucius only briefly.

"What do they do?"

"Ah . . . well, my father has the seed-oil works."

Alucius kept his nod to himself. That explained a great deal. "Do you have any brothers?"

"Yes, sir. Four."

"You're one of the younger ones."

"The youngest, sir."

"Did any of the others serve in the militia or the Guard?"

"Yes, sir. Aluard, he's the next to oldest. He was a conscript about ten years ago, when Clyon was the commander. He does some growing these days and helps with the oil works."

"Tell me what you recall about the fights around Pyret when you were with Sixth Company."

A brief expression of confusion crossed Yusalt's face. "Ah, yes, sir. That was a number of years ago . . ."

Alucius waited without speaking.

"We were ordered up there. I was the undercaptain. Captain Tregar was in charge. Majer Dysar headed the whole militia force. We were all crowded into this holding in

Pyret. It snowed all the time. I remember that. The Matrites had this spear-thrower, and it just cut people down . . . like they were overripe oilseeds. I guess that was how they pushed the other companies out of Soulend and farther south. We had this big assault on their camp, except it had been a militia outpost, and we lost a lot of lancers. But we were lucky. When it was all over, their spear-thrower had exploded. Some of the lancers said there were sanders there, but I never saw any. That could have been because I was on road duty, making sure the Matrites didn't have reinforcements coming in from the west. After that . . . well, it got colder and snowed more, and they didn't do so well in the cold, and we pushed them back to the edge of the Westerhills before winter ended." Yusalt shrugged. "Then it got warmer, and the Matrial sent more lancers. That was when Captain Tregar got it, and Captain Cavalat took over. They pushed us back to Soulend, and nothing much changed for almost a year. We fought some, but not a lot, and then they pulled back. That was when everyone thought the Matrial died. But no one knew for certain."

"Didn't Majer Dysar have family or friends near Fiente?" That was a guess on Alucius's part.

"Yes, sir. Both he and Colonel Weslyn visited my family several times. They knew some of the larger growers, too, like Dhafitt and Guiral."

"What did Sixth Company do after the Matrites pulled back?"

"We moved west to the border post—that was the old stead just short of the Westerhills—and we ran patrols through the hills and along the high road. We never saw any Matrites then, though."

"After you served with Sixth Company, you were promoted to captain and took over Seventh Company. How did that happen?"

"I can't say that I know. It was after Colonel Weslyn—except he was a majer then—became the deputy, and I remember that he signed the orders."

"Then you knew Colonel Weslyn fairly well."

"No, sir. I only met him a few times before he became deputy commander. I'd have to say that he was a friend of the family, but it was more business. He was a buyer for one of the old factors—Ostar, I think—and then maybe Halanat, except I think he doesn't run the factoring anymore. Anyway, we sold oil through the factors. Still do, but I don't have anything to do with that."

Alucius nodded. From what he could tell, and what his Talent reinforced, Yusalt was exactly what he seemed—a not-too-bright younger son who'd been placed at headquarters for exactly that reason—and to placate or do a favor for his father. "Thank you, Captain. I appreciate your forthrightness." Alucius stood. "Just carry on with your duties for now. We'll probably be making some changes, but I'll let you know."

Caught off guard, Yusalt belatedly rose. "Ah . . . yes, sir. Thank you, sir." He shifted his weight from one foot to the other. "Ah . . . can I . . . I mean, what can I say . . . about Colonel Weslyn?"

"I'd tell the truth. Right now, all we really know is that the Lord-Protector wanted to replace Colonel Weslyn, and Colonel Weslyn had some golds and goods that belonged to the Guard in his dwelling, and he tried to kill his replacement. Why? That's a good question. That would suggest that there was something wrong that he didn't want known, but at this moment, we don't have all the answers." Alucius offered a wry smile. "As soon as we know, I'll let you know. There's no harm in saying that Overcaptain Feran and I were sent to take over and find out what was wrong, and that both the Lord-Protector and Marshal Frynkel were well aware that there were problems here."

"Yes, sir."

"You have my leave, Captain."

"Oh, yes, sir." Yusalt bowed and hurried out of the study.

Alucius managed a quick reading of Overcaptain Sanasus's file before the graying overcaptain in charge of communications and logistics appeared.

Sanasus sat down, forward on the edge of the wooden chair, pursing and pursing his lips, waiting.

"I'd be interested to know, Sanasus, if you ever saw the ledgers for the supplies."

"No, sir. Not after Colonel Weslyn took over. He said he was reorganizing things, and he put all the disbursements and payroll receipts under Shalgyr. Brought him in from Fiente. Never served before. Made him a captain right off, then last summer, promoted him to overcaptain. Wasn't right, I said, but the colonel said that times were changing and that the Lord-Protector wanted logistics and disbursements separate. Wasn't much I could say to that. Especially not with but a few years before I could get a stipend. This golds business in his house . . . I never knew. I thought maybe he was taking a few . . . but not hundreds."

Alucius could sense the absolute truth behind the overcaptain's words, and that was both a relief and a worry. "I think that, once we go over the ledgers, you'll have to take over both functions once more. I doubt if there's anyone else in headquarters who knows what's required."

"What about the Lord-Protector's requirement?"

"So far as I can tell, there never was such a requirement. Even if there happened to be one, my orders and mandate allow me to change any procedures that are not working. I don't know everything that happened, but the golds, and Colonel Weslyn's reaction and Overcaptain Shalgyr's flight, suggest that things are not as they should be."

"No, sir. Couldn't prove it back then, but I felt we were paying too much for supplies. Then there's the payroll. The colonel decommissioned those two companies, but we were still getting the same payroll from Tempre, and no one's pay that I know of was increased."

Alucius cleared his throat gently. He'd spent more time talking in the last day than he did in weeks on the stead. Or in several days as a majer in charge of a few companies. "You can advise me on how you think the ledgers and accounts should be set up so that any irregularities can be quickly and easily caught."

"I can do that. That was the way Colonel Clyon had it, sir. Fine officer, and a better man."

"He was."

"You'd best be real careful, sir. Leastwise, until you get everything out in the open. I don't know who they are, not for sure, but there'll be more than a few in Dekhron who won't want the Lord-Protector to know."

"That's one reason why we already sent out an interim report."

"Might not be a bad idea to let folks know that."

Alucius smiled. "I can't say much about that, but I certainly wouldn't complain if that word got out."

"I can see that, sir, and, well, it just might." Sanasus offered a grin, the first warm expression on his gaunt and grizzled face.

When the overcaptain finally left, Alucius turned to the window. The snow had stopped, leaving a fine dusting on the roofs of the compound and on the courtyard itself. Then he turned back and picked up the file on Komur.

After he met with the undercaptain, he needed to get Feran and Sanasus together and undertake a count of what was left in the existing pay chests in the strong room, then have Sanasus develop and provide him with a budget for at least the next few months. He also needed to see if the accounts and ledgers provided any clues as to exactly what Weslyn had been doing to amass all those golds.

He still needed to read all the recent reports from company and outpost commanders, and to update himself on where all the current companies were stationed and what the command structure was. For some of that, he could read at night, and he would have to—for longer and later than he'd ever imagined.

108

Dekhron, Iron Valleys

Tarolt looked up as the door to his study opened, and a round-faced trader in a heavy dark blue winter cloak marched in, halting a mere yard from the desk.

"You look rather . . . disturbed, Halanat."

"You said everything would be fine." Halanat glared at the white-haired Tarolt. "You said that he'd fail or get killed in the revolt, or by that spear-thrower. He didn't. Now he's here, and the whole city knows—"

"He's only just taken command—and, as I recall, the initial idea of having him recalled to duty was yours."

"You aren't the one that they'll be looking for."

"Oh . . . and just what will Colonel Alucius do? He has no power over anyone who is not in the Northern Guard. He cannot touch you. There's no proof of anything, except Weslyn's stupidity. Stupidity on two counts. One never draws a weapon on a warrior. It's far better to have someone else do it. Or push him into a situation where he cannot win or where he kills the wrong person. One also should never underestimate an honest man. Especially an honest Talent-steer."

"That's easy for you to say. Word is already all over Dekhron that Weslyn was lining his own pockets and that others might be involved. This . . . Colonel Alucius even found a chest with three hundred golds in the strong room in Weslyn's house. How could he have been so stupid? Where does that leave us?"

"What you do is have Halsant send a letter to the new colonel, welcoming him and promising him the greatest cooperation in providing goods at the lowest fair price, and suggesting that the colonel's reputation for honesty and directness will serve him well."

"Within weeks, he'll see right through that."

"He may do so within glasses or days. What can he do? Call Halsant a liar? The colonel is direct, but far from stupid. He will not do anything that is public and direct without proof. If we do not provide it, he can suspect all he wishes, but he cannot act, except to insist on better prices, and that should not be a problem, not for the short time he will be colonel."

"Weslyn would take great comfort in your words."

"You're not Weslyn, and you're not in the Northern Guard. Every trader and factor, and even the larger crafters, will be watching this Alucius. He's too young. He's arrogant, and he's a nightsheep herder. None of those traits will endear him to those who must supply him and who are tariffed by the Lord-Protector to support him and the Northern Guard. His high-handed search of Weslyn's house will be the first of many actions that will cause him trouble."

"He can do much damage in a short time."

"That's to our gain. Already, people in Hyalt are beginning to murmur that the True Duarchy doesn't sound so bad considering the problems they have now. The same is true in Southgate and Zalt, and Dimor and even Arwyn. If our new colonel drives a hard bargain for supplies, that will increase the anger and unrest. If he does not, he will lose favor in Tempre, because the Lord-Protector is hard-pressed to find coins for his wars."

"And then what?"

"We wait for him to make a mistake. Young and brilliant officers always do. That is their greatest failing, and one that is inevitable. One cannot gain wisdom except by making mistakes. Young and brilliant officers get promoted too quickly and before they can make those mistakes where the consequences are not so great."

"Just what mistake will he make?"

"What particular mistake?" Tarolt smiled. "I have no

idea, but it will be one that lies in his failure to understand that brilliance and skill do not address every problem. Sometimes, there is no substitute for subtlety and treachery." Tarolt paused. "Did you have something else?"

"Something else . . . ?" Halanat stood speechless for a moment. "Something else?"

"If not, you should return to your own dwelling and consider how best to make the new colonel look unbending and unsympathetic to the needs of the oppressed traders and factors of Dekhron."

Halanat's eyes lifted to the purpled orbs of the white-haired trader, then dropped. "Ah, yes, sir."

109

On Quinti, Alucius and Feran spent much of the day just digging out information and supervising the assembly of records from various places. Weslyn had clearly tried to keep information as fragmented as possible so that he was the only one who had access to everything. Again, that was just another indication that far more was wrong than Alucius had yet seen, but there was so much information that Alucius had decided to set that aside for a time and get back to assessing the state of the Northern Guard as a fighting organization and determining what he could do immediately.

By Sexdi morning, Alucius and Feran were in the commander's study trying to sort out the strategic situation from dispatches and maps, outdated as they might be. Alucius could only hope that he'd get updated reports from Majer Lujat in the west. His dispatch to Lujat had offered his full support and his admiration for Lujat's effectiveness under difficult conditions.

Alucius looked to Feran. "No wonder Majer Lujat is barely able to hold any positions. Half of the officers are captains that Weslyn appointed over the past three years. None of them had any real experience."

"I told you that," Feran said.

"You did. That was before I knew I'd have to fix the problem."

"Makes a difference, doesn't it, most honored Colonel?"

"Yes, it does, most honored about-to-be Majer."

"I haven't said yes."

"I won't take 'no.'" Alucius took a long deep breath. "Do you know any of the senior squad leaders of those companies?"

"Some of them."

"We can make Egyl a captain, if you think he can handle it, and if he'll accept it," Alucius said. "Give him Seventh Company here, and, in a week or so, send them to Sudon for training before posting them somewhere west."

"Egyl would be a good captain," Feran agreed. "Faisyn could handle senior squad leader of Fifth Company for a while, and they could train out of here. Wait a few months and make him captain, and move Zerdial up to senior squad leader."

"More like a few weeks for Faisyn. We don't have much time. That's two companies. That leaves sixteen, eighteen when we re-form the Nineteenth and Twentieth."

"You've got a couple of decent captains. Koryt still has the Third. And Cavalat with the Sixth."

"What ever happened to Vanas?"

"Matrites got him early on in that first campaign. Dysar sent the Thirteenth against three Matrite companies."

Alucius looked at the Thirteenth Company roster. "Zaracar's the captain now." He went through the stack of officers' files, not all that many, and quickly leafed through Zaracar's file. "He's another one that Weslyn appointed— just last year. He's from here in Dekhron." Alucius wrote down the name and the company number on the tally he was keeping.

"Haven't heard of him."

"Is Estepp still around?" Alucius frowned, then answered

his own question. "I thought I saw his name somewhere. The training company at Sudon, maybe?" He went through the rosters. "Yes. I thought so. He's still a senior squad leader. He should have been made a captain years ago."

"Maybe he didn't want to be."

"And maybe Weslyn needed someone to train lancers . . ."

"Good lancers, but captains who aren't that bright?" suggested Feran.

"That's what it's looking like, isn't it?"

"What about Overcaptain Culyn?"

"He's not on any of the rosters, and there's no file on him. The head of training at Sudon is Overcaptain Dezyn." Alucius paused. "I remember him. He was here at Dekhron when we came back."

"Oh . . . the blond captain. He was like Yusalt—didn't seem to know that much."

Feran and Alucius exchanged glances.

"Maybe we should promote Estepp to captain and leave him in charge of training for a while," suggested Alucius.

"That might be better. He knows what he's doing. With the Regent still in power in Madrien, we're going to need more and better lancers."

"We aren't going to get that many more," Alucius pointed out. "Let's hope Estepp can keep giving us better ones. And some more foot troopers. Weslyn pared down the foot to just three companies, and they're all split into squads for basic stationkeeping at the outposts."

"They're useless that way." Feran snorted. "Like a lot of those captains. It probably took Yusalt years to figure out which end of a rifle to use."

"He's a nice young man who has no business being in the Guard." Alucius had originally thought that Weslyn had just been trying to squeeze all the coin he could from the Guard, but now he was getting a far darker impression, and one that suggested to him that Weslyn had been used, either as a tool or directly, by the ifrits to weaken, if not to gut, the Northern Guard. But that wasn't something he

could say, not about the ifrits. "It's almost as if he were trying to destroy the Guard."

Feran nodded. "It looks that way. Do you think that the
traders were paying him off?"

"There's not much doubt about that. It might be hard to
prove, and we don't know why." Even if the ifrits did want
to weaken the Guard, why would they want the Matrites
running all over Dekhron? "It doesn't make sense for them
to weaken the Guard so much that the Matrites would take
over the Iron Valleys and Dekhron."

"Maybe they don't want either side to win," Feran suggested. "So long as the fighting goes on, no one will be
looking at how they operate."

"That does make sense." In more than one way, Alucius
realized. "But we can't let them keep doing it."

"Stopping them will be hard. You're just the Guard commander. You've got your hands full fixing the mess Weslyn
left you."

Alucius grinned. "What do you mean by putting it on
me? *We* have our hands full."

"I was afraid you'd say something like that, most honored Colonel." Feran shook his head.

"I think the next item is your promotion. You're getting
the grief; you should get the coins."

Feran snorted. "They're not enough."

"They never are. Now . . . about that promotion . . ."

110

In midafternoon on Septi, Dhaget rapped
on the doorframe to Alucius's study. Alucius looked up
from the draft of the Northern Guard reorganization plan
he and Feran had worked out. "Yes?"

"This just came, sir," said Dhaget, extending an envelope.

"Thank you." Alucius took the envelope and opened it. Dhaget slipped back out of the study.

The envelope held a formal dispatch, with a small square of paper folded inside the dispatch. Alucius read the short dispatch.

Colonel Alucius—
In Captain Dezyn's absence, I am reporting that the training company at Sudon has been informed of the change of command in the Northern Guard. I have informed all squad leaders and trainee lancers, and we await any orders that may be forthcoming.

The signature was that of Estepp.

Alucius nodded and unfolded the second sheet. It had but a few words and no signature.

We're behind you. Take care of this group of brig-ands like you did the last.

His smile was rueful. Those words were the Estepp he recalled, but the formal dispatch was all that Captain Dezyn would see. Of that, Alucius was certain. He was also certain of the message that Estepp was sending. He pocketed the second and unsigned note. Feran would certainly want to see it.

He glanced out the window at gray skies that seemed to be lifting. He hoped so. Then he went back to the plan on his desk. The plan itself wasn't that complex, but figuring out which transfers to make in what order and what officers' resignations to ask for first were still things he needed to work out. He had decided that he wanted to complete the reorganization in two steps. He'd thought about doing it all at once, but Feran had pointed out that having more than half the companies without captains or captains in transit at one time was likely to be too unsettling.

Then, too, he still had to deal with the logistics problems. Although Sanasus had implemented a new set of ledgers, reconciling the accounts was going to take days, if not weeks.

Another knock on the door interrupted his concentration, and he looked up.

"Sir . . . there are some folks to see you." Fewal was grinning as he stood in the door. "I thought you'd want to know. They've come a fair piece."

Alucius could see a feminine figure, holding an infant, and an older man. He scrambled to his feet and through the doorway past Fewal, who was still smiling broadly. For a long time, how long he couldn't even tell, Alucius held Wendra and his daughter. He could sense how three lifethreads almost intertwined in a swirl of green. His eyes blurred, and she reached up and brushed away the tears.

"I'm so glad you're here," he murmured in her ear.

"I'm so glad you're safe."

Kustyl cleared his throat.

Alucius flushed as he released his wife. Tears streaked her cheeks as well as his. Alendra merely gurgled.

"Couldn't tell that the man missed you or anything," Kustyl observed.

Wendra said, her voice low, "Do you have quarters here? Grandpa Kustyl said you did. I can go up there and feed Alendra. You need to talk to Grandpa. He says it's important."

Alucius nodded. "Fewal . . . if you could escort my wife to the quarters . . ."

"Yes, sir. I'd be pleased to."

Alucius and Wendra exchanged smiles before she stepped back, and Alucius nodded to the older herder. "I understand you have some information for me."

"That I do, Colonel. That I do." Kustyl's eyes twinkled, and there was the slightest emphasis on the word "colonel."

Alucius watched for a moment as Wendra left, then stepped into his study. Kustyl followed and closed the door. Alucius gestured to one of the chairs.

"Hope you don't mind if I stand, Alucius, but it's been a long ride, and I'm not so young as I used to be."

The younger man laughed. "Not if you don't mind if I sit. I'm still sore in places." He eased into the chair behind the desk.

"Wendra didn't say, but you were hurt pretty bad, weren't you?" Kustyl's eyes narrowed.

"I didn't tell her in my letters. Feran said no one thought I'd live."

"And you're walking around now."

"Nightsilk helps."

"Some." Kustyl smiled. "She brought you new sets of nightsilk undergarments. And a new vest. Said even nightsilk couldn't keep taking the beating you gave it." He studied Alucius. "You almost look old enough for this job. Gray hair helps." Then he smiled. "Anyone any younger, the troubles'd kill 'em."

"What can you tell me?" asked Alucius.

"Might help if I knew what you know and what you need to know."

"Here's the problem. I'm sure that Weslyn was lining his own pockets, entering higher charges for goods and pocketing the difference. We found three hundred sixty golds in his cellar, mostly the kind that are sent from Tempre—"

"Three hundred sixty? The sandsnake skimmed off that much?"

"I can't yet link the amounts, but that's what it looks like. He also replaced any officers who might question him with captains who seemed to be the younger sons of factors and merchants who sold goods to the Guard. Oh . . . and he also disbanded the Nineteenth and Twentieth Companies, and I think he pocketed that payroll, but I don't know. I haven't had a chance to go over all the ledgers in any depth. We've been working on letting everyone know about the change in command and that Weslyn tried to kill me." He pointed to the chart on the desk. "Feran and I have been trying to work out which officers to remove, and what senior squad leaders we can promote to captain or undercaptain to take over. We've just about got that figured out, not just who but how and in what order so that we can get someone who's good in charge in the important posts as quickly as we can."

"Your grandsire always thought you'd be good at this. Your mother made him promise not to tell you." Kustyl coughed. "You've figured out what Royalt and I suspected was going on, but there are some things that you ought to know. First off, all the old traders that backed Dysar, then Weslyn, are dead. Except for two. One's Halanat, and the other's Tarolt. No one sees Tarolt much at all. He doesn't trade or factor anymore, and all his business is handled by Halanat's outfit. No one sees Halanat much, either. His son, young fellow by the name of Halsant, is the one who does all the factoring, and he's the head of this new Traders' Council. Probably the youngest of them all, but he's still in charge. He's not much older than you are, maybe thirty, but they all do what he wants. Has to be because Halanat and Tarolt are behind him. Don't know why everyone backs off 'em, but they do."

Alucius nodded. "There has to be some connection with Weslyn."

"Oh . . . everyone knows they were friends. Ate together, even over at the Red Ram. Weslyn was the friendly type, met and ate with most of the big factors. Already . . . some of them are saying that you were sent back to break up their trading combine so that the factors from Tempre and Borlan can move in."

Alucius snorted. "From what I've seen, the southerners can't even handle trading in their own land—in lower Lanachrona, I mean. Those that can are more worried about what's happening in Deforya and in Southgate."

"Doesn't matter what's really happening, Alucius. You have to deal with what the traders in Dekhron think."

"I know. So what do I do? I'd thought about meeting with them and telling them exactly what happened." Alucius gave a twisted smile. "One problem is that I haven't figured it all out yet."

"Set up a meeting now, but for a week away or so. That

way, they'll hold off saying their worst. They'll still talk, but they'll want to know what you have to say before they act."

"That makes sense. What do you think they'll try to do?"

"I don't know. Not for sure. Some of 'em have to be thinking about paying brigands or some of the old-time Reillies to take you out."

"That's a comforting thought. And if I get rid of them, I'll be a high-handed butcher sent by the Lord-Protector."

"After what you did in Hyalt, they're already saying that."

"How do they know what I did in Hyalt?"

"I don't know, but word's out that you butchered thousands of men and turned the city and the trade over to the women."

"The prophet had used Talent to enslave maybe a thousand men into his forces. They kept attacking us, and when they did, we killed them. I'd judge that we killed something like eight hundred. No more than a thousand. We had to turn the city . . . well . . . it's really only a big town . . . we had to turn it over to the women. The men who were left were either ten years older than you or not quite right in the head from what they'd been through."

"Doesn't matter."

Alucius sighed. "I know. Are my choices to try to do what's right and try to survive assassination attempt after attempt, or will I have to wipe out all the factors here in order to have a chance to keep the Iron Valleys from being taken over by the Regent of the Matrial?"

"Regent?"

"She's the one who took over in Hieron. From what I've seen of their lancers, she's even worse than the Matrial was. They've got those torques working again. We did get rid of their crystal spear-throwers, and the Lord-Protector has pushed them back north for now. If I can get the Guard reorganized, we might be able to keep them in check in the north as well."

"In check?"

"With half the captains hardly competent, and without the Nineteenth and Twentieth Companies, I'll be fortunate to do that. Dezyn doesn't know much about training—do you know what happened to Overcaptain Culyn?"

"There was talk about it, say a year and a half ago. They found him dead in the quarters here. Not a mark on him. Figured his heart just stopped."

Why hadn't Alucius heard that? Or had he been so relieved not to be in the Guard then that he just hadn't paid attention?

"You don't think it was that, I take it?" asked Kustyl.

"Looking back . . . no. No more than Clyon died of the flux."

"You got your hands full." Kustyl shook his head. "Every herder's behind you, but there aren't many of us left."

"You have any more suggestions for me?"

"Don't enter any narrow ways and never leave your back bare. And if you've got any ways to have folks die of flux or in their sleep, Halanat and Tarolt wouldn't be bad places to start." The older herder shrugged. "And don't wait very long. They won't. That's for certain." The lanky gray herder looked toward the closed door. "That'd be all I've got right now. Except to spend some time with that wife of yours."

"I don't need a reminder for that." Alucius smiled as he rose. "You'll let me know if you hear anything else?"

"That I will. Be talking to a few folks I can trust here in Dekhron. Not that many, anymore, but I'll stop by tomorrow."

"Do you have somewhere to stay? We could—"

Kustyl shook his head. "Be staying with Renzor— Mairee's cousin's boy. Works better that way."

"Thank you." Alucius opened the study door for Wendra's grandsire.

After Kustyl left, Alucius took another look at the charts and planned company rosters, but his eyes wouldn't focus on the names or the descriptions. He shook his head and walked back out of the study.

"Sir?" Dhaget looked up from the table where he was sorting lancer files into piles by company.

"If Overcaptain Feran comes back, tell him that my wife just arrived, and that I'm up in my quarters getting her settled in."

"Yes, sir." Dhaget kept the smile off his face, but not totally out of his voice and eyes.

Alucius did not run up the steps to the commander's quarters, but neither was his progress sedate. He found Wendra on the large bed in the main bedchamber, propped up with pillows and feeding Alendra.

After a moment, he eased onto the bed behind her shoulder, then kissed her neck.

She turned her head, and their lips met.

After several very long moments, Wendra eased her head back and readjusted Alendra. "You don't have to act as though every moment will be the last," she said with a grin. "I'll be here for several days, maybe longer." The grin turned to a frown. "How did you get that scar?"

"That was from the prophet."

"You didn't mention that."

"It didn't seem important." He paused, almost afraid to ask the next question, with his desire to have her in Dekhron for more than an afternoon or a day. "What about the stead?" He kissed her neck again.

"It will do without me for a few days. While I've been with Alendra . . . your grandsire . . . he had to take the flock." Wendra shifted Alendra into the crook of her left arm and switched the infant around, readjusting her clothing to let her daughter nurse on her other breast.

"Did he . . . have trouble?"

"No. He never saw those creatures. Alucius . . . they're attracted just to you and me. It has to be. Have they ever appeared anywhere besides where one of us is?"

"There were the pteridons of Aellyan Edyss . . . but, as for the wild ones . . . no."

"Why are they attracted to us? Because we show more Talent?" asked Wendra, readjusting Alendra in her arm again.

Alendra began to suckle in earnest.

Wendra winced slightly. "She's strong, and she's a little piglet. She must take after you."

"Me?"

"You," she said firmly. "Now . . . why do those things show up when we're around?"

"That we have Talent might be part of it, but it can't be all of it. They have to be coming from somewhere, and that has to be from wherever the ifrits are coming from."

"Where is that? Is it truly another world, as you said?"

"It must be. There's nothing that looks like those creatures anywhere in Corus, and there never has been, except in the days of the old Duarchy." He paused. "Except maybe the ones that look like black dustcats." He shook his head. "It's like nothing quite fits. But the soarers said the ifrits were from another world, and so far, what the soarers have said . . . it's been so." Alucius bent forward and kissed her neck, easing one arm around her.

"Later . . . dear man. Later. When not every lancer is speculating on what we're doing, and when Alendra is asleep. I've missed you, and I'd like to have some time to enjoy being with you." She turned her head.

Alucius enjoyed the kiss—enormously—even knowing that he would have to return to charts and rosters and other matters. But only for a time, and only until later.

111

Hieron, Madrien

The Regent rose from the wooden armchair set behind the conference table and took several steps toward the north wall of the private study that had once been that of the Matrial. She stopped short of the built-in shelves, filled with ancient tomes that covered the entire wall, shelf upon shelf, running from the floor to the four-yard-high ceiling. A small walnut book ladder rested in the middle of the shelves, a single volume balanced on the third step.

For a time, she looked at the volumes, unspeaking.

Then she turned from the volumes on the shelves and walked back to the conference table, where she reseated herself. Her violet eyes fixed upon the marshal in a purple and green uniform tunic on the other side of the circular conference table. "Have the engineers made any progress with the drawings I supplied?"

"They have yet to discover how to duplicate the crystals necessary for energy storage," admitted the marshal.

"Then they scarcely deserve the title of engineers."

"They have begun to grow the crystals that focus and create the spears. The storage crystals are harder. They are much more complex than those for light-torches, and you know how long it has taken and how hard it has been to create those. Even the . . ." The marshal broke off.

"Even the Matrial, you were about to say?"

"Yes, Regent."

The Regent offered a cold smile. "I suppose that is fair. She did have more experience than I have at present."

"Do you know how the Matrial became . . . the Matrial?"

"Changing the subject, are you, Aluyn?"

"Yes, Regent." Aluyn's voice carried a rueful tone. "It seemed wiser."

A sharp laugh was the Regent's reply. "You are honest. I've always admired that."

Aluyn waited.

"I suppose it cannot hurt to tell what I know," admitted the Regent. "There were a few notes that I found. She was not from Madrien. She was born in Aelta."

"She was Deforyan?"

"She was a pleasure girl in the palace of the Landarch, if what she wrote was correct, and then she cut her hair and became a lancer in the time of troubles with the nomads—the old troubles, four centuries ago. She was proficient enough with rifle and blade to survive. Then . . . according to the notes, she discovered her destiny and brought it with her as she made her way westward . . ."

"Discovered her destiny," mused the marshal, "and brought it with her. Almost as if it were something she held in her hands."

"I'm sure that she thought of it in that fashion," replied the Regent. "At times, destiny can indeed have a tangible form."

"A tangible destiny? And is that destiny now yours, Regent? Will you soon be the next Matrial?"

"There has been but one Matrial, and that is all that there ever will be." The pale-faced, violet-eyed, and dark-haired Regent smiled enigmatically. "We shall leave it at that, and you will offer great encouragement to the engineers—if they wish to remain engineers."

"Yes, Regent." Aluyn offered a discreet head bow. "I will do so."

"You may go."

Only when the marshal had departed both the study and the Regent's private quarters did the Regent stand. She left the study, then crossed the main sitting room and stepped through the arches and out into the enclosed garden.

The Regent glanced at the row of daisies, green and seasons from flowering, before turning to light upon the miniature redflower tree in the northwest corner. Her violet eyes darkened.

Abruptly, the small red flowers browned, then dropped onto the dark soil of the narrow flower bed. In turn, pointed olive green leaves darkened, blackened, and fell. The smooth brown trunk blackened in turn, and, but for an instant, blue flames played over the blackened remnant of the ancient miniature tree. Within moments, all that remained was a circle of black on the soil.

The Regent smiled coldly, then turned and left the enclosed garden.

112

Wendra had persuaded Alucius that she could stay a few days, and that she could certainly look over the ledgers to give him a hand while she was there. He had not protested excessively strongly about either proposition, and he had enjoyed Octdi greatly, taking more time off from his work than he should have.

On Novdi, when he came upstairs for a quick midday meal, he saw that Wendra had laid out three ledgers across the single couch, open at different points. She sat in one of the overstuffed armchairs, burping Alendra.

"Alucius . . . there are things really wrong with these ledgers . . ." Wendra looked up, a smudge of dirt or ink over her left eye. She rose, holding out Alendra. "I need to show you."

Alucius took his daughter, still amazed at her, for so many reasons. Already, Alendra's lifethread was close to half green, a promise of strong Talent, yet she was still so small, or so it seemed to him, no matter how often Wendra told him that she was good-sized for a child less than two seasons old. And her eyes—a deep green with flecks of gray. Over the years, Alucius had not seen many infants, but never had he seen one so young with eyes of such strong and striking color.

Wendra picked up the first ledger and carried it to where Alucius could see without setting down Alendra. "This is the one for outpost supplies. That's what it seems to be. Look at these lines here."

Alucius looked, taking in the words: Cooperage, fifty full barrels [slack/oak].

"The barrels . . . that was what caught my eye. Father never charges more than a silver a barrel for slack cooperage—that's for oak. The Guard is paying two silvers to Halanat and Sons, but they're buying from Father at less than half that."

"A tidy profit—more than five golds for just that one lot of fifty barrels."

"It's worse than that," she said. "Father has asked to bid on barrels. He's always been told that his bids were too high."

"But he sold them to Halanat for what, less than five golds, and Halanat resold them for ten?" Alucius shifted Alendra higher on his shoulder.

"The ledgers don't say what price Halanat got. Between Weslyn and Halanat they skimmed off more than five."

"How many times has this happened?"

"There are five times that I've found in this ledger. I don't know that I've discovered them all. Or even most of them. There are also some purchases of buckets and some flour that look like the same thing. I can only trace the things where I know the costs."

"Still . . . just on the five-barrel lots, that's more than a half year's pay for a colonel."

Wendra grinned. "Do you get that? We could buy another ram and get a better outbreeding."

"You don't get the bonus on my pay anymore." Alucius wasn't sure about that, but he doubted that the Lord-Protector would pay it once he was back in Dekhron, even if it happened to be looking almost as dangerous as battle duty. He frowned. That was overstating matters.

"What's wrong?"

"Nothing. I was just thinking that . . . well . . . no one's going to like what I'm finding. Even after the golds Weslyn was hiding."

Wendra set down the first ledger and brought a second one over. "All this feed. It comes from a grower named Aluard in Fiente. The amounts are twice what we pay for it for the town sheep, and we're paying for almost a hundred vingts of cartage when we buy it in Iron Stem. The Guard can't be paying but half that, not if it's coming from Fiente to Dekhron. And there's a lot more feed sold to the Guard than barrels."

Aluard—that was the name of Yusalt's brother. Were there two Aluards who were growers in Fiente? Somehow Alucius doubted it.

"Weslyn had more than a few ties to Fiente. I'd wager that any oil the Guard bought was purchased on the same basis."

"What will you do?"

"For now, I'll have to meet with the factors and traders and tell them about what Weslyn did and suggest that it appears as if he pocketed a great deal. I'll probably have to let it go at that—unless I find evidence otherwise from here on in."

"Oh . . ." Wendra set down the ledger. "You need to eat, and I haven't done much."

"There's bread and cheese, I think, and a few other things."

"That's not enough—"

"It will do. It's what I was eating before you came. Besides, what you found already is more important than food." Alucius smiled. "So is your being here."

"I'm glad to be here."

Alucius turned sideways, then leaned forward and brushed her cheek with his lips. "You don't know how glad I am."

She grinned wickedly. "You showed me last night."

Alucius couldn't help flushing.

"Grandpa Kustyl came by a while ago." Wendra's voice sobered, a serious tone.

"When are you leaving?"

"Tomorrow morning. I don't feel right leaving you, but I don't feel right leaving everything on the stead to your grandsire. He gets tired, really tired, if he has to take the flock out more than two days in a row."

"You didn't tell me that."

"You've had enough to worry about."

That was true enough, and now she had told him.

"We need to get you something to eat." Wendra turned. "I can do it if you'll keep holding Alendra."

Alucius readjusted his daughter against his shoulder. Alendra squirmed, as if protesting the change in position, as Alucius followed his wife toward the kitchen.

Still . . . he was back down in his study in less than half a glass, and Wendra had promised to write down, as she could, all the instances of obvious overpayments. He'd redrafted his request to meet with the Traders' Council on the following Sexdi to discuss matters of mutual interest and concern. After he signed and sealed it, he had Fewal take it to Halanat's factorage, since he had no idea where else to send it.

The lancer returned within half a glass to say that the factor Halsant had accepted the letter with little more than a nod.

Kustyl arrived less than a glass into the afternoon, while Alucius was drafting letters requesting the resignations of various officers, mostly captains placed by Weslyn. Interestingly enough, Alucius had already received a letter of resignation from Yusalt. That indicated that either someone had passed the word to the captain or Yusalt had not been quite so clueless as he had first appeared. It also suggested he was far from guiltless.

Kustyl walked into the study, closing the door behind him. This time he did settle into the chair across the desk from Alucius. He smiled. "You got 'em worried. That's for sure."

"Who? The factors?"

"Mostly the folks with golds. Even Renzor's heard, and he's just a coppersmith. They're talking about your facing down Weslyn. Some of 'em claim you're part sander, with skin like theirs. Say that nothing else could have survived the shots you took. A couple say that Weslyn was a crack shot. Maybe three years back, he shot a cutpurse running away from thirty yards in the dark. 'Course, no one knew the cutpurse, and only Weslyn said he was a thief."

"Anyone know any more about that?"

"There was some captain who claimed the fellow had been a lancer working in headquarters who deserted, but nothing came of it."

Alucius nodded. Like so much he'd found, it was suggestive, but hardly proof of anything. "What else?"

"It's what's not happening. No prices are changing. No one's stocking up on things, and folks don't think you'll be colonel that long. Figure someone'll shoot you, or that you'll go back to being a herder, or the Lord-Protector will order you back into fighting the Matrites."

"That's not good."

"Nope. Not all that bad, either."

"Why do you think that?"

"If they were all into this, you'd see more happening, one way or another. People leaving town. Goods being sold."

"That . . . or they're all in it."

Kustyl shook his head. "Too many loose lips in Dekhron. Way I figure it, it has to be Tarolt and Halanat, and everyone else is trying to stay out of their path."

"What sort of goods do Halanat and Halsant handle?" asked Alucius.

"Pretty much everything except nightsilk. Heard they've been shipping more wine from the south out east, and sulfur to Deforya lately," Kustyl said.

"The sulfur sounds like trouble."

"Your grandsire said you didn't much care for the Landarch."

"He wasn't as bad as the nobles around him. They're in charge now. Before long, the Praetor of Lustrea will be trying to take over Deforya. The Lord-Protector would like to, but he doesn't have the lancers to do it."

"You're getting less cheerful these days."

"Wouldn't you?"

Kustyl laughed. "Never have been. Mairee had to be twice as cheerful."

"I need someone here local to look over the ledgers. Someone who's honest and won't take advantage of the information, but I'd like them to be someone whose word most factors would trust."

"Don't want much, do you?"

"I never do," replied Alucius dryly.

Kustyl laughed again. "I'd say you ought to try Agherat. He's the most honest of Dekhron's usurers."

"A usurer?"

"Who else knows ledgers and coins? You don't need a usurer. Guard doesn't borrow. Means he doesn't gain much by it. He's a cousin of Mairee's—she's got lots of cousins. I can ask him after I leave here."

"If you would."

"I can do that." Kustyl stood. "That's what I've got. Talked to your Wendra. She tell you?"

"You plan to ride back tomorrow morning." Alucius rose from behind the desk.

"Quite a woman, that granddaughter of mine."

"More than anyone knew," Alucius said.

"Except you. You saw that right off, didn't you?"

"I'd like to think I did. I knew she was special. I didn't know why."

Kustyl nodded. "Glad to see she's on the stead. Best herder in the whole family, and she had to get a stead from your family. Glad it was your grandsire's. Almost family, anyway."

"I'm glad it worked out."

"You and all of the north valleys. See you in the morning." Kustyl opened the door and slipped out.

Alucius looked down at the unfinished letter on the desk. Sometimes, the writing that followed the decisions seemed as bad as the decisions themselves.

113

In the grayness before dawn on Decdi, Alucius opened the door to his quarters. He carried Wendra's saddlebags, stuffed full, mainly with clothing for Alendra, but also with his old nightsilk undergarments. He hadn't realized how fast infants went through clothing in cold weather, at least, if parents wanted them to remain relatively dry and odor free.

Wendra followed him, with Alendra in the carrypack across her chest, a pack designed to keep the infant snug, warm, and slightly to the left, positioned so that, if necessary, Wendra could use her rifles. Their breath trailed them like white fog as they made their way down the steps to where Kustyl and Wendra's mount waited. Alucius had saddled her chestnut earlier. The chill was more of midwinter than late winter, and more what Alucius would have expected on the stead, rather than in Dekhron.

At the bottom of the steps, Alucius gave Wendra a last, one-armed embrace and kissed her cheek, then bent and kissed his daughter's forehead. "I wish you could stay. Or that I could have put my other plans into effect." Alucius had already told Wendra that he had asked for permission to move the Northern Guard to Iron Stem, and that the Lord-Protector was considering it. Wendra had understood that he was reluctant to say more until he had a firm commitment.

"I wish I could stay, too. You know it's not for the best."

Alucius did. In many ways, Dekhron was looking to be less safe than the stead, and there was also the problem of Royalt. According to Wendra, Alucius's grandsire was beginning to show his age, and if he were left too long to handle the stead without Wendra—or Alucius—the strain would be too great, and in the end, both Alucius and Wendra would suffer more. Given all he owed to his grandsire, Alucius did not want to place too heavy a burden on Royalt. "Just be careful on the way back, and on the stead."

"I will. I always am." Wendra smiled warmly at him.

For a long moment, their eyes and lifethreads intertwined.

Then Wendra turned, and even with the carrypack, mounted easily. After she mounted, Alucius checked the rifles at her knee, making sure—once more—that the actions were clean and that the magazines were full.

He stepped back. "Just be careful," he said again.

"We'll be fine." Wendra looked down at him. "You're the one who needs to be careful."

Kustyl cleared his throat.

Alucius looked at the older herder.

"Agherat said he'd be glad to help," Kustyl said from the saddle of his roan. "No charge. That's something from a usurer, but he didn't care much for Weslyn. He's across and up from the chandlery nearest the bridge. Sign with two coins."

"Thank you."

"Glad to ask for you." The older herder glanced to the north. "Cold but clear on the way back. Wendra'll take care of us both. Better shot than anyone except maybe you, Alucius."

"Let's hope you don't have to shoot anyone."

"Being prepared to shoot's better than hoping you don't have to," Kustyl replied wryly, easing his mount around to face the gates.

Alucius walked beside Wendra's mount until they reached the gates and the sentries, where he stopped, watching as they turned northward. Then he started back toward his quarters.

Behind him he heard the sentries.

". . . Colonel's wife . . . pretty woman . . ."

". . . herder like him . . . she can run a stead alone . . . rifles there aren't for show . . ."

". . . heard tell she was as good a shot as him . . ."

". . . tough folk up north . . ."

". . . could use more of 'em, especially now."

He could use more of just about everything, Alucius reflected, except crooked factors and ifrits—and inept captains. He made his way back to his study.

Once in the study, cold because the coal stove in the main part of the headquarters building had not been fired up for the day—and would not be until he did, since Decdi was end day, when lancers had a day off, except in the field—he sat down behind the desk, thinking over what lay ahead.

He'd promoted several senior squad leaders, and now Egyl was the captain in command of Seventh Company. Feran had taken Egyl and Seventh Company, as well as the two Southern Guard companies, to Sudon, with another promotion order for Estepp to captain and the order dismissing Captain Dezyn. Seventh Company would stay there for some intensive training. Fifth Company, with Faisyn as senior squad leader, had remained at Dekhron to support Alucius.

Alucius still hadn't received any word from Majer Lujat on the situation in northern Madrien, and only about half the northern and western outposts had reported back. So far, thankfully, the reports had been positive and seemingly appreciative of the change in command. That would not last, not if the Northern Guard had to deal with an attack by the Matrites, not when supplies and effective officers were both low.

He took a deep breath and looked at the stacks of paper and charts before him. He could only hope that Sanasus was almost finished setting up the new ledgers and revamping the accounts and disbursing systems.

114

Lundi and Duadi passed without incident—and without dispatches from anywhere. Alucius and Sanasus checked the inventories of everything against the ledgers, then began to go over the ledgers line by line, sorting out what they calculated had been paid to various crafters, growers, and factors, and what had been recorded as being paid. They'd gone back only two seasons, and the discrepancy was far larger than Alucius had originally thought—more than a hundred golds in four months. At that rate, Alucius calculated a difference of two hundred fifty golds a year. If Weslyn had been diverting that much, where were the other five hundred or so golds that had been "overcharged" in the past four years? Had they gone to Halanat?

He'd brought in Agherat late on Duadi, and the old usurer had clucked and mumbled and muttered, then found almost ten more places where Weslyn had concealed overcharges. "Never liked him. Too friendly. Kind that smiles while he cuts your purse." Those had been Agherat's only words about the late colonel.

After the usurer had left, Sanasus and Alucius had both taken deep breaths.

Alucius might suspect, but the more they looked, the clearer it was that there was no evidence within the Northern Guard records that pointed to misdeeds—except by Shalgyr and by Weslyn. Alucius had no doubt that others were involved—or that, barring some mistake or disclosure, he'd never find proof of his suspicions.

Feran returned to Dekhron on Tridi, striding into headquarters in midafternoon and settling into the chair across from Alucius.

"How was Sudon?" asked Alucius.

Feran grinned. "Captain Estepp said you were the only colonel who'd dare to make him a captain. He also said that he'd even volunteer to take a company against the Matrites, if you needed it."

"Dezyn?"

"He should have been waiting with a letter of resignation." Feran laughed harshly. "Instead, he asked when he'd be promoted to overcaptain because all the heads of training had been overcaptains before."

"How did you break it to him?"

"Not well. I told him that he was lucky you hadn't assigned him personally to a suicide attack against a crystal spear-thrower, and that he could consider himself fortunate to be able to resign, rather than being dismissed or court-martialed for incompetence."

"He protested, of course. That kind always does."

"Not for long. I'd made sure Estepp was promoted first, and called him in." Feran's grin widened. "I've never heard such a detailed listing of incompetence. Never heard one so well presented, either. I did ask Estepp to write it up and send it here."

"To you, I hope. As deputy commander." Alucius handed Feran a sheet of parchment and a set of insignia. "It's official, now. You are number two."

"You rushed that."

"No. I should have done it within the first day, but I dated back to then, so you'll get paid for it."

Feran shook his head. "You do know what lancers think is important."

"I hope so. Put on the new ones."

"Here?"

"Here."

Feran took off the overcaptain's bars.

Alucius looked at the majer's insignia on Feran's uniform collar. "Those look good. Unlike some of us, you look old enough to be a majer."

"That's another legacy I have to bear," Feran snorted.

"You'll handle it fine," Alucius insisted. "Better than I do."

"Not better. Differently. We make a good team."

"As a team," Alucius began, "we still have to figure out how to strengthen all the companies in the west. We haven't heard from Lujat."

"He's cautious. He's probably gathering information on his own, to make sure that you're really in charge."

Alucius hoped so. Again, he was hoping too much.

115

By Quinti morning, dispatches were flooding in from all the outposts and companies. Alucius walked into Feran's study and handed several more to the majer. "I think these are the last. It's almost as if they'd all cross-checked with each other."

"They probably did. Once they saw senior squad leaders getting promoted and Weslyn's flunkies getting sacked, they decided it was real. Estepp sent a note with his report on Dezyn's incompetence. He got a note from Sawyn— he's senior squad leader with Twelfth Company—wanting to know if you were really colonel."

"You think Sawyn . . . ?"

Feran shook his head. "Senior squad leader is where he belongs. He can get anything done, but he's never had an idea of his own in his life. Captains sometimes have to think."

"I'll be glad when we get the last of the new officers in place."

"Except that's when they've got to get to work." Feran glanced at the reports. "Are you finished with all that work on the ledgers?"

"We had to go back over things after everything that

Agherat pointed out, but we did find a number of other discrepancies. Sanasus has some loose ends, but it's done. At least, everything that we could do."

"And?"

"We figure—it's a guess—but we think Weslyn diverted close to twelve hundred golds. Who got the other eight hundred or so . . . who knows? The house was only fifty golds, and even with that matched pair of his and the carriage . . ."

"Only fifty golds for a house? Imagine that. I'd have to save every copper for three years. And that's at the munificent pay of a majer . . ."

"Then there was the wine. Agherat told me some of the bottles cost a gold apiece. There were two hundred and five bottles."

"A mere hundred golds more," suggested Feran. "That leaves seven hundred. You think it was Halanat?"

"That's my guess, but there's not too much I can do. There's not a shred of proof."

"That hasn't stopped you before."

"Not knowing why, what they did with the golds, or the reasons just might stop me." Alucius cleared his throat. "Anyway, I'll have to be careful. I've got to meet with this Traders' Council tomorrow. They've suggested some place called the White Bull."

"An old tavern on the river. That's not so bad. Things have quieted down. If you don't accuse anyone, they'll probably stay quiet."

"That's what bothers me. I get a cordial letter from Halsant, promising cooperation. Sanasus says that we're getting solid and lower bids for flour and feed. It's as if nothing ever happened."

"You think something is about to happen?"

"Yes. They could be waiting to hear what I have to say, or they could already be planning something." Alucius paused. "What did you think of Majer Lujat's report?"

"He thinks the Matrites are waiting for warmer weather to attack."

"So do I," replied Alucius. "I just hope we can get those

companies reinforced, and the new captains have time to get settled and ready."

"That's already happening. We've got good lancers. You wouldn't believe the difference in Seventh Company under Egyl even in a few days. We can send them out to Wesrigg in a week, and they'll be a big boost."

"When does Estepp think we'll have enough trainees to reestablish Nineteenth Company?"

"Midspring. I'll need until then to find the seasoned squad leaders, and a nucleus of decent lancers from other companies."

Alucius was glad that he had Feran as his deputy because he'd been able to leave the military organization side of things to the older officer while he concentrated on unscrambling the logistics and disbursement mess, although he had doubts that all the questions would ever be resolved.

116

The White Bull was indeed an old tavern, on the river and less than a quarter vingt west of the high road and the ancient eternastone bridge over the River Vedra, set in the middle of a block of even older structures. The wooden front had been slathered with so many coats of brown that the paint doubtless had more strength than the wood beneath. The windows were clean, but the panes were blued with age, except for the handful that had been replaced. Fewal and Roncar rode with Alucius, but remained mounted outside the tavern as he walked in.

About twenty men sat at the tables in the public room. All looked at Alucius. No one said a word. Alucius took several moments to survey the group before he finally spoke.

"I appreciate the chance to meet with you. I'm afraid

that I don't know any of you. At least, I can't say that I recognize any of you, and if I should, I must apologize."

The sandy-haired and heavyset man who walked forward to greet Alucius looked far older than the thirty years suggested by Kustyl. He carried the aura of purpleness that bespoke some ifrit contact, an aura stronger even than that which had surrounded Colonel Weslyn. His eyes scanned Alucius before he spoke. "I'm Halsant. I suppose . . . well, normally Tarolt would be doing much of the talking, but he couldn't be here today."

"I see. Do you know why he couldn't?"

"No, Colonel. I don't ask other factors their business."

Alucius offered a smile. "I wasn't suggesting that. Sometimes, people explain why they can't be places. I certainly wasn't prying. If the honorable Tarolt didn't say, then that's his business, and I certainly respect that."

Halsant nodded. "There have been stories of all sorts about what's happening with the Guard . . ."

"That's one reason why I suggested that we meet. Another reason is that the militia and then the Northern Guard have been so closely tied to the traders and factors in Dekhron." Alucius turned slightly so that he faced all the traders. "I don't know if Halsant shared what I wrote, but I was asked by the Lord-Protector to become colonel because an inspection of the Northern Guard last year had revealed some serious problems." He took the sheets of paper he had had prepared and laid them on a large circular table to his left. "These are some papers outlining what we've discovered so far. When you have a moment, feel free to look at them." Alucius paused, hoping that someone would ask a question or move and look at the documents. He really didn't want to do all the talking to a silent audience.

"Some folks are saying that you were ordered to take care of Colonel Weslyn, just get rid of him."

Alucius shook his head. "I was sent from Tempre to replace the colonel. The documents on the table show that there were no orders and no hints to do him harm. The Lord-Protector had accepted the colonel's resignation—"

"Weslyn didn't resign."

Alucius smiled pleasantly. "That was a polite way for the Lord-Protector to allow the colonel to save face. If the Lord-Protector had wanted to be harsher, he could have dismissed the colonel or ordered a court-martial for malfeasance."

"We liked the colonel. He was a friendly sort," offered a dark-haired man to the rear of the group. He seemed to bear little trace of the ifrit purple aura.

"I'm certain that you did. He was a pleasant man. But the colonel never fought in a pitched battle, and he never commanded lancers in battle, and it has been clear to battle-tested officers in both the Northern and Southern Guard that it was time for a change. As most of you should know, I did not seek this position. I only accepted it under duress, and at the personal request of the Lord-Protector. I accepted it because the war with Madrien is far from over, and because the Iron Valleys would suffer greatly with the Guard in the condition left by Colonel Weslyn."

"Why did you have him shot?" That came from another factor, a ginger-bearded and balding man.

"I didn't. He shot me. Only after he and Imealt fired at me did my men return fire. I was unarmed at the time. There were more than ten witnesses, and a number of them were not my men, but the colonel's."

"He must have had a reason."

"He did. He was afraid that if I survived, he'd be punished after I discovered his crimes."

"You broke into his house. Why?"

"To recover the golds he'd stolen from the Guard accounts."

"You took his savings, according to his boy Lynat."

"We found a chest with over three hundred fifty golds in it. Colonel Weslyn did not come from a wealthy family. Nor did he marry wealth. He'd been a buyer for Ostar after he'd first left the militia. In fact, according to those who knew him, he had almost no coin when he returned to the militia as Colonel Clyon's deputy. In the less than six years he was with the militia, then the Northern Guard, his total pay was less than one hundred fifty golds. Would any of you care to explain how an officer who was coinless managed to purchase a large house, with a stable, costing over fifty golds, a matched team and a carriage, and still come up with more golds than twice his pay?" Alucius swept the room with his eyes.

Not a single trader even met his gaze.

"What he was doing, so far as the ledgers show, was to get a good price from you and from other traders and crafters, then charge the Guard almost twice that. He pocketed the difference. He disbanded two companies and never told the Lord-Protector, and pocketed the extra payroll as well. The Guard's not exactly in the best position because of this. And neither are you and your businesses."

"So . . . you're going to increase our tariffs?" suggested Halsant.

"No. The Lord-Protector was most specific. I have no powers beyond those that Colonel Weslyn had. Tariffing still rests with the Lord-Protector. My authority extends just to those matters affecting the Northern Guard."

"Why do we have to get involved? Either as factors or as people in the Iron Valleys?" That came from the dark-haired man in the back.

"You might recall," Alucius said quietly, "that the Matrial invaded the Iron Valleys several years ago, and it was a hard fight to push the Matrites back. Now, the Regent of the Matrial has refused any terms with Lanachrona and demanded all of the south back and all of the north, and ten thousand golds. I'd imagine, since the Iron Valleys have an eighth of the land area of the rest of Lanachrona and less than a tenth part of the population, our share might only be one to two thousand golds. Whether we like what was done in the past or not, we are involved, and the only question is how we deal with it from here on."

Several traders exchanged glances.

". . . never should have gotten into this . . ." came a whisper from the back table.

Alucius refrained from pointing out that their unwillingness to support the militia years earlier had created the problem. "We've changed the ledger system back to something resembling the older system, and we will be asking for various bids in the weeks ahead. We've also been strengthening our forces in the west because it's likely that the Matrial will attack in the spring. As I mentioned a moment ago, Colonel Weslyn was indeed lining his own pockets. I've asked several respected traders and crafters to look at the Guard ledgers as well to attest to what we have discovered. Some of your goods were involved. Because of the way in which the colonel arranged for purchase of the goods at your standard prices, you would only get your normal price and would not know of this."

Alucius was lying here, because there was a strong suggestion, both in the ledgers and from the fear emanating from a number of the traders, that more than the colonel had been involved, but he could not prove it and doubted that he ever could, not in a way to be laid before a justicer or the Lord-Protector.

"Unless other problems arise, of course, I see no reason to dig into the past. We certainly can't recover coins already spent. We can only make sure that both you and the Guard get value for coins in the future." Alucius offered a smile.

"You've been most forthcoming, Colonel," Halsant finally said.

Alucius could sense the worry from the man, worry and an aura of fear that intensified the purple miasma that drifted around him.

"After all I've said," Alucius went on, "I'm certain that you'll all wish to look at the documents here, and I'll wait in case you have any questions."

As Alucius had suspected, there were few questions indeed, but more than half the traders did stop to examine the papers and documents. None asked him anything new.

After less than a glass, he was on his way back to Northern Guard headquarters, still musing over the meeting, and why Halanat and Tarolt had not been there. Was it because they were closely connected with the ifrits and didn't want Alucius to know? Or because they thought he was just beneath notice? Or because they intended to act against him and didn't want to alert him, knowing that a herder could sense that?

He didn't know and couldn't come up with any more plausible reasons on the ride back to Northern Guard headquarters. But he needed to find out. That thought remained with him as he dismounted and turned the chestnut over to Fewal.

"I don't think I'll be riding out this afternoon."

"Yes, sir."

Alucius had been back in his study for only half a glass when Feran appeared in the doorway and stepped inside.

"Lujat sent another dispatch," offered the older officer, as he sat down on the edge of the chair across from the young colonel.

"About what? That he's short of supplies, payroll, mounts, equipment, and experienced officers?" replied Alucius dryly.

"It wasn't that bad. He has enough payroll and mounts. He also expressed his appreciation of the recent reorganization—that's the way he wrote it—of the officer corps. He said that would be of great help, especially if the Matrites did not attack in the next few weeks."

"I'm glad someone thinks we did something right."

"He also wrote that they found several Matrite deserters—dead, without a mark on them."

"The torques. They've got them back working, maybe all of them." Alucius still didn't know how, but it wasn't something he could explain to Feran.

"Can't say that I like that." Feran paused. "How was your meeting with the traders?"

"I'd guess we've reached an unspoken truce, of sorts, except with Halanat and Tarolt. Tarolt wasn't there, and Halsant was doing the talking for him and for his father."

"You think that the two older traders not being there means something? That they don't want to agree or meet with you? Or that they're guilty and know that because you're a herder, you'd know if you met them?"

"That's my guess. I was willing to let it go, if they'd have come, but without seeing them . . ."

"You could always just go see Halanat first," suggested Feran. "From what you've said, he's the one who's been supplying more of the goods to us. Then if he won't see you in person . . . you do what you have to."

"I'd already thought that, but I was interested in what you think. I don't like the idea of the two most powerful factors in Dekhron avoiding me, as if I didn't even exist, or that the Northern Guard doesn't matter."

"To them, it probably doesn't, except for the coins they get." Feran's laugh was low and harsh.

Alucius nodded.

"If you go, I'd suggest an escort," Feran added. "Four lancers, at least."

"That's too many. Two. Two makes it look as though I'm just self-important. Four suggests I'm afraid, and that's not good."

"Fear is sometimes wise," Feran said sagely, before his somber face broke into a grin.

"I'd agree, but showing it is not."

"You are wearing nightsilk still, I hope."

"Wendra brought me two new sets and a stronger vest. She said I'd worn out the old ones."

"You probably did."

Alucius nodded. Wendra had made that point by putting her knife through the chest of one of the older undergarments. She'd also packed the old ones in with Alendra's clothes so that Alucius wouldn't be tempted to wear them. She'd said that she could use the heavy shears and tailor the unstressed nightsilk into a jacket for Alendra. They both had understood that need, because Alendra would have to accompany Wendra out on the stead at least some of the time. Alucius worried about that as well. It seemed that the older he got, the more worries he had.

"When will you try to see Halanat?" asked Feran.

"Tomorrow. The sooner we find out where we stand on all this, the sooner we can work out a better budget and plan for the rest of the year and next year."

"I'm glad you got all that herder training on how to handle coins." Feran shook his head as he stood. "It's easier to deal with the Matrites than ledgers. For me, anyway." He gave a last smile as he left Alucius's study.

Alucius looked at the stacks of paper. He hoped he could finish up with them in the next week. Then he could get back to working with Feran on more ways to improve the Guard. But . . . without coins and supplies, they couldn't do that, either.

117

On Septi, under a clear silver green sky, promising spring, with the sun nearing midmorning, Alucius rode out of the Northern Guard headquarters. With him rode Roncar and Dhaget. He wished he could ride alone, but he'd promised both Feran and Wendra that he'd take an escort when he could.

He was glad to be out and riding. After only two weeks as colonel, he was restless. Was he too young to be a headquarters officer? Too much of a herder to spend so many glasses behind a desk? He snorted. Did nightrams have sharp horns? Was the Aerlal Plateau high? Was winter at Blackstear cold?

For all his restlessness, though, he had a job to do, and if he didn't do it and do it well, he might never get back to being a herder. He shifted his weight in the saddle and continued riding toward the river.

Halanat's factorage and warehouse were just opposite the wharves on the River Vedra, almost a vingt west of the White Bull. Whether he'd find Halanat there, he didn't know, but it was likely that if he didn't, he'd learn more by visiting the warehouse. He might even find out more from Halsant. Although Alucius had his doubts about that, he thought he should try if Halanat didn't happen to be there.

Once beyond the headquarters gates, Alucius turned the big chestnut to the right and followed the unmarked avenue toward the trading district, one part of Dekhron that he had never visited.

The factor's warehouse was clearly marked—HALANAT & SONS—with a recently painted signboard over a building that was old but had been kept in repair. A heavy wagon was being unloaded through the dock on the west side. Both the signpost and the wagon bore a painted image of a silver wheel.

A silver wheel—the design mentioned by the women in Hyalt. That gave Alucius a most uneasy feeling as he reined up in front.

"Do you want us to accompany you, sir?" asked Fewal.

"No. Just wait here. I don't think I'll be that long." Alucius dismounted and handed the chestnut's reins to Fewal.

Alucius stepped up onto the narrow porch, opened the heavy oak door, and paused. Inside the cavernous warehouse there was little light, save that coming from the open loading door on the north side of the west end and from the pair of barred and narrow windows flanking the front door. Pallets, bales, and amphorae were neatly placed in rows along the stone floor, but without signs or labels. While there was a slight mustiness to the air, there was surprisingly little dust.

Alucius caught sight of several figures beside the loading door and started down the space between two rows of bales toward them. Two men were rolling a hogshead farther inside the warehouse. The third, who had been watching the unloading, turned—Halsant.

"Colonel . . . I can't say I expected to see you here. Unless you're on stead business, and, in that, I certainly can't help you. You know we don't handle nightsilk."

"I understand that you never have," Alucius replied. "But that's not why I'm here."

"Oh . . . ?"

"You seem to be doing well these days." Alucius gestured back at the goods stacked in the warehouse.

"As well as can be expected." After a pause, Halsant asked, "What did you want?"

"Actually, I was looking for your father."

"You know . . . he's not that involved in the factoring these days."

Alucius smiled politely. "I understood that as well. A number of people have suggested I should talk to him."

Halsant's eyes flicked from Alucius toward the windows though which the two lancers could be seen and back to Alucius. "Oh?"

"Yes." Alucius waited.

The trader shook his head and shrugged. "That's your business, then. He should be in his study at the house."

"Thank you." Alucius started to turn, then stopped. "I didn't want to ask when I met with the Traders' Council the other day, but could you tell me something about it? Why it was created?"

"Not much to say. Once the Lord-Protector dissolved the old council, none of us really met. We decided we still needed to tell each other what was happening . . . the way the traders do in southern Lanachrona. We were stumbling all over each other . . . cost a lot of golds. It's more like an exchange, not really a council."

"I take it you become one of those most involved with it?"

"I've been going to the meetings. Most of us have. I suppose I have more to say than some. We've had to go farther and farther in our trading."

"I noticed the silver-wheel emblem. Is that just yours, or

do all the traders in Dekhron use that? I could have missed it, but I don't recall seeing it before."

"It's ours, but it's new in the last few years. Once we started going south, we decided we needed an emblem, something that would make us easier to recognize. It's not a name, not something tied to the north, you know?"

"That makes sense," Alucius said.

Halsant looked toward the loading dock. "If you'll excuse me . . ."

Alucius smiled. "I'm not that familiar with Dekhron. I've spent most of my time in the Guard and militia out fighting. Could you point me in the direction of your father's house?"

"Oh . . . take the avenue north one block, then follow the street west almost to the end. There's a wagon carved in a plaque by the door." Halsant nodded and turned.

Alucius watched for a moment before walking back along the row of bales and leaving the warehouse.

Fewal and Dhaget looked at their colonel as Alucius left the warehouse and remounted the chestnut.

"We're off to see his father, another trader called Halanat. I hope he's where he should be." Alucius eased his mount back up the avenue, then westward on the next street.

That street extended a good half vingt to the west before it ended, but even from several hundred yards away, Alucius could Talent-sense the purplish feel that seemed to envelop the two-story dwelling set slightly farther back from the street than the houses on either side. The ornamental shrubs that flanked the wide front porch seemed to droop lackadaisically, as if winter had been hard on them. The grass was sparse and dying, and not from winterkill.

With no hitching posts in front, Alucius dismounted and handed the chestnut's reins to Dhaget. "I shouldn't be all that long, but I'd guess this Halanat might have more to say than his son did."

The two lancers acknowledged the words with a nod.

Alucius took the two steps up to the covered porch,

glanced up at the ancient carved wagon plaque beside the door, then lifted the heavy brass knocker and let it fall. The *thud* echoed harshly in Alucius's ears. After several moments, a thin-faced and graying woman, without a dual lifethread but with a heavy purple aura, opened the door. She frowned quizzically.

"Alucius, madam. Halsant said that I could find Halanat here." He smiled as warmly as he could manage.

"He doesn't handle the factoring anymore. That's Halsant, and he's down on the river."

"I'm not here about trade," Alucius replied politely. "I've just talked to Halsant, and he suggested I needed to talk to his father . . ."

"If you must . . ." With a resigned sigh, she stepped back into the foyer and held the door, inclining her head toward the closed door to her right. "He's there. As always."

"Thank you." Alucius bowed his head briefly, then stepped to the door, behind which he could sense a well of purple. For just a moment, he paused before depressing the door lever and entering the room. He closed the door as he stepped inside.

Halanat sat behind a wide table desk, with stacks of parchment and paper set across the side facing Alucius. The herder saw not one image, but two. His eyes took in a round-faced trader with nondescript brown hair wearing a dark gray tunic trimmed in brilliant blue. His Talent-senses showed him another sight entirely—that of a man whose lifethread had been possessed by an ifrit. That lifethread was not the normal brown or tan or yellow, or even that of a herder—black or black shot with green, or even black shot with purple or pink, or the dual pink and black threads he had seen with the torques of the Matrial. Instead, there was the thinnest of brown threads, a lifethread of Corus. Entwined and twisted around that thin brown thread was a pulsing purpled rope of an ifrit lifethread, and that purpled ropelike thread dwindled southward into the distance, but not all that far, Alucius felt.

Although Alucius had suspected as much from what he

had sensed already, he still had to restrain his total shock at seeing the trader so possessed.

"You are bold, Colonel—or should I call you herder?"

"Titles don't matter. You should know why I'm here."

A momentary expression of puzzlement crossed Halanat's face. "I must say that I cannot imagine why—especially alone and without a company of loyal Northern Guards with you."

"There are several outside." Alucius nodded slowly. "Even more might have been more prudent after your last effort of some years ago." He had no proof that the trader had been involved in the attempted assassination effort with more than twenty bravos just after Alucius had been released from the Northern Guard some two years before, but it was worth suggesting.

"What effort?"

"The one that cost you more than two hundred golds," Alucius replied. "Or have you forgotten? Did all those golds mean so little?"

A cool smile crossed the trader's lips, but did not reach his eyes. "And you let it pass for so long before suddenly appearing to accuse me of whatever this might have been?"

"I'm not suggesting anything. You know what you did, and I'm saying it."

"You can say whatever you want," Halanat stated. "That doesn't mean it's true."

"It's true enough, and now there are wild pteridons roaming the steads. That is also your doing—or that of those working with you. As were the supplies you sent to the prophet, and the excessive number of golds you received in return."

"That is to be expected. Supplying a rebel can be dangerous . . . and costly. You expect a factor to risk that for normal rates? Surely, you are not that naive, Colonel."

"And the wild pteridons?"

"Times are changing." Halanat rose, still smiling coldly.

"Do you wish to leave? You might prevail here, but you cannot stand against what will be."

Alucius could feel the chill inside himself. How many more of the ifrits had invaded Corus? And how? "Seldom is anything inevitable."

"Ah . . . the arrogance of youth." Halanat continued to smile.

Why didn't the ifrit attack? Because he knew Alucius could win? Because he was waiting for assistance? What had Alucius done before? After the slightest of hesitations, he sent out a slim Talent-probe, the strongest he could muster.

In return, the Halanat-ifrit hurled a blast of purplish life-force at Alucius.

Alucius slipped the purple force aside, in a fashion similar to the way in which he might have handled a sabre slash.

The trader slammed back with another blast of intense purple Talent-force.

Again, Alucius slip-parried it. Then, recalling his training with the soarer, he concentrated on seeking the nodes beneath and within the ifrit lifethread, the thread that was linked to something to the south.

The trader threw up a purpled shield, blocking Alucius's probe, and reached for a drawer in the table desk.

Alucius formed a golden green wedge of life-Talent and let the force flare around him, then struck once more, aiming at the most prominent node linking the ifrit lifethread to the trader.

Halanat froze for a moment, perspiration bursting out all across his forehead in droplets that flew from his face in all directions.

Alucius slid his probe under the purple shield, twisting and unraveling the smaller lifethreads within the node. As he did, he could sense heat rising in and around him, and sweat popping out on his own forehead. His efforts felt like clumsy fumbling and as though time all around him had slowed to a crawl as his Talent-probe knifed into the node of the ifrit's lifethread.

Suddenly, the trader's ifrit thread vanished in a spray of tiny purple threads, and Halanat stood there, wavering on his feet, his eyes widening. His hand twitched, and he pulled a double-barreled pistol from the now-open drawer.

Unable to reach the trader in time, Alucius slashed a second Talent-probe at the trader's now-unprotected and remaining lifethread node, keeping his lance of golden green tight and focused. With a spray of brown and green, Talent-threads and Talent-shards vanished as they flared into the air.

The pistol clunked dully as it struck the rich Hyaltan carpet. After a moment, Halanat pitched forward and crumpled against the table desk. His lifeless body slid sideways and sprawled across the carpet, covering the pistol.

Alucius stood stock-still, breathing hard. He'd forgotten just how much effort Talent-battles took. He took several more deep breaths before slowly turning. He opened the door to the entry hall carefully, but the foyer was empty. Closing the study door behind him, he crossed the foyer and stepped out onto the porch, then made his way down the stone walk to where the lancers waited with the chestnut.

"Sir?"

"Dealing with factors can be . . . trying. Everything is in coins. He admitted that they supplied the prophet and was proud of it."

"Sir?"

"He said that profit was necessary for a trader. I had to tell him that he could no longer expect excessive profit from the Guard. There wasn't much more that I could say." Alucius wiped his still-sweating forehead, then took the reins from Dhaget and mounted. "He was rather agitated when I left. Most agitated." Alucius forced a crooked smile. "That was the least I could do under the circumstances."

He guided the chestnut back eastward on the long street, back toward Northern Guard headquarters. Much as he disliked the idea, he needed to find Tarolt before long, but he had no idea exactly where to begin.

He'd have to claim, if anyone accused him, that he and Halanat had argued, and that Halanat had pulled the pistol and gotten so agitated that his heart had just stopped. But, somehow, he doubted that anyone would say anything.

Alucius took another long breath and blotted his forehead once more. He'd hoped otherwise, but he had known that there was always the possibility that the ifrits would return. And it was clear that their return was linked to the prophet—and possibly to the Regent of the Matrial. He just didn't know how—or how many ifrits there were, or where.

118

Northeast of Iron Stem, Iron Valleys

Wearing her vest over a long-sleeved shirt, although with nightsilk undergarments, Wendra stood in the equipment room of the maintenance barn, careful not to inadvertently swing the carrypack that held Alendra into any of the heavy machinery. She lifted the handle of the antique crusher out of the housing, setting it and the attached iron piston carefully on the oak workbench that seemed equally ancient. Tilting the crusher's housing slowly, she poured out the fine granular powder that she had just ground. She measured out a half cup of the powdered crushed quartz and used a funnel to ease the powder into the bottle she had brought from the main house.

She'd have to go back to the kitchen and the cooler to add the goat's milk and heat the makeshift formula before she fed the orphaned nightlamb that was bleating mournfully in the crib pen beside the main barn. Even with the goats supplied by Kustyl, feeding and caring for the lamb had been hard, but none of them wanted to see the lamb die—early unseasonal birth or not—and especially not after losing four nightsheep over the fall and winter. That the lamb was the second that needed hand-raising in less than two seasons didn't help, either. After she fed the lamb, she needed to check the spindles in the processing tank to see if they were ready for spinning.

Something murmured outside the closed windows of the workroom. Wendra cocked her head and listened, wondering if Lucenda had come back for something. Royalt had taken the flock, after having let her take the nightsheep on the previous two days.

She smiled to herself. No one on the stead ever turned back for anything, especially Alucius, and she'd come to understand why after living with Lucenda and Royalt. She tilted her head. There was a greenish sense outside, almost like that of her husband, and the silence of a still day, which was welcome because the winter had been long and blustery and cold.

"Yes, it has been, little one," she murmured to Alendra, who was neither quite sleeping nor quite awake in the carrypack.

Wendra replaced the crusher handle and piston, then picked up the bottle and stepped out of the maintenance barn, carefully closing the door behind her. With everyone gone for the morning, she couldn't go around leaving doors open.

Out on the stoop of the stone building, she thought she heard a song without words, a haunting song that enfolded the stone building. It was definitely a song and not the wind. The melody was not quite recognizable.

The herder looked eastward, squinting from under the edge of the eaves into the early-morning light. Already, Royalt and the nightsheep flock were well out of sight, beyond the nearer ridges.

A glittering flash of golden green washed over her—

from her left. She turned, and her mouth opened as she beheld a soarer hovering at the end of the porch, closer than she ever had seen one. The green-tinted wings blurred the light, wings that appeared almost crystalline one moment and diaphanous the next. The soarer's face was that of a beautiful girl child with short golden and translucent hair. An expression that might have been a smile crossed the small mouth. The silver green eyes remained fixed on Wendra. The soarer wore no garments, but the golden mist that surrounded her feminine figure served just as well to conceal her shoulders and torso.

Only once had Wendra seen a soarer from closer than a vingt away, and this one was less than five yards from her. There was an enormous difference in seeing one from two thousand yards or even fifteen—and from five. So Wendra watched, listening, as the soarer hovered.

The soarer was beautiful, not as any woman might be, but of itself, and Wendra drank in that beauty, entranced.

For a long moment, she stood there.

Then, out of nowhere, a hand grasped her right shoulder, a hand that felt like warm stone, a hand that belonged to a squat figure less than two-thirds her size. The sander was tan, and its skin sparkled in places, as if diamonds or crystals shone through its rough skin. Like a person, it had two arms and two legs, hands and feet, a pair of eyes, and a mouth and nose. It wore no clothes. Sanders never did.

Wendra jerked her head around and tried to pull away from the sander. Although the top of its head came but to her shoulder, its hand held her arm so tightly that she could not break free. She lashed out with her knee, driving it into the creature's body. Her knee felt as if she had rammed it into a stone wall, and a wave of pain seared up through her thigh and down to her toes simultaneously.

As she tried to pull back from the sander, a second ironlike grip took her left shoulder. Another sander had appeared from nowhere, seemingly sliding out of the sandy soil and leaping onto the porch.

Trapped and held tight by the two sanders, Wendra glanced toward the soarer, who still hovered in at the end of the porch.

"What do you want?"

Neither the sanders nor the soarer answered.

"Why are you doing this?"

Again, none of the three replied.

"Why?" Wendra demanded. "Why me?" She gathered together her Talent-force and began to reach out for the life-node, as Alucius had taught her.

Do not . . . The soarer wrapped a greenish force around Wendra's probe. *We mean you no harm, but you must come.*

The two sanders said nothing, but then, Wendra had not expected that. Not even as they lifted her—each using but a single arm and hand—and carried her down the steps as if she were a lamb or a child. They walked northeast—toward the Plateau—and away from the southeast, where Royalt had ridden out a good glass earlier.

Wendra did not scream or yell. There was no one within vingts who could have heard her.

119

Slightly more than a glass after morning muster on Octdi, Alucius returned from the strong room, where he and Sanasus had counted out and checked the payroll. Normally, and once things were more settled, that would be handled almost entirely by Sanasus, but Alucius still felt that he needed a better understanding of some of the mechanics of how headquarters worked.

Not for the first time, he was beginning to see why Royalt had never even entertained the idea of making a career out of the militia—and probably would not have, even if he had not had the stead to return to. Everywhere Alucius looked, there were reports, and accounts, and he couldn't do much of anything himself—just order and advise and wait . . . and hope that things were done right.

With a deep breath, he picked up Sanasus's report on logistical needs for the next two seasons. He was not looking forward to reading it, but he needed to know, especially if he wanted to carry out his project of moving the Guard to Iron Stem.

A chill, bitingly cold, slashed across Alucius's wrist. He looked down, even as his Talent enfolded the black crystal of the wristguard. Although the wristguard remained chill, not quite unbearably so, he could sense that Wendra was healthy. But why the chill?

Had something happened to Alendra?

For a moment, he felt that he could not breathe, but he pushed that thought away. The chill had to be related to Wendra. He swallowed. It felt almost like the times when he had used the ifrits' Tables. But there weren't any Tables in the northlands. Were there?

He just looked at the wristguard. The chill continued. That it did told him that, whatever was happening, it wasn't a Table, because the Table transport was faster. But what could it be?

He just sat there behind the desk, looking at and sensing the crystal, but the chill continued.

After a time, he looked down at Sanasus's careful handwriting and the column of figures below. The letters danced before his eyes, and they made no sense whatsoever.

Finally, he stood up and walked to the window, looking out at the hazy sky.

Abruptly, as suddenly as it had come, the chill lifted from the wristguard, and the pulse from the crystal remained strong—and somehow warm. That was only slightly reassuring for the young colonel.

Alucius looked at the wristguard, but it offered no answers beyond indicating that Wendra was healthy. He did feel that, had anything happened to Alendra, there would have been some continuing sign of distress from Wendra.

Beyond that, he could only hope and trust that Wendra and Alendra were not in danger.

He couldn't just ride out—not when what he did with the Northern Guard might affect their future as well—and even if he did, it would be a long day and well into the night before he could reach the stead. And if Wendra had been transported by a Table . . . going home wouldn't help at all.

But the chill, and what it might have meant, nagged at him.

120

Dekhron, Iron Valleys

At the sound of the knocker on the door, the white-haired man in black left the study and walked across the foyer. He frowned as he looked through the side window and saw the figure standing outside in a heavy winter coat. After a moment, he opened the door and stepped back.

The younger man stepped inside the foyer, ushered in by a wintry blast of chill air, and Tarolt closed the door. He did not offer to escort the newcomer beyond the foyer. "Yes?"

"Tarolt . . . I know I should have come earlier. I felt I had to come," began Halsant, "but . . . I didn't find out until late last night. I was working late on the ledgers at the warehouse . . . and it was only when I came by the house and saw the lamp on. You know . . . Father got most angry if anyone entered his study, even with Mother."

"Halsant. What happened?"

"Father's dead. It must have happened after the colonel came."

"After the colonel came? Could you please tell me what

happened? In order, if you could manage that?" Tarolt's firm words verged on cold and cutting.

"Colonel Alucius came by yesterday morning. By the warehouse, I mean, and he was looking for Father. He said several people had suggested he talk to Father, but he didn't say who. I told him Father was at home. He thanked me, and he left." Halsant blotted his brow, sweating despite the chill from which he had emerged. "Mother said he— the colonel—came to the house. He didn't stay long. Mother heard a thump, but she didn't think much of it, because Father threw things sometimes. Especially when he was angry, and the colonel would make any trader angry these days. Anyway . . . Father hadn't left the study, and she was worried, but . . ."

"But what?"

"She wouldn't go in. So I did. He was dead. There wasn't a mark on him. I think . . . whatever the colonel said must have made him so angry that his heart stopped. You know what a terrible temper he sometimes had." Halsant blotted his face once more. "Anyway, I thought you should know, but it was well after dark last night. So I came first thing this morning."

Tarolt nodded slowly. "I appreciate your riding out here to tell me. It must be a terrible loss to you and to your mother."

"She doesn't know what to do."

"I'm certain you can take care of everything, and I will certainly offer any advice and support you need."

"Thank you."

Tarolt looked toward the door. "I wouldn't want to keep you from your family right now. They'll be needing you, and once you're more settled we can talk. We will talk."

A faintly dazed expression crossed Halsant's face at Tarolt's last words.

"You'll talk to me before you do anything with his study, of course."

"Of course."

"Now . . . you need to see to your family."

"I need to see to my family." Halsant nodded dazedly and turned.

Only after Tarolt had watched the young trader ride back eastward toward Dekhron did he return to the study.

"What was that all about?" asked the pale and stocky man in a maroon tunic.

"We had a visitor, Sensat. He had to tell me something. Most important." Tarolt glanced around the oak-paneled study, his eyes flicking across the hundreds of books shelved there before dropping back to the other. "Have you found anything else?"

"No. I doubted that there would be even before you purchased all those volumes from Borlan. I told you that. Those who wrote books wouldn't be the ones who knew where the scepters might be. Or even where the old maps would be."

"There must be a hint . . . somewhere . . . about the scepters."

"You said we did not need them. Rather firmly, I recall."

"That was not quite what I said, Sensat. I said we would not need them *if* the ancient ones and the herder colonel did not become involved. More precisely, we do not need them, but they could be dangerous in the hands of the herder."

Sensat's fine black eyebrows arched as he tilted his head and placed the volume bound in burgundy leather on the long table beside which he stood. "And they have suddenly become involved?"

"Halanat was killed earlier today. His son and widow say that he was visited by the colonel just before that."

"Murder's still a crime. That would solve dealing with the colonel."

"It would be hard to prove. Halanat's heart stopped. There wasn't a mark on him. He had a heart attack. They all think he was so upset by the colonel that it happened after the colonel left."

"It didn't, of course."

Tarolt snorted. "His lifethreads were severed, I'm sure.

That was what the colonel did to Enyll. Even for an Efran, that's hard to tell unless you're present. The traces are faint and vanish soon. No one here would be able to tell anything except that his heart stopped. It did, of course, but not in that order."

"You don't think it was an ancient one?"

"No. It had to be the colonel. I would have felt it, even from here, if there had been a lifeforce drain, at least from them. So it was just a severing."

"What do you plan? Are you going to see Trezun and use the Table?"

"I think I'll wait until the colonel comes to see me. He will, sooner or later, and it is always better to deal with Talent from a position of strength."

"What if he does not come to you, the way he did to Halanat?"

"Then one way or another, we'll ride to Salaan and entice him into following. He might anyway."

"You want him to know that there is a Table in Salaan? He has no reason to suspect that, and you want to let him discover that?"

"We cannot assume that he is that ignorant. Not now," Tarolt pointed out. "He destroyed one Table. Besides, he will sense a Table there, and that will be a great temptation."

"He destroyed the Table in Tempre."

"That was an ancient Table, one weakened by age and misuse. We would have had to replace it shortly, in any case. Waleryn and you are supposed to be working on that, are you not?"

"Waleryn should be in Norda, but he has not finished rebuilding the Table there. You had said he was to work on the Table in Tempre after Norda."

"You *hope* Waleryn is in Norda?"

"There is no way to tell, Tarolt. You know that."

Tarolt offered a cold smile.

Sensat frowned. "Do you think it is wise to let the colonel near a Table? That could be risky."

"Only to him. Besides, where could he go? To Prosp? Or

to one of the inactive Tables? Translating there could kill him. In any event, one fully translated Efran should be more than enough, even to deal with an ancient one. I would rather deal with him here, but if he does not come close here, we will not take chances. We will deal with him from even greater strength in Salaan." Tarolt glanced toward the door to the study.

"While we wait, might I continue perusing these?" Sensat gestured toward the burgundy volumes on the table.

After a moment, Tarolt laughed. "You will have plenty of time. The colonel has begun to learn patience, though it will avail him little."

121

The Hidden City, Corus

Wendra woke. She was lying on a bed wide enough for two, in a cramped fashion, looking up at a ceiling of amberlike stone. She scrambled upright, looking for Alendra. The carrypack on her chest was empty. She bolted for the doorway, but the silver door lever was unmoving, as solid as if it had been carved from amberstone in one piece with the door itself.

She turned, forcing herself to take in the room around her. The walls were of the same polished amber as the ceiling. The room's single window showed the cloudless silver green sky of Corus. For a moment, she looked dully at the window. Then she realized that she had never seen glass so clear, and that it was set not in wood, but in a shimmering silvery metal that could not have been silver.

Wendra hurried to the window. She pressed the flat bracket to one side and slid the window open. A blast of winter-cold air whipped around her, and as quickly as she had opened the window, she closed it. So cold was that air that even her nightsilk undergarments, her winter shirt, and vest were insufficient to offer much protection against that rush of frigid air.

Standing at the closed window, she looked out. Immediately, she could see that she was in a tower. Below were other buildings that extended a good vingt from the tower. The buildings ended at a circular wall, and both wall and buildings were of the same amber stone. Beyond the wall was white sand that shimmered and glittered in the afternoon sun. Even farther to the west was a rampart of dark rock, along the top of which ran green-tinted crystal oblongs.

Wendra turned from the window, looking back into the room, wedge-shaped and far narrower at the end with the door. She walked to the door, golden wood without windows or peepholes, and a single lever handle of the same metal as the window casements.

Extending her Talent to the door, she tried to move the door lever, but it did not budge. Was there a lock somewhere? Alucius had mentioned something.

She could sense a greenish radiance behind her and looked toward the window. When she looked back, the soarer had appeared within a yard of her. The soarer's shape was shrouded by the golden-tinged green mist that acted as a garment, but her form was feminine. Her brilliant green eyes were clear, and deep . . . and very old, so old that Wendra took an involuntary step backward—until Wendra saw that in the soarer's arms rested a smiling Alendra. From the lifethread, Wendra could tell that her daughter was healthy and happy, but she rushed forward and swept Alendra into her arms.

"Why am I here? Why?" Wendra's words echoed through the tower room. "Why did you take my daughter?"

The hidden city. It is not for you. Not once you are prepared to do what must be done. We only took your daughter because she awoke before you, and we did not wish her to be distressed. Although the soarer did not speak her words aloud, they were as clear as if she had.

"But why?"

Because it is necessary.

"Necessary?"

We will teach you all that we taught your mate, while he searches for you.

"Why did you take me?"

You are the key to whether your people survive, and we would have you survive, if only for our own foolish pride. Dry humor colored the words. *Pride is what little remains to us.*

"Me? How can I be key? Alucius has the great Talent. Not me."

You have the same potential as does he. The ifrits must be stopped. They should not be allowed to destroy world after world. Your mate will do only what he must. He would not have acted in time, had we not taken you.

"That is evil . . ." Wendra protested.

Well that may be, but it is an evil less ill than watching our—and your—world be bled to death.

"What if he doesn't find me?"

He will not find you.

The certainty in the soarer's words chilled Wendra.

You must learn greater use of your Talent. We will try to teach you. If you learn, you may rejoin him in his efforts against the ifrits.

"How do you know he will fight them?"

He has no choice.

"What if I cannot learn what you want?"

Then, in time, you also will perish, for the ifrits will seek you out and use your body and expunge your mind. In greater time, all that you know and love will also perish.

Wendra was silent, trying to assimilate what the soarer had said. If she did not learn, she and all she loved would be lost?

Now . . . you will learn more about the threads of life,

*and how they may be mended—and unraveled . . . and how
you may do so more quickly . . .*

Wendra swallowed. But she listened, and she held Alendra tightly.

122

Alucius had heard nothing about Halanat
on Septi, nor during the day on Octdi. Nor had the feeling
from the wristguard changed. He tried not to pace too
much in his small study, but he couldn't help but worry
about Wendra—and about Tarolt, the shadowy trader that
everyone followed but was never seen. Alucius had to believe that Tarolt was another ifrit, but he was hesitant to
confront another trader immediately. He had the feeling
that the meeting would be just like the one with Halanat—
and that only one person would leave. Having two traders
drop dead after meeting with him within days wasn't
something he wanted to deal with, and the alternative was
worse. At the same time, he worried about what might happen if he didn't do something fairly soon. He didn't want
to deal with an attack by the Regent and whatever Tarolt
might be planning at the same time.

He struggled through more inventories and planning,
and reports, all the while trying to reach some decision on
how to deal with Tarolt. Finally, late on Octdi, Alucius
looked into Feran's study for the third time in less than a
glass, but this time Feran had returned.

"Yes?" asked the older officer. "Did you need something? I was out going over some things with Faisyn, and
the schedule for replacements from Sudon."

"How about some supper at the Red Ram? I'll pay."

"That's a hard offer to refuse," Feran replied with a grin,
"even for a newly affluent majer." He set aside the dispatch

he had been reading and stood. "That can wait. It's basically a report from Soulend saying how cold it's been and how nothing has happened since harvest."

"What does Sordet want?"

"Replacement lancers for those whose terms are up, and some assurance for two squad leaders that they can actually get stipended."

"The Lord-Protector pays the stipends these days, but Frynkel's been delaying them by a season. He hasn't said whether that applies here. I don't like doing that . . ."

"But you're thinking about it?" asked Feran.

"I worry that we don't have enough experienced squad leaders and that the ones we promoted to captain need all the experienced squad leaders they can keep for at least a month."

"So that just before the Matrites attack, we get rid of the stipended ones?" Feran's voice was dry.

"You're right. Do you think we ought to promote early, and overlap?"

"That might not be a bad idea." Feran reached for his riding jacket. "You'd better get your jacket. It's as cold as Soulend outside."

"Winter's supposed to be ending."

"Tell the wind out there that."

Alucius reclaimed his own riding jacket, and the two walked out of the headquarters building, across the courtyard, and through the narrow archway in the south wall, turning west toward the tavern.

Despite the signboard with the ram upon it, more a nightsheep painted in red than a town sheep, most of the Guard officers called the old redstone building on the corner after the proprietress—Elyset's.

The graying Elyset was the one to meet Alucius and Feran. Her eyes sparkled, and she looked at the insignia of both collars. Then she smiled. "You two have come up in the world—especially you, Colonel. The last time you were here . . . was it majer?"

"It was." Alucius couldn't help grinning. "The last time I

was here, you told me about the chicken, but I'd been hoping for quail."

Elyset laughed, but the sound died away quickly. "I didn't remember last time, but you were the one who stopped the barbarians in Deforya and got decorated by the Lord-Protector. Right?"

"Unfortunately. Then, after a couple of years, he ordered me south, then back here."

"Good thing. Guard hasn't done so well since then."

"That's what I heard." Alucius paused, then added, "Might just be me, but I missed Colonel Clyon."

Elyset snorted. "So did the few old-time officers left. Got word that they're happy to see you."

"So far."

The proprietress turned to Feran. "You should have come here more often. Gheravia was asking about you."

"Now that I'm a majer, you mean?" parried Feran.

"She liked you when you were a captain, Majer."

Feran shook his head, as if to deny it.

"She did, but . . . I'd better get you two settled." Elyset turned and escorted them to a corner table, one adjoining the hearth, in which several large logs were burning on a deep bed of red and white coals. "Good table here for a chill evening."

Alucius settled himself into one of the four armless wooden chairs, the one of the two that afforded a view of the front entrance. Feran settled into the other one.

"Don't have quail today, but the noodles and fowl are good. Cutlets are tough. Wouldn't even have 'em to serve, except some of the senior rankers, they won't eat anything else."

"Habits." Alucius laughed.

Elyset bent down, leaning toward Alucius, and lowered her voice. "Tarolt and Halanat been talking about you, I think . . . herder majer and then colonel . . . Don't know why . . . thought you ought to know."

"Thank you. Can you tell me what Tarolt looks like?" Alucius kept his voice low.

"White-haired, sturdy, eyes sort of purple, white skin—got little hands and a mean smile. Always wears black. Built a new place out on the point. Only house there, now that Hanal's place burned down. Didn't tell you that." Elyset shrugged and straightened.

"Appreciate the tip about the cutlets," Alucius said loudly, winking and managing to slip a silver from his wallet and into Elyset's hand.

"You don't like something, and you don't come back. We always need people to come back." She grinned. "Even if it takes some herders years and becoming a colonel."

"But they remember," he returned.

"That's what we hope. Grenna will be along in a few moments."

Despite the banter that had surrounded Elyset's warning, the whole exchange left a cold feeling in Alucius's guts, especially since the proprietress had no sense of purpleness. He glanced around the Ram, but only two other tables were taken, one by a grizzled crafter with a woman clearly not his wife, and the other by two bravos in brown.

"What did she say?" asked Feran.

"Told me that Tarolt and Halanat had been talking about me."

"Speaking of Halanat . . . Sanasus said he died yesterday. Found him dead last night. Didn't you go see him yesterday morning?"

"I did. He was the trader, or his wagons were, who was supplying the prophet. They had the same silver-wheel sign. I found that out. We exchanged a few words, and then I left. I don't think he was very happy with me." Again, everything Alucius said was true, but not the whole truth.

"Must not have been. Word is that he got so angry his heart stopped."

"It couldn't have happened to anyone who deserved it more," Alucius said dryly. "Not that it will stop his son from doing the same sort of trading if he gets the chance. I also think Tarolt's tied up in it all, but there's no real proof there. I'll have to look into that before long."

"Like everything else?"

"What'll you have?" asked Grenna as she stopped at the table. Despite her obvious physical charms, the server was a woman barely out of girlhood.

"What do you have?"

"Drinks are same as always—wine, ale, lager. Today, the stew is boar, better 'n usual. Vedra chicken with the thick noodles. Lamb cutlets . . . and lymbyl."

Alucius could do without the lymbyl. "The ale . . . and . . . ah . . . fowl and noodles."

"Make that two," added Feran. "Ale also."

"Be three coppers for the chicken, and one for the ale."

Alucius showed a silver, leaving it on the table.

"Be back with the ale, sirs." With a nod, Grenna moved away from the window table.

The day had been long, and Alucius was tired. The chill with the wristguard bothered him, especially because he didn't know what it meant or what had happened. The silence surrounding Halanat's death wasn't all that good, either, he thought. And spring was coming, with all the possible problems with a Matrite attack. He looked down at the surface of the table.

"Rather deep in thought, aren't you?" suggested Feran.

"I've been thinking—about a lot of things." Alucius paused. "What do you think about moving the Guard headquarters to Iron Stem?"

"You want it closer to home?" Feran grinned.

"That makes it harder to do, in a way. It's more because of the way things have changed. We really don't have to worry about the Vedra as a boundary, but it takes a day longer to get dispatches from the west here, and more than a day longer to send supplies west."

"And you wouldn't have to worry so much about the factors and their plots."

"I won't be colonel forever," Alucius said. "It would make things easier for whoever follows me."

"You thinking about riding off?"

"No." Alucius shook his head. "I'm just trying to get things to work better."

"Your ales, sirs."

Alucius looked up. He'd hadn't noticed Grenna's return—and that wasn't good. "Thank you." He offered the silver.

"I'll take them when I bring the chicken."

Alucius took a swallow of the ale. He hadn't realized how thirsty he'd been until he was looking at a half-empty mug.

"Little thirsty there," said Feran.

Alucius looked at Feran's equally depleted mug.

Both men laughed.

Alucius saw Grenna approaching and watched as she set a crockery platter with a full half chicken and a pile of noodles smothered in a cream sauce before him, then before Feran, along with a basket holding two small loaves of still-warm bread.

"Be four coppers each, sirs."

Alucius tendered a silver and a smile. "Thank you—and two more ales."

She handed back two coppers. Alucius left them on the table.

From the first bite, he liked the chicken. He almost could put aside his concerns about the ifrits and how to deal with Tarolt. His worries about Wendra were something else, and he could only hold to the fact that his herder's wristguard had shown no sign of injury to her. But he still worried.

Two more mugs of ale arrived before he'd even gotten a third of the way through the chicken. Alucius sent Grenna off with five coppers.

"Being colonel, it's not like what you thought, is it?"

"I think I knew, but *being* colonel is harder than just knowing."

"True of everything," Feran mumbled. "Don't get shot at as much here."

"Maybe you don't."

"You're the kind that gets shot at everywhere," Feran pointed out.

In time, Alucius and Feran finished their meal and their ale.

As he rose from the table in the tavern that was becoming more crowded with faces he didn't recognize, Alucius glanced out through the narrow window onto the darkening and chill street outside the Red Ram. He left another copper on the table, then began to walk toward the doorway, followed by Feran.

Alucius nodded and moved aside as two well-garbed men he did not recognize stepped inside the tavern.

Elyset appeared from the other side of the foyer and smiled at Alucius. "Have a good evening, Colonel." She offered a broader smile to Feran. "Majer."

"Thank you, Elyset." Both officers inclined their heads.

As Alucius stepped outside he could hear part of the exchange.

"Colonel . . . didn't expect to see him here . . . just him and the majer . . ."

". . . say he's brave . . ."

"There's brave, and there's foolish . . ."

The words didn't exactly help his feelings or his mood as he began to walk back to his too-empty quarters and a night when he would sleep restlessly at best, worried about all too many matters, and especially about Wendra.

123

Novdi, as an end day, was a half day at headquarters, but Alucius was still in his study in early afternoon. Earlier, he'd inspected Fifth Company, the barracks, the armory, then spent some time with Feran discussing the possibilities for changing the basing positions of

Northern Guard companies, especially those around Harmony and those that might be able to provide reinforcements, if necessary.

He kept checking the wristguard. From what he could tell, Wendra was fine, but the uncertainty nagged at him.

At Dhaget's knock on the doorframe to his study, where he had left the door open, Alucius stiffened.

"There's a young fellow here to see you, sir. Says his name's Korcler."

Alucius could feel a chill run through him, down to his bones. "Have him come right in." He stood.

The brown-haired youth, a young man almost old enough for conscription, hurried into the study and began to speak even before he lurched to a stop on the other side of the desk. "I said I'd come, Alucius. I've been riding since well before dawn. Brought two mounts. Your grandsire insisted. That's because . . ."

"What happened to Wendra? You wouldn't be here otherwise, would you?"

"No, sir. No one knows, sir. She's just gone. Royalt and Grandpa Kustyl . . . they've been searching everywhere. They said you'd know if she was all right."

"She's alive and healthy, but something happened yesterday morning," Alucius said. "Before midmorning. No one knows where she is?"

"No, sir. Your grandsire, he took the flock yesterday," Korcler said. "Wendra'd been out the two days before. Said she didn't see anything, not even a sandwolf. Your ma, she came to town. When she got back in the afternoon, Wendra was gone. So was little Alendra. No mounts missing. No tracks. Only thing they found was a bottle, filled with ground quartz, for that lamb born in midwinter. It was lying on the porch of the equipment building. No goat's milk with it, just the quartz." Korcler stopped, catching his breath. "Your grandsire said no one else had been there. Leastwise, there were no signs. Her herding jacket was still in the house. She . . . she just . . . vanished."

Alucius stepped forward and put a hand on Korcler's

shoulder. "Thank you. I'd worried. I didn't know. I appreciate the long ride, and your coming to tell me." He didn't know what else to say. Wendra gone? Vanished? Without a trace? But how? The questions swirled through his scattered thoughts.

"I didn't want to be the one, but . . . there wasn't anyone else." Korcler looked up at Alucius, then fumbled inside his jacket, coming up with a folded paper. "Your grandsire wanted you to have this."

Alucius took the paper. For a moment, he looked at it blankly, before he finally unfolded it, and began to read.

Alucius—
By now, Korcler has told you of Wendra's disappearance. I wanted you to know that it is most unlikely that she was kidnapped or taken by riders. There are no hoofprints in either the snow or the dirt, or even the dust on the porch where she vanished—just some smudges. There are no signs of boots, and nothing is missing. I cannot tell you where to seek her, or how, save that it appears most unlikely that she remains nearby, and likely that Talent will be required.

Nor do I know if you dare to leave your duties, or if doing so will prove useful. I do fear that all is connected, but I could not say why.

All our hopes and thoughts are with you, and with her and Alendra.

The signature was that of Royalt.
Alucius lowered the message.
"What did he say?" asked Korcler.
"What you told me," replied Alucius, his voice heavy. "More or less."
"What are you going to do?"
"What I have to," Alucius said. "We'll get you settled in

my quarters, and you can ride back in the morning, once your mounts are rested."

"You're not going to tell me?"

"No. How could I? I'm not even sure." Alucius turned and took his heavy winter riding jacket, the one doubly re-inforced with nightsilk, off the peg on the wall and pulled it on. "We'll get your mounts into the stable, and ready mine. You can rest in the guest chamber."

"I can go with you."

"No. Not this time. Your horses are tired, and it wouldn't be a good idea. Not at all."

"You won't tell me."

Alucius shook his head and motioned for Korcler to leave the study. "Go on out. I'm right behind you."

In the main area, he looked at Dhaget. "I'll be leaving for my quarters, Dhaget, after we get young Korcler's mounts stabled for the night. He's my wife's brother, and he'll be spending the night in the quarters before he leaves in the morning. You can go now."

"You're sure, sir?"

"You spend more than enough time looking out for me." Alucius forced a laugh. "Go."

He and Korcler led the two mounts to the officers' end of the stable and stalled them side by side. After that, Alucius took Korcler up to the quarters, where he sat the young man at the table in the kitchen with bread and cheese and some slices of ham shoulder.

Alucius went to his chamber and changed into his riding uniform, with the new nightsilk undergarments and the new vest under his tunic, and the heavy winter riding jacket. He also took out both rifles and his ammunition belt.

"You won't let me go?" Korcler stood in the doorway.

"No. It might not be dangerous, but it could be. You're not trained for this."

Korcler looked down.

"I should be back later, I'd guess around sunset, but it might be longer. Just rest until I get back. If . . . if anything happens, and I don't get back, you're to ride back to Iron

Stem tomorrow. No matter what. Do you understand?" Alucius projected total command. "Don't talk to anyone about this except Majer Feran and my grandsire. No one except those two."

Korcler backed away a step. "Yes, sir. I will, sir."

"Good. Now go back to eating. You haven't had enough."

While Korcler finished eating, Alucius wrote a brief note to Feran, saying that he was going to investigate something he had heard about Tarolt and hoped he would not be that long. On his way back to the stable, he left it on Feran's desk.

Then he made his way to the stable, where he saddled the chestnut. In less than a quarter glass he was riding out the gates.

"You're going out alone, sir?" asked the sentry, a lancer from Fifth Company whose name and face he couldn't put together.

"Just for the afternoon."

"Yes, sir."

As he turned westward, Alucius considered whether he should have left a note for Royalt with Korcler. He decided that his decision not to was the right one. If . . . if Tarolt was an ifrit, there was little Royalt could or should do. If not, Alucius should be back before long.

He wasn't certain, but he couldn't afford to wait to be certain. He worried that he'd already delayed too long. The more he'd thought, the more he felt that the ifrits had to have something to do with both the problems with the prophet and the Matrites and the torques—and with Wendra's disappearance. The most disturbing thought was that somehow he had created the problem. The morning after he'd killed Halanat, Wendra had vanished. That coincidence seemed unlikely. Far too unlikely, and that meant he had to act quickly, especially since he hadn't, but then, he reminded himself, he hadn't known that Wendra had vanished. He'd fretted that something had been wrong, but hadn't even guessed that.

From Elyset's directions, he could doubtless find Tarolt's place—but then what could he do? He wasn't certain, but the puzzlement that Halanat had expressed was a good indication that the ifrit-possessed trader had been surprised at Alucius's appearance. That, in turn, suggested that he had not known about Wendra's disappearance—or had not connected it to Alucius. But Halanat had clearly recognized Alucius. Then again, Alucius had no idea whether Tarolt was also ifrit-possessed, although it seemed likely, but from what Alucius had gathered, Tarolt was the real power behind the traders, and he might well not have told anyone if he had acted against Wendra, nor talked about anything else he might have done.

There were so many unanswered questions. What if more than the one ifrit had been behind the attempted assassination after Alucius had first left the Northern Guard? What if Tarolt had also been involved? But what if he hadn't? Then who else could have been, and how could Alucius discover who the others were? What if they were not responsible for Wendra's disappearance?

He shook his head. There had to be a link . . . somewhere . . . somehow.

Perhaps he could learn more by following Tarolt, at least for a time, or by spying on his actions or his household.

He continued to ride westward. After a quarter vingt or so, he turned the chestnut left onto another street, continuing southward. He rode less than half a vingt, past a mixture of older dwellings and shops, until the street ended at the river road.

He followed it westward, along the southern edge of the low bluffs overlooking the River Vedra, and before long, on his right, the houses gave way to cots, and then the cots vanished. Beyond were overgrazed and snow-dotted meadows with sparse and scattered trees, lands that sloped downhill in rolling rills to the north. To his left were the rugged and rocky slopes that dropped to the river.

Almost a vingt ahead he could see the point of land that Elyset had mentioned—a triangular bluff that jutted southward into the path of the river, so that the river curved around it before once more returning to its westward course. The road did not follow the edge of the bluff as before, but cut directly across the flat. A second road, more like a lane, veered to the left and toward the single walled dwelling set just north of the apex of the point. From the rear of the dwelling, Tarolt must have had a marvelous view of the river, which lay a good fifty yards below, and of the lower hills on the far side of the Vedra. Another half vingt beyond the walled complex were the blackened remains of another large dwelling.

As Alucius rode closer to the point, he glanced around, searching for some position from where he could observe the bluff and the single dwelling, one where he could rest the chestnut and from which neither he nor his mount could be seen. More than a hundred yards ahead, Alucius could discern a line of scrub bushes and several low, winter-bare trees, possibly lining the sides of a wash or dry streambed. While it was farther from Tarolt's than he would have preferred, there did not look to be anything closer that offered any cover.

The vegetation that rose out of the scattered snow and winter-browned grass did indeed mark a dry streambed nearly ten yards wide in spots and three to four in depth. Unfortunately, Alucius had to follow it almost fifty yards north of where it ran under a narrow timber bridge to find enough cover for both him and the chestnut. After tethering his mount to a thick root in a flatter section of the wash, Alucius took a swallow from a water bottle—one of a pair—before slipping one of the heavy rifles from its saddle holder and easing his way back southward along the wash. He found a spot some twenty yards north of the main road, where he could peer through the sparse branches of a scrub oak and see both the road and Tarolt's dwelling.

As he studied the dwelling, the portion of it he could see above the stone wall, Alucius could sense a haziness to the air, a purplish fog unseen to the eye but all too clear to his Talent-senses. The intensity of the purpleness suggested to him that either Tarolt was ifrit-possessed or that there were others in the dwelling who were.

After perhaps a quarter glass he shifted his weight, wondering if his vigil would prove fruitless. How long should he wait? Finally, he decided that, if no one left the dwelling, once darkness fell, he would move closer to see what else he might be able to discover.

Just as he reaffirmed that decision mentally, he saw the gate in the wall surrounding the dwelling open. Four men rode out, and a pair of guards on foot closed the gates behind them.

Alucius waited as the four riders came northeast along the lane, and then turned eastward on the river road back toward Dekhron. As they neared the bridge over the small wash, through the branches of the scrub oak, Alucius could see that only one wore black and was white-haired—presumably Tarolt, although the black was that of a heavy coat.

Even from close to thirty yards away, at a single Talent-glance, Alucius could see that Tarolt was not a man possessed by an ifrit. He *was* an ifrit. He did not have two lifethreads, with the purpled one dominating one anchored in Corus. Tarolt's single lifethread was an ugly dark purple, stretching somewhere to the southeast. Did it run to a Table?

With Alucius's concentration on Tarolt, it was a moment before he realized something else. Not only was Tarolt an ifrit, but so was the dark-haired man in a maroon riding jacket who rode beside him. Like Tarolt, he had a single purple lifethread running to the southeast.

Alucius's fingers tightened around the rifle, but he did not lift it, much as he was tempted. He needed to find Wendra far more than he needed to kill ifrits. And that was assuming that he could kill them.

Once the four were well past him, Alucius eased his way back up the wash to where he had left the chestnut. He waited a time longer before he mounted and set out to follow the riders. He doubted he would have too much trouble, not when his Talent could pick up the purpleness from over a vingt away.

The men whom Alucius followed remained on the river road all the way into Dekhron. As they entered the outskirts of the trading town, Alucius eased the chestnut closer, although he fretted that the four might realize that someone was following them. Tarolt and his party stayed on the river road, riding past the warehouses and wharves on the river, not turning until they reached the causeway that crossed the Vedra and led into Salaan.

Once across the ancient eternastone bridge, the four continued past the lane just on the south side of the bridge, the lane that led to the Southern Guard fort.

When Alucius passed the lane, a good half vingt behind Tarolt, he looked to his left at the dilapidated and abandoned fort. As he continued through Salaan, he glanced at the narrow-windowed houses. It seemed to him that every time he passed through, they looked even poorer than the time before, and certainly more run-down than the first time he had been there more than two years earlier, on his way home from Tempre and his previous encounter with the ifrit-possessed Recorder of Deeds.

Slightly farther southward, Tarolt turned west on a road almost as wide as the eternastone highway but constructed of winter-hardened clay that led, as Alucius recalled, to the bluff on the south side of the river that held the few traders' dwellings in Salaan.

After more than a vingt, the riders turned left, down a lane that split a stand of apricot trees, toward a low ridge south of the sprawling orchard. Alucius hung back even farther before following.

When he finally reached the southernmost part of the orchard, he reined up the chestnut beside one of the last apricot trees and looked ahead. Less than a hundred yards away, at the end of the lane, he could make out a squat stone building set on the lowest point of the saddle between two modest ridges. Snow had drifted against the north side of the building in places, and the limestone blocks took on a greater purplish hue with each moment that Alucius studied them. To the northwest were a stable and an outbuilding, both of timber and plank.

As he watched, with eyes and Talent, another figure stepped from the stone building to greet the four riders. Tarolt made an abrupt gesture, and the group split, the two ifrits and the one who had greeted them going into the squat building, the guards waiting with the mounts. Alucius could sense that at least two of the lifethreads were anchored within the structure. That meant that the building most certainly held a Table. But the structure was relatively new. Were the ifrits constructing more Tables? Was there one in the north through which Wendra had been taken or captured?

Since he had no answers, Alucius continued to watch.

A single stable boy or ostler appeared, and the guards followed him with all the mounts, taking them into the long, shedlike stable. After a time, the three left the stable and entered the other outbuilding. Before long, the dusty open space before the stone building looked deserted, with neither grooms nor guards.

Alucius shifted his weight in the saddle. There were at least five men there, and at least two were ifrits—and the ifrits were in a building that most likely housed a new Table.

Now . . . what was he going to do?

124

Salaan, Lanachrona

The three figures sat around a circular table in the anteroom off the Table chamber. Despite the chill radiating from the north-facing walls, the penetrating heat from the stove set against the outside wall made the room more than pleasantly warm. A decanter of wine on a silver tray was equidistant from the crystal goblets set before Tarolt and the Recorder, and a tray of cheeses and fruit rested in the precise center of the table. Sensat sat beside Tarolt, also with a goblet before him.

"The herder-colonel is somewhere nearby. I can sense him," Tarolt said mildly, pausing to take another small swallow of the red wine. "He was watching the house on the point, and then he followed us."

"You let him?" asked Sensat. "He could have shot at us. He could have injured someone, or killed one of the guards."

"Let him? I tried to project enough vulnerability that he would follow us. Besides, had he decided to attack, he would have waited until nightfall and slipped into the compound. He wanted to know where we were going. And why, I would judge. Curiosity is a fatal flaw with most Talent-steers."

"He may be more than that," suggested the Recorder.

"That is hardly likely, my dear Trezun," replied Tarolt.

"Are you sure it is the colonel? Could it not be an ancient one? Their threads are also green." The Recorder set his goblet on the polished wood.

"The ancient ones seldom come this far south. But . . . does it matter? We must deal with both, and we have the means to do so . . . now."

Both Sensat and Tarolt smiled; the Recorder did not.

"Have you determined whether any of the inactive Tables can be reactivated?" asked Tarolt several moments later.

"The one in Blackstear is in perfect condition. It will take but one translation from here or another Table."

"That one has little use except to strengthen the node grid. What else?" inquired Tarolt.

"The Table in Soupat will require someone to travel there physically, but its repair will be relatively quick."

"Could we not try a translation to it?" asked Sensat.

Trezun shrugged. "We could, but that is risky to whoever is being translated. Would you like to try a translation there?"

"Ah . . . we could arrange for a trading trip there," mused Sensat. "Sometime."

"I hesitate to send an Efran when we're still so hard-pressed." Trezun frowned, his fingers stroking the crystal stem of the goblet before him. "Especially with Waleryn being alone in Norda without a fully working Table."

"I thought he had the Table in Norda working," Tarolt said.

"He can communicate, but not translate," Trezun explained. "The cold affected some of the crystals. It will be a few more days, he says."

"You see?" asked Tarolt. "He is working with all the resources of Lustrea behind him, and it may be almost a year to reactivate one Table and reconstruct another. That is why I asked about the inactive Tables. How else can we build a fully functioning node grid quickly? Even if it takes half a season, that will be far less time than building a Table from nothing at another nodal matrix. And that does not count travel time." Tarolt glanced toward the window on the north side of the room.

"But the Soupat Table, like the one in Blackstear, is useful only in supporting the strength of the entire grid," observed Trezun.

"We will need all the strength that we can build," replied Tarolt. "Remember . . . there are twenty-three thousand Efrans who expect to make the long translation . . ."

"The population here is not large enough to support that many," murmured Sensat. "Not without tapping the world itself."

"The fieldmasters know already that the support limit is between five and seven thousand," replied Tarolt. "So you can count yourself lucky that you are already here."

Trezun nodded politely. "Whatever the number, we will be ready."

"Why is it that those Tables that are the easiest to reestablish are the most remote?" Sensat snorted, going on before the other two could reply, "I know. That is precisely why. They are so remote that no one suspected they were there, or that they retained power."

"Exactly," agreed Trezun with a laugh.

"Now that the Table in Prosp is operating, if Waleryn can reconstruct a Table in Norda, and we can send some-one to repower the one in Soupat, we could rebuild the Table in Dereka, could we not?" Sensat looked to Trezun. "The location still retains enough energy and identifica-tion to be a portal, even if it is not so powerful as the one at Hieron."

"The portal in Hieron is an anomaly. Only a fully trans-lated Efran can use it, as you know, and most infrequently. We cannot spend the effort and energy on portals, not when we need Tables."

"We need to make deliberate haste, then," added Sensat.

"Deliberate haste? That has been the watchword for years."

"We have less time than we thought," Tarolt replied. "Fieldmaster Lasylt has calculated that the translation tubes will endure no more than another five years at most. That is when the nebular field webs will reach the under-space clear-lines linking Efra to Acorus."

"Another curse upon the ancient ones," muttered Trezun.

"We were fortunate that they were not stronger," Tarolt said. "At least their barriers have been weakened enough that we can resume our work. Would that our brethren on Efra truly understood the urgency."

"They fear leaving the warmth and comfort of Efra, and they do not wish to be the ones to deal with the cold and the crudeness of Acorus," Trezun observed.

"Let someone else make the sacrifices," Tarolt snorted. "That's how they feel. We have, and we will reap the bene-fits."

"What about the tubes to Ejernyt?" asked Sensat.

"Twenty years at best," interjected Trezun. "Ejernyt will not be ready for colonization for at least a hundred years, but we can continue that effort from here on Acorus."

"That means finding and removing the ancient ones," Sensat said.

"And their tools—like the colonel outside," suggested Tarolt, smiling coolly.

"What do you suggest?" inquired Trezun.

"He has a curiosity about Tables. We should let him see a fully functioning one—one with a single translation tube directed to Soupat." The white-haired ifrit trader laughed. "That will solve two problems."

The other two nodded. After a moment, a crooked smile crossed the lips of the Recorder.

125

Alucius had tied the chestnut to one of the trees farther back in the apricot orchard, taken his topmost rifle, and eased forward from tree to tree until he stood just behind one of the trees closest to the stone building and the surrounding outbuildings. While he studied the stone building for close to half a glass, he saw no one outside, and it did not appear that anyone would be leaving.

He didn't like the idea of approaching the Table building, not with the ifrits within, but perhaps he could learn something from the outbuildings and even overhear what the guards and the ostler might be saying. He could wait forever, but if there were ifrits holding Wendra, he dared not wait long. They might try to possess her the way they had Halanat and the Recorder of Deeds in Tempre. He'd tried not to think about that, but he couldn't avoid it, not after what he had seen in the last few glasses.

He waited a bit longer, then slipped westward from tree to tree, careful not to step in the patches of snow, until he was directly opposite the stable. From where he now stood, even the apricot tree behind which he had placed himself could not be seen from the stone building, shielded as it was by the stable and another outbuilding.

He took a deep breath, then concentrated, pressing the darkness of lifeforce into the five cartridges in the magazine of the rifle. He did not try that with the fifteen cartridges in the leather loops of his heavy belt. With his sabre at his side and the heavy rifle in his hand, he hurried across the winter-flattened brown grasses of the meadow toward the stable. The back of the stable had no windows—just a blank timber wall that had been painted within the last year. So long as no one left any of the other buildings, he would be out of view.

Once close to the stable wall, he listened, but could hear nothing as he made his way westward. When he reached the end of the stable, he turned the corner and darted along the side wall, then across the open ground to the rear of the next building, one that looked almost like a barracks, with high windows. He kept close to the planked wall, moving back eastward until he was underneath a high window, open but a narrow crack.

When he could hear voices, he paused to listen, trying to sort out the words.

". . . how long, you figure?"

". . . could be a couple of glasses . . . less once in a while . . ."

"What do they *do* in there?"

". . . can't say as I know. Mostly talk. Don't talk like most   folk, either . . . use words no one else does."

"Like Madrien or nomad?"

"Not like that. They'll be talking just like us, and then they use strange words. Sound normal, but they're not."

"Like what?"

"How would I know? They're strange. Take my word for it."

There was a round of laughter.

". . . spend most your time with the horses . . ."

"They're better company . . . that Trezun . . . something odd about him . . . now . . . the mare . . . like to get her bred to Durwad's stallion . . . foal'd be something . . . said that to Trezun . . . told me breeding was important in everything . . . be especially important in years to come . . . laughed when he said it. Didn't seem funny to me . . ."

". . . that girl . . . Kara . . . she ever come back?"

Alucius continued to listen, but the guards and ostler kept talking about horses and women, and finally he edged to the corner of the building, where he chanced a glance at the limestone structure that his Talent-senses told him had to house the Table—or something like it. The building was as much dug into the low hills as built upon them, so much so that the rear wall of the structure rose out of the hill and the roof tiles at the rear were but a yard or so above the hill. From what he'd learned in Tempre, that confirmed his belief that the structure held a Table.

He watched for a time, with intermittent glances around the corner. Almost half a glass later, as the sun touched the western horizon, the door to the Table building opened, and Tarolt and two other ifrits walked outside. They turned onto a path that angled northwest, in front of the outbuildings, and in the direction of the River Vedra.

While he wondered where they were going and why in the evening chill, Alucius waited until the three were a good hundred yards from the Table building before he concentrated on making himself seem like only a vagrant breeze before he stepped from behind the outbuilding and walked quickly southward.

There were no yells or shouts, and none of the ifrits even turned.

When Alucius opened the door to the Table building and stepped inside, he could sense the presence of a Table, one seemingly more powerful than either of those he had encountered before. Rifle in hand, he glanced around the entry hall. The foyer was hexagonal—and empty—with two double doors leading from it.

Both doors were wide-open, and Alucius stepped through the archway to the right, which led into a conference room. A tray with a few small wedges of cheese and half an apple remained in the center of the table, and to one side was a crystal decanter half-filled with a red wine. There were three empty crystal goblets on the table, and warmth flowed from the stove against the wall, but Alucius could discern no one nearby. The sense of the Table was far stronger, clearly emanating from beyond the archway on the far side of the room. On the walls were light-torches, and not ancient remnants of the Duarchy, but ones recently fabricated. The sight of them chilled Alucius.

He eased around the conference table and toward the archway, totally alert, but he neither heard nor sensed anyone. As he stepped through the archway, Alucius found himself in another small foyer, with a staircase headed downward. At the foot of the staircase, he could see a door, slightly ajar. His Talent sensed a well of purpleness beyond the door, but nothing resembling an ifrit—or a guard.

After a momentary hesitation, he started down the stairs, as quietly as possible, trying not to let his heavy boots resound on the stonesteps.

The Table room was empty.

Alucius stepped inside, glancing at the Table, a solid structure with its sides covered in dark wood, running a yard and a third in width and length, and a yard in height. As he had expected, the entire surface was composed of a shimmering mirror. The Table looked to be slightly larger than those Alucius had seen before.

After a glance over his shoulder, he stepped closer to the Table, studying it with both eyes and Talent. Up close, the sheer power and *presence* of the Table was far greater than had been the case with the one in Tempre. Alucius frowned. The Table had to be new—or, at most, constructed within the past two years.

Alucius suddenly felt the presence of an ifrit—as if the room around him had filled with an even deeper shade of purple, although that was merely a sensation received through his Talent.

He turned quickly.

The white-haired Tarolt stood in the doorway, blocking any escape, and the power of the ifrit filled the doorway, a shimmering cloak of purple radiance. "Your attempts at illusion are useless."

Alucius released the breeze illusion. "I thought you'd gone . . ."

"Appearances can be deceiving. You of all Talent-steers should know that." The air wavered around Tarolt, and instead of a white-haired trader, there stood an ifrit of the type depicted in the ancient wall pictures of Deforya—and in Alucius's dreams—a figure a good head taller than Alucius with flawless alabaster skin, broad shoulders, shining black hair, and deep violet eyes. He wore a tunic and trousers of brilliant green, both trimmed in a deep purple, and his boots shimmered as if they were silvered black, so highly polished were they.

"I had no doubts of what you are," Alucius replied, trying to calculate how best to deal with the ifrit. After he learned what he could.

"Then . . . even what is may be deceiving," said the ifrit who was or had been Tarolt.

A section of stone wall to the right of Tarolt slid open, and a second ifrit stepped into the Table chamber.

"You seem to know so much," offered Alucius. "Tell me why I'm here."

"Curiosity . . . a fatal flaw of your kind," suggested the Tarolt-ifrit.

"You don't know much if that's what you think," Alucius snorted. "I already know about your kind. The great ifrits of the past . . . the sandoxes and the pteridons, and none of it was enough to prevent the soarers from thwarting you."

"'Efran' is a more accurate term, in so far as definitions are ever accurate," replied the second ifrit.

"Efran or ifrit . . ." Alucius forced a shrug. "Sooner or

later someone was going to ask about all the strange deaths of traders."

"If they did? What would they discover?" Tarolt smiled and took a step toward Alucius.

"That they shouldn't have died, not all in the same year." The colonel stepped back and to his left, so that the Table was between him and the two ifrits.

"Death happens to you mortals. Does it matter when?"

"It does if it alerts people to your schemes."

"Who else would even care? Your *people* are more concerned about food, golds, and how to procure women and other pleasures."

"Not all of them."

"Most of them, and there are few enough like you that you can be converted or otherwise taken care of. Or used in other fashions."

"That doesn't include the disappearances of herders," Alucius pointed out. "Especially in the north."

The momentary hesitation of Tarolt and the actual fleeting look of puzzlement on the face of the shorter ifrit told Alucius that the two knew nothing about disappearances. If anything, there was a moment of concern.

"The wild translations will feed and destroy what they find," the second ifrit said. "Surely, you do not think that any but herders will fret about a few missing nightsheep?"

Alucius suppressed a nod.

The purplish mists thickened around Tarolt and a pair of Talent-arms appeared, moving through the air toward Alucius.

He brought up the heavy rifle with a smooth motion. He squeezed the trigger, then recocked and fired again.

The Tarolt-ifrit staggered backward, but straightened almost immediately. Alucius fired two more shots at the second and smaller ifrit. The colonel sensed the shredding of the purple shield around the smaller creature, and fired his last shot, following with a Talent-probe, aimed at the main lifethread node.

A flare of purpled energy exploded away from the stricken ifrit—a wave of force that flung Alucius against the stone wall behind him. He barely managed to hang on to his rifle, and it was several moments before he could see through the watering of his eyes. There was no sign of the second ifrit—none at all.

Alucius could see that even Tarolt had been driven to one side of the Table room, but the ifrit had already regained his footing and turned back toward Alucius. A blast of purplish force flared toward the herder colonel.

Alucius managed to block-parry it and send forth a Talent-probe. The ifrit slapped it aside, and another wave of force slammed into Alucius's chest, driving him back against the wall once more. He struggled forward, wishing he'd brought a second rifle. The darkness-infused shells had at least driven Tarolt back.

Breathing hard, he formed a Talent-probe and drove its golden green force toward the ifrit's lifethread node.

The probe shattered into a spray of greenish gold, and Tarolt took another step toward Alucius.

He circled around the Table and away from the ifrit.

"You *will* serve your masters, Talent-steer—one way or another," stated Tarolt.

Alucius sensed two pairs of pinkish purple arms—one from the ifrit and the second from the Table—growing and moving to encircle him.

The herder created his own shield to ward off the arms, even while jabbing another Talent-probe at the arms coming from the Table.

The arms from the Table shattered into a spray of purple.

With a satisfied nod, Tarolt moved farther into the room.

Alucius eased around the Table, hoping to make a dash for either the main door or the passageway through which the second ifrit had appeared.

At that moment, a third ifrit appeared in the main doorway.

"You see . . . you cannot escape."

Alucius scrambled onto the Table, willing himself beyond the glassy surface.

"Then you will serve us in another—"

Tarolt's voice was cut off.

*Purplish blackness swirled around Alucius, bearing him
away from a dark green arrow. The blackness was that
bone-chilling cold that he had hoped never to brave again.
He could neither move his body nor see, except with his
Talent. Even worse, unlike his earlier experiences, when he
had been able to direct his course with his Talent, he felt as
though he were being propelled in one direction, as though
in a tight tube, much like an underground and lightless
stream might have been. The chill was more intense than
winter below the Aerlal Plateau.*

*He tried again to use his Talent-senses to guide him, to
visualize a long thin line of golden green, a guideline of
lifeforce to orient him, but he was carried onward through
the intense cold that seeped into every part of his body. He
tried to reach out for the directions and the arrows that sig-
nified Tables, or the golden green triangular arrows that
represented the portals of the hidden city. He could sense
none of them, only a distant sullen red arrow toward which
he was rushing.*

*More immediately before him, between him and the red
arrow, he could sense a black purple barrier, and he knew
he was being hurled at it. He wanted to swallow, to protest,
as he understood what Tarolt had meant by his serving the
ifrits.*

*Alucius tried to gather all his lifeforce into an arrowlike
shield before him, one with a point that would penetrate the
barrier he was approaching and yet protect him.*

*He slammed into the black barrier, and his entire body
convulsed—or it felt that way—as if he had fallen from a
cliff onto a stone surface.*

Abruptly, silver and light flashed around him.

Alucius found himself standing on a flat surface, but
hunched over. Agony flared through his entire body, and,

convulsively, he jerked upright. His head banged against something hard—so hard that he almost dropped the heavy rifle. Where he stood was lit, but so dimly that for a time he could make out nothing.

He was shivering, and his entire body felt bruised. Yet his forehead was sweating so heavily that he had to blot his eyes with his sleeve to keep the perspiration from flowing into his eyes. His arms and shoulders twitched, and his calves threatened to cramp. Sharp pains ran through his skull, either from his trip between Tables or from the blow to his head.

His eyes focused more.

The faint glow came from a pair of light-torches—set in curved silvery brackets and flanking a door. As his eyes adjusted, he saw that the door had buckled inward. After a moment, he eased his way off the Table. Then he turned and studied it with his Talent-sense, trying to ignore the increased stabbing in his skull created by that effort.

Even as he watched, the purpleness that infused the Table grew more pronounced. It was clearly a working Table . . . now. That also bothered him, because it meant that there were probably more Tables throughout Corus— and more ifrits.

After taking another glance at the Table, Alucius stepped toward the buckled door, the only apparent exit. Through the distended and splintered oak, and the gaps in the timbers that had comprised the door, Alucius could see that whatever room or hall that had lain beyond it was filled with large building stones and broken stone columns. There might have been space for a scrat to wiggle through, but certainly not for a man. Whatever structure had held the Table had collapsed—or been collapsed—over the Table's room, as if to deny it to anyone from outside. Had the soarers managed that during the Cataclysm? Or had someone else done it later? Did it matter?

He slowly surveyed the room, clearly either underground or buried, or both. There were no furnishings in the chamber except for the Table and a narrow chest set against one wall. He could see no other way out except through the blocked doorway. Still . . . there might be another passageway like the one in the Matrial's Palace or the one in the ifrits' Table room.

Span by span, yard by yard, Alucius made his way along the stone walls of the chamber, but neither his eyes nor fingers, nor his Talent, could discover any other exit, although he had looked closely, especially behind the chest. Finally, he stood on the opposite side of the buckled door from where he had begun.

He looked back at the Table once more. The purple glow remained, neither greater nor less than before. With an occasional glance at the Table, he moved back toward the ornately carved chest set against the stone side wall.

There was nothing on the smooth wood of the surface, not even that much dust. He opened the top drawer. Inside was empty. He closed the drawer, and opened the second drawer. Except for several sheets of parchment or paper, it was also empty. Alucius reached for the paper, but as his fingers touched it, the paper fragmented into dust so fine that Alucius's nose began to itch.

For a time, he found himself sneezing, his eyes watering.

He glanced back at the Table, but no one . . . nothing . . . appeared.

He went back to the chest, pulling out every drawer and looking under and behind each. He found nothing more except fragments that might once have been paper.

Then he studied the doorway, but the stones had been packed in so tightly against the ancient and heavy wood, wood that still retained its strength, that he could not budge either the door or any of the stone protrusions.

As he had feared, there was no way out of the chamber except through the Table. At least, there was no way that he could find.

He turned and looked once more at the ancient Table, a dark cube rising out of darker stone and suffused with the purpled life-energy stolen from who knew where. Could he reenter the Table and transport himself elsewhere? His lungs felt tight, and he had to wonder how long the air in the chamber would last.

Or were his lungs tight because he feared he was truly trapped?

He tried not to think about Wendra, or about how easily Tarolt had manipulated him.

He looked at the Table.

After a moment, he began to reload the heavy rifle, thinking that he should have done so earlier, and infused the cartridges with darkness. After doing that, he felt even more light-headed as he climbed onto the Table and concentrated. The surface beneath him dissolved.

Once more, Alucius hurtled downward into the chill purple blackness, but this time there was no current or force driving him. After a timeless instant, he could also sense the arrowlike markers or guides that he recalled—except that there was no sign of those of golden green or silver— the guideways to the hidden city. He could easily sense the dark purple conduits, conduits leading to something far worse than anything on Corus. That he knew without knowing how he knew.

He tried seeking beyond the tube of chill purple blackness, but could sense nothing. Were the soarers gone? Or were there so few that they could no longer maintain their own portals?

With his Talent, he studied the markers—far more than he recalled. There was one of an ancient-looking sullen red over blackish purple, but that, he felt, was the one for where he had already just been. Another was of maroon and dark green, the Table that Tarolt had used to throw Alucius against the barrier. Alucius had the feeling he had been a tool to reopen the Table in the underground chamber, but he had no idea why, since that Table hardly seemed usable.

He struggled to focus his attention on the remaining arrow markers. One was silver, a silver he recalled from his encounter with the ifrit engineer. That wouldn't do, because his departure had brought the walls down around that Table chamber as well. If the chamber had been rebuilt, then there would be more ifrits in it. If it hadn't, he'd be trapped in another underground place. Another marker was a shining cold black, a narrow threadlike arrow that bespoke little use, if any.

With a mind becoming increasingly slow and muddled, he Talent-groped toward the black disused thread, mind-levering himself toward whatever portal or Table it represented.

Once more, he hurtled toward a barrier, but one of thin blackness that sprayed away as he smashed into and through it.

There was more darkness . . . but fresh air, if chill.

That was all Alucius could recognize before his legs buckled, and he fell into oblivion.

126

The Hidden City, Corus

In the amber-walled tower room, the soarer hovered before Wendra—holding the scrat before the herder.

Wendra looked quietly at the creature known to be terribly shy and skittish. It rested motionless in the palm of the soarer's hand, its head cocked, its eyes on Wendra, not paying attention to the child in the carrypack.

Use your Talent. Study its lifethread, but do not touch the thread with your Talent. It is very frail compared to you.

Wendra took the slightest of breaths, letting her Talent observe the scrat.

Look at the nodes. Those are where the threads twist together.

Wendra stiffened, looking down at the black stone of the herder's ring she wore. The sharp chill that had jabbed through her finger was gone, as suddenly as it had come.

She looked at the soarer. "Something happened to Alucius."

It is likely that he translated himself somewhere, using a Table of the ifrits.

"Translated?"

That is how the ifrits travel, both from their base world and also across Corus. They must have Tables or portals at the beginning and at the end of their journeys. Even so, world lifeforces change images. You see the ifrits as the world translates them, and were you on their world you would not appear as you do now. Enough . . . you must learn more about life itself, not Tables. The Tables mean little.

"I thought Alucius had destroyed the Tables."

He destroyed one that had already been weakened, and buried another. One of the ifrits has regained access to that Table and is rebuilding another. They have also repowered other Tables. The "voice" of the soarer sounded tired. *Forget the Tables. There is so little time. So little . . .*

"So little time?" asked Wendra.

You must learn about the nodes. They are the key to all that you must do.

"Alucius might need me."

He might indeed, but you can do nothing to help him until you learn. Observe the scrat.

"How will this help?"

Unless you understand how to untwine the lifeforce of the ifrits, and their massive threads, they will brush you aside as the frailest of butterflies, as the most short-lived of moths. Your Alucius thought his efforts were sufficient. They were not. He ignored the signs on his stead as well.

"You expected him to stand watch over something he knew nothing about? When you did nothing? You expected him to guard all Corus? To have no life at all?"

We have done all we could. You would not be, and your world would be long since drained and dead, had we not acted long years past. We have taken only what was necessary. We did not destroy a world to build cities that will en-

dure forever on lifeless lands. We did what was best for both ourselves and for others. From that forbearance, we have never recovered. Do not speak to me of how one should live a life. We will not live that much longer, no matter who triumphs. If those who can stop evil do not act, then it will triumph. That those with ability are called upon is unfair. The able must always do more. The universe cares nothing for fairness. Beliefs do not matter. Only what is done or not done matters. You and your mate can choose to act against the ifrits. You can choose not to act. Acting without the knowledge you need to change what otherwise will be is futile. How can you help your mate if you know even less than he does?

Wendra could not refute those last words, much as she wanted to, much as she felt Alucius needed her. Nor could she refute the fact that the soarer would not help unless she cooperated. She took a long and slow breath and concentrated on the small creature the soarer held.

Observe the scrat once more.

127

Once more, Alucius found himself on a flat surface, except he was sprawled half across it, and the Table—if it was a Table—was sucking the very heat out of his body. His chest was numb from the chill. With an effort, he rolled sideways. That movement split his skull with an internal thunderclap and sent lines of fire down his arms and legs that left his vision blurring and his entire body shaking. He took a slow breath, then another.

Even after remaining still for a time, his vision was still blurred, his eyes watering, and every part of his body ached.

Was that because he'd burst through two barriers, one practically after another? Or just from the strain of traveling through the dark tubes?

After a moment, he eased himself into a sitting position, although his knees ended up higher than his thighs because there was dirt or rubble piled around what he thought was a Table. There was no light where he was, but he felt that he was in an enclosure of some sort. The room was cold, chill—and dark—but the darkness didn't feel like the previous chamber that had held the buried Table, and there was a definite icy wind filtering in from somewhere.

Alucius slowly moved his head, trying to make out something in the blackness. He stopped. There was an oblong almost directly before him that seemed somehow like a lighter patch in the darkness. He eased himself to his feet, still holding the heavy rifle, and gingerly stepped toward what he hoped was an archway or doorway, or even a window. His boots sank into an oozy substance that felt partly frozen. An acrid odor of decaying vegetation rose in the chill air. Carefully, the herder took one step after another, crossing close to three yards of uneven, unsteady footing until he stood just short of the opening in the dark stone wall.

A doorway of sorts it was indeed, with stone pillars and a lintel. The bottom of the doorway was filled with rubble that had been covered with dirt and possibly moss or something else. He felt the stone, polished into a glassy finish, and with cracks in only a few places. There did not seem to have been a door, not from the smooth-finished edges of the stone.

He studied the corridor beyond the doorway, somewhat lighter, enough that he could make out an incline leading straight ahead and up. It might have been a gradual ramp, although the ramp or steps were covered with dirt.

Before leaving the Table chamber, he glanced back over his shoulder at the Table. Like the previous one, it had also begun to show a purple glow visible only through his Talent. With that glow, he could tell that it was half-buried in dirt and debris.

He turned back and began to make his way up the ramp.

Halfway up, on the left side, there was a gap in the stonework, chest high and almost as wide, through which the wind gusted. Alucius peered through the gap. Overhead, through a break in the roof or ceiling, Alucius could see stars, and they looked familiar, as they might from Iron Stem.

He wanted to shake his head. Of course it was dark. With all the hours he had spent in the one buried Table chamber and the time when he had been unconscious, wherever he was now, the sun had set a long time back. He couldn't help a slight smile at the thought that at least he wasn't trapped underground. Alucius kept climbing the ramp until he reached what he thought might be the ground level of the ruined building. At the top of the ramp, he stood in an antechamber or foyer. Directly ahead of him was a stone wall, with some sort of carving or drawing, but the light was far too dim for even his sight to make it out. To the right and the left were archways. A massive tree trunk had fallen and blocked the archway to the right. Under the trunk were sections and fragments of stone.

Alucius moved slowly though the remaining archway into a long hallway lined with columns. The roof above the columns appeared relatively solid.

Miniature lights or stars flashed before his eyes, and for a moment, he felt weak and dizzy. He stopped and put out a hand to one of the columns to steady himself. For a time, he just stood there, sore and tired and disoriented, various thoughts spinning through his mind.

As little as two years before, he would not have been so shocked at the happenings of the day. But after returning to the comparatively peaceful life of a herder, and then the seasons of battle and riding, it was hard to believe that he was back dealing with ifrits and Tables. Or was that because he wished he were not?

He'd tried to escape the power of Tarolt and been thrown through a Table barrier and ended up nearly buried alive. Trying to escape that fate had led him through another barrier to somewhere else dark and cold, to yet another abandoned Table. Yet his actions, or the power of the ifrits—or both—had rejuvenated Tables that had been dead or inactive.

The ifrits were far more powerful than he'd believed, and he still had no idea who had taken Wendra or where she might be. From what little he had observed, the ifrits he'd encountered hadn't seemed to know. They'd seemed disconcerted or uninterested in the idea of herder disappearances. Alucius also had gotten the feeling that there were far more ifrits in Corus than he'd seen. Far more.

Another flash of dizziness confirmed that he needed to get some rest . . . or he'd end up sprawled out somewhere else, with perhaps even more serious injuries.

Step by slow step, Alucius made his way along the columned corridor, which seemed more sheltered than other parts of the building. Near the far end, through a narrow doorway in the stone wall, a doorway whose door had vanished sometime in the past, he finally found a corner free of most dirt and debris, in what might have been a small room before whatever destruction had visited itself on the place. Setting his rifle close at hand, he curled into the corner.

Everything still ached, but sleep might help. He hoped it would.

128

A flat, silvery light suffused the hallway outside the small room where Alucius was sleeping, reflecting off polished stone walls and into his eyes, bringing him slowly awake. Recalling his awakening from his last Table trip, Alucius opened his eyes and turned his head slowly.

A dull but faint throbbing throughout his skull reminded him of his unwise exploits of the previous day, as did the soreness across his chest and arms. So did the dryness in his mouth and his cracking lips. He thought he'd seen the strength of ifrits before, but he'd had no idea that a true ifrit was so powerful. Then . . . with his rifle and the lifeforce-darkened cartridges, he had killed one. The only problem was that there had been three . . . and who knew many others that he didn't know about.

His breath steamed in the still air, although Alucius judged that it was not quite cold enough to freeze water. Still, he was more than glad he had been wearing nightsilks and his winter riding jacket.

He eased himself into a sitting position and looked out through the doorway at the columns on the far side of the corridor he had traversed the night before. Each was of amber gold stone, like the towers of the soarers or the ancient buildings of Dereka—or of the ifrit palaces about which he had dreamed more than a few times. The light was coming through translucent clerestory panels in the high roof of the corridor.

One thing was very clear. He needed to take care of more than a few bodily necessities, including finding some water.

He rose to his feet, then reclaimed the rifle, checking it over before he stepped into the ancient corridor. His boots had left the only tracks in the span-deep gray dirt that covered the pale greenstone revealed by his own scuffing steps of the night before. He turned to his right, hoping that there might be an exit somewhere ahead, although the corridor seemed to end in a gloomy recess less than fifteen yards away.

Alucius walked forward.

There was an exit—or there had been one—but it had been walled up, with square sections of goldenstone mortared in place. The herder tapped the stone with the butt of the rifle and was rewarded with a dull *clunk*. The stones were definitely solid.

He turned and retraced his steps back along the corridor, checking each of the chambers that opened off it. Every

single one was empty of all furnishings, and every outside
window had been mortared closed.

When he finally returned to the ramp that led downward
to the Table, Alucius was not only thirsty and needing
nourishment and relief, but also more than a little puzzled.
Supposedly, the Cataclysm had been abrupt and without
warning, yet someone had sealed the building carefully,
and in a way that could not have been done in haste. Who
had done it? How long ago? And why? To protect the
Table? That thought alone was even more chilling than the
air in the ancient building.

As he eased his way down the ramp, he could see in the
indirect light that it was covered with a grayish dirt that
had drifted in from the broken part of the wall. He made
his way to the gap in the stonework, where sunlight filtered
around the massive tree trunk. On the upper side there was
a gap between trunk and goldenstone—a gap perhaps half
a yard in width and a yard long.

Alucius managed to lever himself high enough to grasp a
section of stone that looked as though it would break in his
hands. But the jagged goldenstone was as unyielding as
iron, and he had to stretch to set his rifle in one of the cracks
in the stonework overhead, then use both arms to pull himself up. He was panting and sweating by the time he had recovered the rifle and gotten up far enough to squirm into
the opening between trunk and broken stone. The tree
looked as though it had fallen recently, with the indenta-
tions in the bark still clear and fresh. But to his Talent, the
wood felt dead, lifeless. Yet it had not decayed. He touched
the trunk of the tree, a fir of some sort, a good three yards in
breadth, from what he could see. It was cold, like stone.

After a moment, he began to inch his way upward at an
angle and around the trunk until he was on the upper side
and sitting in weak and hazy sunlight, light that offered no
warmth from the biting chill that enfolded him.

He bent and tapped the tree trunk with the rifle butt. It
even sounded like stone. As he caught his breath, he took
in everything around him. In front of him, the fallen tree

rose at an angle above the goldenstones and green tiles that formed the roof of the structure he had just escaped. Neither snow nor ice clung to or touched the tile or the amber stonework—or the tree. Alucius's mouth opened as he realized that even the needles and the branches of the tree had ossified, as if the massive fir had been alive one instant and turned to stone the next—stone that had retained all the color and shape of the original tree.

There were no other trees anywhere in sight. The building itself was situated on a low rise whose slopes were covered with snow. Below the rise—in all directions except north—was a snowy plain with low hummocks irregularly dotting the whiteness. There was not a single sign of any sort of vegetation, nor any rock or stone not covered with snow. To the north, from the position of the sun, the snowy plain extended about a vingt—and ended. The land just dropped away, and beyond and below that cliff edge was a mass of gray clouds or swirling snow, or both. Above was an ever-darker mass of clouds.

Alucius turned and looked away from the clouds and the tip of the stone tree. At the bottom of the rise to the south of the building was an open rivulet of dark water running between snowy banks. A slight mist rose from the water. Alucius resisted the urge to rush toward it. He'd rushed too much lately. Instead, he used his Talent to scan the area around him, ignoring the headache the effort caused.

He could sense a number of birds, a creature he thought might be a snow fox, and some rodents, like scrats, but different. Beyond the low rise on the far side of the small stream, the snow extended as far as he could see to the south.

Slowly, he edged his way down the trunk until he reached the part where bare stone roots jutted upward, blocking any further progress. From there, holding the rifle high in his left hand, he slid off into the snow. The top was crusty, but beneath that crust was white powder that flew up around him, momentarily blinding him.

When the flurries settled, he was standing in thigh-deep snow. His boots, he felt, rested on packed snow and ice, not frozen stone or soil. Step by step he waded down the slope toward the stream, stopping on a flat area short of the water's edge and testing his footing as he edged forward. Finally, he bent down, reaching out and touching the water. Despite the foggy vapor that rose from the surface, the water felt like liquid ice. Alucius could drink it only in very small swallows, and it chilled him all the way through by the time he felt he had had enough.

Alucius glanced around, but the air remained chill and still, with no life except a few birds that skittered across the snow and rodents burrowed somewhere beneath the snow. He needed to get out of wherever he was—and as soon as he could. But it would help to know where he was. From what he had seen, he had to be fairly far north, perhaps near Northport or even Blackstear—although he supposed that, with the range of the Tables, he could be somewhere just as far north, but far to the east in Lustrea.

His one look at the land around him had made one thing very clear. The only way out was through the Table.

In time, after dealing with other needs, and drinking more, he made his way back up the stone tree and wormed his way into the Table building—grateful to be out of a wind that had begun to rise, colder with each quarter glass that passed. The sky to the north was darkening moment by moment, with heavy gray clouds scudding in from the northwest. His head and body still ached, but he didn't see that staying around in the frigid Table building in the middle of a mostly frozen wasteland, with spring yet to approach, would do much to improve his physical condition.

He made another study of every room on the upper levels of the building but found nothing, not even any lighttorches or brackets that might have opened hidden passages. Just walls and columns and floors and ceilings, all of cold stone. There wasn't even a scrap of parchment or a fragment of metal.

Alucius stood at the top of the ramp leading down to the Table chamber and tried to think. The last Table—the buried one—had felt reddish. The one in Salaan had been a dark green, and the one immediately below him had felt black. The one that had existed in Tempre had been blue, and the one where he had faced the ifrit-possessed engineer years before had been silver. The Table in Tempre did not exist any longer, and the one where he'd fought the engineer was probably also buried in rubble. He hadn't fared well against the ifrits in Salaan when he had been stronger. So . . . he had to find another Table, preferably an older one not being tended by ifrits. If there was another Table anywhere.

His breath was steaming more, and he shivered. Was that the cold caused by the storm coming in? Or was it because he was tired and hungry? He pressed his lips together, lifted the rifle that was becoming ever heavier, and retraced his steps back to the lower level.

Once he entered the Table chamber, he noted that the ooze around the Table was firmer, almost totally frozen, except immediately next to the Table. The Table itself held the purplish Talent-glow that indicated it was functioning.

In the dimness, he checked the walls of the chamber, but could find no sign of light-torch brackets or of hidden doorways. By the time he finished, his teeth were chattering.

Alucius took a deep breath, then climbed onto the Table quickly, as if he feared he might lose his resolve. He concentrated on the blackness beneath, on the tubes that led . . . wherever . . .

More quickly than before, Alucius dropped into the purple black chill. In the timelessness that followed, he tried to feel for the arrowlike markers, finding the sullen red one, the dark green, the silver, and the black, somewhere seemingly above him. There were none of the guideways, the golden green threads, that led to the hidden city, not even beyond the blackness, not where he had found them once before.

But there had to be something else . . . somewhere else that he could go . . .

He could sense, nearer now in some way, one dark purple conduit that led to a darkness far worse than anything on Corus—the world from where the ifrits came. Alucius had no desire to go there. Facing an entire world of the creatures was madness when he could barely hold his own against a single ifrit.

Once more, he sought beyond the tube of chill purple blackness, but found nothing. Was there not anything, any kind of marker?

He struggled to find something, anything at all.

Off to the side, or off center, Alucius sensed something else, something faint, a circle of gold and crimson, barely there, yet there, but not flickering or retreating. He thought there might be another, one of hot purple and pink, but that was farther away, and he was tired . . . so tired.

As before, his mind had become slow and confused, and he Talent-probed desperately for the golden red circle, more of a mist than an arrow or a Table. Still . . . it had to represent . . . something. He pressed his being toward that crimson gold, mind-levering himself at whatever it represented.

Before he knew it, he was hurtling through a barrier, but one of silvered gold, whose breaking shards were more like the patter of rain as he flew through it.

129

Salaan, Lanachrona

The two ifrits stood on opposite sides of the Table that dominated the lower chamber. The hidden door had been closed, and the stone facing where it was looked no different from the sections of wall on either side.

"The Table in Soupat is on the grid. So is the one in Blackstear." Trezun looked at Tarolt. "Waleryn thinks he will have the Table in Norda fully operational in a week, no more than two. The cold has hampered some of his efforts."

"It always does. Would that we could work on a warmer world, but the universe does not take note of desires or wishes, only what is."

"Unhappily."

"How did you manage to bring the one in Blackstear into the grid?" Tarolt's voice carried little more than idle curiosity.

"I did not. The herder-colonel did, I surmise, since there was a translation from the Table in Soupat, and none of the other Tables on the grid show another translation."

"That he went to Blackstear proves that he has ability, but not understanding."

"The ancient ones, perhaps?"

"No. Blackstear was at the edge of their reach even when they were more formidable." Tarolt smiled. "They are scarcely that now."

"They could be concealing their strength."

"I think not. Not if they are reduced to using Talent-steers as their agents." Tarolt gestured toward the Table it-self. "The two reaccessed Tables—they will strengthen the grid by how much?"

"A tenth part for now. Another tenth once the Table in Norda is fully operational and can shunt power to them through the grid."

"So we have strengthened the grid, but opened it to an agent of the ancient ones, who, weak as he is, has survived a barrier and made another translation."

"He cannot survive in Blackstear," pointed out Trezun.

"No. But do we know that he will stay there? Warn Waleryn that he is able to use the Tables." Tarolt paused. "You had best begin making translations to Tempre. That is close enough that you should not need a Table there, and the Lord-Protector believes the room is sealed."

"You want me to start rebuilding the Table there?"

"Where else? We need to gain control over the Lord-Protector."

Trezun nodded slowly. "It will take time."

"Everything takes time, and that is what we have too little of. You had best send a message to the fieldmasters about the Talent-steer."

"They will not be pleased."

"No. But they would be less pleased if they discovered it later, and we have not told them. They should also know that we yet face difficulties. Perhaps it will motivate them to . . . encourage greater support for our efforts."

"Most true," admitted Trezun. "Should we request a replacement for Sensat?"

"That would be best—if there is someone willing to take the risk and with enough lifeforce to make the long translation to a marginal grid. But word what you send most carefully. I would rather not upset Fieldmaster Lasylt more than necessary."

Trezun nodded slowly once more.

130

Alucius staggered as he broke out from the purple darkness, and he took two steps before recovering his balance. He glanced around warily, but he saw no one. He stood in an empty chamber, in a square pit perhaps half a yard below the stone floor. Dust raised by his boots swirled up around him and he sneezed—hard—several times.

With his free hand, he rubbed his nose, trying to stop the itching and the sneezing. Finally, he glanced around, noticing immediately as he did that the air around him was far warmer, if not quite springlike. Again . . . he was in a chamber below ground, but this one was lit, if dimly, by light filtering through a doorway to his left. A moment passed before he realized that there was no Table in the chamber. No Table? But how had he been able to appear?

As he stepped out of the pit, he frowned, thinking, even

as he kept looking around the empty chamber. He had not been able to find one of the arrow markers. Nor had he been able to find the golden green circles of the soarers and their hidden city. He had tried to use a misty golden red circle—and he had broken out through some sort of barrier. Did that mean that the Tables were only to make travel easier? He recalled all the Table locations he knew. Each was set on or near stone and deep in the ground. That argued that the Tables could be located only in certain places. Alucius looked back at the Table-sized depression in the stone and nodded slowly.

All that might be, but he also needed food and rest, and before long. He tried not to dwell on the situation he was in. His wife was still missing, and he was, too—at least absent from Northern Guard headquarters at a time when his absence would certainly be noted, a time he should have been there. For the moment, though, he had to deal with more immediate needs.

He considered the chamber around him. There were no furnishings at all, just bare stone walls—except that the walls were gold eternastone. As with the other Table chambers he had visited, there was only a single obvious entrance, but the wooden door and frame that had presumably once filled the doorway had long since vanished.

Rifle still in hand, Alucius moved toward the doorway, then up the stone steps, slowly, because he thought he could hear voices murmuring. With each step, dust swirled around his boots. Halfway up, he paused, listening.

". . . sure be safe . . ."

Alucius tried to make out the words, words that he thought were in an oddly accented Lanachronan.

". . . safe enough . . . Council's armsmen won't be patrolling here tonight . . ."

". . . you know that?"

". . . backhills . . . think this place is still home of demons . . ."

". . . been here before . . . never seen any . . ."

Alucius checked his rifle, then took another step, and

598 L. E. MODESITT, JR.

another, trying to move deliberately so as not to raise too much dust, until he reached the top of the stairs and stood in a small foyer. He could still hear the voices coming from the larger chamber beyond.

The talking went on . . . and on.

Tired as he was, Alucius decided that he would have to try the breeze illusion to move past whoever was in the chamber beyond. If it didn't work, perhaps the rifle's presence would be enough to intimidate them, since those talking sounded as though they were beggars or homeless folk. He concentrated on creating the impression of nothingness, then eased through the doorway out into the larger chamber, moving one step at a time.

". . . heard something . . ." One of the figures in rags turned toward Alucius.

The young colonel shifted his grip on the rifle.

Another of the figures, a bearded man in an armless gray tunic, looked toward Alucius, but his eyes were focused more on Alucius's boots. ". . . over there . . . boot prints . . . see . . ."

"Nobody's there . . ."

"It's a demon . . . or its boots!"

"Run! Run, Nargila!"

". . . no demons . . . you said no demons . . ."

"Run . . . !"

Alucius dropped the illusion once the three figures in rags scrambled through the bare stone archway and out away from him. He walked slowly toward the windows through which sunlight angled. At the low, wide window, which at one time had to have held a frame and glass, he glanced out into late afternoon, where the sun hung low over a city, over dwellings that glowed yellow in the slanting sunlight. He had to squint, trying not to look directly at the sun, but he could see that the dwellings in the distance, to the north, were indeed of yellowstone and dark split slate.

Closer, below the building itself, ran a paved yellowstone road, into which years of wagon wheels had carved grooves almost a handspan deep. The road alone told Alucius where he was—in the city of Dereka, capital of Deforya. To confirm that, he leaned out and looked to the north, where he could see yet another of the gold eternastone buildings, built without visible mortar or gaps between the large and regular stones. Even farther to the north was a greenstone tower.

He stepped back, swallowing. He was relieved, in a way, to be somewhere that he recognized, but also troubled to have discovered just how many Tables there once had been.

After a moment, Alucius turned and made his way in the general direction taken by the fleeing beggars, finding a wide stone staircase. In time he walked from a square arch on the north side of the building, stepping out and turning west.

A vendor at a small cart stared at him, but he did not see anyone else who seemed even to notice him as he walked westward. He took the precaution of leaving his riding jacket closed, so that the insignia on his collar could not be seen. Once he reached the main boulevard, he looked southward, but all he could see of the Landarch's palace was a small section of the main gates and another green tower—the one at the northern end.

From what Alucius recalled, there were no places offering lodging to the south of where he stood. He felt like trudging, but forced himself to walk alertly northward along the main boulevard, vaguely recalling having seen some inns there when he had last been in Dereka. He also remembered to stay out of the center section of the boulevard, reserved for riders and wagons. He worried about carrying the rifle, but he saw more than a few bravos, some looking even more tired and disreputable than he thought he must, also carrying weapons. That was something he had not recalled from when he had been in Dereka before.

The streets were less crowded than he recalled, and few people looked directly at each other or at Alucius. He had to walk almost half a vingt before he reached a corner where, across the side street, he saw a three-story stone structure with the signboard that proclaimed the building as the Red House. Beside the letters was the picture of a house totally in red.

All the shutters, doors, and wooden trim had been recently painted a bright red that stood out against the dressed graystones, stones that had doubtless come from an older structure. The inn was certainly a place more costly than Alucius would have preferred, but it was also likely to be more reputable than a less costly place. He crossed the side street and walked through the stone archway.

A young man with black hair and wearing a red leather vest rose from behind a small desk to one side of the spacious foyer. "Yes?"

"I'm looking for a room . . . and a meal."

The angular young man looked at Alucius, at the heavy rifle, and then at the nightsilk-covered riding jacket. "Be five coppers a night for the room. Seven if you stable a mount."

"Mount didn't make it all the way here," Alucius replied. He hoped the chestnut was all right, but there was little he could do, not when he was some six hundred vingts from Salaan.

"You here to join the Council force?"

"Hadn't thought to . . . When I left my place . . . well . . . Landarch was having trouble, but . . ." Alucius hoped his vague reply would lead to more information.

"He had his troubles, all right." The young man shook his head. "All started after the Lanachronans came in and destroyed the nomads. Two years back. Landarch said the big landowners hadn't met their obligations. He tried to curb their privileges. Landowners . . . they complained . . . plots here and plots there. Woke up a month ago, the Landarch was dead, and the Council was in power."

Alucius nodded. "Think I might just have to think it over."

"You want a room? We have a small one on the third floor. We could go four coppers."

"I'll take it. Need to sleep somewhere. Room have a basin and towel?"

"All the rooms do. You need more water, you can bring the pitcher down here."

"Thank you." Alucius extended the coppers, then offered a tired smile. "What's best to eat tonight?"

"Stew's never bad, but the plumapple chicken's probably the best. Or the Spirnaci noodles with the groundpig." The young man extended a heavy bronze key. "First door to the left at the top of the stairs. Has a red square on the door panel."

"Thank you."

"Sir . . . might be better if you left the weapon in your room. It'll be safe there."

Alucius nodded.

The stairs to the second floor were wide and made of polished stone. Those to the third floor were far narrower and were wood covered with a dark gray carpeting, The key turned the heavy lock easily, and Alucius stepped into the room behind the red square.

Since he'd been expecting a cot in a space more like a barracks cubby, he was pleasantly surprised by the room— a space three and a half yards by four with a narrow window offering a view of one of the abandoned gold eternastone structures. The inside shutters were dark oak, and the bed, while single, had a firm mattress, both sheets, and a heavy blanket. The wash table had two pitchers and a generous basin with two towels.

After slipping the rifle under the mattress, he stepped to the basin and pitcher. Slowly and carefully, he peeled off his clothes to the waist. As he had suspected, he had bruises distributed all across his upper body. Some were still dark, but others were beginning to turn yellow and purple. He slowly washed away the dirt and grime. He would have liked to shave, because his beard itched, both growing out and even when grown out, but all his personal gear had been left in his quarters.

Still . . . cool as it was, the water felt good. And so would some sleep, but that would have to wait until after he ate.

Once he was cleaner, he brushed out the dust and dirt from his jacket and shirt, using a damp corner of one of the towels to remove several obvious spots. He removed the collar insignia, slipping them into his wallet. Then he left the room, locking it behind him, and made his way down the stairs to the public room. He left the riding jacket on, but open.

Only half the tables in the long room were taken, and as Alucius glanced around, a servingwoman—wearing a red apron with a few splotches on it—paused and gestured. "Take any vacant table, sir."

"Thank you." Alucius nodded and moved toward the one corner table remaining.

He had barely seated himself when another server, a squarish woman—also wearing a red apron—appeared beside his table.

"What'll it be?"

"What's on the board?" Alucius asked.

"Spirnaci pig, plumapple fowl, and stew. Four coppers for each. Ale's two, and wine is three."

"Ale and the fowl."

"Coming up."

Alucius surveyed the room but saw nothing out of the ordinary, either with his eyes or Talent. There was absolutely no trace of purpleness in any of those dining or serving them. For that he was most grateful. He wished he had an idea of where Wendra might be and how to reach her. But he doubted he could even search more until he was refreshed and rested, and that bothered him as well. He had always disliked knowing nothing, and when Wendra was involved, that was even worse.

Just as bad was the realization that there were far more ifrits than he had known about in Corus, and that some of them were real ifrits—not just people possessed through the Tables. He had to wonder how many more were placed in other cities, such as Tempre or Hieron, or even Alustre.

He sat back listening, trying not to think of Wendra, or the ifrits, waiting for his ale and food.

"Council's going to raise the road tariffs on the north highway . . ."

"About time . . ."

". . . Praetor of Lustrea won't like it . . ."

". . . he's young . . . army got near wiped out by Aellyan Edyss two years back . . . can't have that many lancers now . . ."

". . . if he does . . . Council can just drop the tariffs . . . worth a try . . ."

"Right about that . . . anything's better 'n more tariffs on us . . ."

Alucius wasn't sure, but the speaker who was concerned about tariffs looked to be a merchant, rather than an landowner.

"Here's your ale. Be two."

Alucius handed over the coppers, and then took a slow swallow. The brew was heavy, a darkish amber, but not bitter, and cool. He kept listening as he took small swallows.

". . . need to be careful . . . say the Council wants to expand the lancers . . ."

". . . no reason . . . not these days . . ."

". . . why we need to be careful . . ."

". . . oh . . ."

"Lord-Protector all tied up with the Madriens . . . say they got a regent now . . ."

"Madrien always been trouble . . ."

". . . wager it'll be more now. Say . . . heard that daughter of yours . . ."

Alucius lost the train of the conversation as the server returned again.

"Here's the fowl."

"Maybe you could help me." Alucius handed over five coppers. "I just got here from the west . . . Heard the Landarch was killed, and a Council's running things. You know who's on the Council?"

The server shrugged. "They say they're all landowners. Don't think anyone rightly knows."

Alucius nodded. "Figured something like that. Thank you."

She offered a polite smile. "Let me know if you want another ale."

"I will."

The fowl was good, as were the plain noodles and bread that came with it, although Alucius's opinion of the fare might have been colored by his own hunger. Even before he finished the last morsels, he found his eyes were so heavy that he was almost nodding off at the table.

The food and the warmth of the public room—and the exhaustion of days—clearly left Alucius feeling more than a little sleepy. He rose from the table and made his way up to his room.

The rifle remained where he had left it, and in addition to locking the door, he slipped the bar standing behind it through the painted iron brackets to make sure his sleep was not interrupted.

Then he sat on the edge of the bed. He pulled off his boots and disrobed slowly. He barely had pulled the covers up when sleep claimed him.

131

Northeast of Iron Stem, Iron Valleys

In the early evening, the young man rode up the last part of the lane to the stead house, a second unsaddled mount following his. Long before he reached the rail at the base of the stairs, the older herder was standing there, bareheaded, with the intermittent flakes of spring snow swirling around him.

"Sir . . . I came as quick as I could."

"You talked to Alucius? You told him about Wendra?" asked Royalt.

"Yes, sir." Korcler swallowed. "He's gone now, too."

For a long moment, Royalt just looked at the youth.

"I didn't do it, sir. I didn't know what he was going to do."

"We'll stall the mounts, and then you can tell us. Did you tell your folks?"

"No, sir. I didn't stop there. They . . . they didn't want me to go to Dekhron. I figured . . . I'd better tell you, first. Might not be going anywhere for a long time, not after this. But I thought . . . someone . . . and now . . . it's worse 'n ever."

Royalt took the tether for the second mount and began to walk toward the stable. Korcler rode slowly after the older man. Neither spoke until they were in the stable and out of the wind.

"You didn't tell me your father had forbidden you to go to Dekhron," Royalt said after stalling the spare mount.

"He didn't say I couldn't, sir," Korcler replied. "I didn't ask. He would have said no. I knew that. And Alucius had to know about Wendra. He just had to."

Royalt took the saddle and racked it, then closed the stall. "We'll finish here after we go up to the house and you tell Lucenda and me everything that you know."

"Yes, sir."

Royalt closed the stable door and began to walk swiftly toward the house.

Korcler had to stretch his legs to catch up. "You're not mad at me, sir?"

"No, Korcler. I'm not mad. Things could be a lot better, but I'm not mad."

Once they were inside the dwelling, Royalt ushered the youth into the kitchen.

There, Lucenda set a mug of hot cider before him. "Have you eaten anything?"

"No . . . ma'am. Not except for some biscuits and cheese Majer Feran sent with me."

"I'll fix you something while you tell us what happened."

"Alucius is gone now, too," Royalt said.

"How . . . ?" Lucenda's mouth opened.

"I told him about Wendra. I gave him what you wrote, sir, and he read it. He turned real coldlike. I almost didn't want to talk to him. Then he helped me stable and groom the mounts and took me up to his quarters and gave me stuff to eat. He wrote something to Majer Feran. I knew he was writing something. Then he rode off. He wouldn't let me come with him. He said he'd be back that night." The young man paused. "Except then . . . he said if he wasn't, I was still to come back and tell you, sir." The youth's look was almost defiant, but his eyes skittered away from Royalt.

"He's gone after Wendra," Lucenda said. "It has to be. She's the only thing that would make him do that. But . . . how does he know where she is?"

"I . . . I don't think he does, ma'am," Korcler said. "He told me he couldn't tell me where he was going because he didn't know."

"It has to be something to do with Tarolt." Royalt frowned.

"That's it," Korcler said.

"What do you mean, young fellow?" asked Royalt.

"Well . . . he didn't come back. Even the next morning. So I went and found Majer Feran and told him. Alucius left him a note. I don't know what it said. The majer said it was Guard business, but then he sort of smiled, and asked me if the colonel had mentioned the name Tarolt. I told him he hadn't and asked who that was. He said he was a trader, and the only one of the old traders left after Halanat's death. Maybe I should have asked more, but that was all he said."

"He said Halanat was dead?"

"Yes, sir. Clear as could be."

"So Alucius thinks Tarolt had something to do with this," mused Royalt. "But he's vanished, too."

"Yes, sir."

"He's alive."

"He said Wendra was alive and healthy. He said whatever it was happened in the morning, but he didn't know what it was."

"He didn't tell you where he was going?"

"No, sir."

"This won't do Alucius much good as colonel," said Lucenda.

"The majer said that everyone knew sometimes the colonel went off and did things for the Lord-Protector, and he'd suggest that was what happened." Korcler took another swallow of the cider.

"Can't purchase friends like that," offered Royalt. "Feran's putting his head on the block and hoping no one's nearby with an axe."

"I'm sorry, sir," Korcler said. "Didn't know as I'd be . . . causing trouble. I just know . . . he'd want to know about Wendra. He would."

Both Lucenda and Royalt nodded.

132

Alucius woke with the first light slanting through the small third-floor window of the Red House. He yawned and rolled over carefully, then swung himself into a sitting position on the edge of the bed. Sleep and food had definitely helped. His eyes no longer burned, and while he was still sore in places, he was better than he had been.

He still had no idea where Wendra was, or how to proceed, and he certainly had no idea exactly how to deal with the ifrits . . . or how he could even get back to Dekhron safely. Whatever he did, or could do, he would need to eat before he set out, and he would also need some small items, if they weren't too expensive—a water bottle that he could hook to his belt and some travel food. He knew he could not get ammunition for the heavy Guard rifle—not in Dereka. That had been a problem when he and the Northern Guard had been in Deforya before.

After dumping the water in the basin out the window and

refilling it with what remained in the pitcher, he washed up. Then, as he was dressing, he checked his wallet. While he had added coins after getting paid the day before, he hadn't planned on traveling all across Corus. Still . . . he had two golds, six silvers, and five coppers left—more than enough for what he needed in the way of food and lodging and some modest supplies . . . for a short time.

Like it or not, he was going to have to try to become more proficient in using the Tables or portals, but if he started in Dereka, at least he'd have somewhere he could come back to without having to confront an ifrit. At least, that was what he hoped, but he certainly wasn't certain, not after discovering the power of a full ifrit in confronting Tarolt.

The sky outside his small window was a grayish silver green when he unbarred and unlocked the door. He left the rifle concealed and locked the room behind him.

Breakfast in the public room consisted of egg toast, so brown it was almost burned, with a berry syrup, two thick slices of tough ham, and a mug of ale. It cost him another four coppers, but he wasn't about to attempt any explorations on an empty stomach.

More than a glass later, he left the inn and began to walk southward along the main boulevard. The morning was cool, not quite chill, with but a light wind blowing out of the north. While the west side of the street was not empty, there were far fewer vendors than there would be later in the day. Most of those seeking to do business with the vendors were older women. Several glanced at him and the heavy rifle he carried, but most paid him little attention.

A block southward, he found a small store, not quite a chandlery, but one with provisions and even a belt water bottle. He spent more than a silver for hard cheese, travel bread, dried fruit and nuts, and the water bottle. He slipped the food into various pockets in his jacket. Then, after leaving the store, he had to retrace his steps to fill the bottle at the public fountain.

He had just left the fountain when a company of lancers

trotted by, heading southward toward the Lancer Prime Base beyond the complex that had served as the palace of the Landarch. Alucius did not recognize the captain and overcaptain leading the column. The uniforms of the rankers at the end of the column were considerably newer than those of the riders leading the column, and several of the trailing riders glanced around them, as if they had not seen Dereka before.

Alucius did not cross the boulevard until he was opposite the ancient gold eternastone building that held the portal. As he walked swiftly across the wide street, he glanced around. His Talent showed no sign of any purpleness or any ifrits. He had not noticed anything of that nature since he had arrived in Dereka. Nor had he felt them when he had been an overcaptain fighting the nomads—except, of course, in his dreams.

Still, several of the vendors had been watching him, and he did not want to have anyone note his return to the structure. So he walked past and then into an alleyway that looked deserted. There, he concentrated on the illusion that he was but a vagrant breeze, occasionally stirring up dust.

". . . see that?"

At the words, Alucius stiffened, but held the Talent-illusion.

"See what?"

"Herder type . . . dark jacket . . . just went away . . ."

"Just seeing things."

"Tell you, he was there. Big gray-haired fellow. Big as life . . ."

Alucius smiled to himself as he eased out of the alleyway and made his way back into the abandoned building, a structure that had to date back to the first ifrit occupation of Corus. He moved quietly, trying to keep his steps from echoing in the abandoned and cavernous interior.

He paused as he heard steps on the stone floor. He flattened himself against the wall of the corridor that led toward the chamber above the portal area, waiting and listening. Two lancer officers walked down the corridor to-

ward Alucius, followed by two rankers. Alucius remained
motionless, hoping that his illusion would prove enough.

". . . you make of it?" asked the captain.

". . . strange . . . boot prints there . . . don't see how they
got there," replied the undercaptain, speaking as he
walked past Alucius without even looking in the colonel's
direction.

". . . you think it was a demon?"

". . . more likely a drunken ranker. Came down there,
fell asleep, dust settled, and when he woke, he left tracks
going out."

Alucius nodded to himself. It was a perfectly good explanation, and one he hoped the two officers reported. He
did not move until the four men reached the end of the corridor and took the short flight of steps that led to the north
exit from the building.

Then he made his made back to the inside stone stairway
that led down to the former Table chamber, moving quietly
and stopping to listen along the way. He neither heard nor
sensed anyone. The chamber was empty, but the dust on
the stone floor bore many boot tracks.

Alucius released his own illusion and looked around the
dimly lit chamber, studying it more carefully than he had
when he had first arrived there the afternoon before. The
walls were all of stone. There once might have been wooden
paneling or more ornate stone facings; but if so, no trace remained. Nor was there any sign of ceiling decoration.

His eyes dropped to the oblong space in the middle of
the chamber floor. Concentrating, and using his Talent, he
could sense a vague purpleness, as well as a crimson gold
circle, in the center of the oblong carved into the stone itself. The stone that comprised the base of the oblong was
darker, and Alucius could sense that it was part of something larger, but not something created by the ifrits, rather
more like a lifeweb, except it was far more vague to his
Talent, almost like the hint of a mist.

Did the world itself have lifethreads—lines that ran
through rock and stone beneath the surface of the earth? It

could be possible . . . He shook his head. The more he learned, the more he found out that he didn't know.

Still . . . the ifrits seemed to follow patterns, and he might be able to discover more if he could use what he knew.

Did the chamber have a secret door, like the one built in Salaan? He walked to the part of the stone wall closest to him. He let his hand range over it, then tapped it, first with his fingers, then with the rifle butt. It sounded solid, and from what he could tell from his Talent, it felt solid as well. He examined the entire wall, but all of it felt the same.

Then, recalling the use of light-torch brackets in the palace of the Matrial, he began to look for places where there might have been brackets. Once he looked, the narrow holes drilled into the stone were obvious. There had been four such brackets, two on each of the side walls, each head high. Alucius looked at each closely. When he reached the third set of bracket holes, he smiled, but he checked the fourth set as well before returning to the third.

Three of the brackets had been anchored by two holes drilled into the stone. The third set had four holes—the two standard anchors, and then two more in the middle, one above the other. Whatever cables had been used had long since vanished, but Alucius had a good idea that there was a door or something like it on one side or the other of the vanished four-hole bracket.

He studied the two center holes, then began to create a Talent-probe—the kind he hadn't tried or used since he'd been confined in the hidden city of the soarers. He began by visualizing a thin golden probe, slipping it into the uppermost of the center holes in the wall. He had to concentrate more, using the probe to feel blindly what lay beyond the stone. There were silvery metal levers, and weights. He wrapped his probe around what felt like a lever and tried to pull it down. The probe slipped off the lever—if that was what it happened to be—as though the metal was heavily oiled. Alucius focused his probe with rougher edges, and greater strength, and sticky as well, almost as if with glue covered with sand. That allowed him to pull down on the lever, but nothing happened. He tried to push, but that didn't work either.

Sweat began to form on Alucius's forehead as he tried combination after combination of pulling on one lever, then another. A quarter glass passed, and then half a glass, and his entire body was shaking when, abruptly, there was a snap, a low grinding, and a section of the wall slid sideways, revealing a passageway beyond—one lit dimly by a pair of ancient light-torches.

Alucius inspected the area on the far side of the passageway, noting the very simple lever. He shook his head. He wasn't very good at visualizing what he'd never seen. Taking his rifle, he stepped into the passageway. He could sense no one in the passageway beyond. After a moment, he eased the lever forward. The stone wall slid back into place, more smoothly and with much less noise than it had made in opening.

He took a deep breath and walked along the narrow stone passage, seemingly cut from the stone itself. After a good five yards, it ended in another chamber—one that looked to be precisely five yards square. Unlike the other chambers or Table chambers, this room had not been touched.

There was a table desk in one corner and an odd settee before it, beside which was a chair with longer legs than most. Against the wall to the left was a wide chest of drawers, similar to the one in the buried Table chamber where Tarolt had hurled Alucius. The light-torches above the table desk shed an even, if faint, glow across the chamber. In a niche carved head high from the wall behind the table desk was a chest or casket of metallic silver and black, although the silver held a purplish sheen. The casket was slightly over a yard in length, and a third of a yard in height and in depth. A key with a triangular head remained in the lock of the casket, although the lid was closed.

A set of clothes lay on the floor, just inside the chamber, a green tunic trimmed in brilliant purple, with matching trousers and black boots. The garments had no dust upon them, and the fabric had a silvery sheen. They were laid out as if someone had been lying down and vanished, leaving the clothing behind. Alucius recalled what had happened in the chamber beneath the Matrial's palace. Had the ifrit been trapped or killed by one of the ancient soarers? Or just been trapped when the soarers had disrupted the ifrits' lines of power?

There was a strange gleam to the garments, and he studied them with his Talent. Then . . . he swallowed. Like the eternastone of the roads and the remaining ifrit buildings, like the Tables, and like the green towers, the garments bore an infusion of lifeforce. The squandering of lifeforce on preserving mere clothing . . . the taking of something that held a whole world together—just for clothing that would endure for eons?

Alucius looked farther into the chamber. The light-torch bracket in the far left corner had been twisted down, and on the polished graystone floor below lay the metal fittings of a light-torch, but without the crystal. Beside the broken light-torch lay a silvery jacket, a pistol-like device, and a pair of boots on their sides.

Alucius nodded. The pistol-like device was like the one the engineer had used, but he could sense with his Talent that its power had long since dissipated. He took a deep breath and hurried back out of the chamber to the hidden door. He pulled the lever down. After a moment, and another grinding lurch, the door opened.

This time, when he returned to the furnished chamber, he left the stone doorway open. He thought he'd rather deal with live intruders than a mechanism that might jam and might well have already trapped two ifrits.

He went to the metallic casket in the wall niche first. As he looked at it, he realized that the casket was not set on the ledge, but actually embedded several spans into the stone so that it could not have been moved without breaking the slab into which it was set. The key had been left in the open position. Alucius lifted the lid. The casket was empty. Inside was a pair of heavy metal brackets, as if the casket had once held something. A purple crystal was set at each end of the casket, and from the position of the brackets, it appeared as if whatever had rested inside the casket had once rested firmly against each crystal. A silvery bar ran from the base of each crystal down through the bottom of the casket and into the stone.

For a time, Alucius studied the casket, but he could not determine what the missing object might have been. From the casket, he turned to the chest set against the wall, leaving the single drawer in the table desk for later.

He opened the top right-hand drawer of the chest. Inside were two greenish crystals. Even as he watched, both disintegrated. What remained in the drawer was a stack of sheets of the same eternal parchment. Alucius picked up the first one. The writing was regular, each symbol precisely the same size as the next—except none of them was familiar. He glanced through the other sheets. All were covered in symbols, without any drawings. After a moment, he slipped them back into the drawer.

The left-hand drawer contained a few odd-shaped coins, including several golds of a type Alucius had never seen, a pair of shears, and a thin coil of wire. He slipped the golds into his wallet and opened the double-width drawer below. Inside was a long shimmering garment of some sort, all golden silver, with large symbols down the front, symbols that Alucius had never seen, but which he suspected matched some of those on the sheets of eternal parchment.

Bending down, Alucius opened the lowermost drawer. It seemed to be empty. Then, in one corner in the back, he saw what looked to be another sheet of parchment, folded over twice. He touched it gingerly, but the substance remained firm to his touch. Slowly, he eased it out of the drawer.

The sheet was neither parchment nor cloth, but something akin to both, flexible and smooth. After a moment, he unfolded it. What he held appeared to be a map of some sort, which could have been drawn recently, with bright colors and clear dark lines. He studied it quickly, noting that it was clearly a map of Corus, although there were representations of parts of the continent that did not match what he knew. The map must have been made a long, long time ago, before the Cataclysm that had changed the world. He glanced back over his shoulder and slipped it inside his jacket and tunic.

He turned back to the table desk and opened the single wide drawer. Inside, he found little enough—a miniature knife with a purpleness to it that prompted him to leave it without touching it, an oblong block of jade with an enameled and unfamiliar seal upon it, and some sort of stylus in the form of a leafy branch. There were also a number of sheets of the eternal parchment, all blank.

Alucius closed the drawer and walked toward the broken light-torch bracket. Avoiding the boots and pistol on the floor and standing beside the broken light-torch bracket, he created another Talent-probe.

This time, as much as he tried, he could do nothing to open what he knew to be another hidden door. He could find no levers, nothing beyond the stone except more stone. Yet . . . once there had been. Finally, with sweat streaming down his forehead, he turned and studied the chamber again.

There were no books, nothing to provide knowledge, except the map inside his tunic and the sheets of eternal parchment with unreadable symbols—too many sheets to carry with him. And then there was the mysterious metal casket—with nothing inside it.

He turned and made his way back along the narrow stone passageway. He stopped under one of the light-torches just a yard inside the open stone door.

There he took out the map he had found and unfolded it. Despite having been folded for longer than he could imagine, once the map—and it was clearly a map—was flat in his hands, there were no creases or wrinkles. Before Alucius was a detailed depiction of Corus. Although he could not read the script that labeled the cities, all the eternastone highways that he knew were laid out, as well as some that he had never seen or heard of.

There were keys to the map—that he felt. One that leapt

out at him was the placement of tiny green octagons. Each octagon had to be the location of a Table—or where a Table had once been. There were octagons in Tempre and where Elcien had once stood and more than half a score across Corus. Each octagon was framed by a colored border edged in purple. Alucius looked more closely. The one in Tempre was blue edged in purple. There was another octagon of purple-bordered silver at Prosp in Lustrea. Had that been where he had fought the ifrit-engineer?

So where was he now? He studied one octagon after another until he found the one with the purple-edged, crimson gold border—and it was Dereka, by its location, although he could not read the symbols beside the city. He kept looking, finding a purple-edged, black-bordered green octagon far to the northwest, just to the west and south of what he knew as the Black Cliffs of Despair. He nodded. The icy and preserved structure had been in Blackstear.

From what he recalled of the sullen crimson Table where he had been sent, that buried Table chamber had to have been the one in Soupat.

For a time, his eyes refused to focus on the map as the thoughts of an entire web of Tables connecting all Corus flashed through his mind. Yet . . . the Tables were not laid out for anything except the travel of a few individuals. Why?

Not that many people—or ifrits—could have had the ability to travel the Tables . . . could they? From what Alucius had learned from the soarer, it was unlikely that anyone who was not an ifrit had been able to use the Tables when they had first been set up. The eternastone highways were what most people had had to use to get from place to place. That also suggested that not that many ifrits had the ability, and that all Corus had been ruled by a comparative handful of ifrits.

Maybe . . . just maybe . . . there was some hope.

He frowned. Was that why Wendra was missing? Because the ifrits were few in number, few enough that he and Wendra might make a difference? But if that were the case, why hadn't Tarolt or Halanat known about Wendra?

He looked at the map before him once more, forcing himself to go over each green octagon, checking the colors of each and trying to visualize what he knew. Originally, according to the map, there had been a Table in Elcien and Ludar, but not in Southgate, and one in Alustre. And in the time of the Duarchy, there had not been a Table in Salaan or anywhere in the Iron Valleys—nor anywhere near the Aerlal Plateau.

After studying the map for a time, he carefully folded it and slipped it back inside his undertunic. His next trip would be somewhere that was hopefully closer to home and less dangerous, but someplace where he hoped he could find out more, either about the ifrits or how to discover where Wendra had gone. The more he thought about it, the less it seemed likely that the ifrits had Wendra—unless there happened to be more than one group of ifrits. But . . . he had to do something . . .

At that thought, he frowned, recalling his grandfather's advice about not acting until he knew enough to do so. But that had been in battle—not when the love of his life was threatened.

He took a long swallow from the water bottle before slipping through the open stone doorway and back into the Table chamber. Turning back, he extended a Talent-probe to the activating lever of the door and pushed it. The door slid back into place, leaving no sign of a second exit from the chamber. Rifle in hand, Alucius stepped down into the depression that had once held a Table, hoping that he could somehow relink to the shadowy web that connected both Tables and portals.

He stood in the circle that he could sense only with his Talent, and ever so faintly even with that, trying to reach to the darkness beyond and beneath. Nothing happened. He was still standing in the oblong space in the stone floor that had once held a Table.

Oblong? For some reason that thought bothered him. He blotted his forehead. Then he realized that if he included the depth into the stone, the Table would have been a cube. All the Tables had to be cubes. Why?

With a deep breath he pushed that thought away, again concentrating, this time not on the idea of purple black conduits running from Table to Table, but a vaguer, more shadowy web on which the conduits seemed to have been imposed.

The stone beneath his boots dissolved, and he was in blackness, a chill blackness, but one that was green-tinged, not purple-tinged. Instead, he could sense that he was somehow resting beside/below the ifrit conduit, and that the conduit wound around the web, much as an ifrit lifethread wound around the lifethread of a person when the person was ifrit-possessed.

Where did he wish to go? To an amber portal, he had already decided, the one that seemed to match with the location of Hyalt. That way, if he could not travel back, at least he'd be in Lanachrona and could make his way to Tempre, and the Lord-Protector.

Travel through the hazy green black darkness seemed to take less effort, and within moments, or so it seemed, although he doubted time was the way he felt it, he hovered underneath an amber portal, one tinged with a faint and distant purple, much as was the portal at Dereka. Did he want to emerge?

For a moment, he could also feel other portals, in seemingly opposite directions, one that was pink-tinged purple, and another, barely sensed, that was blue and maroon.

Alucius decided and concentrated on reaching out of the hazy darkness, to bring himself back into the world of light through the amber.

Silver and amber light shattered away from him.

133

The Hidden City, Corus

Wendra stood in the second tower room, the one adjoining her chamber, looking down at the mirrored square set into the amber floor. In her carrypack, Alendra squirmed. Beside her hovered the soarer.

You must learn to travel the ley lines of the world. Use your Talent. Study the portal.

"Is this like a Table? I thought Tables had to be set into the ground. Is it safe to carry Alendra?"

It is safe for the child now, but only for two seasons or perhaps three. Once she has a firmer sense of who she is, then such travel will not be safe for her.

"Why does that matter?"

Travel is by force of will and self. The Tables are a framework imposed upon the lifethreads of the world itself. We have woven those lifethreads into the buildings of our cities. We once could grow such threads. The ifrits cannot. They can only suck them dry. You could travel from Table to Table now—the few that the ifrits have constructed or re-built. They would soon catch you, because you have not learned enough. That is another reason why we have separated the portals of the Plateau from the ley lines of the world. That way you cannot travel to where you could be taken . . . not until you are ready.

"Why do you want—"

Study the portal. My time and yours is short. I will guide you to another portal in the other city.

"There are two hidden cities?"

Two are but those left. Use your Talent and study . . . I will return. The soarer vanished, leaving Wendra looking down at the mirror-portal set in the amberstone.

134

Once more, Alucius stood in a chamber that had once held a Table. Now the oblong depression was half filled with sand. Through the dimness, he could barely see the smooth stone walls of the room. He stepped out of the depression, almost falling as his left boot skidded on the loose sand that covered the still-polished stone floor.

As with the Table chamber in Dereka, there were no brackets for light-torches, no windows, no furnishings, and no sign of the original function of the chamber except the space cut into the stone that had once held a Table. There was also no obvious way out.

Alucius paused. How could he see if there were no sources of light? From what he could tell, the walls radiated just the faintest hint of light. Or something did. He began to examine the walls, looking for the pattern of holes that might have once held a light-torch bracket. He covered slightly more than half the chamber when he found the telltale pattern.

As hard as he tried, though, he could find nothing to grasp with his Talent, no hidden levers, nothing.

His face coated in sweat, he stopped trying to use his Talent-probes and took a deep breath, leaning back against the smooth stone wall.

"Oh . . ." He stumbled and almost fell as the stone behind him shifted, sliding sideways for half a yard before grinding to a halt. His rifle butt *clunk*ed against the hard rock.

Alucius turned and tried to move the stone door wider. It did not budge. He could not close it either, although his efforts in that direction were not quite so vigorous. There was more of the indirect light in the passage beyond the door, and he squeezed through the opening and into the stone passage beyond, a corridor two yards wide, perhaps two and a half high, walled in redstone. Less than ten yards from where he entered the passage, it ended—or branched into two passages, one heading to the right and one to the left.

Alucius paused, looking first to the left, then to the right. To the right . . . he thought he could sense something, but the left seemed empty. He turned left. Only five yards farther, the corridor ended at what looked to be a wooden door. There was no lever, just a handle. Alucius pulled on the handle and the door opened toward him, swinging out on hinges that squeaked and grated.

His mouth opened, because the other side of the door appeared to be a stone wall, and blocking the opening was a waist-high bench. The room beyond was but three yards in width, and was in fact the prophet's now-empty strong room outside of Hyalt. For a moment, Alucius just stood there, amazed that he had once been so close and not even sensed the tunnel behind. He finally stepped back and closed the door, although he had to lean his weight against the edge, and his feet slipped on the gritty surface of the stone.

He retraced his steps back to the point where the corridor had branched and followed the other branch. The sound of the grit underfoot echoed in the stone-walled corridor, which began to curve after about fifteen yards. The way brightened as he walked the next few yards, and he brought up the rifle, but the source of light was not an exit but a pair of ancient light-torches mounted in antique brackets at head level on both sides of the corridor.

With his Talent, he could sense an end to the corridor at another doorway, and within five yards, he reached another of the handled doors. Gingerly, his rifle ready, although he sensed no one beyond the door, he tugged. It opened easily onto an empty room, four yards wide and three deep, also lit by a pair of ancient light-torches. Opposite the door was an open archway, and beyond it was a wall. Alucius left the door—also stone-faced on the outside—ajar and stepped into the chamber.

He eased toward the archway, its edges finished with

maroon ceramic tiles. At the archway itself, he stopped, studying what lay beyond—a screen wall, no more than three yards high and three wide. Beyond that, his Talent revealed a soaring cavern or chamber, with a stone dais on the opposite side of the screen wall, a dais raised a good two yards above the floor of the cavern.

There was no one on the dais, and no one near it in the cavern, but he thought there might be someone at the far end of the chamber. He could not tell for sure, because there was something about the chamber, almost as if it reflected his Talent back at him.

Rifle in hand, he stepped around the screen wall onto the dais, a stone platform really, five yards on a side. The dimness vanished as a line of light-torches on the screen wall flared into full illumination.

He blinked at the sudden comparative brightness that threw the cavernous area before him into darkness.

"Oh . . ." The moaning sound echoed from more than a score of yards before him, in the darkness well away from the platform.

"One of the great ones . . ."

"Do you bring word of the True Duarchy?"

"We have waited, and we have been faithful . . ."

Alucius immediately called up the illusion of nothingness, of little more than a breeze, and immediately, the cavern amphitheater was filled with the sound of roaring wind. He staggered at the intensity of the sound, before realizing that the roaring was all within his head and that something in the design of the place amplified Talent.

What could he say? What could he do?

He concentrated on creating an image . . . not of an ifrit . . . but of a man, but an image far larger than life, and one that shimmered in green and gold.

"Ohh . . ." The moaning from the worshippers in the back, for that was what they must have been, Alucius concluded, rose, then died away.

He spoke, as carefully as he could, in such unexpected circumstances. "Man must live in the world as it is . . . and tend it with care. The Duarches plundered and pillaged. Do not ask for a return to the Duarchy and those who ravaged Corus! Do not ask for slavery and death."

"The lamaial! It is the lamaial!"

"Lost . . . we are lost! All is lost!"

Alucius sensed the hostility and the lifting of rifles.

He dropped the image of the green and gold figure, and replaced it with . . . nothing . . . an image of nothingness, even as he dashed back through the archway.

A single rifle shot echoed through the chamber behind him.

Back in the chamber behind the screen wall, he stepped through the door he had left ajar, closing it behind him. He retreated back down the stone corridor, around the curves, and back to the chamber that had once held a Table.

He had no idea whether the remaining worshippers knew about the hidden doorway or the passage beyond or whether they would even try to follow, but he could sense that Wendra was nowhere near the portal, and there was little sense in remaining in Hyalt in the ruins of what had been the temple of the prophet—or prophets. He had to wonder why he had not discovered the concealed cavern amphitheater and decided that the Talent-reflective construction might have shielded it. He paused, realizing that also might explain why he had been unable to sense the hidden doors in the Table chambers. Perhaps they had been Talent-shielded.

He stepped down into the depression where once the Table had been. He did not concentrate on the Table, but upon the green-tinged blackness below the faded amber.

He dropped into that chill greenish darkness, but that darkness, chill as it was, did not seem quite so paralyzing as when he had used the Tables. But it was still cold, and he searched for a direction, for the faded crimson gold. As he felt himself moving away from the amber of Hyalt, once more he sensed the blue and maroon portal, still distant, and the closer pinkish purple, noting its familiarity even as he dismissed it.

The crimson-gold-silver shattered away from him . . .

. . . and he stood back in the Table chamber in Dereka.

Alucius surveyed the chamber, his rifle ready, his Talent probing up the stairwell; but there was no one nearby, and he sat down. He took several deep breaths, letting his feet rest on the bottom of the depression that had once held a Table, millennia before. He set the rifle down carefully on a clear patch of stone. Only then did he take a long drink from the water bottle before recorking it and replacing it in its belt holder.

Had he been foolish to try to influence the true believers? He laughed softly, almost hoarsely. He'd known better. He just hadn't thought when he'd been confronted so suddenly with the unexpected.

Also, he'd been almost stunned by the Talent-amplification of the cavern amphitheater. But had it really been amplification? Alucius frowned. As he considered what he had experienced, it had not so much been the amplification of Talent as the total elimination of all other lifeforces, and the comparative feeling of Talent-amplification. Was that so that the ifrits could command greater control—or so that those who were not true ifrits could create the impression of such control?

He wondered if he would ever know.

Every time he ventured into using his Talent, he discovered something else he didn't know. He supposed that was true of life, as well, but with Talent, the dangers could be so much greater.

Just before he had broken through the barrier, and again as he was leaving Hyalt, Alucius had noted the portal of pink-tinged purple, and he had not recalled such a Table octagon on the ifrit map. It was a portal, not a Table. Of that, he had been certain.

Pink . . . and purple . . . was that the Regent of the Matrial?

He scarcely wanted to go there. Where else could he go? He took out the ifrit map of Corus and scanned it, once, twice. His memory had been correct. There had been no pink purple Table, but there had been a maroon and blue Table—in Dulka. So what had created the pink and purple portal if there had been no Table? Something that the Matrial had discovered?

He shook his head. He still needed to find Wendra, and if he could not find her near the abandoned portals, he would have to try the Tables in places where he had not yet been. And . . . if he could not find her, he might have to risk the Table in Salaan in order to return to Dekhron.

For the moment, he pushed that thought away. He had to find Wendra . . . as soon as he had a few moments of rest.

135

As he sat on the stone floor in the former Table chamber in Dereka, Alucius frowned. From what he could tell, he'd been gone three days, and that wasn't good. He had yet to find any sign of Wendra, and he had no quick way to return to Dekhron—except by facing at least two ifrits in Salaan. While they might not always be right at the Table, the only way out was through the area where they seemed to meet and work. Then, too, with the way the one had appeared, he had to consider that they might have a Talent-based warning system. Add to that the fact that he was the commander of the Northern Guard, and he'd effectively deserted, even if he hadn't meant to, and he hadn't solved the ifrit problem. Nor had he found Wendra.

His note to Feran might buy some time, especially since Feran knew the problems created by the traders, but he had to find some answers or some way back quickly—for more than one reason. If Wendra were in danger, the longer she was held, the more likely the ifrits might be able to possess her—or kill her if they could not. Yet . . . he really didn't know whether they even had his wife. Could the soarers have taken her? Only the ifrits or the soarers seemed to be able to travel from point to point without leaving traces. But . . . even if they could, why would the soarers take Wendra? And Alendra? Everything that they had done in the past had protected Alucius. Were they trying to protect her as well? From what? The efforts of the ifrits?

He had no idea exactly what the ifrits were doing, beyond the general description provided by the soarers about the ifrits' domination and eventual destruction of Corus. Had more ifrits arrived from their world? If so, what could he do, especially since the soarers seemed to have cut themselves off from the travel tubes of the ifrits and even from the deeper lines of travel that Alucius had discovered?

He took a deep breath. He was rested, and there were only two portals left that he had not explored—the one in Dulka, and the one that reminded him of the Matrial. What else could he do but explore each, as quickly as possible? If he found nothing . . . then what?

Did he try to return to the Table in Salaan, rifle loaded and cartridge belt filled with lifeforce-filled shells?

He didn't see any alternative. But first . . . the last two portals. Maybe they would reveal something that he didn't know. Each time he tried, he could also see if he could sense a soarer portal.

Alucius stepped into the Table depression, rifle again in hand, taking several deep breaths.

Once more, he sank through the floor and into the deeper and more greenish black misty darkness underlying the purpled blackness of the ifrit transport tubes. The chill, while intense, was not nearly so wearing, and he tried to concentrate on the portal that was blue and maroon, and avoid the purple and pink one until later.

Alucius focused his mind on lifting himself out of the misty blackness, out of the chill and back into the world of light through the blue and maroon. Once more, there was a barrier, one of blued silver. He formed himself into a spearhead of being . . .

*Silver, blue, and maroon mixed in a swirl of chill slashes
that shattered away from him in icy shards.*

The chamber in which he found himself was empty, and
he stood in the oblong depression that had characterized all
chambers that had once held an ifrit Table. For a moment,
Alucius gripped his rifle even more tightly as he saw the
ifrit figures standing on the stone floor around the Table
depression. He relaxed slightly as he realized that they
were statues, but statues such as he had never seen.

The larger-than-life-sized figures were carved of white
marble. All thirteen figures had hair painted black and
wore clothing of the type that the Tarolt-ifrit had worn,
brilliant green and deep purple. Likewise, the sculpted
boots had been painted black. The facial features were similar to those of the ifrit on the frieze in Southgate or those
depicted in the ancient wall paintings he had seen years before in the hidden room in Dereka.

There were six figures on each of the longer sides of
the chamber and a single figure at one end. The single figure was slightly larger than the others, close to three
yards in height, and held a silver scepter topped with glittering blue stones arranged so that the top of the scepter
resembled a blue flame. The facets of the gems reflected
the illumination from ancient light-torches, more than a
dozen.

Alucius immediately used his Talent to scan the chamber, but he was the only living being within it, although he
could sense others farther away. He stepped out of the
Table depression and studied the chamber more carefully.

The light-torches were different. In fact, no one bracket
was the same as any other. Nor were the shapes of the
lights. Likewise, the clothes on the statues, while superfi-
cially identical, varied in fabric and weave, and even in the
more subtle shadings, so that every shade of green and purple varied slightly from every other.

The same was true of the ifrit statues. All twelve of
those along the sides of the chamber were roughly a head
taller than Alucius when he stood beside them, but their

heights varied slightly. Each statue had the left arm by its side, and the right raised as if in a stiff-armed and fingers-pointed salute to the taller figure at the end of the chamber, but none of the arms were quite at the exact same angle as any other. There was no way to tell if the differences were merely the attempt not to have identical statues or inaccurate copying.

Another sweep of the chamber with eyes and Talent revealed nothing besides the statues and the light-torches, and Alucius moved toward the stone door on the side of the chamber. This door was open and had been slid back, revealing a stone-walled corridor.

He could sense the green of Talent at the end of the stone passageway—but how far beyond he could not tell. There were also others in that chamber. But Talent? Could someone have brought Wendra?

He frowned. The Talent was greenish, but did not feel exactly the same. Yet . . . if she had been drugged or restrained . . . If it were not Wendra . . . the Talent was certainly not purple-tinged, not in the fashion of an ifrit.

After a moment, he took a deep breath and eased into the stone corridor that stretched a good ten yards toward what had to be a screen wall beyond the ending archway. The corridor held the odor of burned oil, and he looked up. The entire stone roof was covered in black, as if lamps and torches had traversed the passageway for years, if not centuries. The walls were bare stone, and the floor had been recently swept, although the center of the stone paving was lower than the edges, an indication that many feet had traveled the passage over the years.

As he neared the end of the passage, lighter from illumination beyond, he could see that, as in Hyalt, the archway at the end had edges lined in maroon ceramic tile, but the tiles looked older and the color had faded. Alucius could hear voices beyond the stone screen wall that blocked his view of the chamber beyond.

After a slight hesitation, he called up his illusion of nothingness, moving to the archway, but not beyond. He used his Talent to scan the space beyond the wall screen. As in Hyalt, there was a square platform five yards by five yards beyond the wall screen. Beyond the platform extended a large cavernlike amphitheater.

Unlike Hyalt, there were people on the platform. A man sat in a thronelike chair upon the dais, and on each side of him were two guards, armed with shortswords and rifles. The figure in the chair was not an ifrit, nor ifrit-possessed, but, from what Alucius could sense, all five were garbed in a fashion similar to the garments on the ifrit statues.

In the amphitheater itself were but a handful of people, or so it seemed.

The figure in the chair on the dais wore a black mask across his eyes, a mask with no slits for eyes. Was he blind? Or was the mask to show his ability to act without eyes.

"Silence!" commanded the blind man.

Instantly, the guards froze.

Sensing a faint Talent-probe, Alucius eased back into the stone passageway that led back toward the Table chamber.

"There is an intruder! In the sacred passage! Kill him!"

Alucius turned and ran for the Table chamber. He had to get out of the passageway before they started firing, because the bullets would likely ricochet everywhere, and if they fired quickly and often enough, one could easily hit him where he wore no nightsilk.

He scrambled into the Table depression, standing in the middle, trying to ignore both the statues and his pursuers. Concentrating, he tried to call up the sense of the portal, even as the sound of boots pounding down the narrow stone passageway grew louder and as shots flew out of the passageway toward him. He began to drop into the greenish black mistiness that lay beneath the purpled black of the ifrit tube.

A dull lancelike blow slammed into his shoulder, followed by a second and a third . . .

As he sank into the misty blackness, his whole side and upper body were a mixture of chill and burning pain. What was he doing? He had to think. What was it? Where was he

*trying to go? Back to Dereka . . . but it was so far . . . and
there were no green and gold portals of the soarers . . . and
he was getting so cold . . . so very cold . . . he struggled . . .
trying to orient himself in the darkness . . .*

136

The Hidden City, Corus

Wendra stepped back from the mirror-
portal. Agony and chill flowed from the black crystal on
her finger. She looked at it, although she did not need to.
Within the carrypack, Alendra whimpered, as if in pain.

Wendra's eyes flicked to the soarer. "Alucius needs me.
He needs me now!"

You have not learned enough.

"He's hurt and somewhere in a tube or a ley line. I can
feel it. I'll help him back. You can teach me more then. Un-
block your portals. *Please.*"

The soarer offered a fatalistic sense of a shrug. *It is dangerous. If you fail, then all you know and love may be lost.*

"It doesn't matter! Without both of us, everything is
lost." Wendra squared her shoulders. "Are you going to offer me some guidance?"

*You must use your thoughts to guide you, and to seek not
the places marked with arrows, but those less obvious,
those with hidden circles. He is near the circle that is . . .
blue and maroon . . . as you would see it.* The soarer
seemed to blur. *The portals are unblocked, but you must
hasten.*

Without speaking, Wendra adjusted Alendra in the carrypack and stepped onto the mirrored surface. She began to
drop into the misty black greenness.

Behind her, the soarer sank to the floor, wings drooping,
its gold and green iridescence fading away.

137

Alucius tried to concentrate . . . his thoughts questing for the hidden crimson gold portal, but all he could sense was the blue arrow and the dark green one, the two where the ifrits waited . . . and he knew . . . injured as he was, he would have little chance.

Where was the crimson gold? He would have blinked if he could, but he sensed something, something green and gold . . . so distant . . . and seemingly receding from him. He struggled toward the green and gold, pressing, but he felt as though he made no progress, and all the time, greater and greater chill pressed in around him.

Suddenly, a line of warmth touched him . . . and a gentle pressure . . .

Was it a soarer? Had the green and gold been a portal opening?

He could sense a presence, urging him, pressing him, guiding him, even somehow lending him strength as he struggled toward the green and gold portal that no longer receded. Still, the journey seemed endless.

Then . . . the green and gold shattered into silver shards . . .

Alucius tottered on shaky legs. He could feel dampness running down the side of his face, and there was an iron coppery taste in his mouth. Around him was amber, but he could not see it. He could only feel it, yet everything was amber.

"You're hurt," a voice said.

He knew he should have recognized the voice, but before he could put a name to the speaker, his legs trembled and gave way. A golden redness swept across him, and everything began to spin, swirling around him, faster and faster.

Deep darkness washed over him, a darkness filled with

fire, and purpled visions, and ifrits who stood back and laughed, and ifrit palaces whose walls contracted upon him.

Alucius woke. His eyes opened, and . . . he could see nothing. Nothing at all. There was no amber, no red, no green, just a solid black that revealed nothing. He shuddered. Where was he? What had happened? Why couldn't he see?

"You'll be all right, dearest. Just try to relax."

"Wendra?"

"I'm here." A warm hand stroked his forehead.

"How did you . . . ? Where are we?" The questions tumbled out of his mouth.

"In the hidden city. Or one of them. The soarers took me . . . and Alendra. She's fine. Except she was upset when you got hurt the last time."

"Where is she?"

"She's here. She's finally sleeping," Wendra's voice was gentle.

"I can't see. I can't see anything at all. Are you all right?"

"I'm fine. We're both fine. You'll be all right before long. The soarers said that this sometimes happens when someone is . . . injured and travels the ley lines."

Alucius lay silent for a moment. He wiggled his fingers, and could feel them move against his legs. His toes worked. "Can I sit up?"

"You could," she replied. "You might get dizzy. You've had a concussion. Your head hit something, or something hit your head."

"Stone . . . or bullets. Could be both." He took a slow breath. "I heard you had disappeared . . . I was looking everywhere." Alucius paused. "We're really in the hidden city?"

"There are two of them. I've seen them both. We're in the one where you were. I think we're probably in the same chamber."

"How did you get here?" He stopped. She'd told him. He was having trouble holding on to his thoughts. "Why did the soarers bring you here?" He found himself shivering.

"To teach me more . . . to get your attention."

"I kept trying to find you . . . once I heard. Korcler rode all the way from Iron Stem to tell me. I thought the ifrits had you. The ifrits . . . they're traders, or traitors, or the traders are ifrits . . ." The words seemed to tangle themselves in his mouth, but that could have been because his teeth were chattering and he was shivering violently.

Wendra pulled a cover of some sort up over his chest and shoulders. "You still need to rest. Alendra and I are right here. You don't have to look for us anymore. We're all together."

". . . all together . . ." Those were the last words he heard before he slipped back into the darkness.

138

Tempre, Lanachrona

As he sat in the chair across the low table from the love seat, the Lord-Protector lifted the wineglass and took a small sip. His eyes were directed at his consort, but not focused upon her, nor at the wall beyond her.

"Talryn?"

The Lord-Protector did not respond.

"Talryn." Alerya's voice was a great deal more firm. "You have not heard a word I said. Not one."

"Dear . . . you were talking about how strong young Talus has gotten, and how he managed to turn himself over in his crib."

"You didn't look like you were listening. What is it?"

"Oh . . . nothing . . ." Talryn shrugged.

"It's not nothing. Not when you look through me and around me. I could be in Soupat or Southgate, and you wouldn't notice that I wasn't here."

He shook his head, finally looking at Alerya with his

eyes truly focused upon her. "I'm sorry. There are so many things . . ."

"I know. Yet . . . who else can you tell?"

"This one is trivial. It bothers me. I cannot say why. You know the Table chamber? How I had the remnants of the Table smashed and the chamber sealed?"

"You told me about that." Alerya's words were cautious.

"The servants and the guards claim that they have heard noises there. I had the door unsealed, and there was nothing there."

"Mice or rats. What else could it be?"

"I worry that it is not merely rodents or thieves, not that there is anything left inside. The overcaptain had said that the Tables were a way of transport. He said that the Tables were dangerous."

"He was right, I'm certain. You were right to seal the chamber. What else can you do?"

"I don't know." Talryn paused. "I had the chamber resealed—even more firmly."

"Then, forget that one. You have too many other worries. You worry about everything."

"In my seat, wouldn't you? Waleryn was plotting with Enyll, and Enyll knew how to use the Table. Waleryn vanished into Lustrea seasons ago, and I've heard absolutely nothing. No messages, no reports from scouts or spies. The Regent of the Matrial is massing forces against the garrisons in the south, and Alyniat is uncertain whether he can hold Fola—even without facing the spear-throwers—"

"You didn't tell me that."

"I got the report this afternoon." Talryn sighed.

"Are you thinking about recalling the Northern Guard colonel?"

"If I but could. Why is it that there is only one of him? And a northerner to boot. I could use a score of him. But he is but one, and I cannot recall him. That would cause yet more damage. Weslyn disbanded two companies and pocketed the payroll, and promoted a half score of incompetent captains to cover things up. Colonel Alucius and Majer Feran are trying to rebuild the Northern Guard, and if I pull him out, then I'll have no forces in the north, and the Regent can pull all her lancers out of northern Madrien and use them against Fola and Dimor. It's almost as if someone paid Weslyn to gut the Northern Guard."

"Perhaps they did," suggested Alerya. "That would serve the Regent well."

"It has indeed." Talryn took another sip from the goblet. "It has indeed. I can but hope that the colonel acts well and decisively, and that Alyniat can hold the south . . ."

139

When Alucius woke again, Wendra was by his side . . . and he could see—her golden eyes flecked with green, her brown hair that held a depth of gold, and her wide mouth and generous lips. He couldn't help smiling.

"Are you feeling better?" She slipped onto the edge of the bed, easing the carrypack with Alendra slightly to the side.

"I don't think I could have felt much worse." Alucius slowly eased himself into a sitting position, swinging his feet onto the amberstone floor. The left side of his head still ached, but it was a dull pain, not the stabbing agony he recalled feeling when he had staggered into the tower room. He slipped his right arm around Wendra, holding her gently, trying to avoid disturbing the sleeping Alendra. "She's good, isn't she?"

"Mostly. Except when she's hungry." After a moment, Wendra asked, "How does your head feel?"

"You were the one in the darkness, guiding me, weren't you?"

"I tried. You were so heavy—I know it's not weight, but

that was the way it felt. It felt like I could only urge you to-ward the soarer portals."

"I could feel you. I wouldn't have made it without you," Alucius admitted.

"The soarer didn't want me to go. She said I hadn't learned enough."

"What have they taught you?"

"How to travel the ley lines . . ."

"Is that what they call the misty black lines under the purple black tubes of the ifrits?"

"Yes. I stayed away from the tubes when I went after you. The soarer said they were dangerous."

"I suppose they are," mused Alucius. "I knew that, but until the last few days, I didn't realize about the deeper ways." He looked directly at Wendra. "Why did they bring you here?"

"I told you when you . . . they said you might not re-member. They brought me here to keep me away from the ifrits, to teach me more, and to get your attention."

"Get my attention?"

"She said that you would not act in time against the ifrits. She's very upset. I can feel it." Wendra worried her lower lip. "She's acting like there's not much time left, al-most like a crotchety aunt."

In the carrypack, Alendra squirmed, then made a little sound.

Alucius smiled, but only for a moment. "Why are the soarers worried?"

"The ifrits are rebuilding the Tables. The barriers the old soarers erected have failed. The ifrits are trying to invade Corus once more. Their world is dying. They're close to having drained it of all its lifeforce, and they will come here and do the same."

"If they aren't stopped," Alucius said.

"If *we* don't stop them. The soarers no longer have the strength to hold them off."

Alucius wanted to ask why he and Wendra had to, but

there wasn't any point in asking the question. They were young and had lives in front of them, but they wouldn't be happy lives, not under the ifrits—if they had lives at all. But he did wonder why it had to fall on them, and the only answer was that there wasn't anyone else who had the ability to stop the ifrits—or that anyone else who had that ability hadn't been discovered by the soarers—and there wasn't even any assurance that he and Wendra could do what was necessary.

"Is that why they closed off their portals?" he asked.

"I think so." Her eyebrows lifted in inquiry. "You could sense that?"

"No, not exactly. I could sense that they weren't there. I was trying to make my way to all the portals where the ifrits weren't . . ."

"How did you know where you were?" asked Wendra. "How could you tell which places were Tables and which weren't?"

"I didn't at first," Alucius admitted. "That was how I got into trouble the first time. This time, I recalled where I'd been, but then I found the map." He leaned forward, avoiding his daughter, and kissed Wendra, warmly, perhaps too warmly.

She broke off the kiss. "A map? What kind of map?"

Alucius looked at his wife sheepishly, then slowly stood and walked to the pegs on the wall where his jacket and tunic and trousers hung. After fumbling through them, he withdrew the map. "I've had other things on my mind . . ."

"I've noticed," she said dryly.

"So have you."

Wendra flushed.

They both laughed.

Alucius extended the map to Wendra. "The green octagons show where the ifrits had Tables in the time of the Duarchy. At least, that's what they seem to be."

As she studied the map, Alucius looked at her, thankful

that she was well and safe. He couldn't help worrying about his absence from the Northern Guard, but dealing with the ifrits was of far greater concern—if he and Wendra could find a way. Or if the soarers could teach them.

140

Salaan, Lanachrona

Despite the heavy, fleece-lined, black jacket he wore, Tarolt shivered as he descended from the Table. He moved quickly from the Table chamber up the steps until he stood before the stove in the conference room.

Without speaking, the Recorder followed him, waiting. Finally, Trezun cleared his throat. "What did you find out?"

"What we suspected. There was an accident, and the seals were broached. *You* will clean up the mess in Blackstear and seal the room. That should not take you long, and we might need the Table. The chamber is too cold for regular use as it is now. How they can survive in such chill . . . but then, they are what they are."

"Yes, Tarolt. What of the herder-colonel?"

"He translated to Blackstear and then elsewhere. There were traces there, but he found another Table or portal."

"He must be able to use the portals, then. There is no record of his using any of the other Tables."

"That assumes all the Tables are functioning properly." Tarolt's voice was clipped, cold. "Is that in fact so?"

"The only older Tables are the ones in Soupat and Blackstear. You have inspected the Table in Blackstear. The one here and the ones in Prosp and Norda are new."

"Just five Tables. We need to step up the search for the scepters." Tarolt frowned. "We had best message Lasylt the latest about the herder- colonel. Why can they not understand that we need more support?"

Trezun remained silent for a time, before adding, "Waleryn has been working on the locators." He did not look directly at the fieldmaster.

"You don't sound like you have news I wish to hear."

"They are not quite what we thought."

"Little is," replied Tarolt. "Do they work?"

"They do, but not exactly as Waleryn had expected."

"Explain."

"They were designed to discover the scepters and their assemblies—together. Waleryn has not been able to refine the locations yet. It requires some triangulation. He can only pick up one signal. He thinks the other scepter may have been destroyed."

"They cannot be destroyed. Not here on Corus. One has been removed from its container. It could be anywhere. A map of where the old Tables were would help. We only have an incomplete list."

"But there is some good news," Trezun added.

Tarolt waited.

"With the locators and one of the scepters, the other can be located."

"That is good only if we can find the one. We must hope that the herder-colonel does not discover their importance. Or the ancient ones have not told him." Tarolt's face turned even more severe. "I detest having to rely upon hope . . . or upon the weaknesses or failures of others."

141

The soarer appeared but briefly to Wendra and Alucius in the next two days, saying that her energies were limited and that she would wait until Alucius was able to travel the ley lines before she imparted more instruction. Before either Wendra or Alucius could comment or protest, she was gone, leaving them limited supplies—and the run of the tower. Alucius had tried to soar, the way he had once been able to in the tower, but with the portals closed once more, the lifeforce energies were too weak. That had left them effectively confined to one level of the amber tower.

If he had not been so worried about both the ifrits and his absence from the Northern Guard, Alucius could have enjoyed the time with Wendra and his daughter even more. As it was, he still enjoyed it, although he wished the circumstances had been different.

"We can only take the time we have," Wendra reminded him—more than once.

He thought it was Novdi when the soarer abruptly appeared once more. She walked from the mirror square into the trapezoidal room where the three spent most of their time. Nor did the soarer hover, but stood on the amber floor before Alucius and Wendra. They sat on the ends of the bed, and Wendra cradled Alendra in her arms. Even though Alucius was seated, his head was almost level with that of the standing soarer. The soarer's wings carried but the faintest hint of green and gold iridescence.

The last skill I can provide is the one that will decide whether you can survive while you do what is necessary to stop the ifrits. The soarer paused.

Alucius got the sense that she was panting, but he could not see that she was breathing hard.

You must learn how to anchor yourself. You must link your lifethreads with the threads of all that is around you. The ifrits cannot do that. Watch . . .

Alucius focused on the soarer, who, young-looking as she appeared, also seemed worn and tired. Still, he could sense the thin threads that extended from her lifethread and hooked to the amber of the walls, even to the silvery metal.

As quickly as the threads had seemed to meld, they disengaged, and the soarer stood unlinked.

You must try. When you are so linked, no force brought by an ifrit can touch you or harm you.

Alucius stood, trying to spin off thin threads.

No! The threads are part of you. They must stay part of you. You cast them loose, and you lose part of what you are.

Alucius swallowed. He had sensed both the command and the true fear from the soarer, a fear so real it had frozen him for a moment. Was what they were trying that dangerous?

It is most dangerous. You can link to power and obtain it, but that is even more dangerous. A hint of humor appeared, coloring the words that followed. *Anything that confers power bears danger.* She looked at Wendra. *You also must master this. Your mate cannot protect you, nor you him.*

Alucius tried once more, visualizing the finest threads of his being, almost like hair extending forth, but remaining anchored to him.

Better, but they must be stronger, and there must be more of them.

Alucius watched as Wendra attempted to replicate what the soarer had demonstrated.

Hold the threads to you . . .

At least a glass had passed before the soarer held up a tiny hand. *Enough. If you practice well, you will be strong enough to protect yourself.*

"How will this protect us?" asked Wendra.

When you so link to the world, you cannot be taken by the power of their Tables or their lifeforce. Isolation from the world makes one vulnerable. Linking more tightly to the world creates strength. You will need that ability to save our . . . your world from being drained and destroyed . . .

"Will they use the Tables to drain the world and its lifeforce? Or can they tap the world directly?" asked Alucius.

They must use the Tables to begin with. Once the master ifrits are established here, they will be able to tap the world directly—as they had begun to do before the Cataclysm. They will come as once they did, flooding through the tubes and Tables.

"Did they just add the Tables to the web that already was?" asked Wendra.

It was not . . . it is not a web . . . those lines are part of the lifethreads of the world itself. Were we strong enough, we could travel the threads, as once we did, as you can.

"Without a Table or a portal?"

Yes. The Tables are necessary for the ifrits. That is their strength and their weakness.

Alucius didn't see a weakness. "What weakness?"

They must use a Table, or a location that once held a Table or is otherwise powered, as by one of the scepters. They can also transport those who cannot use the Table themselves. That is a great strength. If you will but learn, you can travel anywhere on the major lifewebs, but you cannot carry another . . . The other weakness is that excessive use of the Tables will drain a world far sooner . . .

Alucius nodded. "Not too many people should use them?"

Use by a handful will not harm the world, but use by thousands or the transport of large weights of metals will wear down a world before its time, and it will die, and then so will everything upon it. Even the existence of many Tables over centuries will wear down a world . . . Enough . . . you must do what is necessary . . . If you wish your children to survive and prosper, you must travel the dark tubes to the world of the ifrits. Only there can you stop them.

"Why didn't you?" asked Alucius.

We could not. We cannot travel the dark tubes. Even entering one will kill a soarer. Nor did we know about the scepters then.

Scepters? The soarer had never mentioned them before, and now she spoke as though they were of great import. He had so many questions. "Why can we . . ." Alucius stopped. "Because they helped form us?" The very thought that he and Wendra were somehow related to the ifrits was distasteful, and he'd shied away from it in the years since he had first learned that.

Wendra's eyes widened, but she did not speak.

You are of this world, of another world, and of the world of the ifrits, and you are of yourself. We are but of ourselves and this world, and that has not proved enough strength . . .

"But you brought me here. You've done so many things," protested Wendra.

I did not bring you. Those with strength did. Our fate was sealed from the first, for we can have either skill or strength. We cannot have both. Skill is not strength. Soarers are most skilled, but you are far greater in strength. Skill can be taught, once the intelligence is there. We have either intelligence or strength. We have never had both. You do. You must use your strength to find one of the scepters and take it to where it can destroy the access of the ifrits to Corus forever.

Scepters again? The soarer's thoughts seemed almost fragmented.

Alucius had never heard any mention of a scepter. Or had he? Wasn't there a mention of a scepter of the day in one of the old rhymes? And there had been the statue in Dulka—it had to have been Dulka—that had borne a scepter tipped with blue flame. "What are the scepters? Where are they?"

They were a symbol of the Duarchy, and they had a function.

"What function?" pressed Alucius.

They made the Tables possible. They created stresses, fractures, in the lines of lifeforce that hold the world together. If they are not either reunited with their source, or one of them destroyed, in time . . . There was the sense of a shrug.

"Then what?" asked Wendra, a trace of irritation in her voice.

The lifeforce webs will shrivel and die, and so will all your descendants. How long this will take, we do not know. Many hundreds of years, but it will happen.

"How did the scepters create the Tables?"

Each contains lifeforce from all the worlds held and drained by the ifrits. Each world contributed a small frac-

tion of its lifeforce. The tension between the two scepters allowed a disruption in the balance of forces on a world. That imbalance makes possible the creation of the translation tubes between worlds, and between Tables and portals.

"And we need to destroy the scepters?" asked Alucius. "Or one of them?"

Need is what one makes of it. There was an impression of a headshake, although the soarer's head did not move. *It gets more difficult to retain lucidity. You need only to destroy one scepter . . .*

"How do we destroy something like that?" asked Wendra. "Where do we find it?"

Find it . . . you must . . . you can . . . it is twisted silver and black, locked in pink and purple, and it cannot be far from a ley line, a world lifethread, and it has its own . . . feeling . . . Its appearance . . . we cannot say. It could look like anything. We have never seen it, only felt what it did . . . The soarer slumped, as if she could hardly hold herself erect on the amberstone. *Destruction . . . that is simply said, and most difficult. You . . . must reunite it with the master scepter on the world from which it was brought . . . find the master scepter on the world of the ifrits and reunite them. You must not wait . . . for in instants . . . will come a great convulsion . . . and you will be trapped there, and die with that world . . .*

Alucius looked at Wendra.

You must practice what I have taught you. And then you must rest before you go. You must be refreshed before searching for the scepters and before you travel the dark tubes.

"We must act quickly?" pressed Wendra.

If you would save yourselves and this world we would leave to you. I must go . . . little time for me remains . . . for any of us . . . Do what you will . . . I . . . we can offer no more . . . No more . . . The soarer walked out into the adjoining room to the square mirror and was gone.

"She didn't say anything more," Alucius said. "She didn't even soar."

"She's dying. They all are," Wendra said. "It's so sad."

"Dying?"

"Can't you feel it? There's so little lifeforce behind her."

Alucius hadn't thought to look. "They always seemed so powerful. So invincible."

"Did she look invincible?"

He shook his head. Inadvertently, he yawned. "I'm tired. I didn't do that much . . ."

"Using Talent is work, and you're still tired from what you've been through."

"We should practice a little more."

"Just a little," Wendra replied.

Alucius stifled another yawn and squared his shoulders.

142

Salaan, Lanachrona

A reddish purple mist erupted from the center of the Table. As the mist vanished, the figure of a tall, muscular ifrit was revealed. His eyes were deep purple, his alabaster face almost translucently white, his shimmering hair black. He did not smile as he stepped off the Table and looked first at Trezun, then at Tarolt.

Trezun bowed immediately.

"Fieldmaster Lasylt? I had not expected . . ." Tarolt inclined his head respectfully, but not deeply.

"Whom else did you expect with so much at stake?" The deep voice reverberated through the Table chamber. "Whom else . . . ?" His eyes caught a glimpse of his visage reflected in the now-silvered Table top. "The dark hair . . . the paleness . . . it . . ."

"It takes some getting used to," Tarolt said. "We stand ready to do your bidding."

"Where are the scepters? Do you have them under guard?"

"We have located but one, and there is no functioning Table at that locale."

"Is there a portal?" demanded Lasylt.

"Ah . . . yes. There was once a Table."

"And you have not attempted to recover it?"

"With but two of us remaining . . ." Tarolt pointed out.

"I see your problem, especially given a strong Talent-steer being loose. Once I have rested, I will procure it, and with it we will locate the other."

"Are the scepters that . . . critical?" asked Trezun.

"You sent word that this Talent-steer had killed a fully translated Efran. Is that not true?"

"Yes, Lasylt. But he used local lifeforce attached to local projectile weapons."

The newly arrived Efran's violet eyes blazed. "You do not understand, I see."

"But . . . a projectile weapon?"

"No . . . any Talent-steer who can bind lifeforce into inanimate metals and minerals—that is the danger, because that ability can direct the use of the scepters. Or have you found this Talent-steer?"

"No. He made a translation to Blackstear, but he is no longer there."

There was a long silence. The senior fieldmaster seemed to shudder, then took a deep breath.

"Can we assist you?" asked Tarolt.

"Assist me? Ah, yes." An ironic laugh filled the room. "You will. If only Talent were linked to intelligence. If only . . . but we cannot change what is and what is not." Lasylt turned to Trezun. "Are there any other Tables that can be constructed or rebuilt rapidly?"

"Waleryn—the shadow-engineer in Lustrea—has been working in Norda to re-create the Table there. He has it operating for communications and believes that he can have it fully operational within a few days. Because of its location, once it is operational, it will boost the grid strength by another fifth."

"That is the first encouraging information I've had from you." A hint of a smile crossed the taller ifrit's face. "With another Table after that, we will have enough to translate third-level Talents." Lasylt nodded. "We could have three hundred Efrans here within a year, then, and we will be able to warm the atmosphere more. In our absence, the planet has reverted toward chill, and we must have greater warmth to boost the lifeforce mass. Even so . . ." The faintest frown crossed the broad forehead. "We cannot undo all of what has already been done."

"What has been done?"

"I will explain . . . after I rest." Lasylt walked toward the doorway leading to the steps.

Trezun and Tarolt followed.

143

When Alucius and Wendra woke, aroused by the plaintive wails of a hungry Alendra, indirect light filled the tower room, creating an amber glow that suffused everything. Alucius put his arms around Wendra, holding her close for a moment. After a time, he sat up and took Alendra, to allow Wendra to move into a more comfortable position to nurse their daughter.

Wendra propped herself into a sitting position on the bed that was narrow indeed for two and an infant. Her head tilted quizzically. Her face stiffened. Then, abruptly, tears began to stream from her eyes.

Alendra began to wail even more loudly, almost despairingly, and Alucius looked from his daughter to his wife. "What is it?"

"She's gone. They're gone. All the soarers. Can't you feel it?"

Alucius stopped, letting his Talent extend into the tower. The mistiness of the ley lines to the mirror-portals remained, but the greenish gold was gone. And for the first time, his Talent was not blocked by the tower. Beyond the walls, there was not a trace of the lifeforce energy that might have been a soarer. Not the smallest trace remained.

Not a trace, as if all of the greenish gold lifeforce that had always been part of the soarers had been removed from the world, as if an entire part of Corus had vanished. And it had.

The soarers had always been there, always a part of Corus, especially of the lands of the Iron Valleys. How could they be gone?

Yet, even as he asked himself the question, he knew that Wendra was right. The emptiness of the hidden city was like a gaping hole in what his Talent sensed. The soarers were gone. Or had there been only the single soarer at the end? Was the wood spirit of Madrien gone as well? "They were here last night. She was." His words sounded empty.

He swallowed. The soarer had been dying the night before, and she had known it. Alucius should have known, should have guessed. But . . . soarers were soarers, not herders. They had always been secretive and private, and there was no way that a soarer would have allowed anyone near. That he understood, even as it saddened him.

"She didn't want us to know." Wendra tried to blot the tears from her face, but they kept flowing. "I think . . . she was the last. She had to be." Several sobs convulsed her. "She didn't want us to know . . . so sad . . . to be so alone . . ."

So alone. Alucius found it hard to imagine what it must have been like, soaring through an empty city, trying to hold on, trying to impart knowledge to others not even of the same race, so that part of the legacy would live on, trying to remember, to tell what was important.

As Wendra's sobs subsided, Alucius kept patting Alendra's back, and her wails subsided into something more like sobbing cries. After a time, looking at Wendra, he spoke again. "She said it was up to us. I knew there weren't very many. I just didn't know that she was the only one. Or that it would happen . . . overnight."

"She was so tired," Wendra said. "So tired. And lonely . . . I didn't see it. I should have."

Alendra whimpered.

"You can hand her to me. She's hungry." Wendra extended her arms.

Alucius eased Alendra into them. "I'm going to wash up and dress while you feed her. Then I'll take care of her while you dress."

Wendra nodded, wincing slightly as Alendra began to nurse, greedily. "Don't be quite such a little piglet . . . that's hard on your mother." She shook her head. "About some things, she's like you. When she gets something on her mind, she's not good at listening."

"You expect her to listen at less than three months old?" Alucius asked.

Wendra forced a grin, despite her tear-streaked face. "In some matters . . . of appetite . . . age doesn't matter."

Alucius could feel himself flushing. "I think I'd better get washed up." He turned to the washstand, realizing abruptly that he needed to be frugal with the remaining water—unless he wanted to try soaring down the narrow shaft that was the only way up and down the tower, and he had his doubts about his success there after his earlier experiments with soaring.

When he had washed and dressed, he turned to Wendra.

"It will be a bit," she said, looking down at Alendra.

Alucius smiled. "I'm not going anywhere without you."

"I should hope not. You get into trouble."

"You got into trouble not going anywhere," he countered.

"Where do we start the search for the scepters?" she asked.

"I have some ideas where they aren't. I think I would

have sensed them—I hope I would have—if they'd been in Blackstear or Soupat or Hyalt or Dereka . . . or Tempre."

"The soarer gave us an idea," Wendra pointed out. "If the ifrits can only travel where there are Tables, don't the scepters have to be where there is a Table—or where there was one?"

"The map would show the old locations of the Tables where I haven't been." Alucius nodded. Where had he put the map? He glanced around, then realized it was on the narrow lower shelf of the washstand.

He retrieved the map and opened it, studying it more closely, looking for a hint of something, anything. He smiled faintly, realizing that the tower room was about the only place where he'd actually been able to look at the map in anything close to full light.

After a time, he finally saw what he had missed on his previous observations. There were two purple dots at the upper vertices of two of the octagons—the ones at Dereka and Lysia. He eased over beside Wendra and lowered the map. "See? Here and here. Those don't appear on any of the other Table octagons."

"There are two scepters, aren't there?" asked Wendra.

"That's what the soarer said." Alucius frowned as he studied the map.

"What is it?"

"I might already have found one of them—except it wasn't there."

Wendra raised her eyebrows.

"There was a hidden room off the old Table chamber in Dereka . . ." Alucius went on to explain what he had seen in the chamber, concluding, ". . . and I'd wager that the casket once held one of the scepters. But the scepter was gone."

"There weren't any signs of anything else missing, were there?"

"No one had been in the chamber in years. There was dust everywhere. Someone might have taken it a long time ago, but not recently."

"So it was taken years ago. Could we travel there by the ley lines and see if we could sense where it might lead?"

There was something, something, but Alucius couldn't quite recall what it was . . . and he felt that he should remember. "It's not there. Not now. We should try Lysia."

"Have you been there?" Wendra eased Alendra from her breast and to her shoulder, patting her back.

"No, but the map says that the colors are yellow and orange. We can concentrate on that."

"Will it help if we hold hands?" Wendra lowered her daughter to the other breast. "She's still hungry."

"I don't know. I don't see how it could hurt." Alucius frowned. "What about Alendra? Do you think . . . ?"

"She comes with us," Wendra replied. "I'm not leaving her. Besides, we have to finish this soon. Alendra won't be able to travel with us for much longer. We don't know how long this will take. Besides, there are too many ifrits around."

Alucius could have argued about that, but then, his wife's mind was clearly made up . . . and there had been far more ifrits in Corus than he'd thought about, and with the translation tubes open to the ifrits' world, there was always the chance that another might appear. Or a whole host of them.

"I won't be that long. Or Alendra won't."

Alucius straightened and walked to the window, looking down and out at the hidden city, a city that had once held much of a race . . . and now held but three herders . . . and the hopes of both soarers and herders.

144

Salaan, Lanachrona

Purplish mist boiled away from the Table, and a tall figure emerged from the mist holding a case in both arms. In the holster attached to the wide maroon belt was a light-cutter whose discharge formulator had been half-melted, half-shattered.

The ifrit slowly and carefully descended from the Table, easing the silver and black case into Tarolt's arms. "Careful . . . barely . . . made . . ."

"Fieldmaster . . ."

Lasylt sat down on the stone floor. Then his eyes rolled up in their sockets, before closing. He slowly pitched sideways. Trezun grasped his garments quickly enough so that he was able to keep the senior fieldmaster from slamming down onto the stone.

Tarolt opened the hidden doorway and carried the metallic case into the strong room at the end of the short corridor, returning quickly—empty-handed. He closed the hidden door.

"What happened?" stammered Trezun.

"Table strain. It's hard to carry something like that through the tubes," explained Tarolt. "He'll recover quickly. We'll just carry him up to his room."

Effortlessly, the two picked up the larger ifrit and carried him up the stairs from the Table chamber, through the conference room, out into the foyer, and up yet another flight of stairs to a corner chamber, where a stove suffused the room with strong but gentle warmth. There, they laid him on the extra-long and extra-wide bed.

Tarolt took the folded sheet of eternal paper from the

fieldmaster's belt, opening it. He smiled as he beheld the map.

"What is it?"

"An ancient map of where all the Tables were." Tarolt fixed his eyes on Trezun. "I will wait. You must guard the Table. Should the Talent-steer appear, use a light-knife before he can use any of his weapons."

"Yes, Fieldmaster."

"Tarolt . . . still."

"Yes, Tarolt." Trezun nodded and hurried back down the steps.

Tarolt seated himself in the overlarge straight-backed wooden chair and waited.

Half a glass passed before Lasylt's eyes blinked, and another quarter before the ifrit coughed and looked around. He finally caught sight of Tarolt. "You . . . have . . . the scepter?"

"It's locked in the storeroom. Trezun is guarding it and watching the Table with a light-knife."

"Good." The senior ifrit slowly eased himself into a position where he sat on the edge of the bed and looked directly at Tarolt. He began to speak, his voice low and gravelly. "We must insist that Waleryn bring his Table up to full power and immediately bring the locator here to Salaan. We can lose no time in seeking out and recovering the other scepter. Then one of you must translate to that scepter. It will act as a portal."

Tarolt nodded slowly. "I will have to make that effort. Trezun is limited to Tables."

"That is not all," Lasylt continued. "As soon as you can, Tarolt, you must use my authority to order the translation of another ten Efrans here. Now."

"Ten?"

"As I was leaving with the scepter, I could sense your Talent-steer moving toward Lysia. We retrieved the scepter just in time. He is far stronger than the ancient ones, and he is searching for the scepters. He must know their purpose.

If we have both here, and there are always two . . . or more guarding the Table . . ."

"We cannot do that without more Efrans," Tarolt said.

"We cannot. That is why we will order ten more here."

"The translation is still dangerous with such a frail grid."

"Order fifteen then, or twenty. Some may perish, but the Talent-steer must not be allowed to take either scepter."

"I told Trezun to use a light-knife on him should he appear in the Table, even before he is fully translated."

"Good. We will still need more Efrans. Go and issue the orders."

"Yes, Lasylt." Tarolt inclined his head, then rose from the chair.

"I will be down shortly." Lasylt paused. "The strong room is Talent-shielded, is it not?"

"It is indeed, and the door is closed."

Lasylt nodded again as Tarolt left the bedchamber and started down the steps.

145

Alucius and Wendra stood at the edge of the silver mirror in the amber-walled tower. Alendra was strapped firmly into the carrypack, and Alucius held his rifle in his left hand. All the cartridges in the magazine had been infused with the darkness of lifeforce, as had the ten remaining in the loops of his belt. He glanced at Wendra, and their eyes met.

"Are you ready?" he finally asked.

"No. But I won't be any more ready tomorrow or the next day." Wendra forced a grin. "And we'll be a lot more hungry."

Alucius extended his right hand and took her left, and the two stepped onto the mirrorlike surface.

"Yellow and orange—those are the colors, and they'll seem misty, almost not there. They might seem hidden behind the blackness," Alucius said.

Wendra nodded.

He began to concentrate on reaching the misty darkness of the ley lines, trying to match what he did with what he felt Wendra was doing.

He began to sink into the silverness of the mirror and along a misty-dark conduit toward the deeper and more greenish black misty darkness beneath the hidden city. He could barely sense Wendra, but she was beside him, in that fashion of closeness that he could not touch or reach. The chill did not seem quite so intense as he recalled, and he tried to concentrate on the portal that was yellow and orange. Yellow and orange, he tried to project to Wendra as he focused his mind on traversing the misty blackness to the far southeast, almost as far from the Aerial Plateau as one could go and still remain within Corus.

So slowly, the yellow and orange drew nearer, or they drew nearer to it, veiled by a purplish shadow of an ifrit tube, one that was but partly there. Alucius continued to send the image of yellow and orange toward Wendra, but he had no idea if she could sense what he tried to project. Finally, he concentrated on lifting himself out of the misty blackness, out of the chill, and back into the world of light through the yellow and orange.

The barrier before him was one of silvered orange, and he formed himself into a spearhead of being . . .

Orange, yellow, and silver mixed in slashing swirls of icy chill a swirl of chill that exploded away from him. . . .

Alucius stood in the Table depression—alone. He glanced around. There was no one in the Table chamber besides himself, not even Wendra. He swallowed. Should he try to go back into the darkness and chill to find her? Or should he wait a moment?

Then, a swirl of dark mist appeared and Wendra and Alendra stood beside him.

He reached out and squeezed Wendra's hand. "I was getting worried."

"I had . . . a little trouble . . . breaking through."

"I'm sorry. You have to imagine yourself as a spear or something sharp."

A rueful smile crossed her lips. "I tried being a hammer. A spear would have been better."

"Or an axe." Alucius studied the chamber more intently. Unlike the walls of the other Table chambers, those of the chamber in Lysia were cracked. In more than a few places, the walls appeared to have been splintered and broken by gunfire or shrapnel. The thinnest rays of light penetrated the chamber through cracks in the stone ceiling, providing a twilightlike illumination.

"I'll get better," Wendra promised, patting Alendra on the back.

Even as Alucius stepped out of the depression that had held a Table many years before, he could sense an aura of purpleness as well. It was the first time he had sensed an ifrit in a place where there was not a functioning Table. He cast out his Talent even farther, bringing up his rifle as he did . . . but there was no one else in the Table chamber, or in the open passageway that led up the stone steps to an upper level. "An ifrit's been here. He's gone, I think."

"Is that the purple feeling?"

Alucius nodded.

"It feels cold . . . worse than a sandsnake or one of those Talent-creatures on the stead."

"They're very strong, and their clothes are like nightsilk. Don't think they are, but they've pressed lifeforce into them, and they act the same way when they're hit with a sabre or a bullet. They might be even stronger than night-silk." Alucius inspected the first set of holes drilled into the stone walls, where once a light-torch bracket had been.

"I think it's this one," Wendra said from the other side of the chamber. "There are four holes here, and there are scuff marks in the dust on the floor."

Alucius walked around the oblong Table depression and joined her. His eyes took in the holes. Again, his Talent revealed nothing. "Do you want to try to open it?"

"Why don't you show me? That will take less time."

He extended a thin Talent-probe, turning the leading end as sticky as drying honey, and sand-rough. He fumbled with what he could barely sense on the other side of the stone wall. His forehead was damp with sweat when there was a *click* and the wall slid aside to reveal the passageway. A mist of purpleness drifted out of the passage and around the two herders, but Alucius could tell that the passageway and the chamber beyond were empty.

Wendra wrinkled her nose. "I know it's something I sense with Talent, but it *smells* bad. Alendra doesn't like it, either."

The two eased into the passageway, almost ten yards long and lit by the faint glow of an ancient light-torch. As Alucius had expected, at the end was another chamber— exactly five yards square. Large footprints stood out in the dust that had settled onto the polished stone floor. As with the chamber in Dereka, a table desk stood beside the wall in one corner, with a long-legged chair beside it. Against the wall to the right was a single-wide chest of drawers.

Stretched on the floor in the corner beside the desk was a set of clothes, the green tunic trimmed in brilliant purple, with matching trousers and black boots. All the garb had a silvery sheen and held embedded lifeforce. On the wall adjoining the one closest to the table desk was an empty niche. Alucius stepped toward it.

Unlike every other bit of stone in the chamber, the stone surface of the niche was rough and uneven, with deeper gouges at each end. Alucius could also feel heat emanating from the stone. He looked down at the rock droplets on the ancient stone floor, then up at Wendra. "The scepter was here. Not very long ago, either. The ifrits used one of their light-knives to cut it out of the stone."

"Now what do we do?"

Alucius stopped. "I think I know where the other scepter

is . . . where it has to be . . ." He couldn't help frowning as the words left his lips.

"Where?"

"It has to be in Madrien, under the Residence of the Matrial. It can't be anywhere else. The soarer said that it was locked in pink and purple, and the entire residence—everything associated with the Matrial—has an energy that is pink and purple."

"But . . . you said you destroyed the crystal." Absently, Wendra patted Alendra, as if to calm the infant.

"I did . . . but what if the crystal was just something created by the use of the scepter? That's the only thing that explains it, and it would explain why the Regent of the Matrial was able to repower those torques."

"Can we travel there . . . by the ley lines?"

"We should be able to. I kept feeling a pink and purple portal, but I'd wager it isn't a portal at all, but that other scepter, and probably the case that held it in Dereka was designed as much to hide it as for anything else."

"Then . . . hadn't we better go and see if we can get it, before the ifrits do?" asked Wendra.

A rueful smile crossed Alucius's face as he realized that he had been trying to avoid returning to Hieron and the Residence of the Matrial. "We should."

"You really don't want to go there, do you?"

"That doesn't matter," he replied. "You're right. We need to get there before the ifrits do." He turned and started back toward the Table chamber. "We can come back here later, if we have to."

Wendra followed, humming under her breath to Alendra.

Once she was out of the passageway, Alucius used his Talent to close the hidden doorway. Then he stepped down into the depression where the Table used to be, all too many years before. Wendra stepped down beside him. He took her hand and squeezed it.

"Are you ready?"

She nodded.

Alucius concentrated.

The three began to sink into the very rock itself, merging into the misty blackness of the worldthread that they would travel westward, toward the pink and purple that marked Hieron—and the second scepter, Alucius hoped.

146

Norda, Lustrea

Two oil lamps set in light-torch brackets illuminated the room whose walls were primarily of ancient stone. On the northern wall, newer stones showed where recent and hasty repairs had been made. The stone ceiling displayed years of soot from torches and lamps.

A single figure stood before the oblong Table that dominated the middle of the underground room. The odor of wood oil and that of the energy that powered the light-torches mixed in the air that hung heavy in the dimly lit chamber.

Waleryn stepped closer to the Table, his eyes fixing on the purplish glow in the center of the Table, a glow that expanded until the entire top surface of the Table glowed purple. Almost immediately, a grid appeared above the surface of the Table. Close to a third of the sections of the grid were purple; the remainder were red.

The shadow-engineer concentrated on the grid, and another grid section changed from red to purple. A moment later, the entire grid vanished.

The engineer turned and walked to the side of the room, lifting a wooden box two yards long but less than a third of that in height and width. Carrying the box, he stepped onto the Table, then began to sink into it, vanishing into the Table, leaving the barred Table chamber empty, the oil lamps flickering but slightly.

After a time, the Table glowed more brightly, and the engineer reappeared, carrying a small pack. He was breathing heavily as he eased himself off the Table and walked to the crude and flat table set against the recently repaired wall. There he set the pack down.

He settled onto the stool beside the flat table. Almost a quarter glass passed before his breathing returned to normal, and he stood and began to remove items from the pack.

147

The purple pink portal became less and less like a portal and more and more like a brilliant point of crystalline light, burning evilly through the misty blackness of the ley line that Alucius, Wendra, and Alendra traveled westward. There was no clearly defined portal, only two rings of pinkish fire. Alucius tried to signal to Wendra that they should try to emerge on the lower level. He could only hope she understood. Silvered purpleness shattered away from him.

Almost before he broke out of the misty darkness, Alucius was looking for Wendra, but, this time, she and Alendra were beside him. The unseen but strongly felt purpleness infused the very air, filling the entire hexagonal stone chamber.

Alucius had his rifle up and ready even before he saw the ifrit holding the scepter. In general shape, the scepter was close to the replica he had seen in the Table chamber in Dulka, a length of silver and black—two metals exuding light and intertwined—topped with a massive blue crystal. The crystal glimmered with energy, a deep and brilliant purple that was almost too bright to look at or sense directly.

A broad smile crossed the ifrit's face as Alucius started to squeeze the trigger. Alucius released the trigger pressure. The pinkish shield had flowed around the ifrit, and

Alucius remembered what had happened when he had tried to strike the first pink crystal of the Matrial.

The ifrit looked familiar.

"You're Tarolt."

"That is not really my name, but yes, I am. It would have been much easier if you had just pulled that trigger."

Alucius concentrated on creating a web of blackness to cast around both ifrit and scepter.

"I don't think so." Purplish energy shredded Alucius's web.

A black javelin of force flew from Wendra toward Tarolt, slamming into his leg. He limped backward, lowering the scepter so that it formed a complete shield. Wendra's second javelin struck that shield, and Alucius could sense the shield weakening.

"How can you believe that turning a world into dead land is good?" Alucius knew there was little point in asking, but wanted to occupy Tarolt as he formed another black lifeforce missile, a hard task indeed, because there was so little lifeforce in the small stone chamber.

"Good is what enables a people to survive in glory and power and dignity," replied the ifrit. "Not surviving, or surviving in squalor and poverty, is bad."

"I can't believe you think that destroying all life on a world—"

"You can believe whatever you wish to believe. What you believe has no effect on the universe, only on yourself." The ifrit smiled coldly. "Beliefs change nothing. Actions do. They change the arrangement of items in the universe. The universe remains as it was and will be. Beliefs have value only to the believer. There is no absolute good in the universe; there is only survival. Those who survive determine which beliefs rule."

"So might makes right?" Alucius hurled another black javelin of darkness, a javelin that shredded off some of the purple shield.

"Has it ever been otherwise? The universe does not need to have meaning. It is. You need the comfort of meaning."

Alucius knew that the ifrit was wrong, but now was not the time to unravel that puzzle. He flung another missile, one that weakened but again did not penetrate the shield created by the scepter.

"Besides, all life that is superior is the same. Have you asked the ancient ones what sustains them?"

"The ancient ones? The soarers?"

"The ones you call soarers are but half the species." The ifrit's smile grew broader—and colder. "They were no different from us, save that they are dying, and we will live. They have but told you what they wish you to know. That, too, is the way of all life." He stepped back into a doorway concealed by a Talent-illusion until the ifrit shredded it. The tall figure quickly backed up the steps.

Alucius hurried after Tarolt, with Wendra almost at his side, throwing up a green golden shield before them and aiming another black missile at the ifrit. Somewhere he could sense Talent-alarms going off, and bodies moving toward them.

No sooner had Alucius reached the top of the narrow staircase and stepped through the upper archway than he and Wendra were enfolded by blinding purplish pink, light that was visible not just to Talent-senses, but to eyes as well. Alendra whimpered and began to cry.

As if it had never been destroyed, there, floating in the center of the stone-walled chamber, rotated a massive, multifaceted crystal. The Talent-like roots of purple energy no longer flowed into the rock, but directly to the scepter held by Tarolt. Even the once-cracked stone walls of the chamber had been regenerated or repaired, so that the stone was smooth and flawless.

Alucius could sense that the ifrit was having trouble trying to translate out of the chamber while still maintaining control of the scepter. As before, Alucius could feel the heat building inside his nightsilk undergarments, as well as Alendra's and Wendra's discomfort. He forced himself to cast another Talent-missile at Tarolt.

Wendra followed with one of her own, then another.

As blackness cascaded around Tarolt, the oak door burst open, and more than a squad of Matrite special guards poured into the small chamber. Their pistols came up, some aimed at Alucius and Wendra, some at Tarolt.

"Shoot them!"

The ifrit raised the scepter, its aura blinding and stopping the Matrites. Then he vanished.

"Link to the earth!" Alucius ordered. "Now!" Even before he spoke, he had begun the linking process, extending thin threads.

Beside them, the massive crystal began to slow, no longer spinning above the stone floor, but beginning to wobble.

Alucius forced himself to concentrate on strengthening and intensifying his links to everything around him, weaving some of those threads around Alendra as well. At the same time, as he began to feel that the links to earth were stronger, he pressed lifeforce darkness around the faltering purple crystal.

He extended that blackness against the resistance, a resistance that suddenly shredded into purplish threads that exploded away from the crystal. Wrapped in its covering of darkness, a darkness added to by Wendra, the crystal contracted, pulsed, and contracted again.

"Shoot them! Now!" commanded someone.

Alucius ignored the commands, Talent-pressing darkness around the failing crystal. A high, whining sound knifed through Alucius's ears, but he crammed more darkness around the crystal. A heavy, leaden, splintering sound echoed through the chamber.

Instantly, huge cracks and rents appeared in the chamber's stone walls. Feeling like an immobile and massive miniature mountain, tied in place, as well as protected by his threads that felt as though they went everywhere, Alucius forced yet more darkness around the crystal.

With a dreamlike slowness, the crystal stopped rotating and tumbled down toward the stone below. Faint purplish light swirled as if it were smoke, providing a trail. All the glass and crystal in the world shattered—that was the sound when the pink purple crystal struck the stone.

A single piercing shriek followed, so high in frequency that while Alucius could not hear it, his very flesh felt as though it were being flayed apart from within. Silver green blackness flared across the underground chamber . . . a blinding wave of color and power . . . drowning Alucius and Wendra—and Alendra.

148

Salaan, Lananchrona

A spray of pink and purple Talent-mist appeared in the center of the Table, concealing for a moment the appearance of Tarolt. The older ifrit staggered off the Table, pitching forward and landing in a large crumpled heap on the stone floor of the Table chamber. The scepter he had carried flew through the air, striking the stone wall to Tarolt's left, then slamming to the floor. A hairline crack appeared in the stone.

Trezun moved forward and quickly scooped up the scepter. It was untouched, seemingly without a mark or a smudge upon it. Transferring it from hand to hand, as if the metal were too hot to hold firmly, he glanced toward the other two ifrits who had appeared in the doorway of the staircase that led back up to the conference room.

"So that's what it looks like," offered the recently arrived ifrit, a woman even taller and more muscular than Trezun. "It doesn't seem that special."

"It is more . . . special . . . than you know," replied Lasylt, stepping forward and taking the scepter from Trezun. "Barylt . . . you and Trezun carry Fieldmaster Tarolt up to one of the beds, where he may recuperate."

"His force levels are low," observed Trezun as he lifted Tarolt's shoulders. "He must have had some difficulty. He could have encountered the young colonel."

"Even if he did, he was successful in retrieving the scepter, and that was what mattered." Lasylt nodded. "Take him up and return immediately."

The senior fieldmaster watched the Table intently, but the Table remained inactive, without a flicker in the unseen purple glow that surrounded its surface. Nor did any other figures emerge from the Table.

Before long, the other two returned.

"Bring out the other scepter, but leave it in its casket," Lasylt ordered Trezun.

Barylt remained standing silently beside the Table, one hand resting on the butt of the light-cutter holstered at her belt.

Wordlessly, the Recorder opened the hidden door to the strong room and disappeared down the short corridor, returning shortly with the silver and black metallic case.

"Put the case beside the Table," Lasylt said.

As Trezun did so, the senior fieldmaster took the uncased scepter and set it on top of the metal case.

"You don't want them in the strong room?" asked Trezun.

"No!" snapped Lasylt. "There is no shield for the one, and it acts as a portal. If you put them in the strong room, the Talent-steer will be able to translate directly in and out of the strong room. We cannot guard both places at once, not effectively, not with but four Efrans, and we must watch continuously until more of the others arrive." Lasylt frowned.

"Are the translations not going well?" asked Trezun.

"Several have already perished in the long tubes from Efra. There is less lifeforce remaining in Efra than we had calculated."

"We may not have to worry about the lifeforce mass here, then," suggested Trezun.

"We may not, and you should consider yourself fortunate to be here," replied Lasylt. "Most fortunate."

Barylt glanced at the Table, then at the bare stone walls and the unadorned stone floors. The slightest shudder traversed her frame.

149

Time passed. How much, Alucius was not certain, but he began to unlink from the chamber around him. He glanced at the cracked stone walls, walls that were beginning to sag inward and would not long last against the pressure of the soil around and the structure above. *Cracking* noises flowed around him, and the stones underfoot felt unsteady. He could not sense much of anything with his Talent, and only faint light filled the chamber, light coming from the doorway that led to the stairs up into the Residence of the Matrial—or the Regent, Alucius supposed.

Only the barest trace of skeletons lay on the stones inside the entry to the underground chamber, and the oak door had disintegrated into dust, while even the iron hinges had vanished into rusty dust that lay heaped at the base of the stone doorframe.

Had years passed? Alucius swallowed. Had they been frozen in time when he had linked to the world itself?

"Everything's . . . dead." Wendra's voice was small.

That was why he sensed little. There was little enough to sense. Between the ifrit's actions, the failure of the crystal, and their defenses, they had sucked all the lifeforce out of everything around them—for yards at least.

"We didn't get the scepter," he said dully.

Wendra said nothing.

Should they have come to Hieron first? Had they failed because Alucius hadn't wanted to return to Madrien, and the place where he'd almost died once before? "I'm sorry. We should have . . ."

"I agreed with you," Wendra said. "We can't do any more here, can we?"

"No. The scepter was the only thing. Well . . . except for the torques, but with the crystal gone, they can't power the torques, and without the scepter, they can't re-create the crystal."

"We need to get something to eat. I do anyway. We're too tired to do anything more without eating," Wendra said.

"There's some travel food in my jacket and belt pouch," Alucius suggested.

"There was. We ate it. The soarer was getting forgetful or tired about meals."

"We could go back to Dereka . . ."

"Do we have to go there?" asked Wendra. "The soarer said that we could travel anywhere along the ley lines."

"I'm sure we can." Alucius's lips quirked into a crooked smile. "But I don't know how to determine where I am . . . or whether we'd end up under several yards of soil and stones? Do you?"

"Oh . . ."

"The Red House in Dereka isn't too far away from the Table chamber . . . and we can check that case that I thought might have held the other scepter at the same time."

"Can we go?"

He nodded, reaching out and taking Wendra's hand. "There's a portal in Dereka, where there once was a Table. It's crimson gold."

They walked down to the lower level, where the stone walls seemed slightly more sturdy. Even so, it seemed to take forever before they could find the misty blackness beneath the stone and drop into the world lifeforce lines.

Deep in the blackness, Alucius wanted to shiver, but he concentrated on the crimson gold and on projecting that image to Wendra. He could sense the growing power of the ifrits' Tables, especially the maroon and dark green of Salaan, the silver of Prosp, and another Table, one of a bright brown, as well as the other older Tables in Soupat and Blackstear. Then, too, he could feel the purple and pink of the scepter, almost on top of the maroon and dark green. Slowly, too slowly, it seemed, they moved closer to the faded crimson gold of Dereka . . . until they burst out of the blackness and through the silver . . .

Almost before he broke out of the misty darkness, Alucius was looking for Wendra, but, once more, she and their daughter were close beside him. Although he had the rifle up and ready, the ancient Table chamber was empty. He could sense someone in one of the chambers up the steps and farther toward the north end of the building.

Alucius stepped out of the oblong pit, and dust swirled around him as he reached down and offered a hand to his wife.

This time, Wendra was the one to sneeze, but far less noisily than Alucius usually did. With his free hand, he rubbed his nose, trying to stop a sneeze before it started. What light there was in the chamber filtered through the doorway framing the bottom of the staircase.

They moved quietly up the steps and came out into the smaller chamber. As he moved to the larger chamber, with the empty windows overlooking the main north-south boulevard of Dereka, Alucius realized that it was late afternoon. How long had he been locked into timelessness? He shivered as he considered that they could have been locked there for far longer. The soarer had not mentioned that problem. Then, there were more than a few items that she had overlooked—and the ifrit had suggested even others. He wondered what else they would discover along those lines.

Wendra walked toward the low, wide window, looking out to the west, where the sun cast a glow over the city. "It looks old, and it feels old."

"It is old," Alucius pointed out. "We need to get out of here. The stairway down to the lower level and the north doors to the street are this way." He turned to the right.

Wendra slipped alongside Alucius as they followed the bare-walled golden eternastone corridors generally north-ward until they reached the wide stone staircase leading down. A single beggar, hearing their steps, scuttled back to the southern side of the structure so quickly that Alucius never saw the man. Before long, they walked through the square arch on the north side of the building. They turned west toward the main boulevard.

Despite the warmth of the afternoon, Alucius left his jacket on to conceal his uniform. Even so, several of the vendors and peddlers took second looks at the two herders, but the looks faded into disinterest as they took in Alendra.

When they reached the main boulevard, Alucius pointed southward. "You can see the main gates of the palace there . . . and the tower."

"It looks just like the one in Iron Stem," Wendra said. "You'd told me that, but it's hard to believe."

"All the green towers look like that. So do the ones in Tempre." Alucius motioned to the left, northward. "It's several blocks that way. And we have to stay out of the middle of the road. That's only for riders and wagons."

The streets remained less crowded than he had recalled from his first trip to Dereka, but, perhaps because he was walking with Wendra, more people looked directly at them. Alendra was beginning to fuss by the time they had walked the half vingt that took them to the three-story Red House.

"It *is* red," said Wendra with a laugh. "Very red. Shut-ters, doors, trim . . ." She grinned. "We could do that to the stead."

Alucius made a face, then laughed. "The food's not bad."

He knew they had to eat, and that they needed rest, but he still worried that they were losing ground with every moment not spent seeking the scepters.

150

Alendra woke up, whimpering with hunger, as the faintest touch of gray seeped through the shuttered second-floor windows of the room in the Red House. While Alucius struggled to find some alertness, Wendra eased their daughter to her breast.

"I must have been tired," Alucius finally said.

"You were. You were snoring. You don't snore unless you're tired."

Alucius managed a smile, easing himself into a sitting position, his bare feet on the plank floor. A solid meal and sleep—even on a most lumpy mattress—left him feeling better than he had in days. He stood and walked to washstand, where he washed quickly, then refreshed the water for Wendra.

"I've been thinking . . ." he began.

"About what the ifrit said about the soarers? I wondered about that, too." Wendra shifted her weight and repositioned the nursing infant. "What do you think that he meant?"

"I think I know. It makes sense. I just hadn't thought of it that way. You know leschec? It has the soarer queen and the sander king, and the soarer mentioned that they had skill but not strength, and that you had been brought by the strength of others . . ."

"You think . . . the soarers are the women and the sanders the men? They're so different."

"There's another thing. The sanders kill nightsheep. Why? They don't eat them, or not their flesh. The sandwolves do, but not the sanders."

"They take the lifeforce, just like the ifrits do," Wendra concluded, lifting Alendra to her shoulder and burping her.

"But there is a difference, no matter what the ifrit said,"

Alucius pointed out. "The sanders or the soarers don't do that to people."

"They don't? Or they haven't in recent years? And what about the amber towers? I hadn't thought about it either, but I'd wager they've got some type of lifeforce in them."

Alucius frowned. "You're probably right. I still feel there's a difference."

"There is. The soarers only used a fraction of a world's lifeforce; they even let themselves die out rather than take too much. The ifrits squander it all within a few hundred or thousand years, then move on to other worlds."

"I wonder . . ."

"We'll always wonder, but maybe . . . if . . . after . . . we can explore the hidden cities and find out more."

If . . . Alucius understood that "if" all too well as he sat and pondered.

After Alendra's needs had been met, and Alucius had to admit that his wife had been most inventive in dealing with such, they left for breakfast in the public room, and then, after eating, made their way down the boulevard on a morning already promising to be hot and dry, heading for the store where Alucius had purchased food and other sundries days earlier.

The morning's purchases also included several squares of cloth for swaddling Alendra, as well as hard cheese, dried fruit, salted nuts, and another water bottle, which they filled at the public fountain a block away.

As Alucius capped the water bottle and handed it to Wendra, he studied the boulevard to the south. Almost a full company of Deforyan lancers was formed up outside the palace gates, and the gates had been closed. "We'd better get moving."

"The lancers?"

"They're expecting trouble, and when that sort of thing happens, strangers aren't welcome."

They crossed the boulevard immediately and walked swiftly southward. Despite their worries, no one even seemed to look at them, perhaps because a couple with a child—even if one of them carried a heavy rifle—did not seem threatening.

As they neared the ancient gold eternastone building that held the portal, Alucius slipped the illusion of nothingness around them.

"You'll have to teach me that," murmured Wendra.

"You could do it now," replied Alucius as they moved toward the north entrance to the ancient structure."

After climbing the wide staircase, they followed the long corridor back, then wound their way to the inside stone stairway that led down to the former Table chamber. Along the way, Alucius did not hear or sense anyone. Once in the former Table chamber, Alucius released the illusion.

"We'll take a look at the hidden chamber first." He walked to the side of the chamber where the special light-torch bracket had been. There, he created the Talent-probe with the grasping edges, wrapping it around the hidden lever beyond the wall. The first two levers he tried did nothing, but with the third came the *snap,* followed by a low grinding. The hidden wall section slid sideways, revealing the passageway beyond—still lit dimly by a pair of ancient light-torches.

"Do all the old Table chambers have these secret rooms?" Wendra absently bounced Alendra. "Just be a good girl now, while your mother and father see what they can do."

"Most seem to, but I didn't try the ones in Blackstear and Soupat. I wasn't in very good shape there." Leaving the hidden doorway open, he led the way along the passageway to the hidden chamber. Once there, he stepped aside and let Wendra survey it.

As Wendra moved toward the empty scepter case embedded in the stone, he stepped around her and made his way to the other ruined light-torch bracket. Again, he tried to use a Talent probe to find a way to open the door, but nothing worked.

"Let me try," suggested Wendra.

For all of her Talent probes, Wendra had little more luck than had Alucius.

She looked at him. "What if we tried to transport ourselves on the ley lines and came out on the other side of the wall? That what the soarers seemed to do."

"If we could do that . . ." mused Alucius.

"Then we could take the lines close to the Table at Salaan," Wendra pointed out, "and we'd be close to Dekhron."

"We can certainly try, but I think I'd feel better if I started at where the Table was," Alucius admitted.

"So would I. The thought of getting stuck in solid rock bothers me."

Alucius offered a crooked smile. "I wish you hadn't mentioned that."

Wendra smiled sheepishly—town sheepishly. "The rock doesn't bother the soarers, but it might take practice."

"We'd better start." Alucius walked back along the passageway, casting out with his Talent to see if anyone happened to have made their way into the lower chamber. While it was unlikely, there had been lancers investigating once before. His Talent—and his ears—told him that the Table chamber remained deserted.

He stepped into the oblong depression . . . concentrating on the misty blackness below. Immediately, he began to sink . . .

The chill washed over and through him, and he tried to edge himself sideways . . . and suddenly he could tell that he was vingts away. He refocused himself on the crimson gold and could sense that he was back close to the Table chamber. Instead of trying to break through the silvery barrier, he tried to sense/see through it without breaking through . . . the image was like a mirror that undulated like a banner in the breeze, and his head began to ache. For a moment, he just hovered in the misty blackness, if hovering was the right term for seemingly being buried in stone.

He tried to extend a thread from himself, one that would serve as an anchor so that the slightest thought would not propel him vingts—or scores of vingts—away. Then he drifted sideways, slowly letting the thread extend from the ley line. Deeper darkness surrounded him, but that passed, and he seemed to be in another corridor. He tried to use the lifeforce thread to tug himself back to the Table chamber, and he found himself beyond the mirrorlike barrier, but in the Table chamber.

With the chill in his bones growing, he eased out the thread ever so slowly, heading down what he hoped was the passage to the first hidden chamber . . . then beyond . . . Silver shattered away from him . . .

He stood in another narrow corridor, one but barely illuminated by a single light-torch five yards away, in a bracket high on the wall. The wall to his right was similar to the ancient chamber beneath the Deforyan officers' quarters, in that it contained murals—three in a row, each three yards long and two high—and all rendered in brilliant colors that had been infused into the very eternastone itself.

The first mural showed a desolate scene of low, rocky hills, mostly covered in ice, and heavy gray clouds, and nothing at all living. Not a tree, a bush, a sprig of grass or even a lichen. Alucius moved before the next panel. It displayed the same location, save that there were patches of grass, a few bushes, and other scattered vegetation across the hillside, as well as a pair of what looked like scrats at the edge of a gray-water lake. The third panel showed a circular lake of brilliant blue below the same hills, and a structure of gold eternastone that resembled the Landarch's palace. Lush grass stretched toward the hills and a herd of antelope grazed in the distance, while nearer were several sandoxes being hitched to an enormous wagon by a pair of ifrits in maroon and green.

Alucius had sensed no life in the corridor or the adjoining rooms, and because he did not wish to alarm Wendra, he walked quickly to the open doorway to the first room. The wooden door had been infused with some lifeforce and swung open at his touch. An ifrit lay upon the wide bed, but the slightest air currents created by the door open-

ing touched the figure—that of a black-haired woman—
and the body shivered into dust, leaving only the shimmering eternal garments.

He watched, openmouthed, taking in the rest of the
chamber—with its carved armoire, the dressing chest, the
graceful table desk of a wood like cherry, a black-bordered
mirror, and the nightsilklike maroon coverlet upon the bed.
As in the outer chamber, the chairs had longer legs than
any that would have been comfortable for Alucius.

He stepped back out of the room and walked to the end
of the corridor, the one that he thought adjoined the chamber that had held the scepter. A small metal stub protruded
from the wall near the corner. The remainder of the lever
lay on the floor. Alucius could not budge the stub, not with
his arms, his legs, or his Talent.

Were the walls closing in on him? He glanced around,
deciding that they were not. Still . . . he was a herder born,
and being surrounded by stone with no way out, except by
Talent, gave him an uneasy feeling.

He concentrated on extending a thread of Talent toward
the darkness beneath. The return seemed much easier, and
so quick that he scarcely felt the chill.

"Oh . . . I was getting worried." Wendra let out a deep
breath.

"I stopped to take a quick look."

"Quick?"

"Fairly quick. I'm sorry. It's just that . . ."

"What was there?" asked Wendra.

Alucius shook his head. "Four rooms along a corridor . . .
I couldn't explain in the time we can go back together."

"Is it safe? How did you do it?"

"It's . . . it's like leaving a thread, one of those binding
us to the world, except that you make it thicker and anchor
it to the ley line. You leave it anchored until you're certain
that you're where you want to be."

Wendra snorted. "How do you know where you want to
be?"

"Just think about it. It's almost like looking through . . .

or at . . . a mirror in the dark. If you're worried . . . try moving just to the open passageway there, first."

"I just might."

Alucius watched as Wendra vanished, then reappeared in the doorway to the passage leading to the scepter chamber.

"You were right. It's not that hard, once you try it."

He couldn't help smiling. "You have a knack for that. It took me much longer."

"That's because all I had to do was start with what you told me."

Alucius had his doubts about that. From what he'd seen, Wendra picked up Talent matters faster than he had.

"I'll meet you in the hidden rooms." Wendra and Alendra—in the front carrypack—turned into a misty image, then vanished.

Alucius followed, ending up beside the wall with the broken lever. He stepped forward, standing behind Wendra as she looked into the room whose door he had opened.

"How terrible . . . to be trapped here. What happened, do you think?"

"The Cataclysm, I'd guess. The soarers disrupted everything, and the ifrits needed Tables. They were trapped. Or maybe the soarers were stronger and jammed the doors around the scepter."

"Why didn't they do that in Lysia?"

"I think . . . I don't know . . . but I think it's because Lysia is too far south and too hot and damp. The soarer said something about that before, when I was in the hidden city."

"Did you look at the other rooms?"

"No. I didn't want you to worry." Alucius stepped back. Wendra followed.

"You open the door. When I opened that one, there was an ifrit in the clothes, but she turned to dust at just the touch of the breeze from the door."

Wendra eased open the second door, but the chamber,

similar to the first, held no long-dead ifrit and no clothing laid out as if an ifrit might have been there. In the third chamber, the body of a male ifrit lay sprawled across a rug with a geometric design Alucius did not recognize, woven in brilliant crimson and shades of silvered gray. Within moments of the door opening his figure vanished into dust as well, leaving but the eternal clothing.

The last chamber was an armory, with strange riflelike weapons racked along the wall on the left side. The barrels were not hollow, but of a solid green crystal. Alucius could sense that whatever energy had once powered them had long since dissipated. On the right wall were pistols with the same crystal barrels, and on the rear wall were what looked to be whips with heavy stocks. The lash of the whips were thin tendrils so sharp that Alucius could appreciate their deadliness without touching them.

"Do you think we could find anything we could use?" asked Wendra.

"We can look."

In the end, even after they had gone through every drawer and desk in the sealed rooms, there was little of immediate use. Alucius had pocketed the few strange golds, but the few devices he had seen either seemed to lack power, as had the weapons, or were incomprehensible.

"We'll have to come back and study some of these later," he finally said.

Wendra nodded reluctantly. "I think the air is getting bad, too."

They held hands and slipped into the mistiness and back to the Table chamber. Alucius set the rifle on the stone and sat down. "I need a few moments to rest and some water."

"That's good. Alendra's hungry again."

Alucius drank some of the water from his bottle, occasionally extending it to Wendra. He also kept using his Talent to make sure that no one crept down the stairs to surprise them.

"I can't imagine living in a chamber like those." Wendra

shuddered. "All that stone around, and no way out if the mechanisms failed. Even if they were ifrits . . ." She shook her head.

"They didn't expect their mechanisms to fail." Alucius laughed softly. "Mechanisms always fail, sooner or later."

Wendra eased Alendra to her shoulder, burped her, and then shifted her to the other breast. "What do you think we should do now?"

"Head back to Dekhron, or as close as we can get. The dark green and maroon Table is at Salaan, and it's on a ley line. It has to be. That's close enough that we can walk to Northern Guard headquarters."

"You're going to use the Guard?"

"We have to. We can infuse all the bullets with lifeforce and have them hold the outside."

"And we'll come in from inside?"

"Do you have a better idea? Sending lancers inside would get most of them killed. At a distance, the ifrits can't do that much. I just hope that they haven't translated too many from their world while we've been learning what to do."

"We couldn't have done it much faster."

Alucius had his doubts. They should have gone to Hieron first.

"You did what you thought was best," Wendra said. "Besides, we can't change what's done."

Alucius knew that, but it didn't keep him from wishing that he could.

Wendra stood, burping Alendra once more. "She's had enough. Let's go."

"To Salaan?"

She nodded.

Alucius picked up the rifle with his left hand and took Wendra's hand with his right. Wordlessly, they concentrated.

The chill darkness welled up around them. Alucius concentrated on the dark green and maroon beacon—and the purple pink portal-like circle created by the scepter. He felt as though they rushed toward the two, and he tried to slow that rush at the end, extending a Talent-thread as an anchor, trying to press that thought/concept to Wendra as he rose through darkness, a brownish darkness that he hoped was the hillside to the east of the Table building. When he sensed light, he focused on seeing beyond the silver barrier, and thought he could see a distorted hillside. He pressed forward, and silver shards flew past and around him.

Alucius found himself on the hillside—or above it, and he barely kept his balance as he dropped several spans onto the uneven slope. He turned, trying to find Wendra, with both eyes and Talent. He could sense that she was nearby, but where?

Then he began to grin.

"That's a nasty trick," he said to the illusion of nothingness she had created.

The illusion vanished.

"Did I get it right?" asked Wendra.

"You did indeed." Alucius turned, and looking down and to the west, he saw the building the ifrits had built to house their Table. "We need to start walking. That's where the Table is, and with only one rifle, I'd rather not have to fight them off."

"We could use the ley lines again," Wendra pointed out. "If we had to."

"We could, but . . . then we'd end up somewhere else, and I think we need to meet with Feran and figure out how to attack them before they bring in more ifrits. That's if they haven't already."

They started walking down the hill, a slope covered with sparse grass, a grayish sandy soil, and scrub brush that Alucius did not recognize. He glanced toward Salaan, a good vingt and a half to the northwest. "It's about four vingts to Guard headquarters."

"The walk will do us good."

"As long as the ifrits don't send armed guards after us."

"They won't," Wendra predicted.

Alucius hoped she was right, but he lengthened his stride. They'd had more than enough delays. Useful as those had proved in some fashion, he couldn't help but worry that he'd delayed too much.

151

Salaan, Lanachrona

The light of a spring sun shining through high hazy clouds oozed through the west-facing windows of the conference room, where four ifrits sat around a table.

Barylt turned her head to look at the window. "Even the sunlight here offers no warmth." She shivered. "Everything is so cold . . . and so crude. There's no sculpture, no art, no music."

"That's what we have to build and create," Tarolt replied. "All worlds are crude before we mold them. They're often cold, as well. It is much warmer in the south, but we were limited by where we could push through the Table tube after the barriers gave way."

"We almost didn't make the long translation," Trezun added.

Lasylt straightened, lifting his hand in an imperious signal for silence. His face stiffened, and his eyes took on a faraway look.

The silence continued. The other three looked at the senior fieldmaster. In time, he lowered his hand, and his face relaxed slightly.

"What was it?" asked Tarolt.

The senior fieldmaster did not reply immediately. Then his eyes refocused, and he looked at Tarolt, seated directly across the polished wooden table from him. "There were two ancient ones, on the hillside to the east. They hovered there for several moments. Then they were gone. Or their use of lifeforce vanished." His lips tightened. "You said they were dying."

"They are less than a handful, Fieldmaster, that is, of those who direct the species. That does not mean that a few may not linger. It might also have been the colonel and the woman with him. She might have been one of the ancient ones. I could not tell."

"Either way, I suppose it does not matter, save that they must be blocked and defeated." Lasylt continued to frown. "But with the Talent-steer still loose, and two with the powers of the ancient ones seeking out the Table . . . we dare not fail. Too much is at stake. We will have to move the master scepter here from Efra in less than a year, and we have far too few Efrans here on Acorus."

Barylt nodded, not quite emphatically.

"Less than a year?" asked Tarolt. "You had said before . . . three to five years."

"It is taking more energy to maintain the tubes than we had calculated, and the supporting lifemass birthrate on Efra is declining more quickly than predicted. The Efran steers are spiritless, worse than those here on Acorus."

"Do you know how many Efrans tried to make the long translation?" asked Tarolt. "In response to your orders?"

"More than twenty," replied Lasylt.

"Yet only eight survived?" Trezun's voice carried a hint of incredulity.

"Ten," replied Lasylt. "Two of them mistakenly translated to the new Table at Norda. Once they recover, they will translate here to help protect the scepters."

"Is the young colonel that strong?" asked Barylt.

Tarolt laughed. "He's survived two translations through barriers, and he almost broached the very shields of the scepter. He has managed to kill three shadow-Efrans and one true translated Efran, and he can translate to both Tables and portals. Yes, I would say that he is strong."

"He is nothing compared to what we offer, but he is strong enough to steal the scepters, if we are not watchful and prepared to defend them. When the others have recovered, we will hunt him down like the cowardly jackal he is. Once our numbers increase, we will have no more of this nonsense. Steers must be steers, and we must rule them to create the order and beauty we bring to a world." Lasylt added, "Shortly, we will seek out the colonel so that he cannot act against us."

"If he is not already," murmured Trezun under his breath.

Tarolt glared at the Recorder.

152

Alucius and Wendra had walked through Salaan and over the ancient River Vedra bridge, then westward in Dekhron along a side street paralleling the river road, because Alucius didn't want to be recognized and have to explain . . . or refuse to explain. By the time they were a hundred yards east of the open gates to the Northern Guard post, it was early afternoon. Even though the day was windy and cool, under high hazy clouds, he was sweating, and his feet ached. He was used to riding long distances, not walking, and riding boots weren't that well designed for walking on hard-surfaced roads.

Alendra was protesting that she was hungry, and a certain odor suggested that other matters needed attention as well.

"It won't be that long," Wendra crooned. "Just a little longer, little girl, and we'll get you cleaned up and fed. Just a little longer."

Alendra's cries suggested that a little longer was far too long to wait.

The sentries at the gate watched as the two walked closer. With the hand not carrying the rifle, Alucius unfastened the riding jacket enough to show the colonel's insignia he had replaced on his tunic collar.

"That you, sir? Colonel?"

"It's me. Things didn't quite go as planned. We've had a long walk." Alucius smiled. "One of you probably ought to go tell Majer Feran that we're back."

"Yes, sir!" The younger sentry turned and ran toward the headquarters' building. Alucius and Wendra kept walking.

Ahead of them, the young lancer's voice echoed through the post. "Majer! The colonel's back! Big as life!"

Feran was standing outside, watching as Alucius limped up to the headquarters. He shook his head. "Couldn't you have found an easier way to spend time with her, sir?"

Alucius laughed, as much at the dryness of Feran's voice as anything else. "I didn't plan it that way. I thought the traders were up to something. They were, and Wendra's disappearance was connected to it. Once we get her settled in the quarters, I'll fill you in on what happened."

Alucius caught sight of a familiar figure in the doorway. "Dhaghet . . . would you help my wife up to the quarters?"

"Yes, sir."

Wendra smiled at Alucius, an almost enigmatic expression, but one that was both warm and a warning to him not to reveal too much.

"I'll be up later," he promised.

"Do what you need to do."

Alucius nodded, watching as Dhaghet escorted her toward the steps to the upper level. Then he turned and walked into headquarters. Once inside, he made his way into the colonel's study—his still, he imagined—and waited for Feran to follow.

Feran shut the door.

"Where have you been?" asked the older officer. "We found your mount in an orchard south of Salaan. A grower reported it. I was holding off reporting your disappearance."

"Thank you. I appreciate that." With a deep breath, Alucius settled into the chair behind the desk, happy to get off his feet.

"Was this . . . the traders? Tarolt?"

"It's worse and more complicated than I'd thought. I

started out tracking down Tarolt because I thought he had to have used Talent to steal from the Guard. He caught me off guard and locked me up, in a special way, and I got shot up some more . . ."

"Why doesn't that surprise me?" Feran asked dryly. His eyes narrowed, and he frowned. "The traders have Talent?"

Alucius had thought out how he wanted to approach that question. "We had it backward. The traders are working with the Regent. They might even be controlling her, rather than the other way around. That's why they don't want anyone to win. Tarolt has more Talent than the prophet did. That's how so many old traders died, and why all the others do what he wants. He's got two or three others with Talent working with him. He probably used Talent to control Weslyn. That could be why he and Imealt tried to kill me."

"I wondered about that. It didn't make sense," Feran said slowly. "Not unless they knew you had Talent. You've always been a target. There have been more bullets aimed at you than at anyone else." He paused, then asked, "Is it because you're the only one who can stand up against that kind of Talent?"

"I didn't think so at first, but that just might be it." Alucius offered a shrug. "You remember the traders with the silver wheel on their wagons?"

"The ones who supplied the prophet? I thought that was Halanat and his son."

"It was. But Tarolt was the one behind it. He's been controlling everything." Alucius leaned forward slightly. "I was scouting out his place south of Salaan, but he'd been watching me, and they set up a trap. I guess I got too cocky. I ended up in a strange place with stone walls all around. The guards there weren't as good as Tarolt and his men, but it took some time to get free, and then I found Wendra." Those words were true in a sense, as true as Alucius dared to make them.

"I won't ask how you managed that." After a pause, the majer asked, "What can we do?" He smiled, crookedly.

"Knowing you, you've got a plan. And knowing you, you'd not be too happy with anyone who hurt your wife."

"I'm not. But I'm even angrier at what Tarolt has done, and all the lancers killed on all sides just so they can get more power and golds. We've got a war between Lanachrona and Madrien, and if we don't do something, before long the Regent will be attacking all our companies in the north."

"You think that stopping Tarolt will help?"

"More than you know."

Feran shook his head. "When you talk like that, it's hard to believe otherwise."

"You've seen it. Weslyn did what they wanted. If we hadn't come back when we did, what would have happened to the Iron Valleys?"

"Nothing good. So . . . what do we do now?"

"We stop Tarolt and the handful around him. Most of the traders have just been controlled by Tarolt and Halanat. Halanat's dead. We take care of Tarolt, and things will eventually settle down. But . . . we'll have to be very careful. We can't storm his stronghold the way we did with the prophet. It would take years for the Guard to recover from that, and the Lord-Protector might want both our heads—or at least our immediate resignations or dismissals. And we'd lose a lot of troopers to Talent, and we don't need that, either."

"I can see that," Feran said. "If it's possible, I'd like to stay in service and alive long enough to collect a stipend."

"I'd like that, too. So . . . Wendra and I will do the dirty work—"

"Wendra? She . . . you've got a child."

"She's also a herder, and I need someone who can resist Talent and handle a rifle." Alucius needed more than that, but that was as much as he was about to admit.

Feran chuckled ironically. "Anything that needs two of you . . ."

"Tarolt and his two assistants can use Talent up close, but not from a distance. We'll take advantage of that. We'll use Faisyn and first squad to keep them pinned inside so that they can't escape."

"Then what?"

"Tarolt and his people are holed up in a building just south of the orchard—it was an apricot orchard, wasn't it, where you found the chestnut?"

"All those fruit trees look alike to me."

"We're just going to sneak in the underground entrance and flush them out."

"Just like that? You and Wendra?" Feran raised his eyebrows. "Are you going to stay in one piece this time, or is this going to be like the business with the prophet?"

"It could be worse," Alucius admitted.

"Can't we just . . ." Feran paused. "They were really behind the Regent?"

"And Weslyn, and the attacks on Twenty-first Company when we were at Emal."

"How many are there?"

"Three that I know of, but there could be more. They were training more people in using Talent. I don't know where they came from, but they could use Talent." Again, Alucius was stretching the truth.

"How about two squads?"

Alucius considered for a moment. "Two would be fine. I don't like the idea of riding an entire company up to a trader's building. Oh, and I need a mount for Wendra, and another rifle for her. I'll pay for them, but she'll need them."

"The man is trying to save his homeland, and he still thinks about not abusing his position." Feran shifted his weight in the wooden chair. "Then, that's another reason why I trust you when you tell me something strange like this. It also doesn't hurt that you're always right. Anyone who wagers against you loses."

"Not always. I did end up in the Matrite forces."

"True. But who else ever escaped, except the ones you brought back?"

"There must have been some," Alucius demurred.

"When do you want to do this?" asked Feran.

"Tomorrow morning, starting two glasses before dawn."

"I could have guessed. You've always had that herder habit of getting up early."

Alucius laughed, once. "I'd prefer to sleep later, but I need the darkness to set up things, and I worry about their bringing in more Talent."

"Tarolt can't be just a trader."

"He's not. But we'll leave it at that."

"So long as you're colonel, that's fine by me."

"So long as I'm the one explaining? I'm not sure I'll ever be able to explain. But it doesn't matter. We have to stop Tarolt before he does any more damage."

"With what he's done already, that's good enough for me. How do you want to approach his stronghold?"

Alucius opened the drawer, looking for paper on which to sketch out his plan, and Feran eased his chair up to the other side of the desk.

It was late afternoon by the time Alucius and Feran had finished working out the details, including briefing Faisyn on the particulars of the next morning's attack. Alucius had only munched on some dry travel bread, and his stomach was growling as he walked up the steps to the commander's quarters.

He had barely closed the door when Wendra met him, draped in one of his tunics.

"It was good to get washed up, but I just had to wash out everything I'd been wearing. I hope you don't mind."

He eyed her appreciatively. "I don't mind at all. Where's Alendra?"

"She's sleeping in the second bedroom."

Alucius grinned widely.

Wendra flushed.

After a moment, they both laughed.

153

Early on Tridi morning, two and a half glasses before dawn, Alucius had finished his simple breakfast of bread, cheese, dried fruit, and water. So had Wendra, and she had just changed Alendra and strapped her into the carrypack.

"You're wearing nightsilk?" asked Alucius.

"I told you I was. That's why I washed it yesterday."

"Are you sure you can use the rifle with her?" asked Alucius.

"I'm sure." A tinge of exasperation colored Wendra's voice. "The carrypack holds her out of the way, and it's nightsilk. I'm used to it. I've ridden the stead and shot sandwolves with her. I've even killed a black sander and one of those pteridons . . ."

Alucius hadn't realized that the wild translations had continued to track Wendra. She'd never said a word.

". . . Besides, it will take two of us. You've gotten hurt every single time you've gone against the ifrits by yourself. And I'm not leaving Alendra. Don't even suggest it."

"She'd be safe here," Alucius ventured.

Wendra looked directly at him. "For how long . . . if anything happens to either of us? I can't help you if I'm worrying about her, and you can't do this without me. We have to do it together."

"I could detail a squad."

"How much good would they be against those ifrits?"

Alucius decided against saying more. "We'd better head down to the courtyard." He slipped on the nightsilk riding jacket. With the vest under his tunic, he trusted that his body was as well protected as possible. Wendra was wearing his lighter nightsilk riding jacket, with the bottoms of the sleeves rolled up. He just hoped that they wouldn't come under rifle fire from the ifrits.

He picked up both his rifles and slung the saddlebags over his shoulder. All that was inside were packages of travel fare, as well as two belt water bottles. All the cartridges in his belt and in the magazines of his rifles and Wendra's rifle were already infused with dark lifeforce, but they needed to do the same for the rifles of the lancers who would be accompanying them.

Alucius waited at the door for Wendra and Alendra, then closed it behind them. It thudded shut with a heavy dullness.

Dhaget had their mounts saddled and waiting, but after putting the saddlebags in place, Alucius took a moment to check everything before slipping the rifles into their cases. Wendra had already mounted by the time he finished. As the two squads began to form up in the darkness, Alucius and Wendra began to infuse the cartridges of first squad with lifeforce darkness.

"That's not tiring you, is it?" he asked.

"Dear . . . I'm fine."

Alucius winced. Somehow, it was different with Wendra accompanying him. She was more capable than most of the lancers, if not all of them, and yet . . . he couldn't help worrying.

"If I fussed over you," she whispered quietly, leaning toward him, "the way you are over me, you'd have removed my head a good glass ago."

He flushed, glad that it was dim enough in the courtyard that she could not see. "I'm sorry," he finally replied, in a low voice.

"You don't have to be sorry. Just don't do it anymore."

Alucius couldn't help smiling.

Faisyn reined up, less than three yards away. "First and second squads are present and ready, Colonel."

"Thank you, Faisyn. I'd like to say a few words to them before we head out."

"Yes, sir." Faisyn turned his mount. "Listen up. Colonel's got a few words for you!"

Alucius urged the chestnut forward, then reined up, waiting for the last murmurs to die away before speaking, using a touch of Talent to boost his voice and project absolute conviction. "As some of you may know, I was on a mission for the Lord-Protector, trying to find out some things. What I discovered is that a trader here has Talent, just like the prophet. This trader was the one who trained the prophet, and he was the one who corrupted Colonel Weslyn. They've been working to weaken the Northern Guard so that the Regent can move into parts of the Iron Valleys. This morning, your job is simple. You're to make sure that no one escapes from the trader's stronghold. These people are like the prophet's lancers. They'll keep coming and try to kill you until they're dead. They're about as evil and as low as anyone can be, and they've done just about everything they can to weaken the Guard and get you and the other lancers killed off so that they could make a few golds. We're going to put a stop to it. When we get where we're going, senior squad leader Faisyn will deploy you so that you can cover all the entrances to the stronghold. Under *no* circumstances are you to leave your group. That's all." Alucius turned to Faisyn. "Let's head out."

"Colonel's detail, form on the colonel."

Four lancers rode forward, headed by Dhaget and Fewal, moving in behind Alucius and Wendra. Once they were in position, Alucius urged the big chestnut toward the gates. Wendra kept pace.

"Squads, forward! Silent riding! Silent riding!"

The small force rode through Dekhron, toward the River Vedra bridge. Outside of insects, and the occasional squalling of a stray cat, or the barking of a dog, the loudest sound was that of hoofs on the street, a clicking that sharpened once they turned onto the eternastone high road north of the bridge.

Selena had set shortly after sunset, but the tiny green disc of Asterta was close to its zenith as Alucius reached the midpoint of the bridge. Was that a sign? With a wry smile, Alucius dismissed it as mere coincidence.

Few as the lamps were in Dekhron, by comparison, Salaan was totally dark, and Alucius had to rely on both his Talent and his herder's nightsight to pick out the side road leading toward the Table building—and the scepters within. All the time, Asterta stood high in the predawn sky, symbol of the ancient goddess of war, a tiny, bright green disc shedding little light.

As Alucius led his force away off the side road and westward along the lane toward the eastern end of the orchard that bordered the Table building, the faintest trace of gray had begun to appear above the eastern horizon. They had ridden only a few hundred yards down the lane when Alucius turned in the saddle and whispered, "Faisyn!"

"Sir . . ."

"Here's where we leave you. You know what to do. Don't let anyone get close to you and the men, and don't let them escape. If you shoot someone, leave them where they fall."

"Yes, sir."

Alucius turned the chestnut to the south, leading the way across the meadow toward the dip in the hillside. Tarolt's Table building was almost a vingt to the southwest from the point he and Wendra had picked out. When they reached the base of the low hills, Alucius guided the chestnut up the swale, extending his Talent sense, trying to seek out the ley lines beneath the clay and rock of the hillside.

Halfway up, he reined the chestnut to a halt. "This is as close as we can ride."

"Yes, sir."

After he dismounted, Alucius handed the chestnut's reins to Dhaget, while Wendra handed those of her roan to Fewal. Alucius took both his rifles from their cases, then looked up at Dhaget. "This could be over in a glass, or it could take half a day. If you see anyone coming from the building to the west, shoot them. Otherwise, just wait."

"Yes, sir." Dhaget's voice held a slight question.

"We're going to try to enter through a hidden underground entrance. You can't do it unless you're a herder or have Talent."

"Yes, sir."

Alucius looked to Wendra and Alendra. Their daughter was awake, peering through the predawn dimness, but making only slight gurgling sounds.

"We'll walk up a ways."

Wendra nodded.

After about thirty yards, Alucius stopped. "Can you feel them?" He hooked the second rifle to the makeshift clip on his belt.

"I think we're close enough."

"We'll try to come out on the east end of the Table room, and you'll have to be ready to fire the moment you can . . . If we don't have time to reload, we drop under and come back here."

"I'm taking whichever side I'm on, and you're taking the other?"

"That's right."

Alucius concentrated on letting a Talent-probe weave through the ground beneath him, seeking a firm contact with the misty blackness of the ley lines beneath. As he probed, he was ever more aware of Wendra's presence. He brought up the rifle into a firing position, knowing that he would emerge in that same position. Wendra followed his example.

Alendra gurgled happily.

"There . . ." he murmured, as his probe touched and linked to the darkness below.

"Me too."

Alucius felt himself merging with the blackness beneath and with the hillside as he dropped down toward the ley line. He could sense Wendra and Alendra as well, even as they reached the chill darkness that they would travel such a short distance. Above them was the purpled hard blackness of the ifrit's translation tube, and ahead were the maroon and green of the Table and the purple pinkness of the

scepter and the portal it created. The silvery barrier wa-
vered before him, and he could make out two ifrits beyond
the Table.

Silver splashed away from him . . .

His finger tightened on the trigger, but he had to take a
half step to steady himself.

Crack! Crack! Wendra had gotten there first and was already firing.

Crack! Alucius's first shot took the ifrit on the left, for
he was to the left of his wife, squarely in the chest. The ifrit
man staggered.

The second shot went through the broad forehead.

The other ifrit dropped.

Another figure in purple and maroon scrambled down
the steps—and dropped as both Alucius and Wendra fired
together.

A fourth ifrit appeared, and a line of blue flame flared
toward Alucius.

Wendra's shot knocked the ifrit off balance, and Alucius jabbed a Talent-probe toward the weapon. The
weapon flared purple, and Wendra's second shot dropped
the ifrit.

"Reload now!" Alucius said.

Wendra deftly slipped the cartridges from her belt into
the magazine while Alucius covered the steps, probing
with his Talent to find how many other ifrits remained. He
hadn't thought that Tarolt had been among those who had
rushed them.

"You now," Wendra said.

Alucius reloaded quickly, but the stairwell remained
empty, although he could sense five other ifrits somewhere
on the upper levels. He edged forward around the left side
of the Table while Wendra took the right side.

"The Table . . ." murmured Wendra.

Alucius didn't have to look. He could sense a well of force
rising from the oblong beside him, force linking to an ifrit.

Pinkish purple filled the stairwell, a shimmering crystalline curtain.

"Don't shoot," Alucius murmured. "Not at the pink. It'll throw the bullet back at us."

"What . . . ?"

"Darkness. Lifeforce darkness . . . we need to surround it."

The purple-pink shield bulged into the Table chamber. Behind it came an ifrit, a male figure taller and broader than any Alucius had seen, an ifrit almost as large as the oversized statue in the Table chamber in Dulka.

"Most ingenious . . . especially for Talent-poor steers. Use your weapons . . ."

Alucius flung a web of blackness across the purple shield, blocking the ifrit from view, but that blackness began to fade, and the purpleness began to shine through the blackness, slowly dissolving it.

"The scepter!" Wendra pointed toward the side of the table. "He's drawing on it."

"Can you use blackness against it?" Alucius asked.

Wendra's face tightened. Alendra whimpered.

A line of purple flame flared toward Wendra.

Both Alucius and Wendra raised green black shields, stopping the jolt of power, but Alucius ended up taking a step backward, so great was the pressure. He glanced sideways to see that Wendra also had been forced back.

Before the ifrit could direct another flare of purple at them, Alucius aimed a black Talent javelin at the ifrit's shield, flinging it with all the force possible. The shield shivered . . . contracted, and then expanded to fling the blackness away from it, back toward Alucius, thrusting him against the wall.

Even wearing nightsilk, Alucius could feel the impact of stone against his back.

"Link to . . . the ley lines," suggested Wendra. "Not to the world, but . . . lifeforce. Draw directly . . ." The words were forced out, as if against great pressure.

Another purple spear flared toward them. Alucius managed to parry it, and the energy slammed into the wall beside him. Droplets of molten stone splattered around him. One burned the back of his hand.

The purple pink shield grew brighter, and hot like a summer sun, then even hotter. Waves of heat surged toward Wendra and Alucius.

Alucius linked to the blackness beneath them, the blackness of the ley lines, with all his Talent, letting the lifeforce flow through him, and around the scepter beside Wendra. He could feel her linking into the lifeforce—all the lifeforce of Corus.

Darkness welled out and through them, creating a wall of blackness that blocked the sunlike blaze that had heated the air in the Table chamber so much that each breath burned.

Alucius found himself coughing while still trying to channel the dark lifeforce of Corus itself from the ley lines and the world into the wall of greenish blackness that he and Wendra had built—a wall of lifeforce that had finally halted the progress of the blazing purple shield. Even so, the air in the Table chamber remained stifling.

The purple shield pulsed.

Alucius and Wendra pressed back.

"We . . . can't let him . . . get to the Table," Wendra panted.

"He's strong."

Alucius pressed more darkness against the shield, and around the unshielded scepter, trying to deny its force to the ifrit. Wendra followed his example.

Sweat poured from Alucius's forehead, and he felt as though he had been carrying chests filled with lead.

Abruptly, the purpleness shivered.

Alucius lifted his rifle, waiting, adding more darkness to the cartridge in the chamber and those in the magazine.

Dark purpleness exploded away from the stairwell and the entry to the Table chamber, revealing the looming purple figure who held a light-cutter.

Alucius fired first, one shot right after the other. Both

slammed into the ifrit's suddenly revealed forehead, and he toppled forward. Flame filled the stairwell with such intensity that the stone walls glowed for a moment.

Holding his rifle ready, and ignoring the other rifle's impact against his knees, Alucius charged past the table and over the bodies of the ifrits. The heat from the stone walls of the staircase was so great that the sweat on Alucius's forehead and neck evaporated instantly before he was halfway up the steps.

As he neared the top of the stairs he saw another figure and fired. Once more, the ifrit's garments stopped the bullet, but the impact staggered the woman. Alucius used the last two shots in the rifle to stop her.

Wendra, following him up the stairs, fired past his shoulder, and yet another ifrit dropped.

There were words in another tongue, coming from the foyer beyond the conference room. Alucius thought he understood them, not knowing how or why. He edged up beside the archway into the foyer, less than three yards from the ifrits, but protected by the internal stone walls of the building.

"The ancient ones!"

"Do something!"

"They can't stand against the light-cutters . . ."

Alucius leaned the empty first rifle against the wall and wrenched the second from its clip, cocking it as he did, and extending his Talent to the foyer, where three ifrits had raised weapons—the ones that used light to cut through everything.

Wendra eased against the wall beside him.

With a cold smile, Alucius extended a Talent-probe, quickly unlinking the crystalline linkages within each weapon. "Can you reload?" he whispered.

"Just a moment."

Even before she had slipped the magazine back into place, Alucius had determined where the three stood.

"We'll try unraveling them . . ."

Two Talent-probes snaked around the edge of the archway, then arrowed toward the three remaining ifrits.

Alucius could feel the jolt as his probe struck the Talent-armor of the ifrit. He just slipped around that and arrowed toward the ifrit's main node. Purple light flared, and the edge of the archway boiled away, rock and glass droplets clinking like rain on the stone entry foyer flooring.

Wendra was far more deft than Alucius, and in instants, one of the ifrits shuddered and toppled forward. Moments later, the second shuddered and fell.

The third turned, and started to wrench the doorway open.

Alucius leapt clear of the archway, lifted his rifle and fired. It took three shots before the last ifrit lay on the floor.

He continued to study the building with eyes, ears, and Talent.

"There's no one left," Wendra said dully.

"We need to move the scepters out of sight. There's a hidden room."

"Like the others off the Table chambers?"

"Yes." Alucius paused. "Are you all right? Is Alendra . . ."

"We're all right. I think . . . she's a little . . . awed . . . stunned . . . something . . . she senses Talent already, I think, but she doesn't know what it is."

Alucius waited.

"You're used to this. With people, I mean. I've killed sandwolves, and sanders . . ." She shook her head. "It was all so fast. There were ten ifrits . . . people . . . and they're dead. I know we had to . . . but . . . they are dead, and they thought they were doing what was right for them."

"They probably thought that." Alucius nodded back toward the staircase back to the Table chamber. Absently, he blotted his sweating forehead. He hadn't noticed it before, but the rooms were hot, almost stifling, and the stove in the conference room was pouring forth heat.

"It is hot."

"The soarers said that their world was warmer." Alucius moved past the circular table, where several crystal mugs remained, half full with a clear liquid. He started down the steps, avoiding the two bodies, and then reentered the Table chamber, moving past the other bodies.

As Wendra had indicated, there were two boxes against the northern side of the Table. One was metallic black and silver—a match to the empty casket still embedded in the rock in Dereka—and the second was a simple wooden case, through which Alucius could sense the purple-pink pulsing power of the scepter that had been the basis of the powers of the Matrial and the Regent.

"Can you open that door?" Alucius asked. "The hidden one?"

Wendra moved to the light-torch bracket and twisted it. Nothing happened. She frowned, then concentrated.

"There's some sort of Talent-lock on this," she finally said. "They've wrapped Talent around it."

"Can you undo it? Dissolve it with darkness?"

"I think so . . . I've got it." The section of stone wall silently slid open.

"Wait a moment." Alucius used his Talent to check the passageway and the chamber beyond, but he detected no one.

The two eased into the two-yard-wide corridor and followed it to the single chamber at the end. A weapons rack, holding a single light-cutter and brackets for twelve more, was the only thing affixed to the walls. A sturdy long table, holding five chests, was set against the wall to the left.

Wendra opened one of the chests, then stepped back. "It's filled . . . with golds."

"I thought there might be something like this." Alucius set his rifle against the wall. "I'll carry the chests out, and the scepters in, then we'll close this up." He looked at Wendra. "Once I do, could you put Talent around it, in the way that the ifrits or the soarers did? A Talent-lock of sorts?"

"I can try."

Alucius lifted the first chest, carrying it out, then returning with the black and silver scepter casket, far heavier than it looked. He was sweating profusely by the time he had finished moving chests and scepters. After that, he reclaimed one of his rifles and watched with his Talent as Wendra closed the secret stone door and Talent-locked it, so that merely turning the light-torch bracket would not open the hidden door.

"Now . . . we'll have to tell the others."

Wendra started for the steps.

"No. We'll have to go back the way we came."

"That's right." Wendra offered a wan smile. "You left orders to shoot anyone who left the building." She took a deep breath.

Alucius started to link with the ley blackness before realizing that he was still linked.

He and Wendra dropped into the chill, almost welcome after the heat of the Table building. With each use of the ley lines, the world lifeforce lines, Alucius was becoming more aware of what lay outside and above—and of where Wendra was. They eased themselves to a point that looked—through the wavering silver barrier—to be behind a stand of scrub brush less than forty yards uphill from the waiting lancers. The silver flashed away from them.

They stood in the slanting light of the first glass past dawn, dew still on the shadowed sparse grass and the leaves of the scrub oak. Just a glass. Alucius was always amazed at how quickly some things happened and how slowly others did.

"Ahhhh . . ." The first syllable was Alendra's.

"She's hungry," Wendra said wryly. "She's had her adventure, and it's time to eat."

"Let's let them know we're back."

They turned downhill and stepped out from behind the brush.

"Dhaget! Fewal!" Alucius called.

"Sir. We heard shots. Are you all right?"

"This time."

"That's because you didn't do it alone," murmured Wendra.

Alucius could hear the smile in her words. "You don't have to remind me."

"Oh, yes, I do. We still have to deliver some scepters."

Alucius felt a chill run down his spine at her words. "As soon as we get some respite. And you feed our little friend."

Wendra nodded.

Wendra's words had reminded Alucius of how little time they had. Days before, there had only been four ifrits. They had found ten, and he had no idea how many were elsewhere, in Prosp or Norda.

Dhaget and Fewal rode uphill and met the two herders halfway.

Dhaget looked at Alucius for a long moment, then at Wendra. So did the other three lancers. Alucius glanced at his wife. He didn't see any great difference . . . except . . . he thought that she seemed somehow . . . more alive . . . a little larger than life.

There wasn't much Alucius could do about that. He took Wendra's rifle, checked it, and slipped it into her saddle case while she mounted.

"You're missing a rifle, sir," observed Fewal.

"I left it inside the stronghold. I'll get it when we go back." Alucius mounted the chestnut. He turned to Roncar. "I'd like you to ride back to headquarters and have Majer Feran join us. We'll also need a heavy wagon to move some gear back to the post."

"Yes, sir." Although a puzzled expression crossed the lancer's face, he nodded acknowledgment and turned his mount back toward Salaan.

Alucius and Wendra rode slowly back across the meadow, then turned west on the lane through the apricot orchard, followed by the remaining three lancers.

Faisyn met them near the end of the orchard—almost at the spot where Alucius had tied the chestnut when he'd first investigated the Table building.

Like Dhaget, Faisyn studied Alucius for a moment before speaking. Then he gave the minutest of headshakes. "Sir? We heard shots a while back . . . but no one came out. I had second squad order the ostler and the folks in the other building to stay inside."

"Thank you. I should have thought about that," Alucius admitted.

"If I might ask . . . sir."

"Oh . . . they're dead. All of the Talent-twisted ones."

"Talent-twisted?"

"You'll see. Talent can be used for good or evil, just like most abilities. Those who use it for evil . . . it does something to them." As he spoke, Alucius realized that, for some reason, he seemed to be sitting higher or straighter in the saddle. He didn't recall looking down at Faisyn quite so much. He glanced sideways at Wendra, realizing that she was larger . . . all over, not by that much, but enough so that she probably stood a half a handspan taller, yet her garments did not seem tighter. Alucius concealed a frown. How could that have happened? "Oh . . . send Roncar to get Majer Feran and a supply wagon. There's equipment in there, and some other things that belong to the Guard."

"Yes, sir."

Alucius looked at Wendra, who was patting Alendra, and gently bouncing her, clearly trying to mollify a hungry child who was unlikely to be pacified much longer. "Where do you want to feed her?"

"Out here. For now."

Alucius understood. He turned back to Faisyn. "Why don't you come inside? You can see what happened." He turned in the saddle. "Dhaget, if you and the others would stay with my wife?"

"Yes, sir." Dhaget's expression conveyed a definite impression that he doubted Wendra needed much protection.

Alucius wondered at the reaction, because Dhaget hadn't seen Wendra even using weapons, not that the lancer's impression was totally wrong, but Wendra would be slower to react while breast-feeding.

Faisyn and Alucius rode toward the Table building, trailed by a half squad of lancers. They reined up just short of the stone walkway to the door. The senior squad leader dismounted, following Alucius. Alucius carried his rifle toward the entry, although his Talent sensed no one in the building. Still, so long as the Table was operational, other ifrits could appear.

As he neared the half-open doorway, Faisyn's mouth opened as he saw the dead ifrit.

"That's what the Talent-twisted look like when they don't hide behind a Talent-illusion," Alucius explained. "There are more inside. They're dead." He opened the door and stepped over and around the dead ifrit.

Faisyn looked at the two fallen ifrits in the foyer before his eyes drifted to the ravaged side of the archway, and the once-molten and since-hardened drops of stone and ceramic on the floor.

The two walked into the conference room, where the heat continued to well out from the iron stove against the wall. Alucius blotted his forehead again. "They like it warm."

"It is hot." Faisyn looked to the side wall behind the archway, where Alucius's other rifle rested. "That's yours, isn't it?"

"I left it here. I didn't see any sense in lugging it back."

The squad leader's eyes dropped to the two bodies on the far side of the conference room.

"There are five more on the stairs and in the lower room," Alucius said.

Faisyn stopped. "Looks like you scarcely needed us, sir."

"You saw the one by the doorway. If there had been more . . ." Alucius left the rest of what he might have said hanging. "We were lucky."

Faisyn shook his head. "Sir . . . Colonel . . . I'd not be arguing with you, but . . . if you'd been counting on luck, you'd have been buried long ago." He straightened up, surveying the room, then walked to the staircase and looked down. "Pretty big fellows . . . even the woman there." He paused. "Your wife shot some, too, didn't she?"

"About half, maybe more. She's very good."

"You wouldn't have brought her if she wasn't."

"I didn't want to," Alucius admitted.

Faisyn shifted his weight from boot to boot.

"You can go outside, if you want," Alucius said. "I need to wait here, just to make sure someone else doesn't try to sneak in through the underground entrance down there."

"You want two of the men here?"

"Two should be enough." Alucius walked to the window and opened it wide. Then he pulled out one of the chairs and seated himself. "If you'd leave the front door open."

"Yes, sir."

On his way out, Faisyn dragged the one ifrit back into the foyer.

Shortly, two troopers appeared. "Sir?"

"In here."

Alucius recognized only one of the two, the generally hapless Sylat. "You can sit down. We're just here waiting for Majer Feran . . . and to make sure none of the Talent-twisted sneak in from down there." He inclined his head to the stairwell.

More than a glass passed before Alucius heard the wagon drive up. During that time, he drank almost an entire water bottle.

Alucius could sense that Wendra accompanied Feran. He stood as his wife and the majer entered the room. "Sylat . . . you two can report back to your squad leader."

"Yes, sir."

The two lancers inclined their heads to Feran and slipped out.

Feran waited until the three of them stood alone. He studied Alucius. "It's still you, isn't it?"

"Same man who played leschec with you in Emal, when you complained that you didn't see why you bothered," Alucius said dryly. "Same officer who watched you go off griping about protecting an oilseed works . . . owned, as we later found out, by Yusalt's esteemed father."

Feran nodded. "You're different. The same, but different."

"Come on down the stairs. You'll see why."

Feran looked at the dead ifrits more closely. "Those . . . what are they? I've never see people like that."

Alucius caught the amused smile that flitted across Wendra's face. "That's what someone truly twisted and possessed by Talent looks like. The one second from the end was Tarolt. He just projected an illusion when he met people. That was probably why he didn't meet that many people. It took too much effort. There are five more down below." Alucius led the way. Feran followed, and Wendra came last, patting Alendra with one hand, her rifle in the other.

Once in the lower room, Feran gestured toward the black lorken-framed oblong. "Is that one of those Tables?"

"Yes. Tarolt built one here. That's how he knew where people were."

"Can you use it?"

"Probably," Alucius said, "but using it for long turns people into . . . those."

An expression of distaste crossed Feran's face. "The more I find out about Talent . . . the less I like what I discover."

"Talent's like any other form of ability. It's easy to misuse, and the results are ugly when it is."

Feran gestured toward the body of the largest ifrit. "Never seen anyone that big before. You think he was someone important?"

Alucius looked at the dead ifrit. "He was the most powerful one. I don't suppose we'll ever know who he was." After a moment, he walked over to the five chests set in front of the Table. He opened each of the lids in turn, revealing the contents.

Feran surveyed them. "There must be thousands of golds . . ."

"Close to ten thousand, I'd guess," Alucius said.

"They had that much . . . and they let . . . the Council . . . ?"

"Some of it they got later, I think, but they never would have let the Council know."

Feran's lips tightened. "They make hogshit smell sweet."

Alucius nodded.

"What do you plan to do with the golds?"

"I'd like to buy back our independence, but it's too late for that. We'll send a third of it to the Lord-Protector and we'll keep the rest to pay for moving the Northern Guard to Iron Stem—and for equipment and supplies. We'll be honest. We'll tell the Lord-Protector. He'll be happy to get three thousand golds. He's already agreed to the move, and now it won't cost him."

"You don't think he'll want more?" asked Feran, skepticism evident in every word.

"After what we've done? I don't think so." Alucius laughed. "Besides, who would he send to collect it?"

In turn, Feran laughed. Wendra smiled.

The silence drew out.

"You're not finished, are you?" Feran said slowly.

"No."

"I didn't think so. You have that . . . air."

"I'm going to ask you for yet another indulgence and favor," Alucius said. "I'll need a guard posted around the building. They're to stop anyone from leaving until Wendra and I return."

"Where are you going? How long?"

Alucius gestured to the Table. "They can be used for travel. With Talent. There are two more of these." He gestured to the dead ifrits. "And a number more of those Talent-twisted."

"And I suppose you two need to save Corus from them?"

Alucius forced a laugh. "Something like that." He paused. "Do you want another bunch like the prophet's lancers or the Matrial's torques?"

"These . . . did that?"

Alucius nodded. "And more. They brought those pteridons and skylances we fought in Deforya." Alucius didn't
mention that they'd brought them millennia earlier. They
had brought them, and it didn't matter when.

Feran was the one to laugh. "If it were anyone but you,
anyone at all . . ."

"Thank you."

"When are you leaving? How long will you be gone?"

"As soon as we can. We won't leave until we eat, and until the lancers have dragged out the bodies, and until you're
ready to take the golds back and lock them up. I think it
would be better to get some oil and burn the bodies."

"So do I. But I'd like all the squad leaders to see them."

Alucius nodded. "Post sentries outside. Don't let anyone
out but Wendra or me."

"They couldn't create an illusion like you?"

"It wouldn't be very good. Any of them who knew me
are dead. I don't think any of them even know about Wendra. Not yet."

"It's been quite a month, Colonel. Quite a month."

Not nearly so much of a month as it would be, reflected
Alucius—one way or another.

154

Just after late midmorning in Salaan, Alucius and Wendra stood between the archway to the stairs
and the Table. Each had one of the heavy scepters recovered from the ifrits, but each scepter was strapped to an
empty sabre scabbard, secured with a tie around the leg
just above the knee. The power of each scepter, black and
silver, seemed to cast light and shadows, but light and
shadows seen only with Talent.

"You think the scepters will show us where the master

scepter is?" asked Wendra. "The one the soarer told us to find?"

"I don't know, but if it's a master scepter, it has to be stronger than these, and we could sense these halfway across Corus, once we knew what we were looking for."

"If it's not in a case, or shielded," Wendra pointed out.

"We'll have to risk that."

"Risk what?" asked Feran, coming down the steps from the conference room.

"Not being able to do what we have to," Alucius replied.

"You look . . . armed." Feran's eyes went to the scepters. "Those . . . they don't feel right."

"They aren't. That's why we need to return them."

"You're not going to explain more, are you?"

"It's better that we don't."

Feran raised his eyebrows, but didn't reply.

In addition to a scepter, Alucius and Wendra each carried a herder's rifle. All the cartridges they carried had been heavily infused with lifeforce. Alucius had strapped a cartridge belt over his nightsilk herders' vest. He had decided against wearing the heavy riding jacket, based on the heat in the Table building and the soarer's statements that the ifrits' world was far warmer than Corus. Both he and Wendra carried water bottles as well as travel food within their garments, and Wendra had folded extra cloth and clothing for Alendra around and inside her jacket and tunic.

Feran stepped to one side. "All you want is a guard around the building?"

"That's right. Not in here."

"How long will you be gone?"

Alucius shrugged. "I don't know. A day, a week . . . If we're not back in a month, then you'll have to worry about the . . . Talent-twisted ones yourself." He'd almost said ifrits, but the word would have meant little to Feran. "Their clothes are like nightsilk, except stronger. Head shots are best. Right now, I don't think there are any left west of the Spine of Corus. There are two Tables in Lustrea, and an old

Table in the ruins of Blackstear, not that there's any way
for the Northern Guard to reach any of them."

"What do we do here, if you . . . ?" Feran didn't finish
the statement.

Alucius understood. "Use enough powder to fragment
the entire building and drop it around the Table. Explosives
won't destroy the Table, but rock piled deep on top of it
will keep it from being used."

"Hope it doesn't come to that," Feran replied.

"So do we."

Wendra offered a tight nod of agreement. Within the carrypack, Alendra waved a small fist.

Alucius jumped onto to the Table, then offered a hand to
Wendra. She took it, and they stood side by side on the
Table. Alucius nodded to Feran, then concentrated on the
darkness of the translation tube beneath them. He and
Wendra began to sink into the Table.

*The purpled blackness of the ifrit tube was every bit as
chill as Alucius had recalled, a bone-biting cold that combined with a sense of foreboding. He focused on the deep
and long purpleness that stretched endlessly into a faraway
depth lost beyond the reach of his thoughts. He pushed
away the idea that, once they pursued that purple tube, they
would never return, and concentrated on reaching whatever lay in the distance, a distance that the soarers had
suggested was farther away than some stars. In the chill of
the purple tube, he sensed warmth—Wendra and Alendra—
streaming with him.*

*The chill blackness of the tube walls contracted, then
twisted, and even though Alucius knew that his body could
not move, he felt as though he were being pummeled by the
sides of the tube, as though the very walls had projections
that reached out and struck him, buffeted him, twisted and
turned him. With each timeless instant, the chill that permeated him grew deeper, crept further inside him, slowed
his thoughts. Yet he concentrated on that distant purpleness, a landmark, much as the Aerial Plateau had once
been for a herder youth.*

Time passed in the timelessness of the translation tube, instants, years, both, neither . . . time unmeasurable by sluggish thoughts. Alucius clung to the goal, and to Wendra's warmth and presence, as he knew she clung to him and to Alendra.

More time passed, and the intolerable chill of the tube and the purple blackness that surrounded the herders warmed slightly, and the purpleness became brighter. In the near distance, Alucius began to sense Table arrows, not just the handful of those on Corus, but a comparative plethora, as many as fifty.

They had decided that they would simply try to get as close as they could to whatever resembled the scepter and showed great power, probably purple pink power. Except . . . Alucius couldn't sense anything like that. For all of the Table arrows, there were none of great intensity, none even as strong as the golden green portals of the soarers had been. All the Table arrows were faint—and none were of purple or pink. Yet all were close, and there seemed to be no way to tell which of them might be close to the master scepter.

Feeling the chill again creeping into his bones, Alucius pressed toward the purple gold arrow, trying to convey that sense to Wendra. As his thoughts carried him toward that near yet faint arrow, he could sense Wendra's presence moving beside him.

A thin shimmering veil of silvered purple rose before them. Alucius formed a spear of lifeforce, enfolding him— and Wendra and Alendra.

The thin purple silver barrier shattered . . .

155

Norda, Lustrea

Waleryn frowned, then hurried down the stone steps to the Table. Behind him came two ifrits in their shimmering green and maroon garments, each a good head taller than the shadow-engineer.

The former Lanachronan lord and heir stepped up to the Table, ignoring the ifrits, his brow furrowed in concentration. The ruby mists replaced the mirrored surface, revealing the empty Table chamber in Prosp. Waleryn nodded. A second image replaced the first, and that was the Table chamber in Salaan—also empty.

For several moments, the shadow-engineer just stood before the Table. Finally, a long tube appeared, projected into the space above the Table. Each end of the tube connected to webs of purpled darkness, although the web at one end consisted of but five branches.

Waleryn studied the web of purpled darkness projected above the Table, his eyes fixing on a point on the tubular segment glowing a luminescent shade that appeared black, gold, and green, in turn, and yet none of those colors precisely.

"Is something wrong?" asked the young muscular ifrit who stood at the former lord's left shoulder.

"Someone's making a translation. They're using energies I haven't seen."

"Isn't that good?"

"They're translating *back* to Efra. It has to be the lamaial. I warned Trezun and Lasylt. The fieldmaster said everything was under control."

"Can't you stop them? You have to."

Waleryn shook his head. "I'd have to depower the entire

grid, and we don't have the master scepter here. The only way to do that is Table by Table. No one can do that in time. And if we did . . ." He looked at the ifrit.

"We'd all die, is that it?"

Waleryn nodded. "So would Efra . . . or all Efrans, because there isn't enough lifeforce to repower the long translation tube, and the master scepter hasn't been moved. The lamaial or the ancient ones might even be wagering that we would depower the tube, thinking that we would not know what would happen."

"They wouldn't do that."

"How do you know that?" countered Waleryn. "In their day, they were far more ruthless than we are. They sacrificed most of their people—and thousands of the Talent-steers—to sever the great translation tubes."

"You're not supposed to know that."

"About history? Or about the master scepter and the power requirements? Or as a mere shadow-Efran, you mean?" Waleryn snorted. "It's obvious from studying the flows of lifeforce."

"You have to do something," insisted the other ifrit.

"Tell me what," suggested Waleryn. "Does one of you want to try a reverse translation?"

The two offered no reply.

Waleryn released the projected image and stepped back from the Table. "The fieldmasters on Efra will have to stop him. If they can."

"You doubt that they can?"

"It will not be easy. He must have the scepters. Otherwise, why would he attempt the translation?"

The two ifrits exchanged glances, but did not speak.

156

Purpled silver flowed away from Wendra *and Alucius like mist and . . .*

. . . where they stood, the air was warm and humid. Frost boiled away from both Alucius and Wendra. Around them was a Table room, but one unlike any Alucius had seen. The walls were not just blank expanses of polished stone, but works of art, with carved friezes illuminated from within the stone and illustrated so well that the images seemed caught in midstep, or in midaction. Above the friezes were wall murals, similarly colored, running all the way around the chamber.

Seeing two figures through the mist dissipating from around them, Alucius brought up his rifle. A bored-looking ifrit with silver blond hair turned, and his mouth dropped open. Agonizingly slowly, his hand fumbled for the light-cutter hand weapon holstered at his belt.

Crack! Alucius's single shot struck the ifrit in the chest, exploding through the man.

Alucius turned, but the second ifrit, also blond, who had begun to run toward the archway opening onto a set of steps, went down from a single shot from Wendra.

The two herders looked at each other.

Alucius gaped, for the Wendra who viewed him was not the Wendra with whom he had stepped into the portal. Nor was the child in the carrypack the same Alendra. Wendra was more angular; her brown hair had turned black, and her eyes had gone from gold-flecked green to violet flecked with green. She looked more like the Matrial than she did like his wife. Yet . . . her lifethread was the same brilliant green.

"You look like an ifrit."

"So do you," she replied. "Your hair is black."

"Yours, too." He paused.

"The soarer," Wendra began, "she said something about a world affecting someone who translated."

"We'll have to worry about that later. I just hope we look normal when we get back." *If we get back.* Alucius scanned the Table room once more, a chamber that looked more like the Landarch's palace than what he thought of as a Table chamber. His eyes skipped over the friezes and the murals, which depicted ships such as those he'd seen in the murals in Dereka years before, and pteridons, and sandoxes—but the colors and proportions were different—and all the ifrits had blond hair, not black.

He looked sideways, taking in the light-torches on the wall. Then he scrambled off the Table.

"The one in the other corner," Wendra suggested.

Alucius hurried toward the torch she had suggested, using a twist of greenish lifeforce to break the Talent-lock, before he turned the bracket. Absently, he noted that he didn't seem to have to reach up as far. Were the brackets lower?

The stone doorway slid open. Alucius sensed no one inside.

"I'll cover it." Wendra dropped off the Table and moved toward the open doorway, turning so she could cover the room, the archway, and the staircase beyond.

Alucius hurried into the passageway, so like those on Corus, finding a chamber at the end of the corridor. He rifled through the chest against one wall, but found nothing resembling a map or anything else. Nor was there anything in the drawer of the table desk that resembled a map. The papers he did see were covered with angular and incomprehensible writing. Alucius left the rack of light-cutting pistols untouched as he hurried out.

He had sensed nothing of power, nothing similar to a scepter. "There's nothing here. The soarers said that they had to be close to lines of power."

"Then let's try another Table," Wendra said.

"There are fifty."

"If it takes fifty, it takes fifty," she snapped, moving back toward the Table. "We'll try the one that's closest and strongest."

Alucius had to hurry to catch up with her, bringing his rifle into the ready position as he took his position beside her on the Table.

Again they dropped into the purple-chill blackness.

The chill was colder than that mistiness of the Corean ley lines, but warmer than the purple chill of the long translation tube. Wendra moved toward a bright blue Table arrow, bright, yet somehow faded. Behind them the purple gold Table arrow flickered . . . and vanished. Alucius would have frowned if he could have.

Ahead in the darkness was the bright blue arrow, with yet another purpled silver barrier that dissolved away from them as they burst through.

The mist that swirled away from the two herders was much fainter at the second ifrit Table, and Alucius had to take a half step to hold his balance.

The single ifrit guard was faster than the first, but still only had the light-cutting pistol halfway up when the heavy cartridge tore through him, exploding a quarter of his upper torso and shoulder away from his body.

A second ifrit jerked out of the normally hidden but now open doorway. Before she could move, Wendra's rifle barked once—with results as devastating as those from Alucius's shot.

Alucius could sense no one else in the chamber, although there were ifrits in the rooms up and beyond the staircase. He pointed as he scrambled off the Table. Wendra nodded, but remained standing on the ancient Table—set amid more murals and carvings of graceful and exquisite beauty, beauty that Alucius had no time to take in and even less to admire.

Rifle ready, he scrambled into the chamber at the end of the passageway. The layout was reversed from the first chamber, but with the same furnishings and weapons racks as in the previous chamber. He'd finished a furiously quick search of the chest and was just flicking through the few papers in the table desk drawer when he heard the report of Wendra's rifle. He forced himself to finish the search—which revealed no maps and no Talent-signs of a scepter or anything like it. Then he was hurrying back to the Table.

Another ifrit's body filled the stairwell, downed by Wendra.

"Did you find anything?" asked Wendra.

"No."

"Hurry. There are more of them coming down the stairs."

Alucius vaulted back onto the Table. He brought the rifle into a near firing position, even as he began to concentrate on entering the ifrit tubes once more.

Chill washed around them, a chill that was welcome after the steamy heat of two Table rooms and the hot frustration of having found nothing. Wendra guided them toward a chartreuse Table arrow. Behind them, Alucius could sense the bright blue arrow fading, seemingly shriveling away. The gold and purple arrow had not reappeared, either.

Again, they reached a purple-tinged silvery barrier, seemingly more transparent than those they had encountered previously. Beyond the silver, Alucius could see a pair of ifrits, each beside the archway that presumably led to a staircase. Then . . . the silver streamed away from the two herders seeking a scepter . . .

The ifrit who had been looking toward the Table grabbed for her light-cutter.

Crack! Wendra was faster than either Alucius or the ifrit, and the single bullet exploded through the guard's torso.

The second guard's hand didn't quite reach his weapon before Alucius's single shot took him down.

Alucius vaulted off the Table and hurried toward the light-torch bracket to his left. Behind him, he heard a faint wailing from Alendra. Either his feelings were correct, or he was lucky, because he could sense the Talent-lock even before he started to turn the bracket. The lock dissolved, and the hidden door slid smoothly open. As before, there was no one inside.

Also as before, there was no sign of a scepter, nor were there any papers or maps that might have led them to the master scepter emphasized by the soarer just before she died. Alucius hurried back to the Table and scrambled back up beside Wendra, who remained with her rifle trained on the archway.

"Reload while I catch my breath," Alucius suggested. "We need a better approach." Sensing even greater warmth from his right side, he glanced down. The heavy scepter strapped to his empty scabbard was glowing a faint pinkish purple and radiating heat. Yet he could sense nothing like a scepter. He looked toward Wendra. Her scepter was doing the same.

"We're safe just so long as we keep ahead of them," Wendra pointed out as she slipped cartridges from her belt into the magazine.

"We can't go through all fifty Tables," Alucius protested. "Not without resting somewhere along the way. And we don't have enough ammunition for that. We don't have enough Talent-strength to fight that way, either."

As Wendra raised her rifle, he took a moment to reload his own weapon.

"Both scepters are glowing," Alucius said.

"I think they've begun to glow a little more with each Table we've visited. Do you think they're picking up energy from them?"

"That could be. We'll have to watch and see."

"Did you notice that there are only five really bright Table arrow markers?" asked Wendra.

"No," Alucius admitted. "But the two Tables we visited first . . . they're gone."

"It could be the scepters. Or it could be that the soarer was right," Wendra said. "The links are fading. That's why the guards. They don't want them used."

"Or both," suggested Alucius. "You think that one of the brighter markers holds the scepter."

"It has to," Wendra said.

"You keep picking where we're headed. Can you do some more?"

"I have to. We can't stop now," she pointed out. "We do, and they'll have guards everywhere. Through the Tables, we can move faster than they can."

"As long as we can keep it up."

"We have to." Wendra looked at him. "Are you ready?"

Alucius nodded, lifting his rifle and ignoring the sweat beading on his forehead.

The almost-welcome chill settled over them as they dropped through the surface of the Table and back into the purple darkness of the ifrit tube. Alucius could sense the brighter markers that Wendra had mentioned and let her guide them toward the nearest—one of pinkish silver.

Behind them, the chartreuse Table arrow collapsed in upon itself, shriveling away into nothingness. Neither the bright blue arrow nor the gold and purple one had reappeared. Was their transit disrupting or shutting down those Tables, or was it because they carried the scepters?

Through the next purple-tinged silvery barrier, Alucius could see/sense a single ifrit, not even looking toward the Table. As they flashed through the thin barrier, silver billowed like mist before them, vanishing almost instantly . . .

The single blond ifrit looked at the pair on the Table, his mouth opening ever wider, as if he could not believe what he saw.

Alucius fired, almost hating to do so. He was off the Table before the figure sprawled across the mosaic floor, a flowing design of interlocking geometric forms so beautiful that, for an instant, Alucius just stared, before he jerked himself back into action, moving toward the light-torch bracket whose hidden energy outlined it as if by a sign posted below it on the stone wall, a wall covered with the brilliant murals showing graceful blond ifrits in peaceful settings.

Alucius turned the bracket, his rifle ready as the doorway slid open.

An ifrit bolted upright.

Alucius fired, and she fell, half her upper body blown away. Relieved that his Talent showed no one else in the hidden chambers, Alucius swallowed the bile that threatened to erupt into his throat and charged into the end chamber.

His search was as fruitless as the first three had been, and, as he hurried back to the Table, he could feel the scepter growing warmer and exuding more of the purple lifeforce-related energy.

Without a word, he vaulted onto the Table.

He and Wendra dropped into the darkness below . . .

. . . and found that more than half the Table markers had vanished. Why?

Because the ifrits knew that they were using the Tables? Or because they had disrupted the links so badly that some twenty Tables no longer functioned?

Wendra moved through the chill darkness, a golden green beacon blazing in the dark, moving toward a crimson arrow marker. Alucius had to force himself to keep pace . . . even as she shattered the silvery barrier . . .

157

Norda, Lustrea

Waleryn scanned the image appearing in the Table's mirror. The Table chamber in Salaan remained empty. He concentrated. The next image was that of the conference room above, where he watched for a time, but neither of the goblets on the Table moved.

"There's no one there," offered the ifrit by his shoulder.

"The Tables won't show the lamaial or us, unless we're actually using the Table," Waleryn replied, "but they will show the motion of non-Talent-objects once they're no longer touched. No one has moved anything."

Another image appeared—that of the Table chamber in Blackstear—followed by the audience chamber of the Lord-Protector, and by others in rapid succession. Waleryn finally let the Table blank for a time and blotted his forehead. "There's no sign of anyone . . . not anywhere . . . except Tyren. They've vanished."

"Or they're immobilized or dead," suggested the third ifrit.

"Lasylt? How could any mere Talent-steer have killed him?"

"Whatever happened," snapped Waleryn, "he isn't making his presence known." He took a deep breath, calling up the image of the full translation tube web. No sooner had the replica image appeared above the Table than a purple section of the more heavily webbed section at one end of the translation tube faded—and then vanished.

"Three are already gone," said one of the ifrits at his shoulder. "How can he . . . ?"

"What is he doing?"

"He's shredding the Efran Table grid," snapped Waleryn.

"Can't you message the fieldmasters?"

"I'm trying, but the lamaial has created so much interference that . . . I'm not getting through, or he's blocking us."

"Why is he doing it?"

"He hasn't been able to find the master scepter, but somehow the resonances from the scepters he has to be carrying are weakening the transport links."

"No one can carry two scepters," protested the closer ifrit.

"Tell that to him." Waleryn snorted. "I knew he was dangerous. I *told* Trezun. But no, no mere Talent-steer could be that threatening. No simple herder-mercenary could pose that much of a threat to Efra."

The three watched the image above the Table.

Another section of the grid shriveled and vanished.

158

The Table onto which Alucius and Wendra emerged was twice as large as any that they had seen before, its square top a good four yards by four. Nor was there any billowing of mist or splashed silver. Alucius looked for stone walls and light-torch brackets. There were neither.

The Table stood in the center—or the base—of a chamber that was a small amphitheater, rising up a yard above the surrounding stone floor, in the center of an oval area a good thirty yards across, enclosed by a yard-high wall of green eternastone. The arched pink marble ceiling was a hundred yards above Alucius's head, and lights of all colors played over it. Somewhere, musicians played, a melody that was stirring, soothing, and sensual, all at the same time.

Beyond the first wall rose dais upon dais of green eternastone, and upon each dais stood the blond ifrits, all in different garb—some bearing weapons and some empty-handed. Alucius realized, almost instantly, the "ifrits" were incredibly lifelike statues—except for the four pairs of guards stationed equidistantly around the lowest dais.

"There!" said Wendra.

Alucius turned, still holding his rifle ready, to see halfway up the daises in the middle of the long side of the oval an enormous scepter, shimmering purple, with light playing across it.

He could sense no power, and no response from the scepter he carried.

"It's false. It's not a real scepter."

Alucius caught sight of movement and whirled.

Two of the tall blond ifrit guards aimed their light-cutters toward Alucius and Wendra. An instant before the beams of the light-cutters slashed toward them, Alucius flung up a shield of greenish black.

When the light-knife beams splattered away from the shield, Alucius was more surprised than the openmouthed guards.

"There's no scepter here! We'll try the next Table," Wendra said.

"Let's go."

Light flashed around them as they dropped back into the darkness beneath the Table.

The chill was greater, more oppressive, and Alucius could sense no Table arrow markers at all. None. Had all the Tables been deactivated? How could the tubes remain? Except they had to be ifrit world ley lines, and the master scepter had to lie along them . . . somewhere.

In the chill darkness, Wendra blazed even more brightly, a figure of green and gold, and Alucius could also sense the purple pink brilliance of the scepters they carried.

Ahead, or so it seemed, was a pinkish purpleness, not an arrow, not a marker, but something more like a portal, like the portal created by the scepter they had sought on Corus. Alucius would have laughed had he been able. The ifrits, believing that he and Wendra could travel only from Table to Table, had shut off the Tables, and that had revealed the location of the master scepter. Yet . . . would there be guards waiting there? How many? With what kinds of weapons?

Alucius forced himself to move faster to sweep in beside Wendra.

The darkness was deceptive, for they seemed to move so slowly.

Was the scepter like the portals of the soarers, outside the ley lines?

Alucius reached beyond the webs of darkness, somehow off to the side, and the portal blazed brighter. Wendra . . . had she tried to pulse an inquiry? Alucius reached once more, and he could sense Wendra reaching with him.

With that effort, Alucius and Wendra surged toward the purple pink portal, so quickly that they were through what-

ever barrier that might have existed even before they were aware of any such membranes separating the world lifeforce lines and the world above.

Waves of pulsing purple light flashed over them, light so bright that Alucius could see nothing.

Alendra shrieked, a thin cry lost in the silent light that was, impossibly, louder than thunder, a light that seemed to paralyze all thought, blind all vision.

Alucius cast out a dark Talent-probe, sending it forth almost as a shade against the source of the light. That Talent-shade dimmed the intensity enough that he could see, through eyes streaming tears, and only perceiving blurry objects at first, that they were in an empty chamber—empty except for a silver scepter three times the size of those they carried, set in a framework of silver bars that descended through the solid stone floor into the depths of the earth below. Above the scepter was a massive spinning purplish crystal, easily a dozen times the size of the one that had powered the Matrial's torques.

Alendra's cries continued, but Wendra and Alucius exchanged a quick glance.

"Someone's coming," she said. "How . . . what . . . do we do?"

"What did the soarer say? Reunite the scepters . . . wasn't that it?" As he spoke, Alucius set down his rifle, reached down with both hands, and began to undo the clips that held the scepter to the scabbard.

When he had loosened the first clip, the silver scepter snapped the second clip and surged toward the master scepter. All of Alucius's strength was barely sufficient to hold it. "Wendra. Drop your rifle and get rid of the scepter. Quick!"

Wendra did not even look at Alucius as she bent and released the first clip. The second snapped.

A roaring filled the chamber, and the intensity of the light began to multiply once more.

Alucius glanced at his wife, his vision blurring under the

searing brilliance. The metal of the scepter was *bending*, yet she was holding it. He glanced down. He was also holding a scepter that was bending, the metal elongating as the crystal surged and struggled toward the master crystal.

"On three," Alucius yelled. "Release it, and grab hands, and drop . . . all the way back to Corus. One! Two! Three!"

He released his scepter, and his fingers closed around Wendra's wrist, even as he tried simultaneously to cast up a green black shield and struggled to reach the darkness of the ley lines beneath the chamber.

A splintering impact rocked the chamber, and Alucius and Wendra were flung backward against the wall. Splinters of stone, of crystal, flew past and around them. Alucius could feel his shield crumpling as he/she/ they forced their way into the blackness beneath the stone, a blackness beneath the stone chamber.

The blackness was neither totally dark nor chill. Lines of purple pink flared past them and around them, with waves of heat that alternated with a deeper chill. Alucius felt blistered and frozen by those waves, buffeted one way, then another.

Wendra turned, seeking the long translation tube.

Alucius followed, as much tracking the cold and sensing the tube as knowing where he and Wendra were headed. Behind them rippled waves of pink and purple. The scepter portal flared brighter, then fragmented into pink sections that disintegrated into smaller sections, and ifrit ley line after ley line began to shrivel.

As if sensing the urgency, Wendra began to press, her thoughts pulling her, Alendra, and Alucius toward a darker, stronger, greener blackness at the end of the purple tube that they traveled, a tube that seemed to be cracking, letting in even deeper cold, and disintegrating behind and around them. The foreboding he had felt on the out-translation was stronger, the chill ever deeper, and Alucius focused on reaching the Corean end of the deep and long purpleness that stretched eternally beyond the reach of his Talent, a star-great distance that he knew they could cross, that they must cross. As in the outward journey, he sensed the warmth of Wendra and Alendra—joining in that combined strength against the star-deep chill as the tube walls, even as they began to separate—began to split—contracted, twisted, pulled, and pushed at the three of them.

Instants, years, seasons, moments—measurements of time—meant little except that they passed so slowly, yet instantly, in the timelessness of the translation tube. As the timeless instants stretched out, Alucius focused his being on the stead, on the timelessness and the openness, and upon the Corus that could be, that would be . . .

A huge convulsion ran through the tube, and Alucius felt that he and Wendra had been tumbled, head over heels, even though they had moved not at all, and he reached out, seeking the heavier, stronger ley lines of Corus . . .

. . . and found them as they dropped into a greenish black chill that was steadier, and merely uncomfortable, a ley line that was of Corus. For all of that, there were no Table arrow markers, no portal markers, just the long darkness.

Alucius concentrated, thinking about the "memories" of portals, and a faint image appeared, the faintest hint of maroon and green. He seized on that, and they sped toward that faint indication. As they traveled, Alucius began to sense what lay beyond the ley lines, above and beyond, a sensing he had never had before—the land, the River Vedra to the north, and the Plateau farther to the northeast. Had the ifrits' tubes blocked those senses?

Then . . . they neared what had once been a Table, now only a block of stone framed in wood . . . and they stepped out of the blackness, without even a barrier barring the way . . .

159

Norda, Lustrea

Waleryn slowly picked himself up, looking around the unfamiliar room, a room he knew he had never seen and yet knew. A pair of light-torches illuminated the stone-walled underground chamber, but while the room was similar to the Table room in Tempre, it was not the same room. There was something that looked like a Table, but the surface was dull black stone.

He looked down. An angular tall figure, not quite like a man, lay beside the wall. As he watched, the figure and its garments shimmered, then dissolved into dust. After a moment, the dust vanished as well.

"Engineer, sir?"

Waleryn turned.

A man in the uniform of a Praetorian Guard stood in the doorway, a doorway that showed a staircase behind it. "Sir? The whole building was shaking. Are you all right?"

"I'm a little confused. Where am I?"

"In Norda, sir. Where else would you be? You and the Praetor ordered us here."

Waleryn nodded slowly, but his expression was not one of comprehension, and his eyes did not meet those of the guard.

160

Alucius and Wendra stood at the end of the Table chamber in Salaan. Alucius turned and looked at her, but she was the Wendra of Corus, with brown hair and golden eyes flecked with green, with the same generous mouth. And yet . . . she was more, with a presence that radiated power and a lifethread that was both a more brilliant green and yet darker, more somber. He found her looking at him, equally intently.

"We're us," he said.

"Mostly. You look . . . more powerful . . . dangerous."

"So do you."

"I don't know if I like that," Wendra said.

"It's who you are, who you were meant to be."

Wendra cocked her head for a moment, thinking. Then her eyes fixed on the dark block of stone, framed in lorken, that had once been a Table. Now it was only dark stone surrounding shattered and vanished crystal. Whatever crystalline structures had once powered it were gone, gone with the ifrit transport tubes.

"They're gone," Wendra said. "All of them."

"But there are light-torches." Alucius walked to the light-torch bracket and turned it. The hidden door opened. He turned it again, and it closed.

"Whatever was truly made here, that will remain. The soarers had light-torches. Maybe the ifrits took that from them, rather than the other way around." Wendra's nose wrinkled. "All this has taken a toll on our little friend here. Let's go upstairs and see if we can find some water."

Alucius could only hope that there were no surprises waiting, or none that couldn't be handled by Talent, because both rifles were somewhere on the ifrit world, and his scabbard was empty. Still, as he stepped toward the doorway to the stairs, he could sense no one.

He made his way up the steps carefully, but the main level was deserted.

"I said that no one was here," Wendra offered with a smile.

"I thought that was so, but . . . these days, you never know." From the outside light, Alucius thought the time of day was late afternoon, but while it could have been the same afternoon as the day they left, the light felt different, as though it were not. Given his instructions to Feran, it had to have been less than a month.

He nodded and kept looking.

There was a washroom in the rear, and before long, Alendra was cleaner . . . and hungry.

Sitting in one of the chairs in the conference room, Wendra began to feed their daughter.

Alucius walked over to the iron stove set against the wall. The metal was cold. In fact, the room was cool, almost chill, and with the heat that had filled the structure before they had left, the coolness was another indication that more than a few glasses had passed, that at least a day had gone by. Alucius doubted that it had been only a day.

He took out his water bottle and offered it to Wendra. After she drank, he finished it, then fished out a package of travel bread and hard cheese. He alternated between eating some and feeding Wendra as Alendra nursed.

"Our rifles . . . the bullets," Wendra said slowly. "They didn't act like that even against the dark sanders or the wild translations."

"No. They didn't do that to Tarolt or the ifrits here. It must be the lifeforce. The ifrit world was dying—"

"And we used the lifeforce from Corus," Wendra said. "But why didn't it work that way here?"

"I'm just guessing," Alucius replied, "but the ifrits who came here were drawing on the lifeforce of Corus through the Tables, not that of their own world. All their lifethreads were tied to the Tables, and their tubes were linked to the ley lines. So they were drawing lifeforce all the time."

"They would have bled Corus dry." She paused. "But . . . how could they think a mere handful could—"

"They did once before," Alucius pointed out, "and against seemingly greater opposition."

"But the arrogance . . ." Wendra paled. "How did you feel against those poor ifrits in the Table rooms? Strong? Almost invincible?"

"Linking to power, the ley lines? Does it do that to everyone? Is that another temptation we face? Is that what you mean?"

She nodded slowly. "They had so much . . . and it wasn't enough. There was so much beauty there, in just those few rooms. If we had seen their world . . ."

"They created beauty here, too, before," Alucius pointed out. "That kind of beauty has a high price. Like the Matrial's order and beauty."

"We'll have to make sure we don't do that."

"Avoid that sort of temptation," Alucius added. Yet that would be bittersweet, he knew, because he *had* been moved by those brief glimpses of surpassing beauty.

Wendra eased Alendra to her shoulder, patting her back. "We'll have to be very careful with Alendra. She won't have seen and felt what we have."

Alucius wasn't so sure that he wouldn't have to be careful with himself first. Another thought occurred to him. "I need to visit the Lord-Protector. It won't take long."

"You've said that before." But she smiled.

"It's not to another world," he countered, returning her smile with one of his own. "Besides, you're still guarded. I can feel the lancers out there."

"If you won't be long . . ."

"I don't think so. Not this time."

She nodded. "Be careful."

"I will."

Alucius walked down the steps to the chamber that held what had once been a Table. He suspected he could have contacted the ley lines with his Talent from the upper level, but it was easier on the lower level.

Almost immediately, he was in the misty greenish blackness, searching for the trace of the blue that had once been a Table in Tempre. At the same time, he was seeking other landmarks, knowing that in time, the portal/ Table traces would vanish as the ley lines healed from the imposition of the ifrit tubes.

The blue shadow was located where three lines came together south of the flow of life that was the River Vedra— and Alucius could sense all three. Extending himself on a Talent-line from the ley line, he drifted shadowlike from the Table room to the private chamber off the audience hall— empty—to the Lord-Protector's private apartments. Through the green silver veil, he located himself in the foyer and stepped through the misty veil.

His boots hit hard on the polished floor. Alucius smiled. He'd been a third of a yard above the tiles, and that was something he'd have to watch in the future. He stepped to the foyer archway, where he looked into the sitting room.

The Lord-Protector sat in one of the chairs, facing Alerya. Her eyes widened at Alucius's appearance.

"Talryn . . ."

The Lord-Protector turned and rose, his eyes widening as well at the appearance of the young colonel in his private chamber. "Colonel . . . this . . . it's . . ."

"Rather irregular. Yes, it is." Alucius smiled. "You'll pardon me if I'm quick and cryptic."

"I thought you were . . . in Dekhron."

"I was, and I'll be returning there after we talk. The Northern Guard had a few more problems than we'd thought. The Regent of the Matrial had some hidden allies there. I wrote you about them before I knew they were working for the Regent. Among them were those traders who were overcharging the Guard and pocketing the golds. They were also promoting incompetent officers and trying to undermine the Guard's ability to hold the north. I ended up having to go to Hieron to take care of the problem at the source. The torques no longer work. This time, they won't be repowered. You should start to receive reports of greater success from Madrien in the weeks ahead, if you haven't already. And . . . one other thing . . . there are no functioning Tables left in Corus. There won't be any more, either."

A faint smile crossed Alerya's lips, but she said nothing.

"We've also recovered a fair sum of golds from those traders," Alucius continued, "and about a third of those are on their way here. The others we'll be using to move the Northern Guard to Iron Stem. That will solve several problems at once."

"Ah . . . Your methods have always been . . ."

"Controversial, but effective. That's true. After I return to Dekhron, you will be receiving my letter of resignation from the Northern Guard, and my recommendation for my successor. Unless matters have changed since I left Dekhron, it will be Majer Feran."

The Lord-Protector frowned. "He's only been the deputy for less than a season."

"I'd greatly appreciate that favor, Lord-Protector. Majer Feran can always call on me for advice." Alucius paused. "Besides, all your colonels and marshals will be much happier dealing with Feran. He's had a more . . . traditional background. He also believes it's time to move the Guard headquarters to Iron Stem."

Talryn spread his arms and provided a helpless shrug. "It seems as though I have no choice, Colonel."

"You have choices. They wouldn't be as good. And you'll still have problems, but they'll be more manageable." Alucius waited.

After a pause, Talryn laughed brittlely. "And you?"

"I'll go back to being a herder. I'm better at that."

The Lord-Protector offered a lopsided smile. "I have my doubts, Colonel, but you've more than fulfilled my request. Will you need an escort . . . to return?"

"That won't be necessary," Alucius replied. "Not this time." With a smile, he bowed and turned, walking toward the archway and the foyer beyond. He stepped to one side, where neither the Lord-Protector nor his consort could see him, and extended his Talent-probe toward the darkness below. Then he entered it.

The ley line's dark chill was welcome, and he could find the former Table building in Salaan with even less difficulty. He stepped through the silver veil almost directly in front of Wendra and Alendra.

He found he was hovering a span or so above the floor, and let himself down before releasing the Talent-link to the ley line.

"That was quick," Wendra observed. "But you don't look like much of a soarer, even soaring."

"I'll have to work on that. I'm an inexperienced soarer." Alucius grinned. "Have you finished feeding her? We need to see Feran."

"And then what?"

"I write out my resignation and make him commander, and then we ride home to the stead."

Wendra nodded. "That might be best. Alendra . . . she's beginning to sense too much, I think."

"I wouldn't mind spending some time just riding and talking to you."

"You'll have that." Wendra stood.

Alucius walked toward the doorway to let the lancers know they had returned.

161

Tempre, Lanachrona

Talryn paced back and forth in front of the sideboard, refusing to look at Alerya. She remained sitting on the loveseat. Her expression was pleasantly composed.

The Lord-Protector stopped, then looked at his consort and wife. "You think it's amusing, don't you?"

Alerya tried to maintain her composure before breaking into a wide smile. "It is, if you think about it, Talryn."

"That man—if he even is a man—has more Talent-power than the rest of the world. He can appear without notice and leave the same way. He radiates power. I'm sure you sensed that. He really didn't give me any choices at all. None at all, and I've been more than kind to him from the beginning."

"You're upset because he told you, very politely, that you were on your own, that you'd have to solve your problems without him. After what he's been through, do you blame him? Would *you* have wanted to do what he's done?" She raised her eyebrows.

Talryn glared at his consort. "I'm glad you think it's amusing."

"It is. You're behaving like a little boy who's had his favorite toy taken away. Or like a child who's discovered that his once-little friend has grown larger, stronger, and quicker. And you don't like it. You like giving favors. You don't like having to receive them."

"Me?"

"You." She laughed. "You said you loved me for my terrible honesty. I'm being terribly honest. He's made sure we could have a son; he's removed Madrien and Aellyan Edyss as threats and gotten rid of that terrible Enyll. He saved Southgate for you, and he's rebuilt the Northern Guard for you. And now, instead of taking your throne, he's leaving you alone." Her eyes fixed on him. "He's also a reminder that you'd better act thoughtfully and carefully, and for that you should be most grateful."

"For that?"

"For that," she repeated. "You don't want to end up like Waleryn or the Matrial, do you?"

Silence stretched out between the two of them.

"I suppose I should be grateful for all that," Talryn finally conceded. "But I don't feel grateful."

Alerya rose from the love seat. "I am. You should be.

You will be." She took his hands in hers. "We owe him. Let him be."

Talryn nodded, then smiled warmly, as she bent forward and her lips brushed his cheek.

162

In the twilight, Alucius and Wendra reined up outside the headquarters building of the Northern Guard.

Alucius turned in the saddle. "Noer, if one of you would see my wife to the quarters . . . Then you can return to your duties."

The lancer looked at the gray-haired figure who had led the half squad from Fifth Company back from Salaan—and the woman beside him. In the dim illumination of twilight, both stood out, almost as if the faintest of light-torches shown from within them.

"Yes, sir." Noer nodded.

Alucius dismounted and tied the borrowed mount to the post. "I need to spend a few moments with Majer Feran."

"I'll be in the quarters," Wendra replied.

Alucius climbed the steps effortlessly and opened the door, stepping into the building and closing the door after him.

"Colonel! You're back!" Roncar jumped to his feet.

"Like a clipped coin," replied Alucius dryly.

Feran appeared at the doorway of his study. A half smile crossed his face.

Alucius gestured. "We have a few things to discuss."

"I imagine." Feran followed Alucius, closing the study door behind him.

Alucius settled into the chair behind the table desk and waited for Feran to sit down. Then he looked at Feran. "Congratulations, Colonel. Or Colonel-to-be."

"You're still colonel."

"Not for much longer. I'll be writing my letter of resignation. It's better this way. I never wanted to be colonel. I just want to go back to the stead. You can blame all the bad decisions on me, and everyone will be far happier with a solid career officer at the head of the Northern Guard. You can serve for another five or ten years, get a good stipend, and probably find a lovely woman in the process. And the only truly daunting chore you'll have is to train a successor. Since we got rid of the worst of the captains and overcaptains . . ."

"You herders . . ." Feran shook his head.

"Do you really think anyone wants me back?" Alucius asked. "Besides you, maybe?"

"You're a hero. I don't know what you've been doing, but whatever it was, I'd wager it worked."

"Oh, it worked," Alucius admitted. "You won't have any trouble with any of the traders or the Talent-twisted. The Lord-Protector has agreed to let you move the Guard to Iron Stem. The torques of Madrien don't work, and they won't ever work again. The Lord-Protector has promised not to change the customs in Lanachrona. Lustrea and Deforya are still a mess . . . but they're far enough away that they won't be a problem for a while. Oh . . . and none of the Tables work, and they won't."

"How did all this come to pass?" Feran's tone was dry and detached.

"It just happened," Alucius said blandly.

"I don't think so. You're the hero. The one in the old poem."

"I doubt that," Alucius replied. "But even if I were, heroes don't make good commanders. Neither do herders. We're loners by nature, and everyone can tell that. I've created enough unrest. After we finish, I'll write out my resignation as colonel, and my recommendation that you succeed me. It will be accepted. If you have trouble . . . send me a message."

Alucius saw no point in saying that the Lord-Protector had already agreed.

"Just like that?"

"Just like that," Alucius replied.

Feran laughed, a sound filled with humor, irony, and sadness. "You've done great and terrible things, Colonel. You've done them in ways that no one who wasn't there will ever believe."

"That's probably for the best," Alucius replied.

"What will you do?"

"Run the stead, and whatever else needs to be done." Including exploring and learning from the Hidden City. And spending time with Wendra and Alendra.

"I suppose it really is for the best," mused Feran. "For you, too. You're changed. I can see it. Whatever you've done, even just what I've seen, being a mere colonel would be a letdown." Feran smiled sadly. "In a way, I suppose it's almost a tragedy."

"A tragedy?" questioned Alucius.

"It is when you've been covered in glory, saved three lands, and defeated every foe in battle, and probably done more that I don't know, all before you've turned thirty years."

"You mean before I had a chance to truly grow up?" Alucius's words held gentle irony. "It may be better that way. I don't have to spend the rest of my life seeking glory . . . or whatever." He smiled at Feran. "You don't either, you know? Just be solid in the way you are."

Feran smiled in return. "I can always threaten to call you back." He paused. "For Fifth Company, maybe for all the Guard, I'll be Colonel Feran. You'll be 'The Colonel.'"

Alucius shrugged helplessly. "After I write the resignation, we'll get Wendra and go over to Elyset's for supper."

"So long as you pay. You're still colonel until the Lord-Protector accepts that resignation." Feran grinned at Alucius.

163

Twilight had just fallen across the Iron Valleys when Alucius, Wendra, and Alendra reached the point on the high road where they turned off onto the lane leading to the stead. When Alucius and Wendra had stopped at the cooperage in Iron Stem, Kyrial and Clerynda had been glad to see Wendra and Alendra, and even Alucius. But there had been a reserve, far more than with Feran . . . or with the Lord-Protector.

Alucius had considered that reserve as they had ridden northward on the ancient high road, and finally he spoke. "Your parents were relieved to see us, but almost as relieved to see us off."

"Of course . . . they never thought their daughter would marry the hero or the lamaial. They just thought you'd be a good herder who would give back the heritage of the land to their daughter, and that we'd just be a good little herder couple. They don't know what happened, and they don't want to know, and they're afraid they might learn. They can tell that I've killed people, and worse, and it frightens them. Daughters aren't supposed to do that." Wendra patted a complaining Alendra. "It isn't that much farther, little one, not that much farther."

"Feran said the same thing, when we met while you were tending Alendra. Before dinner. He said I was the hero. I never did understand that poem. Not really," Alucius said. "I certainly wasn't a hero. I did what I could, and I was fortunate."

"There were more than a few who wanted to be the hero, dear one," she replied. "The barbarian in Illegya, the Matrial and the Regent, the Praetor, even that ifrit . . ."

"Tarolt," Alucius supplied.

"That wasn't what the poem was about," Wendra continued.

"What was it about?" asked Alucius. "Besides a dream about restoring the faded glory of the past, a glory that wasn't really ever there?"

"What is a hero?" she countered.

"Heroes are the people that everyone recognizes."

"That doesn't define a hero."

"You tell me."

"Someone willing to sacrifice himself for other people. In a way, the soarers were heroes. They sacrificed themselves for us, for all of us. We didn't make any sacrifices like that," Wendra pointed out.

"What's the point of sacrificing . . ." Alucius suddenly broke off as he understood. "That's it."

"What is?" This time Wendra looked puzzled.

"The ifrits believed that survival justified any action, and they would sacrifice any world and any people for their way of life. The soarers believed that no sacrifice was too great to maintain life as it had been. They were both wrong."

"You're saying that the poem was wrong, too."

"Maybe . . . it was meant to be wrong." Alucius shifted his weight in the saddle, looking ahead toward a stead still out of eyesight. "It doesn't ever *say* whether the hero or the lamaial was in the right, now that I think about it."

Wendra laughed. "We won't ever know that."

"In a way, in one way, the ifrits were right," mused Alucius. "So were the soarers, and neither really saw it."

"Oh?" Wendra's tone was light.

"There's no one living who is not but a lodger upon the land. We are born, we strive, and we pass. You can only tend and pass on the land."

"So philosophical."

"So much a herder," he countered.

"That's why we're riding home, instead of using the ley lines. But, for all that, your mother was right. You are the soarer's child."

Alucius looked at Wendra. "The old song—it's Alendra's as well." Before Wendra could reply, he recited the last part of the words, slowly,

> "But the soarer's child praise the most,
> for she will rout the sanders' host,
> and raise the lost banners high
> under the green and silver sky."

"You say that well."

"You said I was a soarer. So are you. What does that make her?"

Wendra turned in the saddle, her smile and eyes bright. "Ours. The land's."

In the darkening sky to the east, just above the Aerial Plateau, both Asterta and Selena shone full across the Iron Valleys, and across the stead just ahead of the three riders. Three riders coming home.

1

Fitzhugh

At times, every professor believes that his classroom represents the abnegation of intelligence, if not absolute abiosis. This feeling has been universewide since long before the Tellurian Diaspora. Lughday was no exception, especially not for my fourth-period class, Historical Trends 1001, the introductory course, one of the core requirements for undergraduates.

I walked through the door into the small amphitheatre classroom and toward the dais. Forty bodies sat waiting in four tiers, arrayed in a semicircle—all avoiding my scrutiny. At times such as the one before me, I could only wish that the university did not require all full professors to teach one introductory course every year, at a bare minimum. I'd drawn fourth period—right after lunch, and that made it even more of a challenge.

I stationed myself behind the podium, the representation of a practice significantly untransformed in almost ten thousand recorded years of human history—and for the last five, savants and pedants had prognosticated the decline of personal and physical-presence classroom instruction. Yet in all instances where such ill-considered experimentation in technologically based pedagogical methodology had been attempted in an effort to replace what had worked, if imperfectly, the outcomes and the ramifications had ranged from social catastrophe to unmitigated disaster, even as my predecessors in pedagogy had predicted such eventualities.

Technology and implementation had never constituted the difficulty, but rather the genetic and physiological strengths and limitations of human cognitive and learning

patterns. From a historical perspective, successful technological applications are those that enhance human capaci-
ties, not those that force humans into prestructured
technological niches or functions.

As I cleared my throat and stepped to the podium, the
murmurs died away. I glanced down at the shielded screen
before picking a name, smiling politely, and speaking.
"Scholar Finzel, please identify the single most critical aspect of the events leading to the Sunnite-Covenanter Conflagration of 3237."

"Ser?" Finzel offered a blank look.

For the second class of the first semester, blank looks
were not exactly infrequent, not for beginning students,
especially for those from nonshielded continents or from
the occasional off-planet scholar. "I realize neolatry pre-
cludes your interest in matters of past history, but since the
Conflagration resulted in the devastation of Meath, exten-
sive damage to the Celtic worlds of the Comity, and significant taxation increases for the entire Comity, and since
both the Covenanters and the Alliance have continued to
rearm and rebuild their fleets, with a continued hostility
exemplified most recently by the so-called pacification of
the Mazarene systems and the forcible annexation of the
Walden Libracracy . . ."

That not-so-gentle reminder did not remove the expression of incomprehension, but only added one of veiled
hostility. I used the screen to check his background. As I'd
vaguely recalled, he was from Ulster, where he could have
netlinked and been provided the answer.

"Scholar Finzel," I said politely, "Gregory is a shielded
continent, and the university is a shielded institution. You
are expected to read the texts before class. For some reason, you seem unable to comprehend this basic requirement. I suggest you remedy the situation before the next
class." I turned to a student with a modicum of interest in
her eyes. "Scholar MacAfee?"

"According to Robertson Janes, ser, there were two
linked causes of the Conflagration. The first was the mal-

function of the communications linkages of the Covenanter fleet command, and the second was the widespread perception among the population of the Alliance worlds that the Covenanters intended to spread a nanogenevirus that would transform all herbivores into hogs." A hint of a smile crossed Scholar MacAfee's lips.

"You're in the general area," I replied, "but I don't believe that Janes said the Covenanter fleet's command communications malfunctioned. Do you recall exactly what he wrote?"

MacAfee frowned.

"Anyone else?"

"Ser?" The tentative voice was that of Ariel Leanore, a dark-haired young woman who looked more like a girl barely into seminary, rather than at university.

"Yes?"

"I think . . . didn't he write something . . . it was more like . . . the expectations of instantaneous response resulted in the ill-considered reprisal on Hajj Majora . . . and that reprisal made the Sunnis so angry that they passed the legislation funding the High Caliph's declaration of Jihad. There were rumors about the Spear of Iblis, but those were noncausal . . ." Leanore paused, her voice trailing away.

"Very good, Scholar Leanore." I stopped and surveyed the faces, seeing that most of them still hadn't grasped the impact of Janes's words. "The expectations of instantaneous response . . . what does that mean?"

All forty faces were blank with the impermeability of incomprehension. When I had been in the service, I had believed that such an expression was limited to those of less-than-advanced intelligence. The years in academia had convinced me that it appeared upon the visages of all too many individuals in the adolescent and postadolescent years, regardless of innate intelligence or the lack thereof.

"What it means . . ." I drew out the words. ". . . is that instantaneous communications and control preclude the opportunity for considered thought and reflection. The Covenanter command had the ability to order and carry out an immediate reprisal. They did so. They did not think about the fact that the Covenanter trading combines on Hajj Majora had, within the terms of their culture, acted responsibly against those Covenanters who had manipulated the terms of exchange in a manner that could be most charitably described as fraud." I cleared my throat. There are definite disadvantages to auditory lectures, especially without even sonic boosting, but my discomfort was irrelevant to those who had enacted the shielding compact. "Now that you know that, why did I initially suggest that there was only one critical aspect to these events?"

"You suggest that both events listed by Janes share a commonality, ser?" That was Scholar Amyla Sucharil, one of three exchange students from the worlds of the Middle Kingdom.

"Not only the events cited by Janes, but those cited by Yamato and Alharif."

"Isn't it communications? They all deal with communications, ser," suggested Leanore.

Young Ariel might have been tentative, but at least she was thinking, unlike most of the others. "Exactly! Both the events cited by Janes were the result of misunderstanding and misapplications of the use and function of communications, if in different societal aspects. If you apply the same tests to the examples of Yamato and Alharif, you'll find a similar pattern." I smiled, not that I wanted to, because it was likely to be a long afternoon. "History illustrates a pattern in communications. In low-tech civilizations, only immediate personal communications can be conveyed with any speed, and those are often without detail. As more detail is required, communications slow. As technology improves, there is always a trade-off between speed and detail, because improving technology results in greater societal and infrastructural complexity, which requires greater detail. Until the development of fullband comm and nanoprocessing, this trade-off existed to a greater or lesser degree. For the past millennium or so, however, the limitation on communications has not been the technology. What has it been?" I surveyed the faces, some beginning to show apprehension as they realized that they did not know the answer, and that I might indeed call upon them.

"Would it be understanding, ser?" ventured Sucharil.

"Precisely! Just because you have the information, and even a hundred near-instantaneous analyses, doesn't mean that you truly know what to do with it, particularly when the analyses may be conflicting, depending on the background assumptions and the weight of the evidence. This was particularly true in the case of the Conflagration, because of the cultural imperatives of both the Covenanters and the Alliance. Even today, any analyses dealing with the interaction of those cultures are problematical."

"Ser? Why does it matter that much?" That was from Emory David. "The Comity has a thousand world members, and the Covenanters have less than two hundred. There can't be more than seventy Alliance worlds."

"What is the first rule of interstellar warfare?" I replied.

"No planet can be effectively defended against a determined attack . . . ser . . ." replied Scholar David.

"And what are the beliefs behind a jihad?"

Finally, comprehension began to illuminate a few faces.

"You mean, ser, that they don't care because they'll go to paradise?"

"Or Heaven, if they're Covenanters doing the Will of the Divine, and seeking to ensure that we do not recover the Morning Star," I replied dryly.

"But . . . that's a myth without foundation . . ."

I could not ascertain the source of that incredulous murmur.

"Not to true believers, it is not. Not even in this so-called enlightened and rational times, and certainly not upon the Worlds of the Covenant. The Morning Star, or the Spear of Iblis, the Hammer of Lucifer, whatever the specific term, is a symbol of forbidden knowledge, knowledge that is considered only the province of Iblis, Satan, or their demon children. If there is one aspect of all true-believer religions that remains constant across time and history, it is that certain aspects of technology or science are forbidden by the deity because use of that knowledge usurps the powers and privileges of the deity. Such theocracies will therefore commit great violence over issues or scientific practices that would appear common to many of you." I inhaled slowly, for a pause. "With regard to this, even if the Comity is more secular in outlook, once the theocracies have used force against our interests, such actions require force in response, or the perception of weakness will cost even more in the long run. We lost the populations of ten worlds. The Covenanters lost thirty and the Alliance nearly forty. It has taken close to ten centuries for them to recover, half that for us, except that a dead world remains that for longer than we or any other humans will be around to recolonize. A hundred worlds scoured . . . would you like it to happen again, on Ulster, or Lyr? Or perhaps Culain or Liaden?" I paused. "Or perhaps the Covenanters are somewhat sensitive to the power of position, in which case, what happens to be the other leading secular polity? The one with whom they share the closest stellar congruencies?"

"The . . . Middle Kingdom?"

"Correct. Now . . . my skepticism is almost without limbi, but most recently the First Advocate of the Middle Kingdom died in circumstances resembling assassination—right after he had delivered a series of addresses severely critical of the theocratic expansionism of the worlds of the Covenant. What might happen if the Middle Kingdom were reputed to obtain some forbidden knowledge, something resembling the Spear of Iblis? To borrow an ancient metaphor, how long before the sabres began to rattle? Again . . . just over, if you will, information?"

There was silence in the room, although I could hear someone murmur, "It couldn't happen again . . ." I refrained from suggesting all too many people, particularly politicians, had said those words, or some variation, over hundreds of centuries, generally to everyone's regret.

"Now . . . I'd like each of you to take a moment to reflect. I would like each of you to come up with an example from history where information and how it was handled was critical in determining the fate of something—an army, a fleet, a nation, a world." I held up a hand to forestall the objections. "I know. Once you're away from Gregory, you can netlink and get a reply, ordered by whatever parameters you suggest. The point of this exercise is to develop your judgment so that when you do that in the future, you will have a greater understanding of what that information actually means."

This time the majority of expressions were those of resignation. I supposed that was an improvement. If they thought what I was requiring was difficult, they hadn't even considered what was going to be required in the later stages of applied manual mathematics. I'd learned, years earlier, that if I leaned on the students hard in the opening classes, the classes got easier and more rewarding toward the end. Unfortunately, doing so, and maintaining a cheerful demeanor in the process, was arduous in the first weeks of the semester.

I didn't quite breathe a sigh of relief when fourth period was over and I left the classroom, walking down the ramp to the main level. There were times I could feel my hands tightening, wanting to throttle certain students. The best ones cared for knowledge as a tool, and the worst only sought a degree with marks that would guarantee entry into some multi or another or into the Comity bureaucracy, which was worse, from what I'd seen, than that of academia. I could not help but wish, at times, that I were back teaching in the days prior to the Disapora on Old Earth, where everything had been broadband and without the direct face-to-face student contact that reminded me all too often of how little most of them cared for knowledge itself.

But . . . that time on Old Earth had been before the discovery of the subtle but far-reaching effects of broadcast energies, even at extraordinarily low power, on neonatal and prematuration mental development. The Comity had banned wide-scale public and private broadcast of information and power, and relied on monoptic distribution systems, unlike the more conservative governments, such as the Covenanters and Sunnite Alliance, for whom cost-benefit analyses included individuals with environmentally damaged attention spans. I couldn't help but snort to myself. My students had short enough attention spans without additional technological assistance in shortening them further. The continent of Gregory, as many other continents on Comity worlds, had even more stringent requirements than the baseline regulations in force throughout the entire Comity of Worlds.

Once back in my office, little more than an overlarge closet three meters on a side, I settled myself behind my console and keyed in the codes to call up my in-comms— there were no personal direct-links at the university, or for that matter, anywhere on the continent.

The first message was from the provost—just a message, and no text.

> Congratulations on being nominated for a senior fellowship with the Comity Diplomatic Corps. Your continued diligence in seeking outside validation and recognition of your talents, accomplishments, and credentials has not gone unnoticed . . .

I just looked at the message. The last thing I wanted was a senior fellowship with the CDC. Years back, my service tours had convinced me of the futility of government service. I certainly had not applied for such a fellowship. Had the provost nominated me? Why? Had I been that much of a thorn in his bureaucratic side? It didn't matter. In the unlikely event I happened to be selected, I'd politely refuse. There were more than enough brilliant junior professors who wanted such empty honors and would be happy to accept.

I moved to the next message.

2

Goodman

The five-story building in New Jerusalem was identified as the Zion Mercantile Exchange. It wasn't, although there were legitimate trade and commerce offices on the main level. At the end of the east corridor, I stepped through the gate to the lifts, cleared by a minute sample of my true DNA. My destination was on the second level. At the third doorway on the second level, I offered my wrist once more to the DNA-coder.

"Request clearance codes."

"Kappa seven-eight-nine-six, Josiah three, Walls of Jericho, Hatusa version."

"John Paul Goodman, cleared." The endurasteel portal irised open, long enough for me to enter one of the sanctums of the Covenant Intelligence Service.

One of Colonel Truesdale's bright young men looked up from his console at me. "The colonel will be with you in a few minutes, Operative Goodman."

I was a senior CIS operative, not just an operative. I didn't correct him. Instead, I settled into one of the straight-backed chairs to wait.

Fourteen and a half minutes passed before the aide said pleasantly, "You can go in now, Operative Goodman."

"Thank you." I offered a warm smile and walked through the door that opened as I neared and closed behind me.

The inner office looked to have a panoramic view of New Jerusalem through a wide expanse of glass. That was an illusion. Two men awaited me. Colonel Truesdale sat behind a table desk, and a dark-skinned man with gray hair sat in a chair to his left, facing me.

Colonel Truesdale's eyes were hard and glittering blue. They didn't match the genial laugh and the warmth of his voice. "Operative Goodman, you've heard of Major Ibaio."

I nodded politely. "Yes, sir." Who hadn't, after his exploits in pacifying the Nubian Cluster? Or rooting out the followers of the antiprophet among the Mazarenes? He hadn't had much to do in the ongoing annexation of the Walden Libracracy. He wouldn't have been needed. The Waldonians didn't believe enough in anything to fight that hard.

"Take a seat."

I sat in the remaining chair.

Major Ibaio's dark eyes scrutinized me from an even darker face. After a moment, he spoke. "The Comity is undertaking an unusual expedition. They have refitted a former colony supply ship. The *Magellan* is the largest possible vessel that can fit through a Gate. The AG drives are the most powerful ever installed and have been under construction for the past three years. The shuttles are larger than couriers. The vessel is heavily shielded, and armed with the weaponry of a standard Comity battle cruiser, and it will be part of a scientific expedition."

A colony vessel with beefed-up drives armed like a battle cruiser for a science expedition? That made no sense. Why were they giving me that kind of mission? What I knew about any science besides weapons and the general basics wouldn't enabled me to pass for a lab tech, much less a scientist. Or was it a way to get rid of me?

"The Comity government has seldom invested heavily in any research exploration, but it seems more than probable that their scientists have located a planet with alien forerunner technical artifacts—or a renegade Technocrat colony that escaped the Dirty War, then failed." Ibaio smiled coldly. "You understand the possible value."

"In thousands of years, no one has found any alien artifacts—not anywhere in the Galaxy. It's unlikely that any of the renegade Technocrat scientists escaped."

"Exactly." Ibaio's voice was colder than before. "The

Comity would not expend such funding if they were not absolutely certain. They may even be seeking the Morning Star."

The legendary Hammer of Lucifer, the Spear of Iblis? Had they ever even existed? I wasn't about to ask that question. "I'll do whatever is required, sir, but I'm not a scientist—"

"Your job is both simple . . . and very difficult," interrupted the colonel. He smiled warmly once more. "We don't expect you to bring back scientific discoveries or artifacts. That would be asking far too much of any operative."

That didn't reassure me much.

"What you are to do is to leave an AG signaler that will allow our ships to locate the planet or station or locale independently."

AG signalers didn't exactly float in orbit off strange planets. That I knew, but I wouldn't have recognized one if it had been set before me.

"Needless to say, you cannot carry such aboard the *Magellan*. That means you'll have to build it from scratch."

I was getting a very bad feeling about what the colonel had in mind.

"We don't intend to confront the Comity directly. That would be . . . unwise, but it is difficult to monitor an entire planet, even for the D.S.S." The colonel smiled once more. "You'll be given an in-depth indoctrination for both your cover and for your mission. Your cover will provide you access to the equipment you need. You will spend the next month in a regime of forced nanite education and indoctrination. By then, you'll look and act like your cover."

More surgery and forced nanite education? What stories I'd heard about them hadn't been good. "How many operatives are you putting through this?"

Truesdale ignored the question. "You will be William Gerald Bond, Comity armorer second class. He has been assigned to the *Magellan*, but will be late in reporting for cadre training because he is currently finishing a patrol cruise on the *Drake*. That will allow us time to prepare you. Along with other techs of lower rank, armorer Bond has been under surveillance for some time, and we have his DNA. Because this is a long mission, we will have to alter the medical records at Hamilton base and those carried on board the *Magellan*. We cannot risk changes to the main databases, but the subroutines should hold unless there is a deep audit. Even so, that will require your escape relatively soon after the ship returns. Any other information you can supply will be most useful as well."

"Might I ask why an armorer?"

"There are several reasons," Ibaio replied. "First, scrutiny of mid-and lower-level techs is somewhat less. Second, armorers have access to AG-driven message torps and regular armed torps. The torp drives have the components that can be converted to the necessary signaler."

"Do we know anything about where this place is?"

"Distant enough to require several Gates to reach it. The details will be covered in your briefing and indoctrination, Senior Operative Goodman," Truesdale said smoothly as he stood. "I wish you well, Goodman. You're in Major Ibaio's most capable hands now."

Ibaio had risen as well. Unlike the colonel, he wasn't smiling.

The Morning Star—the Hammer of Lucifer, or what the Sunnis called the Spear of Iblis? Why was the colonel sending an operative? Why not a crusader who was deep-programmed? I could see why he didn't want to send a fleet directly against the Comity, especially when too many ships were tied up in finishing the pacification of the Libracracy, but a single operative?

Look for

⤞ ALECTOR'S ⤝ CHOICE

Fourth Book of the Corean Chronicles

Now available!
from Tom Doherty Associates

Look for

⸙ DARKNESSES ⸙

Second Book of the Corean Chronicles

Now available!
from Tom Doherty Associates

Look for

⤝ LEGACIES ⤞

Book One of the Corean Chronicles

Now available!
from Tom Doherty Associates

Look for

✴ **ORDERMASTER** ✴

Now available!
from Tom Doherty Associates